W9-CEG-881

THE ACCIDENTAL EMPRESS

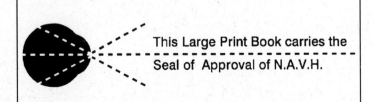

This Large Print Book carries the
Seal of Approval of N.A.V.H.

THE ACCIDENTAL EMPRESS

ALLISON PATAKI

THORNDIKE PRESS

A part of Gale, Cengage Learning

GALE
CENGAGE Learning·

Farmington Hills, Mich • San Francisco • New York • Waterville, Maine
Meriden, Conn • Mason, Ohio • Chicago

GALE
CENGAGE Learning®

Copyright © 2015 by Allison Pataki.
Interior map by Jeffrey L. Ward.
Thorndike Press, a part of Gale, Cengage Learning.

Thorndike Press® Large Print Core.
The text of this Large Print edition is unabridged.
Other aspects of the book may vary from the original edition.
Set in 16 pt. Plantin.

LIBRARY OF CONGRESS CATALOGING-IN-PUBLICATION DATA

Pataki, Allison.
    The accidental empress / by Allison Pataki. — Large print edition.
        pages cm. — (Thorndike Press large print core)
    ISBN 978-1-4104-7882-5 (hardcover) — ISBN 1-4104-7882-3 (hardcover)
    1. Elisabeth, Empress, consort of Franz Joseph I, Emperor of Austria, 1837–1898—Fiction. 2. Large type books. I. Title.
PS3616.A8664A64 2015b
813'.6—dc23   2015000791

Published in 2015 by arrangement with Howard Books, a division of Simon & Schuster, Inc.

Printed in Mexico
1 2 3 4 5 6 7 19 18 17 16 15

To my parents,
Libby & George

Like thine own sea birds,
I'll circle without rest.
For me earth holds no corner
To build a lasting nest.
— Empress Elisabeth "Sisi" of Austria

"So quick bright things come to confusion."
— William Shakespeare's
A Midsummer Night's Dream,
Sisi's favorite play

CONTENTS

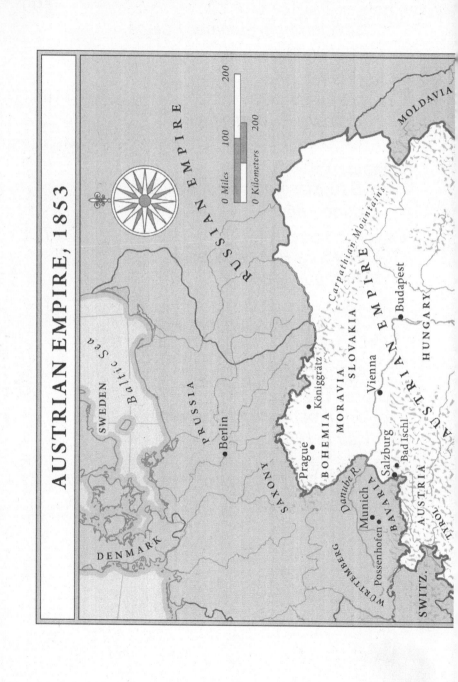

AUSTRIAN EMPIRE, 1853

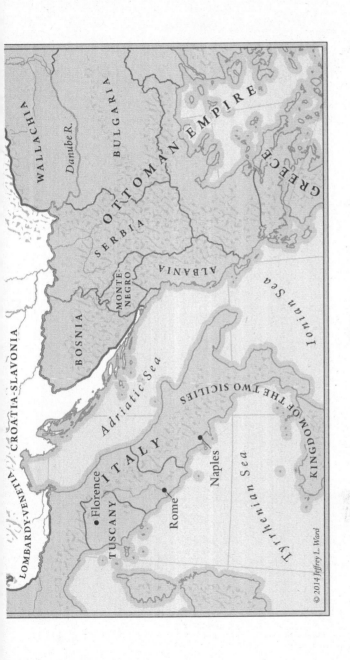

LOMBARDY-VENETIA / CROATIA-SLAVONIA

WALLACHIA

Danube R.

BULGARIA

OTTOMAN EMPIRE

GREECE

SERBIA

ALBANIA

MONTE NEGRO

BOSNIA

Ionian Sea

Adriatic Sea

KINGDOM OF THE TWO SICILIES

ITALY

Naples

TUSCANY

Florence

Rome

Tyrrhenian Sea

© 2014 Jeffrey L. Ward

INTRODUCTION

The year is 1853 and the Habsburg Empire covers much of Europe, stretching from the Russian border in the east to Italy in the west, from northern Germany south to the Balkans.

Emperor Franz Joseph, one of the most powerful crowned heads in the world, rules over more than 35 million souls, including Catholics, Protestants, Jews, and Muslims. His people are of Austrian, Hungarian, German, Czech, Croatian, Italian, Gypsy, and other descents.

Austria is the quintessential multiethnic empire, a polyglot patchwork held together not by a unifiying nationality, religion, language, or even a feeling of mutual affection. One thing alone unites these divergent lands, people, and interests: Franz Joseph. A handsome young man in his early twenties, with auburn waves of hair and serious blue eyes, Franz Joseph rules by divine right, a blessed figure, an institution more than just a mere man.

Franz Joseph ascends to power in the year 1848, the year that revolutions roil across Europe, toppling crowns on a wave of liberal idealism and nationalistic fervor. Nowhere is that revolutionary zeal more fiercely espoused, and then crushed, than in the Austrian Empire. Quashing revolts in both Hungary and Italy, Franz Joseph takes the throne from a weak uncle and solidifies his grip over the government in Vienna and the entire kingdom.

But a few years into his reign, a Hungarian nationalist attacks the emperor while he strolls through Vienna, lodging a knife blade in the young Franz Joseph's neck. The empire trembles and prays as the emperor lies in a hospital bed, recovering from the wound. The need for a Habsburg heir has never been more apparent.

With his good looks, his charming personality, and, not least of all, his glittering kingdom, Franz Joseph faces no shortage of young ladies eager to be his bride.

But Franz Joseph's most powerful advisor is not some stiff-necked general or mustached bureaucrat; the person from whom Franz Joseph most often takes his counsel is his mother. Archduchess Sophie is, after all, the very person who has groomed him all his life for this role and has found the way to thrust him onto a throne that hadn't belonged to him. And she already has a bride in mind.

Heeding his mother's advice, Franz Joseph sends an invitation to Bavaria, where his pretty young cousin, a girl named Helene, is cowed and flattered to receive such a summons. When Helene's younger sister, a spirited young girl of fifteen named Sisi, joins her elder sister, no one involved knows how deeply their lives — and indeed the world — are about to change. . . .

PROLOGUE

BUDAPEST, HUNGARY
JUNE 8, 1867

"Empress, we are ready for you."

She turns, a small nod and a flourish of her hand. "Time to assume the role." She slips her arms through the sleeves. The silken fabric, expertly stitched and tailored, molds around her curves. My, but she has never quite grown accustomed to how heavy these things are. Heavier, it seems, than her own tired frame.

All around her, nervous footmen and chattering attendants fuss, bickering like frantic bees in the hive that encircles their all-important leader.

"Fluff her skirt!"

"Mind the trim!"

"Time to go!"

"Can't be time already, can it?"

"Ready, Empress Elisabeth?" The imperial hairdresser stands before her, the ancient crown poised between two fingers, its diamonds catching a glint of candlelight. As delicate as

19

the wisps of a spiderweb. And yet, durable enough to have survived the centuries, to have persisted longer than the royal heads on which it has rested. Heads now embalmed, hairs now gray and fallen out.

"Ready." She nods, lowering her chin so that the diadem can be nestled into her chestnut curls — curls that have been named the most valuable crown jewels in all of the Habsburg collection. The curls, they say, that won her the emperor's heart.

The crown in place, she glides forward and glances at herself in the full-length mirror. She does make an arresting vision; even she has to admit it.

The gown is of white and silver brocade, laced with rows of diamonds and stitched to hug her narrow figure. A long cape of white satin drapes over her shoulders before tumbling to the ground. But it's her face that they always want to see, more so than any imperial stitching or ancient tiara. They've all heard of her slanting, honey-colored eyes. Her smoothly sculpted cheekbones. Her lips, the lips that the emperor once declared as "fresh as strawberries." The emperor. Her heart lurches clumsily in her breast. God, but she is tired. Will she have the energy to survive this day?

A knock, and her heart trips once more. She glances up, her eyes darting to the heavy oaken door. Which one of them will it be on the other side? Will it be the emperor? Or will it be . . .

him? Her cheeks grow warm at the thought, and she chides herself. Even after everything she has been through, she still reddens like a girl of sixteen at the thought of him, the mention of his name. Her own husband doesn't pull such a scarlet blush to her cheeks.

The door lumbers open, groaning like a sluggish guard woken from his midnight watch after too much ale. In an instant, she sees him, and he sees her. He takes her in. She can tell from his face that she has succeeded in beating the breath from his gut; he wears the look of a stunned animal.

"Sisi," is all he manages to say. He throws his arms up, wide, as if to pull her into him. But he checks himself, takes note of the servants bustling about.

"Your Majesty." He clears his throat. "Are you ready?"

She inhales, considering the question. Is she ready? No. She never really was ready, she supposes. That was the problem, wasn't it? But she lifts her chin, throwing her shoulders back.

"I am," she answers, one quick nod. She glides forward. The dress drags — its splendor too heavy for her exhausted body. But she sighs and continues across the room.

She can already hear them on the other side of the walls. Not so much the individual cheers and cries, but a dull, persistent throb. Constant. Like the crush of the sea waves on the earth: unyielding, unceasing.

He offers his arm and she slides her own through it, her soft flesh pressing into his heavily starched uniform. The doors open wider now. She blinks, longing to pull a gloved hand upward. To shield herself, to hide her face from all of those direct, inquisitive eyes. . . . Eyes that will study her and take her in, as if she is theirs for consuming. She seethes with that instinctive, familiar desire to flee, to escape. But she checks her impulse. Stands a bit taller.

And then she hears it. "Sisi!"

A breath inward. A moment to fortify herself as she turns to him. "It is time." And it was. At last, it was time.

PART ONE

CHAPTER ONE

POSSENHOFEN CASTLE, BAVARIA
JULY 1853

Sisi crouched low, peering over the wall of brush. Her gaze was alert, her legs ready to spring to action, her heart pumping blood throughout her veins with a speed that only the hunted can sustain.

"Come out, you cowards!"

Just then Sisi spotted the figure crossing the meadow, a dark silhouette piercing the backdrop of the crenellated white castle and deep-blue sky, and she ducked once more out of sight. Her brother Karl had not yet found her, and he yanked on his horse in frustration, as if to remind the beast of the authority his sisters so brazenly flouted.

Sisi watched Karl, her contempt thickening as she discerned his thoughts: clutching the reins, he imagined himself a Germanic warrior atop a stallion, ready to ride on the Hungarians or the Poles and seize glory from the battlefield.

"Karl the Beneficent, Duke of Bavaria, demands that you come meet your lord and surrender!" He scoured the woods, his words finding Sisi even as his eyes failed to locate her. "Kiss the ring and I shall show you mercy — more mercy than you deserve. But if you continue to run and hide like rodents, I shall have to flush you out. And when I do, you shall wish you had surrendered!" The horse pawed at the ground, agitated under Karl's grip.

Sisi was fed up with being the prey. The odds were not just; if she had had the chance to mount her own horse, Bummerl, she would chase Karl all the way to the Bavarian border, and he knew that. But she hadn't expected to have to fend off her brother when she had wandered toward the wooded lake shore with her sister, Helene, to pick wildflowers.

"We should surrender, Sisi." Helene crouched beside her, worry pulling on her sharp, dark features. "You heard him. Otherwise, he will make trouble for us."

"Nonsense, Helene."

Two years younger than Sisi, her brother was nearly twice her size, his thirteen-year-old body robust from adolescence, beer, and bratwurst. But though she lacked his girth, Sisi knew she could best Karl with wit.

"We'll show Karl the Beneficent what a formidable foe he really is." Sisi nodded at her sister, picking up a cool, smooth stone. Helene responded with a whimpering sound.

"So be it," Karl hollered from outside the woodline, on the far side of the meadow. "You have chosen your own fate. And that fate is — *pain!*" Karl dug his leather boots into the sides of his horse. The beast whinnied in response, and then Sisi felt the earth begin to vibrate beneath her.

"Now we're really in for it, Sisi." Helene paced in their hiding spot like a wounded animal as the sound of hoofbeats grew louder.

"Hush, Néné." Sisi quieted her elder sister. Oh, how she longed to be atop Bummerl! "Helene, when I say 'run' — you run. Understand?"

"Run where? Right into the lake?"

"No." Sisi shook her head. "In the other direction. Across the meadow, toward home."

"Toward *Karl?*"

"Trust me, Néné, all right?" After a pause, Helene nodded her reluctant assent. Sisi poked her head out once more from behind the brush and saw that her brother had almost cleared the entirety of the meadow. He rode toward the woods where they hid, his eyes narrowed to two slits as he scoured the brushline. But he had not yet discovered their hiding spot. Sisi took aim, raising her hand and the rock in it. The hoofbeats were like cannon blasts now as Karl barreled toward them. She waited, patiently, allowing him to come still closer. When he was within striking distance, Sisi released the rock, hurling it with as much precision as she could manage.

"Ouch!" Karl yelped in pain, halting his horse and sliding out of the saddle before collapsing into a heap on the ground. From the stream of blood curling downward from his nose, Sisi knew she had hit her mark.

They had to seize their opening. "Helene, *run*!" Sisi ordered, pushing off from her crouched position. She charged toward home on the other side of the field.

"Why, you little witch!" Karl yelled at Sisi's passing figure, but he remained prostrate on the ground, stunned by her assault.

Heart flying in the heady moment of victory, Sisi raced across the meadow toward the large house. Her own legs might not carry her as swiftly as Bummerl's could, but they were strong, agile from years of skipping up the mountains, swimming in the lake, hopping across the fields in search of plants and small animals. They would be enough to deliver her to safety.

Glancing over her shoulder to ensure that Helene followed, Sisi cried: "Hurry up, Helene!" She grabbed her older sister's arm, forcing her to keep apace. They shared the same parents, but little else. Helene thrived indoors: studying languages, reading philosophy, knitting, or writing quietly in a shadowy corner by a fire. Sisi always took charge when they were out of doors.

A few more steps and, hands linked, they cleared the meadow. Panting, Sisi rushed past a startled footman and flew into the front hall of the castle, Helene following behind her. Through the latticed window she saw that her brother had regained his mount and now trotted away from the lake toward home.

"Papa," Sisi cried, running into the large drawing room. "Oh, thank goodness you're here, Papa!"

Duke Maximilian's inanimate frame occupied a large, overstuffed chair in the corner of the dark room. At his feet, beside his mud-licked boots, reclined two snoring hounds, their own paws caked in dirt. They lifted their heavy heads in a perfunctory greeting as the girls ran in, but the duke continued to snore. A lit pipe sent up a curl of smoke where it burned in Duke Max's lap, forgotten.

"Papa, wake up." Sisi removed the hot pipe before it singed a hole in his woolen pants, and placed it on the side table. "Wake up!" The duke choked out one last snore before he emerged from his deep slumber, his breath overripe with the sour stench of beer.

"Papa, Karl is chasing Néné and me. Please, wake up."

"What's that?" The duke rubbed his eyes, bloodshot and droopy-lidded.

Sisi heard her brother barking a question at

the startled servants outside: "Which way did they go?" The front door opened and she heard Karl step into the great hall, his boots landing heavily on the stone floor.

"Ah, Sisi." Now Duke Maximilian shifted in his armchair, staring at her through glassy eyes, the same honey color as Sisi's, though not lucid this afternoon. "You've arrived just in time. I was just learning a new tavern song." The duke looked at his favorite daughter with a drowsy grin, lifting an index finger as he began to sound out a bouncy, peasant tune. "But have the others left? Gone home, already?" Duke Max looked around, his gaze listless.

Sisi's frame sagged as she heard Karl's footsteps outside the drawing room. "Papa, please —"

"You little wretch, you'll get it this time." Just then, her brother appeared in the doorway. His nose seemed to have stopped bleeding, but a sheen of crimson had caked into a muddy line between his nose and lips. "You hit me in the face with that rock."

Sisi straightened up, turning from her father to face her brother. "You deserved it."

Helene began to simper. "Papa, please." But their father stared into the sputtering flames of the fireplace, his empty beer mug tipped toward his lips in an effort to sponge any last drop.

"Sisi, what do we do?" Helene backed away

30

from Karl. Sisi cursed under her breath as her victory turned to failure. She should have heeded Helene's pleas and mollified Karl; her own reckless pride had led them to this.

"I'll teach you sneaky whores to defy me." Sensing weakness, Karl lunged first toward Helene.

"Get off her!" Sisi tightened her hands into two hard fists and prepared to land the first blow before what would undoubtedly turn into her own beating. She shut her eyes, so that she didn't see the figure emerging just then through the doorway.

"There you are." Duchess Ludovika swished into the drawing room, an imposing figure of black silk, crinoline-hooped skirt, and thick brown curls. Karl instantly recoiled at the sight of their mother, retreating into a shadowed corner.

"Good, you're all here." The duchess crossed the room in two quick strides and yanked open the drawing room curtains, setting free a cloud of dust. "Helene, Elisabeth, I've been searching everywhere for you girls."

"Mamma!" Sisi ran to her mother, falling forward into the duchess's long, slender frame. She shut her eyes, dizzy with relief.

"Sisi, my girl. Whatever is . . ." But the duchess paused as her eyes moved from Sisi toward her husband's reposing frame, and the large slicks of mud darkening the carpet. "Look at this mud!" The duchess sighed, her

31

shoulders rising and falling with each irritated intake of breath. "I suppose the servants will have to clean the carpet again." Then, under her breath, she murmured, "And I'll have to ask them to dust in here, as well. And this curtain needs mending. And I must remember to ask how the chickens are doing with eggs . . ." Ludovika sighed, tugging once more on the tattered curtains. Unlike her husband, who seldom concerned himself with the managing of their home or the petitions of the local peasants — and certainly not with the concerns of his children — Ludovika always had too many tasks, and too little time in which to complete them.

The duchess looked to her daughters now, the two of them cowering beside her like frightened kittens, and then to Karl's bloody face. Understanding spread across her features. She let out a weary sigh, looking out the window, as if longing to escape this dark, mud-stained room.

"Gackl," Ludovika spoke, her tone suddenly sharp. "Is that your horse I see in the garden, untethered?" Their mother used the familiar nickname for Karl, the name they had given him in his cradle because of the noises he had made. *Gackl* was the local Bavarian term for a dirty, barnyard rooster. Sisi thought it suited Karl just fine.

"Well, is it?" The duchess repeated her query when Karl didn't respond. Karl looked out the window, fumbling for a reply. She cut him off.

"Go get that animal immediately and take it to the stables. If you can't care for your horse properly, you shall have no horse at all."

"Yes, Mother." Karl answered, his ink-colored eyes burning with a warning to Sisi: *This is not over.*

"That boy." The duchess turned from her departing son to her daughters. "And look at you girls — no better. As dirty as a pair of reapers." The duchess scowled at Sisi, surveying the tracks of mud that lined her daughter's skirt. Yet she never forbade them from wandering into the woods to pick flowers, or down to the lake to fish.

"Quiet down, Ludovika, I can hardly hear Frau Helgasberg speak." Their father looked up at his wife from his armchair, momentarily pausing a conversation he appeared to be conducting in his head. Sisi felt herself cringe at the name. Frau Helgasberg was one of her father's favorite mistresses. That he uttered the name now so unashamedly was nothing new: everyone in the home knew of her existence. Everyone in the duchy knew of her existence. And yet the brazen and frequent reminders of her father's infidelity never failed to infuriate Sisi.

Ludovika, for her part, was unflappable, not faltering for a moment. "Max, how about a walk to the lake?" The duchess glided to her husband's side and lifted one of the empty glasses to her nose. She sniffed disapprovingly and swept the other empty mugs into her hand.

"Up you go, Max, you've squandered enough of this day." Ludovika pulled at the wool blanket covering her husband with her remaining hand, but he pulled back, keeping his arms on the cover.

"Away!" He growled, a loose dribble of slobber slipping out the side of his mouth.

"Max, I beseech you," Ludovika kept her voice quiet, controlled. She was the picture of composure, even if she did feel the same frustration that now caused Sisi to seethe. "Get up. Please."

"Stop this at once, Ludovika. And do not talk to me this way in front of our distinguished guests! The baron and I will finish our conversation."

The duchess studied her half-lucid husband, apparently weighing the efficacy of arguing further. She sighed, and, turning to a footman, said: "Coffee for the duke. And quickly, please." Turning back to her two daughters, she clapped her hands. "You girls had better go wash up. Change your dresses and come down for supper in something more fitting. Your father and I" — now the duchess threw a perfunctory glance in the general direction of her husband — "have news for you."

"Sisi, my wild girl! Helene! Come sit, we are waiting on you two, as usual." The duke appeared more alert at dinner, no doubt thanks to the mug of Turkish coffee his wife had placed before him.

The family was gathered in the castle's formal banquet room, surrounded by the stuffed heads of the large caribou, reindeer, and bright orange fox that decorated the walls. The spoils of her father's countless hunting expeditions. Watching him now, his frame jittery and his eyes bloodshot, it was difficult for Sisi to imagine Duke Maximilian hunting his way through Bavaria. But tales of his skill as a sportsman were well known; he was seldom at home in Possenhofen for more than a few months before fleeing on another such trip. He, like Sisi, loved the wilderness. Perhaps even more than he loved women and liquor.

"Your mother insisted that we all clean up for this dinner. What do you think she has afoot?" The duke grinned at Sisi, his amber eyes twinkling with teasing, and Sisi's disdain for him lessened ever so slightly.

In their unstructured household, such formal dinners were a rarity. The duke was seldom at home in the evenings. Their mother, though she tried valiantly to impose some sort of order over a masterless household, found it hard to wrangle her brood of wild and free-spirited children. This time of year, with the days stretching out as they did, long and mild, Sisi's evening meal was often little more than a bowl of cold soup whenever she wandered indoors, sun-kissed and dirt-stained, from a day spent in the fields and woods.

Sisi presumed that the formal dinner had to do with the news to which her mother had alluded earlier in the day. Was it possible that there was another baby on the way? What with the four siblings that had come since Karl — the little girls Marie, Mathilde, Sophie-Charlotte, and the baby boy, Max — Sisi had grown accustomed to such announcements. It seemed that, however much enmity existed between her parents, they both submitted willingly, and often, to the task of producing heirs for the duchy. Each one of Papa's long absences was inevitably followed by his unexpected return: a chaotic, confusing family reunion; weeks later, news of another baby.

But Sisi did not suspect that that was her mother's news this time; not when Mamma's busy behavior lately had been so unlike her past pregnancies.

Sisi took a seat now at the large mahogany table beside Helene. She had dressed, according to her mother's wishes, in a simple gown of black crepe, and the maid, Agata, had brushed and styled her long hair into two plaits.

"Black dresses again tonight. Always black." Sisi had lamented to her sister and the maid while dressing before dinner.

"Hush, Sisi. Don't let Mamma hear you complaining about the mourning clothes yet again," Helene had chided her. Like her mother and Helene, Sisi's wardrobe was limited these days, on account of an unknown aunt's recent passing.

"But I'm tired of black. I didn't know Great-Aunt . . . whatever her name was . . . and I want to wear *blue*. Or green. Or rose." Sisi yanked her head in opposition to Agata's tight braiding.

"Hush now, Miss Elisabeth," the round-faced maid replied, speaking in her wiry Polish accent as she adjusted the tilt of Sisi's head. "Always so impatient. Try to be sweet like your sister."

Karl, opposite Sisi at dinner now, wore a fine black suit and cravat. He had wiped the blood from his wound, but a light-purple bruise had begun to seep along the flat ridge of his nose. As he gulped his beer, scowling at his sisters and tugging on the too-tight cravat around his thick neck, he appeared more like a schoolyard menace than the heir to the duchy.

The younger four siblings, under the age of twelve, did not dine with the family, but ate

37

in the nursery with their governesses.

"Wine, Master Karl?" Agata circled the table, pouring wine into goblets while two footmen stepped over the snoring dogs to deposit platters of hot bread, potatoes, and cabbage slaw.

"No wine for me, Agata. More beer." Karl proffered his empty stein for refilling. Sisi noted how Agata replenished Karl's drink while keeping her body a safe distance from his; her brother's hands — like his father's before his — tended to wander when an unsuspecting woman got too close.

"Now that we are all here." Duchess Ludovika sat straight-backed and alert, her manners impeccable, a foil to her husband's tired slouch across the long table.

"Before you begin" — Duke Max waved a finger in the air — "I have something very important to say."

"Oh?" Ludovika eyed her husband. "What's that, Max?"

"I think the servants have been touching my mummies again." Max ignored his wife's sudden scowl, continuing on with words that strung together like pieces of sloppy linen hanging on the laundry line. "I don't want them touching —"

"Max, they have been told countless times not to touch your Egyptian memorabilia. I assure you they have not." The duchess, at the opposite end of the long table, speared a link of bratwurst with her fork and deposited it onto her plate.

"But I think they have been. I swear that my mummy's arm looks off balance."

Sisi had witnessed this exchange enough times to know that her mother had to suppress the urge to offer an impertinent reply.

The duke continued to grumble: "I can't have the servants meddling with such priceless treasures." Sisi knew that her father, when he was not off stalking wildlife, drinking his way across Bavaria, or fathering illegitimate peasant children, cared about nothing more than the collection of artifacts he'd assembled in his study at Possenhofen Castle — chief among them the relics with which he'd returned from Egypt decades earlier, on a trip to the Temple of Dendur. Sisi had always lived in fear of the mummified young female body kept in her papa's study — especially after Karl had taken the time to explain in vivid detail about the dead girl's corpse, just about the size of her own, preserved under the crusty, yellowed wrappings.

"Well, Max, if you are certain." Ludovika sipped her wine through tight lips, exchanging a knowing glance with Sisi. "I will have another word with the servants to remind them not to touch the mummy."

"Or the stones . . . I don't want them touching the temple stones either."

"Or the stones, then." The duchess managed a quick, taut smile. "Anyhow, girls" — she turned her gaze from her husband to her daughters, seated beside one another — "as I told you, I . . . we . . . have big news."

"What is it, Mamma?" Sisi glanced at Helene. While dressing for dinner, they had tried to guess, but neither of them had come up with a reasonable theory as to what their mother's announcement might be.

"Perhaps Karl is betrothed," Helene had guessed, a contemptuous smirk on her face as she had helped Agata braid Sisi's mass of dark golden hair.

"Poor girl, if that's the case," Sisi had answered, laughing with her sister and her maid.

To Sisi's surprise, however, the news seemed to have nothing to do with Karl. "Your father and I have been thinking about your futures." Ludovika lifted her knife to cut into the link of wurst. "Isn't that right, Max?"

Sisi sat up, her back stiffening against the chair.

"Surely you girls remember your Aunt Sophie?" The duchess fed herself slowly, eyes flitting back and forth between her two daughters.

"Aunt Sophie, the Austrian?" Helene asked.

Sisi remembered the woman she had met five years earlier, during a trip to Innsbruck in Austria. Aunt Sophie had been strong and tall and thin, in many ways resembling her mother. But unlike Ludovika, Aunt Sophie had had a sharp edge that permeated her entire being — her voice, her mannerisms, even her smile.

It had been 1848 — the year that the uprisings roiled throughout all of Europe. Vienna was burning and Austria's royal family, the Habsburgs, had been at risk of losing their ancient hold on the crown. Aunt Sophie, who had become a Habsburg when she married Emperor Ferdinand's younger brother, had begged Ludovika to come support her at the royal family's emergency meeting in Innsbruck.

They met at the imperial retreat, high atop the stark Austrian Alps. Sisi, then ten years old, remembered the trip well; she had grown up in the mountains, but had never seen anything quite like the snow-capped scenery into which they traveled.

"We are at the top of the world," Helene had gasped, as the carriage had climbed higher and higher. Sisi remembered wondering at what point the sky stopped and the heavens began.

On the first night in Innsbruck, her mother had left them in a dark nursery, rushing away beside her elder sister and a crowd of men in clean, crisp uniforms. The adults had all seemed very busy and very cross — tight-lipped whispers, creased foreheads, darting eyes.

Innsbruck passed, for Sisi, as interminable hours with stern, unknown governesses in that quiet nursery. Karl had been perfectly pleased; the imperial nursery was well-stocked with candied nuts and their cousins' trains and toy soldiers. But Sisi had longed for her mother. At home, they were never separated from her for more than a few hours. And they seldom spent summer days entirely indoors, but rather conducted their education by climbing the mountains around their beloved "Possi," fishing the lake, riding horses, and studying the local flowers.

Sisi had spent the hours of that trip staring out the glistening windows of the nursery at the mountains, wondering where the birds that flew overhead landed in the rocky, barren vista.

On one such afternoon, restless and aching for a glimpse of her mamma, Sisi had slipped unnoticed out of the nursery. After a fruitless search, Sisi found herself wandering the long, empty halls, lost. Now she had no idea how to find her mother, or how to get back to Helene and the stern imperial governess, a woman by the name of Frau Sturmfeder. It was then that Sisi had stumbled upon the familiar figure of her aunt, the woman's heeled shoes clipping down the long hall.

"Auntie Sophie! Auntie Sophie!" The resemblance to her mamma had been such a relief that Sisi had flown toward the woman, arms outreached and expectant of a hug.

Sisi was met, instead, with a cold slap to the face. "Calm yourself, child." Sophie scolded her, the skin around her lips creasing into a patchwork of well-worn lines. "You do *not* run in the palace, and you do *not* accost adults. My sister is more determined to raise a pack of wild things than to groom you into civilized little nobles. Now, why are you alone? Back to the nursery at once." With that, the woman had straightened her posture, patting down the place where Sisi's tiny hands had pressed into her skirt, and continued her determined march down the long hallway. She did not glance back toward her niece again.

"That's right, Helene." Her mother's response to Helene's query disrupted Sisi's remembrances, bringing her back to the dinner table and the duchess's announcement. "My elder sister, Sophie, the Archduchess of Austria."

"You know what they say about your Aunt Sophie?" The duke glanced at Sisi, a mischievous grin tugging on his lips.

"Max, please, it's really not appropriate —" The duchess lifted a hand, but failed to quiet her husband.

"They call your Aunt Sophie *'the only man in the Viennese Court.'* " The duke erupted in laughter, pushing his coffee mug to the side as he opted instead for wine.

The duchess, her lips pressed together in a tight line, waited for her husband to finish laughing before she addressed her daughters once more. "It has been extremely difficult in Austria since the emperor, Sophie's brother-in-law, abdicated the throne."

"Didn't that happen when we were in Innsbruck?" Sisi asked, recalling once more that unpleasant trip. Her parents seldom discussed politics, and the remoteness of Possi was such that Sisi's indifference toward the topic was allowed to go unchecked. But still, she knew that her aunt occupied a powerful position in the Austrian Empire.

"Yes, Sisi," her mother replied, nodding. "You remember that trip?"

Sisi nodded as her mother continued: "My sister has had to rule, more or less, to keep the throne safe for her son until he grew old enough to assume power."

Sisi remembered her cousin from that same visit to Innsbruck: a stern teenage boy, his hair the color of cinnamon. He had been too old for the nursery, but it had been his trains and toy soldiers that Karl had hoarded. Sisi had only seen her cousin a handful of times, always in the company of his military tutors, attendants, and his mother. Sisi recalled how Franz, a narrow-framed boy to begin with, had seemed to shrink whenever his mother had spoken, looking to her for cues as to where to stand, awaiting her subtle nod before answering a question posed to him. Why had that reserved and taciturn boy been selected as emperor to replace his deposed uncle? Sisi wondered.

Ludovika turned now to Sisi, as if speaking only to her younger daughter. "My sister, Sophie, has managed to survive in Vienna where men have failed. Though perhaps she has at times exhibited a strength which some have called unladylike, she has preserved the empire and always maintained the . . . how should I say this?" — and now Ludovika cast a sideways glance at her husband — "*decorum* that is expected of her high position."

" 'Spose you're right, Ludovika. Let's drink to good old Soph. She's got more stones than the rest of us." The duke took a keen swig of his wine, oblivious of his wife's scowl.

"So, is Cousin Franz old enough to assume power now?" Sisi asked, turning to peer at her sister. Helene sat quietly, nibbling on a small bite of potato. Helene never had much of an appetite.

"Indeed, Sisi," the duchess said, her expression brightening as someone took interest in her narrative. "Your cousin, Franz Joseph, has ascended to the throne. He is emperor of Austria."

"And doing a damned good job so far, too." The duke spoke with a mouth full of meat and cabbage slaw. "The way little Franzi fought at the Italian front — that was baptism by fire. That's the way a boy becomes a man, Karl my boy. Those Italians threatened to leave his empire." The duke landed a fist on the table, sending some of his son's frothy beer over the brim of its mug. "And once he finished them off, he did the same to the upstart Hungarians. Crushed them, with the help of the Russians. 'Course, I'd never trust a Hungarian, that's the truth."

The duchess interjected: "Your father is referring to the fact that your cousin, the emperor, has preserved his empire even as, in recent years, several territories have risen up in revolution."

"How did Cousin Franz become emperor when it was his uncle's crown?" Sisi asked, trying once more to picture that timid, red-haired boy on a throne.

"The people demanded that his uncle step down," the duchess explained. "I give my sister Sophie much credit for putting her son forward as the viable alternative that would please the people and keep the Habsburgs in power, while managing not to upset the rest of her family."

"Probably why all the men like to point out the stones on that one, that Sophie," the duke muttered, grunting out a quiet laugh. Ludovika threw a pointed glance at her husband. Sisi shifted in her seat, looking sideways at

Helene as a tenuous silence settled over the table.

Her mother continued after several moments: "Now that Franzi — Franz Joseph — is in power, he faces one task of the utmost importance. A duty which his whole empire wishes to see fulfilled."

"What's that?" Sisi asked.

Ludovika breathed in a slow inhale, tenting her fingers on the table as she assumed a thoughtful look. "He must marry, of course."

Sisi swallowed, unsure why this simple statement caused her stomach to flip as it did.

Duchess Ludovika turned to her eldest daughter now, eyebrows arching in a quizzical expression. "Franz must find himself a bride and produce an heir to the Habsburg dynasty."

But why was Mother staring at Helene like that? Sisi wondered. A shadow of a suspicion took root in her thoughts, like a shapeless form barely detected through a fogged window. No, Mother couldn't possibly mean *that*. The room was silent. Karl tugged on his cravat and ordered more beer. Helene, her cheeks as colorless as the table linens, kept her eyes down.

The duchess pushed her plate away, crossing her hands resolutely on the table. "Néné, I never allowed myself to hope for such a fate for my daughter." Duchess Ludovika's voice caught on the words, and Sisi was surprised at the moment of rare sentimentality in her usually composed, stalwart mother. Before Sisi could untangle the meaning of these words, her mother continued.

"To think . . . one of my girls sitting on the throne in Vienna."

Helene struggled to utter even the quietest of replies. "Mother, surely you don't mean . . ."

The duchess nodded. "My sister has asked for you, Helene. *You* are to be Emperor Franz Joseph's betrothed."

Helene dropped her fork to her plate with a jarring clamor.

"Helene, you are to be Empress of Austria!" The duchess beamed at her pale daughter, but no one else at the table spoke. Sisi understood Helene's mute shock. Her own sister, Helene, the girl who had just returned with her from picking wildflowers. The sister who slept beside her at night, burrowing her cold feet under Sisi's warm legs. The painfully shy girl who loved philosophy and religious instructions, but pled sickness to avoid her dancing lessons. Helene, Empress of Austria? Presiding over the Imperial Court at Vienna?

"And just think, Néné," the duchess continued, undaunted by her daughter's silence. "Once you give birth to a son, you shall be the Imperial Mother, the most powerful woman in the world."

The duke raised his glass and took a celebratory swig of wine. "To Helene."

"To Helene," Sisi echoed halfheartedly, still probing her sister's features for some hint of a reaction. But Helene's face was blank.

"We are moving up in the world, the House of Wittelsbach, eh, Karl? You won't have a hard time running this duchy with a sister sitting on the Habsburg throne!" The duke was now in a full celebratory humor.

But the reaction elsewhere at the table was mixed: Sisi sat in silence, mining Helene's face for clues as to her thoughts; the duchess, exuberant at first, now appeared incredulous, stunned by Helene's expressionless quiet; and Karl seemed far from joyous over the news of his sister's elevation.

Eventually Karl broke the silence. "Helene, a bride. You know what he'll expect you to do?" He speared a long link of meat with his fork and held it toward Helene, letting it hang menacingly before her. "How about some sausage?"

"Karl! Have you no shame?" the duchess hissed at her son, staring at him until he lowered the outstretched fork.

Sisi reached for her sister's hand, clammy and cold, under the table.

"Helene, it is the greatest of honors, and we are all proud of you for being chosen." The duchess turned back to her food, which she began to cut with quick, jerky motions.

"But, Mother," Helene spoke at last.

The duchess looked up at her daughter. "Yes?"

"Mamma, I . . ."

"Out with it, Helene." Ludovika had little patience for Helene's timidity, a trait which surely had not come from her side of the family.

"I don't want to marry Cousin Franz." With that confession, Helene dropped her face into cupped hands. Across the table Karl sniggered.

The duke, eyes watching over his raised beer stein, looked to Sisi as Helene's translator. "What's wrong with your sister?"

Sisi lifted a hand and placed it gently on Helene's shoulder, whispering a small conciliatory remark about how she ought to let the news sink in. Then, to her father, Sisi answered: "It is such momentous news, Papa. Perhaps she is just overcome by the shock."

"You presume to know my thoughts, Sisi?" Helene turned to her sister, her tone uncharacteristically sharp. "You're not the one being given away like chattel."

This remark, a rare instance of causticity from the usually sweet Helene, served to quiet Sisi. Helene was correct. Sisi was not the one whose fate was being discussed before her, the one who had no say in her own future.

The duchess sat observant, weighing how to respond to this unexpected turn. Finally, she spoke. "Helene, I don't understand. Every girl wants a fine husband."

Helene shook her head. "Not me." She wept, noiseless tears slipping down her cheeks.

The duchess sighed. "Why, Helene, you knew you would have to marry someday. It might have been a Saxon count, a Venetian prince . . . and yet you weep over the emperor of Austria? That is the best match you could hope for."

Again Helene shook her head. "Please, Mamma, I beg you not to make me do it."

The duchess let loose a heavy exhalation. "Helene, Franz is a good boy . . . *man.* He will treat you kindly. And you'll have Aunt Sophie to help you settle into your new life at court."

"But I don't want to marry him!" Helene insisted.

"Surely you knew this day was drawing near, Helene? You *are* eighteen." The duchess looked to Sisi, as if seeking assistance.

"But, Mamma, I don't even know him," Helene said.

Sisi noted her mother's mounting exasperation. "What does that have to do with anything? When I was sent to your papa for my wedding, I had never met him before." The duchess looked to her husband, who drained

51

his beer mug in reply. Her jaw set, her eyes expressionless, she continued: "Why, I spent my wedding night in tears. But I did my duty."

The duke did not look at his wife, nor did he reply, but Helene erupted into fresh sobs.

"For heaven's sake." The duchess rose from her seat and approached her weeping daughter. "Helene, my foolish, scared little girl, you must not be so upset. This is the best fate that a girl in your position could possibly dream of. Your husband will be the emperor of Austria, and a good, kind man. What more could you ask for in a match?"

"But I don't wish to marry — at all." Helene allowed her mother to wipe the tears from her cheeks.

"Hush, Helene. Surely you understand that to avoid marriage would leave you with no option but to enter a nunnery," her mother reasoned. "You cannot possibly want that for yourself. Don't you want a nice home of your own to manage? And babies?"

Helene's silence was her answer. Now Sisi felt the same surprise that she saw reflected back from her mother's face. She, Sisi, who knew Helene better than anyone in the world, had not suspected that her sister dreamed of such a solitary future. Eventually, her voice barely a whisper, Helene said, "I *had* thought often of the nunnery, Mamma."

Sisi saw two emotions battling for supremacy on her mother's face: in one moment there appeared sympathy for a shy, scholarly daughter. A daughter who remained quiet whenever in the presence of more than just the smallest of crowds. But then, there it was: the stronger of the two emotions chased sympathy away, and her mother's face set with a look of stony resolve. One must do one's duty. How many times had Sisi heard those words uttered by her mother's lips? A lady must accept the role that is required of her. Hadn't she, a duchess of Bavaria, always lived according to that creed, however unpleasant Papa had made it for her? This was how things were done.

When she spoke next, Mamma had regained her composure. "Helene, it's a noble idea. But the eldest daughter of the duke of Bavaria will *not* be allowed to waste away behind the walls of a nunnery. One does not simply send the emperor packing. You will marry Franz Joseph and you will be empress — it has been decided between our two houses."

"Just let her come round to the idea, Ludovika." Her father, Sisi could see, had grown bored of this discussion. "She's such a shy, scared little thing. Imagine if we married her off to some rough Prussian Count von Something or other . . . she wouldn't last a fortnight." Experience had shown the duke time and again that women would do what was expected of them. With an air of finality, he took a swig from his wine cup.

But Helene now lifted a hand to her face, concealing a fresh sob that set her narrow frame atremble. "God, why must I . . ."

The duchess put a hand on Helene's shoulder, though her face maintained a mask of composure. "My girl Néné, there now. No more tears, please. You have always been an obedient girl. You will see. You will love Vienna."

Lowering her hand, Helene looked up: "But I love it *here,* Mamma."

Sisi saw an instant's hesitation, a flickering hint of softness in her mother's eyes; the duchess was stricken. But Ludovika pushed that aside with masterful self-control. With a sigh, she pulled her hand from her daughter's shoulder and stood up taller, her shoulders drawing back. "We all must do our duty."

The two men continued their dinner while the duchess returned to her seat, her face pale but expressionless as she picked up her own fork. Sisi had lost her appetite. So, too, had Helene.

"There now, Helene," their mother said, breaking the taut silence. "I haven't told you the second part of the news."

"I don't wish to hear any more news, Mamma."

"But this you shall wish to hear. You shall not be going to court alone."

Now Helene looked up.

"Wouldn't you like a companion at court?" Ludovika's eyes darted from her eldest daughter to Sisi, who sat beside her, still clutching her hand. Sisi looked to her mother, her heart suddenly pounding as she felt the faintest embers of hope.

"Sisi and I shall accompany you." Their mother said, her voice upbeat. "Won't that make you feel better?"

Helene considered this and, after a long pause, nodded.

For her part, the thought thrilled Sisi, sending her heart on a gallop within her breast that made it hard to breathe. Leaving Possi. Traveling to the imperial court: a place of power and fashion and courtiers who exemplified both. A world entirely unlike her simple life in Bavaria. It was petrifying news, but it delighted her.

"How does that sound, Sisi?" The duchess looked at her younger daughter.

"I'd love to go," Sisi answered, her voice too eager, too full of enthusiasm. She squirmed in her chair, leaning toward Helene now. "Oh, Néné, won't we have fun together?"

"Fun?" Her mother knit her brows together, her tone turning to sternness. "Elisabeth, this is not some adventure for you, like those romances you read about."

Sisi felt her joy retreat, just slightly, at the

bite in her mother's tone.

"You understand that your role at court shall be to help your sister settle in. You will serve her as a lady-in-waiting serves a queen, do you understand?"

Sisi nodded, suppressing the smile that wanted to tug her lips upward. "Yes, Mamma." But inside, her heart leapt. She was to accompany Helene to her new life. Helene, Empress of Austria! She, Sisi, would be there to witness it.

"You must always make Helene look good," the duchess continued. "Do you understand?"

"I can do that," Sisi promised, wrapping her arms around Helene's thin, spindly shoulders. "Helene, do you hear that? I will be there with you!" The sisters held one another, and for the first time since the announcement, Helene managed a feeble smile.

"And" — the duchess leaned close to her younger daughter now — "I hope I do not need to remind you that there are plenty of ways to get into trouble at court, Elisabeth. Aunt Sophie is far less indulgent than I am, and she will be watching. You shall be there to serve your sister, and that is all. I do not wish to hear that you have fallen in love with some Hungarian count." The duchess frowned and Sisi flushed, avoiding Karl's burning gaze.

"I will be watching you, Elisabeth."

"I understand, Mamma."

"Good girl." Duchess Ludovika nodded, her stern expression softening into an approving smile. "No suitors for you. At least, not until you have helped your sister settle into her role."

Helene was excused from dinner and Sisi allowed to retire to the bedroom with her. They climbed the stairs in silence, both of them sorting through a tangle of thoughts and questions.

The Habsburg Court! For Sisi, the news had quickened her curiosity and stirred her restless spirit. Her mind raced into the imaginary scenes she'd witness beside her sister, the empress — the high-ceilinged halls where the waltz had been invented, the banquets, the dances attended by women in skirts so wide they looked like the bells of a cathedral. And her, Sisi, experiencing it all at the age of only fifteen.

"What a relief that you shall come with me." Helene clutched her sister's hand as they reached the top of the stairs and walked the candlelit hallway to their bedroom. Her sister's thoughts, Sisi noticed, seemed of a much less enthusiastic variety.

"Shall I call Agata for some wine?" Sisi pushed the heavy bedroom door, leaving it slightly ajar.

"No, Sisi. Just sit with me for a moment."

Helene lowered herself onto the large mahogany bed that they shared. "I am in such a state of shock."

"I will be with you, Néné." Sisi opened the curtains, allowing in the last delicate rays of summer sun. She stared out the window, looking over the quiet dusk that settled over Possenhofen. The woods beyond the meadow, skirting the border of Lake Starnberg, glowed an indigo blue under the descending veil of night. In the meadow, a farmer cut a slow path toward the village, pulling a tired horse beside him. The smoke of distant hearths coiled skyward in the background, issuing from the barely visible homes that dotted the wooded foothills of the Bavarian Alps. It was such a familiar tapestry; a beloved view, one Sisi could have re-created with her eyes shut. And tonight, knowing that she would be going far away, she savored it with a newfound affection. How many more times might she behold this view? Sisi wondered.

"You'll only be with me until you get a husband of your own. Then what happens?" Helene's worry tugged Sisi from her twilight reverie, and she turned back to her sister and the darkening bedroom. "He'll probably insist on taking you back to his own palace in Prussia or Saxony or Hungary. Then what shall I do?" Helene's lip quivered with the threat of fresh tears.

"You heard Mamma" — Sisi walked toward

her sister — "I will be at court to attend to you. I promise, I won't even *think* of marriage until you are settled and happy with at least half a dozen fat little Austrian crown princes and princesses." This promise appeared to temporarily assuage Helene's panic. But only for a moment.

"Marriage does sound awful, doesn't it?" Helene thought aloud, slipping out of her heavy dinner gown and allowing it to drop to the floor. Sisi couldn't help but notice her sister's figure, now exposed in just a thin shift and undergarments. It looked so pale and thin and fragile. And yet this would be the body that would be tasked with producing Austria's next emperor.

As if on cue, Karl appeared at the bedroom door, which Sisi chided herself for having left ajar.

"So that's the emperor's view on the wedding night?" Sensing that the power dynamics had somehow shifted in the household, Karl appeared reluctant to too directly challenge his sisters, but rather hovered at the threshold of their bedchamber.

"I heard you talking about your husband." He grinned at the partially undressed Helene, who quickly retreated behind a dressing screen.

"Go away, Gackl," Sisi snapped, tossing Helene's discarded shoe in his direction.

Karl ducked the shoe but remained in his

spot in the doorway. "No, not me. It's you two who are going away. Helene is off to Vienna to get pricked by Franz Joseph's Austrian wiener." Karl sniggered. "Poor innocent little Helene will likely catch syphilis from one of Franz's palace whores."

Sisi ignored her brother, speaking only to Helene. "And Gackl will probably never prick a single girl in his life. Who would ever want his pockmarked face and sour beer breath?"

This insult only further enraged Karl, who struck back. "I wouldn't look forward to my wedding night if I were you, Helene. Franz Joseph is the emperor, you know, and therefore he gets whatever he wants. How do you think *you* shall compare to one of his well-practiced courtesans?" The sight of Sisi wincing seemed to encourage Karl. "And Sisi, who knows who you'll get plucked by? Neither one of you even knows what must happen, do you? Why do you think Mamma always talks about how she cried on her wedding night?"

Cowed, but even more so infuriated, Sisi stood to her full height and crossed the bedroom toward Karl. When she spoke, it was with more authority than she actually felt. "And how do you suppose the emperor will look upon the brother who has tormented his beloved bride? I will be sure to tell him about our brother, named after a rooster, and deserving of a good pecking."

Surprised by the vehemence of her anger, by the command in her voice, Karl turned and left their room.

"Who taught him to be so vile?" Sisi wondered aloud, slowly unclenching her fists as Karl's figure receded. She heard the sound of faint whimpering behind the dressing screen. "For goodness' sake, Néné, come out from behind that screen." Sisi flopped onto the bed, already exhausted in the role of supporting her sister. It would be a demanding position at court. "Do not take a word of that to heart — Karl is just jealous that we have an invitation from the emperor, while he's stuck here with the babies."

Helene emerged from behind the dressing screen, her black eyes round with horror. "It does sound awful, though, doesn't it?"

"What does? Ruling an empire? Wearing the finest crowns and gowns in all of Europe? Dancing to the imperial violins all night?" Sisi ran her fingers through her hair, removing her braids and allowing her heavy waves to tumble loose around her shoulders.

"No. What Karl said . . . the wedding night," Helene whispered.

"I don't know." Sisi paused. Their mother had only ever implied things, offering scanty scraps about what the ordeal of the wedding night actually entailed. Insinuations that both frightened and confused Sisi. Words such as "duty" and "submission." Actions that required "forbearance," that must be "endured for the sake of one's husband and family." But then the maid had given Sisi quite a different account. "Agata tells me that she's heard that it can be . . . well, *nice.* That it's not all bad."

"How did she hear that?" Helene asked, eyes widening.

"Oh, they talk about that sort of stuff all the time in the kitchen. It's only those of us in the front of the house who know nothing about it." A ludicrous arrangement, Sisi thought, when it was the girls in the front of the house whose bodies were burdened with the important duties of dynasty-making.

Helene thought about this. "Karl seems to know an awful lot."

Sisi tilted her head. "Not from experience, of that much we can be certain."

Helene allowed a pinched laugh before once more deflating. "Do you think, when I become Franz's wife, that I will have to . . . you know . . . ?"

"Yes, Helene," Sisi said, toneless. "You will."

Helene appeared freshly demoralized. "I hope we have a very long engagement."

Sisi attempted a cheerful manner, speaking as she undressed for bed. "Don't fret. You won't have to do it much, Helene. Just until you give Franz some sons."

Helene considered this. "Think about our

family — there's me, you, Karl, Marie, Mathilde, Sophie-Charlotte, and baby Max. Can you believe that Mamma and Papa have done it *seven* times?" Helene asked.

"No, that shocks me," Sisi answered, shaking her head, and the two of them erupted in giggles.

"Well, I'm glad to see you two girls in good spirits once more." Duchess Ludovika appeared at the doorway with fresh candles for her daughters. "Hopefully you've resigned yourself to the ghastly fate of marrying an emperor, Néné?"

"Mamma!" Sisi waved their mother into the bedroom. The duchess deposited the candles on the nightstand and kissed each of her daughters on the forehead. "Don't stay up too late, girls." She made her way to the door, pulling its handle as she exited. "And don't forget."

"We know, we know," Sisi chimed in response. "Our prayers."

"Good night." Ludovika smiled, her head disappearing behind the shutting door.

Sisi climbed into bed and kicked the covers back, her body warm from the excitement of the evening and the balmy summer air. She sighed, watching her sister where she combed her dark hair before the streaked mirror.

Sensing that Helene's initial panic had dissipated a bit, that her spirits might even be lifting, Sisi broached the topic once more.

"Really, Helene, the news is not that terrible. An emperor? You would have thought they had told you that you were betrothed to marry the local butcher, the way you responded to the news."

Helene thought about this as she replaced her ivory comb on the nightstand and joined Sisi in bed. "At least if I married the local butcher I could remain close to home. I could come home to Possi for dinner every Sunday."

"Yes, and you and your butcher-husband could bring the slaughtered animal for the dinner meal," Sisi added.

"And Karl would leave me alone, lest he fear that he might end up in the stew," Helene added, reluctantly joining Sisi in a giggle.

After several moments Sisi spoke, adjusting her long hair that fell around her on the pillow. "I will miss it here, though."

Helene nodded, her features knit in an anxious expression as they reflected the flickering of the candlelight.

"I wonder what Franz is like," Sisi mused, remembering the shy, cinnamon-haired boy of years ago. "It's all so surreal." Sisi envisioned the meeting — Helene and this cousin who had grown into the emperor. Meanwhile all of the jilted princesses, countesses, and marquesses of court would gather round, looking on, sniffing for any sign of weakness on Helene's part, any opening through which to launch a counterassault. Would Helene summon the nerve to charm this young ruler — Europe's most powerful, most desirable young bachelor? She'd have to. Helene had no other choice.

"Just think about it," Sisi thought aloud, "Helene, born as Duchess of Bavaria from the House of Wittelsbach, becomes Empress of Austria."

Helene offered no response to this, burrowing under the covers even though the night was a warm one.

"Néné, you're awfully quiet." Sisi reached across the bed, snuggling into her sister's frame. Oh, how she would miss her. But she swallowed that sadness. Wasn't her job now to be strong for Néné? "Come now, talk to me. How are you feeling?"

After a pause, her sister spoke. "I'm not feeling very . . . imperial."

"Oh, Néné. My shy, quiet sister. I won't allow you such self-doubt. You don't even realize how sweet you are. Or how lovely." Sisi's voice was jarringly loud compared to her sister's as she declared, determinedly: "You shall be splendid. We shall present the emperor with a bride so lovely, he will say he has never seen her equal."

Later that night, after Helene had slipped off into a fretful sleep, Sisi rose from bed and stared out the window, enlivened by her thoughts and the low-hanging moon that cast a bright glow over the fields and hillsides. Sleep eluded her, as it often did. And on the other side of the window, the night waited, warm and serene, luring her out of the house.

Sisi fumbled in the dark for her dressing gown, careful not to creak the wooden floorboards as she did so. She slid her feet into her favorite slippers, a pair of plush, red-velvet clogs. These tattered dressing shoes, a gift on her fifteenth birthday, carried her across the earth whenever she set out on these solitary midnight adventures. These slippers were stained by pieces of the Possenhofen earth, its grass and mud permanently stuck to the soles. Sisi decided, in that moment, that these red slippers would come with her to court. In that way, she laughed to herself, she might always be able to tread on her beloved Bavarian soil.

Outside an owl droned its melancholy melody. The crickets in the fields serenaded one another, their bodies like small violins whose nocturnal waltzes had existed long before Johann Strauss had begun composing in Vienna. The frogs in nearby Lake Starnberg belched and blurted out their familiar amorous rhapsodies. Sisi spread her arms wide and looked up at the moon, laughing, reveling in and embracing everything about this night.

Sisi's parents had not raised her to be strictly religious. Spiritual, yes, but not dogmatic. Her father had even shown himself to be lenient when it came to the Reformers in the duchy, the Protestants who so brazenly flouted the Catholic Church and received punishment for doing so elsewhere.

But they had imbued in Sisi an appreciation for the Almighty and His presence all around her. While God felt elusive and difficult to find in some of the dank old churches — His words garbled in impenetrable Latin — Sisi felt His undeniable presence in the majesty of the mountains, in the inevitability of sunrise and the softness of moonlight. God was the unseen power that set in motion the natural world; the seasons that ripened and shifted, each one beautiful in its own way; the chamois that leapt uphill without tiring or the stallion that outran the wind.

Oh, how she would miss Possi!

Sisi remained outside, tracing the perimeter of the squat white castle in silence for quite some time, when suddenly her musings were interrupted by a rustling noise. A sound decidedly different from the crickets and the owls. A human sound. She turned and saw him: a figure gliding across the meadow, in the direction of the village. It was dark, but Sisi knew immediately whose retreating shape she saw. "Papa," she said. Quietly, so he wouldn't hear her. Off, most likely, to see some female consort of his. Sisi sighed.

"Please let Franz be more faithful to Helene than Papa has been to Mamma," Sisi begged, sending the prayer out into the warm, still night.

II.

Once I was so young and rich
In love of life and hope;
I thought nothing could match my strength,
The whole world was open to me.
      — Empress Elisabeth "Sisi" of Austria

CHAPTER TWO

*IMPERIAL RESORT AT BAD ISCHL, UPPER
AUSTRIA
AUGUST 1853*

Sisi found it hard not to grow disheartened
when she watched her sister, sitting beside
her in the coach and trembling like a frightened doe before the archer's bow.

"You're going to be lovely, Néné. But you
must *smile!*" The duchess seemed to be
wrestling the same anxiety as she spoke to
her elder daughter. Helene offered no reply.

"Just a few more hours now, then we'll be
able to stop and freshen up. We'll change our
clothes before we arrive at the imperial
resort." The duchess managed an upbeat
tone, but Sisi noticed that her mother did
not attempt a smile. Did not mask the sever-
ity of the headache that had plagued her for
most of the journey.

Her mother had spent most of the long
hours in the coach with her eyes fixed shut
— wincing at each smack of wheel against

the rutted dirt road, massaging her temples with weary fingers. When at last Mamma did open them, her eyes were uneasy, darting back and forth between her two daughters. Was Sisi imagining it, or was Ludovika studying them, as if comparing her two girls? Was that merely a jostle of the coach, or did Mamma shake her head ever so slightly, sighing, as her eyes moved from Sisi to Helene?

Their resemblance had seemed to evaporate the instant they had set out from Possenhofen Castle. Sisi, invigorated by the journey and eager to meet her aunt and cousin, had grown more wide-eyed and merry throughout the weeks-long trip. The fresh air along the Alpine road agreed with her; her cheeks flushed a rosy hue, her honey-brown eyes shone alert and vibrant, and her voice was cheerful as she remarked on the fields and villages they passed.

Beside her slouched Helene, who had been too nervous to either eat or sleep very well on the journey, and whose ashen skin appeared almost translucent against the drab black of her mourning clothes.

"We'll get out of these black mourning clothes first thing," their mother said, repeating herself. As if a wardrobe change would somehow transform Helene into the imperial bride she needed to become.

Sisi kept herself occupied in the nerve-fraught coach by staring out the windows and

71

imagining what life must be like in each Alpine home she passed. While the farms appeared idyllic, the goat herders had it the best, she decided. For the goat herders were free to set out each morning from their cliffside chalets and march into the hills. Armed with a block of cheese, a loaf of bread, and a skin of wine, they could wander and explore the mountains and creeks with no one to answer to. Or they could find an open, sunlit field and lie down on the grass, passing away the hours under a sky so close that Sisi longed to reach up and pull some of its blueness down into her hands.

"Bummerl would love these fields." Sisi thought of the horse she'd left behind and felt a stab of longing for home. "We could get lost in them for hours." Neither her mother nor her sister replied. "Mamma, will I be able to ride in Vienna?" Sisi asked.

"I don't know, Sisi." The duchess answered dismissively, her head tilted back against the upholstered wall of the coach. "I would imagine that you will be much too preoccupied to be thinking about your own leisure activities. You will have an entire court to meet, and years' worth of etiquette to learn. You think the Austrian aristocracy gives a fig about your riding? No. They expect to receive a well-mannered, well-spoken young lady. You and your sister must concern yourselves with learning the ways of the

Habsburgs."

"I don't know how I will bear it if I'm not able to ride," Sisi mused aloud. But it was a mistake to say it, and she knew so immediately when she saw her mother's eyes flash open.

"You shall do whatever is expected of you," her mother snapped.

"Mamma," Sisi started, taken aback by the duchess's recent irritability. Her mother sighed by way of reply, shutting her eyes once more. A tense silence rocked with them in the coach.

Eventually, the duchess spoke. "I apologize, Sisi. It's just that . . . well, I fear that . . ." She hesitated, then said, "I only wish for you two girls to succeed."

Sisi considered this. How different could court life be? They were, after all, the daughters of a duke. And besides, such obvious worrying on her mother's part would not help Helene gain confidence before the important meeting with her groom. Speaking with more self-assurance than she felt, Sisi answered: "Don't be nervous, Mamma. Of course we shall succeed." She looked determinedly into her sister's eyes as if to convince Helene of this statement's inevitability. "Besides, as you said, we will have Aunt Sophie to help us."

The duchess now opened her eyes, and the equivocal look she gave her daughter did not offer any reassurance. "Let's *hope* that we have Sophie's backing," was Ludovika's response.

Sisi felt for her mother, because she knew that it was on her two daughters' behalf that the duchess worried so acutely. Ludovika's initial joy following the invitation to court had been whittled down over the past month, replaced now by a sharp tongue and scrutinizing stare. Sisi's and Helene's previously permissible — even customary — behavior now seemed to elicit harsh chidings. Like when, on the road, Sisi had gotten out of the carriage to help the groom water the horses, and had unwittingly splashed her dress.

"You do not water the horses like a stable boy!" It had been just the latest in a recent litany of unanticipated rebukes and censures.

"You will not answer back when your Aunt Sophie speaks to you."

"You will not gallop down the hallways at court like a wild ruffian."

"You will not appear at dinner dirty, like a country peasant."

The duchess, usually so measured, seemed to wrestle with some undeniable fear when it came to her elder sister. Days before they'd set off from Possenhofen, Sisi had overheard her parents whispering in her father's study.

"But what if they inadvertently say something to offend him? Or worse, to offend Sophie? They know nothing of the stringency

74

of court protocol."

"They aren't farmhands, Ludovika, they are perfectly nice girls," the duke had replied. "And of aristocratic birth, might I add."

"Yes, but they are so naïve, Max. Instead of language and dancing lessons, we let them ride horses through the fields and hook fish in the lake." Ludovika, pacing the cramped study, had spoken with an urgency that Sisi had rarely heard in her mother's authoritative voice. "They've hardly seen the world outside of Possenhofen. Sophie will have their game in less than half an hour."

"That's precisely what your sister wants." The duke shrugged, staring wearily into the fire. "Sophie wants a wife for her son whom she can control. She'll see Helene's naïveté as a positive — something she can use to her advantage."

Ludovika had considered this in a brooding silence. Eventually she sighed, saying: "Max, I'm beginning to think this is not the best fate for our daughter. Perhaps we thought too much of the opportunity, without considering what such a future meant for Helene. And *Sisi.*"

Sisi's spine stiffened at the mention of her name — at the fact that her mother's voice now carried outright panic. She crouched closer to the study door. "I shudder to think how Sisi will appear at court. Why, she is just a child. And a wild, free-spirited one at that.

Why, she can barely string five words together in French. And she's *never* danced with anyone other than her tutor."

Sisi bit on her lip, irritated by this. She was young, yes. And what her mother was saying wasn't inaccurate. But surely she wouldn't prove such a disappointment. In fact, she decided right then to prove her mother's fears wrong.

"One does not say no when the Imperial Mother comes and asks for one's daughter for marriage," the duke reasoned. "They'll be fine."

"Max. We have found so many faults with our own parents over the years. Putting us together in this . . . *marriage.* I know perfectly well that you were in love with another woman. And you know that I was terribly homesick, and cried every day. Aren't we now doing the same thing?"

Sisi couldn't help but peek her head around the opened doorway now, eager to see her father's response to such a raw, unguarded question. "What choice do we have?" The duke shrugged his shoulders, taking a long inhale from his pipe. "When you have daughters, and a title, that's what you do."

Sisi had remained there, just outside the door, as the moments passed, her parents sitting in silence beside a dying fire. Eventually, her mother had said: "How I shall miss them. If only we could keep Sisi a few more years.

She is just a child."

"I shall miss them, too," the duke had sighed, and Sisi had been surprised — even touched — to hear the confession. "But it is what's best for them. We must try to be happy with the opportunity."

The duchess, still perched on the arm of her husband's leather chair, remained silent.

"Helene will do better than you think, Ludovika. And Sisi will take care of her. That one is smart. Perhaps a little wild, you're right. But Sophie will rein her in. Baptism by fire, that's what I call it."

Word spread like a plague, as gossip tends to do in a small town, and the entire population had turned up to see them off. Some of the peasants and townspeople had smiled, some of them had wept, but all of them had blessed the Wittelsbach women with prayers, waving small miniatures of the blue and white Bavarian flag.

Sisi, her trunks loaded in the second coach, embraced her father and her younger sisters, not knowing how long it would be before she saw them again.

"You're going to win them all over at court, Sisi." The duke pulled his daughter into a hug, holding her longer than she'd ever known him to. Perhaps he had hugged her like this in her childhood, but not recently enough for her to remember it. Sisi, sensing the genuine warmth of his feelings, felt her body soften into his embrace. Suddenly, uncharacteristically, she hugged her papa back, wishing he would not let go.

"I don't know what I shall do without you around here, my wild girl," he said, his voice cracking.

"Oh, Papa." With that, Sisi began to weep, burrowing her head into his shoulder. "Please take care of Bummerl for me, will you? And when she's old enough to ride, Marie may have him as her own horse."

"That's right, my girl." The duke patted her long hair. For the first time in a long time, his eyes were glossy with tears, but not from drink. "You go show those Habsburgs how to ride the stallions they keep in the royal stables."

"I'll miss you, Papa." Sisi held on to his hand, looking up into the hazel eyes that she'd always been told she had inherited. "Will you please take care of yourself, Papa?"

The duke lowered his eyes, nodding.

"You promise, Papa?" She squeezed his hand.

"I promise that I shall try." When he looked at her again, he had regained his composure. "You just remember one thing. The House of Wittelsbach is a proud house. You've got nothing to feel inferior about in front of those Austrians, you hear me?"

"Yes, Papa." Sisi squeezed his hand tighter,

reluctant to let it fall away. Finally, it was the duke who ended the farewell. "Go now, my girl. Go and make your old papa proud. I know that you will."

"Goodbye, little Max." Sisi kissed the pudgy cheeks of her baby brother. "And you, Marie, and Mathilde, and Sophie-Charlotte." She kissed each of the little children, running her fingers through their soft, downy hair. "When I see you all next, you might not even remember me." She wiped a tear from her cheek, hoping that her sadness would not compound Helene's dread.

When Sisi approached Karl for a farewell, he pulled her into a hug. Startled by this gesture of fraternal affection, she put her arms around him. "Goodbye, Gackl," she said. "Take care of Papa while Mamma is with us."

He whispered into her ear: "I won't have to take care of him for long. You'll all be back before the farmers have cleared the autumn harvest."

That seemed more like the Karl she knew. Energized by this challenge, Sisi stiffened her posture and cocked her head to one side. "What makes you say that?"

Karl's glance slid sideways, toward Helene, before he looked back at Sisi. "The emperor is going to get one look at the homely, crying fiancée his mommy picked out for him and send you all back to Bavaria."

If anything, the taunt had only solidified Sisi's determination to achieve success for herself and her sister. Karl would not have the satisfaction of gloating in their failure. No, they would not return to Possenhofen Castle — Sisi vowed to herself — unless it was in the royal coach, emblazoned with the imperial seal of the Habsburgs.

"Girls, look! There's the river." The duchess pointed out the coach window through a canopy of leafy trees. The appearance of the Traun River signaled their approach to the outskirts of the Alpine city of Bad Ischl, where the imperial court was installed for the summer. The coach had begun its descent into the valley.

"The waters in Bad Ischl are therapeutic." The duchess studied the slow-moving current that now hugged the roadside. "That's why Franz chose it for his summer retreat. Wouldn't it be nice if we had time to take in some of the waters? We could all use a little refreshment right now." She rubbed her forehead in a slow circular motion.

The coach rattled onward in a determined course down the narrow mountain pass, sinking slowly into a valley framed on all sides by jagged green mountains. The panorama grew wider and more open as the coach carried them into the broad bowl of the populated valley below. Helene, who had not spoken since her very meager breakfast, looked out the window now. "We aren't there yet, are we, Mamma?"

"We're close, darling. We are outside the town." The duchess pointed farther down the road, where the outline of yellow limestone buildings sat nestled in the valley like a large cluster of edelweiss flowers.

"That is Bad Ischl. The mountain town fit for an emperor," the duchess mused, watching the village as they approached. Individual buildings now began to take shape, and Sisi spotted a church spire rising up above the other structures, piercing the blue skyline like a thin stone finger.

Up ahead on the side of the road sat a modest limestone building, like a roadside tavern or café of sorts.

"Stop the coach!" Ludovika called out the window above the rattle of the horses and wheels. The groom obeyed, and the carriage slowed to a halt. Now the faint sound of birdsong, mixed with the quiet hum of the Traun River, filled the silence around them.

"We'll change our clothes here at this tavern, girls, so we're fresh when we arrive at the imperial retreat."

"I can't wait to get out of this black," Sisi admitted, already removing the dark cap she'd traveled in and shaking her curls loose. "Black is stifling in this heat. And so bland — I want to put on my most colorful dress."

"Don't be immodest, Elisabeth." The sharp look her mother shot in Sisi's direction told her that she'd once more irritated the duchess.

The carriage door opened and the groom extended his arm to assist the ladies out into the sunny afternoon.

"Hans, where is the other coach?" The duchess exited first, looking from the groom to the empty mountain road. Nearby, a short man with a stocky build emerged from the tavern, intrigued by his new visitors.

When Sisi stepped down onto the road beside her mother, she noted that the second coach, the one carrying Agata and the luggage, was not in sight.

"If you please, my lady." The groom, Hans, held Helene's hand as she stepped tenuously down from the coach.

"Well, Hans?" Ludovika looked at the groom. "The second coach?"

Now Hans lowered his eyes. "Madame . . . we lost the others."

"You *lost* them? What do you mean, you lost them?" The duchess, in spite of her headache, appeared suddenly alert, as alert as Sisi had ever seen her. She threw a glance at the tavernkeeper before looking back to the driver. "What do you mean, Hans? How?"

"We got separated, Duchess Ludovika."

"Tell me, Hans, how does one lose sight of a giant coach pulled by four horses?"

The groom kept his gaze fixed on the muddy road as he answered: "You see, my lady, we stopped so many times on the road . . . on account of Your Excellency's headaches, and such." Hans stuffed both hands into his trouser pockets.

"That doesn't explain anything. Where are our dresses?"

"We seem to have become separated a short while ago, my lady. During one of our unexpected stops."

The duchess cursed under her breath, pacing a small circle in front of the coach. When she looked once more at her daughters, their road-weary frames standing opposite her in their drab black clothes, her entire face seemed to sag.

"Not to worry though, my lady," the groom said. "I'm sure the dresses made it safely to the palace already."

"Yes, but we don't need them to be safely at the palace, we need them to be on *us* when we enter the palace!" The duchess fumed, looking from the groom to her eldest daughter.

"Helene, don't cry. Oh please, don't cry." The duchess folded her daughter into a hug, looking to Sisi with eyes that did not mask her panic.

"I've been in this dress for weeks, Mamma, I can't wear this to meet him."

"You look lovely, Helene."

"Rubbish, Mamma."

"The emperor will commend you on the fact that you are so dutifully mourning a relative. And he will find you modest and humble. Isn't that so, Sisi?" Ludovika, frantic, looked to her younger daughter.

"That's right." Sisi nodded, picking up the line started by her mother. "Néné, it is my sister's good and gentle spirit that I want Franz to see — not a head and neck full of jewels."

"Precisely," the duchess concurred.

But Helene was unconvinced. Her eyes fixed on the ground, she moaned: "Oh, why did I have to be born first?"

"Helene." The duchess, exasperated, gripped her daughter's narrow shoulders. "You cannot change the order in which you were born any more than you can change the configuration of the stars. You must not lament such a thing."

"But it's rotten luck, Mamma. I don't *want* to be the empress."

"Helene, do you think I spent my life complaining that my elder sister got to marry a Habsburg and I had to . . ." Ludovika paused, looking to Sisi. "Well, never mind that. All I mean to say is that we must live the lives that are intended for us. And we must live them well."

"I'm ill suited for the life that was chosen for me," Helene answered, chin jerking to the side. "I wish you could have just lied and said that Sisi was the elder."

Sisi exchanged a look with her mother over the top of Helene's head. It was worse than just Helene's pinched frowns and unflatteringly drab wardrobe; if her sister continued in this despondent mood, Sisi was certain that Franz's eyes would look elsewhere.

The church bell tower chimed three times as their carriage lurched and lumbered down the cobbled village streets, sounding the hour as if to welcome the duchess and her daughters to Bad Ischl.

The town itself was a hive of activity, swollen with the influx of Austrians who had descended on it in the hopes of glimpsing the visiting emperor. It was certainly more crowded than the small, sleepy square in Possenhofen. Through the carriage window Sisi spotted rows of clean village shops painted in crisp shades of white and yellow. Hausfraus yelled to small children as they crossed the streets, arms burdened by cargo of crispy bread loaves, links of meat, and fresh fruit still warm from the summer sun. Small boys bearing red cheeks and short-cropped lederhosen britches weaved between passing carriages and horses, more preoccupied with the candy shop windows than the calls of their mothers or the foot and horse traffic that swerved around them.

"We're close now." The duchess observed the scene through the window, stitching her hands into a tight knot in her lap. "Helene, when we arrive, you must smile. Especially when you meet Franz, understood?"

Helene nodded, once. An indecisive, noncommittal gesture.

As the carriage turned off the main esplanade, the traffic thinned and the structures changed from commercial to residential. Modest homes lined the cobbled lane, their windows ajar and their light-colored walls trellised with climbing ropes of ivy. The afternoon sun still hung high in the sky, pouring down over the residents who sat perched on their stoops in front of overstuffed flower boxes and drawn curtains. They watched the modest carriage roll by with only moderate interest.

A heavy wrought-iron gate waited at the end of the esplanade. If the townspeople hadn't taken much note as Sisi's coach had passed, the dozen armed imperial guards stationed at the gate appeared as if they surely would.

The Kaiservilla, or Imperial Palace, was a sprawling complex set off from the main esplanade, just at the seam of where the village seeped into Alpine wilderness. The complex hugged the base of the stark, craggy mountains that framed the valley fields on one side before gently sloping down to the banks of the Traun River on the other side. The main structure of the Kaiservilla, a building of creamy-yellow limestone, had been a nobleman's home, constructed in the popular neoclassical style.

Sisi had been told by her mother that when the young emperor had first visited the thermal waters of this town, he had declared the spot to be "heaven on earth." Hearing her son's pronouncement, Sophie had swiftly bought the largest home in the area and had relocated the court there for the warmest months of the year, swapping thermal waters and clean mountain air for city stink and the threat of fever.

"Here we are, girls." The duchess barely breathed the words as the coach rolled to a halt outside the gate.

Sisi studied the waiting guards in their white uniforms, starched to impossible stiffness and trimmed in red and gold silk. Imagine, she thought to herself, having a group of soldiers like this always stationed outside your gate. Must one answer to them every time one wished to leave or return home?

Barking out a quick order to Hans the driver, a mustached guard now approached the coach, eyes darting between the three road-weary women who sat on the other side of its window. "May I?" He signaled with a gloved hand that he wished to open the carriage door. Ludovika nodded.

"Good day." Sisi's mother sat up as the guard opened the door, her chin angling upward. Sisi marveled at the air of authority her mother had so suddenly summoned, as if the anxiety of the preceding days and hours had been merely a bothersome cloak that the duchess now shrugged off.

"I am Her Majesty Duchess Ludovika of Bavaria, from the House of Wittelsbach and sister of the Archduchess of Austria, Sophie of the House of Habsburg-Lorraine. My two daughters, Their Majesties the Duchesses of Bavaria, accompany me on the special invitation from His Imperial Highness, Emperor Franz Joseph, and his mother, the Archduchess Sophie."

"Your Grace." The young soldier saluted, clicking his heels together. "We have been expecting you."

"If you please." Her mother raised a hand, as if struck by an idea. "Has our other coach arrived before us?"

The guard nodded. "Yes. Less than an hour ago, Madame."

"Please direct us to it," Ludovika said, her tone brightening a bit as she looked to Sisi and Helene. "It carries our trunks, and we must change before we enter the palace."

The guard raised a gloved hand, his tone courteous but unmoving. "My apologies, Duchess Ludovika. We have been instructed to direct you immediately into the front hall, where Her Majesty the Archduchess Sophie awaits your arrival." With that, he looked at the driver, a tight nod of his chin, as he stepped back. "Drive on!"

Ludovika scowled, whispering to her daughters as the door shut and the carriage rolled forward onto the property, "I tried."

The horses' hooves clopped heavily across the cobblestoned forecourt as the walls of the castle complex absorbed the coach, pulling them into a cold hug of limestone and brick. Though the property was spacious enough, Sisi did note with mild surprise that the home was not any larger than Possenhofen Castle.

Regardless, it was not the size of the structure that mattered. Sisi sensed, when rolling through the front gate, the imperial presence. The numerous and intangible indices of Franz Joseph's power hung over the property like a mist or shadow that loomed all around — difficult to touch or point to, yet impossible to deny. The flags of Franz Joseph's many kingdoms colored the front wall: Austria, Hungary, Croatia, Bohemia, Venetia, Lombardy, Galicia. Clusters of guardsmen, rigid in their white and red uniforms, marched determinedly on various errands across the grounds. It felt more like a miniature city than one man's home. Servants hustled, dogs barked, secretaries and valets hurried around the yard as they administered their tasks. A general air of busyness filled the forecourt and its surrounding buildings, reminding the visitor that this remote mountain town was now suddenly the heart of the empire — and all because one person was in residence.

And they, too, were here on the emperor's business. The ruler of all of this had requested that a young girl and her family come to him, traversing grueling roads from Bavaria to Bad Ischl, prepared to wed a stranger. And they had obeyed. Surely not because that shy, rust-haired boy from years earlier was powerful enough to impose a fate on any of them, but because the position he now occupied imbued him with an almost otherworldly authority. And Helene, his bride, would now possess that same, deified status. The magnitude of her sister's new role suddenly overwhelmed Sisi, and she fell silent, cowed before this daunting specter of imperial authority.

The horses heeled and the carriage stopped, signaling the end of their journey and the beginning of their work. "All right girls, here we are." The duchess seemed to have shaken her burdensome migraine, for now she sat tall and spoke in short, clipped commands. "You heard the guard — Sophie . . . the Archduchess . . . is waiting for us." Ludovika stepped out of the carriage. Seeing that her daughters did not follow, she paused. "Come now. Helene?"

Helene remained seated. "Mother, I can't . . ."

"But you must. Come now."

Helene shook her head, the rest of her body unmoving.

"You are here to see your cousin, Franz, and your Aunt Sophie," the duchess replied with an impatient sigh. "Think of it that way."

"Yes, my cousin and aunt who happen to be the emperor and the archduchess of Austria."

The duchess glanced around, ensuring that no one listened, before she leaned close and whispered into the coach. "Helene, *they* chose *you.* You are *their* guest, responding to *their* invitation. You have more right to be here than any other person inside this complex."

Helene closed her eyes, shaking her head once from side to side. The most timid, most modest of protests.

"Helene, we've made it this far. You *will* go through with this." The duchess looked once more over her shoulder, offering a curt smile to a secretary who passed, his suit jacket emblazoned with a golden crest of a double-headed eagle. Sisi guessed this to be the Habsburg family crest.

"Néné." Sisi took her sister's hand in her own. "We'll be together."

Helene latched on with cold fingers, her

grip stronger than usual. "Don't leave me, Sisi."

"I won't." Sisi squeezed her hand back, an unspoken communication. "Now, let's go meet your fiancé, Néné."

"That's another thing, girls." Ludovika leaned close, whispering so that a passing guard wouldn't overhear. "No more of this *Néné* and *Sisi*. From now on, you are Helene and Elisabeth — daughters of the Bavarian Duke Maximilian, House of Wittelsbach."

"Really, Mamma?" Sisi asked, stepping out of the carriage and pulling her sister with her. "Even when we are alone? It seems a bit —"

"Yes, even when you are alone, Elisabeth," Ludovika hissed. But even more stinging than her tone was the look she fixed on her younger daughter. "And you will *not* shame our house by arguing with your superiors, do you understand?" Ludovika patted her skirt with a jerky, impatient hand, making a futile attempt to undo days-old wrinkles. For her part, Sisi was cowed to silence, and offered nothing more than a feeble nod.

"You are now two young duchesses at the imperial court, and you shall act accordingly. That means no more childish names." The duchess said this with a stern, clipped tone, but Sisi thought her mother's eyes betrayed a hint of sadness. "And it means no more whining, Helene. And no more answering back, Elisabeth, *especially* not to your Aunt Sophie.

Am I clear?"

"Yes, Mamma," they answered in unison.

"Good," Ludovika nodded. "Now, let's not keep the emperor waiting. I'm sure he is quite anxious to meet his bride."

The guard at the front shut the door behind them, closing them into a cool, high-ceilinged hall. Sisi squinted, her eyes slow to adjust to the darkness of the room after the stark sunlight of the outer courtyard. The din of the yards was now blocked by the thick walls of the palace, and they stood in silence for several moments, a hesitant trio wondering how to proceed.

A wigged secretary clipped forward and startled Sisi as his voice rang out. "Duchess Ludovika," he said, bowing. "Please, if you and your daughters would be so gracious as to follow me?"

Without a word, the trio fell in line behind the secretary as he led them across the hall. They moved next into what appeared to be a receiving area, its cream-colored walls bare except for the same array of flags that Sisi had seen outside — the many kingdoms of Franz Joseph's realm.

They cleared this room by way of a high-ceilinged doorway and immediately stepped into a much smaller room. This one was flooded with light, walled in by floor-to-ceiling windows, and Sisi blinked, her eyes having already adjusted to the dark, cool hallway.

"Your Majesty, Archduchess Sophie, may I present to you Her Royal Highness, the Duchess Ludovika Wilhelmine, wife of Duke Maximilian of Bavaria from the House of Wittelsbach."

Sisi's eyes followed the direction in which this secretary projected his voice, and she noticed, for the first time, the seated figure of her aunt. Sophie was tucked in at a small table, a man on each side. Their faces were lit by the splash of afternoon sunshine that seeped in through the French doors and floor-to-ceiling windows. The male companions, one quite young, the other quite old, must have been a military officer and a minister, Sisi guessed. There were others in the room, too. Sisi's eyes moved next to the corner where, removed from the seated party, stood a gray-haired woman, her complexion chalky and her face pinched. Unlike the standing footmen sprinkled around the room, wigged men who kept their eyes diverted and expressionless, this gray-haired woman studied the three Bavarian newcomers unashamedly, rendering her verdict with a tight jaw and a mistrustful gaze. Who was she? Sisi wondered.

Sisi's eyes turned back toward her aunt, who looked on the newly arrived trio with an appraising expression, one of curiosity, but not delight. At the secretary's introduction, Ludovika stepped forward, fanning her black skirt wide and curtsying low with a grace that surprised Sisi.

"And her daughters." The secretary, seemingly unsure of which girl was which, waved them forward simultaneously. "Their Royal Highnesses, Helene Caroline Therese and Elisabeth Amalie Eugenie, Duchesses in Bavaria, of the House of Wittelsbach." The two girls followed the example set by their mother and curtsied in unison. Sisi found it odd, even slightly entertaining, to hear herself referred to with such a lofty string of words.

An almost imperceptible flicker of Sophie's forefinger signified that they were to enter the room and approach her at the table. With the duchess leading, the three of them crossed the threshold and moved toward where Sophie sat.

"Slowly, girls," Ludovika whispered between Helene and Sisi. "Heads down," she reminded them.

But Sisi could not resist the temptation to steal a glance upward at the figure she approached. The archduchess was as Sisi remembered her: a more sharp-featured version of her mother. Like Ludovika, Sophie wore her hair so that her face was framed by tight ringlets — light brown laced with wisps of gray — that met in a low bun at the nape of her head.

Sophie's salmon-colored gown draped over a broad crinoline hoopskirt; emerald earrings danced beside her rouged cheeks as she jerked her head tightly from side to side, eyeing each visitor in turn. She had narrow eyes that seemed more probing and less inclined to smile than Ludovika's.

Sophie was to speak first, according to Ludovika, but the woman did not appear in any rush to break the silence, so that the only sound in the room was the coordinated clicking of the visitors' heels as they crossed the marble floor. The three of them paused several feet before their hostess. Sisi was close enough now that she could smell Sophie's perfume, a potent mixture of sweet floral scents. Up close, Sophie was wider than Ludovika in the bosom and hips, most likely as a result of the imperial banquets she now enjoyed with her son. In fact, the table at which she sat was cluttered with teapots, biscuits, miniature cakes, and platters of nuts and fruit. It struck Sisi how hungry she was after their hours on the road.

A small cream-colored dog sat in the imperial mother's lap, haughtily observing the three silent visitors from his perch before the tea service. Sophie's ringed fingers stroked the pet's thick fur, and at one point she picked up the small animal to whisper an inaudible phrase of affection into its pointed ear.

Ludovika cleared her throat, and Sophie turned from her tiny dog to look at them once more. "So, the Bavarians have arrived." As this statement left little opening for a reply, the three visitors remained silent.

"What is this?" Sophie continued, "Ludovika, are you so interested in my palace floors that you won't even look up at your old sister?"

At this remark, Ludovika lifted her eyes and smiled at her sister. "Hello, Sophie. It's good to see you."

"Hello, Ludie. It's good to see you, too. I was beginning to think you didn't recognize me, these imperial cooks have caused me to get so round."

And with that, Ludovika let out a laugh, gliding toward her sister's chair and reaching forward in a greeting that was half a bow, half a hug. The two women embraced, and the display of affection served to noticeably slacken Sisi's frayed nerves; Sisi hoped Helene found the same effect.

Would this be her and Helene someday? Sisi wondered. Sisters meeting like strangers after decades of prolonged separation? Babies, and husbands, and different homelands pulling them apart as if they had never shared a bed and nighttime whispers and a childhood home? No, Sisi decided. Helene would never become remote. She'd never be the type to use her authority and power as a perch from which to look down upon her former life. And Sisi would never let so much time lapse without the two of them seeing one another.

Sisi used the distraction of the reunion to study her surroundings further. As she'd noticed before, Sophie was flanked by two men, both of whom had stood upon the entrance of the ladies. On one side stood the older of the two, a wigged man wearing a suit of dove-gray silk and tight white curls: a minister of some sort, Sisi guessed. He did not watch the meeting taking place before him, but kept his eyes fixed forward at the table in a look of cool disinterest. On Sophie's other side stood a young man in the full military uniform. Apparently a military aide or advisor, though young, by the looks of it. Young and quite handsome. The officer had pale-blue eyes, auburn hair with just a hint of a wave, and a thin mustache. He had a narrow frame, but Sisi had to admit that he made quite an arresting impression in the sturdy red and white uniform, its details trimmed in gold thread. The young officer looked up in time to catch Sisi staring at him. Quickly, she averted her eyes, but not before her cheeks had grown warm. Oh, how she would have to watch herself at court, suddenly exposed to all of these handsome men! No, she could not allow herself to be distracted by Aunt Sophie's military aide, or any other man, when she had to help Helene secure her place as the emperor's wife.

The two sisters now separated from their embrace. Sisi noticed that both women had tears on their cheeks, though Sophie quickly brushed hers aside and sat back down in her chair.

"Well, Ludovika, step aside so that I may see your beautiful daughters." The cold edges of Sophie's authority had been thawed, slightly, by the display of familial affection. But an intangible sternness still clung to her unsmiling features.

"Of course, Soph. This here —"

"Tut, tut, so you've taken it upon yourself to disregard my royal title?" The archduchess leaned her head to the side, staring at her younger sister with a quizzical purse of her lips. "So comfortable, already?"

"Oh." Ludovika cleared her throat. "Am . . . am I to call you . . ."

"I'm only teasing," Sophie said with a flicker of her wrist as if to swat away a fly. "A joke."

But was it? Sisi wondered.

"Step aside, Ludovika."

"Yes, of course." Ludovika slid backward, like a skittish mare unclear of the trainer's instructions, fearful of the whip. Now Aunt Sophie's eyes fell fully, for the first time, onto her nieces. "Ludovika," her eyes narrowed, "why are they in black?"

What happened next was quick, an instantaneous exchange, and one Sisi might not have noticed had she not been watching her aunt so closely. Sophie's eyes darted to the young man, the officer standing beside her, as if to ask him something. A wordless communication. And then she turned back to Ludovika, her gaze cold and censorious. "Why have you not changed out of this awful black, Ludovika?" Sophie crossed her arms in front of her.

"We intended to, Sophie. Truly, we did. But it's just that —"

"You should have changed on the road."

"We tried, Sophie. But the coach carrying our trunks got separated."

"That was poor planning on your part."

"And once we got here, we were ushered immediately inside."

"For a meeting like this, you should have been more prepared."

To Sisi's astonishment, her mother fell silent at Sophie's words of rebuke. Eventually, Sophie sighed.

"Fortunately they have their youth and their health to recommend them," Sophie said, speaking of her nieces as if they were not present. "Let me guess, this is your eldest, Helene? I see the strong family resemblance. She is a beauty."

"No, Sophie, that is my second girl, Sisi, I mean . . . Elisabeth," Ludovika answered, stepping in front of Sisi and putting her arms on Helene's shoulders. "*This* is our Helene. Our sweet, tender, obedient Helene, and our eldest daughter."

"Oh?" Sophie turned from Sisi to Helene, pausing a moment to register her error. "Oh! *That* is Helene?" She said it as if she wished to be corrected. When Ludovika nodded, Sophie's exhale was audible. A sigh of . . . what was it, disappointment?

"My word, I would not have guessed. It's been so long since I've seen you girls."

Sophie studied Helene now without modesty or shame, as she would inspect a horse she considered acquiring for the imperial stables. "But you seem . . . I don't know . . . younger than the other one."

Ludovika shifted on her feet, attempting a half-coherent reply that mentioned something about a dainty, feminine figure. Both Helene and Sisi had dropped their eyes so that they each appeared very preoccupied with the hemlines of their black dresses.

"What's the age difference between the two of them?" Sophie asked.

"Elisabeth is but fifteen. Helene just turned eighteen, the perfect age for matrimony," Ludovika answered.

"Indeed?" Sophie cocked her head, unconvinced. "She still has the figure of a girl. She doesn't look eighteen."

Ludovika shrugged, a polite smile clinging

to her face. "Well, I can assure you, she is. I was there when it happened, after all."

"And how old did you say the other one is?"

"Elisabeth will be sixteen in just a few months."

"Ah! Still a child." After a long pause, Sophie continued. "You've had a few more since these girls, right?"

"That's right," Ludovika answered. "They have a brother, Karl, who is heir to the duchy. And then four younger siblings — three girls and another boy — all of whom are at home with their father, the duke."

"All of those girls to marry off," Sophie sighed, still studying Helene through narrow eyes. "But of course, with the eldest one becoming a Habsburg, I doubt you'll have a shortage of young men calling on the rest."

Ludovika nodded. "You are correct, I'm sure."

"Will she be fertile? She looks as thin as a maypole."

Ludovika laughed, a short, nervous titter, and Sisi sensed her mother's irritation. "Why, Sophie, I've never had a problem with fertility, and my daughters will not either."

At that moment Sisi caught once more the eye of the auburn-haired soldier beside Sophie and, in spite of herself, felt herself smile at him. He smiled back, a secret communication that she hoped only she had noticed as she lowered her eyes again. Her cheeks, indeed her whole body, flushed warm.

"Let us hope. But I don't like the black, Ludovika, it doesn't suit her." Sophie's tone remained flat, unimpressed.

"As I tried to explain, Sophie, we have not yet had time to change from our mourning clothing." Ludovika kept her lips close together as she replied. "I do hope we shall be able to locate our dresses quickly."

Sophie nodded. "Step forward, my girl." Sophie lifted a hand from her dog's downy white fur, waving Helene closer. Helene obeyed. Sisi watched her sister approach, peeling her eyes from Helene only for a minute to glance once more at the young soldier. He still studied Sisi, and their eyes held one another's for a moment too long before Sisi forced herself to look back to her sister.

"So tell me, niece, how was your journey?" Sophie awaited a reply, but her eyes were already roving over Helene's figure, riffling through a hundred additional questions: Would she really be fertile? Would she be pleasing to her son? And certainly there was no need to worry about her maidenhead being intact when the girl was so small and meek? Helene wilted under the intensity of this visual inquisition.

"Well? I asked you a question: How was your journey, niece?"

Helene, gaze still tilting downward, made no reply. She gnawed at her lower lip, a nervous habit that Sisi would always remind her she *must* break before her formal introduction at the Viennese Court.

"Helene, your Aunt Sophie is asking you a question." Ludovika nudged her elder daughter, but still no reply issued from the timid girl.

Sophie laughed at her niece's reticence. "Nerves?"

"I suppose." Ludovika smiled with her lips only. "Helene is such an intellectual girl. She astounds all of her tutors. Perhaps a bit serious — but then, the art of conversation can always be learned. And of course, your court here is much more imposing than our Bavarian duchy. She simply requires time to grow comfortable."

"Ha, this is nothing! This is a small summer retreat. Just wait until we move back to Vienna." Sophie sat, petting her little dog, her jeweled ring momentarily catching in the tangle of its fur. "I remember when I first arrived to court. I didn't *allow* myself to show my nerves. Helene, you know I'm Bavarian originally? Like your mother?"

"Yes, Your Majesty." Helene nodded and Sisi could have sung in relief. At least that minor communication had been transacted.

"Tell me, Helene, how do you find Austria compared to Bavaria?" When Helene did not answer yet another question, Sophie continued. "I, for one, should never like to return to that dark, cold land. Surely the beauty of our Alps and the open Austrian vistas were a welcome sight after the oppressive pines of your forests, nay?"

A clamorous silence now stretched between the seated woman and her three visitors, the only sound in the room being that of the little dog snoring in the archduchess's lap. The young officer, still standing, cleared his throat.

Sophie took a slow sip of tea and then tried again. "Well, what do you have to say to that, Helene? Do you find Austria beautiful?"

Speak! Sisi wished to yell to her sister. She threw a sideways glance in Helene's direction, urging her sister on with her eyes. But Helene, still chewing on her lower lip, remained as mute as the guards positioned at the doorways throughout the room.

Sophie arched her eyebrows now. "Did you lose your tongue on the journey at the same time that you lost your trunk of fresh dresses?"

A quick glance toward her mother confirmed to Sisi how dismally Helene was performing. Ludovika scowled, her hands clutching the black folds of her skirts, her tight lips finding no words with which to intervene.

Reacting as she had done so many times

before, Sisi instinctively stepped forward to stand beside her sister.

"Indeed, Your Highness, my sister was so enthralled by the Alpine scenery that she's grown extremely tired." Sisi bowed low before her aunt, noticing that the young officer stood up straighter, fixing his eyes firmly on Sisi as she spoke.

Sisi forced herself not to look in his direction as she continued: "I can't tell you how Helene prattled on about how beautiful her new country was! Why, Mamma and I felt that she had already forgotten her Bavarian roots in her eagerness to embrace her new homeland."

"Is that so?" Sophie, slowly stroking her dog, turned her gaze on Sisi. "Your sister prattling on? I can hardly imagine it."

"Well, it is hard not to become effusive when beholding the views of Upper Austria," Sisi answered.

To the combined relief of the three visitors, Sophie's lips curled upward into the hint of a smile. "And how do *you* like it, Niece Elisabeth?"

"It is unimaginably beautiful here," Sisi answered honestly. "I should think there is no life more glorious than that of the Austrian goat herder."

Now Sophie erupted in laughter, her sharp features creasing in delight, and the sound cleared the tension in the room like a thunderstorm clears the oppressive summer heat. "My goodness, Ludovika, you sure have raised up a spirited girl in this one, haven't you? A little duchess longing to be a goat herder — I've never heard of such a thing." Sophie turned to her young officer and they exchanged a chuckle.

Sisi, too, caught the eye of the young guard and she felt herself flush. His gaze was so intensely fixed upon her, she felt as though he wanted something from her.

"Well, are you going to sit, Ludie? You and the girls must be eager for some refreshment. Tea, tea" — Sophie waved her hand and three footmen descended on the table, helping the ladies into their seats and filling porcelain glasses, painted in a delicate, vinelike pattern, full of steaming tea. Sisi settled in beside her sister, joining her aunt and the others at the small round table. The gray, pinch-faced woman still stood silently in the corner, motionless. She could have been a statue, if not for the slight rising of her bosom that indicated she was breathing.

"Come now, Elisabeth, how can the fate of the Austrian goat herder be superior to that of the Austrian emperor?" Sophie seemed to have forgotten entirely about Helene as she spoke now to her younger niece.

"Of course my aunt knows that there is no fate more glorious than that of the Austrian emperor." Sisi looked longingly at the biscuits spread before her on the table. Must she wait until the archduchess invited them to partake of the food? She turned back to her aunt. "But I would never allow myself to imagine what such a life is like — for that role belongs only to God's chosen vessel, my dear cousin Franz Joseph, and therefore it is not for us commoners to covet."

"You are not a commoner, you are a duke's daughter." Sophie lifted a small lemon cake to her lips, taking a bite, but not inviting the others to do the same. Ludovika took measured sips of her tea. Helene sat perfectly still.

"Indeed, but next to Emperor Franz Joseph, we all feel common." Sisi bowed her head once more, casting her eyes humbly toward her lap.

"True," Sophie said, a crumb of lemon cake clinging to her chin.

This was easy, Sisi thought to herself. All the woman wanted to hear were compliments about herself, her country, and above all, her son.

"She's quick, this one." Sophie turned to the aged minister dressed in gray silk, sitting beside her. And then, as if her two nieces were not in the room, she addressed her younger sister. "Ludovika, it's a shame that Elisabeth is not your eldest. She has the appearance and the disposition much more suited for the crown."

Sisi winced, not daring to raise her eyes

108

from the floor for fear that she would scowl at her aunt. How dare that woman utter such an insult in front of Helene?

"You are kind to compliment my Elisabeth, Sophie." Ludovika spoke through a tight jaw, her tone more submissive than Sisi had ever heard it. "Elisabeth is spirited, but nowhere near as well-educated as Helene. And Sisi . . . *Elisabeth* . . . has promised to devote all of her energy to the assistance of her sister, as Helene prepares for this most august role with which you have honored her."

"Is that right?" Sophie looked from one niece to the other as if comparing two reams of silk — her gaze, like the blue-eyed stare of the officer beside her, lingered on Sisi. With a final sigh of resignation, Sophie turned back to the girl intended for her son. "Helene, I will allow that the journey was fatiguing. But please get out of that drab clothing. You would benefit greatly from some rouge to those cheeks, and perhaps a smile once in a while? And for God's sake, stop chewing and gnawing on your poor lip as if you would eat it off. You've come for a marriage proposal, not a funeral."

Ludovika leaned forward, her tone almost plaintive. "We intend to go locate our trunks and change immediately, Sister. As soon as it is your pleasure to excuse us. In fact, I would very much appreciate it if we could change before meeting the emperor."

"Meet the emperor?" Sophie smiled at her sister, a cake held between her ringed fingers. "Well, you're too late for that, I'm afraid. He's right here." Sophie jerked her chin to her left, toward the handsome young officer sitting beside her. The man whom Sisi had assumed to be a military advisor or aide.

"Your Majesty!" Ludovika gasped, hopping from her chair before bowing forward. Her eyes fixed on the ground, she spoke in barely a whisper. "My sincerest apologies. I had no idea. Why, you have grown and changed so much, I did not even recognize you."

This young man in the army uniform was the emperor? Their host and the owner of this palace? Helene's groom? And then Sisi remembered a young boy with delicate features and hair the color of cinnamon. Her mind careened, and she was certain that her face betrayed her surprise. But she quickly recalled herself. Responding like her mother, she too lifted herself from her chair to curtsy before him. Poor Helene wobbled next to Sisi as if she might faint.

The young man smiled at them, speaking for the first time. "There is no need to apologize, Aunt Ludovika." His blue eyes, softer and kinder than his mother's, fell on each of them as he addressed them. "Please, rise, rise, all of you. You are my family, not my subjects."

"Why, you made no introduction, Sophie,"

Ludovika said, looking at her sister with a bewildered expression.

"It's a little game we like to play. It allows Franzi to observe for a change . . . something the poor boy can never do when he is always on display."

"But I feel quite ashamed that my daughters and I did not offer the proper respect." Ludovika still stared at her sister, her tone betraying discomfort and even slight irritation. "One does not enter the presence of the emperor without a suitable show of humility."

"It is quite all right," Franz said, his voice lighthearted opposite his aunt's. "I rather like being inconspicuous once in a while. Being able to watch without being watched." Franz looked from his aunt to Sisi, his light-blue eyes holding hers, like a patch of cloudless sky. "Won't you please rise? I cannot have you all on your knees after the punishing journey you've undertaken at my request."

"My goodness, Franz." Ludovika beamed toward her nephew as she sat down once more. "What a handsome emperor you make."

Franz reached forward, shocking his aunt as he took her hand in his own. "Aunt Ludie, it is so good to see you. And welcome to Austria. I can't wait to get to know your daughters better."

He was engaged to marry Helene, but Franz's eyes lingered on Sisi as he said it.

III.

As the doors open, Sisi is stunned by a blast of color, an eruption of trumpet notes. Hundreds of courtiers line the route, waving flags as they look on, eyes wide and lips moving in indistinguishable shouts and prayers.

They stand plumed in their finest robes and suits, the women with meticulously coiffed hair. Behind them, the common people jostle and elbow and cheer, a wall of merchants, peasants, children, and tradesmen. All of them swarm the processional route with one purpose: to catch a glimpse, however fleeting, of the queen.

In front of Sisi, noblemen hoist their banners, charting a course for the cathedral where it waits atop the hill. Imperial musicians press glistening trumpets to their lips as guards stand stiff and erect, lining the path now walked by royal feet.

Sisi keeps her eyes down as she processes, just a few steps behind him. She listens as the people cry out, uttering her name like a holy incantation: "*Éljen Elisabeth!* Long live Queen Elisabeth!"

The only noise louder than the cries of the crowd is the roar of the cannons, jarring and bone-thumping as a summer thunderstorm. The barrels fire off a steady salvo as the monarchs make their way up the hill.

As they reach the massive doors to the cathedral, the bells clang so uproariously overhead that it sounds to her as though the bell tower might crack. The organ blares deafeningly loud as its pipes contend with the trumpets.

"Here we go." He turns to her, adjusting his cape one final time. Sisi nods.

"Yes, here we go." Her body trembles, as it had on her wedding day, but she forces out the hint of a smile. Today shall be nothing like her wedding day. She is nothing like the girl who made that wedding march.

CHAPTER THREE

*IMPERIAL RESORT AT BAD ISCHL, UPPER
AUSTRIA
AUGUST 1853*

Their moods lifted markedly when they arrived in their rooms to find their trunks awaiting them.

"Agata!" Sisi ran toward the Polish maid, falling forward into a hug.

"Hello, misses!" The round-faced young woman laughed. Before her sat the trunks, opened and spewing out heaps of bright clothing.

"Agata, we've missed you." Sisi hovered beside her servant, savoring her familiar presence in this foreign place. "And we've missed our *dresses!*"

"Miss Sisi, don't you seem merry." Agata leaned back and took in Sisi's figure. "No, you don't seem a bit weary from your journey. And you, Miss Helene, how are you feeling?" Agata cast a nervous glance toward the more subdued Helene.

Helene shrugged her shoulders. "Tired. It's good to see you, Agata."

"Oh, our dresses. Helene, look!" Sisi picked up the dress atop the opened trunk, an afternoon gown of rich emerald silk, and completed a wide twirl with it across the room. "Agata you have no idea how tired we are of black."

"I can see that." The Polish maid giggled, her ruddy cheeks spreading out over her wide face.

"And how are you, Agata? How was the rest of your journey?"

The maid turned back to sorting, retrieving a riding jacket, which she placed beside its matching skirt. "Shall I tell you honestly, Miss Sisi?"

"Of course, Aggie."

Agata paused, considering her words. "The journey was long. I had no idea we would be so far from home."

"It is far from Possi, isn't it?" Sisi agreed. "Oh, but I recognize these!" Sisi dove into the trunk and retrieved her red velvet dressing slippers, still stained with the mud and grass of home. She bent over and slid off her heeled boots, slipping her feet into the plush red velvet. "Much better. Now I feel as if I have a bit of Possenhofen. Do you suppose the Archduchess Sophie would mind if I wore these to supper?"

"Miss Sisi!" Agata lifted a hand to cover

her laughing lips.

"Helene, what are you doing resting on that bed, you must come look. Fresh clothes at last!" Sisi reached into the open trunk and this time retrieved an indigo evening gown.

Helene walked toward the maid and her trunks. "Hello, Agata," she said, hugging the maid with her thin, irresolute arms.

"That's better, Miss Néné." Agata returned the embrace.

"Not allowed to use that name anymore," Sisi said, half-serious, half-plaintive, as she examined a formal evening gown in shimmering ivory silk. "Mamma's orders."

"Is that so?" Agata asked.

"We are to be Elisabeth and Helene from now on. Proper little duchesses." Sisi sighed. And then, turning to her sister she said, "What do you say, *Duchess Helene,* shall we get you out of those mourning clothes?"

Helene scowled as the maid laughed.

"What should we wear to dinner this evening?" Sisi now held up a yellow gown with cream-colored trim, draping it in front of her figure.

"Whose room will this be?" Agata asked, still sorting through the clothing and forming two piles for each of the girls' gowns. Helene's pile was twice the size, given her preeminent status on this visit.

"We're going to share," Sisi explained. Though the Kaiservilla had more than

117

enough rooms for them to each take their own quarters, Helene had asked Sisi to sleep in her bedroom with her.

"Can't say that much surprises me." Agata smiled. "And is your mother the duchess situated in a room as well?"

"Yes, Agata, she is just down the hall." Sisi pointed in the direction where the grim-faced old woman from the tearoom had escorted their mother. "Countess Gray-Hair took her there."

"I'd better go help your mother get settled," Agata said. "The two of you can finish unpacking these gowns, yes? If not, I'll ring for help. There must be more than a thousand servants in this palace."

"We'll be fine." Sisi nodded. The last thing she wanted at the moment was a stranger in here, snooping and adding to Helene's nerves.

"I'll be back to help you girls dress for supper, if I have time."

"Yes, please come if you can. I'd like you to braid my hair." Sisi smiled at her maid.

"You won't be needing me to style your hair much longer . . . now that Helene is set to marry the emperor. Why, I imagine you'll each have scores of hairdressers and valets and maids to yourselves."

"Don't be jealous, Aggie. You'll always be our favorite," Sisi said. Agata giggled and exited the room.

The bedroom in which Sisi and Helene were installed was mercifully adjoined by a small water closet, complete with a large porcelain tub. Some faceless servant had already filled it with balmy fresh water, and the experience of bathing was a welcome one after several weeks on the road. Sisi enjoyed how the scent of the perfumed water stayed on her skin even as she slid into one of the soft silk robes that hung on the nearby hooks, also provided by a faceless Habsburg servant.

The bedroom itself was large and bright, with floor-to-ceiling windows that donned a view over the back gardens of the palace complex. Sisi, hair still wet from her bath, pressed her forehead to the clean glass of the window.

Staring out over the yard, she watched the dizzying hive of activity. Half a dozen wigged secretaries cut intersecting lines, carrying papers and books and other parcels. Armed soldiers drilled in crisp rows. Their commander's shrill orders rose up above the barks of nearby dogs, their tails wagging as maids carried baskets heaped with vegetables toward what had to be a kitchen.

"What do you think they are all doing?"

Helene, in the bathtub, could not have heard Sisi's question, nor did she answer. How much activity went into the household of one man — and a bachelor, at that! Sisi sighed, her warm breath fogging up the windowpane, as she remembered the persistent looks of her cousin.

Across the yard, behind a cluster of small administrative buildings, Sisi spotted a broad flat building that most certainly looked like stables; her heart sped up at the thought of taking off into the surrounding hills on horseback. Once Helene had settled into her role, Sisi decided, she would look into taking a ride. Not until Helene was settled, though. "Don't be selfish, Sisi," her mother had repeated throughout the journey. Once more, the handsome face of her cousin popped before her in her mind's eye. Sisi blinked, forcing his image away.

Sisi turned from the window back toward the bedroom. Though the Kaiservilla had only recently become Franz's summer home, this room lacked for no small comfort. A fire blazed in the fireplace even on this warm August afternoon. Wooden parquet floors were covered by a dark, ornately patterned carpet, and a four-poster bed much like their bed at home was piled high with downy pillows and a hand-stitched silk bedcover.

Just then Helene emerged from the water closet, her hair wet and her face appearing somewhat refreshed after her bath.

"Helene! You're looking revived. Let's pick something for you to wear this evening." Sisi crossed the room and peered into her sister's open trunk, removing the few dresses Agata had not yet unpacked.

Helene slipped behind the dressing screen, its thin silk panels covered with delicate butterflies, and slid out of her robe.

"So, Helene." Sisi ventured to speak to her sister now that they were alone and feeling more comfortable. "What did you think?" Sisi stared into the full-length mirror, considering a gown of navy-blue silk for her sister. Not bright enough for this balmy summer night, she decided.

"Of what?" Helene emerged from behind the dressing screen, wearing bloomers and her shift.

"Of your fiancé, of course." Sisi arched her eyebrows, catching her sister's gaze through the reflection of the mirror.

Helene shrugged her shoulders. "I don't know." She sifted through her mountainous pile of dresses.

"Helene, come now," Sisi sighed, lowering the navy-blue dress. "It's me. You may answer truthfully." She picked up the yellow gown once more and now held it out to consider it against Helene's complexion.

"Not that one." Helene swatted the dress away. "I didn't get much of a chance to form an impression of Cousin Franz."

"Well, then, I'll tell you what *I* thought," Sisi offered, holding the yellow gown up against her own reflection once more.

"All right." Helene looked at her sister, half-amused. "And what did you think, Sisi?"

"He's very good-looking."

"I suppose." Helene let her eyes slip from Sisi's gaze.

"Even *you* must have noticed that."

Helene shrugged. "If you like the military uniform."

"He seems to have a very kind and approachable demeanor, Helene. Why, the way he told us not to bow to him. He seems much less preoccupied with his position than his mother is."

Sisi thought back to her good-natured cousin, still finding it hard to believe that he was the same young boy she had met years earlier. In spite of herself, she blushed as she remembered the multitude of occasions in the tearoom during which their eyes had locked. "I was certainly surprised that *he* was the emperor," Sisi said, revealing only half of her thoughts. Surprised, certainly. And perhaps a little bit disappointed, as well. But she blinked, shaking that thought away before it could take root. "He looked nothing like I remember him. Though Aunt Sophie was largely unchanged."

"Sisi, don't you think it was sort of duplicitous of our cousin and Aunt Sophie to conceal who he was?"

Sisi thought about this, wishing that her aunt and cousin had not played this trick on them. Had she known from the beginning that it was her sister's fiancé she looked upon, Sisi never would have conceded to herself how good-looking he was. But of course, she could never admit this to her sister.

"I was too shy, wasn't I?" Helene joined Sisi before the mirror.

"Perhaps you could have spoken up a little more," Sisi admitted, replacing the yellow gown in the trunk.

"But conversation does not come naturally to me."

"You do not know that. You haven't tried."

"What if I appear a fool? —"

"What did Goethe say?" — Sisi turned to face her sister — "Hmm? Come now, you're the scholar."

"But you're the romantic. Tell me."

"Leap, and the net will appear."

"I don't quite feel like leaping," Helene said, raising a gray gown up to the mirror to examine it against her figure.

Sisi leaned toward her sister, removing the gray gown from Helene's hands. "Néné, you are not wearing gray. You just arrived in black. How about some color?"

"But I like gray." Helene reached for the dress, which Sisi withheld.

"How about something brighter?"

"This one suits me just fine." Helene leaned forward and snatched the gray gown from her sister's grasp.

"You're not even going to try to look happy

to meet your groom?" Sisi sighed, growing increasingly frustrated with her sister.

"I cannot hide my true nature," Helene stated, her tone as emotionless as her face.

"It's one thing to hide your true nature. It's quite another to flatly refuse to show any of your lovely and appealing qualities. Come now, I've *never* in all our years known you to be so stubbornly mute as you were at tea today." It was true. It was as if Helene, beginning with the moment her engagement had been announced, had become impermeable, even to the sister who knew her best in the world. Helene, usually shy and timid, yes, but still charming and warm, had suddenly become aloof, ornery, and obdurately mute.

"If Franz refuses to marry me because I choose to wear gray to dinner, I'd rather have it be done with sooner rather than later, Sisi."

Was Helene trying to forfeit Franz's interest? Or was this simply her timidity crippling her? Surely her sister was as kind and good and loving as any girl in the entire Austrian Empire, and just as deserving as any Prussian princess or Hungarian countess. Sisi fortified herself, refusing to drop the argument. Her sister *would* marry the emperor.

"We never had much occasion in Possenhofen to meet young men, did we?" Sisi tried a new tack. "We were so often alone, just our family, in that castle. I can see why this would be terribly daunting."

Helene looked at her sister now, her gaze softening just the slightest bit. Sisi continued. "But, you know, Helene, Mother is right. Most young ladies would line up through the streets to have a chance to win a man like Franz. He seems kind. And he's much more handsome than I had imagined he would be. You are not so unlucky as you think you are."

"If there are young ladies lining up for him, why can't one of them have him?"

"Néné, I could search this entire kingdom and I know that I'd never find a person as kind as you. You must see that you deserve this."

"You don't understand." Helene turned to face her sister, the look in her eyes alluding to tears that seemed imminent.

"What don't I understand? Explain to me." Sisi calmed her tone, taking her sister's cold hand in her own.

"I miss Possi," was all Helene managed to say.

"Of course you do." Sisi sighed. "I do, too. But Helene, Possenhofen is exactly as it was when we left, and it shall remain that way." Sisi wrapped an arm around her sister's shoulders. "There was nothing in Possen-hofen. No one for you to marry. No one for you to even talk to, except for me. And Mamma. Weren't you ready for something larger? More adventure?" Sisi urged her sister with what she hoped would be contagious

125

enthusiasm.

"No," Helene answered, her voice remaining flat.

"So you were content, then? When all our days looked the same: lessons and walks to the lake and meals with our parents? Days in which the only young man we ever saw was our brother Karl?"

"Yes, I was satisfied with that." Helene nodded.

For her part, Sisi could not understand how her sister was not enthralled by this new life for which she was intended. She had always known that her restless spirit would likely carry her somewhere far, far away. The highlights of her days in Possenhofen had been when Mamma had allowed her to saddle up Bummerl and run free through the woods and fields. She wanted adventure. She wanted love; love like the love she read about in the books she stowed away and carried up to the tops of the mountains. Love that devoured, like what Isolde experienced in her tragic tale. Or love like what Shakespeare's young women felt; women who braved ship-wrecks and battlefields and villains and the damning hand of fate.

As if reading her sister's mind, Helene said, bluntly: "Sisi, I'm not like you. I never have been. I've always admired you for the ways in which you are different from me, but I've never wanted the same things as you. I don't

126

want a life like this —" Helene waved her thin arm toward the large windows, outside of which the hive of activity buzzed as madly as before.

"A life with all sorts of strangers to meet, and dinners to attend, and a groom to impress." Helene shook her head. "No, I want a quiet life. A life of solitude does not scare me. In fact, it seems quite nice."

Sisi had known this about Helene: that her sister possessed reserved — almost hermitic — tendencies. That the boundaries of Possi would be enough to contain her for life, and happily, too. But as a young woman, Helene did not have that luxury; Helene could not forgo marriage to remain in her father's isolated Bavarian duchy. Helene had to marry the man who chose her. Or rather, the man who was chosen *for* her.

The fact that that man was kind and good and handsome — and happened to be the emperor of Austria — seemed, to Sisi, to be uncommonly good fortune.

"I had hoped that Mamma would allow me to enter a nunnery," Helene confessed after several moments, her shoulders wilting as she said it. "And I was planning to ask them. But this all happened so quickly."

Sisi cut her sister off. "My sweet Néné, we know how impossible such a fate is. You heard Mamma explain."

"Yes, I did." Helene slowly slipped into the

gray dress.

"Well, my sweet Néné." Sisi stepped into her petticoat now, and she walked toward the window, gazing out once more at the household that her elder sister would have to manage. "This is your new life, and I know that you will make the best of it. You will be such a sweet wife that Franz will adore you, as I adore you."

"You look lovely, Miss Elisabeth." Agata admired Sisi, whose long hair she had just fashioned into her favorite style: two plaits woven into a thick bun. "Miss Helene, are you certain that I cannot fashion your hair for dinner?"

"I'm certain. Thank you, Agata." Helene, following her aunt's orders, was applying a meager amount of rouge to her cheeks, but her black hair she insisted on wearing in her customary style — parted down the middle and pulled back into a sensibly tight bun.

"We must give her credit, Agata." Sisi looked at her sister in the mirror's reflection. "My sister will never be the type of monarch who changes to suit the fancy of the times."

Though her sister was adamant about wearing a muted gray gown, Sisi had selected a dress of soft blue with white lace and pearl trim for herself. She felt a rush as she gazed in the mirror, seeing bright color once more, and she couldn't help but smile.

128

"Well, let me see my girls in their fresh clothing." Ludovika swirled into the room, a blur of raspberry brocade and tightly pressed dark curls.

"Hello, Mamma." Sisi ran to the duchess.

"Sisi, how nice you look. Wasn't it a relief to have a good bath and a change of clothes?" The duchess's spirits seemed higher than they had been following the afternoon's initial introduction. That was, until she spotted her elder daughter. "Oh, Helene, gray? Must you wear something so colorless?"

"What's wrong with gray? I like gray," Helene repeated her earlier justification, standing up from the dressing table.

"Gray is fine for mass during Lent. But can't you put on something a bit merrier to have dinner with your groom?" Ludovika riffled through the pile of gowns her daughters had unpacked. "How about this nice yellow gown? Or perhaps something in peach? Or why don't you borrow the one Sisi has on?" Ludovika gestured toward her younger daughter. "Sisi, let Helene wear the blue."

"But, Mamma, I am wearing this one," Sisi answered, folding her arms protectively over her dress.

Ludovika shot Sisi an aggravated scowl. "Yes, but perhaps your older sister should wear it instead."

"I don't want to wear that one." Helene shook her head.

Ludovika slouched, the buoyancy with which she'd entered the room suddenly gone.

When Franz Joseph's name was announced, he entered the receiving area flanked by men wearing the same white and red uniform. Everyone waiting in the anteroom bowed.

"Cousin Helene, Cousin Elisabeth." He approached his cousins first. "Please rise. And please, allow me to say how lovely you both look this evening."

Helene offered nothing by way of reply, but instead threw furtive glances around the room, her dark eyes avoiding the curious stares of the guards and whispering courtiers. Sisi could sense her sister's panic at the thought of speaking with these strangers. For fear of their appearing rude, Sisi answered their cousin. "Thank you, Your Majesty."

"Please" — he raised a gloved hand — "it's Franz."

Sisi smiled, surprised — yet flattered — to find the emperor speaking to them especially. As she lifted her eyes from her curtsy she noticed, a bit guiltily, that his stare rested on her, and she hoped that he did not notice the reddening of her cheeks.

Franz had not changed out of the white and red military uniform he had worn earlier, but his hair had been combed back and he smelled fresh with the scent of eau de cologne. His stiff, high-necked coat made him appear impeccably dignified.

A gong sounded, announcing dinner. Extending an arm toward each of them, Franz smiled. "May I escort you ladies in to dinner?"

Sisi waited so that Helene could take his arm first and thereby enter into some pleasant conversation. But she noticed, as they walked into the dining hall, that Helene did not speak.

They left the antechamber and proceeded through a candlelit hallway, illuminated by crystal chandeliers and bordered on each side by a column of imperial footmen.

Sisi stared from side to side at the two rows of footmen, each figure identical in a crisply pressed livery of black and gold, eyes unblinking, mustaches trimmed tidily, much like her cousin's. "They are so serious," Sisi observed, watching them intently. They kept their gazes fixed ahead on some unmoving point, so that even though Sisi walked between them, they did not seem to see her.

"Don't be afraid of them, Cousin Elisabeth. They appear more intimidating than they are," Franz whispered to his cousin.

"How do they stand so still?" Sisi wondered aloud. "Like statues."

"Lots of training," Franz answered. "You could do the same if you needed to."

"I very much doubt it," Sisi laughed.

Franz kept his attention fixed on Sisi as the

three of them made their way toward the banquet hall. "Are you pleased with the Kaiservilla?"

"Oh, indeed." Sisi nodded, turning from the motionless figures back to her cousin. When their eyes met, Sisi forced herself not to smile at him. And then, to look away. There was no good reason to be staring into the clear, light-blue eyes of her sister's fiancé.

The sound of violin music now floated delicately through the air, and Sisi peered through the open archway into the dining hall. In spite of herself, she gasped at the candlelit splendor of the room they now approached. "My word."

The dining hall was flooded in amber light, festooned with a line of overhead chandeliers, each one ablaze with several dozen candles. A long central table beneath the chandeliers ran the length of the wood-paneled room. Sisi admired the scene, not sure how they would fit any food on the table between the heaps of silver candelabra, ripe summertime flowers overspilling the china vases, and hors d'oeuvres of pâté, butter rolls, and miniature pickles.

"It's like a painting," Sisi whispered, more to herself than to anyone else.

Franz turned once more to Sisi beside him, his features aglow in candlelight, softening into an affable smile. "I think that one of my cousins is happy. How about you, Helene?"

Franz turned now to his fiancée, standing on his left.

"This is nice." Helene's response came out sounding forced, but at least agreeable. How Helene could be anything but delighted by now was difficult for Sisi to understand, but she suppressed her desire to once again interject herself into the scene.

"Here we are. Franz, girls, come sit." Sophie, who had been escorted to dinner by a man in uniform slightly older than Franz, moved toward the head of the table on the far side of the room. She took her seat there, as several solicitous footmen hovered about her.

"Come, to your seats, everybody. We won't bite." Sophie's miniature dog was placed in her lap by another footman. It took Sisi a moment, but she soon deduced that it was the same minister from earlier who took the seat to Sophie's right; he had shed the formal white wig so that his natural, black hair flew wildly from his scalp. An empty chair waited on Sophie's left.

Sophie beckoned the three of them forward, a flourish of her heavily ringed hand. "I hate to be kept waiting, especially when I'm hungry." A full plate of hors d'oeuvres — slices of goose liver pâté, veal dumplings, Viennese sausages, and pickled herring salad — was now placed in front of her.

"Elisabeth, come sit by me." Sophie summoned Sisi across the room to the empty chair beside her. "Franz, let go of your pretty little cousin's arm, I demand that she be my dining companion this evening."

"Best to do as she says," Franz spoke softly to Sisi. "Enjoy your dinner." They exchanged a smile and Sisi slipped free from Franz's arm. Sisi crossed the room toward her aunt, aware that the eyes of the ministers already seated at the table now rested upon her. "Hello, Mamma," Sisi whispered to the duchess as she walked past her.

Franz kept Helene on his arm, escorting her to a chair on the opposite end of the table from Sisi. When Helene was situated, Franz took the seat at the head of the table farthest from his mother and immediately adjacent to his fiancée. Ludovika was placed to his other side, across from her elder daughter.

"Gentlemen, this is my niece, Elisabeth of Bavaria." Sophie spoke to her end of the table, turning to the black-haired minister from earlier in the day.

"She is so entertaining, is she not? Why, she actually told me earlier that she would love to be a goat herder!" Sophie broke into laughter as the men looked at Sisi with expressions ranging from keen interest to befuddlement. At that introduction, Sisi accepted a footman's outstretched arm and lowered herself into her chair.

"Elisabeth, meet some of my . . . Franz's,

the emperor's . . . ministers," Sophie prattled, picking at a lump of foie gras with her jeweled fingers.

"This is Minister of the Interior Baron Alexander von Bach." Sophie pointed toward the minister beside her, across from Sisi. "I let the minister shed the wig for dinner, it is so ghastly hot in this house." At that complaint, a servant appeared and began fanning the archduchess.

Sisi smiled a greeting to the minister. "Baron von Bach" — she nodded — "it is an honor to meet you." Just then a footman arrived beside her, proffering a crystal flute filled with bubbling champagne.

"Duchess Elisabeth." Bach nodded once in reply. Without the wig, he appeared decades younger, his unruly tufts of black hair falling loosely to the side, matching the same dark shade of his abundant mustache. Though Bach may have shed the wig to counter the summer heat, he still must have been warm, Sisi noted, for he wore a white shirt and vest under a heavy black suit coat and a wide black cravat around his neck.

"And this man next to you, to your right." Sophie was the only one picking at the plate of appetizers before them, nibbling on a veal dumpling. About the uniformed man who had escorted her to dinner Sophie said: "This is one of my son's generals and closest advisors, Count Karl Grünne."

"Count Grünne, a pleasure to meet you as well."

"Your Majesty, Duchess Elisabeth." Count Grünne nodded his head, offering just the hint of a smile.

"You'll want to win him over, niece. For he's the one whose opinion Franz heeds. Isn't that so, Count Grünne?"

Sisi marveled at the familiar manner in which her aunt conversed with these men — much more forward and assertive than when her mother addressed officers and ministers.

"Of course, whatever opinions I might humbly submit to the emperor fall second to those of his most faithful and admirable mother, the archduchess," Grünne replied, flashing a charming grin. Even though he was advanced in years, much more so than Franz, he was not unattractive.

"Nonsense. Your humility does not serve you, Grünne. Grünne here is the type of man you want around when you're under attack," Sophie added, raising her eyebrows suggestively to Count Grünne as she fed herself another large bite of dumpling. Sisi found it an interesting way to describe someone, but she did not question her aunt further. "And across from Grünne is His Excellency Pyotr Kazimirovich Meyendorff." Sophie now fed her little dog a bite of dumpling. "Ambassador from the Russian Empire to Austria. A special friend and most distinguished guest."

"Your Excellency." Sisi nodded, staring into the wide face of a dark man, his broad forehead made even more expansive by a receding hairline and faint fringe of thinning brown hair. The man's features were not attractive, but they were striking: he had bulbous lips and a thick nose under even thicker eyebrows.

"Pleasure to meet you, Duchess Elisabeth." The ambassador offered a curt nod. He, unlike Grünne, spoke with a strong accent that confirmed his foreign roots.

"And this —" Sophie pointed farther down the table, and Sisi spotted the same stern, pinch-lipped woman she had seen earlier in the day, at tea. The one whom she had nicknamed "Countess Gray-Hair."

"This is the Countess Sophie Esterházy," Sophie explained. "The countess shares not only my name, but happens to be my closest friend." Sophie beamed at the woman, who returned the remark with a solemn nod. And Sisi deduced, from that limited interaction, how the friendship went: the archduchess spoke her mind, and the Countess Esterházy agreed, unflinchingly.

"I understand you come from Bavaria, Duchess Elisabeth?" The Russian ambassador's dinner clothes appeared to Sisi more suited for a Siberian winter than a summertime dinner in Austria. He wore a heavy, high-collared black suit, with gold leaves embroidered around the neck. Dangling from his left shoulder were three heavy medals. "Your father's castle is called Possenhofen?"

"Indeed, Your Excellency," Sisi answered.

"Would you call that a castle?" Sophie smirked, tipping her glass for it to be filled with champagne.

"I've heard it described as a place of great beauty," Grünne said.

"I certainly think so." Sisi smiled, ignoring her aunt's slight against her home.

"Max's castle? A place of great beauty?" Sophie put a ringed hand to her lips as if to conceal giggling lips, exchanging a meaningful look with the Countess Esterházy. "Oh, but I see what you mean. You must mean the *surroundings* are beautiful. Yes, I suppose Bavaria does have its appeal. I find the manners there a bit too . . . countrified . . . myself. At least when compared to Austria."

"Was it a long journey?" Count Grünne had the good taste to interject, his eyes fixed politely on Sisi.

"Poor Ludie." Sophie broke off into a splintered conversation with the Countess Esterházy, one which Sisi couldn't help but overhear. "How happy she must be, to be away from *him.*"

Sisi blinked, taking a moment to regain her focus. Her stomach seized to hear the mockery with which her aunt discussed her father. But the Count Grünne had asked her a question. What had he asked?

"It must have been a tiring journey," Grünne prodded her, his gaze kind and leading.

"Oh, yes. Indeed," Sisi stammered. "We only just arrived, this afternoon."

"They lost their trunks along the way," Sophie said, an eyebrow lifting as she looked still at Countess Esterházy.

"A long way." Meyendorff's gaze held Sisi. "But not as far as St. Petersburg."

"Speaking of St. Petersburg, Pyotr, here, you must taste the herring first." Sophie leaned forward to pick up the plate of fish, garnished with onion, pickles, beans, and a sauce of egg yolk and vinegar. "A Russian specialty — we made it in your honor, of course."

"Ah, herring! You are most gracious, Archduchess." Ambassador Meyendorff accepted the plate and served himself a modest portion.

"You know, Niece Elisabeth, that Russia is our most important ally?" Sophie spoke loudly and slowly, as if to ensure that the ambassador would hear.

"I see," Sisi answered.

"Do you speak Russian, Duchess Elisabeth?" Countess Esterházy asked, her light eyes expressionless.

"Well, no." Was she expected to speak Russian?

"Wine, Duchess Elisabeth?" A footman hovered over Sisi's shoulder; yet another question coming from another direction.

"Oh, no, thank you. I have the champagne."

"But you must have wine as well," Sophie interjected. "After all, we are celebrating. How long has it been since I've had my sister and her two girls with me?" Sophie peered down the long table at Ludovika.

Once all the glasses at the table had been filled, Sophie raised her champagne flute and the conversations that had sprouted up around the table, along with the violin music, ceased. "To the emperor's health." Sophie looked down the long table at her son. "Long live Emperor Franz Joseph."

"Long live Emperor Franz Joseph!" The ministers and courtiers at the table echoed in unison.

At that, Sophie raised her glass to her lips. "I've asked them to serve the vintage from the year of his birth. I've been saving it for twenty-three years. Almost exactly, since your birthday approaches, Franzi. I thought we should drink it, finally. After all, we have so much to celebrate this evening." Sophie beamed at her son before touching the crystal to her lips and sipping.

Sisi was prepared to do the same when she noticed that the ministers, and even Franz, appeared to be waiting to drink. The men at the table watched Sophie in silence, as if mining her features for some reaction.

As Sophie drained the last remnants of champagne from her glass, she lowered the empty vessel, smacking her lips with a satisfied sigh. "A vintage fit for an emperor," she remarked, handing her empty glass to the footman for a refill. The diners around Sisi laughed good-naturedly, as if some barrier had been cleared, and with it, the tension lifted. The violins resumed their waltz and the diners raised their own champagne flutes, sipping their drinks and resuming conversation.

Sisi took a sip from her glass and savored the chilly sweetness of the drink, a welcome sensation in the warm room. Footmen now descended upon the table, bearing the first course, a Viennese beef soup. The broth seemed too heavy for the evening, but Sisi accepted her bowl.

Sophie, sipping her second glass of champagne, was speaking loudly to the Russian ambassador. "But the Turks are threatening war, Pyotr. Is that a war for which the tsar is prepared?"

The ambassador, chewing on a bite of herring, considered the question. "The Blessed Tsar has never run from war, especially when it is God's own work at stake, Archduchess Sophie."

Grünne leaned in toward Sisi, speaking softly so that only she might hear. "What the archduchess is speaking about is the Turkish response to the Russians. You see, Tsar Nicholas has just marched his Russians into the Turkish territories of Wallachia and Moldavia."

"Of course." Sisi nodded, but she was certain from his grin that she had not fooled Grünne. She had never discussed politics at a table such as this. In fact, she had never sat down to dinner at a table such as this. She took a generous sip of champagne.

"We are ready for war, Archduchess," Ambassador Meyendorff spoke louder now, perhaps irritated at Grünne's side conversation. "We have become convinced that war with the Turks is the only way to resolve the Eastern Question."

Sisi watched with surprise as more food was now deposited onto the already-full table. Footmen reappeared and delivered a plate of *Tafelspitz,* boiled beef with apples and horseradish. Next came a dish of potato noodles soaked in butter and poppy seeds. There was *Rindfleisch,* Franz's favorite cuts of beef, and *Salzburger Nockerln,* dumplings which Franz greeted with delighted clapping. And finally came several plates of fresh produce from the villa's kitchen gardens — sliced tomatoes in oil and vinegar, cucumbers with carrots shredded thin like paper, and potatoes garnished with peppers and onions.

Before she could make any progress in her

champagne, Sisi's flute was refilled, as if the servants had been instructed to replenish her glass after every sip. The drink cooled her from the inside like a fizzy balm, a feeling that she welcomed after the long journey and tense arrival. After several more sips, she felt confident enough to initiate further conversation.

"Pardon me, Count Grünne, but what is the Eastern Question?" Sisi whispered to her dinner companion as she accepted a plate from him, heavy with stewed pears and walnuts.

"The Turks ruling the Ottoman Empire are weak, and getting weaker each day." Count Grünne wiped his mouth with his napkin. "Russia wants to ensure that, if and when the sultan loses power, he recognizes Russia as the rightful ruler of the Christians within the Turkish Empire."

"But Russia is right there. Who else would expect to rule those subjects?" Sisi asked.

"France has gotten a little too bold lately, under that new Napoleon. The nephew of the first one, and he fancies himself like his uncle. Russia simply wants to remind Turkey that the tsar will deal with the Ottomans going forward. Not the Western European powers that have no place in Turkish lands."

Sophie's voice overpowered Grünne's and Sisi listened in. "You are absolutely right, Pyotr. That little Napoleon imitator has no right meddling in the Eastern lands. That is Russia's sphere of influence."

"If you allow them to take over the subjects that are rightfully Russia's, then what is next?" Count von Bach interposed. "This nephew of Napoleon, this upstart, will fancy himself commander of the waterways and the trade routes next. It's the Turks today, the Black Sea tomorrow."

"It's like what we . . . what my *son* . . . did in Hungary. They were getting too bold. What did we do? We went in there and reminded them that *we* were the power." Sophie took a self-satisfied sip of wine. "And no problems from those Hungarians since."

"The Blessed Tsar feels similarly." The Russian Ambassador nodded. "He would not run from his duty as Blessed Father of His Peoples."

"That is perhaps why the two of us are such good friends." Sophie also nodded, leaning toward the Russian ambassador. Her eyes, beginning to droop, blinked at him as she took another sip of champagne.

Sisi extricated herself momentarily from this foreign policy discussion, peering through rows of vases and candles to catch a glimpse of Helene at the far end of the long table. Her sister seemed to be listening politely to some of Franz's good-natured chatter. Listening, even if not contributing much, Sisi noted.

"But enough of this foreign policy. Let's

talk of something light now." Sophie pulled Sisi back into her orbit. "Let's talk of my visitors. Isn't this one pretty?" Sophie, flushed from the generous servings of food and wine, peered at Sisi with an amused smirk. "Be careful, Niece Elisabeth. You are so young. So fresh and innocent. The men at court shall like what they see."

Sisi didn't know who felt more mortified at that remark — these staunch ministers or herself. She took a gulp of champagne. Sophie, however, appeared to feel no discomfort.

"You know why I like you, Niece Elisabeth?" Sophie stuffed another bite of sausage into her mouth.

"You are too kind, Your Majesty."

"I like you because you remind me of myself," Sophie continued, a morsel of half-nibbled sausage slipping undetected out of her mouth. "When I was younger. Why, look at your beautiful hair — does it not resemble mine, Bach?" Sophie looked to the minister beside her.

"Indeed, your niece is lovely, and very similar in appearance to you," Bach answered dutifully, seeming to know that the sooner he replied, the sooner the topic might change.

"Your hair looks especially fine tonight, Archduchess Sophie," Countess Esterházy interjected, somehow making even a compliment sound stern.

"And you're a quick wit, too, Elisabeth." Sophie served herself a second portion of herring, showing no sign that her appetite was yet sated.

"Thank you, Your Majesty," Sisi said. Now she knew how Helene felt, when the words suddenly dried up and could not be forced out.

"You may call me Aunt Sophie. Or even Auntie, if you prefer." Sophie dabbed the corners of her mouth with the white tablecloth.

"Thank you, Aunt Sophie."

"Do you like the champagne, Elisabeth?" Sophie asked.

"Indeed, Aunt Sophie."

"Twenty-two years old, about to be twenty-three. Just like my Franzi." Sophie sighed. Silence hovered around their end of the table, with Sophie breaking it: "The French got one thing right, though it pains me to say so. I'll take our beer, and the Italian wine, but nobody can make champagne like a Frenchman. Drink with me." Her aunt raised her glass of champagne. "To Austria!"

"To Austria, and to you, my aunt," Sisi replied. They tipped their glasses in unison. Sisi realized she must slow down, and cringed as she saw that a footman had appeared and already refilled her drink.

"She has what I would call a 'regal bearing,' does she not?" Sophie turned to Bach now, her lips tripping over the edges of her words. Though she lowered her voice to a whisper, her next words were still easily heard by those seated near her, including Sisi. "It's a *shame* she's the younger. Between you and me. But Franz is a good boy; he knows there's more to picking an empress than just a pretty face." And with that, Sophie switched from her champagne to her wine, taking a slow sip and staring wistfully toward the musicians in the corner.

At the opposite end of the table, Helene did not appear to be enjoying her dinner companion any more than Sisi did. Mercifully Helene was far enough away not to have heard this latest exchange. And now, even though she strained her ears, Sisi could not determine what it was that Helene and Franz discussed. Her mother, beside them, was laughing gaily at everything her nephew said, and though Ludovika appeared to be enjoying the dinner immensely, Sisi noticed that her mother had hardly eaten a bite from her plate.

"Elisabeth, you will travel with us to Vienna when we leave Bad Ischl, isn't that so?" Sophie sat back from the table, handing her little dog to a servant so that she might fold her hands across her full belly.

"Indeed, Aunt Sophie."

"That will be within the month. The workers need to get started on the renovations of this home. It's dreadfully small; we've been so cramped this summer. But next summer it shall be a proper palace fit for an emperor."

"I am certain that it will be the finest summer retreat in all of Europe."

"Do you know why I bought it?" Sophie asked.

"Why is that, Aunt Sophie?"

"As an early wedding present for Franzi. Now we just need to have the wedding." With that, Sophie threw a probing glance at the opposite end of the table. "Now now, what are the two lovebirds talking about at the end of the table?" Sophie spoke so loudly that all conversations around the table ceased.

"Hmm?" Sophie rapped her knuckles on the table, impatient for an answer. "Don't keep her all to yourself, Franzi. What are you and your bride talking about?"

"I had asked my cousin —" Franz paused. Sisi saw his language as a troubling sign; if Franz felt affectionately for Helene, wouldn't he also have referred to her as his bride?

"I had asked my cousin Helene what she likes to do in her leisure time," Franz answered.

"Ah, and what is the answer? How do you amuse yourself, Helene?" Sophie arched her eyebrows, burping through closed lips as she awaited Helene's reply.

Helene kept her eyes on her plate, where a pile of noodles had been pushed around but barely eaten. "I like to read, Your Majesty."

Here Aunt Sophie did not offer the same correction she had just made to Sisi, granting Helene permission to forgo the royal title. "And what do you like to read, Helene?"

Helene paused, thinking, before she offered a quiet answer: "All sorts of things. Philosophy. History. The Bible."

Sophie laughed to herself. "A pious bride you have, Franzi. And what else do you like to read, Helene?"

"Saint Thomas Aquinas," Helene answered.

"Ah, a pious girl *and* an intellectual." Sophie shot her sister a disdainful smirk and Ludovika winced. The appropriate answer for Helene could have included dancing, or singing, or playing the piano. Reading dry philosophical and religious texts could hardly be seen as a suitable way for a young noblewoman to spend her time. Almost as bad as Sisi's preferred pastimes of riding, fishing, hiking, and composing poetry.

Sophie wasn't done, though. "But I said for *amusement,* Helene." Sophie turned back toward her niece, her eyes glassy from too much champagne. "What do you do for *amusement?*"

Helene thought about this. Sisi knew intuitively that her timid sister wished to slide under the table, to slip away from the attention being heaped upon her. But, she noticed with relief that Helene responded. "I talk with my sister." Helene looked up at Sisi, her eyes pleading to be rescued.

"Ah!" The archduchess, her face brighter now, turned her gaze back on Sisi. "Yes, talking to Elisabeth here certainly is amusing." Now it was Sisi's turn to feel the burning discomfort of Sophie's stare — and the looks of all the other diners around the table.

"Tell me, you funny girl, what do *you* do to entertain yourself?"

Caught by surprise, Sisi knew not how else to answer this question but honestly. "A great many things, Aunt Sophie." Sensing that her aunt somehow preyed off of the perceived weaknesses of others, Sisi straightened up and continued with a strong voice. It helped, too, that the champagne had lessened some of her previous shyness. "I love to ride my horse. I love to walk the fields in search of wildflowers. I love to read poetry, and compose my own lines."

"You love to ride?" Franz interjected.

Sisi turned to face her cousin at the far end of the table, grateful that he had wrested the conversation from his mother's grip.

"I do, Your Majesty."

"As do I." His light eyes shone with genuine interest. "Especially in these mountains."

"Don't we all know?" Sophie rocked her head back and forth, her features loose from the wine. "Franzi thinks there's nothing more attractive than a young woman with a fine seat atop a horse."

Franz ignored his mother's remarks, his eyes still affixed to Sisi. "We have a whole stable full of very fine horses here, Cousin Elisabeth."

"Yes, I believe I saw the stables from afar, earlier today."

Franz continued. "They are not as fully stocked as the imperial stables in Vienna, but they have been sufficient for the summer. I can show you them tomorrow, if you'd like." Though he was an emperor, and could have easily stated it as an order to which anyone would have acquiesced, there was nothing forceful about Franz's tone. No, in fact, it was almost timid. As if he were beseeching her. As if he worried she might not accept.

"Oh?" It was barely a reply — more of a measure to stall, since Sisi felt as uncomfortable with the development of this dinner as her mother now looked. And yet, the invitation also filled her with a thrill she could not completely deny.

But then Sisi noted Helene's downcast eyes, the desperate look of her mother, and she understood how she must redirect this invitation.

"Helene, wouldn't that be fun, to accompany our cousin?" Sisi looked to her sister, trying to pull her into this exchange. Helene shrugged her shoulders.

Turning back to Franz, Sisi pasted an innocent smile on her face and answered: "Cousin, if you don't mind my joining, I would love to accompany you and my sister to the stables tomorrow."

Franz turned from Sisi to Helene, stammering for a moment before regaining his well-rehearsed composure.

"It's so nice of you to include me to join you and Helene," Sisi pushed further. "Isn't that nice, Helene?" Sisi widened her eyes at her sister.

"I'm not sure that I was invited," Helene answered frankly.

"Oh, yes, of course you may join." Franz nodded at Helene, forcing out an awkward smile that did not include his eyes. "Nothing would make me happier than for you to accompany us, Helene."

Sisi hoped that the others around the table did not have the same thought that weighed on her own mind throughout the remainder of dinner: If the thought of Helene's company made Franz so happy, then why did he look so disappointed?

IV.

"How could anyone not love that man?"
— Sisi discussing Franz Joseph,
Bad Ischl
August 1853

CHAPTER FOUR

IMPERIAL RESORT AT BAD ISCHL, UPPER AUSTRIA
AUGUST 1853

"Perhaps I better not go." Sisi paused on the broad stairway. The idea of this morning's outing made her uncomfortable; it had been an invitation to *her,* first, leaving Helene as an afterthought.

And yet, the thought of Franz last night at dinner, his earnest hope made plain across those handsome features as he had looked at her . . . Sisi reached for the banister, waiting a moment for that wobbly feeling to subside.

"Of course you must come, Sisi. You know perfectly well how little I care for horses," Helene replied, tugging on the sleeve of her sister's gown.

Sisi inhaled, speaking slowly. "But I think this might be a good chance for you and Franz — the emperor — to spend time together."

"Sisi." Helene reached for her sister's hand

and gave her a smile. What was that quizzical look? "It was *you* he invited in the first place."

That was precisely what made Sisi so uncomfortable.

She glanced sideways at her sister. "That's simply because I'm the only one who will talk to him. Can't you please try to be pleasant to your fiancé?"

"I *am* trying," Helene answered, a rare edge to her voice.

Sisi lowered her voice, peering into the large, dark rooms they passed to ensure they were free of eavesdroppers. "Well, perhaps you might try a bit harder?"

Helene sighed, her eyes looking straight ahead.

"Come now, Néné." Sisi took her sister's arm. "You'll try harder than you did last night?"

"Goodness, are you my sister or my mother?" Helene shook her head. "I'm surprised *she* didn't find a way to join us on our outing to the stables. You know, to supervise the courtship. I wish she would just stop fretting so. She makes me even more nervous."

"She only wishes for you to succeed."

"Well, it's not as easy as you and Mamma would have it seem, Sisi. I'm sorry I don't share Mamma's slavish devotion to *duty*. That I don't have the same gift of frivolity, the same fanciful notions of romance as you."

Sisi turned to her sister now, stung by the

sharpness of the remark. Helene kept her own eyes fixed stubbornly forward, and in a tense silence, the sisters proceeded out the back door of the villa.

The girls blinked in the bright summer morning, and Helene lifted her plain straw hat to her head. Eventually, Helene spoke. "I don't like being scolded by you now, as well."

Sisi considered her words for a moment before responding. "I just don't understand why you must be so opposed to this marriage. Can't you see that many would consider it a great fortune to have such a —" But Sisi cut herself off, swallowing her next words, aware that they would give her away if she allowed herself to utter them. Instead, Sisi busied herself with her own hat. Her bonnet was decidedly less plain than Helene's — she had found a patch of wildflowers in the gardens that morning and had strung a ring of them around its brim.

"Let's not argue, Sisi, please. I can't bear it." Helene sounded as though she might cry, which would make this morning's outing even more awkward than it already promised to be.

"Fine," Sisi agreed. "You know I can't stay cross with you, Néné."

"That's a forbidden name, isn't it?"

Sisi laughed. "Then, *Helene,* allow me to pay you a compliment: you look very nice this morning."

"Thank you, *Elisabeth,* as do you."

"Your groom ought to be very taken with his bride."

"Sisi!"

"Sorry, sorry."

The two of them clipped across the courtyard toward the stables, passing a file of uniformed guards who marched past, their boots landing heavily on the cobblestones. In their wake walked several maids, their eyes lilting toward Sisi and her sister with inquisitive, probing gazes.

"So many people, always bustling about," Helene grumbled, lowering the brim of her hat as if to shield her face from the questioning stares.

Sisi turned, stealing a furtive look at her sister as they walked on. It was Helene they all wished to see — the woman whom they knew to be the emperor's intended. She had meant her compliment: Helene's plum-colored riding coat and matching skirt suited her. For herself, Sisi had selected a riding outfit of emerald-colored silk.

"There he is," Helene spoke quietly. Sisi shielded her eyes from the strong morning light and peered toward the stables. There he stood — a slender silhouette against the shadows cast by the buildings.

"Hello!" Franz spotted them, too, and called out, waving. "Over here!" Franz looked comfortable this morning, even relaxed.

Rather than the stiffly starched uniform, he wore hunting breeches and a dark-green jacket. His auburn hair caught flecks of the morning sunlight, shining warm and golden around a cheerful face. In spite of herself, Sisi smiled at him.

"Good morning, cousins." Franz bowed his head as they approached.

"Your Majesty," they responded with coordinated curtsies. Another figure emerged just then from the stables.

"You remember Count Grünne from last night's dinner?" Franz introduced his companion. Sisi and Helene both greeted the count.

"I trust you were comfortable in your chamber last night?" Franz asked them both, but his eyes fell upon Sisi.

"Indeed, thank you, Your Majesty," Sisi answered. "Isn't that so, Helene?" She looped her arm through her sister's.

"Yes." Helene nodded.

"Cousin Elisabeth, I saw that Mother kept refilling your plate. I confess I worried — did our rich Viennese food overwhelm you?"

"Oh, you are kind to ask, but it was quite the contrary. I enjoyed myself immensely." Sisi smiled. "We had a merry discussion at our end of the table, did we not, Count Grünne?"

"We certainly did. I think your cousin Elisabeth has a rare ability."

"Is that so?" Franz looked from Grünne to Sisi, his interest piqued. "And what might that be?"

"Elisabeth has the skill of pleasing your mother, Your Majesty." Count Grünne nodded.

"Ah! Yes, that much I deduced." Franz shifted his weight from one foot to the other, allowing a brief silence to settle between the four of them. "Well, shall we?" Franz offered his arm, and Sisi noticed with relief — and a twinge of something far less pleasant, something involuntary — that it was to Helene to whom he made the gesture. She, Sisi, accepted Grünne's arm and the foursome proceeded into the stables.

It was the smell that struck her first. That familiar, heady smell — that pungent medley of hay, leather, and polished wood. Even in a stable like this, easily twice the size of the Possenhofen stables and still gleaming under a recent coat of lacquer, the horses and their trappings had conspired together to fill the space with their uniquely familiar odor.

It was the aroma of her favorite pastime, the smell of Possenhofen: the summer nights before dinner when she'd brush Bummerl's shimmering coat until Mamma called her into dinner. Immediately, her body felt at ease.

Given that this was not Vienna's imperial palace, the stables were perhaps not as fancy as she had expected. But what they lacked in splendor, they made up for in buffed and scrubbed orderliness.

Sisi studied the tack wall, taking in the presence of so many bits, bridles, steel snapples, wool blankets, grooming boxes, leathers, and saddle pads. Why, everyone in the palace, servants included, could have ridden at the same time given how much equipment and how many horses were housed in this stable. The saddle collection alone was probably worth more than Sisi's entire stable at Possenhofen: saddles fashioned in sleek brown leather with soft supple curves to fit the shapes of the strong backs upon which they rested.

But the best feature of these stables was its collection of horses; rows of stalls stretched before Sisi, each filled with a specimen that alone might have cost an ordinary family its entire year's wages.

"Look at these horses." Sisi walked the corridor of the stable, absentmindedly breaking free from Grünne's arm to gain a closer look. How she longed to reach through the ornate wrought-iron gates and touch the horses. Each stall presented a new occupant that appeared even stronger than the one before — clearly the imperial stables only housed horses in peak health and condition. There were mares: their frames long and light, bred over centuries to run without growing weary.

There were stately Thoroughbreds, haughty and skittish. Several stalls were filled with Hanoverians, the German horses bred for their indomitability at war, with their broad muscular chests and thick, barrel-shaped necks. There were the lithe hunters and the golden chestnuts, these daintier breeds probably preferred by the women of the court.

Toward the back stood half a dozen Lippizaners, the Austrian prancing horses cloaked in beautiful dapple-gray — a white mane with small black and gray freckles. This group occupied Sisi's interest the most, as this was the same breed as Bummerl.

Sisi approached a medium-sized female Lippizaner, reading the name scrawled on the wooden gate. "Diamant," she noted aloud. "Hello, Diamant." She removed her riding glove and extended her hand, allowing the horse to acclimate to her foreign human smell before running her fingers over the soft, spackled fur of its nose. "Oh, you are a beautiful one, aren't you?" Sisi cooed as the horse welcomed her attention, cocking its head into her caresses.

"Ah, yes, this one looks like she has a coat full of diamonds." Franz had approached undetected, and Sisi started slightly at the sound of his voice, jerking her hand away from the horse.

"I named her myself when she was born. She's the daughter of this one." He pointed to the adjacent stall that housed a Lippizaner similar in build and color to Diamant. "This here is Blume. But her proper name is Dame von Blume."

"Lady of Flowers." Sisi couldn't help but chuckle at the name, looking at the mother horse. "Hello, Blume."

"Because of this, do you see?" Franz took Sisi's ungloved hand in his own and pointed her fingers toward Blume's chest, where a small cluster of white fur seemed whittled out amid a constellation of gray freckles. Sisi's heart leapt, keenly aware of the soft touch of Franz's skin on her own.

"It looks like edelweiss, does it not?" Franz's voice was quiet, his lips close to her ear. Just then, the horse offered its snout, nestling against Sisi's and Franz's hands for a caress.

"It does. She is beautiful," Sisi replied, smiling at the sudden familiarity of the horse. She noticed, dizzily, that Franz still touched her ungloved skin.

"You are a great admirer of horses?" Franz let go of her hand but remained close, his gaze still locked on her.

"Very much."

"Then I hope you will make yourself comfortable in here. Please treat these stables as your own."

"You are too kind, Your Majesty."

"Please." He waved his hand. "I beg you to

call me Franz."

Sisi glanced down the length of the barn and noticed Helene and Count Grünne speaking cordially in front of a wall of saddles. How was it that Helene could be perfectly agreeable with a stranger such as Count Grünne, yet she froze whenever she interacted with Franz?

Franz had followed Sisi's gaze. "Your sister told me last night that she doesn't enjoy riding. Not as you do."

Sisi pulled her gaze back, looking once more at Franz. She was grateful that, in the shadowy stable, the flush of her cheeks might appear less obvious.

"Let's go," Franz said, quietly, "just you and I."

"Go where?" Sisi asked, taken aback.

Franz pointed at the horse. "For a ride."

"Oh, I'm sure that Helene would like to join us," she said, turning her focus back on Diamant, feeling guilty at even having heard the suggestion.

"Come now, Elisabeth. May I call you that? *Elisabeth.*"

She nodded absently, her words stuck in her throat.

"Please, Elisabeth. I so rarely have time off for my own leisure. I would love to take you riding. I know how you love it. You can ride Diamant. Or would you prefer Blume? You may have your pick." He waved at the stables, his eyes still fixed on her.

She hesitated, but he continued, insistent. "I'll have them saddle up my horse." He stared with an intensity that was foreign and uncomfortable to Sisi — she had never been the recipient of such an expectant stare by an attractive young man. Much less an emperor.

"I'm not sure that it is a good time," Sisi answered, her voice sounding as feeble as her half-formed excuse.

"Why not? You're dressed for riding. I have had Count Grünne clear my calendar this morning. The horses certainly are not otherwise engaged."

Sisi shifted her weight, her fingers touching the flowers strewn around her bonnet, a distracted, girlish gesture.

"Let's take a ride," Franz insisted once more.

"Well, perhaps Helene would like to join us." Sisi stammered, throwing an irritated look at her sister, who seemed oblivious to this exchange.

Franz, too, looked down the long corridor of the stable toward Helene. And then, without a moment's pause, he called out: "Grünne, you don't mind escorting my cousin Helene back to the villa, do you? I'd like to take my cousin Elisabeth for a ride."

Sisi saw how, in the shadowed corner of the stable, Helene's mouth fell open, her eyes fixing on her sister. Sisi, frantic, returned her gape: *Forgive me, Néné. I didn't mean for this to happen.*

Franz continued, his tone effortlessly affable: "I've been hearing from Elisabeth what an avid rider she is. I'd like to see it for myself." Looking from one sister to the other, he continued: "Cousin Helene, you said yourself that you do not enjoy riding, isn't that so? I'll put Count Grünne here entirely at your disposal for the morning. You may do whatever you'd like. Perhaps a walk through the gardens? Or a carriage ride into town? Her wish is your command, Grünne, do you understand?"

Grünne, looking between the two sisters, seemed to understand the situation with perfect clarity. The consummate diplomat, Grünne replied in a pleasant tone, "Of course, Your Majesty."

"Good, it's settled then." Franz nodded his approval and turned back to Sisi. "I'll have them saddle up Diamant immediately. I think you shall find she has a pleasantly smooth gait."

Helene, still having offered no reply, stared at Sisi as if her younger sister were complicit in this crime. Sisi felt her own guilt like a stab in her gut. *I would switch places with you, Néné.*

"Shall we, Duchess Helene?"

Helene, without a word, accepted Grünne's

outstretched arm and turned to exit the stables. As she crossed the threshold of the shadowy barn into the splash of determined sunlight that lit up the yard, Helene glanced back over her shoulder. What was that look? Sisi wondered, reeling. Hurt and anger? Envy? Or, Sisi wondered, could it possibly be relief?

"Here, you'll need this," Franz crossed the stables toward the tack wall, retrieving a black *bombe,* a riding helmet fashioned in lush velvet.

"Pardon me?" Sisi blinked, turning from the place where her sister had just exited, back toward Franz. She stared at the helmet he offered her, mute, before she understood his point. "Oh, yes, of course." She reached to remove the straw bonnet she currently wore, offering a perfunctory "thank you."

Franz lifted the helmet, unfastening the front buckle. "May I help you into it?"

"Oh." Sisi fumbled, removing her straw hat. As she did so, her hair came loose, her thick, dark-blond curls tumbling down around her face and shoulders. She gathered her hair, refastening it into a quick, sloppy braid, aware that Franz watched her intently as she did so.

"It goes just like so." Franz leaned close, placing the helmet gently on her head before clicking the buckle under her chin. The tips of his fingers grazed her cheeks, then the top of her neck. Sisi felt a shiver that could not have been caused by the balmy morning air, and she closed her eyes.

"All set." The buckle clipped into place, Franz allowed his fingers to linger just a moment too long under her chin. Try as she could to block it out, the warm touch of Franz's skin made itself obvious against hers, and Sisi realized yet again that this was the closest she had ever stood to a young man.

"Thank you," she managed to say, looking away from Franz toward the horse. A stable groom appeared and she was grateful that it was this stranger who helped her into the saddle, and not Franz.

Franz mounted his horse, a thick Hanoverian with a coat as smooth and rich as chocolate. "This is Sieger." He leaned forward to stroke his horse's thick neck.

"Hello, Sieger. An appropriate name, he looks every inch the champion." Sisi nodded, admiring the appearance that Franz and the stately Sieger made together.

"So far, we have never lost together," Franz answered. "Isn't that right, Sieger?"

The blanket Sieger wore under the saddle was of plush velvet in deep cardinal red, embroidered with a coat of arms in golden thread. Sisi studied the crest, finding it difficult to determine the meaning of the elaborately stitched design.

Franz followed her eyes. "Do you speak Latin?"

Sisi read aloud the words scrawled beneath the crest: "*Viribus Unitis.* Something about . . . being one. Oh, I'm afraid my Latin is poor. Forgive me." Sisi averted her eyes, embarrassed. She could tell him the Latin name of any wildflower. Could quote any number of lines of Shakespeare or Goethe from memory. But ancient Latin translations? She had never found a passion for something referred to as *dead;* no, she wanted to concern herself with that which was *alive.*

" 'United Strength,' " Franz said, looking as if he were trying to suppress a grin. "The Habsburg family motto."

"The crest above it is . . ."

"Yes?"

"Interesting," Sisi said. "I see the crown on top of the eagle, and the eagle certainly looks very proud and regal . . . but, why does the eagle have two heads?"

Franz grinned knowingly. "It's because we Habsburgs have beheaded so many of our subjects that we believe everyone ought to be born with two heads."

Sisi gulped, responseless.

"Cousin Elisabeth!" Franz laughed heartily. "I am joking."

"Oh." Sisi smiled, softening. "Thank goodness."

Opposite her, Franz seemed entirely at

ease. "But you really should have seen the look on your face."

Sisi lowered her eyes, flushing with the warmth of the morning, the warmth of Franz's gaze. "Then tell me the true meaning of it."

"When Maria Theresa — my Great-Great-Grandmamma — became Empress, she married Franz Stephen, Duke of Lorraine." Franz slid his boots into the stirrups as he explained. "The two of them not only lived together happily married, but they ruled together happily as well."

"An admirable accomplishment," Sisi said, thinking of her own parents' union. *Happily* would not have been the word she would have used to describe their manner of living together.

"Indeed. More difficult than it sounds, I'd imagine," Franz said.

Sisi nodded. Something she had seen in her poetry books, only. And yet, surely such unions existed.

"Since their marriage, the Lorraine branch has been a part of our House. So I am Franz Joseph, from the House of Habsburg-Lorraine."

"That explains the double-headed eagle."

"Precisely. Two families, one House." Franz nodded.

Now settled atop her horse, Sisi's discomfort lessened noticeably; after all, this was where she was most at ease.

"And now, I believe we are ready for our ride." Franz clucked at his horse and led Sisi out of the stables, away from the villa. At a back gate an imperial guardsman saluted and let them pass. Sisi blinked, her eyes adjusting to the flood of sunshine.

"But Maria Theresa was not entirely lucky, in the end." Franz picked up his history account as he trotted Sieger farther away from the villa toward the open field.

"Why is that?" Sisi asked, intrigued, as her horse kept apace with Franz's.

"You see, Maria Theresa had a favorite daughter, for whom she made an excellent match; it was a marriage envied by every girl in Europe."

"Who was that?" Sisi wondered aloud.

"This daughter was married to a certain King Louis. And her name was Marie Antoinette."

"Marie Antoinette? The French queen?" That name came from a history lesson that Sisi was certain she would never forget.

"The wife of King Louis XVI. They both met their unceremonious ends at the guillotine, I'm afraid."

Sisi had never connected this history lesson to her own cousin's family. "My goodness, she was a great-aunt of yours."

"She was." Franz nodded.

"It makes one think twice about longing

for the crown, I would say," Sisi mused aloud, before she realized the poor taste of her remark. She really must learn to tame her tongue, she chided herself. "That is . . . forgive me, I would never mean to imply . . . surely you are beloved by all —"

"It's quite all right, Cousin Elisabeth," Franz interrupted her, adding a wave of his hand. "I understood your meaning. And I do plan to keep my head where it currently is — neck and all."

They rode in silence for several minutes, and Sisi noticed, with a mounting sense of discomfort, that Franz's expression had turned serious, even brooding. Still cringing over her own thoughtless remark, she did not speak. Eventually, Franz broke the silence between them. "I intend to be a monarch who works for his people and serves them well. Hopefully I will never give them reason to wish to send me to my death." Franz looked to her with an earnest expression, and Sisi was struck once more by how good-looking her sister's fiancé was.

"And they shall love you, in return," she answered. She was sure of it.

"Love is not my primary concern," Franz answered matter-of-factly, looking out over the field. "Let them love their queen. Their crown princes and princesses. But the emperor must have their respect. That's of the utmost importance."

Sisi frowned at this curious statement. "But . . . surely you'd long for both? Their love *and* their respect?"

Franz turned to her now, speaking as if he were reciting an edict that he had memorized long ago, in his earliest days as a boy in the imperial nursery. "I rule by divine right. If they love God, then they love me. But to rule . . . to rule, a king needs respect."

Sisi considered this, twisting the reins in her fingers. "Do you not believe that people are motivated primarily by their hearts . . . by their love . . . more so than by anything else?"

Franz turned now, staring at Sisi with an intensity that made her long to squirm in her saddle. But she forced herself to hold his blue eyes with her own. After what felt like an interminable silence, he looked away and said: "Perhaps you're right, Cousin Elisabeth."

But Sisi was not sure whether he actually believed that.

Franz shrugged his shoulders, assuming a lighter tone as he redirected the conversation. "Enough politics." Gesturing out over the scenery before them, he observed: "The vistas are not bad, are they?"

Sisi stared across the wide fields and admired the miles of rolling, uninterrupted green. Past the fields, the craggy mountains rose toward the sky, and Sisi spotted a small farmhouse tucked into the very seam where the mountains split from the fields. Franz led them toward this spot now. As they approached the farmhouse, Sisi spotted several girls chasing a homemade kite while their mother stood nearby, hunched over a small vegetable garden.

"Hello," Sisi waved at the girls as they passed. Oblivious of their imperial visitor, the little girls continued to pursue their kite as their mother looked up from her gardening.

"Your Majesty!" The woman gasped, allowing the vegetables collected in her apron to tumble to the ground. "Girls, stop! Bow to the emperor!" The girls caught the kite and stood still, dumbstruck, as Sisi and Franz rode by.

"Lovely day to fly a kite," Franz called out, allowing a smile to soften the impact of his impossibly stiff posture.

Within several minutes they had crossed the field and began a slow ascent toward the nearby foothills. Sisi looked back, glancing once more over the meadow they had traversed, and noticed a cluster of horses trailing them. Uniformed men sitting with rigid uprightness atop thick-chested war horses. The group now passed the same farm at which Sisi and Franz had just been greeted.

"Your Maj— Franz." Sisi studied the group, its formation like that of a small army. "I think we are being followed."

"We most certainly are." Franz glanced sideways at her, unfazed.

"Who are they?"

Franz leaned his head to the side. "The imperial guard."

"Your bodyguards?" Sisi narrowed her eyes to gain a better look; there were about a dozen of them, all riding identical brown Hanoverians. She spotted the Habsburg-Lorraine crest on the side of each horse's blanket. "Do they follow you everywhere?"

"Everywhere except the privy closet and the bedroom," Franz answered, looking straight ahead. Sisi flushed.

"Let's ride up a little. The view gets better the higher you climb." Franz pressed his heels into Sieger's side, picking up his speed and breaking stride with Sisi and Diamant.

"All right," Sisi answered, spurring Diamant forward.

She caught up with him and they galloped uphill, side by side, for a while. When she did steal a view of her cousin, she noted to herself how good Franz looked atop his horse: his face was relaxed, his seat confident.

He turned to catch her staring at him, and he slowed the pace to a trot. Sisi matched him. "You ride well, Elisabeth."

"Thank you," she answered, her breath uneven. She remembered Aunt Sophie's words from the night before: *Franz thinks there's nothing more attractive than a young woman with a fine seat atop a horse.*

Franz interrupted her thoughts: "It's rare for a young woman to ride as skillfully as a man, is it not? Mother always tired long before the men in our riding parties."

Sisi reddened, not sure whether his observation also carried with it a tinge of judgment, even disapproval. "My father was . . . well, less traditional, you might say." She neglected to add that, at times, he had been so unconventional that he had encouraged his daughter to ride bareback, like the peasants with whom he mingled and caroused. "Papa cared very little for the conventions that restrict young girls. He thought there was nothing more ennobling for us than to spend time out of doors."

"I had heard that. From Mother."

He had heard that? What did that mean? Perhaps he been *warned* about their unruly upbringing? Sisi wondered this to herself, remembering the disdain with which Sophie had spoken of her father the evening before, bristling at the thought.

"Your father encouraged you to ride often, then?" Franz continued.

Sisi felt the need to come to Papa's defense now. "Papa did not believe all of the conventional wisdom that women are somehow the weaker sex," Sisi answered. "My parents were perhaps more lax with our upbringing than others of their station are. But I am grateful of it."

Franz looked at Sisi appraisingly, as if entertained by her defiance. "The girl they have raised can keep apace with the emperor himself. I suppose that's perhaps the best piece of evidence yet that women should be allowed to exert themselves."

So he was not disappointed with her after all, Sisi noted. In fact, he seemed appreciative of her strength.

"So there was to be no keeping you indoors with your needlepoint and dance lessons, Cousin Elisabeth?"

"You've seen my inadequacy when it comes to Latin." Sisi grinned. "No, my favorite classroom was always the outdoors." She thought back to Possi, to days spent in the woods with her father. Perhaps it was homesickness. Perhaps it was the exposure to Franz's entirely different upbringing. But from this distance, the duke stood in Sisi's mind as a glossier, more attractive version of himself. Less shaky, bloodshot, and erratic, and more of a free spirit, like herself. "Papa would take me hiking, and I would skip and hop about like a chamois as he taught me about the plants and wild animals. My history lessons were the tales he would tell me while we rode, side by side."

Franz nodded, listening. "But your sister, Helene, she does not like to ride as you do?"

It was the first time that Helene's name had been spoken between them, Sisi realized, noting the lump of guilt in her stomach. "I'm afraid not," Sisi answered. "She had a bad fall once when we were younger. She's never wanted to get on a horse since then."

"Ah, so you were lucky. You escaped a similar trauma?"

"Oh no, I fell all the time. Scared Mamma nearly to death. But I refused to give it up. Papa liked to joke that, had we not been born noble, he and I would have been performers in the circus."

Franz laughed at this and Sisi couldn't help but smile. She was enjoying his company more than she had expected to. Below them, farther down the hill, the imperial guard continued to trail her and Franz.

Franz looked from his bodyguards to Sisi, a mischievous flicker in his pale-blue eyes. "Shall we give them some exercise?"

"Pardon?"

"Try to shake them off our trail?" Franz said, leaning his head to one side as he smiled at her.

Sisi sat up a bit straighter, excited by the challenge.

"If ever two riders could manage it, it's us," Franz said. "What do you say?"

Sisi nodded.

"Come on, Sieger, let's ride!" Franz clapped the reins against the horse, and Sieger set off into a forceful, determined run that propelled his imperial cargo straight up the mountain.

"Diamant, let's go!" Sisi followed suit, spurring the horse to the challenge. Diamant was as strong as a young horse in her prime could be, and her gait was smooth and sure. It was a thrill unlike anything Sisi had ever experienced, and she surrendered to the welcome rush of the pine-tinged breeze in her face, the thunderous pulse of the hooves beneath her. Her breath heaved in and out in labored, heavy panting, and before long she found her arms and legs aching, a feeling of fatigue that she found familiar and incredibly comforting. This was the feeling of exertion she had always sought in her rides, and her heart beat in a wild, carefree rhythm.

Eventually the trail flattened slightly and Franz slowed his horse's pace. "Slower now, Sieger. We lost them. Good boy, good boy."

Sisi reined in Diamant to keep Sieger's pace. The horses, like their riders, were short of breath, and coated in a glossy sheen of perspiration. "I think they must be a mile behind us," Sisi panted.

"There's a stream here, let's have some water." Franz pulled Sieger to a full stop and dismounted. He tied Sieger and then reached for Sisi's hand, helping her down from Diamant. Warm from the weather and the ride, Sisi unclipped her helmet and removed it, allowing her hair to fall freely around her shoulders.

"I hope that was not too strenuous." Franz studied her, taking her arm and guiding her upstream from where the horses were drinking.

Sisi smiled. "Not at all."

"I'm impressed, Cousin Elisabeth. You didn't grow weary?"

"Just thirsty," she answered.

"Well, we are in the right spot."

The clearing was just wide enough to allow the slow stream to carve a narrow path through the pines and the mossy earth. The trees that bordered the clearing were amply stocked with birds, carefree creatures who now trilled out the arrival of these two new visitors. It was a lovely setting. Too lovely, in fact, and Sisi felt it once more: that troublesome lump of guilt in her gut. What must Helene be doing now, at the bottom of this hill?

Sisi pulled her eyes away from Franz and pointed at the spring, its waters collecting in a clear, shimmering pool before them. "So, is this some of the famous Bad Ischl water?" She asked it in what she hoped was a casual, lighthearted tone. The tone used between friends.

"Indeed. You said you were thirsty?"

Sisi nodded.

"I personally doubt all of the tales about

this water being therapeutic, and having curative powers. But it certainly tastes good." Franz knelt on the soft ground and bent forward toward the spring. "Mother claims it was this water that . . ." He paused suddenly.

"That what?" Sisi asked, noting with humor that her polite cousin's cheeks were now flushed a deep crimson.

"That . . . er . . . allowed her to have me."

"Then perhaps I had better not drink it, after all," Sisi chirped, an impulsive response that struck her as far too forward the moment it slipped from her lips.

However, to her relief, Franz erupted in laughter. "I believe there were other variables involved." He looked down, his cheeks growing even more deeply colored. Sisi averted her eyes, trying to suppress her own giddy, even girlish laughter.

"Anyhow" — Franz tossed his shoulders back, regaining his practiced composure — "you must try the waters, Cousin Elisabeth. I insist." Dipping his fingers, Franz ruptured the calm glassiness of its surface, sending rippling rings through the water. When he lifted his cupped hands, he had captured enough to drink. Sisi did the same.

"Cheers." Franz smiled at her.

"Cheers," Sisi replied. "To your health, Cousin Franz."

"No, to yours, Elisabeth." They sipped the water, its cold sweetness sending a welcome chill through Sisi's body. She dipped her hands back under the surface and helped herself to a second drink.

"You work up quite a thirst when riding in the middle of the summer heat. And an appetite. I should have thought to bring some wine and cheese." Franz reached for a second sip.

"This water will do just fine for now," Sisi answered, wiping her mouth before leaning forward to take another sip.

As she did so, she detected a noise in the distance. It was faint at first, two voices. Sitting upright, she looked deeper into the forest. Franz had heard it now, too, and he rose to his feet.

Just then two people emerged from the brush, arguing loudly.

"I told you, we'll get a bit lower, the spring is too cold up 'ere!"

"I'm thirsty *now,* Marga." The man appeared on the trail first, but not from the lower direction of the imperial guards. They were coming from above, descending the mountain from an even higher point.

"Well, pardon me, my fine gentleman and lady." The gray-haired hiker paused, looking to his female companion. Sisi supposed them to be man and wife.

Their clothing betrayed that they did not belong in the court, nor did they belong in the village of Bad Ischl below. No, they looked like they came from some remote mountain chalet. The man wore simple black pants and a gray sackcloth shirt. The woman, sweaty and browned from the sun, wore a faded dress covered by a linen apron that looked as if it hadn't been new for years.

Though their wrinkled skin and thinning hair spoke to their advanced age, they emerged on the trail with a spry nimbleness that indicated their familiarity and comfort in the hills. The woman held a basket, filled with what looked to Sisi like mushrooms, and the man carried a satchel across his back stacked with kindling wood.

"Look, Gunnar, fellow hikers." The woman studied Franz and Sisi, placing her basket of mushrooms down beside the spring. "And of a noble sort, by the looks of it. Good day, sir and lady."

"Taking some of the waters on this fine morning?" The old man chattered good-naturedly, bending over to take a sip for himself. When he had finished drinking, he looked up once more, directly into the face of Franz. Understanding spread across his face. "No." He kept his eyes fixed on Franz. "Can't be. Is it you?"

Franz smiled, looking to Sisi before answering. "That depends on who you think I am."

"But you can't be . . . His Holy Grace? The Emperor?" The old man turned to his wife, speaking at barely a whisper. "Marga, you think it's really him?"

The woman shook her head decisively. "All the way up 'ere? And without his guards? Don't be daft, Gunnar."

But the old man was not so easily convinced of his error. Turning back to Franz he asked: "Are you . . . the . . . Emperor hisself?"

"I am," Franz said; his smile was kind and unassuming, even shy, Sisi marveled.

"God Almighty!" The old man reached for his wife's rough hand, clutching it as he lowered them both into a bow. "Marga, it's him. Emperor Franz Joseph, in the flesh!"

"Majesty." Marga crossed herself several times, bowing her head. "Forgive my rudeness. I'm not used to seeing kings up in these hills. Come to think on it, I'm not used to seeing kings *anywhere.*"

Sisi had to laugh at the guileless confession.

"Please stand, please." Franz shifted, looking to Sisi as if uncomfortable.

"Your Grace!" Gunnar kept his eye fixed firmly on the forest floor between them. "I climb the mountain thinking I'll get some firewood and a sip from the healing waters, and I get to see the Emperor hisself." The man called Gunnar now had tears in his eyes, and he dropped his wife's hand to cross himself. "Do you believe it, Marga?"

"Tell him about Rolphe. Tell him!" The old woman nudged her husband.

"Majesty, if you please, our son, Rolphe, he's terribly sick. Would you mind saying a prayer for him?"

The old wife continued. "Only reason I come up 'ere anymore is to get these here mushrooms — they are Rolphe's favorite, you see. I'll do anything to give that boy a bit of comfort."

"I'd be honored to pray for your son." Franz nodded at the elderly pair, his voice courteous yet formal. "Rolphe is his name?"

"Aye, Majesty." The old man nodded.

"And who is this pretty companion?" The old woman turned to Sisi, flashing a gummy smile. "I hadn't heard of you taking a wife — 'scuse me, an empress — yet. Course, news is slow to reach us up in these hills."

"Oh, no." Sisi lowered her eyes, shaking her head.

"This is my cousin, Duchess Elisabeth of Bavaria," Franz answered.

"God Almighty, didn't know they made them that pretty in Bavaria. I fancy I'm going to have to take me a trip to Bavaria when you expire, Marg." Gunnar nudged his wife.

"Such bawdy talk! You can't talk like that in front of the Emperor and his cousin." Marga slapped Gunnar on the shoulder. "Manners, Gunnar."

"No, it's quite all right, I assure you." Franz couldn't help but laugh. "It's true, she's certainly pretty." He turned to Sisi, prompting her cheeks to redden involuntarily.

"Well, we're praying that you'll find your empress soon, Majesty," the old woman continued. "We all want a baby for Your Grace."

Now it was Franz's turn to demur, and he shifted his weight from one foot to the other, mumbling a quick response: "You are kind to pray for me."

"I think this one would be a good choice," Gunnar whispered to his wife, not at all quietly.

"Hush, Gunnar, they can hear you!"

Sisi and Franz looked at one another, sharing an embarrassed grin.

"Well, if you don't mind, I was going to take my cousin Elisabeth farther up the hill. So we will be moving along."

"Of course, Majesty," Gunnar bowed low. "Marga, can you believe I just stepped aside to make room for the Emperor hisself?"

"My sister will never believe it." Marga still stared at Sisi, crossing herself once more. "If only I could show her a picture of how beautiful you are, Madame Elisabeth."

"You enjoy your day, Your Graces. And if you ever fancy some of Marga's mushroom stew — it's the best there is. She puts in the wild rabbit, and some of her spices." The old man smacked his lips as he spoke. "We live just an hour's way down this hill, less if you're atop the horses. Come any time you like,"

Gunnar offered, his face earnest.

Franz nodded. "Thank you. And we will pray for your son, Rolphe, and for his recovery."

"You're too kind, Your Majesty." Gunnar leaned forward and bowed once more, and his wife did the same.

"Good day." Franz helped Sisi back onto Diamant before mounting Sieger and leading her toward the trail up the mountain. Gunnar and Marga stood transfixed, watching the retreating figures like a pair of pious supplicants.

They rode in silence for several minutes. Sisi felt humbled, suddenly, having witnessed the exuberant display of adoration for her cousin. Their awe at beholding Franz had reminded her of the weight of his position; they viewed him as a deity among them.

"That must happen to you all the time," she remarked, breaking the silence. A bird trilled out in reply from a nearby bough. "People coming up to you and recognizing you. Treating you as if you are a god."

"It does." Franz leaned his head to the side, thoughtful. "But I rarely speak to them. They rarely have the chance."

"Why is that?"

"If I am with my guardsmen, or my attendants, or Grünne or Mother, they aren't allowed near. Mother would never have allowed such an exchange."

Sisi frowned; in Bavaria, Papa was constantly mingling with the peasants and villagers. Perhaps more than he should have. But it made him a beloved ruler. "Don't you crave contact with your people?" she asked. "To hear firsthand of their hopes and woes? I thought that was quite nice."

Franz thought about this. After a pause he answered, his words sounding more like a recitation of an oft-repeated lesson than a statement of any true conviction: "One must keep to one's station."

Sisi let the subject go at that, retreating into her thoughts. She conceded that she could not truly know what it must feel like for Franz — being recognized and pursued everywhere he went. To be so instantaneously known and gawked at by every commoner he passed. To be set apart from every person who saw him, a living icon, aware of his own frailty, and yet invested with all the love, praise, pain, and suffering of every citizen. The burdens her cousin must have shouldered suddenly overwhelmed her. She was about to say so when Franz spoke, interrupting her thoughts.

"Mother has always made known to me the importance of my bearing. That there ought to be a certain distance between the ruler and the subject. A ruler ought to inspire awe, and even fear."

Sisi considered this logic once more. It did

not surprise her that Aunt Sophie advocated for a hard leadership style — that was, after all, the fashion in which she herself seemed to live her life. But she could not agree with her aunt's opinion. Franz, Sisi suspected, had a more sensitive character than his overbearing mother. Sisi felt a strong conviction that, if he could shake his mother's indomitable influence, he would be a magnanimous ruler, beloved by his people.

"You are lost in thought, Cousin Elisabeth."

Sisi looked up at him, shaking her head, realizing that she had not heard a word of his latest remark. "Sorry."

"Won't you share them?"

"Pardon?"

"Your thoughts? Would you share them with me?" He stared at her, his eyes impossibly earnest. "Of course, that's not a command," he said, turning back to the path before them, twisting the reins in his hands. "More just . . . a request. If you would . . ."

"Yes, of course," Sisi answered. "It's just that . . . one who imposes fear can easily become hated, and worse, deposed. But love, that must be won, and once won, need never be lost."

Franz thought about this, looking straight ahead at the path. He seemed unconvinced.

Sisi spoke, repeating a phrase she'd studied often: *Nothing is so strong as gentleness, nothing so gentle as real strength.*

"I like that," Franz looked at her. "Where did you hear that?"

"I read it. It's Goethe."

"Goethe," Franz repeated the name. "Perhaps I should read some more of his works. I can hardly recall them."

"I think anyone would benefit from it," Sisi said. "I'd be happy to loan you my copies, Franz."

"Oh, no need, I'm sure we have dozens of copies in our imperial libraries."

"Yes, of course." Sisi reddened. How simple she must have appeared, offering her books to the emperor.

"So then, is that one indoor activity that you *do* enjoy? Reading Goethe?"

Sisi lowered her eyes, pursing her lips to prevent the smile that tugged on them. "Who said that one must read Goethe indoors?"

Franz looked at her, studying her features.

"But yes, I do love Goethe," she said, shifting in the saddle under the intensity of his gaze. "I take his books, and my poetry books, and I go out of doors and I can happily pass an entire afternoon on a patch of sunny grass."

"How lovely that sounds. I can just imagine you doing it, Cousin Elisabeth." Still he looked at her. "I should very much like to do the same. With you."

Sisi let that remark go unanswered, noting as she did so how her heart leapt in her breast. A companionable silence settled between them. They rode on, the only noise being the sporadic call of the tree lark, the gentle whisper of spring water slipping over smooth rocks.

"Peaceful up here, isn't it?" Franz looked to her.

"Lovely," she agreed. And it was. They seemed entirely alone, entirely removed from all other people and all other places.

"We're almost to the top now, just a bit farther," Franz said.

They proceeded up the mountain. The trees grew thicker now, forming an impermeable wall of forest and shading them in a cool, damp cocoon. The breeze, gliding through the tree boughs, carried with it the sweet scent of pine and sap.

And then, suddenly, the steep ascent leveled off. The trees cleared, opening up before them. Sisi gasped as she beheld a view of cloudless blue sky at the top of the world. The horses, without orders, stopped, as if they, too, were overcome by the beauty sprawled out before them.

"Look at how high we are!" Sisi hopped off Diamant, quickly tying her to a thin sapling before running to the ledge. There, she surveyed the expanse of green and blue. "The entire world is below us." She sputtered out a laugh, fanning her arms out as if to pull the whole scene into her embrace. Franz fixed the haphazard knot she had fastened for Diamant and tied Sieger as well.

Sisi skipped along the edge of the precipice, looking down on the lower mountaintops and the fields far below.

"Please be careful, Cousin Elisabeth." Franz approached, stepping cautiously toward her.

"Come see this view!" She waved him forward.

"It is something, isn't it?" Franz was beside her now, bracing himself with the support of a flimsy branch. "Look, there's the Kaiservilla." Franz pointed at a minuscule shape far beneath them, a dollop of yellow surrounded by green.

"I can barely see it." Sisi looked down, marveling at how tiny the massive complex had become.

"And that's the farm we rode past. Can you see the kite flying over the girls?"

"No, I can't see it at all." Sisi marveled, squinting her eyes.

"And that's the village of Bad Ischl." Franz pointed toward a cluster of buildings that sat nestled into the valley, the church spire now the only identifiable structure.

"We are above the world," Sisi exclaimed, spreading her arms wide. "This must be the view of God."

Franz was beside her, close now. "Or the emperor."

"Or Gunnar," Sisi quipped, edging forward even closer to the ledge. "Only he climbed this on foot, while you and I, we needed our horses."

"I think you might make me jealous, the way you praise Gunnar." Franz was so close to her now that she felt his breath on her cheek.

"How could a duke's daughter make an emperor jealous?" She turned to face him. Her heart stumbled involuntarily, as if careening over the edge on which they stood, when she noticed how keenly he looked at her.

"You'd be surprised," Franz answered, cracking a smile as his light eyes held hers. She was aware that they approached a dangerous precipice. Their words, their glances, their physical closeness were taking them somewhere that she knew they ought not to go. How easy it would be to flout the border of friendship, to step headlong into some unknown territory that, while frightening, felt natural. Inevitable, even.

They stared at one another in silence, this unspoken thread weaving between them, pulling them closer in this wordless moment. But before one of them could do something they might both regret, Sisi turned, snapping the thread. She edged away from the ledge and walked toward the spring. Her tone light, she said, "Let's have a drink."

Franz followed her with his gaze, but did

not reply.

Sisi fixed her eyes on the pool of water. "Pity that Helene missed out on all of this." She swallowed hard, forcing the words out. "Next time you'll bring her here."

"Not if she doesn't like to ride," Franz answered, joining Sisi beside the stream.

"You're the emperor," Sisi answered, turning to hold his gaze. "You'll find a way to get your bride up here."

"I suppose." The manner in which Franz shrugged his shoulders confused Sisi. She was grateful when he changed the topic. "It's terribly hot. Do you mind if I remove my coat?"

"Only if you don't mind that I remove mine," Sisi answered. Had she been riding alone in this summer heat, or with Papa, she would have shed her outer layers hours earlier.

"It's settled then." Franz tugged on his jacket sleeves, slipping out of the heavy riding coat. Sisi unbuttoned her silk riding jacket and removed it, enjoying the breezy lightness of only the white blouse on her skin.

"Much better," Franz sighed, placing his jacket beside him on the ground. He looked at her, seeing Sisi in her blouse. His eyes remained fixed on her. She fidgeted. It occurred to Sisi for the first time that she was not wearing a corset. Not only was it impossibly uncomfortable to wear one under a riding suit, but the presence of one would render her favorite activity, riding, completely miserable. Having shed her riding coat, all that stood between her and Franz on her upper body was a thin blouse and her skimpy undergarments. She crossed her arms.

"Water?" Franz arched his eyebrows, gesturing toward the brook.

"Oh, yes."

Franz leaned down once more to sip from the spring. As he did so, Sisi noticed a thick gash across the back of his neck. The skin was discolored and raised, a scar that had healed but would never fully disappear.

"Franz," Sisi said. "What is this?" Instinctively she reached forward. She didn't realize what she had done until it was too late — until her fingers touched the soft raised flesh on the back of his neck.

"Oh, this?" He stiffened, reaching his hand for the spot, grasping her fingers before she could retract them.

"You have a scar," she said, now more preoccupied with the feel of his hand atop her own than the raised skin of his wound. They stared at one another, their hands still touching, his palm warm against hers. After a pause, he released her hand and she dropped it to her lap.

Flustered, she tried to clear her head and remember her question. "What is it from?"

Franz fingered the spot, his expression

clouding over. "A would-be assassin."

"Truly?" She gasped.

"A Hungarian, by the name of Libényi."

"He . . . he tried to kill you?"

Franz nodded.

"How?"

"I was walking the walls in Vienna, examining the fortifications, when this Libényi came up behind me and stabbed me in the neck."

Sisi put her hand to her own neck in a reflexive gesture. "Horrific," she said.

"I was saved by two things. First, my uniform. The one you saw me in last night. It's god-awfully heavy and unforgivably hot, but it's sturdy. Sturdy enough that it protected against the blade."

Sisi looked at the coat lying on the ground between them, the more casual riding coat. It was heavy, but nowhere near as heavy as the white uniform had appeared. Franz, sensing her thoughts, added: "I only ever wear this thing when I'm here. Back in Vienna, I wear the uniform every day. You'll see. Things are very . . . *different* . . . in Vienna."

Sisi couldn't help but scowl at this curious remark, wondering what he meant by it. But she didn't probe. Instead, she asked: "You said you were saved by two things. What's the second?"

"My men. The loyalty of my men. They fought that Hungarian back."

She nodded. "And thank God. But that

sounds" — Sisi stammered — "horrendous."

Franz sighed. "Mother was terribly shaken. It made her hate the entirety of Hungary even more. And she kept repeating that it showed the importance that I be married. Produce an heir. And soon." Franz laughed, but not a lighthearted laugh. "In some ways, however, I was almost glad that it happened."

"Glad?"

"To be wounded made me feel . . . I don't know. More worthy. Like I could finally understand what all of the soldiers I command are facing. It makes me more like them."

Sisi blinked heavily, turning her gaze on the pool of water beside them. "That's one way to see it."

"Ever since then, the imperial guard has been like my shadow."

"Maybe it was unwise of us to lose them," Sisi pointed out, looking around at the woods in which they sat, alone, with no sign of the bodyguards.

"I feel safe here. Don't you?" Franz smiled, turning so that his upper body angled toward hers. "But you're as pale as a ghost, Elisabeth. Did my story upset you?"

"It is horrific to think . . ." Sisi let her voice trail off.

"You are upset by the idea of me being hurt?" Franz's eyes stared expectant, hopeful.

Sisi nodded. "Of course."

Franz smiled, putting a hand softly on top of hers. She let it rest there, though she knew she should pull away.

"Then I'm doubly grateful it occurred," he said, his voice quiet now. "It granted me the opportunity to win your sympathy."

Not sure how to respond, Sisi merely sat beside him, thinking about this confession. And about how terrifying it would be to have people in the world who desired to kill you. What immeasurable pressure her cousin lived with.

Franz interrupted her troubled musings after several minutes. "Heavens, it's hot." He pulled his hand back from her to wipe his brow.

"Indeed," Sisi agreed, her own head feeling fuzzy. She was not sure if it was from the heat and the exertion, or from something else entirely. From Franz. From the image of Helene's face that kept passing before her mind. From her frenzied, frantic, confused thoughts.

"I'd like to go swimming," Franz said suddenly, staring at the water.

"I'll take Diamant and begin walking down the hill, if you'd like to swim," Sisi offered, beginning to rise. "You can meet us on the trail."

"No, no, no," Franz shook his head, pressing his hand against her arm, holding her beside him.

She turned, her gaze flying to Franz's hand where it held her. He dropped it, releasing her.

Sisi swallowed, speaking in a light tone. "Why not? Take a swim, you've earned it."

Now Franz looked away, lifting a loose blade of grass and releasing it into the breeze. "This is the source of the drinking water. One is not supposed to bathe in it. It would taint the supply for the villages below."

"Oh, I see. Yes, I suppose as the emperor, you aren't able to be reckless. Perhaps you, of all people, ought to honor the rules."

Franz thought about this a moment, plucking more grass from the carpet of green beneath them. His hands seemed restless, as did his thoughts. "What if we did decide to be reckless?" He posited, staring into her eyes once more with a new, alarming intensity. "What if we did the reckless thing? Didn't think of the others first, but thought of what we wanted? If we did what was right for us, just you and me?"

And suddenly Franz was no longer talking about swimming in a spring.

"But we can't," Sisi answered, her reply barely a whisper.

"Why can't we?"

"Because . . . you belong to your people." *And you belong to Helene.* Her throat was dry, so scorched that all the water in this brook wouldn't cool it down. "Your decisions aren't just made for you. Or for me. They are for the empire." What had her mother raised her on? *"One must do one's duty."* Her duty was to support Helene.

"Isn't an emperor entitled to happiness?"

"Of course he is."

"What's the point of being emperor if I can't have the one thing I most want? The one thing that will make me happy?" He stared, eyebrows knit, into the reflection of the small, smooth pool. Eventually, he slapped the ground and rose up, walking back toward his horse. Sisi guessed that their excursion was over.

They descended the hill in a strained silence, Franz's mood clearly darkened. When they arrived back at the stables, Franz handed over the reins of his horse to a groom and left Sisi with a quick, "Excuse me, Cousin Elisabeth."

"Thank you for the ride, Cousin Franz," she called after his retreating figure.

He paused, glancing over his shoulder in her direction. "I shall see you at dinner, Elisabeth?"

"Yes."

"Good. We are having a cotillion." And now, his tone was laced with frustration. "A dance, in *my* honor. I turn twenty-three at midnight."

"Oh," Sisi said, "that's right."

Franz wavered. "Very well. Good-bye."

With that, he turned and was gone, walking briskly across the courtyard, leaving Sisi in a troubled, confused silence.

Franz's abrupt departure was as difficult to understand as his behavior had been all day. Why had Franz insisted on spending time with her, speaking to her in these vague insinuations and indecipherable declarations? What was the point of it? she wondered. It was maddening, the way he had allowed his fingers to graze her skin. The way he had smiled at her, affixing her with those light-blue eyes filled with — what was it? Hope? Affection? Why couldn't he have saved all of these charming and quizzical looks for Helene, the one to whom he was betrothed?

It was like sitting before a grand table, a table laden with every delicacy she could have ever hoped for — smelling the sauces and anticipating the sweets — only to pick up her fork and be told she was not allowed to taste it.

Why did he have to be so maddeningly wonderful? So good to others? So handsome? So attentive to her? Her heart felt joyful, even giddy, when she recalled how his fingers had sought hers. How she had felt the soft skin on his neck.

What was worse was that she suspected that he felt the same for her. And that irrefutable realization gnawed at her, aching like a rotten tooth that evaded extraction, but from somewhere deep inside her.

She paced the courtyard, unwilling to reenter the house. *His* house. And her bedroom, which she shared with his fiancée. His fiancée, who happened to be her beloved sister. Helene, her closest confidante and only friend.

Helene. Sisi pitied Helene, and yet, she was furious with her sister. How could Helene be so carelessly cruel as to squander this, to not appreciate the unparalleled gift she had been given in being matched to Franz? Hadn't her very disinterest paved the way for Sisi and Franz to find the affection that existed between them? *Oh, Helene, how I envy you! And yet, I hate myself for doing so.*

She was also angry with Franz. She resented him for his reckless kindness and veiled remarks, when he knew full well that he would never be hers. Was he just toying with her for his own amusement? He, who could have any girl in all of Europe, was he just enjoying her as his latest conquest?

But underneath all of that, more potent than her anger toward Helene or Franz, there brewed a deep self-loathing that was directed at no one but herself. How could she have allowed herself to waltz so recklessly into this situation? To enjoy his kindnesses so much? To return his smiles, allowing them to turn into laughter? Why had she felt the need to speak up for her sister, and in doing so, to pull attention away from Helene? Why had she allowed herself to go riding with Franz, and worse, to enjoy it as much as she had? And how, oh how, had she allowed herself to fall in love with her sister's fiancé?

V.

They look into one another's eyes, a silent communication passing between them. Even after all the years, all the hurt taken and doled out between them, only the two of them can go through this. What awaits on the other side of the doors is something they must face together.

"It's time." A short priest enters the antechamber, his silken robes aflutter with the haste of his gait. After the requisite bow, he stands tall and rattles off their instructions.

They both nod. He rises from his chair, standing beside Sisi. She takes his outstretched hand and squeezes it, one last gesture of support.

"Are you ready?" he asks her.

"I am. And you?"

"Is one ever ready to divide his empire in half?"

"Franz," she says, squeezing his hand. "You are keeping your empire whole."

Franz looks forward, his lips pressed together in a tight line. When his eyes slide back toward her, he holds her gaze. Her breath stops short,

fearful of what he might say next. And then he
sighs, asking, "But what of us?"

CHAPTER FIVE

"Duchess Elisabeth, would you do me the honor?"

Sisi stared up into the broad, smiling face of Count Grünne. The officer, dressed in his starched uniform and clean-shaven, stood over her.

Sisi couldn't be certain, but it seemed that the hand held out toward her was an invitation — inexplicably — to dance. "I . . . I beg your pardon, sir?"

Helene fidgeted in the seat beside Sisi, avoiding her sister's eyes as she had done all night. On Helene's other side, Ludovika watched, her face stitched tight in nervous confusion.

In reply, the count merely waved his gloved hand and offered a grin. "May I have this dance, Your Highness, Duchess Elisabeth?"

"Oh, but I . . . I don't know the steps

205

to . . ." Sisi's words trailed off as the cluster of nearby violins struck up a waltz. Men and women paired off, taking their places in the middle of the hall.

In truth, Sisi had never before danced at a cotillion. Had never even *been* to a cotillion. The only partner with whom she'd ever stood up was her dance instructor back at Possenhofen, the stern Herr Hausmann, who appeared at the castle for irregular visits, trying to wrangle her and Helene into some familiarity with waltzes and quadrilles and polkas.

"I would look foolish." Sisi demurred, feeling her cheeks glow with a conspicuous blush. Even more painful than Count Grünne's expectant stare were the curious stares that had landed on her from around the hall. Courtiers and ministers and attendants all looked on, their lips whispering behind gloved hands and fans that offered little concealment. And there, across the crowded room, Franz Joseph sat, watching. Bach and Sophie hovered beside him, with Sophie alternatively chattering with passing courtiers and looking out over the floor as if to supervise the dancing.

The uniformed advisor leaned closer to Sisi now, his hand still extended. He arched an eyebrow as he spoke: "I will help you."

Sisi rose, giving her hand but no reply. As Grünne directed her toward the center of the dancers, she felt as if the fixed eyes of the entire gathering could have scorched a hole in the silk of her gown, such was the intensity of their collective observation.

Grünne leaned close, his manner like that of her dance instructor. "Forgive me, Duchess, but I must put my arms on your waist." Sisi blushed as he did so. "And now, we commence." His feet began to step to the three-count tempo, and she followed. Grünne's hold on her was so firm that, after a few steps, she realized that she could have picked her feet up off the floor entirely and he would have carried her through the waltz.

"The archduchess asked that I dance with you."

Sisi looked into Grünne's eyes for the first time now. "I beg your pardon?"

Grünne smiled. "Come now. Surely you know that everyone in this room was waiting."

"For what?"

"Why, to see you dance, of course."

"But . . . why?"

"Because the emperor plans to ask you to close the ball with him."

Sisi swallowed hard — certain that, if Grünne had not been holding her upright, her legs might have given out beneath her.

This was not how she had intended the night to pass. Earlier, following her ride, she had collected her warring, mangled emotions and had returned to the Kaiservilla resolved:

Franz was Helene's betrothed. She, Sisi, was here to support Helene, her beloved sister, and that was precisely what she would do.

Entering their chamber, Sisi had found Helene in bed, wrapped in covers with the shades drawn.

"Néné." Sisi hovered on the threshold of the room.

Her sister looked up, a noncommittal glance, before turning her pale face away.

"Oh, Néné, forgive me. Please." Sisi flew to her sister's side. "It was nothing, Néné, just a ride." Sisi perched herself on the edge of the bed, tenuous. Uncertain whether Helene would tell her to leave. But Helene did not.

"He knew that you don't enjoy riding. He was merely being a courteous host."

"Courteous indeed."

"Please, it was nothing more than —"

"Stop." Helene held up a hand, silencing Sisi. "Just stop, won't you? It's not your fault," her sister said eventually, but her voice had an edge to it. "I know that he asked you to accompany him." Her black eyes held Sisi's now and, though they were eyes into which Sisi had stared her entire life, they looked different somehow. Inaccessible, veiled and impenetrable.

"Yes, but, Helene, it means nothing," Sisi lied, taking her sister's limp hand in her own. It would *have* to mean nothing. She would do everything in her power to steer Helene into Franz's attention and affection. She would make this right for her sister, somehow. As much as it pained her.

Helene had listened, quietly, as Sisi had described their ride in the blandest of terms. For Helene's benefit, Sisi left out all mention of the smiles they'd shared; of the ease of their companionship and conversation; of the fleeting moments in which her skin had touched his; of the tense, fraught manner in which Franz had left her.

Helene had slowly thawed beside Sisi, listening to the story of the afternoon. Sisi's repeated assurances that it all meant nothing. As the minutes passed, her black eyes had softened, slightly.

Sisi ached from the inside, comforting Helene with these omissions, coaxing her with half truths. She hated misleading her beloved sister, but she also ached because she knew she was forfeiting the claim that she had come to feel she had over Franz. *But it is a claim to which she is not entitled,* she kept reminding herself.

And so, when eventually Néné had accepted Sisi's emphatic declarations that it all meant nothing, Sisi could have collapsed in relief. Néné had agreed to make another effort; to win the fiancé that she had come here for. She had even agreed to dress for her part.

Sisi was certain that she herself looked plain

in a pale, rose-colored frock beside her sister's elegant ivory gown ornamented with elaborate ostrich plumes. While Sisi had fashioned her hair in her customary loose braids and combs, Helene had allowed Agata and Sisi to wreath her head of dark hair in a delicate crown of ivy. She looked regal in silver slippers and kid leather gloves.

Outside their bedroom window, the sun set over the castle complex and adjacent hills. As they finished dressing, the moon rose over a clear night, with just the faintest hint of the crisp air that nipped on the heels of summer. It was the perfect evening for Franz's birthday celebration. And, Sisi had decided, it would be the occasion for Helene to finally assume her role beside the emperor. Reconciled, the girls had left their bedchamber that evening hand in hand.

And yet, when they had arrived in the dinner hall, Sisi had been ushered to the seat beside Franz. Helene, a stunned look on her face, had been seated at the opposite end of the room, farther away from the emperor than the boiled cabbage. Where Sisi should have been.

The dinner had been a terribly uncomfortable affair, with Franz turning constantly to Sisi, seeking her opinions on everything from the food to which sort of music she enjoyed for dancing. It had been too much. Sick over the unwanted attention, Sisi had barely touched her food. She had not been able to bear glancing down the table to where her sister sat, flanked by the pinch-faced Countess Esterházy and the humorless Count von Bach.

And now, here she was, dancing opposite Franz's aide-de-camp, a confidant of the emperor who warned her that he was merely the introductory act. That Sophie, recognizing her son's clear preference, had begged this seasoned officer to guide the nervous and inexperienced Sisi through her ballroom debut.

When the song was over, Sisi turned to make her way back toward her seat, but was forced to pause in her steps.

"Elisabeth?" Franz stood before her, wearing an expectant smile, like the one he'd shown her earlier that day, on their ride.

"Yes?" Sisi paused before him, her heart protesting against the suffocating cages of her ribs and corset. Oh, how she hated wearing this vile thing! Suddenly, she felt as if she could not breathe, and her hand clutched her abdomen.

Franz, oblivious of her discomfort, or perhaps mistaking it for an appropriate measure of well-mannered timidity, kept smiling. "Would you do me the great honor of dancing?"

Sisi, her mouth dry, her eyes wide with panic, looked from Franz to Grünne. Then she looked back toward Helene, and her mother. Sophie. Every set of eyes in the hall watched her. Young women, women whose names Sisi did not even know, had splintered off into clusters of two and three to watch and whisper.

Franz smiled at her, undistracted.

And so, seeing no other option before her, Sisi gave him her hand and forced herself to smile.

The violins began, and two dozen couples filled in the space to the left and right of the emperor and his chosen partner.

Sisi moved her feet in time with his, following Franz's lead, as she had done with Grünne. Franz did not hold her as tightly, did not lead as assertively as her previous partner, but the song was clear and upbeat, and she grew more comfortable as the steps unfolded.

"You do me a great honor, Cousin." Sisi swayed with him, very much aware of his hand on her waist. Aware of the different emotions that chased one another, wrestling and fighting within her. How happy she was to be standing this near to him. How natural it felt to be close to him. And yet, how far from natural this whole assembly truly was. How probing and curious were the eyes affixed on her from around the hall, causing a swell of discomfort, the urge to flee and hide. And then there was the guilt. The awareness of her sister who sat, watching, her hopes surely crushed by this latest blow. *It wasn't supposed to be me.*

"Once again, Elisabeth."

Her eyes slid upward, toward his. "Hmm?"

"You are lost in thought, once again." He watched her with an appraising smile. "Won't you share?"

"It's simply that . . . well, you do me a great honor. But I'm not certain why."

Franz continued to look down at her, his features alight, his auburn hair catching the flicker of candlelight that glowed around them. "Isn't a man entitled to dance with the lady of his choosing on his birthday?"

Sisi avoided Helene's eyes as their steps took them gliding past her seat. No one had asked her to dance. Not once. Sisi swallowed hard, hating herself, yet soaring on the elation of Franz's attention. How was it possible to experience such conflicting feelings at the same time?

"I think . . . I very much hope" — Franz's voice interrupted these thoughts of hers — "that it shall be a happy birthday for me. A birthday to remember."

Sisi looked into his eyes but found it impossible to hold his stare. To ask him what he meant. As her gaze slipped away, she caught a glimpse of Sophie, who watched with her own eyes narrowed. And then, inexplicably, Sophie flashed a broad smile. But it was not a look of delight. It was a communication. A message: *Everyone is watching you. Smile! You're standing opposite the emperor!*

Sisi reacted with a valiant effort at a smile. Her lips quivered. And then, abruptly, the song came to an end.

How could she return to her seat, how would she face Helene? But there were footmen surrounding her, bearing baskets full of flowers — roses, poppies, edelweiss — which they held out toward the emperor. The music had stopped, its sound replaced by the tittering of whispers that filled the hall. It took every speck of her willpower to remain in place rather than to flee.

The whispering ceased as Franz plunged his hand into this fragrant pile of petals and grabbed two fistfuls of blooms. Sisi looked on, as did the rest of the court. It was so quiet now that she did not know if anyone in the room even breathed. There was some ritual being performed, but she could not comprehend its meaning.

And then, Franz took his full hands and bowed before her, dropping the petals so that they rained down in a fragrant shower at her feet, dappling the pink of her simple gown. The entire court erupted in uproarious applause as Sisi looked on, dumbly.

What was this? Why was everyone clapping? Why were people calling out her name? Unsure of what to do, but certain that to weep in public was the worst of her options, she mumbled: "Cousin Franz, please, excuse me."

And with that, while the applause still drummed around her, Sisi fled from the hall. She did not look back into the room — did not wish to see the bewildered face of Franz or the unapproving grimace of Sophie. She couldn't bear to see the dashed hopes of her mother. But, above all, she had no idea how she would ever face the confused, stricken look of Helene.

Sisi flew down the long hallway past guards and footmen. She ran quickly up the steps, her lungs protesting as her breath grew uneven. It wasn't until she had regained the dark privacy of her bedroom that the dam burst.

Sisi felt her self-control drain from her, and, collapsing onto her bed, she allowed herself to weep. She surrendered completely, finding release in the long, despairing sobs that burst forward from the pit of her insides. She wept like a child. A petrified girl. A confused girl. A girl who felt overpowering hope, and, at the same time, immeasurable guilt.

The sobs racked her frame, pressing up against her corset, causing her to wince and gasp in pain and shortness of breath. Clutching her breast, she welcomed that pain. It was just a small penance to be paid for the selfish, inexcusable act of falling in love with her sister's groom. And what was worse, for feeling happy at the indisputable fact that *he* seemed to love her in return. Loved her, *Sisi,* even when Helene was meant to be his bride. And so, in the darkness, she cried.

Much later the door opened and Helene appeared. "Sisi?" Helene tiptoed into the room, closing the door behind her. "I would have come sooner, but Mother insisted I stay. Your leaving caused such an uproar. Sophie flew to our sides and tried to put on a brave face. She told us to smile and chat as if nothing were amiss. I was forced to stay. Oh, but Sisi, are you all right?"

"Helene," Sisi answered, toneless. "Oh, Helene. I am so sorry." Those were the only words she could choke out before she began to weep anew.

"Sisi. You should have seen the look on his face when you left."

Sisi stared, blankly, at her sister. Amazed that Helene could even stand to be in her presence.

"He appeared as if he himself felt pain, Sisi. He asked if he might send his physician to attend to you."

Sisi shut her eyes, wishing she could vanish under the layers that were piled atop the bed.

"He kept insisting that it was his fault. That he had taken you on too strenuous a ride earlier today. And then, forced you to dance.

He thought perhaps you had overexerted yourself."

"Helene, how you must hate me. I promise, I never intended —"

But Helene lifted a gloved hand, silencing her sister as she pressed on. "He seems to care for you, Sisi."

"No." Sisi's voice was faint, and she swallowed hard. "He is kind to worry, but he need not trouble himself with me. Helene, it's not too late. You can still . . ." But her voice faltered. What could Helene do? What could either of them do?

Helene exhaled, looking at her sister as she sank down into the bed beside her, both of them still in their gowns. "Sisi, it's clear to everyone. Especially me."

"What is?" Sisi asked, hoping futilely that her sister wasn't about to say what she suspected.

Helene grinned, that kind, open grin. The grin that Sisi had been searching for, ever since they had arrived in Bad Ischl. It broke Sisi's heart to see it now.

"Sisi." Helene reached for her sister's hand and looked her directly in the eyes. Sisi's palm burned, all the more so against the cold, clammy flesh of her sister's skin. "Why, the bouquet of flowers? Mother said that it is some tradition in which the emperor tells the court which lady he favors. Sisi, it is clear to all of us that Franz loves you."

"Helene." Sisi erupted into a fresh sob. It took her several moments before she could even form the words through her tears. "Helene." She squeezed her sister's cold hands. "I am so sorry. I really am so sorry. I don't even understand how this happened."

Helene moved closer, nestling her head into the crook of Sisi's neck. "Don't be sorry."

Sisi kept crying.

"Sisi, hush. Don't be sorry. I'm not sorry."

Sisi shook her head.

"Sisi, come now." Helene offered her sister a handkerchief.

Taking it, Sisi asked: "How can you even bear to look at me?"

"I had a lot of time to think. First, when he didn't invite me on the ride. And then when he didn't ask me to dance." Helene flashed a soft smile, lifting her hand to stroke Sisi's braided hair. "I'm not a good match for him." Helene paused, pulling her hands back into her lap. "He knows it, and I know it. I'm not right for him. But . . . you are."

"Helene, please do not say that." Sisi shook her head, astounded that Helene did not despise her.

"Sisi, hush." The way Helene looked at Sisi seemed odd — as if Helene was not disappointed at all. In fact, Helene's eyes glowed as if she were happy for the first time in days. Weeks, even.

"Helene, why are you looking at me like that?"

The elder sister only smiled. "Seeing you, standing up there opposite him tonight." Helene threw her head back, shutting her eyes. "God, but the thought of having to do that makes me tremble. But you, Sisi? You looked just right. And he . . . he looked at you with such affection."

"Helene, no, it's not too late — I can still make this right. I didn't mean to ruin —"

Helene raised a finger, silencing her younger sister as she pressed it to Sisi's lips. "I tried my best. As much as you don't believe me, I *did* try. I confess, I was even quite cross with you. But I'm not blind. I can see that there is someone better suited for him. Better suited for his life. It's his choice, don't you see?" Helene leaned forward now, her features brighter than they had been since Bavaria. "And that means . . . I'm *free.*"

Sisi absorbed this in silence, her lower lip falling away from her mouth. When Helene spoke next, she leaned close. "You really do make quite the pair — you with your dark golden braids and lively smiles, him with his auburn hair and military uniform. Sisi — the way he looks at you."

"Helene, really." Sisi wiped her eyes, her mind racing.

"Do you . . . love him?" Helene's eyes were filled with genuine curiosity, but as far as Sisi could tell, held no trace of anger or jealousy.

She could not lie, not to Helene. Not anymore. "I . . . I fear that I might."

"Well, that's good. Then you must be feeling the same thing he is."

"But my feelings don't matter. And besides, I am not good enough to be his queen. You, my sweet Néné, would be the perfect queen. So tender and good — your subjects would adore you, just as they adore him."

"The thought of having *subjects* . . ." Helene shuddered. "All those people constantly staring at me? Why, I can barely survive a court dinner."

"Helene, you should see the way they love him. The people."

"I don't know about his subjects, but I can tell that *you* love him." Helene smiled.

"It's irrelevant, though. How many times have we heard that?"

"Not if it's what he wants, too," Helene argued. "He is emperor, after all."

Sisi thought about this, thinking back over her conversation with Franz in the hills. At the dance. "But his mother wants you, Néné."

Helene thought a minute, and when she spoke, it was with a resolve which Sisi had rarely seen in her sister. "He's a good man, Sisi. But I do not love him, and he does not love me. There is another way, and it would involve all three of us getting precisely what we each want."

"Helene, you can't really mean that you will —"

"Tomorrow I must tell Mother that I cannot marry our cousin. I will suggest that you become his fiancée instead, Sisi."

The statement, once voiced aloud for her ears to comprehend, quickened Sisi's heart, but she soon quashed the involuntary hope that it conjured. Foolish hope.

"Helene, be reasonable. We both know that Sophie will never allow it. One does not simply tell Sophie how things will happen. You were the girl she chose as his bride. If you reject her son, she will be done with our family."

"Perhaps not, Sisi. She is a clever woman, and I am sure that she sees what we all see. That her son is besotted with you."

"How many times has she said it, Néné? *If only you were the firstborn.* I am the younger daughter of a minor duke. My dowry and prestige are much too small for the emperor."

Helene sighed, thinking this over. "What does that matter to a man so very much in love?"

"What does love have to do with kingdom making?" Sisi asked, reiterating the cold, glum realism of their upbringing. Of the truth that her sister refused to accept.

Helene did not have a retort, and the two of them lay beside one another in silence. Eventually, Helene spoke. "I will have to tell them tomorrow: I do not wish to marry Franz any more than he wishes to marry me."

"Néné, you heard Mother. *One does not send the emperor of Austria packing.*"

"Precisely, Sisi." Helene rose to undress. "Which is why I expect you to accept his hand when he offers it. I am certain he will."

Sisi remained in bed, puzzling over their situation. Tomorrow, her meek, shy sister would do what no other young lady in Europe would have the audacity to do: she would turn down the emperor of Austria's suit for marriage. It was an affront to both Franz personally and to his kingdom. Franz would no doubt take it graciously, Sisi surmised. He was a gracious person, and perhaps it *was* in line with his own desires.

But what about Sophie? Surely she would not abide such insolence. Especially not an insult against her beloved son. And she would not tolerate such disregard for her carefully laid plans. Sisi was sure of it: Sophie would send them back to Possenhofen without so much as a farewell, and they would most likely never hear from her again.

As of tomorrow, their stay at court would be over. Sisi would be forced to forget Franz. She would never see Vienna. She would return to Possenhofen, and with a sister as disgraced as Helene would surely be, Sisi would probably never have a single suitor. No eligible bachelor would ever waste his time on the younger sister of the girl who had jilted the Habsburgs.

Sisi saw her life stretching out before her, the same as it had always been, except now she would know that a man such as Franz existed. A man whom she could have loved, and been loved by in return. And that that love, as warm as golden sunlight when it had shone on her, would never be hers. How, she wondered, was it possible to ache for a life with someone so badly, when, just days earlier, she had not even known him?

And now there would be no way to stomach living with Karl. Her brother would watch with smug, insufferable satisfaction as their carriages returned to Possenhofen, depositing them just weeks after they had departed — their hopes for the future and matrimony dashed. Disgrace and failure their only souvenirs from their brief stay with the emperor. Just as he had predicted. Destined for spinsterdom while Karl would inherit the duchy. They would be at Karl's mercy. If he, or, eventually his wife, decided to throw them out of Possenhofen Castle after the death of their father, that was his right. Probably even his duty.

It was in this dismal and dreary torrent of thoughts that Sisi slipped into a fretful sleep, which, mercifully, brought with it no dreams.

Sisi took her breakfast with Helene in the

bedroom the next day, the day of the emperor's twenty-third birthday.

"You are still planning to do it?" Sisi asked, spreading strawberry compote on a piece of toast for which she had no appetite. Outside it was another clear, warm day. The sounds that floated up to their windows from the courtyard below — hurried footsteps, carriage wheels on cobblestone, barking dogs — spoke of a household staff busily executing its tasks on a sultry summer morning.

"I am resolved," Helene answered. "I'll tell Mamma first, to warn her. And I'll see whether she advises that I should speak to Aunt Sophie, or to Franz directly."

How was it that suddenly her meek sister was so resolute, so determined? Sisi wondered glumly. Sophie would receive this news as an affront and an embarrassment. There was no telling how she might respond, but if their mother's cowed quietude in Aunt Sophie's presence served as any indication, there was reason to fear the woman's temper. She would send them home, to be sure.

Franz would go on to marry some other duchess or princess and lead a perfectly happy life. A life Sisi would read about in the newspapers, and hear about on the Possenhofen villagers' lips. She'd hear when he had royal babies, or when he won new lands for his empire.

Sisi looked down, the toast trembling in

her hands, and she replaced it back on the china plate. Pushing herself away from the table, she rose. She had to see him, one more time. Had to tell him how she felt, even if it was the last time she'd ever speak to him.

She dressed quickly, selecting a gown of soft lilac silk that felt cool against the August heat. It was simple but tailored to her figure snugly, and she complemented it with a thin strand of pearls. She didn't lose any time in braiding her hair, but instead pulled her dark blond waves back in a loose, hurried bun that rested on her shoulders.

The hallway outside her bedchamber was quiet and dimly lit. Sisi descended the broad staircase, her eyes alert for any sign of Franz on the ground floor. But, to her dismay, it was not Franz she found.

"Elisabeth, good morning." Sophie sat ensconced in a plush satin chair in the front drawing room, stroking the little dog in her lap. Spotting her niece, she waved her quiet companion, the Countess Esterházy, away.

"Good morning, Aunt Sophie."

"Come here, niece."

Sisi shifted her weight, pausing outside the threshold of the drawing room. "I did not mean to interrupt you, Aunt."

"It's no interruption. I was just getting caught up on some correspondence." Sophie adjusted herself in the overstuffed chair, sitting up taller. Her eyes narrowed as she looked at Sisi. "Well, you are looking cured this morning. Are you recovered from the overexertion of last night, I hope?"

"Indeed I am. Thank you, Aunt Sophie."

"Franz was worried about you, after you left the ball so suddenly." Sophie's tone turned chilly even though she still wore a smile on her features. "I was forced to remind him that there are matters of much greater importance with which he might concern himself."

"My cousin is kind," Sisi answered. The little dog in Sophie's lap growled as Sisi approached, so she stopped her steps.

"Well, he has put it out of his head, that's for certain. He's gone hunting to celebrate his birthday. He'll be gone the entire day."

Sisi's heart dropped into her stomach. Nevertheless, she forced a polite smile. "How nice for him. We will look forward to hearing about the hunt at dinner this evening."

"No, you won't," Sophie answered. The dog now began barking at Sisi, a bothersome, high-pitched yip. "Hush, Oskar!" Sophie scolded the dog, yet she simultaneously raised the tiny puff of fur to her lips and gave it an indulgent kiss. "Franz will sup this evening with his ministers."

Was Sisi imagining it, or was her aunt scouring her niece's face with more than usual interest? Perhaps searching for some indication that she, Sisi, was disappointed at this news.

Unwilling to be read this way, Sisi kept a mask of calm as her aunt continued to speak. "My son needs time with the men. So it'll be just the ladies dining here this evening. You, me, your mother, and my son's fiancée."

Her son's fiancée? So now Sophie was suddenly feeling a mother-in-law's fondness toward Helene?

"Lovely," Sisi replied. "Well, if you'll excuse me, Aunt, I shall take my leave." With a quick curtsy, Sisi turned and exited the drawing room. As she walked back toward her bedchamber, she forced herself to keep her steps slow and measured, even as her heart raced.

With Franz unavailable all day, Helene decided to postpone her announcement as well. Sensing that perhaps it was wise to have as little contact with her aunt as possible, Sisi spent the day in the gardens and the stables, visiting with Diamant and Blume. It was with a pang of melancholy that she noticed Sieger's empty stall; the horse was out enjoying the day with Franz, just as she had done yesterday.

Dinner was a strained, uncomfortable affair. As there were to be no ministers or men of importance present, the small party of four women ate in a small, dark-paneled dining room. The spread was significantly less extravagant than it had been on the previous nights, but the informality came as a relief. Knowing that it would just be the four of them, Sisi did not bother to change for dinner, but instead kept on the same lilac gown she'd worn all day.

Sophie talked throughout most of the meal, her attention fixed persistently on Helene. She prattled on about the plans for the renovations to the Kaiservilla. "It will never be as grand as our Schönbrunn Palace, but nothing could be, you see? Why, Schönbrunn has more than fourteen hundred rooms!"

Ludovika responded good-naturedly whenever there was an opening, but Sisi and Helene sat in silence, with Helene avoiding Sophie's eyes and Sisi drinking perhaps too much wine to wash down the heavily salted fish.

Dessert became even more uncomfortable when the footman failed to appear with the correct dish.

"Chocolate soufflé?" Sophie looked at the platter in disgust. "Why, we are melting into soufflé in this heat ourselves. I specifically ordered a cold lemon ice."

The fish had been tough and oversalted, the molten cake much too hot for the evening, and Sisi had partaken of too much wine. Leaving the dinner table feeling anxious and overheated, she decided that a sip of Bad Ischl spring water was in order. It would be a welcome refreshment after that long and uncomfortable meal.

Sisi exited a side door, hoping to slip undetected into the quiet night. She found her way in the dark to the small garden behind the palace, where she had seen a small fountain and pump. Once there, she stood alone, thankful for the cool, balmy breeze on her skin. She took a sip of water.

Sisi spotted a cool stone bench and sat. The night was dark and comforting, with the jagged outline of the silver mountain peaks climbing upward toward a thin slice of moon. How nice it would be to sleep out here, she thought, enjoying the soft murmuring sounds of the water trickling from the nearby fountain. She stared up at the moon, allowing herself to be transported back to the lakeside field in Bavaria, the place to which she escaped so often at night to stare up at that same moon. She shut her eyes and heard only soft sounds: water and owls and crickets, the familiar trills and stirrings of the night. From somewhere inside the palace, a waltz played.

And then a voice shook her solitary vigil, jarring in its closeness. "All alone out here?"

Franz's voice. She started, opening her eyes and looking around the garden. Her gaze went toward a glow of gentle light, spilling into the garden from an interior room, and with it the sound of soft music. There was Franz, leaning out of the opened window.

"Franz!" She rose from the bench and

skipped toward him, embarrassed by how ill-concealed her joy was at his appearance. She checked herself, reminding herself not to run to him.

"Good evening, Elisabeth." He too smiled broadly, making no attempt to conceal his delight. Sisi felt herself quiver before that smile.

"Franz, I'm surprised to see you. Your mother had told us you were dining out with ministers."

"Is that so?" Franz looked at her, a quizzical expression on his features. "I was asked by Mother to take my supper in my study. She told me the ladies needed to dine together to discuss important matters."

Sisi looked over Franz's shoulder and sure enough, on his heavy walnut desk sat a tray of emptied dishes, surrounded by several opened books. So he hadn't experienced the same distaste for the salted fish, she noted.

"I used the opportunity to take you up on your recommendation," Franz said, turning to his desk and picking up a book. "I've been reading Goethe."

Sisi couldn't help but smile.

"But I'm afraid I'll need some help on your part." Franz replaced the book onto his desk. "It's quite dense, is it not?"

"I'd be delighted to discuss it with you," Sisi answered, her voice barely louder than a whisper.

"What did you ladies discuss over dinner — this matter of such great import?" Franz was now leaning out the window, his smiling face illuminated in the gentle glow of the candlelit study.

"Nothing," Sisi answered, her tone blunt. "Nothing at all."

Franz erupted in laughter, and before Sisi knew what he was doing, he heaved his legs over the windowsill and hopped down into the garden. Now he stood in front of her. The musicians left behind in the study faltered, as if unsure whether to continue.

"Play on," Franz called, nodding back toward the open window. And, seamlessly, they obeyed. What must it be like, Sisi wondered, to have your own quintet at your command?

Sisi stepped closer toward him, suddenly less interested in the spring water she had craved. He appeared casual — more casual than usual, his uniform jacket discarded and left behind in his study. He wore only a collared shirt, its top buttons undone and the sleeves rolled up to his elbows.

She looked up into his eyes. "So then, did you really even go hunting? Or have you simply been hiding all day?"

"I did in fact go hunting, that much was truthful," he answered. "I can't see why Mother would tell me . . ." Franz shrugged.

But Sisi had a guess: Sophie was trying to

231

keep them away from one another.

"And what brings you out into the gardens all alone?" Franz smiled at her. "A secret rendezvous with some nameless suitor? I'll have his name immediately and banish him from court."

Sisi lowered her eyes, grateful for the shadows in the garden. "I wish it was that intriguing. I just wanted a sip of the water. The dinner was salty."

"Then help yourself." He stepped aside, and Sisi walked to the fountain, dipping her mouth slowly under the gentle trickle of water.

"Good?"

"Yes." She rose from the fountain and wiped her lips. Just then, the most beautiful music began to play, its sound seeping out from the open window of Franz's study. Sisi stood, transfixed, listening to the melody. Its beat unfolded in triple time, filling the courtyard with measures of its light, gay tune.

Franz, noticing her reaction, asked: "Do you know *Die Schlittschuhlaufer-Walzer*?"

"The Skater's Waltz?" Sisi repeated the name. "No, I've never heard it before in my life. But it's the most beautiful song."

Franz lifted a hand, wavering. And then, he extended it toward her. "Would you be so kind?"

Sisi looked at him, silent.

"Oh come now, Elisabeth, no need to be

shy with me. It's much less pressure than last night."

Sisi accepted his outstretched hand, allowing him to pull her body closer. Matching his steps, she began a languid waltz through the garden. He was right — it felt nothing like it had last night. This dance, between just the two of them, felt real. Honest. Entirely different.

He really was an alarmingly good dancer, his steps smooth and sure. Their feet fell in together, their movements as slow as the violins that unfurled the dreamlike melody. They were nearly the same height, so that as they danced, Sisi couldn't help but catch the clear blue of Franz's eyes. She felt her cheeks growing warm, but refused to look away from his expectant gaze.

"This song is meant to call to mind the image of *les patineurs.*"

"Ice skaters," Sisi said, translating his French.

"It's nice to conjure a winter's scene on this hot evening, isn't it?" Franz asked, his smile as cool and crisp as the snow-flecked images Sisi imagined behind the music.

"Indeed." She agreed. "I can't quite decide, though. It's beautiful, and delicate. But also, it strikes me as . . ."

"As what?"

"Sad, somehow."

"Yes." Franz nodded. When he spoke next,

his lips were so close that his breath hovered over the soft skin of her neck, a warm, dizzying mist. "Sometimes, something is so beautiful that when you look on it, you are struck with immense sadness. Either because it can't stay that way forever, or" — and now his face was intense, earnest — "because you cannot have that beautiful thing which you long to possess."

Sisi hoped now that the evening was dark enough to conceal her flush. Franz dropped his hands so that their dancing stopped abruptly. In the pale light she noticed that his expression had grown serious, perhaps even a little bit troubled.

Sisi didn't speak, but instead stared up at the velvety black sky, at the craggy mountain peaks that rose up to meet it, carving into the star-strewn tableau. She wondered which had been the peak that she and Franz had ascended yesterday.

Franz eventually broke the silence: "I needed to clear my head today, you see. That's why I went hunting." A pause. "But it did not work."

Sisi considered this confession, noting the speed with which her heart suddenly raced in her breast. "I am sure that a great number of worries constantly weigh upon you, Franz."

"No, just one, lately."

"Oh?" She was as breathless as she had been while galloping up the mountain atop

Diamant.

"Elisabeth, I wish you had not come."

It was not what she had been expecting to hear, and certainly not what she had *hoped* to hear. His words, toneless, might have been addressed to a servant. Or worse, a stranger. Stung, Sisi took a few steps back.

"I do apologize if my coming displeases you, Franz. Surely you know I came to support my sister."

"Ha. So, you want me as your sister's husband?" Franz sputtered out a bitter laugh. "As your *brother*?"

"I did not arrange it, Franz." It was as bold as she could be without crossing propriety's line.

"Do you love me as a brother?"

Sisi knew the truthful answer, but not how to say it.

"Does this," Franz waved his hands between them, "feel like how a brother ought to feel for his sister?"

"I don't know," she stammered, turning away. "No, of course it does not."

"How could I have fallen in love with Helene with you beside her? How could I?" His tone was different now; it was as troubled as she herself felt. "Perhaps, if I had never met you, Helene and I could have had a chance." He ran his fingers through his hair, tousling the auburn waves that he usually wore so neatly. "But now, now . . . it would be akin to sipping vinegar after tasting the sweetest of wines."

"Vinegar? You do realize that it is my beloved sister of whom you speak?" Sisi answered, an edge apparent in her voice; her defense of Helene was instantaneous, instinctive. But what else was that feeling? Hope? Yes, hope.

"I mean no offense to Helene. She is a lovely girl and will make some man a wonderful wife. But that man is not me. Helene is not the one for me." Franz paused. The gurgling of the fountain was suddenly roaringly loud, and Sisi did not know how she could stand his silence a minute longer. Finally, he looked at her. He took a step closer. Her heart clamored so wildly that she felt it between her ears.

Franz, opposite her now, lifted his hand. His eyes, lit by the soft glow of the moon, searched hers. He took her chin in between his thumb and forefinger, angling her face to his. And then he spoke, his voice quiet. "Don't you see, Elisabeth?"

What? She longed to ask.

"You have ruined me," he said.

She shut her eyes, trying to steady herself. When she opened them again, she felt a single tear slip down her cheek, and then the touch of his hand as he wiped it away.

"How must I feel, Franz?" She lifted her hand to rest on his where it held her cheek.

"So then, I am not wrong, Elisabeth? But — you left the ball so quickly last night. And after I had made my intentions so plain. So then, I am not a fool for hoping that you feel the same way that I do?"

She could have laughed. Or wept. How did he think that anything about their situation was *plain*? "No, Franz, you are not wrong."

She saw understanding spread like daybreak over his darkened features. And without further consideration, she leaned forward and met his lips with her own. A moment of shock, as she stood, suspended, registering what she had just done. He tasted like brandy and salted herring, and the novel act of kissing a man struck her at first as slightly odd. But the longer she rested her lips on his, the more pleasing this strange new sensation became.

He didn't seem troubled by her impulsiveness. Rather, his whole frame seemed to awaken opposite hers, answering her with equal interest and longing. He lifted his hands and cradled her head in them as he kissed her, gently at first, but then with a hunger and an ardor that caused her whole body to warm. Now their embrace no longer felt odd or disagreeable to her. No, kissing Franz felt like the most natural, most desirable thing that Sisi could ever do, and she allowed herself to soften entirely into his arms.

When he seemed like he might eventually

pull away, she reached forward, drawing him back to her, not allowing him to end this perfect moment. Eventually, he tried again, lifting his face from hers, and she realized that she stood before him breathless.

"You have ruined me." It was a gentle whisper, his exhale almost louder than his words. But she liked it less the second time she heard it. Why was it ruination? Why couldn't it be salvation?

Before she could summon the courage to ask this of him, he stepped back. His body suddenly out of reach. Standing tall, rigid, he declared, "I must go."

"Franz." She reached for his hands, clutching them in hers. How could he leave her just now? "Please, wait."

"No," he spoke forcefully. "I must go."

"But —"

"Good night."

As she faltered, grasping aimlessly for the right words, he turned, leaving her in the quiet garden, even more alone — even more lost — than before he had come.

Sisi passed a sleepless night, but the thought of seeing Franz at breakfast filled her with small splinters of hope. At least she might possibly steal a moment to speak with him. What had last night meant to him? Hadn't he confessed to feelings similar to her own? Then why had he left suddenly? And without explanation?

Perhaps, Sisi thought, she had offended him with the abruptness of her kiss. But then, he certainly hadn't seemed offended as he had kissed her back. Then perhaps it was all just a game to him; perhaps now that he had had his fun with her, he would move on to the next conquest. Perhaps now that she had confessed to her own feelings, she was less desirable to him. But that certainly didn't seem like Franz. Did it? Then again, did she even really *know* Franz?

She left her bedroom resolved, certain that she wouldn't untangle these troubled thoughts until she spoke to Franz directly. But when Sisi and Helene entered the breakfast room the next morning, she noticed with a stab of despair that only her mother sat eating.

"Good morning, girls." Ludovika looked up when they entered. They had not told their mother of their own private conversations. And yet, surely Ludovika knew that something was amiss; she had, after all, been witness to the past few days.

Sisi sat down at the table in silence.

Ludovika studied her younger daughter, eyes narrowed in keen interest. "You look tired, Sisi."

Sisi forced a smile, a shrug of her shoulders as she turned over the cup before her for coffee.

"How did you sleep?"

"Fine," Sisi lied.

Ludovika looked appraisingly from one daughter to the other as she spread soft cheese on her toast. Her eyes took in their clean, formal gowns. "You both look very nice this morning." It was more like a question than a statement.

They had each dressed with care, as if to prepare for a tumultuous series of battles. Helene wore a gown of gray charmeuse with black trim. Sisi wore a soft silk gown of pale rose, a dress that complemented her coloring and hugged her figure. A dress like the one she had worn to the ball, when Franz had asked her to dance.

"And you, Helene? How are you this morning?" Ludovika took a second slice of toast from the breakfast tray. "I've seen you girls less than I've seen Agata."

But before Helene could answer, another voice spoke. "Ah! I'm surprised you are awake this morning." Sophie hovered at the doorway. "I would think you would be exhausted after your rendezvous last night."

Ludovika and her daughters turned confused stares on the archduchess, who now swished into the room. She paused before the table, knitting her hands in front of her waist. Her gown, belling out to each side, made her appear as wide as she was tall.

"Breakfast, Archduchess?"

Sophie answered the footman with a dismissive flick of her wrist: *No*. With that, the servants holding the pastry trays and coffee seemed to retreat backward, hugging the brocaded walls of the room.

Sophie didn't sit. Sisi watched her, uneasy, as Sophie smiled; an expression of calm, yet forced, cordiality. Pressing her two hands onto the table, her fingers laden with rings, she leaned forward. Her voice, though sweet-sounding, was just as unnatural as her smile. "I'm just impressed you were able to do it. How have you managed it? After everything I have taught him about self-control, and duty, and honor. What must you have said?"

It became clear to all three at the table that the query was directed at Sisi, but Ludovika answered.

"What is your meaning, Sophie?" Sisi's mother continued to slowly spread the cheese across her warm bread, attempting a measured tone, but her face had tightened in concern. Or fear. Yes, Sisi realized, Mamma had known this was coming. She had braced for it, probably since the moment Franz had asked Sisi to dance.

"You know perfectly well what it is, Ludovika, and please don't think you can deceive me. Why, the whole thing was brought about by you and your daughter."

"Please explain yourself, Sophie." Ludovika gently placed her knife down beside her plate, her voice as artificially calm as Sophie's.

"You never could accept it, could you?" Sophie leaned forward now, her voice quiet. "That I was the archduchess, and a Habsburg? You always regretted that you had made the worst match of us sisters. Why, Elisa is queen of Prussia. Marie Anna is queen of Saxony. My son is the emperor. While *you* — you wallowed in that beggar's household at Possenhofen. No, you saw your daughter and you thought of my son, and you set your sights on my throne."

Ludovika lowered her gaze, absorbing the sting of these words with stoic calm. "Sophie, I don't understand your meaning. Please recall: *you* are the one who asked that my daughter be engaged to your son."

"I wanted *that* one!" Sophie pointed at Helene, looking at her for the first time. "But you, you knew that the elder one was weak. You knew it, just like we all knew it. You brought her here, looking homely and plain . . . dressed in *black*!"

"We were in mourning," Ludovika mumbled, barely audible.

"And you brought this one in — chirping like a little bird. Going on and on about her love for horses. Her hair in braids, her childish eyes, smiling at my son from the moment she entered the hall." Sophie now turned toward Sisi, staring at her as if to size up a foe. "You don't think I saw your designs?

How you trotted her out, even though she's just barely out of the nursery and knows nothing of the life my son leads."

Ludovika turned to look at Sisi, her expression clouding over with — what was it? Pity for her younger daughter? Surprise? But Sophie had not finished.

"This one is wild and unruly, and I will not allow her to disrupt my . . . Franz's court." Sophie still spoke quietly, but her neck and chest had turned as pink as the strawberry pastries on the table. "None of you know the first thing about surviving at court. You have no idea what it takes."

After several measured breaths, Ludovika answered, folding a napkin in her hands as she did so. "Sophie, if there is some attachment which has formed between your son and my younger daughter, it was a result of a natural and unanticipated affection. Nothing was engineered or . . . designed." And now Ludovika threw a sidelong glance at Sisi before turning back to her sister. "But I must say that I find your response to these unplanned developments troubling."

"*Unplanned?* Don't act as if you didn't plan this," Sophie said, a short laugh escaping her tight lips. "I will not be derailed — not after everything I have done to secure my son's position in a treacherous court."

"Sophie, I beg you to remember that we are your family. We would never come here with designs on your —"

Sophie lifted a hand, silencing Ludovika. "My own sister, a guest in my house, acting as though she has no schemes of her own."

"That is correct, your own sister," Ludovika said, nodding. "And I can say, as your sister, I, too, want what is best for your son. Why should he not make this choice for himself?"

Frustrated by her sister's soft yet persistent opposition, Sophie turned toward her niece.

"Elisabeth, surely you know that you have no legitimate right to marry my son. You are the second daughter of an inconsequential duke." Sisi winced at this insult, but Sophie continued on. "Something as important as an emperor's marriage really ought not to be left up to a momentary fancy. Just because my son might be . . . *besotted* . . . does not mean you can be his queen. You are no more than a child. I won't see our Habsburg ministers forced to become tutors, our state rooms filled with the frivolity of a nursery, do you understand that?"

Sisi did not answer. Sophie, seeing Sisi's silence as an advantage to press, leaned forward, her voice gentle.

"Elisabeth, you are a smart girl." Sophie's face drew up into a smile now, but her upper lip quivered. "I've been very good to you since you arrived here, and I will continue to esteem you highly. I will even make you a fine match . . . something way beyond what you could have previously expected." Her tone was laced in condescension. "I will do that for you. I just need your guarantee that you will not accept my son's hand, should he be foolish enough to make you an offer." Sophie reached forward, taking Sisi's hand in her own two and pressing them together, her palms clammy. "Can I trust you on this?"

Sisi, repressing the urge to pull her hand away, did not need long to consider her response. "I apologize, Aunt Sophie, but no."

Now it was Sophie's turn to be stunned. She dropped Sisi's hands, her smile slipping from her face. "What is this?"

"No, I cannot promise that I would decline your son's proposal. If Franz wished to marry me, I would happily say yes."

"What? Oh, but this is utter nonsense." Sophie, mouth agape, stared from Sisi to Ludovika to Helene. Turning back to Sisi, she stammered: "But you can't possibly be serious. You, with your countrified manners? As wild as your boor of a father? Am I really to believe that *you* imagine yourself the next empress of Austria?"

Sophie turned her gaze on Helene now. "And you? You, who have barely spoken two words together since you stepped out of the coach. You would allow your sister to snatch away your groom? Your title? To steal the life for which I . . . *we* . . . have chosen you?"

Under the table Helene took Sisi's hand, giving it a squeeze. It was just what she had needed, and Sisi inhaled, prepared to defend herself. But before Sisi could answer her incredulous aunt, she noticed a figure in the doorway. Franz. He had appeared, undetected, and her heart leapt involuntarily at the sight of him. He looked every inch the emperor, dressed in his starched uniform, his hair brushed back smartly, his face calm.

"Mother?"

Startled, Sophie turned to see her son. "Oh, Franzi! Why, I wasn't expecting you." Sophie smiled, her eyes flashing momentarily to Sisi before she lowered her wide figure into a chair at the table, as if overcome.

"I was wondering, Mother, if I might have a word with you?" A muscle in Franz's cheek twitched, but he retained complete mastery of his emotions, his eyes fixed on his mother.

"I was just talking to your cousins, Franzi. Give us a moment. Why don't you go —"

"Please, Mother." Franz lifted a gloved hand and his mother stopped speaking. "I'm afraid it can't really wait." His eyes darted toward Sisi, resting on her for only a moment. But it was long enough for both Sophie and Sisi to notice.

For the rest of the day, Sisi, her mother, and her sister were ushered and escorted through town on a never-ending itinerary of guided activities by a palace secretary named Herr Lobkowitz. It had been at Franz's suggestion, a thinly veiled excuse to draw them out of the palace. The thought of the girls staying back to hear — even participate in — the discussion of their futures had not been an option.

They were shown the village cathedral, the market square, and the riverside. Though none of them felt up for much conversation, they listened politely as this palace guide, this Herr Lobkowitz, accompanied them to lunch and then for a walk to one of the lowland water springs.

All the while, Sisi's mind wandered back to the Kaiservilla, where she hoped Franz was winning the right to dictate his own future. Did he stand any chance against the iron will of his mother, a well-known negotiator who had won her son the crown with nothing more than her words?

They arrived back at the imperial complex that evening, where they were greeted by the unwelcoming scowl of Countess Esterházy and ushered directly into a small, windowless dining room. There, the three of them were served a generous dinner of Viennese potato soup, followed by veal dumplings in a sauce of garlic and parsley. None of them felt much like eating, or talking.

Afterward, when they retired to the drawing room, Sisi noticed that, though they were treated as honored guests, they were accompanied by the same two palace aides: Countess Esterházy, with her fixed frown, and the same Herr Lobkowitz, a short, monocled man of vaguely middle age. The two of them stood at the ready, lingering in the corners of the room and watching the ladies like officious governesses.

After-dinner drinks were served. Cards were offered for playing, and declined. A court musician entered to play the piano. Outside night fell, and inside the room grew dark. Sisi paced the salon, restless, wondering how she might slip this guard to find Franz. After a while, Herr Lobkowitz stepped forward, a solicitous smile on his face. Looking at Ludovika, he asked if she and her daughters "might like to be escorted back to their bedchambers now?"

"Yes, fine," Ludovika answered, draining her wineglass and placing her napkin crossly on the end table. Under her breath, but loud enough for the aide to hear, she muttered, "Now I know what house arrest feels like."

They had neither seen nor heard from Franz and Sophie since breakfast, and Sisi couldn't bear the thought of returning to her bedroom with no idea of where things stood. But as they were guided toward the front staircase, she detected the sounds of a muffled conversation occurring in Franz's study. Sisi knew those two voices and she paused, rooted in place.

"But she is not fit, it is as simple as that. She is too young — a child really, too giddy. Unable to fulfill the role and all of its obligations."

"Doesn't my love for her make her more fit than any other, Mother?"

"Love? *Love* has nothing to do with it." Sophie's tone was pleading, a tone that Sisi had never heard her use in public. A tone reserved only for her precious son. "Why, love is nothing more than a passing fancy. Come now, my dear Franzi. You've always made the right choice. You always do what is best for the empire. Surely, in this case, you must see that she is entirely ill-suited for the —"

"Mother, isn't what's best for the empire a happy emperor?"

"But you are mistaken to think that *she* is the one to make you happy. Her? With her wild character? No, you are being impulsive, and refusing to listen to me." Sisi could hear that Sophie's tone was taking on a pitch of mounting desperation; she was not used to hearing her arguments opposed. "One does not make such an important decision as to whom to marry based on *love*. I have never known you to display such rash and incautious —"

"Miss Elisabeth, if you please?" The diffident palace aide, Herr Lobkowitz, stood beside Sisi, sticking to her like a pesky fly.

Waiting. Insisting that she continue up the staircase with greater haste. Sisi longed to protest, to tell this man that *she* was the young lady whose fate was in question on the other side of the door, and that that afforded her a right to listen. But a stern look from her mother told Sisi that she had better oblige, and she glumly assented to climbing the stairs.

"Please have them bring some wine to the bedroom," Sisi told the short, monocled man. If she hoped to sleep at all, she would have to numb this thickening anxiety somehow.

They were served breakfast in their bedroom the next morning. Before they had finished their coffee, there was a knock on the door. Sisi clutched Helene's hand. "Come in."

It was a familiar face that appeared at the door.

"Agata!" Sisi rose from the table, running to greet her maid.

"Miss Sisi!" Agata quickly entered the room, staring at her young mistress with an appraising look. "Miss Sisi, you are causing quite the stir in this household. It's all anyone can talk about in the kitchens. How the emperor is going head-to-head against his old mum over you."

"Agata, we've been completely isolated. What are you hearing?" Sisi whispered.

"Just that they've been arguing for days,

since you arrived. It's very unusual for them to argue so. But the emperor won't drop his suit." Agata turned to look over her shoulder nervously. Footsteps sounded from the carpeted hallway.

"Someone's coming." The maid ran toward the bed and retrieved the chamber pot, picking it up just in time. Countess Esterházy appeared at the open doorway. The tall, pinch-faced woman spied Agata and cast a skeptical look toward her, but let her pass with the chamber pot. Poor Agata would probably be scolded later for venturing upstairs when she was supposed to remain below in the kitchens.

The lady-in-waiting turned from the exiting Agata toward Sisi. "Excuse me, I've been sent to summon you, Duchess Elisabeth."

Sisi nodded, walking toward the frowning matron. Helene rose to join her.

"No, I do apologize." The countess lifted a hand before Helene, sounding very unapologetic. "Just the Duchess Elisabeth."

To what fate was she being marched? Sisi descended the stairs behind her aunt's ally, wishing she might walk faster. She was ushered into the large dining room.

"Please be seated, Duchess Elisabeth." Countess Esterházy gestured a gloved hand toward a carved chair at the table.

"Thank you." Sisi waited for what felt like an interminable length of time. She glanced

251

often at the mantel: the hand of the marble clock marched evenly on, covering three-quarters of an hour. Restless, Sisi rose from her chair and began to pace the large space.

As she walked to the window, she noticed an unexpected figure in the courtyard. *Franz!* Mounting the saddled Sieger. Instinctively, she rapped on the window, trying to get his attention. But he didn't hear her. He nudged the horse with his heel and they sped across the forecourt, past Sisi, past the guards at the front gate, and out of the complex.

Just like that, he was gone. Left the palace. Surely this did not bode well, Sisi thought, her heart aching. Franz had surrendered.

"Excuse me, Duchess Elisabeth?" Countess Esterházy reappeared. Did her features know how to fold in any way other than a look of perpetual disapproval?

"Yes?" Sisi still stood beside the window.

"I am to escort you back to your suite."

"But . . . but I have seen no one," Sisi protested. "What is happening?"

The lady-in-waiting shrugged, offering no scrap of additional information.

Sisi sighed and followed the countess out, marching back up to her bedchamber.

"Sisi!" Helene waited for her, pacing the room. "What news?"

"None at all." Sisi dropped wearily onto a chair. She noticed, with considerable sadness, that Helene had packed up their trunks while she had been downstairs. "You've packed?"

"Just in case. Not because I think . . ."

"No, you were correct to guess at the outcome. I saw no one. But Franz has left the palace, that much I know."

Midday came and passed but they were served no luncheon, nor were they informed what had happened to Sophie or Franz. In the early afternoon, when Sisi poked her head out the door, she noticed Countess Esterházy pacing the hallway like an indefatigable sentry. So that was why Mamma had not come to them.

Sophie must be relishing her victory. Once more, she was the devoted mother and advisor, willing to do whatever it took to protect her son. Not only had she saved her son from such an unfathomably ill-suited match, she'd also reasserted her power as the most powerful woman in his life. She'd proven, once more, why *she* was referred to, by many, as "the Empress."

"Excuse me, Duchess Elisabeth." This time, Herr Lobkowitz appeared at the door.

"Yes, what is it now?" Sisi grumbled, her patience long expired. If Franz had lost, then couldn't she just be allowed to go home without further punishment?

"Would you accompany me, one more time, Duchess?" The aide touched the monocle, a nervous gesture, where it perched on the bridge of his nose.

"Oh, very well," Sisi frowned, exchanging a look with her sister. "It's not as though I have anything else to do."

Again she was deposited in the large dining room, and again she was shut in, alone, with nothing but the sound of the clock to divert her thoughts.

The wait was shorter this time. The door opened without a knock and Sisi was stunned to stare into the face of her aunt.

"I shall dispense with all formalities, as you know very plainly how I feel." Sophie swished into the room and sat herself at the opposite end of the table. It was the same slick oak table where they had dined together with such merriment the first night.

"The wedding will be in eight months."

Sisi went numb, certain that she had misheard her aunt. Or at least misunderstood her meaning.

"Enough time to quiet the rumors that you have become . . . *pregnant.* Though that is hardly enough time for you to learn how to become empress." Sophie stared at her niece with ill-concealed disapproval. "It takes a lifetime to prepare for this role. It was risky enough inviting Helene, knowing what sort of . . . *upbringing* you had in that household. Your father, behaving as he did. Your mother doing nothing to teach you any discipline." Sophie twisted the rings on her fingers, catching the sunlight on the large stones.

"But Helene at least had the temperament for it. She was reserved, and dignified, and she knew her place. And she was more mature than a *child*. But you? You have exactly the wrong disposition." Sophie's voice was thick with annoyance, and her gaze slid away from Sisi toward the floor. The next words were spoken under her breath, a catalogue of the flaws she detected in the young girl opposite her. *"Willful. Independent. Far too opinionated."* Sophie turned back toward Sisi now, addressing her once more. "And you did no favors for yourself by crossing *me* on your quest to steal my son's heart."

Sisi tried to answer, to defend herself. But before she could, Sophie lifted a hand, silencing her: "Let me finish. He seems determined to move forward with this" — Sophie paused, pursing her lips, as if the words tasted bitter — "match." Sophie exhaled, a sigh. "You will be married in April. In Vienna, at *Augustinerkirche*. The church where all Habsburgs are wed."

Sisi's lips pulled apart in a stunned smile, while Sophie's scowl made it clear that she was loath to bestow this honor on her niece. "If you aren't a virgin on your wedding night, I will know, do you understand? And I will have a priest on hand to nullify the union before you've even sat down to breakfast the next day."

Sophie kept talking, laying out a list of warnings to Sisi: her French must be flawless by the time of the wedding. Her dancing skills were glaringly insufficient. Her wardrobe was lacking. And she had better have her teeth straightened and whitened, or they would be the cause of endless ridicule in Vienna.

But Sisi had stopped listening. These insults and threats slid over her like slippery raindrops. There was only one bit of information in this barrage to which she clung — the announcement that she would marry Franz. And with that realization, happiness. Franz had won. She, Sisi, had won. She would be Franz's wife! Relief and joy seeped through her until she was so recklessly glad that she couldn't help but cry out in a peal of laughter.

"What is so funny, girl? This is no laughing matter."

It wasn't funny, but Sisi continued to laugh.

"Stop that this instant." Sophie's eyes widened, staring out from a pale, pinched face. "This is highly undignified."

It was just such beautiful news — such unexpected, incomprehensible news: *she* was going to marry Franz. She, Sisi, was to be Empress of Austria.

Sophie still looked on disapprovingly. "Now, you had better go and change. We are to meet my son at church within the hour.

We will go and pray. You will need God on your side against the court at Vienna."

PART TWO

VI.

I have awakened from a rapture.
— Empress Elisabeth "Sisi" of Austria,
1854

CHAPTER SIX

Sisi had never imagined it possible to awake one day and look upon a life so entirely foreign. Unknown. As if, now that she was engaged to marry Emperor Franz Joseph, the first fifteen years of her existence had been nothing more than a dream. A memory belonging to another girl.

When Sisi returned that autumn from Bad Ischl to Possenhofen, it was to an unfamiliar way of life; her days were no longer her own. The fall, usually her favorite time of year for getting lost in the woods atop her horse, was not hers to enjoy. "There isn't enough time!" became her mother's daily, frantic refrain.

The imperial tutors descended on Possi first, with their heavy books, their impeccably glossy spectacles, and their stern, mustached lips. They were with Sisi from the moment she awoke until long after supper. Her Italian was deplorable, her Hungarian was non-

existent, and her French *had* to improve —
on that score, everyone seemed to agree.
Even her grasp of German, her native tongue,
presented concerns; Sisi needed to know not
simply how to *speak,* but how to *converse.*
Additionally, she needed to become an ex-
pert, in a matter of months, on the topics of
Austrian history, the Habsburg family, and
life at court. On this last topic there existed
voluminous pages of protocol to be learned,
never-ending lists of nobles and courtiers
with whom to become familiar, and scrolls
on all of her various new homes, territories,
and responsibilities.

Franz Joseph had been schooled and
groomed for his role since his first days in
the nursery; he had known no other companionship than that of royal relatives, fashion-
able courtiers, and attentive tutors. For Sisi,
fifteen years of a relaxed, provincial upbringing now had to be unlearned and remedied
in just a matter of months. Nobody around
her seemed to believe it possible.

Sisi's dancing skills, as Sophie had repeatedly pointed out, were also glaringly insufficient. Vienna had given the world the waltz;
now Sisi would be expected to take her place
at the fore of the imperial ballrooms opposite
the emperor, a famously good dancer, and
she must not embarrass the Habsburgs. So,
rather than tiring her legs out on the lengthy
rides and hikes through the Bavarian moun-

tains that she had always relished, Sisi wore her feet raw that autumn with countless hours of practicing waltzes, polkas, and quadrilles. She heard violins keeping three-quarter time in her sleep.

Even Sisi's body no longer seemed to be her own; she was poked and prodded and measured as she had never before been. Dentists were sent from Vienna to pull on and straighten the young bride's teeth, and to apply a paste that her Aunt Sophie hoped would render them an appropriately pristine shade of white. Milliners and tailors and shoemakers and seamstresses from throughout Bavaria arrived at Possenhofen, stitching and sewing from sunrise to sunset. None of the snappish, harried craftspeople believed it possible to complete the imperial trousseau by the time of the bride's departure for Vienna. Urgent word went out to all the neighboring nunneries throughout the region: the cloistered sisters *must* help their young duchess prepare a wardrobe worthy of an emperor's wife. They must pray for Sisi, yes, but even more important, they must *stitch* for Sisi. Even God, it seemed, was enlisted to help this ill-prepared girl.

When Sisi wasn't learning history, or practicing the art of speaking, or dancing, or nursing an aching tooth, she was sitting. She sat for countless hours as the imperial artists sketched and studied and re-created her likeness. The people were ravenous for a glimpse of the girl who had enchanted their emperor: a girl whose beauty was already being heralded by those who had been fortunate enough to meet this unknown duchess in Bad Ischl. Her face, the imperial artists told Sisi, would be the most recognized face in all of Vienna before she herself ever set foot in the capital.

All that fall and winter, the gifts came. At first it had excited Sisi immensely. She had loved reaching into the velvet pouch and retrieving a small portrait of her groom. She had gasped in surprise and delight at the diamond bracelet that had accompanied it, so that she might wear Franz Joseph's likeness around her wrist at all times. He was doing the same with her miniature portrait, her smitten groom wrote her.

Sometimes, while opening these new packages, sharing their contents with her excited mother and her quiet elder sister, Sisi would catch a glimpse of something difficult to decipher on Helene's face. Was it a look of envy? A look of longing? Noting the strange tug on Néné's features, the quick way in which her sister found a reason to leave the room, Sisi decided that perhaps she had better not be quite so rapturous in her joy while her sister was present.

Each day it seemed that some new gift arrived. Franz sent a silver breakfast set emblazoned with her new initials. Franz sent a cape of plush blue velvet trimmed in ermine. He sent her a brooch of jewels in the shape of a rosebud, along with fresh roses, even though it was the dead of winter and roses were nowhere to be had. He sent her gloves of kid leather in every color, and ceremonial robes embroidered in gold trim, and winter gowns and summer gowns and hats decorated with apple blossoms and ostrich feathers. She received capes and purses and mantillas and satin slippers. Her favorite gift was the pet parrot Franz sent her, along with a note declaring how eager he was to show her his own private zoo at Schönbrunn Palace.

Franz wrote dutifully, gushing to Sisi about how his thoughts drifted from his government papers, wandering from Vienna back to their "divine sojourn" together in the mountains. He assured her of his mother's excitement for the coming wedding. Perhaps in an effort to earn back her son's good favor, or else to ingratiate herself with the young bride who would inevitably be moving into her home, Sophie's demeanor had changed entirely. According to Franz, his mother now raved to anyone who would listen about the "divine little lady" her son had chosen. Sophie had even decided that the new wing on the Kaiservilla would be laid out in the shape of the letter *E,* in honor of her son's bride.

For her sixteenth birthday, the night before Christmas, Sisi received a letter detailing her aunt's efforts to prepare the imperial suite that the newlyweds would occupy after the wedding. Sisi's opinion was not sought, but Sophie wrote that she was certain that the future empress would be perfectly delighted. Everything, Sophie assured her, was being done with Sisi's comfort and pleasure in mind. Sophie had bought her niece a toiletry set of pure gold. The bed and windows were to be draped in pale-blue lyonnaise silk. Sophie had arranged for her niece to have Chinese porcelain, hand-stitched carpets, custom furniture, and portraits from the Habsburg family's own collection.

Also for her birthday, Sisi was given a tiara inset with diamonds and opals — the same tiara Aunt Sophie had worn on her own wedding day. It came with matching earrings and a choker, as well as a note beseeching Sisi to take extreme care when transporting the collection to Vienna. The objects were some of the Habsburg family's most treasured jewels, and the consequences of their loss or damage would be unfathomable. Sisi wept on receiving this gift, along with its officious warning; now, on top of everything else she had weighing on her, she had to ensure the safe passage of these priceless Habsburg crown jewels?

■ ■ ■ ■

Sisi felt a great many things as the wedding day approached. Excitement. Fear. Gratitude. Exhaustion. But the emotion that remained with her at all times, never wavering even as the others ebbed and flowed, was incredulity. Had Franz really picked *her*? Were all of these people really working to help and prepare *her* for this role? Were all of these dresses of silk and brocade and tulle and satin for *her*? Were these mobs of villagers — lining the streets of Possenhofen on the day of her departure, waving the blue and white provincial flag and showering her in flowers — really there to bid *her* farewell?

It was a departure entirely unlike the previous one, when she had ridden in a humble carriage to Bad Ischl as the younger sister joining in on some fanciful adventure. Now she was the imperial bride, traveling in state to a capital city ravenous for a glimpse of its new empress.

Sisi was loaded, speechless and pale — along with her twenty-five trunks — onto the steamship *Franz Joseph.* The journey down the Danube took three days. They had the water to themselves, as all other river traffic had been expressly forbidden. The steamer glided deliberately forward, covered in garlands of fresh roses while the banks of the river swarmed with tens of thousands of onlookers. Everything they passed was now *her* land: the orchards blossoming with early spring fruit; the ancient ruins crumbling in the medieval towns; even the people who lined the river the entire way, the peasants picnicking and the impromptu bands serenading her in her national anthems, new and old. Bells clanged in every town, and the crowds waved the Austrian and Bavarian flags while Sisi waved back to them, fluttering her lace handkerchief the way her dance master had instructed her. She heard her name extolled from dawn until sunset, and she stood on the deck, performing her duties until her arms ached and her smiling cheeks quivered.

Always, she was performing. It grew so exhausting that at night, alone in her cabin, as Sisi peeled off the painful corset and slid her feet into her familiar red slippers, she wept. She wept from exhaustion. She wept for Possenhofen. She wept for her childhood bed and Néné's comforting presence and the servants she had known since birth — servants she had been forbidden to bring with her. She wept for the carefree frivolity of a ride on her horse in a simple gown and dirty leather boots. She wept for the lenient, easy manner of her parents, a style entirely opposite of that expected by Aunt Sophie. She knew it was foolish to weep — she, the luckiest girl in all of Europe, had no right to weep. She, who had won the heart of the kindest, most handsome emperor, ought to feel only joy.

And so, each morning, she would dress once more, dutifully sliding into a too-tight corset and wobbly heels, reminding herself that all would be well. She was in love with Franz. Once she saw him, once she was reunited with her groom, all would be well.

The wedding day dawned clear and chilly, a perfect April morning, confirming to everyone in the capital — from the lowliest bar sweep to the emperor himself — that God smiled down on the imperial pair.

All of Austria, it seemed, had descended on Vienna, ready to welcome the bride with a crushing embrace. Sisi's picture appeared everywhere throughout the capital: hanging in the windows of the coffeehouses in Stephansplatz and painted on the porcelain plates in the bistros on Kärntner Strasse. Blue and white, the colors of Sisi's native Bavaria, blanketed the city, from the awnings of the posh hotels, to the hats on display in the milliners' windows, to the flower markets' choicest bouquets.

Sisi awoke early to the sound of the church bells, feeling weary before the day had even begun. Her mother and Néné, who had arrived in the capital shortly after her, came to her room to help her dress.

"Happy wedding day, Sisi." Néné said it quietly as she entered. Again, there was that indecipherable look on her sister's face, like a grimace that Helene did her best to mask with a smile.

"Good morning," Sisi said, feeling too tired to smile at either her mother or sister. They ate a small breakfast, nibbling on the corners of toast and exchanging only a few words. Afterward, it was time to dress. As Sisi stepped out of her nightgown, her new lady-in-waiting, the stern Countess Esterházy, arrived in the bedroom.

"Good morning, Your Royal Highness." The old woman bowed low before sweeping into the room without invitation. This was yet another new daily occurrence, and one to which Sisi had definitely not grown accustomed.

"Good morning, Countess Esterházy." Sisi now pulled the nightgown back up, covering her figure as she exchanged a look with Néné.

"Carry on, continue dressing," the old woman said, her voice like the pecking of an old hen as she made herself comfortable in one of Sisi's chairs. "I won't be in your way. I shall read to you as you dress." And with that, the countess began reading aloud from one of the voluminous tomes that had been prepared for the new empress. These materials included the *Ceremonial Procedure for the*

271

Official Progress of Her Royal Highness, the Most Gracious Princess Elisabeth, along with a pamphlet on wedding procedure, titled *Most Humble Reminders.* And finally, the material with which Sisi felt the least comfortable was the massive *Book of Royals.* It was a seemingly endless registry listing the name, rank, and exact greeting for the thousands of guests who would congratulate her on her wedding day.

As tedious as Sisi found these texts, Countess Esterházy seemed to relish them, pausing her reading every few sentences to quiz Sisi on some fact.

"You *have* reviewed these materials, have you not, Your Majesty?" Countess Esterházy sighed, as Sisi fumbled through a family of Prussian counts.

"Yes, I have. I promise. It's just that . . ."

"Never mind. Let's just continue on with the Austrian history," Countess Esterházy said, her lips pressed tight in a disapproving scowl as she fingered the pages. "Please, Duchess Elisabeth, be so kind as to tell me your future husband's full title?"

Sisi inhaled, thinking, as Néné and her mother buzzed about her, preparing her combs and jewelry and toilette. She had studied this. She knew the answer. "It is . . ." her palms were sweaty, made worse by the Countess Esterházy's impatient tapping of her heeled boot.

"I know this," Sisi said, ignoring the noble-woman's censorious stare. "It is: Franz Joseph the First, by the Grace of God, Emperor of Austria; King of Hungary and Bohemia; King of Lombardy and Venice; Grand Duke of Tuscany and Kraków; Duke of Lorraine; Grand Duke of Transylvania; Margrave of Moravia; Duke of Upper and Lower Silesia, of Modena, and Parma, and Piacenza —" Sisi faltered. That was as far as she remembered. She looked to her mother.

"I think that's quite enough." Ludovika stepped forward, having pried open the row of pearl buttons lining the back of her daughter's wedding gown. "Quite impressive that she made it that far. Now, my darling, let's get you dressed."

"She can*not* be too prepared." Countess Esterházy stood up, clearing her throat. "This is her kingdom now. And Her Royal Highness Elisabeth will be expected to know this," the woman said, her tone imperious. "Now, Duchess Elisabeth, please. If you would be so kind, we must continue. Please tell me, how many souls inhabit the realms of our blessed emperor?"

"Approximately forty million souls," Sisi answered, noting Helene's approving nod. Her elder sister had been her most devoted tutor these past few months.

"And, from where does the name *Habsburg* come?" Countess Esterházy asked.

"From Habichtsburg Castle, the imperial family's first seat."

"And tell me about Habichtsburg Castle?"

"It mean's Hawk's Castle. It was in Switzerland."

"Where in Switzerland?" the countess asked, the only movement on her face being a lone eyebrow that lifted beneath an impossibly long forehead.

Sisi's spirits faltered. She didn't remember that part. Countess Esterházy made a disapproving noise, like a purr in the back of her throat. "It was in Aargau, Switzerland, Duchess Elisabeth." And with that, the old woman riffled her way through the book, scouring for her next morsel of trivia.

The countess cleared her throat. "Oh! This is important. Tell me, who was the first Habsburg ruler?"

"Charlemagne!" Sisi exclaimed, exchanging a triumphant look with Helene where she stood. "Crowned in the year 800." With that, Sisi crossed her arms. She did not feel that she was performing *that* poorly on this first test of her preparedness.

"Wrong!" The countess snapped, as if thrilled to say so.

"Wrong?" Sisi asked, the smile sliding from her face. "But I'm certain that Charlemagne was a Habs—"

"He *was* a Habsburg, yes. But the *Austrian* Habsburgs trace their reign back to Count

Werner, who ruled around the year 1000."

"But that is tricky," Sisi began to protest, but her mother cut her off.

"I think we've had enough." Duchess Ludovika put her hands up, stepping in between her daughter and the countess. "We must dress you, Sisi, or you shall never be ready."

"The most essential part," Countess Esterházy interjected, throwing a barbed look toward the bride's mother as she clutched her procedural book like a precious relic, "will be the names and greetings for each of the court ladies. Your Majesty will have a special time to visit with them during the Kissing of the Royal Hand Ceremony. It would be highly . . . indecorous . . . to err on any of their names, as they are all most eager to meet you. Their good opinion is of the utmost importance."

Sisi nodded, cowed by the severe look on the countess's face, as well as the thought of the day's duties. Plus her body felt entirely too fragile to bear the weight of the wedding gown now held before her by her mother.

"Enough of this. She will be fresh and lovely and charming, as she always is." Ludovika stepped in front of Countess Esterházy, lifting the ivory gown like a shield. "And let's not forget, Franz chose *her,* and not any of those other *court ladies.*"

The countess answered with a raised eyebrow, as if to challenge Ludovika. But whatever barbed remark she had thought of, she refrained from uttering it, instead pinching her lips and burrowing back into her tome of Habsburg trivia, though Sisi was certain that the old woman already knew every word of that book.

Sisi's wedding gown was the heaviest, most ornate gown she had ever beheld, even after the hundreds of gowns that she had received in recent months. It was trimmed with gold thread, embellished with lace and crystal and stitched roses. She was sewn into it, the neckline and sleeves draping below her shoulders, allowing the ivory skin of her neck and shoulders to peek out, rivaling the pure, creamy color of the gown itself.

Her waist was squeezed to an impossibly narrow dimension, and her hoopskirt was so wide that, when the time came, she struggled to fit into the carriage that was to carry her to the cathedral. She was loaded in by several footmen, clutching the hand of her mother, who would ride along with her. A stiff-postured footman gave the signal and eight prancing Lippizaners pulled them forward, the horses' manes braided and trimmed in gold thread and scarlet tassels.

Sisi rolled through the Hofburg gate reserved only for members of the royal family, plunging into a crowd so vast that she could not see its end. The Augustine Cathedral was less than a mile from the palace, but it took

Sisi's coach several hours to make it there, so packed were the boulevards with thousands of revelers crying out for a view of the empress. Her passage was heralded by trumpeters, footmen coifed in impeccable white wigs, and banner men bearing the Habsburg flag. Imperial guards lined every step of the way, and even the horses pulling the coach appeared haughty, seemingly sensing the importance of the procession in which they took part.

"There now, Sisi, how about a smile?" Ludovika, who huddled beside her daughter in the coach, looked tired. Sisi turned and stared into her mother's eyes — her throat dry as she considered her response. But this was her mamma; surely she could be honest.

"Am I the only one who finds this frightening?" Sisi trembled, a lone tear sliding from the corner of her eye. Ludovika sat up tall, wiping the tear from her daughter's cheek before its existence could be detected by the hordes surrounding them.

"Nearly there, Sisi. Just remember — Franz is waiting for you at the end of all of this. Think of him."

Sisi nodded. "Yes." Once she saw Franz, all would be well.

When Sisi arrived at the church, a legion of attendants descended on her to fluff her gown, inspect her jewels, and approve of every strand of her hair. They adjusted the buttery satin that draped over her with layers of crystal-encrusted lace. They adjusted Aunt Sophie's opal tiara, perfecting her dark blond curls that had been trimmed with diamonds and pearls. Sisi marveled, remarking how much more beautiful a woman became when she had the full backing of the imperial court, with all its seamstresses, tailors, and artists stitching, sewing, and conspiring to make her a figure worthy of the empire into which she married.

Augustinerkirche, the medieval cathedral built by the royal family in Vienna's Josefsplatz Square, was swollen with more than a thousand guests and lit up by more than ten thousand candles. Seventy bishops stood before the altar dressed in gowns of gold thread, solemn and eager to assist in blessing the divine union.

Sisi was ushered to her father. Together they stood at the back of the cathedral, staring up at the staggeringly high gothic ceilings, propped up by white pillars that seemed as fragile as wishbones. Gilt chandeliers created an ethereal, glittering canopy over the length of the aisle. Delicately carved and lacquered pews were filled with courtiers, nobles who temporarily forgot their highborn manners as they elbowed and craned, vying to catch the first glimpse of Franz Joseph's beloved. Thunderous organs mingled with the fanfare of trumpets and horns to stun all in the audience, to overwhelm them with the august power of the Habsburg dynasty.

"Ready, Sisi?" Her father took her hand in his, waiting to commence the long march toward the altar. She nodded. Yes. Even though she was certain that one was never *ready* to make this walk.

"Then let's go, my girl." Duke Maximilian looked dignified in his old military uniform, presenting a stoic face even though his hands trembled as he kissed his daughter one last time.

Through the haze of the tiring, chaotic afternoon, Sisi felt cowed by the sense of awe that was stirred inside of her: the same awe that she now saw reflected back to her on the faces of her wedding guests. This was not about a sixteen-year-old German girl marrying the young man she loved. This day was about empire and the continuation of the Habsburg-Lorraine line.

The one memory that Sisi was certain she would savor from that day was the way her groom had looked at her. *Franz is waiting for you at the end of all of this — remember him.* How Franz had waited for her before the gold-leaf altar of the church, his eyes fixed on her with such earnest love and longing that she had almost felt bashful in front of the congregation. How he'd kept that gaze locked on her, immutable, as she processed down the aisle, her narrow satin shoes and heavy gown forcing her to walk more slowly than she would have liked. How he had smiled in the moment after they had exchanged their marital vows. And how, in that moment, a battalion of grenadiers outside the church fired off a salvo of cannonfire. All of Vienna knew, in that moment, that God's anointed vessel on earth had joined his hand to a Bavarian beauty named Elisabeth.

"Goodness," Sisi jumped at the sound, the cannons mingling with the roars of the crowd assembled outside the cathedral. "I think they've just heard the news of our marriage all the way to Russia."

Franz smiled down at her, taking her hands in his. "If they haven't yet, they very soon shall."

Back at the Hofburg Palace, a dozen aides and attendants were on hand to ensure that the newlyweds stepped gracefully through the procedure and protocol that was expected of them. The imperial couple made their first appearance as man and wife on the main balcony above the palace's grand staircase. Below, a crowd of hundreds of courtiers — dressed in their most formal regalia — stared and waved, elbowing one another aside in an effort to get a better look.

"*Repräsentazions-pflicht,*" Franz whispered to his bride, through close-knit lips. He, like her, was waving down at the courtiers.

"Pardon me?" Sisi asked, breaking protocol, turning her glance from the crowds to look at her husband.

"Keeping up the front. That's what this is. We play our roles today. And then, tonight, I may finally be with you."

Sisi turned back to the crowds below, hoping that they assumed her sudden smile and blush to be for them, and not in response to her groom's whispers.

Next, in the state receiving room, the couple was to grant their first private audience as man and wife. This honor was given first to the generals who had led Austria victoriously against the Hungarians in the uprisings of 1848 and 1849. Next came the court envoys and ambassadors, as well as Franz's ministers. Sisi had a special smile for Count Grünne, the only man whose face she remembered. The count leaned forward and bowed, whispering: "You are ravishing, Empress."

Last, in the position of least honor, marched in the Hungarian noblemen. Sisi marveled at these tall, dark-mustached men, proud and disinterested, bedecked in leopard skin cloaks and spurred boots. Sisi noted, with interest, that Sophie excused herself from the hall upon the entrance of the Hungarian lords, as Franz greeted them with cordial hospitality.

With these meetings over, the pair entered

the Hall of Mirrors to begin the portion of the afternoon Sisi most dreaded. This was to be the sacred Kissing of the Hand ceremony, the first moment in which the noble ladies of the court, hundreds of them, would have the opportunity to step forward, one at a time, to meet their new empress. At this time, the aristocratic ladies would be granted permission to do something that no one else in the kingdom, save the members of her immediate family, would ever again be able to do: touch Sisi. More precisely, on this wedding day, the highborn ladies were permitted to place a kiss on Sisi's now-imperial hand.

"Is this the Kissing of the Hand?" Sisi whispered to Franz as the noblewomen swished in, their heads plumed in feathers and fruit, their faces fixed with probing looks of appraisal and scrutiny. "Or the Parade of Broken Hearts?"

Franz laughed at the joke, but Sisi caught her mother-in-law scowling. Nowhere in the protocol guide did it say that the newlyweds were permitted to whisper to one another. And certainly, there was to be no giggling on their wedding day.

The first few women stepped forward without incident. Countess Esterházy stood at Sisi's side, whispering the names so that Sisi could maintain the illusion of preparedness, her hand resting and ready on a plush, velvet cushion. She sat still, her spine stiff against the high-backed chair, as the ladies filed past: some nearly as young as she, some as old as grandmothers. All of them bowed obsequiously as they stole furtive glances at their empress. Sisi noticed, too, the sideways looks some of them angled toward her husband. The young ones, the pretty ones, flashed quick smiles to Franz. When he returned their smiles, that's when Sisi realized: he knew them. He'd come of age mingling with them. She sat up taller in the uncomfortable, high-backed throne, suddenly keenly aware of how many other women had wished to sit in this same chair.

After more than a dozen ladies had been met, Sisi spotted a familiar face in the line. "Helene!" Sisi did not wait for her sister to approach, but instead rose from her chair and ran to her sister for a hug, dropping the cushion to the ground as she did so. "Oh, Néné, I am deliriously happy to see you!" Sisi nearly tripped as she folded into her older sister's arms.

"Sisi! Oh, Sisi!"

Immediately, the sisters heard gasps popping up from around the hall, like small puffs of gunfire. Sophie appeared by their side.

"Empress. You forget yourself." Sophie's voice was barely a whisper.

"Oh, Aunt Sophie." Sisi pulled away from the hug, wiping a tear from her eye. "But it's my sister. Surely I am allowed to hug my sister on my wedding day?"

"Empress . . ." — Sophie stared, her lips pinched and her face as stonelike as her posture — "this is *not* how things are done."

Sisi dropped Helene's hand, swallowing hard. And there it was, Sisi saw it again; that same look on Helene's face. That was when Sisi realized. It was not a look of envy or bitterness that had flickered behind Néné's familiar features all of these months. No, it was a look of *pity*. Her sister did not covet this role, or these jewels, or this groom, or this life. Her sister pitied Sisi for the fate she had willingly stepped into.

Realizing this, Sisi stepped back from the line, avoiding Franz's gaze, avoiding the gaze of her sister, the gaze of her new mother-in-law.

Helene was ushered out, her turn having come and gone, and the next woman approached, bowing before Sisi's hard, high-backed chair. But Sisi's vision was suddenly blurry as she watched her sister's receding figure, like a lifeboat drifting away from the flailing limbs of a drowning swimmer. *Néné!* Her heartbeat quickened, and Sisi found herself longing to leave the room with her sister. *Come back, Néné! Please, don't leave me!*

It struck Sisi, then, that she had not had a bite of food since the early morning, and she felt suddenly overcome by hunger. She tried to inhale a deep, fortifying breath, but her stomach met the resistance of her too-tight corset, and instead, she felt suffocated. Before her, the noblewoman still waited, bowing and expectant. Waiting to be addressed by name and to be invited to kiss the royal hand. But Sisi's ears were pounding. If Countess Esterházy had whispered the lady's name, Sisi had not heard it. And now, her vision was so blurry that she could not even see the face before her, and there was no chance of her knowing whom to address.

Sisi, hands clammy with perspiration, heart hammering against her corset, turned to Franz. He sat expectant, waiting for her to perform this simple task that was required of her. But she didn't know the woman's name.

And then, breaking protocol for perhaps the tenth time that hour, she muttered: "Excuse me." And with that, her vision still patchy and her steps unsteady, she rose from her chair and wobbled across the room. She had just cleared the door, entering a small anteroom, when the tears burst forward.

Sisi doubled over, clutching her waist, her gasps of breath breaking against the boning of her corset and her too-tight wedding gown. She gripped the wall to steady herself, feeling her vision recede in dizziness as a film of sweat rose to her face.

"Elisabeth! My darling, are you ill?" Franz burst into the room after her, a look of concern fixed tightly on his features. "My word, you look as white as a ghost. We must fetch a doctor, immediately." Several aides scurried off to dispatch the imperial will.

Sophie entered in the next moment, her face drained of color, her lower lip quivering. "What is the meaning of this? Do you not hear all of them whispering in there?" Sophie put a hand on her son's uniformed shoulder. "This was the *one* moment that was most essential. You know how word spreads on the lips of those ladies. Their opinions become fact. Elisabeth, did the Countess Esterházy not tell you that countless times?"

Sisi lowered her head once more, sliding down the wall until she collapsed in a crumpled heap of silk, diamonds, and goose-pimpled flesh. "I'm . . . I'm . . . terribly sorry," was all she managed to reply.

"Elisabeth is ill, Mother."

Sophie sighed. "I don't care if she *is* ill. I don't care if she has caught the plague! She has a role to play. She *must* come out and finish the ceremony."

Franz turned from his mother toward his bride, the worry plain on his face. When he spoke, his tone was decidedly softer than Sophie's, yet it carried with it the tinge of an urgent entreaty. He had been trained for this — he would never have imagined running from a formal receiving line, and his bride should not have, either. "Elisabeth . . . do you think you can manage it?"

Sisi took a moment before answering, gulping in small sips of air. Eventually, she nodded.

"Good girl," Franz said, a look of relief breaking across his features. "I promise, once this is over, we have only the banquet and the dance left."

Sisi shut her eyes, willing herself to breathe. This was only her first day as empress, and already she felt as if she would never make it.

That night, the evening of her wedding, Sisi was happy to put her troubling thoughts aside: to forget the months of training; the lectures by obsequious attendants and her disapproving mother-in-law; her failure at the Kissing of the Hand ceremony. She had muddled and fumbled her way through the day, but at least now, it was over. She was Franz Joseph's wife. And she was certain that protocol would be the furthest thing from her new husband's mind this evening.

Her mother and Aunt Sophie led her from the wedding ball to her new suite of rooms shortly after midnight. There, the two women, in solemn silence, had helped Sisi out of her wedding gown, unfastening the pearl clasps and peeling away the layers of silk, hoopskirt, petticoat, and corset. Sisi had flushed red as she had stepped out of the gown, her body revealed before her mother-in-law's inquisitive gaze.

Agata was the one servant whom Sisi had been allowed to keep, after much begging. She now stood on hand, plucking out the dozens of combs and pins and pearl strands woven into Sisi's dark golden curls. Finally, she helped Sisi into the delicate satin sleeping gown that had been commissioned especially for this night.

"I'll go and get him." Sophie slipped from the bedroom, leaving Sisi alone with her mother and Agata.

Sisi felt as if, at last, she could exhale. "I wish she had left long ago," Sisi sighed, once the door was securely shut on Sophie.

Ludovika frowned, the skin between her eyebrows crinkling like white paper. "I suppose you shall have to get used to her company, Sisi." When Ludovika took her daughter's hand in her own, the flesh was cold. Ludovika's eyes pleaded as she spoke to her daughter. "Allow her to help you. Obey her. Please do not set yourself up as a rival."

Sisi's eyes looked to the floor. "Please, Mother. Not now. Not on my wedding night." There was enough weighing on her mind about the night to come without having to fret over her new husband's mother.

"All right, all right." Ludovika nodded. "Let's get you into bed."

"This way, Empress Elisabeth." Agata gestured with her hand, a somber look on her face as she and Ludovika helped Sisi up into the massive four-poster bed. Sisi slid in where the heavy covers had already been peeled aside, where the holy water had already been splashed by a priest, blessing the imperial newlyweds even as they slept — or didn't sleep.

"I suppose this is it." Sisi felt so overcome by a throng of emotions that she could not resist reaching out to take her mother's ice-cold hand once more. It felt like an urgent request: *Please, don't leave me.*

Ludovika was perfectly composed, taking the empress's outstretched hand and doing something illegal: kissing it. Agata bowed and slipped from the room, leaving just the empress and her mother alone in the candlelit space. Ludovika settled quietly into a nearby chair as Sisi burrowed into the plush bed and waited for her husband to knock.

As the wait continued, Sisi's stomach coiled more tightly into a tangle of nerves. It was her first night as empress, her first night in her new bedchamber in her suite of imperial rooms. She looked around from the large bed, with its deep pool of down pillows and immaculate canopy of icy-blue silk, at the space that was now to be her home.

It was nothing like Possi. Whereas Possi had been familiar in its shabbiness — with its threadbare sofas, its chipped porcelain — everything about the Hofburg Palace was gilded and gleaming and fine. The walls, filled in with creamy silk brocade, were pierced by sparkling floor-to-ceiling windows that opened out over the imperial gardens. The furniture, polished and buffed, creaked when Sisi sat on it, giving her the impression she was always about to break something. Chairs and end tables had been arranged in a small, tidy seating area before the bay of windows, and an imperial-sized armoire had been loaded with the dresses she had brought with her, plus the many, many new ones which she'd received.

Adjacent to her bedchamber, her suite continued into a bright, airy sitting room, where she was to receive her most intimate guests. Here, silk-embroidered settees and armchairs huddled around a varnished tea table, and the high ceilings were painted with pastoral scenes that looked more likely to have occurred in the Garden of Eden than Vienna.

Beyond that room was an unnecessarily large hall, from which Sisi would dictate correspondence, read her mail, and accept guests of a less intimate variety. She would do so, all the while surrounded by the many faces of the Habsburg sons and daughters whose likenesses stared out at her, occupying every spare inch of the wall in their gilt portrait frames.

Their additional apartments included a

dressing room, a mirrored room, a dining room, and an anteroom. It was surely a suite fit for an emperor and his bride. Now, Sisi thought, she just had to get used to the idea of being that bride. Her stomach tumbled at that thought — that *she* was Franz Joseph's empress. That all of this was hers. That *he* was hers.

Finally, a knock on the door to the bedroom. Sisi's eyes darted toward the entrance of the room, her heart hammering against her ribs. Ludovika stood up from the chair, flattening her skirt as she threw a sideways look at her daughter.

"Come in," Sisi called, tousling her hair one final time so that it tumbled down around her shoulders, just as her husband liked it. She threw a glance at her mother, then back toward the soft sound of the knocking.

Franz pushed the door open, carrying with him two glasses and a half-empty pitcher of brandy. He didn't wear his uniform, but rather a cream-colored dressing robe and leather slippers. Sisi smiled at the sight of him, at the intimacy of this simple act of appearing before one another in their sleeping clothes. Immediately, her stiff shoulders softened, just slightly. Franz looked tired but happy.

And then, behind him, Sophie entered the bedroom. The woman's eyes landed squarely on the reclining frame of her new daughter-in-law. Sisi nearly gasped in horror at being spotted in her marital bed by her aunt, and she slid down into the bedcovers, turning her head so that her flushed face was concealed by her hair.

"Sophie, shall we?" Ludovika crossed the room in several brisk strides. "I think they are entitled to some privacy, at last." Sisi could have leapt up and hugged her mother in gratitude. But she stayed still, cowering in her bed. The two women left, the heavy door silencing the whispers that passed between them as they did so. Sophie threw one more gaze toward Sisi, before shutting the door.

Finally, they were alone. An emperor and his empress. A groom and his bride. Silence filled the room.

"Good evening, Your Royal Highness." Franz walked closer, his eyes fixed on Sisi's reclining figure, and Sisi resisted the urge to pull the bedcovers even higher around her shoulders. Her silk shift suddenly struck her as embarrassingly insufficient. How she longed for a woolen nightgown!

Sisi took a deep breath, forcing herself to answer him. "Good evening, Franz." How strange it was to look upon him. He was the man, the emperor, for whom the day's feasts and parades and crowds had been assembled. He was the center of this entire empire. And yet, here he was: her husband. Appearing before her on their wedding night in his bedclothes, like any other man might do. Sisi felt dizzy with the twin emotions of love for this man and quaking fear at the position he held. At the position that she, his partner, was now expected to assume.

"Don't you look cozy in that big bed?" Franz walked toward her, his slippers sliding across the floor. He paused before her. "Join me in a toast?"

Sisi took the glass he held aloft and allowed him to fill it with brandy. She noticed, as he poured the drink, that it was not only her hand that trembled.

"To us," he said, pressing his glass to hers. She could not bring her eyes to meet his.

"To us." She nodded slightly. They both drained their glasses. Franz sat slowly onto the edge of the bed, kicking his slippers off. He was still, silent for a moment before turning to look at her. She willed herself to look at him now. As she caught sight of his blue eyes, the involuntary trembling of her frame subsided. Just a bit.

"So, Mrs. Habsburg-Lorraine." Franz paused, refilling her glass and his, too. He kept a respectful distance between her reclining body and where he sat, his posture stiff, on the edge of the bed. "What did you think of your wedding?"

Sisi's head spun at the question. "So many people," she answered honestly, sipping her second glass of brandy. "I shall never remember all their names, and I'm sure I shall offend more than half of them before we've been married a month. That is, the *other* half . . . those whom I have not already offended today."

Franz laughed at this. "Too many people indeed." He finished his drink and leaned toward her, his breath sweet with the scent of it. "I much prefer the size of this crowd." Slowly, Franz pulled the covers down, revealing more of her silk shift and her barely covered body. He sat frozen for a moment, and Sisi did, too. Leaning forward, he kissed her bare shoulder, resting his lips against her skin.

"Alone at last," he whispered, breathing onto her neck and causing goose bumps to rise involuntarily to the surface of her flesh.

"Alone," she answered, nodding. Still seated, he took her empty glass and placed it with his on the bedside table. She stared at him, breathless. He had never been more handsome, and she had never been more terrified. Suddenly, the crowds lining the Viennese streets and the cathedral and the palace halls seemed manageable.

"May I join you?" he asked, his face suddenly bashful. Sisi gulped, nodding.

Franz moved slowly, scooting himself up onto the bed so that he was now beside her. He faced her. His voice with a slight tremble to it, he asked: "Are you afraid?"

"No," she answered. A lie. One that she had been prepared for and schooled in, just as she had been schooled in the protocol of a Habsburg wedding day. The wedding night was something to be endured. The bride's most important task in the entirety of the wedding celebrations was to please her husband on the night of the wedding. Especially when that man was the Habsburg emperor.

"Good." He studied her facial features before letting his eyes move toward her body, her figure reclining on the bed. "Neither am I."

Franz leaned forward and kissed her lips now, gently, but with a deliberate firmness. Sisi closed her eyes — he had not kissed her like this since their evening in the garden at Bad Ischl. She remembered how pleasant it had been that night, and noted how pleasant it was now, as well.

Franz sidled his body closer to hers, as he moved more fully onto the bed. He pulled his lips from hers and spoke, his face just inches from hers. Sisi opened her eyes and saw that he looked at her.

"I've wanted to hold you like this since the moment I beheld you. Do you remember when you first arrived at Bad Ischl?"

"Of course I remember." She traced the contours of his face with her fingers, his light eyes visible in the glow of candlelight. She found herself, suddenly, less nervous. If this was supposed to be something to be endured — tolerated — then why was she enjoying his closeness so much?

"You didn't even know it was me, the first time we met. That *I* was the emperor."

"But I noticed you, Franz."

"Did you, Elisa?" *Elisa.* So that was to be his name for her? Sisi smiled, approving of it.

"Of course, Franz. I noticed how dashing you looked in the uniform. I thought surely you were some imperial guard."

"Would you have loved me, even if I had been a guard?"

Sisi smiled, nodding. "Of course. Perhaps even more."

"Come now, you don't like all of this?" Franz waved a hand, gesturing toward the oversized bedroom, at the windows that opened over their imperial gardens and grounds.

Sisi considered the question. "I find it . . ."

"Yes?"

"A bit, oh —"

"A bit what?"

"Excessive."

Franz laughed, kissing her nose, still holding her in his arms as he spoke. "Perhaps it is. But it's all yours now. Remember that, my love. There is nothing you cannot have."

Sisi swallowed, thinking this over as he

kissed her.

He pulled his face away, looking down at her now, his eyes holding hers. "I remember how I felt my hopes dashed when your mother explained that you were the younger sister."

Sisi sighed, thinking back over the battle they had fought to be together. "Do you believe that my heart broke, as well? When I learned that you were my sister's fiancé."

"As loath as I am to think of your heart breaking . . . I *am* happy to hear that you felt that way."

"Franz." She rested a hand on his cheek, because looking at him wasn't enough. She longed to feel him, to know that he was hers. "Was your mother very angry? When you opposed her, and picked me instead?"

His body stiffened beside hers; a small, barely perceptible movement, but Sisi felt it like a recoiling from the intimacy they had enjoyed just a moment earlier. Franz exhaled before answering. "All of that is in the past now. Where it belongs. I'm much more interested with the present, with the matter in front of me." Franz kissed her neck, causing her to shut her eyes once more in surprised delight. She had never known that a kiss could be so powerful — mighty enough to knock the breath from her gut, and yet soft enough to slacken her coiled nerves, to slow her frantic thoughts. And just like that, she was entirely his, folded into his arms and powerless to resist him. But why had her mother told her how miserable this experience was to be?

Sisi had been warned that Franz would not come to their marital bed as a virgin; her mother had prepared her for this inevitability as well. Men had certain rites of passage to which they were entitled as young noblemen, especially a young man who happened to be the emperor. He had clearly done this before, as was evident in the skillful manner in which his hands knew where to rove under her shift. Part of her mind, a distant part, wondered, with a twinge of jealousy, who these women were. Would she meet them at court? Had some of them kissed her hand earlier that day in the state room? Would they smile at her, knowing that they had known her husband, too, in this most intimate of ways?

But at this moment, Sisi forced herself to push those troubling thoughts aside, to forget her jealousy at the fact that her husband had performed this act with other women. Clearly, she was the woman he now longed to be with, as he covered her skin with kisses. It was as if he longed to taste every inch of her.

"You know, as emperor, I'm not always as patient as I ought to be." Franz's lips now traced a course from her lips to her neck. Sisi sighed, encouraging his caresses.

"But I think I have been very patient. Yes, I

think I have waited quite long enough." His lips were now traveling down her neck, and he slid the strap of her nightdress off, kissing her shoulder. When he continued to slide the satin away, replacing its touch with his own soft lips, she gasped with pleasure, running her fingers through his hair.

"Franz," she called his name out to the room, delighted that she could do so with no modesty or shame. Formal title be damned, she thought, laughing aloud. Countess Esterházy and Sophie and all your protocol be damned. Her mother, too, had been wrong. Her mother had clearly never known caresses like these. And Sisi found herself, for the first time all day, actually enjoying herself. Pleasantly surprised. He was her husband, and she abandoned herself entirely to him, every inch of her body crying out with the desire to be his wife.

But she didn't become Franz Joseph's wife that night. At least, not according to the strict definition. He had *seemed* amorous and impatient, and yet, he did not cross the threshold that she had been preparing for. Instead, he approached and then retreated, hopping out of bed and telling her that he wanted another drink. Then he scooted up beside her and — incomprehensibly — told her that he preferred to talk.

On the second night, after a day filled with

banquets and meetings and an interminable parade, he asked if they might simply hold one another. Sisi complied, as she had been ordered to. And yet, as she lay there in his arms, feeling his desire for her like a charge between them, she couldn't help but be perplexed. Frustrated. She was perfectly willing, even eager, to become his wife. What was she doing wrong? Was she disappointing to him?

"Please forgive me, Elisa." His words broke the silence of the dark room, disrupting her ruminations on that second night. "I'm just so terribly . . . tired." Franz sighed, stroking her arm with his index finger. And so, as her own thoughts raced and questioned — Was she not making her desire plain enough? Or was she making her desire so apparent as to put him off? — he slipped off into sleep.

The mornings were, as a result, terrible. They were woken and dressed by servants, then joined at breakfast by their mothers. During that time, Sophie would ask if the union had been consummated, and Sisi couldn't help but feel the heat rise to her cheeks as she lowered her eyes and shook her head. The way Sophie stared at her, her eyes like two icy marbles, confirmed to Sisi that *she* was somehow failing. That she had clearly proven herself unqualified for the task she had been assigned. That Franz must surely be disap-

300

pointed in his selection of a bride.

The following evening, after two nights of this unpredictable and incomprehensible evening routine, Franz came to Sisi's room carrying a half-finished pitcher of wine.

"Hello, Franz." Sisi lay in bed, her hair loose, her body exhausted and yet humming with jumpy nerves.

Franz didn't say a word as he poured himself a glass, drank it in two gulps, and poured himself another. Finally, when the pitcher was emptied, he turned and climbed into bed. He smelled of the drink but his movements were fluid, without any of the lethargy that Sisi might have expected.

Sisi lay still, unsure of what to expect. Her heart clamored. Franz blew out the candle and slid toward her in complete darkness. His hands found her under the bedcovers and he pulled her toward him, his lips uttering no words as his body told her what to do. That night, on the third night of their marriage, Sisi became Franz Joseph's wife.

The next morning, Sisi awoke triumphant. She yawned, looking out the windows at the splashes of sunshine that slipped in through fluttering curtains. She rose to dress, hoping that she would find her husband alone at the breakfast table. Instead, as she entered their small dining room, she saw that she was the fourth person to arrive at the meal. Sophie,

Ludovika, and Franz already sat, drinking coffee and passing platters of pastries and cheeses between themselves.

Sisi's cheeks burned as all three pairs of eyes landed on her. These communal breakfasts struck her as painfully embarrassing. Being plucked from bed and dressed by her ladies-in-waiting — a group of relative strangers — was difficult enough. But then to see her husband for the first time each day under the probing gaze of Sophie and the mortified glances of her mother proved even more intolerable.

"Good morning, everyone," Sisi said quietly, her eyes slanting downward.

"Good morning, my darling." Franz rose upon her entrance and smiled at her, his features bright and enlivened this morning. Meeting his eyes, Sisi was transported back to the previous night and her body flushed warm at the memory. If only they could be alone now to smile and whisper about the evening they had shared.

"Please, join us, Elisa." Franz rose and extended a gloved hand — another one of the new court rules she had learned: gloves at all meals — toward the empty seat at the small, crowded table.

At Sisi's place waited a leather pouch. She looked down at it as she was helped into her chair by a liveried footman. "What is this?"

No one answered her. Her mother's eyes

stayed fixed on the plate before her.

Sisi held the pouch aloft, peeking into it. It was filled with money. "Franz?" Her eyes widened in confusion.

Franz cleared his throat, chewing on a piece of toast. "It's . . . a gift."

"A gift?" Sisi looked from her husband to her mother, confused. "For what?"

"It's your *Morgengabe,*" Franz said, offering little by way of clarification.

"My *morning gift*?" Sisi repeated the words, her brow crinkling.

"For your gallant efforts last night," Sophie said, stuffing a piece of thickly buttered toast into her mouth. "The bedsheets have been examined and Countess Esterházy has confirmed what my son swears to me: that you were indeed a virgin. That is . . . before last night."

Sisi let the pouch slip from her fingers, landing on the table with a clamor. She turned from the direct and immodest gaze of her aunt to the earnest blue of Franz's eyes. *Franz, you fool!* She longed to scream at him. How could he have put her in this position? And how, she wondered, was it that her husband was so willing to include his mother in even this most intimate moment?

Sisi had come to this breakfast feeling joy and relief, confident in the knowledge that she had finally proven herself capable of her new role in at least one way. Why then, was it

303

Sophie's haughty smile that shone the most triumphant at the table that morning?

VII.

The walk to the altar takes an eternity, and Sisi reminds herself to keep her eyes down, her features composed. The image of humility, even if the people packed into this cathedral believe her to be, in some way, divine.

When they reach the front of the church, two thrones await them. There they will sit, side by side. Two flawed mortals forever memorialized, together, in this moment. How strange, she thinks, to be a part of what would surely become history, and yet still worry that she might trip on her heavy skirt.

Her dress is cumbersome and he helps her as she hoists her skirt up to the altar. And then she turns to look out over the cathedral, her eyes combing the scene so that the sea of a thousand unique faces blends into one fuzzy tableau.

But there is just one face she seeks, her eyes roving hungrily down the columns of onlookers. Don't let them read the longing on your face, she reminds herself. She breathes out, slowly.

Has he come?

The noise throbs so loudly around her that she longs to stop her ears, to drown out some of the din, but she knows she must not. A deity does not quake simply because the crowd yells. An empress stands fixed, immutable; the calm that continues on even as the world rages. Even though, all along, she has known the opposite to be true.

CHAPTER SEVEN

HOFBURG PALACE, VIENNA
APRIL 1854

Sisi could have wept in relief when Franz told her, on the fifth night of their marriage, that he would be taking her away from court.

"What do you think of taking a *Flitter-wochen,* Empress?"

"A honeymoon?" Sisi shut her eyes, melting into the pillows as the candle beside the bed expired. A chance to get away from the endless and exhausting days. A reprieve from Sophie's unsought advice and pinch-lipped looks of disapproval. And mostly, a break from the constant crush of people who encircled them — watching, whispering, observing. Not just at the state lunches and banquet dinners, but all day.

They were always accompanied by at least half a dozen in their retinue — Sophie, to be sure, as well as Countess Esterházy and Count Grünne, and many of the other aides and ministers whom Sisi had met in Bad

Ischl. The short, monocled palace secretary, the man whom Sisi had come to know as Herr Viktor Lobkowitz, had become her constant shadow.

There were others, too. Women, who, in just the short weeks' time, had become regular fixtures in Sisi's daily routine. She now had, through no choice of her own, an entourage. Ladies-in-waiting. Beautiful young women whom she'd first beheld at the Kissing of the Hand, but who spoke as if they were old friends of Franz's. She'd inherited this group almost at the same time she'd been given her suite of rooms, and the small party included Countess Paula Bellegarde, Countess Marie Festetics of Hungary, and Countess Karoline of Lamberg.

It was yet another expectation of her new role under which Sisi bristled; how odd, she found it, that these noblewomen, the rising stars of the court, had been the same women who had previously hoped to win Franz Joseph's hand. And now she was to trust them with dispatching her letters, organizing her wardrobe, and helping her rise and bathe each morning?

Yes, a break from it all was precisely what Sisi needed. She opened her eyes, looking at Franz in the dark room. "I quite like the idea of a honeymoon. To where?"

"Not far, I'm afraid." Franz propped himself up on his elbow to look at her. They lay, side by side, in bed. Sisi savored this time, the few hours of solitude they could steal once all attendants and servants had been dismissed. "To one of my . . . our . . . castles just outside of the city. Laxenburg Castle."

"Laxenburg Castle." Sisi repeated the name. "Can't we go farther?"

He laughed, a surprised look, as he shifted his weight on his elbows. "I would love to take you farther," he paused, shaking his head, "but things are unstable abroad."

Sisi crinkled her nose, making a face to ask: *What does that have to do with our honeymoon?* "Then we'll stay within Austria. But let's just go somewhere far away."

Franz shook his head, continuing. "Russia has declared war on the Turks. And England and France have jumped to challenge the tsar. All the while, Hungary is still threatening revolution from within the empire. I'm afraid I can't be away too long — world politics will not wait for us to honeymoon."

Sisi put a hand on his cheek, touching the skin that had become flushed while he catalogued these problems.

"I would take you to Paris. Or Florence, if I could. But . . ."

She interrupted him, pressing her finger to his lips. "Laxenburg sounds just wonderful, Franz, my darling."

In truth, what she meant was that anywhere away from court — anywhere away from her new role — sounded wonderful. The first week of their marriage had been an endless stream of banquets and parades and introductions and waltzes. Frenzied days followed by sleepless nights. Communal family breakfasts and then more busy days. Always, they were accompanied and trailed by a horde of expectant faces.

Sisi didn't think she could learn one more name or manage one more quick-paced dinner conversation, filled with smiles so permanent that her cheeks ached and stares so probing that she felt that her guests could see beneath her shift. All Sisi wanted in a honeymoon was a reprieve, a chance to spend time with her husband and no one else. A chance to speak without having to smile; to wake in the morning without meeting a legion of faces as soon as she opened her eyes.

But Laxenburg did not afford Sisi that opportunity.

The first morning there, Sisi stretched in bed, in a state halfway between slumber and waking. A splash of soft morning sunlight filtered in through the opened curtains, and the notes of several birds trilled from a nearby beech tree. If she kept her eyes shut, Sisi might have imagined herself back at Possi — far away from Vienna and the Hofburg and the unwanted servants and unknown courtiers. She yawned, reaching for her husband.

She had, at last, slept well. And now they had the day to themselves. But as she rustled the sheets, Sisi's hand did not find Franz's warm, reposing body. She opened her eyes. Franz's half of the bed was tousled, its pillows and sheets haphazardly tossed aside. Empty.

"Agata?" Sisi called out to the empty room, aware that someone always lurked on the other side of the door, regardless of the time. The maid, awake and dressed since dawn, would be summoned, informed that her lady called.

"Good morning, Empress." The Polish maid swished into the room several moments later, her hands laden with a porcelain vase of fresh-clipped snapdragons and lilies. She was the only maid Sisi had brought from the Hofburg. "Did Your Majesty sleep well last night?"

Sisi nodded, sitting up. Agata deposited the vase on the bedside table before reaching for Sisi's red slippers, holding them forward to her. "Thanks, Aggie." Sisi yawned. "But where is Franz?"

Agata's smile wilted, but before she could answer, another figure burst over the bedroom threshold. "Good morning, Elisabeth!" Sophie entered without invitation, her loud voice unsettling the previously peaceful room like wind stirring up dust. "Why, you've slept quite late, I was wondering if perhaps I should come in and rouse you. But Franzi

311

had ordered me to let you rest."

Sisi sat up straighter in bed, tugging the bedcovers so that they concealed her flimsy sleeping shift. She crossed her legs, as if to hide her worn red velvet slippers, knowing that they were a part of her old self and her former life — a life of which her aunt vehemently disapproved.

"Aunt Sophie . . . why, hello. You've come from Vienna?" True, it was only a short carriage ride to Laxenburg from the capital — she and Franz had made the journey in just over an hour the previous evening. But Franz had never mentioned that they wouldn't be alone on their honeymoon.

Sophie nodded, tugging on the curtains to allow in more daylight. The day would be a warm one.

"Franzi . . . the emperor, has gone back to the Hofburg to tend to his papers and meet with his ministers for the day." Sophie turned and looked at her niece now, a haughty smirk pulling her lips upward. "The empire needs running whether a man is on his honeymoon or not. And my Franzi is not one to shirk his duties."

Sisi's shoulders dropped. "When . . . when will he return?"

"Don't pout so." Sophie waved her hands, busying herself by crossing the room toward Sisi's wardrobe. "Your husband will be back for dinner. He wouldn't hear of being away from you for longer than that."

Then that was some small relief. Sisi had just the day to get through. That night at supper she would speak to him, beg him not to leave her again the next day.

"Now, how about you dress and we will ask Countess Esterházy to join us for a walk in the gardens?" Sophie clipped toward the bed now, her hand outstretched with a gown of pale violet for Sisi. "I've ordered us veal schnitzel for dinner . . . his favorite."

Sisi's breath caught in her throat. "You are planning to stay, then? For supper?"

Sophie stood up tall, throwing her shoulders back. "Not just for supper, my dear. Franz is going to have a busy few weeks, what with traveling back and forth between Vienna and Laxenburg every day. Someone's got to keep you company. I offered, of course. It was such a tremendous relief to Franzi to know that you wouldn't be here alone every day."

As expected, Franz returned to Laxenburg that evening for supper. What Sisi had not expected, however, was that the newlyweds were joined at the table by the Archduchess Sophie, the Countess Esterházy, and Count Grünne.

Franz greeted Sisi with a kiss. "How was your day, my darling? Did you and Mother enjoy yourselves? Aren't the grounds lovely? I thought you might enjoy walking outside."

But before Sisi could answer, Franz had turned to Count Grünne, who sat to his left at the dinner table. "Grünne, did you receive the reply from Paris yet?"

Franz spent the remainder of dinner discussing France's declaration of war on Russia. Sisi sat in silence, barely touching the schnitzel that her mother-in-law had ordered for her first honeymoon dinner, as the Countess Esterházy droned on to Sophie about some Hungarian count's recent marital troubles.

Later, Franz knocked on the bedroom door. "Elisa?"

"Come in." Sisi sat before the mirror, unweaving her braided hair. It was late, as Franz had spent several hours after dinner with Grünne.

"Hello, my bride." Franz entered the room carrying two glasses and a bottle of champagne. "I'm glad you are still awake."

"Of course I'm awake. I did not intend to miss my one chance to see you all day." Sisi turned to face him. If Franz noticed her barbed tone, he did not acknowledge it.

"Good. Because I thought perhaps we should celebrate."

"Celebrate what?" Sisi stood up from the vanity, kicking off her red slippers as she walked toward the bed.

"Why, what do you think? Our honeymoon." Franz poured the bubbling drink into each glass, a small amount of the white fizz overspilling and wetting his fingers. He poured a glass for himself, and then a second. "For you," he said, handing her the drink.

She avoided his glass, outstretched to clink against hers, before lifting the drink to her lips and taking a big gulp.

"Do you like it?" He leaned past her to blow out several of the candles.

She nodded, placing her glass down.

"Good, because I've ordered a hundred more bottles. As a gift for you. It's my favorite vintage."

Sisi did not thank him. She didn't need any more gifts. She needed him.

"You seem quiet tonight, Elisa. You barely touched your supper." He smiled, leaning toward her. "Not a fan of our Viennese schnitzel?"

"The dinner was fine." She angled her body away from his.

"Are you missing your mother again?"

"Franz." She sighed. Why was she so nervous to speak the truth to her own husband? "I missed *you* today."

Franz finished his drink and poured himself a refill, avoiding her eyes now. She watched him, his features traced in shadow against the glint of candlelight. "I know," he said, eventually.

"I was quite sad to see you gone this morning."

"I left before you awoke so that I wouldn't upset you with a goodbye."

Sisi couldn't help but scowl at his logic. "But I was upset to awake and find that you'd —" She shook her head, trying to remain calm. "This is our honeymoon, is it not?"

"Elisa, I'm sorry. I told you, the situation is very unstable at the moment." He filled his glass once more.

"But perhaps tomorrow you don't have to go? As you said, the gardens here are lovely. And I have yet to ride since arriving in Vienna. Perhaps tomorrow you and I could —"

"It's bad enough that I've left court, Elisa. But I can't be entirely removed. Mother was not happy when I told her that —" Franz's eyes darted at hers, a quick flicker of hesitation, before he paused, sighing. "I can't entirely abandon my duties."

Sisi sighed. "Well, then, can I come with you?"

"Oh my darling, you'd be terribly bored. I simply work all day. No, no, no. Stay here. You are exhausted from this past month. Rest. You can manage without me during the days. At least Mother has kindly offered to be here with you."

He leaned forward, and before Sisi could object, he kissed her, his lips chilly and sweet from the champagne. His kiss was not soft like usual. He seemed agitated, restless, even.

316

He made love to her quickly. Afterward, they lay side by side in silence.

"Franz?" Sisi propped herself up on her elbow.

"Hmmm?" Franz was staring at the ceiling, his eyes devoid of the usual glimmer with which they beheld her each night.

"Is anything . . . is everything all right?" She didn't understand. His letters to her before their wedding had been page after page about how he longed for their time in Bad Ischl. How, once they were married, they would ride together as they had last summer. How, whenever she was not beside him, he ached for her. And now, he had her here, and he was planning to leave her each day of their honeymoon?

Franz sighed, bringing his hands to his temples as he shut his eyes. "This war in the Crimea . . . it's a bloody mess. The Russians expect us to declare war on England and France along with them. And I should. I know I should. Russia is my closest ally. But can I afford to make an outright enemy of both France and England?"

After a long pause Franz clapped his hands, opening his eyes as he sat up. When he spoke, it was with a forced merriment in his voice. "Oh, but never mind. I swore I would never discuss politics with you." He put his hand on her cheek. "I will not furrow this beautiful face with my burdens of the State."

"Franz, you can talk to me. Of course you can talk to me about your affairs. I long to know what you —"

"No," he answered, his voice suddenly firm. A tone that she'd never heard him use before. And then he smiled, as if to soften the impact of his declaration. "No, my darling." His voice was hushed now, even contrite. His fingers grazed her cheek, trailing a line down to her neck and into the dip in her collarbone. "You are pure to me, Elisa. My source of goodness."

Sisi stared at him, her mind swinging along with his rapidly changing moods. As she studied him, she saw that his features had a pinched quality, a look that somehow aged him. She considered what he had just said. If he needed her to be his antidote, the counterpoint to his harried and onerous days — could she be that?

"Please, Elisa." He leaned forward, his finger under her chin. He looked weary, even wearier than she herself felt. "Please, let me escape to you."

She sighed. "All right, Franz." She took his hand in hers and placed a kiss on his fingers. "Then let's talk about something else. What would you like to talk about?"

He thought about this. "My grandfather," he said, pouring them each another glass of champagne.

"Your grandfather?" Sisi asked. "What

about your grandfather?"

"Do you know what a good emperor he was, Elisa?" Franz handed her the refilled glass. Already, she felt her head spinning with the familiar effects of the wine. She suspected that these late-night drinks with her new husband were the cause of the headaches with which she now awoke each morning.

"His name was Emperor Franz, as well. I was named after him. *Franz der Gute.*"

"Franz the Good," Sisi said, repeating the epithet. "As I am sure you shall be someday, as well."

"He was more like a father to me than a grandfather. I remember when he fell ill." Franz's voice was quiet now, his expression far off, as he stared at the wall across the bedroom. "I was only five. The court physician told him that all he could consume was tea. You know what I did?"

"What?" Sisi propped herself up onto her elbow, allowing her hair to cascade around her body as she angled herself to listen to him.

"I told my governess that I, too, would have nothing but tea. And I kept to it. I had nothing but tea until my grandfather . . . passed."

"At age five? My word. How long did that last?"

"Only a few days. Fortunately my dedication as a grandson was not tested too extremely. Otherwise Mamma might have intervened."

Sisi looked at him, her finger brushing away a loose wisp of hair that fell across his eyes. "Do you remember him well, Franz?"

"I do. I remember that he would come to the nursery and watch me while I played with my toy soldiers. I remember how he used to take me outside the palaces to watch the imperial guards conducting their drills. And that he gave me my first military uniform. When I was just four."

Sisi thought about this. At how many years of a head start her husband had had on her in preparing for his role as emperor.

"I remember there was one night . . ." Franz was in full storytelling mode now, his voice wistful with remembering. "Grandfather had not come to my nursery that day. He had been out hunting, I believe. There was to be a great ball that night. I was crying and carrying on in the nursery, telling my governess, the Baroness von Sturmfeder, that I missed Grandfather terribly. That I could not possibly go to bed until I had seen him. Well, the good Frau Sturmfeder tried to tell me that Grandfather was giving a ball that night, and that I would see him the following day. But I would not be appeased."

"So what did you do?"

"Frau Sturmfeder put me in a dressing gown and snuck me out of the nursery into the hallway. She led me to the balcony above the *Redoutensaal,* the Great Hall, and there I stood, looking down on the ball. I remember seeing Mother looking beautiful in a plumed headdress, and Grandfather appearing very dignified in his military uniform. I remember the courtiers queuing in line to pay their respects to him. I remember thinking then . . . now *there* was an emperor."

Franz paused, swallowing. Silence hovered between them in the dark bedroom. After a moment Franz spoke: "Sometimes I still feel like that little boy, looking down. Cowed by it all. As if the *real* emperor is somewhere else, and I am just standing in for him."

Sisi sighed, considering her answer to this confession. She longed to tell Franz that there was nothing more understandable than that feeling. That she felt the same way, and had, since the day he had asked her to marry him. That he was only human, even if more-than-humanness was expected of him. She parted her lips to say these things, but he spoke first.

"Which I know is a silly way to feel, since I am, after all, the one God chose for this role." Franz said it matter-of-factly. He looked at her now, the blue of his eyes unburdened, in control once more.

Did she agree with that? She wasn't sure. Certainly it was how Sophie felt. And everyone else in Vienna. But if kings really ruled by divine right, why were they so often

321

toppled?

"Oh, Elisa, my beautiful bride." He leaned forward and kissed her forehead, this time more slowly than before. "Your brow creases when you are deep in thought. Where have you gone? What are you thinking about?"

But for a reason she couldn't quite explain — not to him, not even to herself — she didn't answer.

He leaned toward her, asking, "Have I overburdened you with my heavy thoughts?"

"No, darling, of course not," she said, smiling innocently. "I'm just thinking of how much I love you."

Sisi felt him sliding his body on top of hers under the sheets, his desire for her evident once more as he kissed her. Sisi knew that a good wife was not supposed to encourage a man's excessive physical advances. She was to accommodate his needs, yes. But she was not supposed to encourage him. And she was most certainly not supposed to reciprocate his longing.

She broke that rule, however. After entire days apart from Franz, and with all of their waking minutes harried and overcrowded, these precious moments were the only ones Sisi had in which Franz was entirely hers. In these moments, at last, they communicated with a language that was meant for the two of them. In the dark of the night, Sisi knew that Franz wanted no one else with him, only her. And so she welcomed his kisses, knowing that at least in his physical expression, he was telling her that he loved her.

In spite of the fervor with which she cherished their nights together, Sisi couldn't help but admit to herself that she found the actual marital act to be somewhat disappointing. It always started out well enough. She loved the way Franz looked at her when he joined her in bed. The way he kissed her. The way he appeared like a captive in his love for her.

But instead of quenching some desire deep within her, when it was complete, it only seemed to leave her with further longings, prompting her to suggest that they continue their lovemaking. What, precisely, she was seeking, she did not know. Only that her body clamored to still be joined with her husband's, and that when he pulled away from her so quickly after his own needs were satisfied, she was filled with a gnawing dissatisfaction. Some unmet craving. She'd go to sleep feeling this way, knowing that, in the morning, he would be gone from his side of the bed before she awoke.

As the honeymoon wore on, Sisi began to notice a change in Franz that happened each night. After his needs were met, he would withdraw to the far side of the bed, pleading an excuse of fatigue, or sometimes even a headache. And suddenly, in that moment, he was different. She would reach for him, would ask him if she had offended him in any way, and always he would smile and say, "Of course not, my darling." But he was different, somehow. Different than the supplicating, affectionate, wide-eyed lover who had come to their room and their bed at the beginning of the evening.

After several weeks had passed in this pattern, Sisi grew increasingly frustrated. Laxenburg had come to feel less like a honeymoon and more like a sentence. She found it harder to bite her tongue when Sophie offered unsolicited advice on how Sisi ought to dress. She found it hard not to scowl when her aunt and Countess Esterházy spent the entire lunch meal exchanging court gossip — discussing names she didn't know, and scandals she didn't care to hear about. She found Franz's daily absence increasingly unbearable. And she found herself fuming when Sophie repeatedly rejected her requests for a ride, insisting that the three women undertake some other activity instead.

Sisi was bored in spite of having her every minute scheduled; lonely, in spite of being in the constant companionship of her aunt and Countess Esterházy. She was, to her own surprise, eager to return to the Hofburg, if only for a change of scenery. There at least she could slip out into the imperial stables and saddle up Blume or Diamant and escape into the nearby woods.

Franz had told her that Laxenburg was to be her break — an escape from the court and a chance for more relaxed days. But it did not feel like a honeymoon when she never saw her husband. Each day, he rode back to his ministers and their papers before five o'clock in the morning. At night, he didn't return until it was time for a crowded and hurried dinner. The excuse he always offered was politics, but he would explain no further.

Troubling as this was, Sisi hoped that things would improve when they returned to Vienna. That was, after all, where Franz would feel more at home. And there she wouldn't have the physical distance away from him each day. She begged him to take her back to the capital with him. Eventually Franz complied and their honeymoon came to its end.

"Let's be quick about it." Sisi looked on, watching as Agata sorted her trunks from Laxenburg. "I would like to finish before Countess Esterházy arrives. If she sees you unpacking, she's going to insist she stay and oversee."

Sisi was back in Vienna and settling in, along with the rest of the court, at the summer residence of Schönbrunn Palace.

"Where would you like these, Empress?" Agata asked, holding up a pair of leather gloves.

"Give those to me," Sisi said, tucking the gloves into her pocket. She intended to ride later.

"Would you like me to tidy those papers, as well, Empress?"

Sisi turned from her trunks to the pile of papers on her rosewood desk. The majority of the stack came from Europe's various ruling families and aristocracy: wishes for a happy wedding, a blessed marriage, a child-filled home. Letters that — as onerous a chore as it was — had to be answered. But at the bottom of the pile awaited two precious notes.

"Ludwig!" Sisi smiled as she said the name aloud, recognizing her cousin's familiar handwriting. "Agata, you remember my cousin Ludwig, don't you?"

"Of course, Empress. How could I forget Ludwig?"

Sisi smiled; it was a well-known fact that all of the female servants at Possi had favored her charming cousin. Ludwig, several years younger than Sisi, also came from Bavaria, where he happened to be the crown prince.

"Oh, I'm delighted to hear from Ludwig." Sisi sighed. "Summertime always makes me think of him." Ludwig was a kindred spirit of sorts, and had been since their childhood. He'd often spent his summers staying in their household at Possi.

The second note came from Helene, surely

detailing the return trip from Vienna and whatever other news she had from home. Sisi's heart soared. "Oh Agata, notes from both Ludwig and Néné! Can you oversee the rest of that trunk by yourself? I'd like to get to my letters."

"Of course, Your Majesty." Agata nodded, riffling through a pile of silk scarves.

"Good. Then I shall take these into my office and find Herr Lobkowitz to help me on my responses." Sisi hopped up from bed. Looking for her slippers, she peeked under the bed.

"Agata?"

"Hmm?" The maid was elbows deep in silk.

"Agata, where are my slippers?" Sisi squatted beside the bed, her corset pinching her stomach as she peeked under the bedframe. "The red velvet ones I brought from Possi?"

Agata averted her gaze, suddenly staring into the trunk before her.

Sisi narrowed her eyes, fluent, after all of their years together, in her maid's body language. "Agata — what is it? The red slippers?"

But the maid had assumed an air of stubborn and frustrating reticence. Just then, Countess Esterházy swept into the room, her hands filled with even more letters necessitating replies. Sisi clenched her jaw but barely acknowledged the woman's entrance, instead keeping her eyes on her maid. When she spoke, it was quietly: "Agata, what is the matter? I'm asking you where my slippers have gone — have you seen them while unpacking?"

"Slippers?" Countess Esterházy interjected without invitation. "Does Your Highness refer to those tattered red . . . *clogs*?"

"Yes," Sisi answered, stiffening to a stand as her gaze met that of the countess. "The slippers my father gave me for my fifteenth birthday — the very same ones I brought from Possenhofen."

"Yes, I'm familiar with them," the countess said, staring directly at Sisi.

"In that case," Sisi continued, a feeling of irritation nagging at her, "have you any idea where they might have gone?"

"The archduchess has ordered me to . . . dispose of them."

Sisi's pulse quickened, but she forced herself to remain calm. "Dispose of them?"

"Get rid of them. When I was packing up your apartment in Laxenburg."

Sisi walked slowly toward Countess Esterházy. "And why would she order you to do such a thing?"

Countess Esterházy pointed toward one of the immense volumes on Sisi's bedside table, the book titled *Ceremonial Procedure for the Official Progress of Her Royal Highness, the Most Gracious Princess Elisabeth.*

"Surely by now Your Majesty has come to

the section on slippers?" The countess lifted a lone eyebrow, her facial features spreading into a servile grin.

"Please be so kind as to refresh my memory, Countess Esterházy, on what that *book* says about slippers."

"Yes, of course." The countess stood undaunted, braiding her long fingers together before her waist. "Etiquette dictates that the empress is not to wear a pair of slippers more than once."

"And why is that?"

The countess exhaled a short puff of laughter. "Why, they would get dirty, of course. The empress cannot be seen in *dirty* shoes! The archduchess believed that, now that the honeymoon was over, you ought to begin abiding by court procedure. You are, after all, an example to the entire palace."

"Countess Esterházy." Sisi's voice trembled with the threat of tears, but she did not wish for this woman, with her condescending grins, her whispered quips, to relish such a display of weakness. "Please excuse me, Countess Esterházy. I'd like to rest. You are dismissed."

Countess Esterházy bowed, her lips still curled upward in a smile. "As you wish, Your Majesty." She turned to walk slowly toward the door. "If Your Majesty should require me for anything, I shall be sitting along with the Countesses Paula and Karoline, just outside your door."

"Yes, I know." Sisi forced a smile, even though her tone was far from jovial.

With Countess Esterházy gone, Sisi ran to the bed and collapsed, her face pressing into the pillows. Her eyes burned hot with tears of frustration. One of the last remaining pieces of her former life — gone! And without her permission or knowledge.

"Forgive me, Your Majesty." Agata approached the bed, her voice meek. "I wanted to tell you. Really, I did. But I never got a chance alone in the bedchamber with you. Not without that . . . woman . . . in here with us."

Sisi turned and looked at the maid. "Oh Agata, you know how I loved those slippers! I wore them all over Possi."

"I know," Agata said, her own eyes welling with tears.

"And all because of some silly rule. Who cares how many times I wear my slippers?"

"I know, Your Majesty." Agata reached forward, breaking protocol as she took Sisi's hand in her own. She sat herself on the edge of the bed. "But you mustn't allow yourself to get this upset."

"Oh, but it makes me so terribly homesick." Sisi wept, squeezing the maid's hand.

"Of course, Sis — Empress. But please, try not to weep like this. It can't be good. Not in your condition."

Sisi looked at the maid directly now, her tears momentarily halted. She wiped her cheeks.

The maid's face had flushed a deep burgundy. "Your Grace, surely you have noticed . . . ?" Agata paused.

"Noticed what?" Sisi leaned forward.

"Your Grace." Agata lowered her eyes. "You didn't bleed this month."

Sisi paused, thinking about this. When had she experienced her last monthly courses? Now that she asked herself, she realized that she did not remember. She had been so preoccupied since her arrival in Vienna that this fact had completely slipped by unnoticed.

"You're right, Agata." Sisi frowned, puzzled.

Agata's lips spread into a smile, her round cheeks like two red apples. "Madame, you're carrying a baby."

"A baby?" Sisi gasped, her hand rising to her opened mouth. "But we only just got married." Surely she and Franz had been performing the marital act with regularity since the wedding. And she had noticed that her breasts had felt tender, a fact that she had attributed to the painfully constricting corset. But pregnant, so soon? The thought shocked her. And yet, she could not deny that it also filled her with delight.

"A baby?" Sisi said it again, as if to confirm her condition. "Agata, I'm pregnant . . . I'm going to have Franz's heir!" Sisi leaned forward, pulling Agata into a hug. They both laughed, tossing aside any concern for protocol.

"A baby." Sisi said it again, nodding. She placed a hand over her flat stomach, where the baby had not yet betrayed any sign of its existence. But somewhere inside there grew Franz's child. Perhaps a boy, the next emperor of Austria.

"Oh Agata, I am so happy. Forget the slippers. Forget the letters I must write to England and Bohemia and Prussia. I must write Mamma and Helene at once!" She hopped up from the bed and ran to her desk, overjoyed at the news she'd now be able to share with her family back in Bavaria. Perhaps Mamma would even return to court to help Sisi with the confinement and the labor.

Standing over her desk, Sisi quickly scrawled: *"Dearest Mamma, I am thrilled that you shall be the first to know —"*

And then a thought struck Sisi, and she paused her writing. "Agata?"

"Yes, Empress?"

"Agata, how did you know that I . . . well, that I was expecting a child?"

Agata's facial expression confirmed Sisi's sense of dread.

"Does she . . . do others know?"

The maid's shoulders sagged. "Empress, I'm so sorry." The maid looked stricken. "It was Countess Esterházy. She came in, snooping around each morning, after you'd gone to breakfast. I told her not to concern herself with the bedding. That it was my job, as chambermaid. But she always found a way to be in here. Always talked about something she had to do . . . court procedure."

"So she's been checking my sheets?" Sisi clenched her teeth, attempting to remain calm. Forcing her pulse to slow its rapid pace. "It's not your fault, Aggie. I should have expected as much." She took the note in front of her and tore it up, her hand rending the paper apart in two swift, angry motions. She refused to let this upset her; not when she had so much about which to be joyous. "Change of plans, now."

Sisi scrawled a quick note, which she handed to her maid. "See to it that this is delivered to the emperor. He may meet me in the imperial chapel. I shall go there directly to pray for my baby. Tell him to come at once."

"Yes, Empress."

Sisi grabbed her rosary beads and her devotional book and swept from her bedroom, pausing to examine herself in the mirror first. She forced herself to smile. She looked tired, yes. But whether it was her imagination, she did believe that there was a glow to her cheeks, a new warmth in her honey-colored eyes. She was to have Franz's baby! Surely this would bring them close in the way that she had craved. Surely he would be happy with his choice of bride, seeing how quickly she had conceived. Forget all the snooping ladies — this was something she and Franz would share together. She clasped her hands and giggled, sending up a private prayer of gratitude for such blessed news.

In the antechamber sat her ladies-in-waiting, their forgotten embroidery projects languishing in their laps. Several guards stood nearby and Sisi found the group engaged in the usual palace activities of gossiping and flirting.

The Countesses Esterházy, Paula, and Marie all stood to attention upon Sisi's entrance. Karoline of Lamberg remained seated, whispering to a nearby guard: "I would never take a Russian for a lover — the stench of vodka makes me ill."

"Well, then, lucky for me I never drink the stuff," the guard answered Karoline.

Countess Esterházy cleared her throat and the two of them ceased their banter as the guard stiffened to attention.

"Your Majesty," Countess Esterházy said, and all four ladies lowered their eyes, curtsying with well-rehearsed — if not entirely authentic — submissiveness.

Sisi folded, then unfolded her hands, assuming an artificial air of imperiousness. "Ladies, I am off to the Habsburg Chapel. We shall go pray for — His Majesty the

Emperor."

Karoline of Lamberg, a gossipy brunette, and Paula of Bellegarde, the ash-blond waif who stood beside her, exchanged an insinuating glance. Countess Esterházy, who was so much older than these women that she could have been their mother, flickered a knowing grin. Only Marie Festetics, the Hungarian countess, kept her pale eyes discreetly down on the floor, and Sisi made a mental note that perhaps Marie was the one lady whom she could trust among her attendants.

"As you wish, my lady." Karoline nodded with a sugary grin. "And how is Her Majesty feeling this morning?"

Sisi's heart dropped; Countess Esterházy must have told them. All of her ladies-in-waiting knew she was carrying Franz's child. Which meant these guards surely did as well. And Agata had plainly told her that the servants' quarters were abuzz with the news. Was nothing to be private? Would she and her husband be the last two people in the palace to know their own personal affairs?

Sisi clutched the folds of her skirt in a tight grip, maintaining her composure as she said: "Let us go." She led the ladies through the palace to the nearby church, her own assembly of imperial guards trailing them closely.

The quiet, stony chapel was cooler than the warm day outdoors. The space was empty, reserved for members of the royal family. The domed room was marble and bright, the walls painted with scenes from the lives of the saints, as well as subtle reminders of the Habsburg family's magnanimity — and power. Inside, the scent of burning incense struck Sisi as more potent than usual, even repugnant, and Sisi remembered her mother's confession that pregnancy heightens a woman's sensitivity to smells.

Sisi dipped her fingers in the basin of holy water and crossed herself, kneeling on the creaky, velvet-covered pew before the altar. Clutching her rosary beads to her lips, she kissed the cross and began to give thanks for the baby she carried. From the main nave of the church came the muffled sounds of the organist practicing for the midday mass, and the music lulled Sisi into a tranquil, pleasant vigil. Oh, how her life would change once she had given birth to the heir of the Habsburg line! How had she been so lucky to conceive so quickly? She, who had been warned by her aunt so many times about the disasters of barrenness?

The whispers that issued from the pew behind her soon distracted Sisi's prayers, and she turned her head to throw a barbed look at Karoline and Paula. They bowed their heads and returned to silence. But within moments, they were giggling again.

"Ladies." Sisi turned, attempting but failing to mask her irritation. "If you won't pray, then I ask that you take this pouch and go give alms to the beggars outside the gates. You are distracting me."

"We'll pray, Your Majesty." Karoline lowered her head in exaggerated contrition.

"Sorry, Your Grace." Paula followed Karoline's example. Sisi exchanged a knowing glance with Marie, who seemed as put off by her companions' behavior as Sisi was.

"Elisabeth!" Another voice soon distracted her, this one a familiar and welcome sound. Franz burst through a side door into the chapel, the pounding of his military boots reverberating off the cold stone walls.

"Elisabeth, I came as soon as I saw your note! Is it true?" Franz was panting as he ran toward her, and she rose to meet him.

"Your Majesty." Sisi bowed before him, as she had been taught to do when greeting her husband in public.

"Oh, you are not alone." Franz paused, spotting the four attendants in the pews behind Sisi. "Countesses." Franz greeted them each with a polite smile. Karoline and Paula tittered behind Sisi's shoulder.

"Your Majesty." The four ladies bowed in unison behind their queen. Sisi turned just in time to note the meaningful look that passed from Karoline to Paula. Their familiarity struck Sisi once more as entirely inappropriate: the way they stared directly into her

337

husband's eyes, flashed furtive grins back and forth between one another, looks they assumed Sisi didn't notice.

Franz turned to his wife, pulling her attention back to himself. "Oh, Elisabeth, I don't care who hears. Is it true?" He placed the palm of his hand on his wife's stomach, his eyes holding Sisi's with unchecked hope.

"It's true." Sisi rested her hand atop his. All she could feel at this point was the boning of the corset beneath layers of fabric. But she leaned forward to whisper: "We will have a baby."

Franz let loose a whoop that seemed more fitting for a battlefield than a quiet chapel. Sisi could not help but laugh at his delight. Without warning, he leaned forward and scooped up his wife, spinning her in a circle through the chapel. "A baby! An heir!"

Now Sisi feared that not only did her ladies hear this news, but that anyone gathered in the main nave of the church would hear, too. "Franz," she chided him, but her tone was indulgent, even tender. "Franz, put me down."

"That didn't take us long, did it? Good God! I sure picked the right wife, didn't I?" Franz turned to the threshold of the chapel, and Sisi immediately turned several shades of crimson when she noticed for the first time that Count Grünne and her husband's guards stood by, witnesses to the entire scene.

"Franz, please." Sisi lowered her gaze.

"I will not be shy about this!" Franz crowed, placing a long, unabashed kiss on Sisi's lips. Though the display was immodest, even more so considering they were in a church, Sisi did not entirely mind her husband's very public affection. Good, she thought. Let those gossips see how enamored my husband is. Maybe they will show me a bit more respect when they see how the emperor dotes upon their empress. Perhaps Countess Esterházy can tattle to the archduchess about this.

But now it was Franz who pulled away suddenly, as another crowd swept into the small space.

"I came as soon as I could!" Sophie swished into the chapel, accompanied by the Russian ambassador, Pyotr Meyendorff, as well as the minister Baron von Bach, and several liveried footmen. "I would have come sooner, as soon as I heard." Sophie panted. "But Meyendorff was giving me and Bach the latest report from Petersburg. And then I wasn't sure where to find you. Never mind, I'm here now. I heard the news!"

"You've heard about Elisabeth, Mother?" Franz asked, a smile spreading across his face. "Isn't it wonderful news?"

"Wonderful indeed!" Sophie clasped ringed fingers together, smiling at her son. "Well done, Franzi. You've done your duty. And you, too." Sophie looked at her niece. "You played a role in this as well, of course."

"How kind of you, Aunt," Sisi answered with a tight smile, repressing the desire to scowl.

"How long have you been . . . well, when do you think it happened?" Sophie asked, feigning ignorance, though Sisi knew very well that her aunt had been examining her bedsheets and no doubt already knew the answer.

"It has been only a month at most," Sisi answered, playing along as much for Franz's sake as her own; Sisi would not reveal to Sophie just how much she knew of her schemes.

"Then you are still very early on. And at very high risk. You cannot be too careful. Franz, we must take very good care of your empress."

"Indeed." Franz wrapped his arms around Sisi's waist and kissed her neck.

"Franz Joseph!" Sophie gasped. "Need I remind you that we are in public, and in a house of God? And that such behavior is entirely inappropriate?"

"Sorry." Franz dropped his arms, allowing them to fall limp as he backed away from his wife.

Sophie pursed her lips together, eyeing her son and his wife. "Anyhow, Franzi, I hate to divert your attention from such a joyous moment, but we've received a response from the tsar, as well as the reply we were awaiting from Hungary."

"And?" Franz asked, his interest suddenly pulled from his wife. "Who sent the reply from Hungary?"

"Count Andrássy." The way Sophie said the name made it plain to Sisi that this Count Andrássy, whoever he was, was not a popular figure in Vienna's imperial court.

"And what did our dear *friend* Julius Andrássy have to say? Was he reasonable?" Franz asked.

"Julius Andrássy's reply was as unreasonable as Julius Andrássy is himself," Sophie answered, shaking her head.

"In other words, no," Franz said.

Sophie nodded. "I've had a chance to discuss these recent developments with Meyendorff and Bach this morning."

"Who is Julius Andrássy?" Sisi asked.

Both Sophie and Franz turned their gazes on her, as if, for a moment, they had forgotten her presence.

"He's, uh" — Franz looked from his mother to his wife, as if distracted by her question — "Andrássy is a Hungarian."

"Never mind, Elisabeth." Sophie stepped between them. "But Franz, you should come back to the council with us now and we'll discuss next steps. That is" — and now Sophie turned her eyes on Sisi — "that is, of course, unless you are not yet finished here?"

"Yes, we are quite finished. Of course, let's convene the ministers and discuss the Hungarian question immediately." Franz took Sisi's hand in his, kissing it quickly. "I shall see you later, my love?" And with that, he left her side.

"I don't know, shall you?" Sisi watched him go, her heart dropping as her husband cocked his head to listen to the hurried whispers of his mother, his face attentive to the report she gave. While she, Sisi, stood still in the chapel, silent once more, with her ladies looking on.

Sisi turned toward them, clearing her throat as she assumed an authoritative tone: "We shall continue with our prayers."

Sisi knelt down once more before the altar and closed her eyes, but her mind was no longer focused on the divine. What was the feeling she had been left with, as she'd watched Franz and Sophie speed away, their heads bowed toward one another?

Perhaps it was jealousy; how could she not wrestle with jealousy, when there were so many sides of Franz that he did not allow her to know, but seemed willing to share with his mother and ministers?

But no, in that moment, Sisi felt something gnawing at her that was more potent than jealousy. What she felt was loneliness: the cold, hard realization that, even when she was surrounded by people, she was entirely alone.

■ ■ ■ ■

Whatever disappointment Sisi had felt after the day's earlier meeting in the chapel, Franz more than made up for it that night when he joined Sisi in their bedroom.

They had made love, tenderly and slowly, with Franz reminding Sisi of his attachment to her with each gentle kiss. The others might be privy to his political affairs and military concerns, but only she joined him in this most intimate of moments. Only she inspired the rapturous joy that he experienced with her each night; he was here with her now, his heartbeat and his body testifying to the fact that he was hers, and she clung to him jealously.

"I love you, Elisa," he whispered into her ear, sounding as if he might cry.

"And I love you, Franz." She ran her fingertips along the soft skin of his neck, lingering on the scar left by the would-be assassin's blade.

"Do you think there is another emperor in all of Europe who loves his queen as I love you?" Franz looked at her now, his eyes at ease.

"Surely it's not possible." She smiled at him, her hair falling in her face as he swept it gently aside.

"Do you know how I adore you, Elisa?"

She closed her eyes, nuzzling into the crook of his neck. "Perhaps not as much as I love you." Even as she said them, the words hurt, because she was paralyzed by the fear that they might be true. But Franz laughed them off.

"That is something you never need worry about, my darling."

"Really?" She heard the desperation in her own voice as she asked it. She wanted to ask more: *Then why do I feel like you are so far away? Why will you speak to me about nothing you do? Why do you allow others between us? Why must I wait all day to see you?*

Before she could say these questions out loud, these worries so close to her heart that they threatened to strangle her, he spoke. His voice had a sound of finality to it. "Let's have champagne. I think we must celebrate." He rang the bell on the bedside table. The footman, dressed in the thick woolen livery even in the heat of summer, appeared, taking the order. Several minutes later he was back, delivering a chilled bottle and two flutes.

Franz filled the glasses. "To our baby," he proposed.

"Indeed," Sisi agreed.

"This one, and many more."

"Let's just get through this first confinement and labor," Sisi replied, chuckling at her husband's enthusiasm. "Are you excited to be a papa, Franz, my darling?"

He sipped from his glass, a casual shrug of his shoulders. "Of course. Every emperor needs an heir."

"Yes." Sisi propped herself up on her elbow, leaning toward him. "But to be a *papa*? To have a baby sit on your knee? To watch our little darling grow?"

Franz lowered his head to the side, quiet a moment. He puffed out his cheeks, exhaling slowly before he spoke: "I suppose I never really thought much about those aspects of the job."

Sisi couldn't help but laugh. "Well, perhaps now is the time to begin thinking about them."

"Don't worry about that, my love," Franz said, tipping his glass upward to take a long sip. "You shall have all the help you need. Our little prince shall want for nothing."

"I'm not worried, Franz." Sisi put a hand on her belly, the flesh more readily available beneath a thin bedsheet than it had been earlier, beneath her gown's stomacher. "I'm rather looking forward to it."

"What shall we name it — the baby?" Franz asked, winding a finger along the ridge of her collarbone. Sisi savored the feel — his skin on her skin — as she considered the question.

"If it's a boy? Franz, of course," Sisi answered.

Franz smiled, taking another sip of champagne. "And if it's a girl?"

"If it's a girl, shall you be very cross with me?" Sisi looked up at her husband.

"Of course not, Elisa." Franz kissed the tip of her nose, laughing at her. "If it's a girl, I shall relish the opportunity of trying again for a boy. And many more after that."

Sisi liked that answer. It was a relief to know that at least *he* would not hold it against her, though she was certain her mother-in-law would find a way to do so. "If it's a girl, I had an idea," she said.

"What's that?"

Sisi sat up, feeling a moment's worth of shyness as the bedsheets fell away, revealing her nude body. But when she saw how completely she held her husband's attention, she resisted the urge to cover herself. "Well, why is it that we are together? What brought us together?"

"Your beauty," Franz answered. "The fact that I wanted to marry you the instant I beheld you."

"No." Sisi giggled, swatting away his roving hand. "How did we meet?"

"Mother. Mother told me to invite you and Helene. So you propose the name Sophie?"

"Not quite," Sisi said, failing to suppress the scowl. After a pause, she added: "My *sister.* Helene is the reason we met."

"Helene?" Franz followed her thought

346

process. "You'd like to name our baby Helene?"

Sisi nodded.

"Helene." Franz repeated the name. "Helene Habsburg-Lorraine, Princess of Austria." He considered it a moment more. "I like it."

"Do you?"

"I think it's a brilliant idea." He kissed the tip of her nose once more, pulling her toward him. She repeated the name, aloud, and then surrendered to his all-consuming kisses.

Though Sisi knew that as the emperor's wife it was practically heretical to wish for anything other than a quick succession of fat baby boys, she couldn't deny that, in private, she longed for a baby girl. A little girl with Franz's auburn hair and blue eyes. A little girl to cover in lace and tulle. A doll for Franz to dote upon, as Sisi was certain that he would. She had no doubt that Franz would be an attentive and affectionate father. Would she be as patient and steady as Mamma had been? Yes, she would be, she assured herself. She and her daughter would be the closest of friends, an example to the women of the court — soft and gracious, yet strong. Sophie's style of brute force and bullying would appear undesirable, and the archduchess's power would wane as the empress's influence would flourish.

Now that she had discussed it as a possibility with her husband, the hope for a little girl consumed Sisi. When she was alone, with no one but Agata in her bedchamber, Sisi referred to the swelling bump as "Helene." Staring at herself in the mirror, watching as her gowns were taken out anew on an almost weekly basis, Sisi wondered: How was it possible to love something that, weeks earlier, she had not known existed?

Sophie's behavior changed entirely over the course of the summer. Suddenly the archduchess sought out Sisi's company rather than pretending she didn't see her. On mornings when Sisi felt ill, Sophie skipped the meetings of the privy council and rushed to her daughter-in-law's bedchamber, toweling Sisi's wan face and holding the basin while her daughter-in-law emptied her stomach. If Sisi felt hot, Sophie ordered Agata and the rest of the maids to fan her; if Sisi felt cold, she demanded to know why they did not cover Sisi with cashmere blankets.

The trade-off was that, while her ladies-in-waiting were largely relieved of their duties ("Their gossip will irritate the baby," Sophie announced one morning after dismissing them rather abruptly), the archduchess was now Sisi's constant companion. Countess Marie Festetics was allowed to stay on, at the request of Sisi, to assist with answering correspondence and responding to the notes of congratulations that poured in from across the empire and the rest of Europe. But other than Marie's specific role, Sophie seemed almost jealous of anyone else who tried to get near her daughter-in-law. On mornings when Sisi received petitioners in her state room, Sophie attended and sat beside her, forbidding the entry of the sick and often answering on behalf of Sisi.

"You must rest, my girl. That baby inside you is a future emperor, and very strongwilled. Best give him what he wants."

Everything that occurred inside Sisi's changing body was, to Sophie, the confirmation of her predictions that the baby would be perfect. And male.

As Sisi grew round much faster than the other expecting ladies of the court had, it was because "Franz had put a strong son in his wife's womb."

When Sisi's appetite at luncheon was much more voracious than usual, it was because "Franz's son already has the appetite of an emperor." And Sophie would promptly order a second helping of chocolate almond pudding for her daughter-in-law.

In late July, Sisi grew fatigued at the feast and services given in honor of St. Anne, the patron saint of fertility, and Sophie excused her. "St. Anne blesses us already."

Sisi was relieved at the shift, though she remained wary of her formidable aunt. But Sophie's overtures continued all throughout the summer. The archduchess sent gifts to Sisi's suite almost daily, so that Agata and the secretary, Herr Lobkowitz, were constantly entering with baskets of fruit, new hats trimmed in the latest millinery fashion from Paris, or new silk gowns, which Sophie instructed Sisi to wear without a corset. Letters from home carried news that Sophie's boasting had spread as far as Bavaria. *"My sister is blissfully happy with her son's choice of bride, suddenly. She seems to have forgotten entirely the obstructive role she sought to play,"* Sisi's mother wrote. *"Bravo, my darling daughter. Based on the reports I receive from my sister, I think you have earned your place and need no longer question the affections of your mother-in-law."*

Sophie insisted, while the summer months stretched out across Vienna, filling the city with festering stink and hot, fetid air, that her daughter-in-law spend her time safely nestled within the palace gates. She ordered Sisi not to visit the palace's petting zoo, where Sisi liked to watch the parrot that had been given to her as a wedding present from Franz.

"You must *stop* looking at that parrot, child."

"Why?" Sisi asked, alarmed by this latest piece of unsolicited advice.

Her aunt pursed her lips, her cheeks reddening. "I've spoken to the doctor about it.

It's dangerous to constantly look at animals. For, however your thoughts take shape, that is the shape that the future emperor will take. It's much better you spend that time staring at the portraits of your handsome husband."

Sisi put a hand to her lips, attempting to hide her laughter. And yet, for the sake of peace, she heeded this instruction.

Riding was flatly forbidden. So, instead of her beloved excursions into the Alps, Sisi spent the summer largely indoors listening to the court musicians and stitching the tiny clothing in which she would soon dress her baby. Sophie would accompany Sisi on daily carriage rides, during which time the horses were permitted to move no faster than at a lumbering walk, but otherwise she restricted Sisi's daily outings. "We can't have you overheating," Sophie would warn.

Sisi took it all in stride, laughing at how attached and doting her formerly prickly mother-in-law had become, even sometimes relishing the fact that her aunt boasted so openly about her and her baby.

"One month, that's all it took them to conceive. Can you believe it? It must be a record for the Habsburgs!" Sophie invited Baron von Bach to dine with them for luncheon one day late in September. "Why, even Maria Theresa with her brood of sixteen didn't become *enceinte* this quickly!"

Sisi nearly choked on her bite of pâté.

Sixteen children!

Sophie continued: "I believe that this union will lead to many, many little princes and princesses. Why, look how fertile she is! Less than five months along and already you can see the swell in her belly."

"It certainly seems that way," von Bach replied, his cheeks reddening beneath gray whiskers. Sisi always had the impression that Baron von Bach was slightly ill at ease with Sophie's blunt, blustery manner of speaking.

"Why, von Bach, if we marry their little ones right, we will have a Habsburg on every throne in Europe."

The minister nodded politely, his eyes fixed on his luncheon plate.

"Elisabeth, my girl."

"Yes, Aunt Sophie?"

"After lunch you must go out and walk the grounds. But be sure to walk past the gates, and *slowly*! We want the people on the *Strasse* to catch a glimpse of your belly. So that they might go home, or to the coffeehouse, or wherever, and report that they saw you grown large with the little prince."

The thought mortified Sisi: the idea of parading around the grounds with her swollen belly. A performer for the crowds who perpetually huddled on the other side of the gates, hoping to catch a glimpse of her.

"Aunt Sophie, I'm not certain —"

"No, no, no arguing, child. You *must* do as

352

I say. We want the whole empire to be abuzz with excitement to welcome the crown prince."

One thing was for certain — if Sophie loved her grandchild even one half as much as she loved her son, then Sisi would never have to worry about her child having a champion at court.

The heat rolled out of Vienna, taking summer's stink and thick moisture with it. Now that the warm days no longer posed a threat, Sophie swore that the autumn chill presented even bigger risks, and she all but forbade Sisi to spend time out of doors unless she wore the heaviest of cloaks.

Sisi laughed at her aunt's perceptions of her frailty. Why, October was her favorite month back in Possenhofen. The harvest being done, the entire village came together to celebrate the Oktoberfest; there were weeks of festivals and musical performances, with both villagers and farmers partaking in the beer that had been brewed and the crops that had been culled.

From the letters she received from home, Sisi knew that her parents were set to welcome an endless stream of guests during this autumn's fest. Cousins, including Ludwig, Bavaria's future king, would travel to Possenhofen to sample the thick beer, dance to the polka music, and meet the beautiful German women the area was known for producing. Perhaps Karl might even meet his future bride during this month's revelry.

Sisi felt a stab of homesickness during this period. As the days passed, she recalled the freedom she had once enjoyed to ride into the village with Ludwig and Néné. There, slipping among the crowds, she was anonymous, just another participant in the carefree merrymaking. And so, at night, Sisi wrapped her arms even tighter around her husband, reminding herself that there was nowhere she'd rather be than beside Franz.

Franz was overjoyed with her swelling belly. He spoke often of their child, detailing to Sisi the titles and lands he would heap upon the future prince. But even though his nightly visits to their bedchamber continued, he no longer wished to make love to her.

"Am I not appealing to you, now that I'm so big?" It was a chilly night in October and they lay, fully clothed, under a heavy coverlet of goose down. Sisi looked down at her protruding belly, finding it hard to believe that she still had months of growing to do. "I worried that I would lose my appeal when I started to get round."

"Elisa!" Franz scoffed at the remark. "Believe me, you have *not* lost your appeal." He pulled the blankets aside, revealing her swollen breasts and belly, her curves barely contained by her tight silk slip. "Just look at you! I don't think you've ever been more beautiful."

"Well then, what is the matter, Franz?" She tried to kiss him but he pulled away.

She sat back, quiet. It was troubling, this sudden retreat from their marital relations.

"I've been warned, Elisa . . . about certain things."

She turned, looking at him. "What things?"

"That it might be hazardous for the baby's health if we continue . . . as man and wife. To . . ."

"To make love?"

Franz nodded. Sisi had never heard that. In fact, she'd heard from Agata some rather bawdy morsels about how coupling during these months was a good thing. That it helped pregnant women find some comfort. "Who told you that, Franz?" But even as she asked, she guessed the answer: "Your mother?"

Franz nodded.

Sisi could not contain the sigh that escaped her throat. "Franz, will you allow her to dictate such a thing?"

"Well, not just her." Franz fidgeted, sliding his body away from hers in bed. "She also had Doctor Seeburger come talk with me. And he urged me against it."

Sisi knew Doctor Seeburger, the emperor's physician, very well. Sophie brought him to pay almost daily visits to Sisi's suite.

"Interesting that she didn't have him tell

me," Sisi grumbled. "Anyhow, I don't believe it. I am certain that Doctor Seeburger told you whatever your mother told him to tell you. And I have heard that many a couple continue to lie with one another well into the —"

"Elisa, please. Let's not be vulgar."

"Franz, it's bad enough that your mother tries to control you in the state rooms. I won't have her dictating your behavior in our marital bed as well."

"Elisabeth, please stop." Franz's tone unnerved her. "I will ask that you do not disrespect me — or Mother — like that again. She does *not* control me."

He was wounded; she realized that as she studied his features.

Sisi breathed out, slowly. "Forgive me, Franz," she answered, reaching for his hand. She hated the thought of quarreling with him.

But he pulled away, still cross. "And secondly, I ask that you exercise some feminine restraint. Showing too great an appetite for such things is unbecoming of a lady. I expected better from you."

Now *she* was wounded. Stung to speechlessness. Never before had Franz chastised her. And worse, made her feel ashamed for expressing her thoughts. She shifted her large, awkward body away from him to the opposite side of the bed and wrapped herself in the blanket once more.

"Come now. Don't retreat from me." Franz tugged on her arm, his tone softening.

"I'm tired," she said, prying her arm from his grip.

Franz scooted his body up behind her, so that he held her in an embrace.

"My sweet Elisa. Please don't be cross with me."

She didn't answer him. She still burned at his censure. He reached around her, cradling her full belly in his hands. After a long pause she turned, her voice sounding jarringly loud in the quiet room.

"Franz, these nightly visits are all that we have. Shall I never see you anymore? What's next? Shall you begin sleeping on the cot in your dressing room, because your mother tells you not to overcrowd me in bed?"

"Hush, Elisa. Why must you fret?"

"Franz, how will you stand it, going the next four months?" She knew as well as anyone that, when men were dissatisfied with their marital partners, they looked elsewhere. Hadn't her entire childhood borne testimony to the wandering of men? What if Franz suddenly found the charms of the other women at court too tempting to resist?

Franz seemed to understand her fear, for his brow creased as he looked at her, his entire manner softening. "Don't you worry about me, my sweet Elisa." He leaned forward to kiss her. "Yours is the only face I care to look upon."

"Are you . . . can you be certain?"

"I'm certain." He kissed her by way of further reply, pausing to look down at her belly. "Besides, it can't be that much longer now. Look at how big you are!"

"Four more months to go," she said, sliding closer to him.

They kissed for several moments, and Sisi could feel that her husband longed for her body.

"We shall have to find something else to do in here every night," he said, sighing as he pulled away, putting several inches between them.

"Like what, Franz?" She stared across the pillow at his restless face.

"I have an idea." Franz hopped from the bed, crossing the bedroom and walking quickly out the door.

When Franz returned, he was followed by several footmen, their bodies hunched over as they wheeled in a large, burdensome cargo covered in a bedsheet.

"Put it right there." Franz pointed toward the fireplace.

"Franz?" Sisi chuckled, pulling the bedcovers close even as the footmen kept their discreet gazes off her. "What is that?"

Franz lifted the draped sheet, pulling it aside with a theatrical flourish. "This, my beloved Elisa, is a pianoforte."

"What are we going to do with a piano in here?"

"What do you think we shall do? Play it, of course!" Franz sat down at the instrument, lifting back the case. "That'll be all, thank you." At the wave of his hand, the footmen bowed and left the room.

"Can you play in the dark?" Sisi asked, lighting several candles adjacent to the bed.

"Indeed." Franz began to press the ivory keys, plucking out a melody with which he hummed along. "My fingers know this song so well, I might as well shut my eyes."

It took Sisi several verses before she too recognized the melody. "I know this song," she said, trying to recall from where. "I've heard this."

"I know you have," Franz continued to play, his head swaying with the slow notes.

"Where have I heard this?"

"With me. In the rose garden in Bad Ischl."

"Yes, it's called 'The Skater's Waltz,' " Sisi recalled. "I love this song."

"Remember that night? It was our first kiss." Franz nodded, playing on. "Can you hear this, Little Helene or Little Franz?" Franz called out playfully. "This is your mamma's favorite song, so you might as well become acquainted with it."

Sisi melted back into the bed, humming along to the waltz, remembering the first time she'd heard it over a year ago. How much life had changed for that innocent, fifteen-year-old girl. A girl who stood in a fragrant garden, staring up at a wall of moonlit mountains and admitting to herself that she had fallen in love. A girl who, having seen nothing of people or the world, had believed that love was all one needed to be happy.

VIII.

They call me the first lady in the land,
whereas I think of myself as the odd
woman out.
— Empress Elisabeth "Sisi" of Austria

CHAPTER EIGHT

SALZBURG, AUSTRIA
DECEMBER 1854

Sisi had never before seen a city come to life with the enchantment of the Christmas Holy Day as the remote Alpine town of Salzburg did during her first winter as Franz's wife. It seemed as though the entire village population, as well as the throngs of people living in the nearby mountain chalets, poured into Salzburg's main square on Christmas Eve, like present-day pilgrims visiting the Nativity, all of them hoping to glimpse the emperor and his expectant wife.

The streets flickered as if under a candlelit halo; the doors were festooned with cranberry and pine boughs; and the aroma of the bakeries spilled out into the city, as still-hot gingerbread and *Pfefferkuchen* cakes tempted the red-cheeked pedestrians who passed by the steamy shop windows.

The imperial visit to Salzburg at Christmas was the largest event to occur for the small village in years, perhaps even a generation, and the townspeople spared no effort in welcoming the royal pair. For Sisi, it was to be her last journey before she entered the final months of pregnancy, and with that, confinement. She was thus determined to savor every last taste, sound, and smell from that merry village, as well as her time with her husband. Surely Aunt Sophie would not allow such stimulation once they were installed back at the Hofburg for the winter.

On the evening before Christmas, a very round Sisi — wrapped in a gown of rich plum-colored velvet with rabbit fur trim — was loaded into a sleigh accompanied by Franz, Sophie, and several dozen imperial guards. They set off from their quarters off the Mirabellgarten, the horses treading through fluffy fresh snow on the route to the Platz and St. Nikolaus Church.

The air outside was cold and snow-flecked, filled with the twinkling of sleigh bells and Christmas carols. Giddy children poked their heads out the windows lining the streets, calling out to their mamas that the empress approached.

"They love you." Franz observed, waving to the crowds swarming the avenue.

"Empress Sisi!"

"God bless Empress Sisi!"

"Long live Sisi!"

Franz listened to these cries from the thick

wall of people, his facial expression a mixture of awe and surprise. "My God, Elisa, how they love you."

"Only because I'm carrying your child, Franz." Sisi cocked her head, ignoring Sophie's disapproving scowl as she nuzzled into the warmth of her husband's neck.

"No. Do you know what they say?"

"What?"

"That you are the most beautiful woman in the world."

She lowered her eyes, blinking away the snowflakes that stuck to her lashes. "But I don't care that they think that." And it was the truth. "As long as it's what *you* think, Franz."

"Well," — he planted a kiss on her forehead, catching a snowflake in his mustache as he did so — "it is."

The ancient stone chapel of St. Nikolaus was cozy with the amber glow of candles and the warmth of the hundreds of bodies packed into the wooden pews. Slowly, Sisi made her way up the central aisle, taking a seat in the front with her husband and mother-in-law. Attendants handed them each their own white candles. Behind them sat the *Burgermeister*, the mayor of Salzburg, and his family, along with Sisi's ladies-in-waiting and Franz's ministers.

Herr Lobkowitz had told Sisi earlier in the day that this was the church in which Europe's favorite Christmas carol, *Stillenacht,* had been composed. After the Eucharist had been shared, the candles lining the church and altar were extinguished, so that the only flames that remained were those held in the hands of the congregation members.

A brief moment of anticipatory silence hung in the air, before the priest began, and the congregation erupted into an a cappella rendition of the song.

Silent night, holy night.
All is calm, all is bright.
'Round yon virgin, Mother and Child,
Holy Infant, so tender and mild.
Sleep in heavenly peace.
Sleep in heavenly peace.

The power of the communal voices poured over and through Sisi. The poignancy of the scene overhwhelmed her: a young mother and her sleeping infant — so tenderly described and so perfectly accompanied by melody. Her eyes filled with tears as she reached for her husband's hand. She couldn't help but feel that, in that moment, she was as happy as the young Mary had felt, all those years ago, while she had cradled her holy little infant in that Bethlehem manger. *A fleeting glimpse of the divine,* Sisi thought, bringing Franz's palm to rest on her belly. Sophie, staring sideways, frowned, clucking her tongue.

Sisi pretended not to notice.

Later that night, tucked into bed beside her, Franz surprised Sisi with a piece of tightly rolled parchment. "For you."

Sisi stared at his outstretched hands. "What is this?"

"Take it," Franz insisted, waving the ribbon-tied paper before her. "It's a birthday present."

"You remembered." She smiled, taking the scroll from him.

"Of course I remembered." Through the haze of the candlelight Sisi saw that Franz wore a satisfied smirk, clearly proud of himself. "What a remarkable Christmas present you must have been when you arrived on Christmas Eve, seventeen years ago."

"What is this paper?"

"Open it," he said, prompting her to untie the golden bow that held the parchment in a tight roll. Sisi looked down at the paper, its surface covered in musical notes. The top of the paper bore a title: *Elisabethklänge.*

"What . . . what is it, Franz?"

"You know how I've just hired a new court composer?"

"Master Strauss?"

"Yes, Master Johann Strauss." Franz nodded. "I've commissioned a new waltz from him, in your honor."

Sisi lowered the paper, looking at Franz as

a surprised smile lit up her features. "You didn't."

"I did," Franz said, sitting up tall. "You see this part?" He pointed to a bar of musical notes, humming as he did so. "The Bavarian anthem. And this part" — he hummed a different tune, more languid than the bouncy Bavarian polka — "the Austrian imperial anthem."

Sisi nodded, singing along with him. "It's like a perfect combination of the two of us," Sisi remarked, looking over the paper once more.

"Exactly." As Franz said it, he put his palm over her belly. "Like our little one shall be."

"I love it," Sisi said, holding the paper in both hands, scanning its entire length. Her own waltz. "*Elisabethklänge.* I can't wait to hear it."

"Unfortunately our bedchamber here is not equipped with a pianoforte, as it is back in Vienna. Can you wait until tomorrow?"

"Something to look forward to." She nodded, carefully rolling the paper up and sliding it back into its golden ribbon.

"Do you really like it?"

"Franz, I love it." She slid close to him in bed, putting the paper down on the end table. "Now if you would only allow me to show you my appreciation." She began to kiss him. He succumbed to her attentions, but only for a moment.

"Elisa! No." He pulled himself away from her.

She sighed. "I don't know how you stand it, Franz. You have far more self-control than I do."

"Not much longer now," he said, patting her belly. "Besides, there are more presents to be opened." Franz sprung out of bed, tiptoeing across the creaking wooden floor of their room in the rented villa. "Goodness, it's cold!" He opened a dresser drawer and retrieved a small package wrapped in red ribbon.

"You will freeze out of the covers. Come back to bed."

Franz ran back toward his wife and hopped down beside her. "Here you go, my darling."

"What is this?"

"Open it."

Sisi took her time unwrapping the gift. Tomorrow, Christmas morning, there would be gifts exchanged in the drawing room. Sophie would no doubt bestow an endless pile of goods upon her son and daughter-in-law — fine clothing, priceless jewelry, sweetmeats and candies. But this gift was different, special, and Sisi savored unwrapping it.

When she tore the paper aside, Sisi saw a necklace with a small gold pendant in the shape of a horse. "Franz, it's lovely," she gasped, admiring the delicate craftsmanship of the gold figurine.

"Diamant was our model. To commemorate your love of horses, and our marvelous afternoon in Bad Ischl — the day that I knew I had to marry you."

"If you would," Sisi unclasped the chain and handed it to her husband. "Put it on me. I shall wear it always."

Franz fastened the chain at the nape of her neck. "Have you missed riding very much?"

"Indeed," Sisi admitted, looking down at her swollen belly. "But it's for a worthy cause."

Franz leaned back and studied the necklace where it fell between her clavicle bones.

"How does it look?"

"Fit for a queen." He winked, pouring himself a full glass of port. "I'm not done, though."

"More?"

"Just one more." Now he proffered a second package in similar wrapping but slightly larger in size.

Sisi opened this gift, ripping the paper aside to reveal a small baby's rattle of glistening silver.

"For our little Helene," Franz explained, sipping his drink. "Her first toy. And here you'll see I've had it inscribed: *With love, from Mamma and Papa.*"

"You really believe it's a girl?" Sisi asked, tracing the engraved letters with her fingers.

"I really do."

"Why is that?" she asked, jangling the rattle to enjoy its crisp, playful ring.

"I am not sure." Franz shrugged his shoulders. "Just a suspicion. I think you enjoy defying Mother so much that you'll have a girl first, just to spite her."

Sisi couldn't help but laugh heartily at this prediction.

"And your final gift," Franz continued, "was something that couldn't be wrapped. Well, I suppose he *could* be wrapped, but that would not be very enjoyable for him."

"Is it a horse?" Sisi guessed, excited.

"A horse? No." Franz furrowed his brow. "Elisa, you have the entirety of the imperial stables at your disposal. You may have any horse in there you would like. Why, would you like a new horse?"

"No, you're right. I don't need any more horses. Besides, I love Diamant," Sisi answered, tugging on her new golden pendant. "Then what is it?"

"I have hired you your own personal hairdresser," Franz answered, a look of satisfaction on his face. He stared at her now, expectant, eager for her gratitude.

"Oh," Sisi said, digesting the news. "A hairdresser."

Franz crossed his arms. "You don't seem excited, Elisa."

"Well, I am." She poured herself a glass of port now, angling herself so as to avoid his

370

gaze. "Thank you, Franz."

"No, Elisa. I can tell when you are happy about something, and you're not."

Sisi sighed, holding the drink in her hands. "It's just that . . ."

"Yes? Let's have it."

"Agata has always done my hair. I like the way she does my hair."

Franz nodded, uncrossing and then recrossing his arms.

"Do you not?" Sisi asked.

"I love the way she fashions your hair, Elisa, of course."

She looked at him sideways, unsmiling.

"Why, I tell everyone I meet that the real crown jewels in the Habsburg-Lorraine family are my wife's dark blond curls. Do not worry about that for a minute."

"Then why change it?" Sisi sipped her port.

"Well, Mother thought that it might be a good idea, now that —"

"Ah," — Sisi nodded, a sour grin affixing itself to her lips — "your *mother* thought I needed a new hairdresser."

"Please, Elisa, no need to be combative. She meant it as a gift, not an affront."

"What is wrong with the way Agata does my hair?"

"Nothing at all. Mother simply thought that . . . that you might want to take on a more sophisticated look. Nothing drastically different. Only that perhaps some hairstyles are beyond Agata's ken."

"So I should start to style my hair like whom?"

"I haven't the faintest idea about these feminine matters." Franz shrugged his shoulders, refilling his glass. "You know how Mother and the rest of the ladies at court fancy all these elaborate hairdos."

"Tell me, is your mother's hairstyle done according to *court procedure*? Why, I am to be surrounded only by people of whom she approves. To spend my days in the manner that she determines. I am forced to wear the slippers of her choosing. Wear gloves at every meal. Am I to begin fashioning my hair like hers now, as well?"

Sisi knew she was being antagonistic, but she couldn't curb the resentment in her voice. Months and months of biting her tongue in the face of Sophie's orders, and Countess Esterházy's insinuations, even Franz's obliviousness, seemed to have swelled into a noxious bile that she could no longer keep down. "Now you'd like me to try to look like your mother?"

"When you put it that way, Elisa. Of course I do not wish for you to look like Mother."

"Can you do me this small favor, Franz — can we have just one evening in bed without your mother entering into the conversation?" She was being petulant. But voicing this anger felt like a relief — like a release of a pressure that had been mounting since before their wedding.

"It's always 'Mother said this,' and 'Mother thinks that' . . . It's bad enough that she has mastery over every minute of our day, but I'm fed up with your damn mother accompanying us to bed!"

"Elisabeth." Franz stared at her, his mouth falling open for several moments before he spoke. "I can't say that I find this sort of language at all attractive. I've asked you to stop insulting Mother. She does an awful lot for you. For me, too. For both of us."

"Yes, *too much,* sometimes."

"Everything she has ever done has been to help you."

"Ha!" Sisi laughed, a sudden puff of air. "I wish she wouldn't *help* so often."

"You will stop this right now." Franz's face flushed a deep red, wearing a foreign expression that made him appear like a stranger beside Sisi.

"No, I will not stop. Not until *she* stops meddling."

"This is the height of disrespect."

"And what respect does she show us, Franz?"

He did not answer, and she, exhausted, fell silent. They sat opposite one another in strained stillness a few moments before Franz moved, sliding out from under the covers. Rising, he walked to the bench at the foot of the bed.

"Franz, where are you going?" Sisi sat up and watched him yank his dressing robe over his shoulders.

"I think I shall sleep in my dressing room tonight."

"Your dressing room?"

"I feel entirely unwelcome in this chamber at the moment." Franz refused to meet Sisi's eyes as he tied the belt of his robe in quick, jerky motions.

"Franz, please." Sisi rose from bed, ignoring the assault of cold air as she hurried toward him, wrapping her arms around him. "Don't go, please."

"I *shall* go!" He shook her off, prompting her awkward frame to lose its balance and wobble backward onto the soft support of the bed coverings. "And perhaps you will think twice next time you feel the urge to carry on like that."

Sisi watched him leave, slamming the door without looking back at her. She stood, shivering. Perhaps she ought to call for a servant to rekindle the fire. But she didn't. All she could do was stand there, motionless, watching the door through which he had exited. When several minutes had lapsed, perhaps even a quarter of an hour, she became certain that he would not return to her that night, and she hoisted her weary frame back onto the bed.

It was the first night they'd passed apart since their wedding, and Sisi cried for every minute of it. The days without him she had gotten used to — even though she hated it — but the night? The night was their time. How alone she felt without him beside her, without his warm body heating the bed and filling the quiet with the familiar sound of his even, steady snoring.

The night crawled on, silent, though Sisi's mind clamored with antagonizing fears, chidings, and self-doubt. The more she thought about their argument, the more she regretted having made an issue of his mother. However much she resented Sophie's meddling, it did her no good to allow those annoyances to alienate Franz. Sophie was an immutable reality in her life. Sisi had accepted that; she had had no choice.

When the feeble dawn came, at last, the winter sun slicing its way through the windows, Sisi rose. Outside, Christmas Day was dreary, a dove-gray sky that hung low, threatening freezing rain or snow. Sisi shuffled toward the fireplace, where she poked the dull ashes in the hopes of coaxing out some last drop of heat. She'd apologize at Christmas luncheon. That was settled. She couldn't bear to have Franz cross with her, couldn't bear the idea of passing another night without him beside her.

The banquet was a festive, drawn-out affair, its merry atmosphere discordant with Sisi's dark mood. The footmen, maids, and imperial cooks must have been awake all of the previous night, for the hall at the rented villa had undergone a transformation. Silver dishes gleamed under coats of fresh polish. Pine boughs filled the air with their crisp, wintry aroma. Plates and saucers and bowls overflowed with gravies and puddings, fowl and meat pies.

Sisi had forced herself to dress for the occasion: she wore a gown of dark emerald that Sophie had given her, and she had placed sprigs of holly in her braided bun. But even in this fine attire, she suspected that she looked horrible. As she entered the room, she hoped that the court would blame her puffy eyes and wan expression on the fatigue of pregnancy.

"Merry Christmas, Elisabeth." Sophie hurried to Sisi's side, handing her a glass of warm mulled cider. "And Merry Christmas to my little grandson." Sophie's pudgy hands cupped Sisi's stomach. Sisi tried not to recoil. "Next year, we shall have a little prince to spoil with toy trains and wooden soldiers and nutcrackers — won't it be wonderful? Oh, my little Franzi used to *adore* his wooden soldiers!"

"Merry Christmas, Mother. Elisabeth." Franz appeared beside them, hugging his mother before placing a cool, obligatory kiss on Sisi's cheek. All around the hall, courtiers had bowed at his entrance. He waved now, allowing them to stand. Unlike Sisi, Franz appeared unbelievably fresh and handsome in his uniform, his hair brushed back and his mustache neatly trimmed.

"Franz." Sisi turned to her husband, away from her mother-in-law, whose eyes observed the exchange. She leaned forward so that she might whisper only to him. "I didn't sleep a minute last night. Please don't be cross with me. I'm sorry."

Franz did not reply, but rather seemed highly preoccupied with Grünne, who conversed nearby with a dark-haired beauty. A lady whom Sisi had never seen before.

Sisi noticed, with a stabbing sensation in her breast, how Franz's eyes traveled from Grünne to the brunette, lingering on her brown-eyed smile. The full lips that whispered some witty remark, setting Grünne off into a peal of carefree laughter.

"Who is that?" Sisi asked, attempting to sound lighthearted. She swallowed hard. "Talking to Count Grünne?"

"Hmmm?"

"Franz, will you look at me?" Sisi tugged on the starched sleeve of his uniform.

"What is it?" Franz turned back toward his wife, his eyes like two cold marbles.

"You're being very aloof."

"I should go say hello to Grünne. I'll see you at dinner."

Gifts were exchanged in the drawing room, and Sophie insisted that Sisi be the first to unwrap hers. Seating her in a chair before the blazing fire, Sophie began with a toast to her daughter-in-law and the baby she carried.

Sophie had stayed true to her affinity for elaborate displays, and her pile of Christmas gifts for Sisi had to be carted into the drawing room by half a dozen footmen. There were four new dresses, all extremely wide in the middle but with the ability to be taken in once the baby came. There was a bassinet of finely carved birch wood, into which the shapes of little animals had been etched around the frame. There were several pairs of furlined booties for the little prince, as well as a wooden sword and a small toy drum. There was a case of champagne to be drunk by the new parents on the night of their son's birth. And the grand finale was a tiara — presented to Sisi on a pillow of purple velvet — of silver, encrusted with a constellation of glistening diamonds.

"From our family's collection. A crown fit for the Queen Mother, to be worn to your son's christening," Sophie explained to the crowded room, which erupted in applause at the archduchess's unsurpassed generosity.

"Thank you very much, Aunt Sophie," Sisi said quietly, feeling overwhelmed, and a bit overburdened, by her aunt's generosity. The pastoral tapestry she had commissioned to give to her aunt suddenly seemed grossly inadequate.

"Please, Elisabeth, call me Mother," Sophie answered, nodding humbly even as she asked the baron beside her if he had ever seen such a crown given to a daughter-in-law.

Next, Grünne presented Sisi with a new lambs' wool cloak, lined with white rabbit's fur. Karoline and Paula had coordinated to buy their queen the matching muff and sleigh blanket. Countess Esterházy had ordered a mirror framed in gold gilt along with a custom leather devotional prayer book. Marie Festetics, aware of Sisi's recent homesickness, presented Sisi with a bound book of Bavarian folk songs and poems. "A reminder of Christmas at home," the Hungarian countess explained.

"I love it, Marie," Sisi said, deeply touched by the thoughtful and personal gesture.

Helene and Ludovika had sent newly knit sweaters in Bavarian wool for the new baby, and Duke Maximilian had sent several prints of Bavarian Alpine landscapes, along with a few barrels of Bavarian beer.

Ambassador Meyendorff gifted Sisi with a

case of fine Russian vodka and caviar, and Baron von Bach gave her a new pair of leather riding gloves. Doctor Seeburger and the aide Herr Lobkowitz, neither of whom had been invited to the formal banquet, had sent gifts of a cashmere blanket and a new wooden escritoire, respectively.

"Well, it looks like Sisi is getting fatigued. Let's finish this up. It's your husband's turn," Sophie said, turning to her son where he stood, quietly, in the corner. Beside him stood Grünne and the unnamed brunette.

"Franz, come out of that corner. What are you doing? Where is your gift for your bride?"

"Oh, I gave her my gifts last night," Franz said, sipping from his wine cup. "Some were more well-received than others." These words hit Sisi like a blow. Franz had not masked his sour tone in front of the entire crowd gathered in the drawing room.

Sisi's skin flushed a deep red as she felt every pair of eyes turn on her. Karoline leaned toward Paula, whispering into her ear. Countess Esterházy scowled, exchanging a look with Sophie. Aware that they all watched, probing her reaction for any sign of distress or weakness, Sisi resisted the urge to show any.

"My husband is so funny." Sisi cocked her head. "And so thoughtful. He knows very well that I loved all of the gifts he presented to me last night. Why, do you know that he commissioned a waltz from Master Strauss, just for me? That was my favorite gift. I loved it so much that I believe I forgot to properly thank him for some of the other gifts."

Sophie's eyes narrowed as they darted from her son to her son's wife, sniffing for any scent of marital discord. Eventually, she spoke. "Franz, you know that we do gifts together as a family. Why would you have your own private exchange?" When Franz didn't answer, Sophie shrugged, a flick of her wrist. "No bother. Who's next to open presents?"

The crowd insisted that Sophie be the next recipient, a suggestion she accepted with much exaggerated protestation. And so the evening progressed, with ample flattery and self-congratulating, and Sisi attempting to participate without too fully revealing her inward misery.

Franz spent the entirety of dinner speaking with Meyendorff to his left. At the conclusion of the meal, he rose and excused himself from the table. Sisi stayed in her seat, struggling to remain composed.

"Merry Christmas, Empress Elisabeth."

Sisi looked up, into the face of her lady-in-waiting, Karoline of Lamberg. Taken aback, Sisi nodded. "Thank you, Karoline. Same to you."

Karoline hovered, shifting her weight. Her

lips were a deep maroon after too many glasses of red wine enjoyed at dinner. After a moment, Karoline leaned forward. "Your Majesty, is everything all right?" Her eyes slid sideways, in the direction of Franz's empty chair.

"I just wanted to make sure that you" — again, Karoline's gaze darted to Franz's vacant seat — "that Your Majesties were enjoying your Christmas together." The words came out a bit too eager; words that betrayed Karoline's hope that, in spite of what she said, the opposite was in fact true.

Sisi's spine went stiff. "Everything is fine, Karoline. Enjoy your Christmas."

"Right, then." Karoline stood back up, angling her body away from the empress. "Good."

"You look pale, Elisabeth." The archduchess approached now, depositing a plate of candied fruits, nuts, and chocolate torte in front of her daughter-in-law. She lowered herself into the seat just vacated by her son. Karoline scampered off, gliding across the room to where Paula stood. Sisi turned to her mother-in-law now.

"Do I, Aunt Sophie?"

"And you barely touched your food. Did you not enjoy the meal? Eat some of this dessert — the torte was the best, though I don't know why they were so stingy on the cream." With that, Sophie forked herself a generous bite of torte from the plate she'd just deposited in front of Sisi.

"I loved the meal," Sisi lied, pretending to enjoy a bite of steamed pears covered in caramelized brown sugar. It tasted sickeningly sweet. She dropped her fork and looked up, her eyes roving around the room, searching for Franz.

"You are exhausted, Elisabeth. This was too much activity for you. You must go to bed. I'll have some wine and chicken broth sent up to you."

"No, I'm fine, Aunt." Sisi shook her head, still scanning the room.

Sophie sat up, bristling at this disregard for her advice. "Elisabeth, the banquet is over. The men are about to retire into the library for spirits and smoking, while we ladies shall go sing Christmas carols in the drawing room. You shall miss nothing if you retire now, I assure you."

Sensing that her aunt would not be refused, and feeling too exhausted to move with the rest of the ladies to the next room for more Christmas merriment, Sisi acquiesced. "Very well," Sisi agreed, nodding. The thought of pretending to enjoy Christmas carols with Sophie was too much to bear.

Sisi found Franz in the corner of the candlelit hall, speaking to Grünne. Nearby, Karoline and Paula huddled with Grünne's pretty brunette from earlier in the evening. Though they pretended to be engrossed in conversation, just the three of them, Sisi noticed the sideways glances the ladies stole, watching her as she approached the emperor.

"Excuse me, Franz?" Sisi nodded at Grünne. "I apologize for interrupting, Count."

"You need never apologize, Empress Elisabeth." Grünne bowed low, stepping back to grant them privacy. He was quickly absorbed into the huddle with Karoline and Paula, and Sisi overheard their gay laughter as she leaned in toward Franz.

"Franz" — Sisi spoke quietly, noticing the way his eyes wandered to the scene behind her, in the direction of where Grünne had just stepped. Sisi shifted, stepping in front of her husband's gaze. "I will retire a bit early. I'm fatigued."

Franz nodded, still not looking at her.

"Will you escort me out?" She heard her voice crack as she asked.

"If you like," he said, offering his arm. Perfectly polite, yet undeniably distant.

"Merry Christmas, Empress Elisabeth," Grünne called out, nodding his head as she turned to leave.

"I'll be right back, Grünne," Franz said. "I shall see the empress out."

"Take your time, Your Majesty."

Sisi tightened her grip on Franz's arm as

384

he escorted her toward the door. "Will you be late?"

A muscle in his jaw twitched. "It's early yet. And it's Christmas. Surely you don't expect me to retire this early?"

Sisi bit her lower lip, then forced the gesture into a smile. "Of course not. I wish for you to enjoy your Christmas." Her mind raced inwardly. When she spoke next, she attempted to sound calm, conversational. "Who is the lady?"

"Who?" Franz nodded at clusters of courtiers as they glided by.

"The dark-haired lady speaking to Grünne. I have never met her."

"I didn't see."

Sisi's glance slid sideways, staring at Franz. "Surely you must have."

He did not return her gaze.

"She was quite pretty."

"Was she?" They approached the doorway. Footmen bowed deeply as they passed.

"Surely you noticed, my darling," Sisi said, her heartbeat throbbing in her throat, between her ears. The woman's beauty was made so much more threatening by the fact that Franz seemed reluctant to acknowledge it to his wife. She inhaled, willing herself to calm down. "Franz, please. Forgive me. I was quarrelsome last night. But I must speak with you."

"Not now, Elisabeth," he said, a note of

impatience in his voice. "I wish to enjoy what remains of Christmas."

"Well . . ." she faltered. "Will you come to me tonight? Please."

After a long pause, his jaw set, Franz answered. "Later."

Sisi was so relieved that she nearly burst into tears.

When she awoke in the middle of the night, Franz was not in bed beside her. Sisi's grogginess evaporated instantly. It was thick black outside, with just the faintest hint of purple. Almost predawn, probably after four in the morning, and no sign of Franz. Where could he be? Sisi's mind wandered back to dinner, when her aunt had told her that the women would retire to sing Christmas carols while the men would smoke and drink. Certainly the men, after several rounds, would have joined the ladies in the drawing room and the party would have escalated to a whole new level of revelry. Drunk on Christmas wine and jolly from the festive mood, the group would have most likely begun dancing. Grünne was courting that young, dark-eyed woman, so he likely would have drawn Franz into his cause.

A troubling thought took hold of Sisi, twisting itself around her like a suffocating cord. Her aunt had been very eager to see Sisi off to bed. Was it concern for her fatigue, or had it been to get rid of her? Had Sophie picked tonight to divert her son's attention, perhaps introduce him to some young, acquiescent lady in the court who would be happy to provide a substitute for the emperor's indisposed wife? Had she picked this night, when it was so apparent to all that Franz, usually so warm and affectionate, had clearly been out of spirits and irritated by Sisi? And wouldn't Franz, having abstained from relations with his wife for months, have been ripe for the temptation?

Sleep eluded Sisi for the remainder of the night, and she faced the dawn in her bedroom with a bitter, frantic resolve. This ridiculous spat, this power struggle for her husband's affection, had gone on too long. And she was losing. She needed to find a way to bring Franz back to her.

Agata's face was a welcome sight when the maid appeared at the door with a breakfast tray later in the morning.

"The entire household is still asleep, my lady," Agata explained, placing the tray on Sisi's lap before moving to relight the fire. "Figured you'd be happy to take your breakfast in bed today, after all of yesterday's activity."

"Quite, thank you." Sisi took a slow sip of the warm tea, the mug shaking in her hands. Two sleepless nights, and she could now feel their effects. She shut her eyes a moment, her nerves addled and her mind as jumpy as an unbroken horse. She exhaled, replacing the teacup and looking at the maid. "Did you have a nice Christmas, Agata?"

The maid turned from the hearth. "Oh, it was lovely, my lady. I'm afraid we were up all night in the servants' quarters." Agata giggled before turning back to the logs.

Sisi watched the maid, humming as she went about her morning activities: stoking the fire, emptying the chamber pot, collecting Sisi's garments from the night before. How was it that Agata, whose life was so much less vibrant and exciting than Sisi's, always managed to whistle and smile her way through the day's tedious chores? Why was it so hard for Sisi to remember how to be cheerful like that — as she had once been?

"Did you get all sorts of lovely presents from the emperor?" Agata asked, her expression guileless, as eager as a child's. Sisi frowned. But then a thought occurred to her. "Oh, Agata, forgive me! In the commotion of the past couple of days, I entirely missed my chance to give you your Christmas present." She reached now into the drawer of her bedside table, retrieving the small parcel she had wrapped for her maid. "Merry Christmas."

"For me?" The maid's round eyes widened. "Oh goodness, my lady, I didn't expect . . .

why, I didn't . . ."

"Don't apologize, Aggie." Sisi smiled, her first true smile in days. "I don't want anything from you — you do enough for me as it is. I just want you to have this."

"Too kind, my lady."

"Open it."

The maid tore the paper, finding a brooch inside.

"Miss Sisi. I mean, Your Majesty. Empress. How could I possibly?"

"Do you know what that jewel is, Agata?"

The maid shook her head, a bashful no.

"It's a ruby."

Agata gasped. "A ruby? But this is far too grand. What place does a ruby have in the servants' quarters?"

Sisi put her hands over Agata's — breaking protocol — and closed the maid's chapped and rough fingers over the jewel. "Nonsense, Agata, I want you to have it. The ruby matches your beautiful rosy cheeks. The smile on them is sometimes the only smile I see all day." Sisi's voice tripped on the confession, and she resisted the urge to tear up in front of her maid. Nevertheless, Agata sensed something amiss with her mistress.

"Miss Sisi . . . I mean . . . Your Majesty, are you feeling all right this morning?"

"No, I'm not."

"You're ill? Shall I fetch Doctor Seeburger?"

"No, it's all right, Agata. I'm not well right now. But I shall be. Just please, I beg you, don't tell any of the other girls in the quarters that I'm sad. Promise?"

"Of course not, Majesty." Agata took Sisi's hand and sat beside her on the bed. Quietly, the maid began to sing Sisi's favorite Bavarian Christmas carol: a simple melody about a father who could not afford the treats with which to fill his children's shoes, but who managed to cut down the grandest pine in the Black Forest, which he decorated with cranberries and pinecones. Sisi allowed herself to be sung to, leaning back against the pillow.

"Thank you, Agata." The maid's simple kindness caused her heart to ache. "And thank you for your discretion in not mentioning it."

"Mentioning what, Empress?"

"Oh, come now, Aggie. You've noticed just as well as I have that the emperor has not been in my room for two nights."

With that, Sisi pushed her breakfast tray to the side and caught her head in her hands. With Agata beside her, Sisi wept.

Outside the sun was no more than a feeble disk of gray behind a wall of thick clouds. At midday, when still Franz had not come, Sisi could bear it no longer. She decided to dress and find him.

As Sisi had suspected, the hallways were still abandoned. That was a good thing, as she was not supposed to walk them without her retinue. *"That is not how things are done,"* Sophie had warned her on countless occasions, when Sisi had tried to slip out to the stables or the gardens. *"An empress does not scurry about, alone. People will talk."*

As if people didn't already talk, Sisi thought, swallowing a bitter groan as she walked the quiet corridor away from her apartments. On this morning, the hallways echoed her loneliness back to her with their own stone whispers. Oh, how she missed Possi at Christmastime! The smell of pine boughs and roasted apple skins. The cozy house teeming with family and servants and red-cheeked peasants, neighbors who had come to share in Duke Max's ale and music. The merry crowd laughing as they bounced babies from hip to hip, singing and dancing with no attention paid to station or protocol.

Sisi had reached the conservatory, a high-ceilinged room with ferns and potted plants, where the courtiers had gathered the day earlier to hear Christmas carols. As she crossed the large room — now empty — and continued toward the drawing room, Sisi detected the sound of a pianoforte. Sighing, she recalled the nights that she and Franz had passed in their bedroom, singing along to his playing. She continued toward the sound of the notes.

It was Franz who played the piano, sitting on the far side of the drawing room. She paused, for the sight of him hunched over the piano momentarily startled her. He wore the same attire as he had to last night's banquet but his hair was tousled and his collar was unbuttoned. He appeared absolutely absorbed in the action of playing this slow, melancholy song, oblivious of his audience.

Sisi hovered in the doorway, silent, following the strands of the haunting melody. The longer she listened to her husband play the song, the more overpowering the desperation that welled up inside of her became: a feeling like she might never be happy again.

Franz stopped playing. The hum of the last notes lingered a moment before fading out, and without turning toward her, he spoke. "Did you like it?"

So he had noticed her.

Caught off guard by the question, Sisi stammered: "It was exquisite, Franz."

He nodded, still not turning to look at her.

"Yet painful," she added.

He snorted out a laugh, short and bitter.

"What's the name of it?"

"Piano Sonata Number 14, by Ludwig van Beethoven," he answered, his eyes still fixed on the piano keys, which his fingers barely grazed. "The *Moonlight* Sonata."

Sisi walked toward the piano, somewhat

lifted by the fact that he was talking to her. "Speaking of moonlight . . . you didn't come to me last night."

"Something came up."

It was a hurtful answer. Vague and riddled with troubling possibility. Had he spent the night with another woman? Paula? Karoline? Grünne's brunette?

"What I like about sad songs" — Franz still looked down at the piano — "they are honest."

"No more of this sad song, please." She lowered herself onto the piano bench beside him. He stopped playing, but still he did not turn toward her. "Play 'The Skater's Waltz,' " she said. "Or better yet, play our new song. The one Master Strauss composed just for us."

Franz didn't begin to play, so she began to hum. All she remembered about her waltz was that it had been a blending of the Bavarian anthem and Austria's anthem.

"All right, all right, I'll play it." Franz touched his fingers to the ivory keys, but paused. "I'll play it, if you promise never to scold me like that again, Elisabeth."

She leaned forward, resting a palm on his arm. "And I'll promise never to scold you again, Franz, if you promise never to abandon me like that."

"What, is my own wife giving me negotiating terms now?" Franz looked at her, sighing.

She was struck by how handsome he was, by how powerful her love for him was. It scared her, because she guessed that her love might not be enough to pull him back to her.

But then his eyes softened, ever so slightly. Not enough to qualify as a smile, but the cool, distant aloofness of the past few days had gone, giving her a small slice of hope.

"You know, Elisa, sometimes I think that you forget that I'm the emperor."

And you forget I'm a girl of seventeen. Here, alone, far from home, all because I love you. Though she felt hurt by him, she reminded herself of the need to win him back, not alienate him further with arguing. "Oh, Franz, do you have any idea how much I love you?" She said it as a sigh, and she meant it. "But really" — she flashed a smile, her head leaning to the side — "even if I do often wish it otherwise, how could I ever forget you are emperor?" Pausing, she lifted a hand, waving at their surroundings. "With all of this?"

"You would wish for me to be something other than emperor?"

She bit her lower lip, reining in the eagerness in her reply. "Perhaps. At times."

He angled his body toward her now, and she saw the fatigue pulling on his eyes, his unshaven cheeks.

"The emperor looks tired," she whispered. She put a finger to his cheek, grazing his whiskered skin.

His hand rose to meet hers, and he brought her palm inside his. "How is it possible?"

"How is what possible?"

"I've won battles in Italy and Hungary. I'm the emperor, for God's sake. And yet you would conquer me with a smile."

She leaned close and whispered in his ear: "I love *you,* Franz, not because you are emperor. I love you because you are the man who snores beside me in bed, and plays the piano for me, and rides up into the mountains with me, and whispers my nickname with so much love in his voice that I never want to let him go." She planted a kiss on the side of his neck, a square of skin usually concealed by his uniform collar, a place that belonged only to her. "Please, my darling, I cannot bear it when you are cross with me."

He waited a moment before he breathed out a long, slow exhale. "And thus, I am won over."

The cord around her heart slackened, allowing her to breathe easily once more, as he wrapped his arms around her, barely making it around her thick midsection.

"Do you still love me, Franz?"

"You know I do, Elisa."

"And I adore you, Franz. But I don't want your mother's hairstylist."

"If I kiss you, will you be silent?"

"Only one way to find out."

He leaned toward her, and from the way he

kissed her, Sisi allowed herself to hope that her husband had come back to her.

"Play me our song, Franz," she asked after several moments.

He rested his fingers on the keys and played the waltz, both of them humming along to the familiar melodies, the two disparate tunes merging into one unique thread. After that, he played her favorite song, the tune from Bad Ischl called "The Skater's Waltz."

Sisi shut her eyes as she listened to the melody. "Franz, how about next Christmas we listen to this song while we ourselves go skating? How about it? We can allow the fountains outside the Hofburg to freeze over and have our own private rink."

He laughed at the idea. "As long as you are not carrying another one of my babies."

"Well, I'm not going to say that's an impossibility. After all, we shall have a lot of missed time to make up for once this baby is born," she answered, and they both laughed.

"Dance with me, Elisa." Franz rose from the bench, continuing the song now through his humming, as he pulled her up.

"I'm too big to dance," she protested.

"You're perfect for dancing," he insisted.

They held one another and swayed for several minutes, but Sisi could not entirely quash the question that persisted in her mind, its presence like a tight knot she couldn't undo. "Franz, where were you last night?"

He looked at her, as if unwilling to answer. "Don't concern yourself with that, Elisa. The past is the past."

She stopped dancing, her hands dropping from his. He tried to take them up once more, but she yanked them free. "Franz, tell me."

"Elisa, I'm not going to —"

"Where were you? I must know." And just like that, an image from her past crept forth and pierced her mind: her father leaving their home. Leaving with no further explanation than to say he was *going into town.* And then, a memory far less distant. The circle of ladies the night before: Karoline, Paula, and the other one. Whispers exchanged, glances stolen here and there. Any one of them would willingly — *gladly* — welcome the emperor into her bed. Wasn't that the highest aspiration for any ambitious young woman at court? — to bed the emperor? Was she, Sisi, destined for the same litany of lonely nights that her mother had known? She began to tremble, her frame closing in on itself as she sat back down on the piano bench. "Franz, were you with another woman?"

Franz put his arms on her shoulders, pressing his hands into her. She shrugged him off.

"No, I was not with another woman, Elisa. For God's sake, must you always pick fights with me?" He lowered himself heavily onto the piano bench, sitting beside her.

"Then why won't you tell me?"

"It was the Hungarians," Franz snapped.

"The Hungarians?" That was one thing she had not been expecting to hear. "What about the Hungarians?"

Franz cupped his tired head in his hands now, his fingers sliding through his unkempt hair. "The Hungarians are clamoring for independence. This troublemaker, Count Andrássy, has vowed to return from exile. He swears he will return to Budapest, and he is getting them all agitated."

Andrássy. Sisi had heard Franz and Sophie speak the name before.

"It's getting increasingly precarious, and now Mother is advising military action against them before they are in open rebellion."

Sisi absorbed this information, dizzy with relief that Franz had not taken a mistress. It was ludicrous, but war seemed like nothing as long as her marriage was still intact. "Why couldn't you tell me that, Franz?"

Franz shook his head.

"But why not? I wish to stand beside you through these troubles. Your mother certainly does —"

"Stop!" Franz turned, holding a hand up, his patience expired. "Enough. I cannot bear it. I cannot be at war with you, too, Elisa-beth."

She was stunned to silence. She sat motion-less beside him, looking down at her feet.

He pointed at her large belly. "I will *not* upset you with talk of war. Not when you are in this condition. Mother told me not to trouble you with this."

Even though the statement made her blood roil, Sisi suppressed the urge to offer a snappy retort. Not after they had just reconciled. Not when he was her only ally, and she needed him. "All right, Franz." She put her palm on his. "I understand."

"Do you?"

"I do."

Franz sighed, leaning his head back. His tired eyelids shut.

"Let's go, Franz, you're exhausted."

"No," he said, fidgeting. "I can't sleep. I've got a meeting with the council in an hour." With that he hopped up from the piano bench, extending a hand toward her. "Now, can we continue dancing and talk of happy things? If I wanted to talk of war, I'd ask Grünne or Bach to dance, not my wife."

She took his hand and allowed him to lift her. They resumed swaying. "But Franz, when would the war happen?"

He sighed, but after a moment, he answered her: "As soon as the snow clears, in the spring."

"Would you have to go?"

"Of course I would go. I am Emperor."

IX.

The imperial guards, sensing that the mood of the crowd is shifting, push back against the rising onslaught of people, threatening to brandish their swords. She reads the discomfort apparent on his face.

But her eyes do not rest for long. Desperately, she combs the crowd once more, looking for another face. Has he come? she wonders. Has he come for her, as he had promised?

Finally, her darting eyes land on him. He stands near the front, his face almost entirely obscured by the ornate headpiece of a bishop in front of him. He appears more dashing than she has ever seen him — his dark eyes aglow, his tall frame outfitted in a fur-trimmed coat. He has been watching her all this time. When they lock eyes she smiles. She does not care who sees.

"Sisi?"

Reluctantly, she rends her gaze from him and turns back to her husband. When she meets his stare now, his expression is quizzical, questioning her. An arch of the eyebrow, a glimmer of understanding in his light eyes. And, in that moment, there is no doubt in her mind: the emperor knows her secret.

CHAPTER NINE

HOFBURG PALACE, VIENNA
MARCH 1855

The labor pains began shortly after dawn. Sisi awoke with a start, believing the constricting ache to have been part of a bad dream. But it continued, gripping her and prompting her to cry out in agony. Franz's face, visible in a sliver of early morning light, reflected her worry back to her.

"Elisa, what is the matter?"

"Franz, I think the baby is coming." At that, Franz sprung from bed to fetch the doctor.

Sophie arrived first, bursting into the bedroom without a knock, her head full of curling papers and nothing covering her frame but a flimsy dressing robe.

"Doctor Seeburger is on his way. How long have you felt the labor pains?" Sophie approached the bed, dispatching her maids on a flurry of errands as she settled down beside her daughter-in-law.

"Only just now. But the bedding is all wet,"

Sisi answered.

"You have released your waters," Sophie explained.

"I have?"

"It's normal," Sophie insisted.

"Mother, where is Doctor Seeburger?" Franz approached the bed, taking Sisi's other hand.

"Coming. Franz, you really mustn't be in here. It's bad enough that you stayed with her through the confinement. Labor is too much for you, on this point I must insist."

"Mother, I told Elisa I would stay throughout the . . ."

"Franz, you listen to me. You must leave *now*!" Sophie rose, and though her frame stood less tall than her son's, it was Franz who cowered. "This is a woman's place, hardly a place fitting for the emperor. Out, out, out!"

"Franz, please," Sisi looked at her husband, clutching his hand, willing him to stay. Hadn't he promised to stay beside her? But just then another contraction began to grip her entire body and all she could do was groan in pain.

Franz turned from Sisi to his mother, his face crumpled with concern.

"Franz! Look how you've upset her!" Sophie railed, her cheeks and neck splotching red as Sisi squirmed in bed, clutching both of their outstretched hands.

"You must go, now! If you want to be useful to your wife and son, go to the chapel and *pray.* Out!"

Before Sisi could protest, Sophie practically pushed her son toward the door, just as Doctor Seeburger entered with four nursemaids.

"We are here." The doctor appeared alert and fresh, somehow dressed and shaven in spite of the early hour. "How far apart are her pains?"

"She has only just begun," Sophie explained, retaking Sisi's hand and sitting beside the bed.

Franz was gone. Sisi began to whimper, looking away from her aunt. But before she could cry out for him, her body was seized by a fresh spasm of pain.

"It is happening quickly," the doctor said, looking from Sisi to Sophie.

From that point on, the activity happening around Sisi was a blur that faded in and out, murky and unimportant compared to the searing pain that seemed to be rending her apart from the inside. The shrill cries originating from her own throat sounded entirely foreign to her, and Sisi wondered how these women and this doctor could tolerate listening to her.

"Well done, my girl, well done." Sophie remained beside her, swabbing her brow with a cool cloth. "It will be over soon. Just keep breathing."

Nurses bustled about Sisi, filling basins with fresh water, threading needles, and swapping out soiled rags with fresh ones. When she spotted the pile of soiled cloths, Sisi gasped in horror; was all of that blood coming from her?

"Almost there now, Empress." A nurse stood beside Sisi, opposite Sophie. "The baby is coming quickly. We will tell Your Imperial Highness when to push."

"Think of your son. You are doing this for your son, Elisabeth." Sophie's eyes were fixed on the end of the bed, where the physician was moving his hands with skilled and steady intention.

Sisi felt the urge to berate her mother-in-law, to tell Sophie to be quiet and bring Franz back in, and she decided to do so. Only, when she opened her mouth, the censure came out as a garbled and incomprehensible groan.

"Bravo, Elisabeth, that's my strong, brave girl." Sophie, none the wiser, urged Sisi on, squeezing her hand so tightly that the pain in Sisi's mashed fingers presented a welcome distraction from the pain she felt below. But only for a moment.

"Now is the time, Empress Elisabeth." Doctor Seeburger's head appeared above the blanketed bulk that was Sisi's lower body. He nodded at the nurse beside Sisi.

The nursemaid leaned close to her now. "Empress Elisabeth, if it would please Your

Majesty to push . . . the baby is ready to come."

Sisi scrunched up her face and clamped down on the two hands she held, pushing from the root of her insides until she was certain that she was forcing the very innards out of her body.

"Almost, almost, almost there!" Sophie yelled.

"Push, Your Majesty!" Doctor Seeburger's voice was urgent over the sound of Sisi's wails. "Push, Empress!" Somewhere in the pain ripping apart her insides, Sisi became disoriented and hazy. She heard the sounds issuing from her own throat, as well as the urgings of those around her, but her mind wandered.

"Empress, push!" The doctor's voice was hoarse, and Sisi turned back to him, as if seeing him for the first time. "Empress, you have done wonderfully. Your baby is coming; would it please Your Imperial Highness to push, one more time?"

Sisi clenched her teeth and moaned, squeezing the nurse's hand as she pushed with all of her strength. She was certain that if the baby did not come this time, she would die. She heard her mother-in-law, and the nurse beside her, urging her on. She heard the low, tortured sound of her own voice. And then, a new sound. The soft, plaintive wails of a new pair of lungs, expressing themselves for the first time in the cold, darkening bedroom.

"He's out!" Sophie gasped, dropping Sisi's hand and running to the edge of the bed. "A boy? Is it a boy?"

Doctor Seeburger stood up, holding a tiny, purple little body covered in blood and fluid, its little legs kicking petulantly. He turned toward the new mother. "Empress Elisabeth, congratulations. Your Imperial Highness has delivered a healthy baby girl."

Sisi absorbed the news, but her body was so spent, and so overcome with the relief of having pushed the baby through, that she dropped her head back onto the pillow without responding.

"A girl," she stammered to herself. "Helene." She began to cry — tears of exhaustion, tears of joy, tears of relief that the entire ordeal was over. Her mind flew to Possi. *"Helene."*

Sophie and Doctor Seeburger took the baby to the corner of the room, where they bathed its tiny pink frame, cocooning it in a blanket.

"I want my baby." Sisi, too tired to lift her head, barely forced the words off of her lips. "I want my Helene. And I want Franz."

"There, there now, Empress Elisabeth." It was the same, soft-featured nurse beside her. She took Sisi's hand in her own once more. "The doctor has got to clean Your Majesty's daughter. Then you shall have the little princess."

"I want my baby," Sisi repeated, delirious. "Please, my daughter. And Franz."

Sisi lifted her head just in time to see Sophie, cradling the clean and newly blanketed bundle in her arms. "My little *chouchou*. My sweet little *chou-chou,*" Sophie cooed to the baby, whose cries were mounting in strength and urgency. "Hush, don't cry. Grandmamma will take care of you, shhh, don't cry."

"Please, Sophie, my baby," Sisi called out across the room, but either Sophie didn't hear her frail entreaty, or she chose not to answer.

"There now, my sweet little girl." Sophie kept her eyes fixed on the pink little face. "What shall we call you, then?"

"Helene," Sisi answered, but Sophie didn't hear.

The archduchess continued, cooing to the baby in her arms: "Wouldn't you like to be named after your Grandmamma? Perhaps we shall call you Sophie?"

And with that, the archduchess glided out of the room, her eyes fixed on her little granddaughter's face, never looking back at the mother who had yet to hold her.

"Elisa, you're awake. Finally!" Franz rose from the chair in which he sat before the fireplace, running toward his wife in bed. "I thought you might sleep for days."

"Franz." Sisi was disoriented as she emerged from her deep sleep, but relieved to tears at the fact that his was the first face she saw. As awareness returned to her, she tried to sit up. But then, feeling how her entire body ached, she decided against it. "Franz, where is Helene?"

"Our beautiful little girl is resting happily in her bassinet." Franz, beside the bed now, took Sisi's hand in his and covered it in kisses. "She is so perfect, Elisa, wait until you see her."

Sisi looked around the room, seeking out the bassinet. She blinked, still disoriented. Her mouth was so dry she thought it might crack. "Where is she?"

"With her Grandmamma, in the nursery."

"With Sophie?"

"Yes." Franz nodded, kissing Sisi's hand once more. "Mother has arranged a perfect wet nurse for her. Oh, Elisa, I'm so proud of you. You did it, my brave darling. Bravo!"

"Franz, I want to see Helene. I haven't held her yet." Instinctively, Sisi reached for her breasts, which were now even more swollen than they had been throughout the pregnancy, and intolerably tender. "I want to nurse her."

"Now, just a minute, Elisa." Sisi did not like the tenuous expression on her husband's face. "You have worked hard enough."

"What? Nonsense; I want my baby."

"There are ways in which we do things in the palace." Franz paused, lowering his eyes so that he no longer looked directly at his wife, but rather at the hand of hers that he held in his own. "The empress does not nurse her own babies."

"What? Why not?"

"I shall have Mother, or the nurses, explain all of this to you. It's not really something I should be discussing."

"Never mind that," Sisi said, too tired and anxious to see her daughter to argue that point. "Well, I won't nurse her then. But I want to see Helene."

"Now, let's not be too hasty to decide on a name." Franz shifted his weight on the bed.

"What do you mean, too hasty? We decided this months ago. There's nothing hasty about it."

"But again, Elisa, there are proper ways to do things in the court. And naming is usually something in which the grandparents have a say. Why, I was named after my grandfather."

Sisi's stomach tightened.

"Now don't get mad, Elisa," Franz said preemptively.

"Your mother wishes to name our daughter?"

"Yes. And I think we ought to allow her to. Just this time. It's the respectful thing to do."

"What does she wish to name her?"

"Mother thought it might be nice to use a

family name."

"Helene *is* a family name, Franz."

"Mother suggested naming her . . . Sophie."

"How surprising," Sisi answered, her tone acidic. "Sophie. After herself."

"Exactly," Franz agreed, not sensing Sisi's silent fury. "We've had the priest draw up the announcement to be distributed to the churches throughout the empire. The entire realm will pray for Princess Sophie at a special mass tomorrow."

"So it's already decided." What else had they determined about her daughter while Sisi had slept? "And did you go ahead and baptize her without me as well? And arrange her marriage?"

"She had to be baptized." Franz laughed, as if it were the most natural thing in the world. "God forbid anything happened to her, we couldn't have her little soul un-claimed."

Sisi's throat seized, swallowing the words with which she tried to answer. "You . . . you baptized my daughter without me?"

"It was nothing. It's never a big affair for the girls. A quick service in the family chapel. Better to have it done with. As you know, those events are much bigger when it's a son. Then, it's a matter of the State."

Sisi felt as though she might cry, except for the fact that her body was so depleted, no tears sprung to her eyes. "I can't believe you baptized my daughter without me." She spoke the words so quietly that Franz did not hear.

"Little Sophie, our daughter." Franz took his wife's hand in his. "Isn't it wonderful to have a baby? And you wanted a girl."

Sisi thought of her younger sister back at Possi, a beautiful, sprightly little girl by the name of Sophie-Charlotte. She would think of her daughter as named after Sophie-Charlotte. "Certainly. It's lovely." Sisi managed a smile. She would not allow the joy of holding her daughter to be tarnished, not even by her mother-in-law's selfishness. "Please, Franz, bring me my little Sophie. I want to hold my daughter."

It took an hour for the little princess to arrive from the nursery, as Aunt Sophie had forbidden anyone to remove the baby from the bassinet until she had awoken naturally from a nap.

But when the baby was finally brought in, carried by a weepy Agata and placed in Sisi's yearning arms, the joy of holding her daughter for the first time overshadowed the pain Sisi had wrestled while waiting.

"My daughter," Sisi cooed, amazed by how instantaneous and compulsory the urge was to love and protect this little being. Tears rose to her eyes like a soft dew, and she wept, happily. "Sophie." Sisi laughed as the baby yawned, and she offered her pinky finger for the little mouth to nibble.

"Agata, can you please fetch Franz?" The maid nodded and quit the room, leaving mother and daughter alone.

"Hello, my little girl. I am so happy to meet you, finally." After several minutes, Sophie yawned once more, spreading wide her rose-bud lips into a tiny circle. "You are so perfect, my little girl. So perfect," Sisi cried, covering her daughter's round cheeks in soft, tear-stained kisses.

Sisi had an idea and she did not care who might oppose it. Quickly, she reached down and slid her nightdress off. "Are you hungry, my little Sophie?" She offered her breast to her daughter. At first Sophie resisted the nipple that was being pressed against her lips. But eventually she opened her mouth and began to suckle happily.

It was a strange, new sensation to feed her daughter at her own breast, but the relief Sisi felt was almost immediate. As her daughter drank, Sisi felt as if both she and her daughter might be lulled into a calm, blissful nap.

"Elisa." Franz had appeared in the doorway undetected. He walked toward his wife and daughter in the bed, an apprehensive look on his face. "You're feeding her?"

"I am, Franz. Just this once. Please, don't oppose me." Sisi began to weep, so overcome was she by a rush of emotions. "I just wanted to know what it felt like to nurse my baby."

"I suppose it's all right, if it's just this once," Franz acquiesced, sitting beside them. They were silent for several moments, both watching Sophie at her mother's breast, and Sisi noticed the same love-struck look in her husband's eyes that she was certain she herself wore.

"She is perfect, isn't she, Franz?"

"I can't believe she is ours, Elisa." They held hands as Sisi wept, both of them looking down on the little girl. A being entirely of their making.

But the peace of this tender moment was pierced by a new voice. "Franz?" Aunt Sophie entered by the same open doorway through which Franz had just come. She, too, had been watching the scene. "We have spoken about this. And yet you flout my — the *doctor's* — orders."

"Mother, Elisabeth and I were just . . ." Franz stood up from the bed, stepping in front of his wife as if to conceal her from his mother's watchful eyes.

"I see exactly what you are doing. Your wife is nursing the child. Elisabeth, this is highly . . . this is not how things are done."

"Why not?" Sisi asked, the sweet calm she had just enjoyed shifting into quiet fury.

"It is custom. An empress does not nurse."

Sisi, infuriated by her aunt's unwelcome presence, as well as the foolishness of "custom" constantly being peddled as the justifi-

415

cation for her unhappiness, snapped her retort. "It is my child, Aunt Sophie. And my breast, furthermore. I think I can decide what to do with each of them."

Sophie, temporarily taken aback by her niece's opposition, blinked. And then, composing herself, her eyes narrowing into two thin slits, she answered: "Elisabeth, perhaps you are *ignorant* in the ways of child rearing in the imperial court, seeing as you were raised in that provincial household, and are little more than a child yourself. Allow me to enlighten you."

Sisi clutched her baby tighter to her breast as her aunt continued.

"It's too much strain on your body. You need to recover. Leave the nursing to the woman whose job it is — the wet nurse. I've found a nice girl from Tyrol. She's stronger than you. You are the empress and your efforts should be focused on conceiving again."

This was so ridiculous that Sisi could not help but laugh. "Sophie, I am just now seeing my daughter for the first time. Please, do not talk to me of the next labor and child." She turned back to her daughter, feeling her anger slacken as she beheld the soft, pink little features.

Sophie stood silent and apart from them, folding and unfolding her hands in petulant fists. When she spoke next, her tone was suddenly composed, even sweet. "What do you think of the name, Elisabeth?"

"It's fine. It's my younger sister's name, and I have positive remembrances of her."

"I've had it carved into her bassinet," Sophie said. "In the nursery. Just adjacent to my bedroom."

Sisi looked up. "Please have the bassinet brought in here. I will have my daughter sleep with me."

"That won't be happening," Sophie said, her tone defiant. When Sisi looked up, her mouth poised to answer back, she noticed Sophie and Franz exchange a knowing look — telling Sisi that something else of importance had been discussed while she had slept.

"Elisabeth, your body has been through a lot." Franz leaned forward, putting a hesitant hand on her arm. "You need to rest, you need to sleep. The last thing you need is a newborn in your bedroom with you, waking you up every hour."

"But that's preposterous. Where will she sleep, if not with her mother?"

"I've had the nursery prepared for her," Sophie said. "She shall want for nothing — she will have nurses with her at all times, and I shall be just next door. They know that they may wake me at any hour."

That was more than Sisi could bear. She did not even care who heard her protest now. "Franz, how can you listen to this? Do you not want our daughter with us?"

"Franz has an empire to rule," Sophie said, stepping toward the bed. "You think he can afford a string of sleepless nights? Absolutely not. You both need your sleep. You both have your roles to fill."

"Mother, please." Franz raised a hand, beseeching his mother to be quiet. Turning back to his wife, he sighed. "Elisa, I want whatever is best for you. The doctor says, for now, that is sleep."

Sophie, now assured of her son's co-operation on the matter, sat down on the bed with them. "My dear girl, you can't just come into the palace and change centuries' worth of customs. This is how things are done." Sophie smiled sweetly at Sisi, like a concerned mother. "Don't worry so, my fretful little fusspot. You shall give yourself wrinkles."

Sisi threw a daggered gaze at her mother-in-law.

"You shall see your little Sophie plenty. You just won't have to wake every hour in the middle of the night. Believe me, my pet." A gentle pat of the hand said: *That is that.* "My child, believe me, I am doing you and your husband a favor."

The remainder of March passed in a blur of doctor-imposed resting and the opening of congratulatory gifts. Cousin Ludwig sent a trunk full of baby dresses in the style of Bavarian tailoring. Helene sent a porcelain

doll with dark golden curls the color of Sisi's.
And Ludovika sent trunks full of the gowns
and sleepwear and bonnets in which she had
dressed her own daughters.

Thanks to her youth and strength, Sisi's
body recovered quickly, so that after several
weeks she felt quite restless and ready to
resume her normal schedule.

It was a gray afternoon in spring. The
palace was quiet, the courtiers observing the
somber rituals of Lent, a time when balls and
concerts and other entertainments were flatly
forbidden. That day, Sisi decided to ignore
Doctor Seeburger's orders of rest and summoned Countess Marie Festetics and Herr
Lobkowitz to her apartments.

"How many letters have we received?" Sisi
asked, sitting down into a blue satin settee in
her office. Her body felt lithe and nimble
once more, with the bulging belly almost
entirely gone.

"Hundreds," Herr Lobkowitz answered, his
brow creased as he studied the stacks of notes
— messages of congratulations from around
the empire and from Europe's leading families.

"Queen Victoria and Prince Albert have just
sent you this." Countess Marie pointed
toward a basket overflowing with chocolates,
pears, and petite macaroons.

"Goodness," Sisi said, eyeing the overflowing bundle. "Take it down to the kitchens,

tell the servants they may divide it up, Marie. And I shall have to remember to add them to the list of thank-you notes."

"Let's remember that Victoria's youngest child, Prince Leopold, turns two on the seventh of April," Herr Lobkowitz said matter-of-factly. "It might be wise to include a small toy horse with your letter, wishing Prince Leopold a happy birthday. He does love horses."

Both Sisi and Marie turned to Herr Lobkowitz, impressed.

"What is it, Your Grace?" The aide fidgeted, adjusting the monocle where it perched on the side of his nose. "Why does Your Imperial Highness look at me this way?"

"You are invaluable to me, Herr Lobkowitz." Sisi smiled, nodding her head approvingly. It was one of the few pleasant surprises she'd had since becoming empress, that this middle-aged man — though perhaps an ally of Sophie's in Bad Ischl — had come to serve her so devotedly.

"It's a brilliant idea, Herr Lobkowitz. Let's include a toy horse and a special message of birthday wishes for the little English prince."

"Her Majesty is too kind." Herr Lobkowitz bowed, flashing a diffident smile.

"Now, we shall start with the letters to my family in Bavaria. I should like to describe everything about my darling little Sophie to Mamma and Helene."

After several hours Sisi's mind began to wander, and she felt as though she dictated the same response over and over again. "Are we nearly done?"

"You see the one downside of being so beloved." Herr Lobkowitz looked up from the rosewood desk, shaking out his cramping wrist. "Too many letters."

"I'd like to go find Sophie. I haven't seen my daughter since yesterday."

"I think we've made good progress today, Your Majesty. If you'd like to stop for the afternoon, we can resume this tomorrow. Marie, will you help me clear these papers?" Herr Lobkowitz and Marie began sealing the envelopes in which the dictated letters sat ready, and Sisi rose to find Agata in order to change into an afternoon gown.

Sisi left her apartments, ordering Countess Esterházy and the rest of her ladies-in-waiting to remain behind.

"But . . . Your Majesty," Countess Esterházy stammered as she heard the order, exchanging a disapproving look with Karoline.

"I know, it's not *custom,*" Sisi said. "But I wish you to stay here. I'm going to find my daughter. I wish to be alone with her." The pinched look on Countess Esterházy's pale lips struck Sisi as, somehow, amusing.

Sisi climbed the steps, seeking out her daughter in the nursery off of the archduchess's suite, as that was where the baby was usually kept when not being paraded around the palace and grounds by her boastful grandmother.

But the nursery was empty, as were Sophie's apartments. Sisi found no one but a timid maid in the archduchess's bedroom.

"Excuse me." Sisi cleared her throat.

"Your Majesty!" The maid dropped the sheets, her face draining of color as she curtsied before Sisi.

"Please, where is the archduchess?"

"The archduchess has taken her baby . . . I mean . . . Princess Sophie, Your Majesty's baby, for a walk through the gardens."

"Thank you." Sisi turned and left the bedroom, grinding her teeth as she marched toward the gardens.

She had argued with Franz a dozen times about this ridiculous arrangement — why was it that Sophie insisted on taking responsibility for their baby? Perhaps the Habsburg empresses in the past had been all too happy to relinquish the tiring and arduous tasks of tending to their newborns. But if Sisi said she was up to the task of waking with her daughter, feeding her daughter, and tending to her needs, then who was Sophie to tell her that she could not? She knew well enough what Sophie was telling people, how Sophie was weaving tales of her inadequacy as a mother. She had forced Agata to tell her, had refused to quit until the maid confessed what she knew from the servants' gossip circles.

"She says that you . . . that Your Majesty . . . is . . ."

"What, Agata? Tell me. I shall not be cross with you."

Agata lowered her eyes; her round cheeks flushed a deep apple red. "Well, she says that you are just a child yourself. Not up to the task, Your Majesty."

Sisi's stomach knotted in anger. But even more so, her heart ached; she was missing invaluable moments in little Sophie's life — those early hints of a first smile, the arrival of new auburn curls. Fleshy rolls appearing in soft, plump skin. Sisi couldn't endure the separation any longer.

Sisi would raise this issue again with her husband that very evening, and she would not drop her suit until Franz had agreed that they get their daughter back.

The garden was damp under a chilly, spring mist. Bright tulips shivered in the parterre flower beds where gardeners had recently deposited the bulbs, fresh from the Habsburg greenhouses. The pebbly walkways were slippery, and Sisi was certain that Sophie would not have remained out of doors with the baby in this weather. She changed her mind, turning to reenter the palace and search the rooms for her daughter.

Just then, Franz emerged on the gravel

path, flanked by a coterie of liveried footmen and stern-faced guards. In his company were Grünne and — to Sisi's dismay — a laughing brunette. The same statuesque lady whom Franz had professed not to notice on Christmas. Sisi's hands gripped the folds of her gown as she stopped, midstep.

"Elisa, there you are!" Spotting his wife up ahead, Franz splintered off from his two companions, trotting toward Sisi.

"Franz, hello." She stood, surprised at this rare midday meeting with her husband. These days, she never saw him before dinner, if then. And yet, here he was, with company by his side. "Where are you coming from?" Sisi's glance slid over Grünne to land directly on the lady.

"Meeting of the council." Franz looked to Grünne, then to the third member of their party. "My darling, have you met Elizabeth, Duchess of Modena? We were lucky to come across her on our way out."

This woman shared her name. Sisi looked upon her, her dark eyes the color of coffee. Full lips that now spread in a modest smile. She bowed before Sisi. "Your Majesty," she said, her voice carrying the faintest hint of an accent. "My most humble congratulations to Your Imperial Highness on the birth of the princess."

Tossing her head back, her tone haughty, Sisi nodded. "Thank you, Duchess. You are too kind." Sisi noticed the faint floral scent that skipped off this woman's skin, the healthy sheen of her glossy dark curls. "You must be new at court."

"I am, Empress." The woman lowered her long-lashed eyes to the ground.

"We shall leave Your Majesties." Grünne stepped forward, extending an arm through which the duchess slid her own. Without another word, the count whisked her away, their heads angling in carefree conversation as they continued on up the pebbled path. Franz and Sisi, side by side, watched them go.

"Shall we?" Franz turned now, offering his own arm to lead his wife in the opposite direction. They walked on, silent, for a moment.

"Is Grünne courting her?"

Franz turned his head. "Hmm?"

"The Duchess of Modena. Elizabeth. Is Grünne courting her?"

"No." Franz shook his head. A bit too emphatically. "Sisi, she is a widow. The Duke of Modena just recently died."

Sisi considered this. "She didn't appear to be in mourning."

"She's just come out of mourning. The duchess is here for a change. Only for a few months. No one is courting her."

It took Sisi a moment to collect her thoughts, scattered as they were, like wisps of a wind-blown dandelion. She blinked, pushing Grünne and the duchess out of her mind. She knew there was a purpose, something of far greater import, for which she sought Franz. And then she remembered: "Franz, you didn't happen to see your mother at the council meeting, did you?"

"No. She rarely comes now, only when little Sophie is napping."

Sisi frowned. "I am looking for little Sophie. Do you have any idea where they might be?"

"In my mother's suite, most likely."

"I've just come from there."

Franz lifted his shoulders, a shrug. "Anyhow, I was coming to find you, Elisa."

"You were?"

"I was. How are you feeling?"

"I am feeling very strong, thank you. I've had a productive afternoon of answering dozens of letters."

"Good." He nodded, still distracted, his mind stretched like a string in too many directions. "Say, are you up for an outing?"

"Perhaps." Sisi cocked her head, intrigued. "But I'd like to see little Sophie. Is it something for which she could join us?"

"Not for this. I'd like to take you to the opera this evening."

"The opera?"

"Yes, they are putting on *Don Giovanni.* They've heard how much you loved your journey to Salzburg, and so they've planned a Mozart opera."

"Salzburg was Mozart's hometown, of course." Sisi smiled at that, flattered. And a bit overwhelmed that the imperial opera house would plan its schedule to please her. "A night at the opera listening to Mozart sounds lovely." Sisi accepted the invitation and her husband's arm and they continued down the gravel path. "Will your mother be joining us?"

"She avoids any Mozart work written in Italian. Doesn't understand why anyone would attend the opera unless it's in German. Flatly refuses to come."

"Even better."

"Elisa!"

"I'm joking, my love," Sisi answered, smiling sweetly to offset the barb.

Vienna's opera house dazzled Sisi anew as she entered it, especially after these many months confined to her own private rooms. The interior, with its high-vaulted ceiling and gold-gilt trim, was illuminated by thousands of candles. Rows of chandeliers hung just low enough to graze the high feathers that burst forth from the ladies' hairdos. A private stairway wove up to the second floor, where Sisi and her husband were escorted via a secret passage into the imperial box, looking directly onto center stage and the orchestra pit below.

When Sisi and Franz entered their box, the entirety of the audience turned to gawk. Here, after all, was the real show. The tuxedoed men and diamond-bedecked women broke out in applause; many of them called out wishes for a long life to the emperor. Everyone craned to get a look at the young woman who had just given birth to Franz Joseph's firstborn.

Come tomorrow Vienna's coffeehouses, newspaper columns, public boulevards, and parks would be abuzz, detailing every inch of Her Royal Highness's appearance. Sisi had dressed for the part. She had selected a wide-hooped gown of rich scarlet satin. Her shoulders were bare, revealed now as Franz helped her out of her cream-colored stole, but her neck, fingers, and ears were covered with Habsburg rubies. She and Agata had spent two full hours pinning her curls, weaving crystals throughout her thick locks so that she twinkled as gaily as the chandeliers overhead.

"You are the most breathtaking woman in here, and every man knows it." Franz took the seat to her right as he waved dutifully, acknowledging his gawking, cheering subjects.

"Thank you, darling." Sisi smiled, tossing her head back so that her crystal-laden curls caught the glimmer of candlelight overhead. She was aware that the entire audience watched. The show about to unfold onstage was of little interest to them when compared to the rare glimpses of the emperor and his wife, and so Sisi made sure to keep the smile affixed to her lips until after the candlelight was dimmed.

The orchestra united in its first notes and the curtain opened on *Don Giovanni* — the scene set in the gardens of the wealthy Don Pedro, Il Commendatore. Sisi gasped in delight, amazed at how the backdrop truly looked like shrubs and flower-lined paths. "The skill of these artists," she whispered to Franz, who sat beside her quietly, his face wearing the stern mask it always assumed in public.

Sisi's favorite melody came in the first act; the duet sung by the despicable Don Giovanni and the unsuspecting Zerlina. Sisi pitied Zerlina, the innocent maiden set to wed another man but somehow seduced by the lecherous don. As he sang to Zerlina, *"Là ci darem la mano"* ("Entwine your hand with mine"), Sisi felt the overwhelming urge to cry out to the young girl, warning her not to fall for this man's honey-laced words of ruination.

Sisi applauded louder than anyone when divine justice took its vengeance on Don Giovanni at the finale, with the spirit of one of his many victims, Il Commendatore, rising from death to drag the don down into the fiery inferno.

"Bravo!" Sisi hollered, thrilled that, in the end, evil had been vanquished. She hoped that Zerlina and Masetto would be able to live their lives together, clear of the unwelcome meddling of Don Giovanni.

"Ready to go, Elisa?" Franz offered his arm. She was not ready to go; she could have sat there for hours more, absorbing the rich melodies and the heart-rending plot twists. But they were to leave first, and the entire audience would remain in their seats until the imperial pair had exited, so she smiled one final time over the edge of the banister and rose to exit the box.

"Let's take the public exit," Franz suggested, extending his arm to her. "They are all salivating to see you. Might as well give them a glimpse of what they came for." Franz winked, and, arms linked, they walked toward the broad, curving staircase that intersected the main hall of the opera house.

"Did you enjoy it?" Franz asked her as imperial guards fanned out before them, lining the steps as the royal pair approached.

"Oh, I loved it, Franz," Sisi gushed. "I could see the opera every night if we had the time. Didn't you think it was incredibly moving?"

Franz cocked his head. "It was . . . impressive, I suppose. Though I have to admit, I find opera a bit . . ."

"What?"

"What is the right word? Tedious? It's all so very dramatic."

Sisi smiled, turning a sidelong glance at her husband. "Come now, Franz. I know that you can be romantic."

Franz turned to look at her. "Only you bring that out of me. But given the choice, I'd rather spend the evening reading a military report than sitting through hours of singing. Opera does not appeal to me."

"Please, Your Majesty, wait a moment?" As they approached the ground level, Sisi turned to see a tall, dark-haired man in a long-coat tuxedo hurrying down the stairs behind them. From just these few words Sisi presumed his accent to be foreign, but she could not have guessed its origin.

Beside her, Franz's frame stiffened. "It's all right, let him approach." Franz nodded to his imperial guards, two of whom had stepped in front of the approaching man. "Hello, Count Andrássy." Franz dropped Sisi's arm, his voice suddenly unnaturally quiet as this man bowed before him. *Andrássy.* Sisi knew the name, but from where?

"Your Majesty." The man stayed one step above Franz, so that he looked down upon the emperor as he rose from his bow. "I was delighted to hear you would be attending the opera tonight. I knew I had to come."

"Pleasure to see you, Count." Though

431

Franz's tone said otherwise.

"And you, Your Majesty, Empress Elisabeth." The man turned inquisitive eyes on Sisi now, holding her gaze for just a moment too long, before bowing his head. His coloring — dark eyes, thick black hair — was entirely the opposite of Franz's.

"Did you enjoy the show?" Franz asked.

"Very much, Your Majesty." The dark-haired man nodded, his expression affable, bearing none of the sniveling servility Sisi saw so often in the smiles of the Viennese courtiers. "I am a great admirer of Mozart's."

"Mozart is one of the many reasons why we Austrians feel such national pride," Franz said.

"Indeed. I especially enjoy his Italian librettos," this man, Andrássy, replied.

Franz did not respond to this, but Sisi guessed that he noticed the barb.

"Your Majesty, I have a message from Budapest."

At this, Sisi felt her husband brace beside her. *Andrássy.* Sisi knew the name now. This was the Hungarian count she'd heard Franz and his advisors criticize. Sophie, especially, had always spoken his name with such contempt. Sisi looked at him now with greater interest, studying him; she'd never before met a political opponent of her husband's, and one so recently returned from exile.

Suddenly, Andrássy's affable confidence,

432

his brazenness in directly approaching them — she saw that it was all an affront to her husband. A lack of respect and submission from a conquered subject. And did he purposely garble his German with such a thick Hungarian accent?

"The Hungarian people wish both of Your Royal Highnesses many congratulations on the birth of your daughter, the Princess Sophie. And we extend our warmest invitation to the whole royal family, hoping that Your Graces can travel to Budapest." Andrássy paused now, swallowing before looking directly into Franz's eyes. Another challenge. "We hope to welcome you to our city of Budapest, and begin discussions whenever you are open to conducting them."

Andrássy did not await a reply, but rather bowed once more and sped back up the stairs, the tails of his tuxedo coat flapping in time with his long steps.

"Insolent. Intolerable." Franz seethed as they exited the opera house and stepped into their carriage for the short ride back to the palace. "The nerve of that man. Coming into *my* opera house, watching *my* artists perform. And then approaching me like that."

"We ought to invite him for a concert of waltzes given by Master Strauss and lose a violin bow down his —"

"Elisabeth, please!" Franz crossed his arms, in no mood for humor. Instead, he stared out the carriage window, his jaw set in a tight line as the horses pulled them down the rain-slicked boulevard. "He invites *me* to Budapest? Why, it's my damned city, I'll go there anytime I want. I'll go there with a conquering army, like I did back in '49, if he needs reminding." Franz, uncharacteristically ruffled, spit out the name now when he said it: "*Andrássy.* Insubordinate traitor. Mother was right — I shouldn't have let him go. I should have hanged him years ago when I had the chance."

Franz was still in a sour mood when they got into bed that night.

"I'm sorry that our night at the opera was ruined." Sisi sat beside him, pulling a comb through her hair, its teeth getting caught on the last few remaining crystals.

"It was fine until I had to be subjected to that filth by Andrássy." Franz looked cross as he sipped from a mug of wine.

"Do you really think that war with the Hungarians is inevitable, Franz?"

"I don't know." Franz creased his brow in a manner that aged him ten years.

"Please, my darling, talk to me," Sisi pleaded, taking her husband's hand in her own. She knew he detested bringing politics and military conversation into his time with his wife, but Sisi longed to know more of the matters that weighed so heavily on her husband's mind.

Franz took a long, slow sip of wine before replacing the mug on the bedside table. Sighing, he looked at Sisi. "We have all this pressure from outside our borders. Prussia is jockeying to usurp our position as the most powerful Germanic state. Friedrich, the Prussian king, is babbling about *unification.*" Franz said the word with disgust. "Talking about uniting the Germanic peoples — in Bohemia, Saxony, even Bavaria — and forming a great power to rival ours."

Sisi lowered her eyes but kept Franz's hand in her own. Her husband, uncharacteristically, continued, and Sisi guessed that he must be very troubled indeed, if he was willing to discuss such matters.

"And then, bolstered by German insubordination, the Italians are now challenging our authority — asserting that they no longer wish to remain under our rule. And France, well, Louis-Napoleon is so unstable that the French are likely to pull us into a war any day now."

Franz paused, reaching once more for his wine. "And Russia . . ." Franz sighed. "Well, Russia was once our closest ally, but the tsar is furious with me. I didn't come to his aid in the Crimea against England and France. And now he despises me. You know what he is saying about me?"

Sisi shook her head. "What?"

Franz's voice was bitter as he answered. "He says that I'm *a man who can't be trusted.*"

Sisi saw now in stark clarity the pressures from which her husband had been shielding her. No wonder he had been so much shorter in his replies, so absent, so quick to become irritable. She took his empty wine mug from his hands and moved toward him, wrapping her arms around him.

"Oh, my poor Franz, my dear husband. The pressures of the world rest on these shoulders." She held on to him.

"Mother tells me not to worry. *We need no one,* that's what she always tells me. But . . ." He sighed again, rubbing his eyebrows slowly with his fingers. "But, you see, I cannot allow those within my borders to challenge me. Not when I face so many threats abroad. We must remain strong internally. A sick man cannot fight another if he himself is not in good health."

"I understand." Sisi nodded, still holding on to him. She thought about Andrássy, about his invitation to visit Budapest. And then she thought back to Possi. Remembered how much the people in the duchy had adored her family. Not because Duke Max was a particularly interested, or even competent, ruler. He was quite the opposite, in fact. Why did they love him? Because he mingled with them. He was approachable. They felt as if he knew them and their troubles.

"Perhaps you should go to Hungary, Franz."

He looked at her now, his lips lilting downward in a frown.

"Think of what Andrássy said." She slid closer to him in bed. "Perhaps you should accept their offer to engage in discussions. Perhaps there is a peaceful resolution possible?"

"Believe me, the last thing I want is to wage war on my own people. War will be avoided if at all possible. But peace might be just a foolish dream."

"Dream no small dreams, for they have no power to move the hearts of men," Sisi answered, quoting Goethe.

"I have no time for poetry, not when I must think of such things."

Sisi sighed, remembering the time when Franz had hurried to find Goethe's book because she had merely mentioned his name. She changed tactics. "Then think of your daughter, our little Sophie. We don't want her growing up in a country at war." Sisi leaned forward and nuzzled into his neck, and she felt his tense shoulders slacken ever so slightly.

Franz turned to her, sliding his head back so that it rested on his pillow. "Yes, let's think of little Sophie. And happy things. Like Bad Ischl." He began to run his fingers through her hair.

"It will be good to get away to Bad Ischl for the summer, won't it, Franz?" Sisi reclined, leaning on her husband's body.

"It will be."

"Imagine riding up into the mountains, like we did two summers ago, when we first met."

"You were such a shy, timid girl, Elisa."

"I was not." She cocked her head, smiling at him playfully.

"Yes, you were. Why, when I asked you to dance at the cotillion, you ran from me in tears."

Sisi couldn't help but smile, remembering that. How overwhelmed she had been by the trappings of the imperial court.

"And now, now look at you."

"What does that mean, Franz?" Sisi propped herself up on her elbows, staring at him.

"Now you argue with me as if I weren't the emperor."

She smirked.

"It's true. You no longer hesitate to speak up."

"Well, I *am* your wife. And the mother to your little girl. I suppose I have earned the right to speak up a bit more, haven't I?"

He reached for a loose curl from where it fell across her brow, wrapping it around his forefinger. "And your hair is darker than it used to be."

"Is it?"

"Indeed," he nodded. "It was golden, back then. Dark blond. Now it's a rich brown. I love it."

"I think little Sophie shall have your hair color, Franz."

"I hope, for her sake, that she inherits everything of yours."

"Speaking of little Sophie, Franz. Do you think there's any chance your mother might be amenable to remaining in Vienna this summer so we can have a few months alone as a family?"

"Elisa!" Franz looked at her, unsure whether she was serious. She met his gaze directly.

"Elisabeth" — Franz sighed — "the suggestion alone would break her heart. You know how attached she is to Sophie."

"So attached that she isn't willing to spare any time away from the girl so that her own mother might hold her?"

"Elisa, I've just laid out the many countries that wish to fight with me. Must I fight with you, too? I beg you, whatever the conflict is with my mother, resolve it. You are both good, reasonable women. I pray, please, stop burdening me with this."

Sisi choked down the words with which she longed to protest. Instead, she forced a tight smile and said, "Good night, Franz."

"Good night, Elisa."

But after several minutes, Franz sat up in

bed. "I can't sleep. Andrássy has me in a foul mood."

Sisi squinted in the darkness, watching him fumble his way out of the covers. "Where will you go?"

"I don't know," Franz said, sliding into his dressing robe, kicking his slippers onto his feet.

"Would you like me to come with you? We could take a walk?"

"No," Franz said, turning back toward the bed, leaning forward to land a quick kiss on her brow. "You sleep."

"Must I? I'll come with you."

He smiled. "No, no. Sleep. Please. That's an order."

But as he left the room, speaking quickly to the footman who waited, always, outside their door, Sisi heard his words. Unmistakable. Franz issuing his most customary, most natural of orders: "Rouse the ministers. Tell them I'm calling a meeting of the council. Oh, and tell my mother I'd like her there as well."

X.

"Then how can it be said I am alone, when
all the world is here to look on me?"
— William Shakespeare's *A Midsummer
Night's Dream,* Sisi's favorite play

CHAPTER TEN

SCHÖNBRUNN SUMMER PALACE, VIENNA
SPRING 1855

They moved shortly after the Easter feast, when Sophie decided that the court would quit the Hofburg Palace for the few warm months before their departure to Bad Ischl. Sisi welcomed the decision, preferring the summer palace with its tall windows, swan-filled ponds, and mazy, flower-strewn gardens to the cold stone walls of the Hofburg.

May waltzed into Vienna with longer days and balmy weather, soft and delicate as the new buds that peeked out on the tree boughs. Master Strauss told anyone who would listen that he was hard at work on a new waltz for the imperial pair. Sisi, relishing the return of pleasant weather, spent as much time as she could out of doors, riding through the sloping hills that held Vienna in a gentle, newly green embrace.

It was a bright morning shortly before their relocation to the summer villa at Bad Ischl.

Sisi sat in her bedroom with Agata, arranging her travel wardrobe.

"It will be several months, so you will need to pack at least sixty pairs of slippers for me. Oh, what a silly rule, wearing a new pair each day," Sisi grumbled, making a note to have Herr Lobkowitz order the shoes. "It was wasteful extravagances such as that which cost our poor cousins in France their heads."

"And gloves, Your Imperial Majesty," Agata said, eyes lowered.

"And gloves, as well." Sisi sighed, looking at the maid. "Another foolish court *custom*. Having to wear those bothersome gloves at every meal. As if dirtying my hands is such a crime."

The maid nodded but did not smile, as she usually would have. "I shall be sure to fetch your gloves, Empress."

"You're awfully quiet today, Agata." Sisi glanced at the maid, handing her a light-yellow gown to pack. "Something on your mind?"

"Majesty." The maid fidgeted, keeping her gaze downward. "I've been hoping to speak with you about something."

"Yes?" Sisi smiled at the maid's uncharacteristic shyness. "You know you can talk to me about anything, Agata."

"I've been wanting to mention it for a while now."

"Then tell me," Sisi coaxed.

The maid stood quietly, fiddling with the trunk buckle and avoiding Sisi's look.

"Come now, Aggie. It's me." Sisi leaned forward and broke protocol, placing a hand on top of her maid's. "No need to be shy."

"I was hoping to tell you about . . . a gentleman."

Suddenly Agata's bashfulness became clear. "I see." Sisi crossed her arms, her head falling to the side. "Go on."

"He's Polish, like me. He works in the palace storerooms."

"And what is this Polish storeroom worker's name?"

"Feliks." Agata's round cheeks plumped into their wide smile as she spoke the name. "His name is Feliks."

"Feliks." Sisi repeated the name. "That's a nice name."

"Feliks has asked me to marry him," Agata blurted out.

"He has?" Sisi felt guilty as soon as she'd said it — the shock in her voice had not been subtle. She'd just never imagined her maid carrying on with a man seriously enough to consider marriage. Come to think of it, she'd never imagined her maid doing much of anything outside of cleaning her rooms and tending to her needs.

This realization made Sisi feel embarrassingly foolish. And how selfish she had grown! Why wouldn't Agata wish to marry? Agata, when not serving in Sisi's suite, was the leading character in her own life. This woman before her had wishes, and hopes, and desires, just like any of the noblewomen in the palace. "Well, that's wonderful, Aggie," Sisi said, sitting up tall. "And would you like to marry Feliks?"

"Aye, Madame." Again, that sheepish grin took hold of Agata's features. "He asked me to dance after the Christmas supper. Since then, I've known he was sweet on me."

"Well, this is joyous news, Agata." Sisi smiled broadly. "I give you my wholehearted blessing — I wish you and Feliks nothing but the best. You will of course both remain at the palace, I hope?"

"Of course, Madame. This is my home."

"Good." Sisi startled her maid by taking her hand once more in her own and placing a kiss on it. "Because I don't know how I'd survive without you. When would you and Feliks like to be married?"

"As soon as it would please Your Majesty to allow it," Agata answered, her apple cheeks flushing involuntarily.

"Well, in that case, we shouldn't keep the love-struck pair waiting. How about when we depart for Bad Ischl in a few weeks, you remain behind? You and Feliks may be married while we are away, and enjoy the summer for yourselves. I shall speak with Herr Lobkowitz to ensure that you are installed in a proper apartment fit for a married couple in this palace."

"Oh, Your Majesty, you are too kind. Thank you!" Agata kissed Sisi's hand. "But, an entire summer . . . away from you? Without work?"

"Consider it my wedding present to you."

"Oh, thank you, Madame. Thank you!"

"There's no need to thank me, Agata. I am just eager to see you happily married — you deserve nothing less."

Agata was still beaming as she turned back to folding Sisi's clothes. "I hope we'll be as happy as you and the emperor are, my lady."

"Indeed," Sisi answered, not sure why the remark caused her heart to lurch, just for a moment, the way it did.

It was a joyous summer for Sisi. Arriving at Bad Ischl after the trying year she'd spent was like opening a window out over a warm afternoon and allowing sunshine to pour in, casting out dust and shadow.

The Kaiservilla felt familiar, even though the complex had been renovated and expanded. She and Franz occupied a large suite of rooms with tall windows, their view that of the Alpine peaks rising up behind a stretch of soft green fields. Away from the multitude of courtiers and without the stringent demands on her time, Sisi was largely free to dictate how she filled the long, sunlit days.

Sisi spent happy mornings walking the

fields with little Sophie on her back, picking wildflowers and packing picnics to be enjoyed along the shores of the Traun River. Though little Sophie was still spending nights in a nursery attached to her grandmother's bedroom, the less formal setting of Bad Ischl allowed Sisi to take her meals with her daughter, and she watched in delight as her daughter evolved each day — sometimes appearing with a new tooth, or a new lock of soft auburn hair, or even forming new sounds that Sisi hoped would soon turn into words.

Each afternoon, while little Sophie napped in the Kaiservilla, Sisi set off to explore the mountains atop Diamant, sometimes with Franz beside her. When they were able to shake the trail of the imperial guards, they sought out shaded coverts in the mountains, where they made love and napped and laughed about the funny new habits and quirks their daughter had displayed that morning at breakfast.

Sisi left Bad Ischl that autumn strong, happy, and pregnant.

"This time it will *certainly* be a boy!" Sophie predicted.

It was a frigid New Year's Day, and Sisi had just returned from mass with the court. Prior to the holy services, Sisi had arranged to have the priest announce to the gathered crowds that they were to pray for their empress, expectant with Franz's second child.

Franz had known, as well as Agata and Countess Marie, but Sophie had been as shocked by the announcement as the rest of the noble congregation. The look on her mother-in-law's face had been precisely what Sisi had hoped to see — already the year was off to a promising start.

"But my dear, why did you keep this news from me for so long?" What Sophie truly meant, Sisi, knew, was *how* had she kept this news from her mother-in-law for so long? How had the archduchess's spies, especially the ever-hovering, always-watching Countess Esterházy, failed to sniff out this most important piece of palace gossip?

It was a feat of which Sisi was truly proud, having concealed her condition for months. She had achieved it with the ingenious help of Agata and Countess Marie.

"There are ways . . ." Marie had suggested, when Sisi had first confided the news to her favorite lady-in-waiting, in addition to her improbable wish that it remain a secret for a while.

"The archduchess will know as soon as you pass your first month without your ordinary cycle. But we could trick her. There are ways."

"What sort of ways, Marie?" Sisi asked, whispering. Paula and Karoline sat in the antechamber and very well might have had their ears pressed to the keyhole. Countess

Esterházy was visiting Sophie for what Sisi referred to as "her daily report." She had only a brief window in which to discuss this with Marie and Agata. "How can it be done?"

"I've heard of people using creative methods. Agata, have you not?" Marie looked at the maid.

"I have, my ladies." Agata nodded. The maid was, herself, brimming with joyfulness lately, perpetually humming in her newly married state.

Marie continued. "There are ways to play tricks on the eye, I hear. Often used so as to convince someone of a bride's maidenhead. But I don't see why we can't do it this time, as well."

It seemed duplicitous and highly risky. But since it afforded her several months in which to celebrate the joyous news with just her husband — months without the prying and prodding of her overbearing mother-in-law — Sisi happily ordered her ladies to enact their plan.

How Marie and Agata had managed it, she had not asked. All Sisi knew was that Countess Esterházy and the maids who changed her bedlinens each morning had reported back for the past few months, as the dutiful spies they were, that the empress was most definitely not carrying Franz's second child.

"Perhaps you don't own as many palace spies as you think you do, *Mother,*" Sisi answered now in the sunny breakfast room following the New Year's Day mass. "Care for more coffee?" Sisi took a slow sip of her warm drink, smiling over the top of her cup.

"Spies? Goodness, child, who do you think I am, the tsarina of Russia? I don't have *spies.*"

"Fine, gossips. Whom you happen to reward with money and favors. Call them whatever you like." Sisi shrugged, smiling at her husband, who sat opposite her.

"You would paint me as a monster." Sophie turned her gaze on her son. "Franz, you let your wife assail your mother like this? When all I've ever done is help you both?"

"Mother, please. Elisabeth, darling." Franz sighed, lifting a soft-boiled egg and depositing it into a small silver eggcup. "We've just come from mass where we prayed for our child. Can we behave in a civil manner?"

"Never mind. I shall endure Elisabeth's abuse, since she is clearly not feeling well." Sophie reached for a roll and sliced herself a glob of butter. "Though I must say, I'm surprised with you as well, Franzi. Why didn't *you* tell your dear Mamma?"

Franz didn't reply, didn't look at either of them as he tapped against the shell of the egg, releasing a rivulet of the bright, runny yolk. His motions were tight, efficient. Perfectly composed.

"Oh, it matters not." Sophie sighed, waving

a hand and the buttered roll in it. "What matters is that you are pregnant, and we shall have a male heir at last."

"At last? Why, we've been married for less than two years. I've conceived immediately both times. My dear lady, patience is a virtue." Sisi sipped her coffee, enjoying this new position of power she suddenly wielded. *She* was the one carrying Franz's child, and he had kept her secret, abiding by her requests, these past few months.

"Oh, you are so argumentative today, Elisabeth." Sophie wrung her hands, throwing a frustrated glance at her son as she finished off the last of her roll and served herself a macaroon. "But never mind, do you think it is a boy?"

"I do." Sisi softened, reaching across the table for her husband's hand. She took it, ignoring the disapproving look that this too-public display of affection solicited from her mother-in-law.

Sophie nodded curtly. "I do, too. I just *know* it this time." How Sophie was so certain, and to what logic she had subscribed, Sisi did not know, but for once, she hoped that her mother-in-law would get what she wanted.

But they were both mistaken. Months later, in the thick midnight hour of July's hottest week, Sisi gave birth to her second daughter. A little girl whom the archduchess promptly swept up into her arms, naming her Princess Gisela, and placing her in the nursery to which she had already laid claim. For someone who had longed for a boy, Sophie certainly seemed delighted at the arrival of yet another little girl, wrapping her in a blanket she herself had stitched and insisting that this granddaughter, like the sister before her, remain with her at all times.

The baby being safely delivered and removed by her cooing grandmother, the doctor had fixed a draft for the exhausted, depleted mother. Too fatigued to protest, Sisi had taken it, slipping into a welcome sleep.

When she awoke the heat had broken. Sisi blinked, noticing absently that a bird sat on her windowsill, trilling a song of puzzling simplicity. "Hello?" She opened her lips to speak, but her mouth cracked with dryness. She blinked again. The sun seeped in, a spear of light slipping through a gap in the gently swaying curtains. Sisi was alone in the room. "Is anybody here?" She blinked again, tugging on the bellpull. And then she remembered: she had delivered a baby. A baby about whom she knew nothing.

"Franz? Franz!" Sisi began to weep, frustrated by the dryness of her throat, by the pain below her abdomen. She didn't understand what had happened — why she felt so weak and why she had awoken alone in this bed in the middle of what appeared to be a clear summer afternoon. When she realized that crying would not bring her baby to her, she attempted to lift herself from her bed. She was successful only as far as collapsing into a kneeling position on the floor. The wood felt hard as her knees smacked the floor.

"Agata? Hello?"

"Your Grace!" Countess Marie swept into the room from the direction of the antechamber. "Majesty, please, you must stay in bed. You are weak still."

Sisi allowed herself to be lifted from the floor and helped back into the bed. Even though it was July, it felt nice when Marie tucked the blankets around her — in just the few moments out of bed, Sisi had caught a chill.

"Where is my husband, Marie? And my baby?"

"Please, Your Majesty, you must rest."

"Marie, please, my baby. Was it . . . ?"

"You delivered a baby girl, Majesty. Wait until you see her, the Imperial Princess is just perfect."

Sisi began to weep.

"She's healthy and strong, just like you soon will be, Your Grace."

Sisi shook her head.

"Don't cry, Majesty. A healthy baby is cause for joy, no matter the gender."

"A girl. Please, Marie, where are they? I must see my baby and my husband."

"The emperor has been called to meetings, Your Majesty. Seems something has come up from Budapest."

"Budapest? The Hungarians?" Sisi's mind raced, dazed by the fact that the world's affairs had continued their forward march as she had slept.

Marie fluffed the pillows behind Sisi's head. "His Majesty only left your suite when the doctor assured us that you were resting comfortably."

Sisi absorbed this news, but didn't feel any less disoriented. "How long have I been sleeping?"

"You've woken a couple of times, though you did not seem to know your surroundings. It's been nearly two days, Empress."

Sisi shook her head, fending off the fogginess that persisted, like stubborn cobwebs. How potent had that sleeping draft been?

"At one point you awoke and asked for your mother and Helene. And Franz. And little Sophie."

"I don't remember that," Sisi said.

"Not to worry, Majesty." Marie rested her palm on Sisi's forehead. "Your body has been through a lot, but you shall be back to full strength in no time. How do you feel now?"

"Cold," Sisi answered. Cold. Alone. Frightened. Angry. She stopped at "cold."

"Yes, Empress. You look pale. I'll alert the doctor that you've awoken, and if he thinks it's all right, I'll have Agata fetch some warm broth for you."

"No, I want to see my baby first." Sisi insisted. Her throat still burned with dryness. "A little girl."

Marie paused, the hesitation apparent on her broad, honest face.

"What is it, Marie?"

"Majesty, I'm afraid your baby . . . the Imperial Princess . . . is not here."

Sisi's heart dropped out of her chest. "What do you mean, not here? But . . . you told me she was healthy."

"Healthy, yes, Majesty." Marie seemed unable to meet Sisi's eyes as she answered. "But the weather has been so hot, and the fever has taken hold of much of the city. The archduchess was fearful that the little princesses might be at risk. She's taken Sophie and Gisela to Laxenburg. Just until we send word that the fever was gone from the capital."

"Gisela?"

"That's the name on which the archduchess and the emperor settled. I'm sorry they didn't wait for you, Madame. I know how you had hoped to name her Helene."

"Never mind that." Sisi shook her head. Why should she be surprised that her mother-in-law had taken the liberty of naming her second daughter, as she had the first? But to leave the palace without Sisi, removing her daughters without her permission? She could hardly believe Sophie's audacity. Sisi's frame began to tremble with fury, compounded by the realization that her babies were out of her reach, and she was completely powerless to fetch them back.

"Franz allowed her to take our babies?"

"I'm afraid the emperor has been so pre-occupied with his council and his envoys, he seemed to think it was rather a good idea."

"How that woman could think it wise to travel with a baby and a newborn . . ."

"She took the wet nurse, and several of the other nurses. And Countess Esterházy."

"So all of those people get to see my baby, and I don't?" Sisi ground her teeth, setting the muscle in her jaw atremble. "That is the final blow. It will end right now."

"Please, Majesty. Just stay in bed." Marie pushed gently against Sisi, stopping her from rising. "I shall go fetch Doctor Seeburger and some of that soup."

"You take this —" Sisi reached for paper and scrawled a quick, biting note — "to my husband right this instant. You tell him to come to me immediately!"

Again Marie's gaze rested on Sisi, a barely perceptible line of — what was that, worry? — knitting her brow. "Madame, I'm not sure if now is the best time to have an audience with the emperor."

"Why not?" Sisi snapped. "You'd have me

wait until tomorrow? When is the best time to berate your husband for allowing your children to be stolen from you in your slumber?"

"You must rest, Majesty, regain some of your color. Perhaps tomorrow might be better for a visit with the emperor."

Irritated, Sisi reached for her small ivory mirror on her dressing table. When she saw the reflection staring back at her, she nearly gasped in horror.

The face into which she stared was pale, almost gray in hue. The eyes, once vibrant and alert, the color of molten honey, now sat deeply in a sunken face, framed by purple rings. Her cheeks appeared like hollow ruts, her cheekbones twice as sharp and prominent as they had been just days ago, and her hair was flat and unkempt. The worst part of all, however, was the frantic, hopeless expression that pulled tight across the haggard features. She had the appearance of a cornered animal — willing to fight, but exhausted and disheartened.

Sisi sighed, her shoulders drooping as tears pooled in her eyes. "You're right, Marie. If Franz sees me like this, he might be inclined to send me to the asylum. I look half mad." Sisi shuddered, placing her mirror back on the bedside table, face down. "Bring me some chicken broth and some wine. And have Agata come in. We must wash my hair."

"Right away, Madame." Marie tugged the blankets so that they formed a tight cocoon around Sisi. Because she could not bear to look once more at the bedroom, empty of her daughter and any sign that the baby even existed, Sisi closed her eyes. Within minutes, she drifted into a merciful sleep.

The sun rose the next day on the heels of a warm breeze that rustled softly through the open windows. After a breakfast of broth and dry toast, Sisi felt achy but strong enough to rise from bed. With the help of Agata and Marie, she dressed and then sent word to Franz, requesting that he meet her for lunch. *"It's a lovely day outside. How about we meet at the Gloriette?"* It was perhaps the most picturesque spot in all of the imperial gardens, a set of stone archways perched atop the hill, overlooking the Neptune fountain and the mazy network of tulip beds below.

She would meet him at lunch appearing chipper and fresh, no matter how she felt. The better way to earn Franz's accord, she had learned, was to charm him, not berate him. He only obeyed a bossy and domineering woman when that woman happened to be his mother, Sisi admitted to herself, her stomach knotted with resentment. Well, if charm was *her* best weapon, then charm him she would.

Sisi selected a light summer gown of pale,

rose-colored brocade. She washed and perfumed her hair, arranging her braids in a
loose coronet that framed her face. Franz's
preferred style. She covered her sunken
cheeks in rouge, and her colorless lips with
painted lard. She splashed a fresh jasmine
scent on her neck and wrists. And she was
certain to wear the gold pendant that Franz
had given her at their first Christmas.

Franz appeared at the table, stepping lightly
up onto the stone path, a pile of oversized
maps and papers tucked under his arm.
"There's the mother of my girls!" He handed
the documents off to the nearest footman and
leaned forward to kiss his wife. "Elisa, my
empress."

"Franz!" She smiled widely, leaning into
the kiss and suppressing the urge to launch a
series of insults at the man who had allowed
her children to be taken from her. The man
whose frame remained so light and agile
through the birth of their children, while hers
felt ruined.

"Good to see you looking well, Elisa."
Franz took the seat beside her, reaching for
her bare hand. She had deliberately kept her
gloves off, flouting Sophie's ridiculous rule.

Franz's eyes traveled now to the low neckline of Sisi's gown, noticing how her breasts,
full from the infuriating ban on nursing,
swelled. He didn't speak for several moments.

"You look . . . very well, Elisa. Very . . .

459

healthy . . . indeed."

"Thank you." Sisi smiled, leaning toward him, allowing him to gape. "I feel as if I slept for days and days."

Franz nodded, his eyes still fixed on her ripe curves. "And when . . . when do you think you shall be able to resume your usual" — he swallowed, stammering — "well, has the doctor told you when you will be ready for . . . back to normal?"

"Soon," she said, smiling as she surmised his thoughts. She looked out over the hillside now, the tidy flower beds intersecting the perfectly groomed grass. The palace in the distance. Turning back to Franz, she cocked an eyebrow. "And I awake to the news that our little daughter was named Gisela?"

"Gisela. Yes." Franz looked up into her eyes now, smiling as he thought of his second daughter. "It's been so hot. Ghastly hot. Fortunately Mother had the wise idea to remove the girls to Laxenburg."

"Yes, I heard that." The hard edge became obvious in Sisi's voice. "I've wanted to speak with you about that, Franz. You must write your mother immediately and tell her that we are all very well back here, and that you want your daughters back. All right, Franz?" She attempted to soften her tone, but even she knew it sounded frantic.

"Let's not be too hasty. Let's just wait and let you get your strength back. The heat might return, and we heard reports that there is fever in the city."

"No, Franz, I cannot wait," she snapped. "I must be allowed to have my own children with me. Can't you understand?"

He stared at her, his eyes unblinking — perhaps growing irritated at his wife's quick displeasure. But just then, Grünne appeared at the edge of the archway.

"Pardon my interruption, Your Majesties."

"Grünne, what is it?" Franz waved his general forward, breaking Sisi's gaze. She scowled, knitting her hands together on the table with a sigh of protest.

"We've received our answer from our envoys in Paris."

"You have the letters?" Franz dropped his fork, eyeing his minister.

"Right here, Your Grace."

"Excellent, take them to the council. Get everyone together; we'll have a meeting as soon as I've finished luncheon."

"Right away. Oh, and we've heard back from Petersburg." Grünne shifted restively from one foot to the other.

"And?"

Grünne shook his head.

"Go on, tell me." Franz barked at his aide in a manner that Sisi had never before seen.

"Our fears have been . . . confirmed."

"What did the Russians say?"

Grünne looked a moment at Sisi, apologizing for conducting the foreign policy discussion in her presence. Then the aide answered: "The tsar is resolved. Russia will pull out of the alliance."

"Can we not convince them . . . is there nothing?"

Grünne shook his head. "We are very much alone, I am afraid."

Franz cradled his head in his hands, and Sisi saw how his auburn hair was traced with thin streaks of silver. Signs of age and worry that she had never before noticed.

"Can't I have one lunch with my wife without the world threatening to collapse around us?"

"I do apologize, Majesty, for the less than preferable news."

"Leave us, Grünne. I shall finish my meal and take this up in an hour. Get the council assembled."

"Yes, Majesty."

"That'll be all, Grünne." Franz turned back to his veal dumpling, a glower now clouding his face.

Grünne bowed and sped from the Gloriette without another word, leaving Franz in a restless silence and Sisi stewing. Was it best to press him now, while he was distracted, or would she just further aggravate him with her domestic petitions? What could her own personal anguish matter when Russia had just declared Austria to be its foe?

But the matter of her two girls being returned to her could not be postponed. For her, a mother, there was nothing more pressing or immediate. Let the Hungarians and the Russians cry for war all they wanted — to her, all that mattered was being reunited with her daughters.

A pair of footmen swapped out the dumplings for plates of breaded perch accompanied by cold potatoes and garden greens. Sisi felt no appetite for the food, but she poked the fish distractedly as she prepared to reinitiate her suit.

"Franz, let's talk of joyful things." She spoke in a chipper tone that belied the gnawing urgency she felt within. "Like our little girls. How I long to see them. Why, I have not even seen Gisela yet. Have not even held my own child. Can you imagine it?"

Franz shrugged his shoulders but kept his gaze fixed on his lunch, which he cut into with quick, efficient movements.

Sisi knew she must continue. "*Gisela.* How did you pick the name? Your mother?"

Franz blinked, dropping the fork onto his plate with a loud clamor. "Elisa, that's how things are done. Why do you always have to be so obstreperous with court protocol? I wish you would just accept how things are done."

Sisi stared at her husband, rendered wordless at the blunt rebuke. At Franz's visible frustration. "Fine." She nodded, reaching across the table to take his hand in hers. "You'll have no quarrel from me. I like the name."

Franz studied her, unsure of whether that was truly the end of it. Sisi offered a conciliatory smile. He picked up his fork once more and began to stab at his fish.

Sisi cleared her throat. "Now, I would just like to see our little Gisela. Franz, I beg you, write your mother and tell her to return with our girls."

"Elisa." Franz lowered his fork again, pushing his plate away. "You just heard a snippet from Grünne. And that's not the half of it. Things are . . . precarious."

"Russia, right? They are angered with us."

Franz snorted, a low, bitter laugh. "They are simply the latest to join the long list."

"Franz, I understand that events have occurred with Hungary as well. I heard that you've been preoccupied with your council, in meetings for days. Before we move on to that topic, please, I need your agreement on our daughters."

"But Elisa, that's precisely it. Things have happened in Hungary and I'm not sure it is the right time to bring our girls back to Vienna."

"What do you mean?"

"I must travel to Budapest."

"Are we at war with Hungary?"

"No. Quite the opposite, actually. We have decided to enter into negotiations."

Sisi sat back, folding her hands before her on the table. She couldn't help but smirk at that. Hadn't she suggested this exact route, months ago, while her mother-in-law had continued to advocate aggressive measures?

"Well" — she leaned her head to the side — "I am glad to hear it."

Franz nodded. "There is so much hostility abroad, with England and France pushing for a treaty with the Russians. And Prussia continues its threats. We are very much alone. Mother might say that we need no one, but we damned well need Hungary. And so I need to shore up Hungarian loyalty from within the empire." Franz paused, as if reluctant to force out his next statement. "I'm going to Budapest to sit down with Andrássy."

Sisi let this news sink in. Budapest. It was to the east, she knew, along the Danube. But she knew little else.

"How long shall you be in Budapest?" She imagined the summer stretching out before her — sweating in Schönbrunn, alone, while Franz was in Budapest. She couldn't stand to be alone with Sophie in Laxenburg, not without Franz there as well.

"Months, maybe more." He reached for her hand across the table. "I shall stay as long as it takes to repair relations with the Hungarians. I cannot have them declare independence. Not now. Not while Prussia and France are threatening us with war."

"Months, maybe more." Sisi repeated his equivocal reply. Her husband was leaving her for an indefinite period of time. As long as he was gone, she stood no chance of regaining control of her daughters.

"I'm sorry, Elisa. It will be difficult, I know. But it will be even more difficult if you oppose me. Please, support me."

The vague outline of an idea began to take shape in her mind — at first as formless and fragile as a cloud. But as she examined it further, the idea gained strength and substance. She reached for it, greedily. Yes, she decided, she had her solution. Now the thought seemed so brilliant that she was hesitant to speak it aloud, for if Franz refused her, she did not know how she would bear it. But it was the only way. "Franz, take us to Hungary with you."

Now it was Franz's turn to be speechless. "Elisa —" he began, but only shook his head. Overhead in the curved ledge of the archway, a bird trilled out a midday carol, mocking the emperor's muteness.

"Franz, hear me." Sisi felt encouraged by the fact that it wasn't a flat refusal. "You say this is a journey to repair a relationship. It sounds as though it will be perfectly cordial. Take us with you. The girls and me."

"Elisa, I'm not sure that you understand the nature of these . . ."

But she had to seize on his surprise, had to further pierce this opening with the merits of her argument. "It will be wonderful for your image, Franz. Just think of it! The young emperor and his wife come to Hungary with their adorable little princesses."

"But you are still weak from the delivery, and besides . . ."

"You will win the Hungarians over. Rather than thinking of you as a foreign conqueror, they will see you for the wonderful family man you are. The girls and I will do everything we can to win them over."

"But it wouldn't be . . ."

"Just think about it, it will be so good for us. And for your image. A family trip to Hungary, imagine it! I've never seen that part of our empire."

"But you are not thinking of the . . ."

"The empress should visit her people, too, should she not?" Sisi flashed what she hoped was her most disarming smile. "Remember how they loved me in Salzburg and Bad Ischl? Perhaps I might win them over in Hungary as well."

"I suppose, but not in this capacity. I don't think —"

"Franz, you know how popular I am with the people. Allow me to help you. Please, I beg you, take us with you." She clung to his hands, her husband looking at her hesitantly.

Eventually, he shook his head. "No, I'm sorry. Not this time."

"Franz, if you ever wanted to do anything to make me happy, do this." The desperation was apparent in her voice now. "Please. I am begging you."

He let out a long, slow exhale, which Sisi did not know how to interpret.

"Oh my love, how do you always manage to do this?" Franz cracked a feeble, acquiescing smile. "You really wish to come to Hungary with me?"

Her heart seemed to momentarily suspend its beat. "If you agree that the girls can come, then yes, I really do, Franz."

"Very well," Franz shrugged. "Hungary it is. To Hungary, with my wild, adventurous wife."

"Thank you!" She leaned forward and landed an assault of kisses on his stunned face.

"Don't thank me, Elisa. The journey will not be a comfortable one."

Sisi smiled. "You forget, Franz, I wasn't always this coddled empress. The thought of a rough journey does nothing to scare me."

"Well, Mother would never consider coming," he said, looking back at his plate, his appetite suddenly returned. "Never mind that she detests the Hungarians, and is angry with me for even going myself."

Sisi suppressed the laugh that threatened to burst forward from her lips. Instead, she leaned forward and put her hand on her husband's. "I imagine I'm going to like the Hungarians quite a bit. When can we leave?"

Sisi swept into her bedroom, panting.

"Empress? Is everything all right?" The maid stiffened to attention.

"Agata, everything is wonderful! We must pack at once. I'm leaving for Budapest."

Sisi was certain that whatever color had drained from her cheeks was back; whatever shine had gone out of her hazel eyes was surely alight once more. The thought of the trip to Budapest had renewed her hope. Just she and Franz and the girls going away together! The family as it was meant to be. And free not only from Sophie, but from Countess Esterházy, and her gossiping ladies, and the rest of the prying, rigid, lonely court.

There was no time to order new clothing — no, she'd have to order her new dresses for herself and the girls in Budapest. Certainly Herr Lobkowitz could find her several talented seamstresses in Budapest. How darling the girls would look, as they sat in the carriage between their mamma and papa, waving out at the crowds of Hungarians as they rolled east along the shimmering Danube. They would win those reluctant Hungarians over, Sisi was certain of it.

To manage and maintain her suite in Budapest's castle she would take Agata. The maid would most likely be less than thrilled to leave her new husband behind, but it would only be a few months, and Sisi needed at least one servant whom she could trust.

Marie would come as well. Not only was Marie a Hungarian by birth, and thus would prove invaluable in translating both Hungarian words and customs, but she had proven very conscientious in overseeing Sisi's correspondence and administrative tasks. Plus the countess was eager to visit her homeland.

Herr Lobkowitz would remain in Vienna to manage Sisi's apartments in her absence — he would oversee her daily correspondences, responding to petitions on her behalf and keeping her abreast of news from court. And hopefully, he would prevent the snooping of bored maids, the fingering of the empress's jewelry box by Karoline or Paula.

Sophie was summoned, and she returned from Laxenburg with a pinched expression on her face. A barely audible line of complaints about a journey to Hungary being "too taxing for the little princesses." About Sisi's unsuitability to have the little girls to herself.

Sisi had been able to hold little Gisela — a sweet little bundle of pink flesh, staring back at her with her mother's honey-colored eyes — when she had first arrived back at Schönbrunn, but Sophie had been miserly with the girls' time since. There was always an excuse, and they were never to be found when Sisi sought them out in Sophie's apartments. The archduchess took them for carriage rides; she brought them to church; she arranged private meetings with the court physician. Imperial guards were perpetually outside Sophie's doors, so that each time Sisi tried to visit, she was sent away before she could knock on the always closed doors. Many times she was told that "the archduchess and the princesses were sleeping," even as she heard little Sophie's giggles within.

The separation was torturous, but somehow palliated by the fact that Sisi knew it would soon be over. It was not worth waging a war, or risking Franz's anger, when she had won the ultimate victory. She and the girls would be departing court with Franz, and that knowledge bolstered Sisi's spirits as the days grew shorter and cooler weather nudged aside the final days of summer.

Sisi found her bedchamber empty when she returned one afternoon, a few weeks later, following a solitary ride through the woods outside of Vienna.

"Agata?" The maid, the mainstay of her royal bedchamber, did not answer when Sisi called. She tugged at the bellpull. "Agata?"

Probably off on a midday dalliance with

471

her husband, Sisi thought with a chuckle. Let the maid have her fun.

The room had been tidied and fragrant flowers, clipped from the imperial hothouses, burst forth from the vases. The bedding was freshly changed, and a lemon-colored tea gown waited atop Sisi's bed, ready for her afternoon wardrobe change. Beside the gown sat a letter.

Sisi reached for the letter, remembering in that moment that she owed a note back to her cousin Ludwig, and another for Helene. Even the mundane tasks of sending and receiving mail somehow seemed so much more enjoyable, now that she knew she would be leaving for Budapest so soon.

Sisi turned her attention back to the note in her hands, unfolding the paper as she studied the unfamiliar penmanship. The note had been delivered unsigned. Intrigued, Sisi began to read.

"The natural destiny of a Queen is to give an heir to the throne. If the Queen is so fortunate as to provide the State with a Crown Prince this should be the end of her ambition — she should by no means meddle with the government of an empire, the care of which is not a task for women . . ."

Sisi's hand trembled as she digested the words, causing the letter to quiver in her grip.

Still, she forced herself to read on:

"If the Queen bears no sons, she is merely a foreigner in the State, and a very dangerous foreigner, too. For as she can never hope to be looked on kindly here, and must always expect to be sent back whence she came, so will she always seek to win the King by other than natural means; she will struggle for position and power by intrigue and the sowing of discord, to the mischief of the King, the nation, and the empire."

Just as Sisi finished this letter, Agata entered the room, humming a merry tune. "Good afternoon, Empress Elisabeth. Didn't realize you had come back so soon."

"Agata." Sisi's voice was unsteady as she turned toward the maid. "Who delivered this letter?"

The maid looked at the paper, confused. "I'm not sure, Madame. I've been in the . . . kitchens." Agata was lying, and this further enraged Sisi.

"You didn't see who placed this letter on my bed?"

"I apologize, Your Majesty, I did not."

"Agata, you are not to leave my room unattended in the middle of the day ever again." Sisi walked toward the maid, still clutching the letter in her grip. "I need you, don't you understand? You are commanded to attend to my rooms at all times, not to go meeting that husband of yours."

"Yes, Majesty."

Sisi noticed the wounded look on Agata's face, and she felt a moment of guilt. But she did not have the time to care. Her mind was racing.

"Where is Herr Lobkowitz?"

"He went to make inquiries about the Hungarian fabrics, like you requested."

"Fetch him, now."

"Right away, Majesty."

Herr Lobkowitz arrived, and he, too, swore ignorance of the letter's delivery and authorship. As did Marie, Paula, Karoline, and Countess Esterházy. But Sisi had already guessed from where it came; there was only one answer.

"I need to see the archduchess." Sisi was stopped outside Sophie's apartments, a guard, stiff in posture and his starched wool uniform, preventing her entry.

"The archduchess is resting at the moment with the imperial princesses, Your Grace." The guard said it with infuriating formality. Did he not know that those little princesses were her two *daughters*?

"I'll wait, then." Sisi glowered at the man, taking a seat in one of the antechamber's creaky wooden chairs.

After several moments the muffled sound of Sophie's voice, doled out in tender, soft coos, slipped through the cracks of the bedroom door. Sisi rose from her chair, her blood roiling. "She is awake."

"Our orders are not to disturb the archduchess and the princesses, Your Grace." The guard's tone was matter-of-fact, his face maintaining a mask of well-conditioned indifference. It only further infuriated Sisi.

"This is ridiculous. I am the empress and I demand to see my mother-in-law."

But the guard stood rooted in place, impassive. "Majesty, I've been ordered that she wishes to have no visitors this afternoon while she sleeps."

"She is awake! I can hear her within the chamber!"

Now the guard shifted his weight, and Sisi sensed his resolve cracking, ever so slightly. He was there to follow orders, not to negotiate a feud in the imperial family.

"Step aside. Please."

"But . . . my orders are my orders, Majesty."

"Well, my orders override hers." Sisi threw her shoulders back, standing to her full height. "The empress counterorders you to disregard the orders of the archduchess. If Sophie punishes you for allowing me in, you shall have an immediate replacement post at my chambers. Or better yet, the emperor's. Now let me pass." Sisi did not wait for the guard's agreement, but rather slid past him and opened the door.

The scene she walked into was enough to cause her knees to crumble beneath her. Sophie was not sleeping. Neither were the girls. The baby, dressed in a crisp white gown, had been sprawled out on a soft pink blanket on the floor. Little Sophie sat beside her sister, playing with a baby doll, while the archduchess reclined, instructing little Sophie on the best way to brush the baby doll's blond hair. It was a tender moment, a beautiful moment, but Sisi should have been in it — it was *she* who should have been playing the role of mother.

The pain Sisi felt only solidified her resolve, so that any deference she might have displayed to her mother-in-law now hardened into a bitter iron in her gut. From the corner of the room, Sophie's small dog looked up from his plush pillow, growling as Sisi approached.

"Sophie, please have the nurse remove my girls. They are to be taken to my apartment."

"Elisabeth! This is a surprise." Sophie looked up from the floor, struggling to hoist her thickening midsection to a seated position. "I ordered that no visitors were to be admitted."

"Mamma!" Little Sophie smiled up at Sisi, reaching her pudgy hands forward.

"Hello, my darling." Sisi reached down and lifted the little girl, planting two long kisses on each round cheek.

"My baby." Little Sophie held forth her doll, proud.

"She is a lovely baby, Sophie," Sisi answered, brushing an auburn curl behind her daughter's ear.

Sisi wept inwardly as she handed the toddler to the nurse. "Please take her out while I speak with the archduchess."

"No!" little Sophie protested, trying to wriggle free from the nurse. "Grandmamma, come with me." Little Sophie threw Sisi a wounded look, stunned by her mother's betrayal, before reaching for her grandmother. The evidence of the little girl's preference stung Sisi like an arrow.

"I shall be right there, my little pet." Sophie rose from the floor, allowing a second nurse to remove Gisela as well. When the two women were left alone, Sophie allowed the feigned smile to slip from her face. "Well, this is something new, Elisabeth — do you think it is appropriate to burst into my apartments and start ordering my servants around?"

"They are all Franz's servants, I believe."

"You've upset the children. What is it, Elisabeth?" Sophie stood just inches from her now, her light eyes meeting Sisi's furious stare in an expression of cool defiance.

"Would you please explain this, Sophie?" Sisi raised the letter in her hand.

Sophie stood, unfazed, as she stared at the

paper in Sisi's hand. "I have no idea who wrote that letter, Elisabeth."

"I didn't tell you it was a letter."

Sophie looked up, her eyes betraying a fleeting hint of fear, but she did not speak.

"I suspect that you know precisely what it is, Sophie. And that you wrote it."

"Believe whatever you want." Sophie turned and walked toward a large rosewood desk, for which she pulled a key from her skirt pocket. "I learned a long time ago not to waste my breath trying to sway you. You are as wild and obstinate as a mule. Just like your father always was."

Sisi followed her mother-in-law toward the desk, teeth clenched as she fought to keep her voice composed. "Sophie, how dare you threaten me with a letter of this nature?"

Sophie unlocked and reached into a desk drawer to retrieve a pair of spectacles, which she now slid onto her nose. "May I?" Sophie pointed toward the letter.

Sisi placed it into her mother-in-law's thick, ringed fingers. Sophie read the words slowly, as if seeing them for the first time. After several minutes, she lowered the page.

"As I said, I did not pen this note. But nothing in it is threatening, unless you see the truth as threatening."

"It threatens to exile me from court if I discuss foreign policy with my husband."

"There are people in this court, Elisabeth,

who find it highly inappropriate that you are attempting to meddle in the relations with Hungary. That you have demanded that you be allowed to join him in Budapest."

"Doesn't the emperor dictate, Sophie? Isn't that . . . *custom*?"

"Of course, but don't think for a moment that I . . . that people . . . don't see how you attempt to sway him with —"

"Then, as long as my husband approves of my joining him, I care not what anyone thinks. You have no right to threaten me like this. How do you think Franz would feel if he read this?"

"I think Franz wants a son. In fact, I know he does."

This point stung Sisi, because she also knew it to be true.

"That's the only purpose of this note, Elisabeth. Someone thinks it necessary to remind you of your place here. And your purpose is to give Franz sons. Not to go gallivanting off to Hungary to ride horses."

This last point took Sisi by surprise: someone in her room, having overheard her confessions of how eager she was to ride along the Hungarian plains, had reported it back to Sophie. Was *everything* she said reported?

Sisi threw her shoulders back, looking squarely into Sophie's eyes. "I have had two of Franz's children in two years."

"Both girls."

"I'm not barren — a son will come. I cannot be banished because it has yet to happen."

"Worse things have happened to emperor's wives before. You wouldn't be the first to fall out of favor when she fails to deliver on her end of the arrangement."

"I remember hearing that it took you . . . how long was it? Six years to conceive your first child?" Sisi snapped, indignant. The stunned look on Sophie's face filled Sisi with momentary satisfaction.

"Well, this is hardly . . ." Sophie stammered, patting the folds of her skirt as her eyes fell to the floor. And then, after just a moment, she stood up tall, jutting her chin out. "No one in this court questioned my utter determination to have my husband's children. I made it plain that that was my primary purpose. You could benefit from doing the same."

"You would disband the union which Franz and I made before God? The union which has produced your two beloved granddaughters?"

"I will do nothing of the sort if you begin to show that you take seriously the business of having a son. But what I will say is that dashing off to Hungary to ride horses and meddle in discussions with the likes of Andrássy is the last thing you should be thinking about. You should be pregnant and you should stay here and rest."

"Franz and I might be a lot happier, and a lot more likely to produce an heir, if you would stop meddling in our marriage. Did you think about that, Sophie?"

Sophie stammered, her face drained of color. Sisi was certain that the archduchess rarely — if ever — engaged in arguments this impassioned. No one would have dared.

"Don't think for a minute, Elisabeth, that you are irreplaceable. My son might be smitten with you. But there are *plenty* of other young women in this court who would happily do your job. And unlike you, they would not spend their days complaining and quarreling."

This latest point was too absurd, too painful, to warrant a response, and Sisi turned on her heels to leave the room. She felt more relieved than ever to be quitting this court for Budapest.

A state of perpetual pregnancy — that was what Sophie expected? And only boys within her womb, as if Sisi could control that? But a thought gave Sisi momentary pause, and she hovered in the doorway, standing tall with artificial confidence.

"Sophie, shall you be sacking this guard who allowed me into your chamber?"

Sophie stared at her daughter-in-law, considering this question. "Yes," she stammered, after a pause. "Yes, I most certainly shall.

You, man, you're dismissed." Sophie pointed a menacing finger at the guard.

"Fine, come with me. You're rehired," Sisi said, waving her hand. "All right, Sophie, I must go. I must finish packing for Budapest. The girls are going to be so adorable with their papa and me — I can hardly wait for the trip."

XI.

Beside her, Franz looks composed. Even stiff. And yet, Sisi detects the weariness that lurks behind his calm mask. The human frailty that persists, even after all of his years of training and emotional mastery.

For a brief flash, she yearns to remove those coverings from him; to free him of his trappings so that he might once again resemble the man she knew, the man whose hopes were once so interwoven with her own that she had not distinguished between the two distinct threads.

But it is too late for that now. He has made his decisions, she has made hers. She cannot undo the past any more than she can retrace the course she has set for the future. She admits that to herself one final time, sadly, as if wishing him farewell. Wishing a version of herself farewell.

All around them now, the crowd packed into the cathedral jostles and applauds, a frenzied horde vying for a spot close enough to touch them.

"My Queen!"

"My Empress!"

"Long live Sisi!"

"Long live Franz Joseph!"

They love her, she sees, but will they forgive her for what she must do next?

CHAPTER ELEVEN

CASTLE HILL, BUDAPEST, HUNGARY
SPRING 1857

"Sit still, little Sophie." Sisi tried to sound stern, though she couldn't help but chuckle as she looked into the eyes of her auburn-haired little girl — tugging on her skirt and begging to be lifted into her mother's lap.

"Up, Mamma! Up!"

"I am holding Gisela, Sophie, my love. You must stand like a big girl. Here, Mamma will hold your hand."

They had been positioned, the four of them, so that Sisi sat in the center, cradling Gisela while Sophie, just two years old, stood grumpily beside her mother. Franz stood behind Sisi, his hand placed proudly on her shoulder.

"Up! Up, Mamma!" Little Sophie stomped a chubby foot on the floor.

"Only a little bit longer, Sophie, my dear one." Sisi longed more than anything to lift Sophie into her lap and smother her with kisses; it was practically impossible to resist her entreaties. "Herr Kriehuber is almost done with the sketch, is he not?" Sisi glanced at the artist.

"If the little princess might stand still just a bit longer," Herr Kriehuber answered, a smile barely masking his frazzled countenance.

"You mind your elders, Sophie," Franz admonished, and Sisi couldn't help but smile at her husband's failed attempt to sound stern with their daughter. "We want the portrait of our family to turn out well, don't we?"

Sophie grumbled, kicking her thick little foot once more on the floor in protest, but she obeyed. She was, physically, her father's daughter. Ringlets the color of cinnamon, clear blue eyes, and cream-colored skin. Gisela looked more like Sisi, with her chestnut curls and eyes of liquid honey. But it was Sophie who had the fire within; a temperament that had been evident to Sisi from her earliest days, and a temperament for which Franz took no credit.

"I was a timid, scared little thing, always clinging to Mother's skirts. Sophie is all you, Elisa." Franz had made this observation in the early days of their trip, when the two of them had enjoyed the process of getting to know their eldest daughter.

While Sisi adored both of her girls more than she had ever thought imaginable, something about little Sophie had captivated Sisi, while she suspected Gisela to be Franz's special little pet. He had told his wife that he liked to imagine Sisi as a baby when he looked upon Gisela's tiny features and darker curls.

"All right, I have what I need." Herr Kriehuber emerged from behind his easel, clapping his hands with a proud flourish. "Your Imperial Majesties are free to go."

Sisi could have sat like this — encircled by her family, playing the central role of mother — without ever growing restless. She would never have her fill of her little girls: the way Sophie's dimpled little hand felt in hers, the powdery clean scent of Gisela's blemishless skin, the new sounds and facial expressions she was witness to on a daily occasion. This time with her girls had only increased her all-consuming need to be with them, her yearning to breathe in their happy, giggly presence. The thought of returning to Vienna, to Sophie being so dominant in their lives, made Sisi feel ill. And for that reason, she never allowed herself to think of it.

Their trip to Hungary had started later than originally planned. The previous fall, little Sophie had fallen ill with a severe cold and had been too weak to travel. Refusing to leave without her girls, it had been Sisi who had suggested that they remain at the Hofburg for Christmas and the cold winter months, when it was risky to travel with a baby and a newly recovered toddler.

They arrived in Budapest in early spring, riding through town in a glass coach on their way up to the castle on Buda Hill. The crowds swarmed, lining the Danube and jostling to get a look at their empress, whose beauty they had heard of since before her wedding day. When they saw that she wore their national costume, a velvet bodice and wide-laced sleeves, they erupted in cheers.

"That was a brilliant idea, wearing the national costume," Franz said, whispering to her as they both waved at the thick wall of cheering onlookers. Even without a translator, both Franz and Sisi knew that the cries were of a happy sort.

"How long have these people been ordered around by Vienna and yet ignored by Vienna's ruling family? They just want your love and acknowledgment, Franz. Give it to them, and they shall love you."

As they settled into the castle so long shunned by Habsburg rulers, Franz complained. He found it dank, less comfortable than his Viennese palaces with their brocaded walls and gold-gilt splendor. Sisi loved it. In its shabbiness, Budapest's castle reminded her of Possi. She never tired of the view it afforded — an unobstructed look at the shimmering Danube

River, with its newly erected Chain Bridge, and, beyond that, green plains that stretched all the way toward Russia.

The rhythm of life in Budapest agreed with Sisi much more than her tedious days back at court. She and the girls took slow carriage rides along the wide, sycamore-lined boulevards that hugged the Danube, waving to the fishermen and schoolchildren and colorfully dressed Gypsies who gawked at the imperial procession, so long unseen on these Hungarian streets.

They attended mass daily at the nearby Mátyás templom, the Cathedral of St. Matthew, sitting in their imperial box. They used the time after mass as an opportunity to ingratiate themselves with the local populace and clergy.

On clear afternoons when there was a blue sky and a determined sun, Sisi and Sophie would set out on foot, winding their way along Buda Hill until they reached the ancient lookout point of Halaszbastya, the Fisherman's Bastion. It was a mazy, white stone complex that looked to Sisi as if it had been plucked from the pages of one of little Sophie's fairy-tale books. There, amidst the arches, the ornately sculpted walls, and the winding staircases that skirted the riverside hill, they looked down over the Danube and imagined themselves like the heroines of Sophie's books, ready to fight off a coming dragon or evil witch.

"In our case, we don't have to pretend we are princesses." Little Sophie looked up at her mother, her big blue eyes earnest and thoughtful. It was a chilly afternoon in early spring, and the crisp air had drawn to Sophie's soft cheeks a bright, rose-colored glow. "I *am* a princess."

"That's right, you are, my love." Sisi squeezed her daughter ever tighter, watching as the breeze that skipped off the Danube pulled on her loose auburn curls, setting them aflutter.

"And you are the queen. Except you're not an evil queen, Mamma. You're the good queen. Or, the beautiful queen."

"Why, thank you, my dear little one."

The words of her toddler overwhelmed Sisi, making her feel in that instant as though she had been dropped down into this life entirely haphazardly. She was the *queen.* Sometimes, in moments when Sisi allowed herself to slip wholly and unguardedly into carefree happiness — moments such as this one — she forgot that fact. She looked out over the majestic city, aglow in the last glorious light of a spring afternoon, and she found it dizzying to remind herself that this was her husband's empire.

"Where is Grandmamma's bedroom, Mamma?" Sophie tugged on her mother's hand, interrupting her reverie.

"Hmm?" Sisi turned back toward her daughter. "What do you mean, my love?"

"If we are pretending that this is our palace and we live here together, then Grandmamma must be here, too. Where is her bedchamber going to be?"

"Grandmamma stays in her palace in Vienna. In this pretend world we are talking about, it shall be just you, and Gisela, and Mamma and Papa. How does that sound?"

"But I miss Grandmamma."

Sisi hugged her daughter, wishing she could silence her with a kiss.

Sophie wriggled away, one more thought left to express. "I suppose it's all right that Grandmamma isn't here, since it is only pretend. She will be waiting for us once this game is over."

As spring bloomed across the city, the air ripening with the scent of acacia, Sisi saw firsthand why that season in Budapest had been memorialized in poetry, symphonies, and paintings. The mountains and plains along the river seemed to burst with new life, the buds appearing like a patchwork tapestry of green, red, and yellow against the blue of the Danube. Outdoor markets, florists, and fruit vendors popped up like new blooms. And the city's wide, stately boulevards luxuriated under the dappled shade cast by leafy sycamore and chestnut trees. For the first time in years — for the first time since Possi, really — Sisi felt that she was truly free to enjoy the arrival and ripening of spring, in all its wonders.

For Sisi there was no better way to pay homage to the season and the signs of new life than to take off into the world around her on horseback. Franz was not up for riding these days; his hours were jammed with papers from Vienna and plans for a rapprochement with Hungary. But that did not stop Sisi, and, in fact, he encouraged her to ride.

It was during this particular moment, this soft and delicate period between early and late spring, a moment as fragile as the new buds and the newly warm sunlight, that Sisi told her husband that she was the happiest she had been since their wedding day. It was the truth.

She was enamored of her daughters, and she finally felt that they returned that same affection to her. She and her husband had enjoyed a reawakening of intimacy as invigorating to Sisi as the May sunshine. Franz had seemed somehow depleted when they arrived in Budapest, disarmed by his status — however unofficial as it was — as visitor and outsider in this land. A severe cold and the discomforts of the journey had seemed to humble him, while the instant love and support of the Hungarian people for his wife had only elevated her high spirits. They seemed to know, implicitly, that she felt like an outsider at a court full of Austrians. That she, like them, was foreign; she would never be a true Habsburg.

Word had spread in the cafés and restaurants that the empress favored her Hungarian lady's maid above all others, that she had brought only Marie Festetics on the journey. They knew of the empress's love for riding on Hungary's plains; they heard of her fascination with Hungarian poetry and history; they smiled as she fumbled and struggled her way through the Hungarian language in public. And, perhaps best of all, they had caught whiffs — whispers and rumors, reports that seeped out of Vienna — of the discord that existed between their empress and their emperor's mother. Sophie, the harshest critic of Hungarians during and since the punishing years of '48–'49, and self-professed opponent to any expansion of Hungarian rights, was not welcome in Budapest. Which meant that Sisi, as her opponent at court, instantly was.

The way the Hungarian people embraced Sisi prompted Franz to look on his wife with a newfound admiration; she became his most important friend and ally. Sisi saw this shift in his behavior, however minor it may have appeared to others, as a miraculous gesture of marital commitment — a gesture that she had craved ever since their earliest days together. He saw her, and needed her. She was finally relevant.

Franz and Sisi became inseparable, close like they had not yet been in their marriage. No longer was Sisi forced to go entire days without seeing a trace of her husband. In Budapest, away from the ceaseless demands of the court and courtiers, they took all their meals together. The girls joined them. They discussed the politics of Hungary together, and Franz, after the period of distance required by two close pregnancies, returned to their marital bed. Sisi enjoyed coupling with her husband once more, not because it brought her any particular pleasure — she still did not understand how to make the act more satisfying for herself — but because it brought him close to her in the most intimate of ways.

Afterward, when they were still, he would lie beside her, his face just inches from hers on the pillow, and she'd enjoy the midnight companionship and conversation that she had cherished in the earliest days of their marriage. It seemed as though the physical distance they had put between themselves and his mother had allowed Franz to put the archduchess out of his mind as well — to focus on his wife as the most important woman in his life. At night, when they shared a bed, he was hers once more; he was open to her loving him and craving closeness. He responded in kind.

Perhaps it was all the time they were suddenly spending with their own children, but, at night, while the rest of the castle slept, Sisi and Franz would share stories of their own childhoods. Childhoods which, when compared, could not have been less similar. Sisi would tell Franz of the excursions her father had taken her on into the Bavarian Alps, where they would hike, and fish, and mingle with local farmers and herders. How, in the summer, her cousin Ludwig would come to stay with the family and they would spend the entire summer out of doors, seldom wearing shoes and often going weeks without formal school lessons.

Franz, by contrast, would tell Sisi of his earliest days in the imperial nursery. Of how, at the age of four, he had begun his formal schooling. Franz spoke of long days, drilling with stern-faced military tutors. Days that began with ice-cold baths before six in the morning. He told her, for the first time, about the void he had felt when the only paternal figure in his life, his grandfather, had died; a void that he had been taught not to dwell upon, for an excessive display of emotion would be very unsuitable. Especially for a future king.

"It's odd, isn't it?" It was the middle of the night in late May. Sisi lay beside Franz, staring at him through the glow of the last candle.

"What is?" Franz appeared drowsy now, and his lips pulled apart in a yawn.

"How different our childhoods were. Though they are sisters, my mother and your mother are nothing alike."

"Well" — Franz thought about this — "they've lived such different lives. They've been apart since they were young girls."

"Yes. But how is it that my mother encouraged us to read romantic fairy tales, and run about outside?" Sisi paused, missing her mother like an ache in her bones. "While your mother, she taught you such stoicism."

"Well, Mother became a Habsburg." Franz shifted restlessly, punching his pillow to fluff the downy feathers inside it. "She knew what was expected of her."

Sisi noticed that whenever she tried to bring up the topic of his mother, Franz quickly changed the course of the conversation, a defensive tone tingeing his words.

"I suppose." Sisi sighed. Frustrated as she was by her husband's unwillingness to address this one particular topic, she was not willing to argue. Not when they had been so happy recently. She changed subjects: "Franz, I've decided something. I'm very poor with languages, but I am going to try very hard to master Hungarian."

"Is that right?" Franz turned toward her now, surprised. "Why? You have the imperial translators at your disposal."

"Yes, I know. But I'd like to be able to speak directly to the people. In their own tongue. And it's such a beautiful language — I can have Marie teach me."

"Imagine that, a Habsburg empress speaking to the Hungarians in their own tongue. It would certainly be a first." Franz's tone had softened, and his sleepy eyes beheld her now with a glow of affection. "They shall love you even more than they already do. And I shall love you even more for making me look so good."

"If I *do* learn Hungarian, can we stay here forever?" Sisi asked, a playful smile tugging on the corners of her lips.

"Forever? You would stay here, in this dark, dingy castle rather than return to our monstrously large and lavish Austrian palaces?" Franz kissed her lips, sliding his body closer to hers under the covers.

"It's just that we are so happy here in Hungary. The whole family, together."

"You are happy, aren't you? Hungary suits you, I can tell." He threaded a finger through one of her loose waves, tugging it gently. "I love seeing you this happy, Elisa."

"Of course I'm happy. I have everything I could ever want. I have you. I have my little girls with me every day. I am free here. My days are my own. In Budapest I don't feel chained by the rigidity . . . the *customs* . . .

497

the rules that dictate life in Vienna." She sighed. "I am blissfully happy and I don't wish to leave." Her brow creased at the thought and she recoiled from his kisses.

"Now, now, Elisa. Let's not think of such troublesome things, my sweet, restless little wife. We are together with our daughters now, aren't we? And I love you."

"I love you, too, Franz." She sighed, allowing him to kiss her again. He was right, for now. They were together, for now, and so she held on to the days in Budapest with greedy protectiveness.

"Van két kislány."

"Which means?"

"I have two little girls."

"Well done, Empress. But you can improve your accent — remember that the emphasis is always on the first syllable."

"Van két KIS-lány."

"Precisely!" Marie clapped.

Sisi was in the middle of a Hungarian lesson when the invitation arrived, a large, ecru envelope delivered by a gloved footman. The cursive lettering was long and elegant, a fine hand, but the note was entirely in Hungarian.

"Well, I may be practicing Hungarian, but I'm nowhere near ready to read this." Sisi handed the paper to Marie. "Can you please translate this?"

Marie took the card in her hand and studied it, her eyes immediately widening. "Very interesting, Your Grace."

"What? What is it, Marie?"

"This comes from Count Julius Andrássy."

Sisi had heard that name on an almost daily basis since their arrival to Budapest; that name was the primary reason they had come to Hungary. The tall, dark-haired man she had met in the opera house. The trouble-making man who had invited the emperor to Budapest, but who had yet to be in the city and available to meet with Franz.

"Oh, so Andrássy has decided to come back and meet with my husband, at last?" Sisi grumbled, taking the invitation back in her hands and staring at it with new wariness. "Tell me, Marie, what does Andrássy want?"

"Count Andrássy wishes to invite you and the emperor to his home for a night of dinner and dancing, according to this invitation."

"Ha! As if we are old friends."

"Will Your Majesties attend?"

Sisi considered this. "If the emperor thinks it wise, then yes, I suppose we will." Sisi turned the card over in her hand. "Quick, Marie, you must teach me how to say: *Behave yourself, Count Andrássy.*"

The two ladies laughed.

"Come, enough studying for today. How about we finish up here and you join me and my girls for tea up on Buda Hill? It's a lovely

day and I'd like them to see the boats floating down the Danube."

"I don't see why we must attend a dinner
with Andrássy. A meeting, perhaps. But a dinner party seems too jolly."

"Believe me, Elisa, there is nothing jolly
about the look on your face."

Sisi stepped out of the carriage, taking her
husband's arm. The night was balmy and she
paused, adjusting and arranging the lightweight silk of her evening attire. She had
selected one of her favorite gowns, a sapphire
blue, with matching peacock feathers orna-
menting her hair.

The two of them lingered in front of Andrássy's home — a stately limestone mansion
surrounded by sycamore trees. The building
sat on a generous lot in Budapest's upscale
Terézváros neighborhood. She studied the
building as their retinue of imperial guards
formed a column around her and Franz.
Violin music and candlelight spilled out of
the floor-to-ceiling windows of the first floor,
splashing onto the lane where she stood, staring up at the glimpses of the gay dinner party
within.

"I dislike the man before I even know him,"
she said, "I do not appreciate how he's
disrespected you, Franz."

"I know, Elisa. Andrássy is not my favorite
person either. But he's the most powerful

man in Hungary. And if we are to reach a peaceful accord, it will only be because Andrássy gives his blessing. Please, be friendly. This is, after all, why we are here."

"I'm here to be away from Vienna . . . and from your moth—"

"Elisa, please!"

"I am only joking. I shall be friendly. Just for the night." Sisi cocked her head, smiling at her husband as they climbed the front stairs. Two roaring lions, frozen in white stone, welcomed them at the top of the stairway.

"Is there a Madame Andrássy?" Sisi asked, adjusting her loose bun one final time so that the sapphires that dripped from her earlobes were visible. They stood before the broad front door.

"Andrássy is married to the cause of Hungarian autonomy. Other than that, I have never known him to mention a woman."

"He sounds terribly dull." Sisi smirked.

A stiff-backed footman pushed open the door and they entered the grand front hall of the Andrássy mansion. There they stood, waiting to be announced. Sisi's eyes darted around the bright, open layout of the first floor, taking it in. The home seemed to sprout out from a centrally located stairway that wound its way up toward a second floor. Veering off from the front hall were four open doorways. To the front right was a spacious drawing room, where clusters of well-dressed men and women stood in small circles, smoking, laughing, and sipping champagne. The floor-to-ceiling windows were open, bringing in a cool breeze that disrupted the heavy aromatic canopy of cigarettes, pipes, and ladies' perfume. Behind this room was a dark and fully stocked library, where smaller, more intimate conversations were occurring, somewhat removed from the violins that played across the hall, in a large conservatory. And to the front left was a dining room, in which servants buzzed about, coming and going from the hidden kitchen with platters of food that would soon be served.

Andrássy's home was pleasant, tastefully decorated, Sisi had to concede that. It certainly did not have the look of a hapless bachelor. Sisi wondered if Andrássy himself had picked out the patterned carpets, the stately grandfather clock and crystal chandeliers, the portraits of mustached, stern-looking men that clung to the walls.

Just then, she and Franz were announced, a clear-voiced attendant silencing all side conversations. "Their Imperial Majesties, Emperor Franz Joseph of Austria, King of Hungary. And Her Majesty, the Empress Consort, Elisabeth of Austria, Queen of Hungary."

All around the ground floor the violins fell silent and side conversations ceased. Each set of eyes fixed on the emperor and empress, two figures unfamiliar to Budapest society. As was required, the entire crowd bowed. Was Sisi imagining it, or were their bows less enthusiastic — more reluctant — than those in Vienna? After a moment, Sisi could detect the hint of faint whispers, hesitant, like new buds after the freeze of winter.

"Well?" Franz looked to Sisi, mouthing it through tight lips, hoping for some cue. They remained at the front of the entrance hall. "What now?"

Franz was always the host, Sisi realized. People came to him, forming lines to be blessed by his acknowledgment; he did not attend dinner parties as a guest. Sisi smiled, tossing her head so that her sapphires and curls bounced as she whispered into Franz's ear. "Where is Andrássy?"

But that question was answered for her.

"Your Majesties." The tall, dark-haired man, dressed in a tuxedo with a coat and tails, swept toward them. Under a dark mustache, his lips curled up into a smile, but it was not the carefree, warm smile that a host offers a guest he truly loves. It was a polite, courteous smile, and nothing more. He bowed before them. "Forgive my guests. You must feel as if you are actors on the stage." Franz bristled at the remark, his figure stiffening noticeably beside Sisi's; not often was the emperor of Austria compared to as lowly a set as actors. "We Hungarians do not often lay eyes on our Habsburg kings and queens. Good of you to come, Your Majesties. Emperor."

"Andrássy, good to see you." Franz stepped forward, nodding at him.

"And Your Majesty, Empress Elisabeth." Andrássy bowed once more, now fixing his dark eyes on her as he did so, and Sisi caught the scent of cigar smoke on his breath. "It is our honor to have you here."

"Indeed," Franz gently directed his wife forward. "You remember the empress from the opera. In Vienna."

"But how could I ever forget?"

"Count Andrássy, it is a pleasure to see you once more." Sisi looked at him with a half smile, making her best effort at haughty formality. It was something she had seen her mother-in-law do so many times.

"Empress Elisabeth, if I may say so, the legends of your beauty have spread throughout our entire country. And yet, they do not do you justice as I see you this evening."

Sisi averted her eyes, irritated with herself for blushing at the flattery of her husband's rival. She had prepared herself for his rudeness, even antagonism; charm was entirely unexpected.

But Andrássy continued his assault, his dark eyes staring at her intently from what Sisi begrudgingly admitted was a strong, attractive face. "Empress Elisabeth, I hear that you are taking Hungarian lessons. How are you finding our language?"

All side conversations had ceased, so that every eye in the room observed this exchange. Now Sisi had to answer, though she was a bit stunned by Andrássy's preparedness for this meeting. How had he gleaned such palace gossip?

"I love the Hungarian people, and their language, Count Andrássy. It strikes me as beautiful and nuanced, as they themselves are."

"And they love you, Empress." Andrássy nodded, running a white-gloved hand through a head of wavy, dark hair. "Why, you know that all the women in the city are now wearing their hair in plaits? They call it *à la Sisi*."

Sisi lowered her eyes, stumped as to how to respond. Part of her wanted to smile, part of her wanted to stomp her foot at Andrássy's cool and commanding demeanor.

He continued: "As any shrewd monarch knows, the best way to win a people's heart is with the softer forms of power: love, words, bread. Not the sword."

"Of course," Sisi answered, wondering, as she did so, if that was a veiled criticism of her husband. A commentary on his brutal response, espoused by Sophie, to the rebellions of 1848.

Andrássy leaned forward, toward her. "In that case, Empress, let me be the first to say it to you in my mother tongue: *Jó estét, felség.*"

"What does that mean?" Franz interjected.

"It means 'Good evening, Your Majesty,' " Sisi said, translating the Hungarian for her husband.

"Very good, Imperial Majesty." Andrássy smiled, a mischievous glimmer in his dark eyes. Sisi could not tell if he was being earnest or if he was mocking her — using her title that he, no doubt, deeply resented. Hungary wanted no part of the "imperial" affiliation. Either way, he made her very ill at ease and she confirmed her intention to feel no fondness for this man.

Sisi stood up tall, tossing her head back with haughty determination, and answered, *"Jó estét, gróf Andrássy."* Turning to her husband she repeated it in German. "I said: 'Good evening, Count Andrássy.' "

"Bravo!" Again, that mischievous, quizzical smile of Andrássy's. "My only critique, if I may be so presumptuous as to offer one to Your Highness, would be that you speak Hungarian with a German accent."

"And you speak German with a Hungarian accent, Count."

Andrássy erupted in a peal of hearty laughter, the type of laugh that prompts everyone in a room to look in its direction, certain that, of all the conversations being conducted, the one that prompted such a laugh must surely be the most enjoyable.

"Please, Your Majesties, you must have wine." With a flick of Andrássy's wrist, a footman appeared, delivering three flutes, chilled and filled with an amber-colored drink.

"It is *tokaji*, our national sweet wine." Andrássy served them and then held his glass aloft, gently clinking it against Sisi's.

"To your daughters, the Habsburg princesses. I hear they have already won the heart of our nation." It might have been a perfectly good-natured toast. Or, Sisi mused, a subtle jab at Franz — the man who had produced two daughters, but not yet a male heir. But perhaps now she was ascribing unjustified villainy to the man.

"Thank you, Andrássy." Franz nodded, apparently assured of Andrássy's well-meant hospitality.

"And to the beautiful mother whom they resemble." Andrássy turned his dark eyes on Sisi once more.

"Thank you, Count." Sisi was furious with herself for blushing at this. "But actually, my eldest is the image of her father."

"Emperor Franz Joseph, as a little girl? What a thought." Again, Andrássy erupted into laughter. She had set him up for that one, Sisi grumbled to herself, clenching her teeth. Franz, meanwhile, laughed stiffly as he sipped his wine. Several other partygoers had moved closer to Andrássy, angling to overhear the source of his merriment.

Sisi understood then just how formidable Andrássy would be in negotiations. This was not a cantankerous man who advanced his side with threats or cajoling. This was a man who won people over. He led because people loved him, they demanded it of him.

He was younger, too, than Sisi had expected. To be a count with such a position of prominence in his homeland, she had expected to find him gray, wrinkled, or at least a man of middle age. But Andrássy was energetic and youthful. Perhaps even close to her own age. He would be a thorn in Franz's side for a long time, if they could not bring him over to their allegiance.

A gong sounded, announcing the start of dinner, and Andrássy led the small gathering into the dining room. There, a spread of traditional Hungarian fare awaited, heaped on platters and overspilling large porcelain bowls and tureens.

The emperor was seated at the head of the long oak table, with his wife to one side and Andrássy's political ally, a lawyer, at the other.

"My name is Ferenc Deák, Your Majesty," the man said, bowing opposite Sisi. His coloring was dark like Andrássy's, yet his hair was laced with threads of silver and white, speaking to his advanced age. "Welcome to Budapest, Empress Elisabeth."

"A pleasure to meet you, Mr. Deák. I thank you." Sisi put on her sweetest smile and reminded herself to keep it on all throughout dinner — this evening was, after all, about making overtures of goodwill.

It angered her, however, as she took her place, that Andrássy sat at the opposite head of the table, in a position of prominence almost equal to the emperor's. *At least now perhaps we won't have to talk to him throughout dinner,* she thought.

Toasts were made by both Andrássy and Deák. Both men commenced by welcoming the emperor and empress to Budapest before expressing their desires that many years of harmony might exist between the Austrian and Hungarian peoples. Always, Sisi noticed, the Hungarians and the Austrians were referred to as two *separate* and *unique* people — not the same, though both lived under the same Habsburg rule.

The dinner was entirely Hungarian cuisine. They began with *husleves,* a light broth with vegetables and thin noodles. Then came *hortobagyi palacsinta,* thin crepes filled with veal and vegetables, seasoned with Hungary's favorite spice — paprikas, spicy chili peppers. The main entrée, *csirke paprikás,* made special use of these peppers. It was a chicken dish in a creamy, peppery stew over rice.

Each dish came with an accompanying Hungarian wine, and Deák, who proved to be softer spoken than Andrássy, turned out to be a perfectly charming conversationalist. By the time she had finished her meal, Sisi felt warm and full; even a little bit more at ease than she had expected to feel.

From the opposite end of the table Andrássy held up his hand and the music in the room stopped. His guests turned to him.

"How was the food?" He arched his dark eyebrows, glancing down the length of table and resting his gaze on Sisi. She averted her eyes, watching as the diners around the table nodded to Andrássy, offering their approval of the meal.

"Good, good. Glad you enjoyed yourselves." Andrássy smiled, proffering a cigar, which a footman promptly lit for him. "And you, Emperor?"

"Compliments to the chef." Franz nodded at his host, rapping the table with his hands.

"You are too kind, Majesty." Andrássy exhaled a wreath of cigar smoke that encircled his dark, relaxed face.

The table was now silent. Several diners accepted cigars from footmen and the rest of his guests looked to Andrássy for some conversational cue. Andrássy sat, content, puffing his cigar. He had the air of a charismatic professor, Sisi decided, more than a political firebrand. He commanded attention.

Even she, in spite of her own efforts, found herself wondering what he might say next.

"I've heard that Your Majesties are great appreciators of music." Andrássy smiled, his dark eyes once again alert as he stared at Sisi. "Your new court composer, Master Strauss, makes Vienna the envy of the rest of Europe."

"Indeed." Franz rapped on the table once more, his body impossibly wooden and stiff opposite Andrássy's relaxed posture.

"I think that, second to the empress, Master Strauss helps to make you the most envied man in Europe, Emperor Franz Joseph." Andrássy held the cigar ever so loosely between his lips, his mischievous smirk darting back and forth between Sisi and Franz. Sisi fidgeted in her chair, uncomfortable with the directness of the remark, the directness of his gaze.

"I heard the *Elisabethklänge,* Your Majesty's waltz."

"That was a gift, from my husband," Sisi said.

"Beautiful." Andrássy nodded, the sound of his voice hanging in the air, suspended like the cigar smoke. "I can't offer you Master Strauss's equal, I'm afraid." Andrássy paused, puffing again on his cigar. "But how about some music?"

"Splendid idea," Deák said. The crowd concurred, delighted to find out what their host had planned. Andrássy clapped his hands and nodded. "Send them in."

Just then, a small cluster of dancers filed in from the kitchen, a burst of color in their traditional peasant clothing. Red and green and black stitching popped from the women's dresses, their hair pulled back behind jeweled headbands that stood upright atop their heads. The men wore vests with matching stitching. They looked like they could have been brothers, with Andrássy's dark coloring and thick, handlebar mustache. But, unlike Andrássy, these men and women were dressed as if they had just arrived from one of Hungary's remotest peasant villages.

Andrássy nodded his approval as his guests applauded. "We cannot have a Hungarian dinner party without some of our traditional Hungarian folk dancing, can we? Emperor and Empress, please, enjoy."

The crowd at the table looked on as the dozen dancers formed a circle. Andrássy's musicians stood ready, their violins poised to begin as soon as their host gave the order.

"Let's begin with a *Moldova,*" Andrássy said, nodding at the lead violinist.

The music began. It was a fast-paced, upbeat violin melody. The dancers dispersed. Men and women alternated, resting their arms atop one another's shoulders as they began to move as one in a large circle. First clockwise, then counterclockwise, their feet bouncing in time with the Gypsylike melody.

As the song progressed, the pace of the violins picked up, and so did the footwork. Sisi watched the dancers, mesmerized by the whiny, meandering tune and the steps that seemed interwoven with the music.

"Great fun." Franz looked on, tapping a finger to the melody. "What are we watching, Andrássy?"

"One of Hungary's oldest dances," Andrássy explained across the table, yet his eyes were focused on Sisi alone. "From a region in our Transylvanian territories." Andrássy sipped slowly on his wine, turning back to the dancing. What did he mean, *our Transylvanian territories*? Hungary's territories? Or did he acknowledge Habsburg dominion over all of those lands?

But Sisi's thoughts were soon pulled back to the music — to the rosy cheeks and agile feet of the men and women dancing before her. The tempo slowed, and so did the footwork. But not for long. After several verses, the pace picked back up. Gradually the music raced faster and faster until the dancers were kicking so quickly that their feet almost became blurred. Finally, when it seemed as if they could not dance any faster, it stopped. The crowd, as well as the dancers, erupted into uproarious cheers, and Sisi could not help but join in.

"Bravo!" Andrássy applauded. "Fantastic." Turning back to Sisi, he studied her, gauging her reaction over the top of his wineglass.

Now the dancers split into two separate circles, the men forming an outer circle, the women forming a smaller circle that revolved the opposite way inside of them. The music began and several servers appeared at the table, bearing plates of cheese and sweets.

Sisi enjoyed a glass of dessert wine, watching the dancers as they completed their circles. Beside her Franz became entangled in a conversation with Deák about the most scenic sites to visit in Transylvania. Elsewhere along the table, the diners, full and at ease after the wine and food, conducted side conversations or sat, watching the dancers. The evening was a sure success, Sisi thought to herself, turning back to the dancers as they finished the last steps of this song. When the music stopped, she felt a tap on her shoulder.

Andrássy was standing beside her. "If you please, Your Grace, would you do me the pleasure of a dance?" His breath was sweet with dessert wine and cigars, and his sudden proximity put Sisi on edge, her spine stiffening involuntarily.

"A dance?"

Andrássy nodded in reply, his features bright, merry.

"Here? Now?" Sisi recoiled from Andrássy's outstretched hand as if he were offering her poison. Then, realizing her rudeness, she answered, "You are kind, but no. Thank you,

Count Andrássy."

"But it is a tradition here. The host may dance at least once with whomever he pleases."

Sisi stared at him, incredulous, allowing his outstretched hand to remain empty. "I'm sorry, I don't know the steps."

Andrássy smiled broadly, undaunted by her excuse. *"Leap first and the net will appear,"* he replied, quoting Goethe. Sisi was so stunned to hear the words of her favorite writer uttered by her enemy that her mouth fell open, making plain her surprise.

Andrássy persisted. "Please, Majesty, I promise to return you to your husband as good as I found you."

"My darling." Sisi nudged Franz, pleading with her eyes for him to intervene.

"What is it?" Franz reluctantly turned from his exchange with Deák.

"The count has asked me to dance."

"Go on, Elisa. I'll watch." Franz waved his approval, turning back to Deák. Sisi suppressed a scowl; now she was almost as irritated by Franz as she was by Andrássy. But, seeing no other option, and feeling the eyes of the diners fixed on her, watching her, she accepted Andrássy's outstretched hand and allowed him to help her from her chair.

"Play a couples' dance," Andrássy ordered as he led Sisi to the space in the center of the dining room.

"I do not know Hungarian dance steps." Sisi protested again, her voice low. She felt the attention of the entire dinner party focused on her, and loathed Andrássy for entrapping her in this situation, as well as her husband, for pawning her off to conduct his diplomacy.

"My job shall be to lead. If I do my job well, it should not matter whether you've danced these steps a thousand times or have never heard the song." Andrássy took her hand and winked down at her. Goodness, he was arrogant, Sisi fumed.

"Be at ease, Empress." He grinned at her and, again, she felt as though he were mocking her. "Loosen your shoulders."

Sisi obeyed, willing herself to relax, if only to deny him the satisfaction of seeing her made nervous by him. She should not allow this man, or any other man, to have that effect. She was empress, after all, and accustomed to being watched. Accustomed to having to perform.

The music began, a slow, languid melody, and sure enough, Andrássy began to pull her into a rhythmic step. His strong, sure arms guided her as they turned a slow circle around one another. "Feel the music." He looked down at her, his dark eyes smiling. *If you don't feel it, you'll never get it.*

"That is the second time you have quoted Goethe to me in just a few minutes." Sisi looked up at her tall dance partner, surprised. "So, you aren't a critic of every German, then?"

"Hardly." Andrássy looked down at her. "And I'd hate it if I'd given you that impression." He thought for a moment. "I often find that whatever I wish to say, Johann Wolfgang von Goethe has already said it better."

Sisi nodded, not wishing to agree too effusively with him. Even if, inwardly, she did.

"But you're doing it, Empress. You're dancing." Andrássy smiled at her, switching the direction of their circle, threading effortlessly through the other dancers in the group.

Andrássy kept his gaze fixed on her. After several moments, he spoke again. "You move with grace, Your Majesty."

"Thank you, Count."

"You see that our steps are very logical. It is our enthusiasm that makes it all exciting. In Hungarian dancing, you can think of the gentleman as the sun and the lady as the moon. The moon dances with the sun, does she not?"

"That seems a bit tiresome for the moon." Sisi allowed herself to be spun, dropping a hand and revolving her body around Andrássy's.

"Not at all. The moon should feel quite special." Andrássy caught her from her spin, taking her waist in his hand once more. "The man has no dance if the woman is not matching his steps, countering him and balancing him."

Everything felt warm: his breath on her neck, his hands holding her, his body just inches from hers. Even her silky summer dress felt heavy suddenly.

"Without the woman, the man merely seems to be jumping about like a madman. But when a woman joins him, harmonizes with him, well, it becomes a thing of beauty."

Sisi shrugged her shoulders, continuing the circle as she fixed her eyes over Andrássy's shoulders. She'd look at the musicians, at the other dancers, at anything to avoid eye contact at this close proximity.

"If you do not like that analogy, Empress Elisabeth, then allow me to explain it in another way." Andrássy dropped her hand once more, guiding her into a circle around him, speaking in a low tone as her body threaded around his.

"Think of the sun as Austria. The leader. The heart. The moon is Hungary." He released her left hand, giving her a long lead with the right, before he pulled her back in toward him, setting off a series of spins that surprised and delighted her.

"We are perceived, at times, as nothing more than a jewel in the already resplendent crown of the empire. Nothing more than an orbiting body, dependent upon the more central sun. But, if we leave, the empire is nothing." Andrássy pulled her close, their frames touching as they wove their way in between the other couples. It felt strange; Sisi glanced around to ensure that all of the other couples stood this close to one another as well, and surely they did. These Hungarian peasants certainly had found a way to turn a simple country picnic into a scene of excitement, Sisi thought to herself.

Andrássy, meanwhile, was still explaining his theory on Hungarian politics. Or Hungarian dancing. Or was it the moon? Her body felt warm and her mind was fuzzy.

"There would be no dance. There would be no harmony. There would be no beauty. The seemingly less powerful piece suddenly becomes the critical piece, without which nothing can survive. Don't you see? That is how the woman is in any union. She is all-important. Anyone who would underestimate her . . . ah, well, it would be a mistake. A grave mistake indeed."

Sisi nodded, swallowing. Her cheeks were warm as he spun her, and then pulled her back into his arms.

"And that is how I like to think of Hungary in our political union. If it is to be a happy union — something you know very much about — we must be allowed to think of ourselves as an equal partner." His voice was low, his face just inches from hers. She angled her chin, looking up into his eyes now, their darkness lit up by the dancing. Or perhaps it was from his passion for the topic. "Now, of course, you see that I mean absolutely no offense to you, a beautiful woman."

The music stopped, leaving them standing close to one another with no more dancing to do, and Sisi realized for the first time that she had been holding her breath. She inhaled, her chest rising.

"Thank you for the dance, Your Majesty." Andrássy brushed the top of her hand with his lips, a fleeting, noncommittal kiss, and turned on his heels, leaving her standing, alone, in the middle of the dance floor. The surface of her skin, the place where he had rested his lips on her hand, prickled. She was unaccustomed to being touched by anyone but her most intimate family members.

Sisi looked toward the table and noticed that every set of eyes watched her, including Franz's. Straightening her posture, patting down the bright sapphire silk of her skirts, she caught her breath and crossed the room toward the table and her husband. Such a thing would never have happened at a dance in Vienna.

"Well done, Elisa." Franz nodded approvingly, pleased with how well his wife had performed.

"Indeed." Deák looked at her from his seat beside Franz. "You're certain you've never danced in the Hungarian villages before,

Empress Elisabeth?"

Franz nibbled on a piece of goat cheese.

"I'm certain." Sisi averted her eyes, draining her wineglass. "That was my first and last time dancing to Hungarian folk music."

The next song was for the men only, and Deák rose to join Andrássy on the dance floor. The violins struck up their fastest tempo yet, and the male dancers formed a half circle behind Andrássy. Deák soon grew tired and excused himself, taking a seat to catch his breath in a chair nearer to the dancing. Matching the frenetic pace of the music, Andrássy began to dance in the center, the men clapping and hollering behind him, urging him on ever faster. It was a quick series of stomps, leg lifts, and boot-slapping, and Andrássy executed the steps with an agility that impressed Sisi.

The guests at the table, as well as the dancers behind him, were cheering for Andrássy, prompting him to move ever faster. He obeyed, and the musicians now hurried to keep pace with his feet.

Sisi looked on, unable to rend her gaze from his dancing. Andrássy was one with the music now, his dark eyes shining out of his flushed face, smiling broadly. Just when it seemed that his body could not move any faster, his legs forced out one final set of stomps, and the violinists dropped their bows, exhausted. The song stopped, and Andrássy, spent, collapsed into a nearby chair.

"I'm not as young as I once was," he cried out to the room, accepting a glass of cold champagne. He panted, his hair tousled, while his eyes shone with a jolly, carefree glimmer. Sisi noticed that every woman in the room, except her, had seemed to somehow glide toward him, each of them hoping that hers would be the hand he sought for the next dance.

Sisi turned back to Franz, who was making his way through his second cheese plate, not in the least interested in rising to dance or mingle with the guests. Besides, the guests were now all hovered around Andrássy, congratulating him on his skilled dancing and his marvelous dinner party.

Instinctively, without realizing it, Sisi allowed her eyes to drift back toward Andrássy, studying him where he sat. She watched as he tugged at the bow tie around his neck, loosening it. She noted his smile as he watched the dancers and joked with the servants that passed. The carefree manner in which he ran his fingers through his disheveled hair, his chest still heaving from his own dancing.

Andrássy turned in time to catch Sisi studying him, and she held his dark stare, her breath momentarily suspended. His eyes flickered, a quick lightning burst of mischief. Then, aware of herself once more, Sisi sat up, rending her gaze from him. "I'm tired," she muttered, looking once more at Franz. "Can we go?"

Andrássy, Sisi decided, would be more trouble than she and Franz had anticipated.

"Go out, go out," Franz said. It was an afternoon in late May. "At least one of us ought to enjoy this day, and it won't be me. Not with this pile of papers."

The windows of the study were open, and the sunlight splashing into the dark-paneled room made Sisi long to heed his advice.

"I hate to leave you."

"Go, speak with the tradesmen, accept flowers from the children. Your charms are just as integral in shoring up support as any discussion I engage in back here."

"Are you certain?"

"Yes. Go, go. You know I can't work when you are restless in here."

With that assurance, Sisi rose from her chair beside her husband and kissed him farewell. "I'll be back for dinner. If you see the girls, tell them I'll bring them flowers."

Once outdoors, she knew instantly that she had made the right decision to quit Franz's dark study. She loved the colors of Budapest in late spring. Vibrant shades seemed to burst forth from every patch of earth — the unruly gardens, the wildflower-laden meadows along the Danube, the blue expanse of sky that spanned overhead, interrupted only by the tall stone bridges and the spires of Mátyás templom. Even the small bouquets presented to her by the brightly clothed schoolchildren and the smiling, wrinkled Gypsy ladies.

Everything about their sojourn in Budapest had been a success. Sisi hadn't seen Andrássy again — mercifully, she told herself, blushing when she remembered how he had coerced her into that dance — but the dinner with him had advanced discussions between Franz and the Hungarian opposition. The little Austrian princesses had become national heroines, prayed for every week at mass and held up before classrooms of Hungarian schoolchildren as paragons of childish virtue. Warnings such as "Little Princess Sophie *always* obeys her father and mother, and so should you" had become commonplace throughout Budapest.

And the empress had become a sort of deity in the Hungarian imagination: approachable and familiar, yet without the human flaws with which mortals wrestled. The tales Marie repeated to her were so grand and exaggerated that Sisi could not help but laugh when she heard them.

Empress Sisi's hair is so long that it reaches the floor when she walks.

Empress Sisi is the best horsewoman in all of Europe.

Empress Sisi never raises her voice at her

daughters.

Empress Sisi bathes in olive oil and warm milk.

Her likeness was everywhere — the portrait that she had posed for just after her wedding had been re-created and dispersed throughout Hungary. In it she sat, hair pulled back in a loose bun that framed a face with bright hazel eyes and a coquettish, innocent grin. Miniatures of this portrait were sold in the merchants' shops, hung over the hearths of the Hungarian housewives, adorned churches and schools and offices and train stations. By the end of May, Sisi had seen this portrait so often that she sometimes forgot that it was her own likeness when she came across it.

The love and loyalty she had felt emanating from the Hungarian people had restored her, given her a new joy in life, matched only by the renewed love she felt from her husband and daughters. But could it last?

Franz promised her that they would stay happy; that they could somehow bottle up these feelings of love and contentment and bring them back with them to Vienna at the end of their summer's travels. And Sisi, finding the other alternative intolerable, forced herself to believe him. Even though Franz refused to give his word that he would keep his mother away from the girls. Even when he refused to explain *how* Sisi would retain control of their upbringing, she believed him.

She had no choice, for the thought of returning to her previous misery was a burden too heavy for her to carry.

Sisi found the palace dark and eerily quiet when she returned home that afternoon. When the door closed behind her, shutting her into the empty front hall, she felt goose bumps pushing up beneath the skin of her arms, but she could not have said why. Something felt amiss, out of balance.

And then she noticed the curtains. They were drawn to shut out the soft light of the spring evening. As a morning dove cooed, a feeling of dread settled over Sisi's body, sliding deep into her bones like the winter's coldest, dampest chill.

Franz had been in his study, so she walked toward that room, calling out his name. "Franz?" But before she had reached it, she found Marie, her short, round frame doubled over as the lady wept. Sisi went numb.

"What has happened, Marie? Is it Franz? Is it the girls?" Sisi dropped the dozen tulips from her hand. "Speak, now! I beg you, Marie."

Marie's eyes were red-rimmed and puffy when she looked up at her mistress. "Empress."

"Has something happened to Franz?"

Marie shook her head.

Sisi pulled a hand to her breast, barely

managing a whisper. "The girls?"

All Marie offered as a reply was a fresh set of tears. Sisi took off at a sprint down the hallway, running toward the stairs. "Where are they?"

"In the nursery." Marie followed behind, climbing the stairs with her.

Sisi burst into the nursery. The room was dark, the curtains drawn, and the sour odor that greeted her was an instant assault on the senses. She swallowed hard, pushing aside the urge to be sick.

In the corner of the room sat a heap of soiled sheets — the source of the intolerable stench in the room. Agata was on the further of the two beds, huddled over a small shape.

"Sophie." Sisi ran toward the bed. "Agata, have you called for the doctor?"

"Yes, Your Majesty." Agata rose from the bed, making room so that the mother could sit beside her unmoving daughter. Sisi took Sophie's little hand in her own. It was as cold as death.

"Sophie, darling, can you hear me?" Sophie now turned her head slightly, tilting her eyes so that they rested momentarily on her mother before listing, wildly, in the other direction.

"It's as though she doesn't even see me." Sisi pressed her hand to her daughter's cold, clammy cheek.

"The fever is severe," Agata said.

"Where is Gisela?" But Sisi knew, for when she turned, she spotted her baby girl in a similarly supine position, resting in the nearby cradle.

"What has happened, Agata?"

"I don't know, Your Majesty. They woke up in good enough spirits from their naps, but just a bit ago Princess Sophie began to wail something horrible. When we tried to find the problem, the princess only wept more furiously."

Sisi looked at the mess of soiled sheets.

"I put them both to bed, noticing the fever that gripped them. That was when they both began to be sick in their beds." Agata's face was terror-stricken.

"You poor little darling," Sisi pressed her palm once more into Sophie's colorless cheek.

"Empress, they've been very ill all afternoon, making a mess of the sheets even quicker than I have a chance to change them."

"Open these windows, Marie, all of them, now. We can't have them breathing in this sickness. It will make them worse."

Marie obeyed, making quick work of the windows, but the rush of fresh air had little impact on the sickening stench hovering throughout the nursery.

"There, there, my little darling girls. All will be well, Mamma is here." Sisi rose and moved to Gisela's bed, looking on at her baby. "Agata, remove the mess of sheets."

"Yes, Madame."

Just as Agata was picking up the pile of sheets to run them to the laundress, Sophie was sick in her bed once more. Exhausted and uncomfortable and sitting in her own mess, Sophie began to cry.

Sisi rushed back to her elder daughter. "There, there, my darling girl, Mamma will clean you up." Turning toward Agata, Sisi said: "I will change her nightgown, you take these soiled linens away from us. And why isn't the doctor here? And where is Franz? Marie, run and fetch the emperor from his study immediately."

The next few hours passed in an odd ebbing and flowing of time. Everything seemed to take an eternity — the wait for the doctor, the wait for Franz, the wait for the water to heat so that they might bathe the little princesses.

But then, before Sisi knew it, it was dark, and she had not noticed the vanishing of the sun, the descent into nighttime.

"What could it be?" Franz stared at the doctor, his hands clutching Gisela's clammy palms.

The doctor was feeling Sophie's cheeks. "The fever worries me. Princess Gisela's seems to have abated somewhat, but I fear that Princess Sophie's has not."

"What can we do?" Sisi asked, her voice hoarse with exhaustion and worry. They had sat, awake, all night.

"I think that the best thing Your Majesties can do now is take care of yourselves. Have some breakfast, rest. You've been sitting in this sickroom for hours."

"I'm not leaving," Sisi replied, toneless.

The doctor persisted. "I must say that it poses a threat to Your Majesties' health, being exposed to the illness."

"Elisa, we ought to listen to the doctor. We can be of no help to the girls if we ourselves fall sick."

"I don't care! Let me be exposed — if they are sick, then I wish to suffer with them." Sisi climbed into bed beside Sophie, cradling her daughter's cold little body against her own in the hopes that her motherly touch might break the fever.

"My darling girl, my darling girl, Mamma is here." Sisi rocked her daughter back and forth in her arms, ignoring the whispers passing between the doctor and her husband. Ignoring the distressed, fretful gaze of Marie, who was terrified at the thought of her queen being so exposed to the fever. Sisi's eyes tuned out every figure in the room except for Sophie. The hours passed.

"My darling girl, my darling girl, Mamma is here." She repeated the phrase, finding some small comfort in its rhythmic regularity. Night fell once more and Sisi ordered the candles lit, refusing when Marie encouraged her to eat some supper.

Sophie kept her eyes open, occasionally looking toward her mother, but the two glassy blue circles of her eyes did not seem to hold on to anything before her.

"My darling, I am here." Sisi kissed her daughter's damp forehead. Surely Sophie had to feel this, even if she didn't respond.

As day broke once more, Gisela was removed to a separate bedroom, declared by the doctor to be on the mend. Inside the nursery, it seemed that the gulf separating Sophie from her mother widened. The fever was both overpowering and all-consuming — it would not allow its little victim to focus on anything, not on the hugs, the kisses, the tears that splashed her cheeks as they fell from her mother's eyes.

The following night, with Franz sitting on the floor beside them, Sisi noticed that her daughter's breathing had become labored, even slow.

"Doctor! Doctor, come here!" Sisi shifted away for the first time all night, allowing the doctor to get close to Sophie's frame. "What's the matter? Why is she having trouble breathing?"

The doctor's hands roved along Sophie's neck and chest, searching for an explanation.

Sisi watched him, clutching her stomach as she waited to breathe. She would not breathe her next breath until her daughter did the same.

But when the doctor turned to Sisi, she saw instantly that his face had shifted from a tight knot of worry to a resigned, sagging sadness. *No,* Sisi thought, *don't say it. Do not say the words, that is an order.* But her orders would fall powerless against a subject as determined as death itself, that much she knew.

The doctor spoke to his assistant first. "Mark the time. Location is Buda Castle, Budapest, Hungary."

Then he turned to Sisi, her breath still suspended, her heart pumping cold blood through her veins. He shook his head. "I'm sorry, Your Majesty. The Princess is an angel now."

XII.

I loved, I lived,
I wandered throughout the world;
But never reached what I strove for —
I deceived and was deceived.
   — Empress Elisabeth "Sisi" of Austria

CHAPTER TWELVE

SCHÖNBRUNN SUMMER PALACE, VIENNA
SUMMER 1857

"It's as I said from the beginning," Sophie whispered, wiping a tear from her cheek with her embroidered handkerchief. It was, Sisi noted to herself, her body numb, the first time she had ever seen the archduchess weep. "You never should have taken the little princesses on that trip. I knew nothing good would come of it."

They were riding home to Schönbrunn Palace from the Kaisergruft, the imperial crypt beneath Vienna's Capuchin Church, where little Sophie's tiny body had been laid to rest beside her Habsburg predecessors. Given the cramped closeness of the carriage, Sisi could only suspect that she was intended to overhear Sophie's remarks. She had braced for this — knowing that Sophie would act while Sisi was weakest, her confidence as a mother most ravaged. And Sisi, too heartbroken to speak, let alone argue, would let

Sophie win. Because perhaps what Sophie was saying was true; perhaps it *was* her fault that her beloved daughter had died.

If the journey to Hungary had been the bright spot of her marriage and adult life, the return to Vienna was the darkest. Sisi wished, futilely, that the fever would return to finish its work, taking her along with her daughter. But, cruelly, she remained alive. Her body, in some vicious trick of nature, remained strong and healthy. And so all that she could do was stay in her apartments and mimic death. She kept the curtains perpetually drawn against the clear sun of the summer. The outside world only mocked Sisi's misery, thumbed its nose at the broken woman inside with its sights of fresh flowers and fat bumblebees, and busy servants catering to a household that still ran in her absence. As if there was still life to be lived.

Franz stopped trying to console her. She refused to join him and his mother for family meals. She refused to grant entry to the courtiers who queued up outside her apartments, hoping to express their condolences and offer their prayers for the young princess. When Franz suggested that she begin riding again, and even offered to buy her a new horse, she laughed at him. A hollow, hoarse laugh that contained no drop of mirth.

Prayers and notes of grief poured in from across the empire, collecting on her desk, unopened and unanswered. Agata, Marie, and Herr Lobkowitz learned to go about their administrative duties without attempting to extract attention or interest from the empress, who spent most of her time in bed, eyes opened but expressionless. Her only outings were the daily coach rides to the imperial crypt, where, veiled in black, Sisi spent hours weeping before her daughter's tomb. Once her tears were exhausted and her head ached, she'd return, black shades drawn around the coach, to the palace.

The only two visitors to whom Sisi granted entry were the painter from whom she'd commissioned her daughter's portrait and the jeweler who carved the small pendant with the princess's likeness. Sisi wore the charm on a chain around her wrist, kissing it often.

When summer finally melted away and the gray, dank chill of November settled over the city, they relocated to the Hofburg, where the palace walls felt cold to the touch and the brightest rooms only ever appeared partially lit. The days grew short, the nights stretched on, fierce and cold, and Sisi felt, at last, that the world was acknowledging the deep, frozen despair she felt within.

Sisi had little interest in eating, and flatly refused to dress. She protested when Agata tried to light a fire in the bedroom. Food, fine clothing, and the warmth of the fire were garish comforts, unwelcome imposters for a body that did not wish to be comforted. She wanted to be cold, hungry, to feel pain, so that she could momentarily redirect her thoughts to that discomfort and forget the much deeper, much more insidious, bottomless misery that throbbed from inside of her.

Even after the official period of court mourning ended, Franz indulged her behavior as that of an inconsolable mother, ravaged by her grief. He was too busy to argue with her, as the return to Vienna had brought with it fresh troubles from Prussia, Hungary, and now Italy. A stoic and unfailingly rational man, conditioned in the dogmas of forbearance and duty, he didn't know how to pull his wife from the clutches of this darkness. And so, he avoided her entirely.

Sophie seemed to view Sisi's secluded bereavement as a long-overdue acknowledgment of capitulation. Sophie took charge of Gisela without further challenge. She did not seek Sisi out, nor did Sisi mind the complete cessation in communications with her mother-in-law. Sisi's ostracism was a just punishment. At last, Sisi and Sophie agreed.

During this time Sisi was, mercifully, excused from her social responsibilities. Franz attended state dinners, mass services, and balls alone. Perhaps not entirely alone. Sophie no doubt noticed the void left by her daughter-in-law's absence, and Sisi suspected that her mother-in-law had happily taken Franz's empty arm, willingly accompanying him to all events, once again held up as the most powerful woman at court.

New Year's Day mass, however, was an occasion from which the empress could not be excused, even if she did feel as though God himself had turned his back on her. The people had been lined up in the frigid weather for hours, days, hoping to steal a glimpse of the empress as she passed through the brightly painted Swiss Gate. And so on the coldest day of the year, with the sun shining as pale and feeble as her wan, joyless expression, Sisi set off for church with her family — the dutiful wife standing beside her husband to pray for a blessed year for the empire. The crowds roared for her. They threw flowers at her passing sleigh, hollered out their wishes that she would produce an heir this year. She wept quietly as she rode, murmuring the words of Goethe's tragic poem about a shooting star: *"Once I blazed across the sky, leaving trails of flame. I fell to earth, and here I lie. Who'll help me up again?"*

Those who joined them at mass had a close enough view to truly see Sisi and the change that had occurred in her over the past months. They stared. Not how they used to stare, hungry to feast upon the splendor she had radiated. No, they looked now with —

what was that look? Concern? Surprise? Gloating? Perhaps it was a little bit of all of it. She knew that her appearance must certainly elicit strong reactions from the courtiers who had seen her in the full glory of her bridal and maternal bloom. That previously soft frame was now shrunken, her chestnut hair pulled back in a tight bun so that her famous curls were in no way visible. And even as she left the church, bombarded by the hordes who jostled to spot her before she climbed back into the sleigh, her features could not form a smile, her cheeks could not manage a girlish blush.

"What did you pray for in the New Year at mass, my darling?" Franz offered his arm to escort her into the formal dinner at the Hofburg Palace following the church service. His tone was upbeat, even cheerful, which Sisi registered with indifference.

"There is nothing to pray for, nothing to hope for."

Franz leaned closer to hear her speak, so low was her voice.

"One daughter is gone, the other now lost to me, the same as if she were dead."

"Elisa." Franz creased his brow, at a loss for how to respond to a declaration so utterly devoid of hope. He, who had mourned the loss of Sophie and then somehow — inexplicably — rallied. Returned to his life and his duties as emperor.

Sisi realized now how terrible she sounded, and she forced herself to rouse, even just a little bit. "What did you pray for, Franz?" she asked, failing to summon interest in his answer. But at least she had asked.

"I prayed for a Habsburg son, Elisa. As I'm sure the rest of the church did."

"Oh. A son." She repeated his wish, her tone indifferent. Did he really expect her to bear more children? she wondered, slightly amused at the thought. Life, for her, was over; did he not understand that? That included living life, enjoying life, and yes, producing life. The thought of carrying a new baby in her shriveled, wasted body was so absurd that she sputtered out a laugh. Poor Franz! How she pitied him! What a wife he had picked for himself; he, who could have had any girl in Europe!

Sisi managed to make her way through the feast without having to offer much in the way of conversation. To her left sat Marie, to her right Karoline. Marie made a valiant effort to draw the empress into her conversations, though Sisi noticed, with gratitude, that Marie did not ever pose a direct question that would have required Sisi to speak. Sisi looked around, noticing with disinterest the lengths to which the palace staff had gone to decorate the Redoutensaal, the magnificent hall with its glittering golden trim and high, frescoed ceiling. She studied the red flowers and berries in the vase before her plate. She watched the fluttering feathers in Sophie's hairdo. She heard, vaguely, as Franz complained that his lungs hurt, that his cough had not abated. She had not known that he had a cough.

Sisi left her schnitzel untouched on her plate, watching as Sophie devoured her own meal and refilled her champagne glass again and again. Perhaps she should offer her schnitzel to her mother-in-law, Sisi thought. Sophie's appetite was certainly as voracious as ever.

"Majesty?" Marie leaned toward her, speaking in a low tone as Karoline rose to greet her latest suitor, a nobleman from Kraków.

"You look very . . . distracted, Majesty."

"Marie." Sisi placed her hand atop her friend's.

"Are you quite well, Majesty?"

Sisi sputtered out a cheerless laugh — how was she to answer such a question? "Oh, Marie. Sweet, loyal Marie. You are so good to me."

"I'm worried about you," Marie said, as if Sisi had not already read that on her attendant's wide, honest face.

"Hello, Countess Festetics." Franz had risen from his seat at the opposite end of the banquet hall and now sat down beside his wife in the seat vacated by Karoline. He accepted a dessert plate of chocolate pastries covered in *Schlag,* cream, and a bowl of candied fruit.

Sisi shook her head at the footman who attempted to offer her the same sweets. "No, thank you."

"Take it, Elisa," Franz said.

"I have no appetite."

"We will help you eat it." Franz looked up at the confused footman, nodding for him to leave the plates. Sisi looked away, eyes landing on the far side of the room where people had begun to dance. Master Strauss stood before the court musicians, his arms waving energetically, the violin bow in his hand keeping the three-quarter tempo.

"Is there anything you'd like to hear tonight, Empress?" Franz leaned toward Sisi. "Perhaps your waltz?"

Sisi shook her head, and the thread of attempted conversation withered to silence. After several minutes, Franz tried again. "So, Countess Festetics, did you have a nice Christmas?"

"Very nice, Your Majesty, thank you." Marie looked down at her own dessert plate but did not touch the food.

"Good." Franz nodded. "I hope you will tell your family in Hungary that I wish them all a very Happy New Year as well."

"You are kind, Your Majesty. They will be most humbled to hear it. And you, Your Majesty." Marie bowed her head. "May it be full of blessings for you and the empress."

"Thank you, Marie. And are you enjoying the feast?"

Marie looked at Sisi, that uneasy expression once more tugging at her features. "It's lovely, Majesty. Thank you."

"What do you think?" Franz scooped up a dollop of *Schlag,* swallowing a mouthful before speaking again. "Do you think we can get the empress back to health in the New Year?" Franz looked at his wife, studying her as he would a painting he did not quite understand. Sisi wanted to tell him that he had a morsel of chocolate stuck in his mustache.

"I certainly hope we can, Your Grace," Marie said.

"Your Majesty, may I wish you a Happy New Year?"

It was a new voice. Sisi looked up, her attention piqued for the first time all night — who was breaking protocol to speak directly to Franz without having first been addressed?

The woman had appeared over Franz's shoulder. A striking woman. Attractive, if not necessarily beautiful. But she had a curvy figure, a sensual, pouty expression. She was older than Sisi and Franz. Sisi didn't like the way this woman angled her chin down, allowing her gaze to rest squarely on her husband's blue eyes. Or the way she had addressed him so directly, even interrupted him in another conversation.

543

"Who are you?" Sisi asked, looking up into this new face, heavily tinted with rouge and lipstick. Like a theater performer.

Franz put his fork down, wiping his mouth and sitting upright. "Oh, hello, yes. Please, meet the empress." He shifted in his seat, looking toward the woman with an embarrassed expression.

"Whom do I have the pleasure of meeting?" Sisi repeated the question, her features expressionless as her eyes stayed fixed on this newcomer.

"Frau Roll." The woman nodded, bowing to Sisi without waiting for the emperor's introduction. "Pleasure to finally meet you, Empress. I've heard so much about you."

"That's funny, I've heard nothing about you." Sisi cocked her head to one side. "When did you arrive at court, *Frau* Roll?" Sisi accentuated the name to remind all present that this woman did not bear a noble title. She knew she was being unacceptably rude, but she did not care.

"Elisa," Franz whispered into his wife's ear. "Frau Roll is not a member of the court."

"Oh?" Sisi turned to her husband, eyebrows arching. "Then what is she doing here?"

Franz fiddled with his uniform coat, as if suddenly it felt too tight. "Frau Roll just arrived this autumn. She's a very talented actress, currently onstage at the Court Theater."

"Is that so?" Sisi turned her gaze back on this woman — this *very talented actress.* Frau Roll kept her eyes on Franz, her expression childish in her complete lack of self-consciousness.

"I really must take you to see her perform sometime, my darling." Franz tapped his fork against his chocolate cake.

"And where do you live, Frau Roll?"

"Right here, in Vienna." Frau Roll stared directly into Sisi's eyes now, her expression almost defiant. She was indeed pretty, Sisi conceded. Yet everything about her physicality gave the impression that it had been painted on her in slippery, thick oil paint; from the fiery red hair curled around her face, to her heavily rouged cheeks, to the raspberry hue of her snug satin dress. Sensuality seemed to seep like honey from out of her too-tight clothing and too-red hair.

"And are you coming from a performance this evening, Frau Roll? You look as though you still have some of your stage makeup on." Sisi was shocked at how bitter, how hateful she had suddenly become, but again, she did not care.

"No." Frau Roll put a palm to her face, her cheeks flushing an even deeper red. "No, I've just come here for the evening. The emperor was kind enough to invite me to dinner."

"He was, was he?" Sisi cocked her head to her husband.

"I invited all of this season's cast," Franz said, too quickly.

But only Frau Roll feels emboldened to come and address you, directly, in front of your hundreds of noble guests, Sisi thought.

"Never been inside a palace before," the woman said, looking around with her long-lashed eyes.

"Well, the pleasure is all mine, Frau Roll. I shall look forward to taking in one of your performances." Sisi smiled, a forced smile, as she thought to herself: *I can be a talented actress as well.*

"Happy New Year, Majesties." Frau Roll spoke slowly, lazily, her berry-colored lips curling over the word "Majesties." As she walked away, Sisi watched her leave. Frau Roll's tight dress hugged her round bottom, so that each step presented a new opportunity to see the moving shape of her ample flesh.

No one spoke for several minutes after she'd gone.

Eventually, Franz exhaled, and it sounded as though he had been holding his breath. "Elisa, you really were terribly rude to that woman."

"And you were perhaps too polite to her, Franz."

Franz snorted, an exhale of laughter. "She's an *actress.* I am an admirer of her work. And you would be, too, if you ever accompanied me to the theater."

"I think I shall retire."

"Elisabeth," Franz leaned forward now, and when he spoke, his voice was uncharacteristically stern. "You have been . . . *indisposed* . . . for a long time. But just because you have decided to forget your duties does not mean I am allowed to. I do not have that luxury." He put a gloved hand on her arm now, angling her so that she was forced to look at him. "Someone must continue to stand at the helm of all of this. I'd very much appreciate it if you'd return to me."

For reasons Sisi could not have explained, when her husband knocked on her bedroom door that evening, she had allowed him into her bed. Perhaps it was because she had lacked the energy to deny his desire. Or perhaps it was because of his words at dinner — his words about his duty, and hers, too. Or, perhaps it was because she had felt the stirrings of jealousy when she had seen the way Frau Roll had looked at him, reminding Sisi that there were women at court whose intentions were to replace her; if not supplant her entirely as empress, then they would at least settle for the role of Imperial Mistress.

As Franz slipped out of his dressing robe, lowering himself into bed beside her with the stiff and formal demeanor of a soldier, Sisi realized that Franz had waited seven months to ask for something that was his husbandly right. He spent every night now in the small room adjacent to his offices. The last time they had been together as husband and wife had been in Budapest. When they had been happy. When their family had been whole. Then they had made love, tenderly, hungrily, Franz showing more passion to his wife than he ever did during his daylight hours.

He was different now. He did not look her in the eye. Considering he had waited patiently for so many months, she expected him to have some urgency, some hunger, but the act was businesslike and not at all memorable. It was her fault, she knew. How could she arouse passion in anyone when she herself felt numb?

If she had known that allowing Franz into her bed once more would have led to her third pregnancy, Sisi would have rejected him. The thought of making a baby hadn't crossed her mind, so ruined was her body and soul. She was as shocked as anyone else that that was how it happened.

"Yes, Majesty, you must be approximately three months along, if I had to guess. You are definitely with child. Congratulations!"

Sisi was barely able to wait until Doctor Seeburger quit her bedchamber to begin weeping. It was early spring, and the signs of the life developing within her were irrefutable: her dresses needed taking out, her breasts felt tender. There was a new baby inside her, growing with the same patient determination as the new buds forcing their way through the frozen earth, the first fragile harbingers of the coming season.

Countess Esterházy played her role as royal gossip, and soon, all around the palace, faces smiled and called out their congratulations. A new baby was just what she needed to overcome the loss of Princess Sophie, they told her. At last, they whispered, the empress would be herself again. How she had managed to conceive, they did not know, but they were thankful that Franz had been so loyal and patient — he really ought to be applauded, they conceded.

For Sisi, the news triggered an even deeper depression. Babies, for her, meant pain. No, not the physical pain of the actual delivery. That was inconsequential. What Sisi dreaded was the deep, intolerable, heart-rending pain that followed. She would have six more months with her baby, and then, when it left her womb, it would be lost to her forever, pulled into her mother-in-law's grasp and henceforth hidden from sight. Knowing this inevitability, Sisi lacked the strength or the interest for anything other than remaining in bed.

If he was worried, Doctor Seeburger did not show it. Rather, he praised her prudence.

"You are wise not to take any risks. You are not as strong as you were during the first two pregnancies. Rest is the best thing for you, Empress Elisabeth."

Franz came and sat beside her bed once a day, holding her cold hand and chattering good-naturedly. He avoided discussing foreign policy with her, because the news abroad was not good, and he did not wish to trouble her. Italy was threatening to fight for independence, Sisi had heard, but Franz would not discuss it. Instead, he told her of Gisela's progress in her dance lessons, and the plantings that were under way at the grounds of Schönbrunn, ready for the imperial family and the rest of the court to move shortly after Easter. He asked Sisi if she missed riding, if perhaps she would like to buy a new horse after her labor.

Did he not understand that she did not care? It seemed the only two people who understood the earnest desire on the part of the empress to self-destruct were Agata and Marie, the two women who spent the days quietly coaxing her, begging her to eat. When they spoke about the baby as if its arrival would make her happy, Sisi wept, asking them to leave her room.

The earth softened and the trees opened up, bringing color back into the gardens. A week before Easter, Sisi slipped into the fever. She felt it coming on and did not care to fight it. In fact, she found herself welcoming the weakness. Fever and sleep would mean a retreat for Sisi. So she slid, wraithlike, into dreams that were disorienting and confusing. But even the nightmares were less painful than her waking life.

Sisi most often found herself back at Possenhofen, a girl of twelve. That perfect age — that moment in which she'd first tasted independence, old enough to wander free, but not so old that she'd had to pretend she was a woman. She sat, high atop Bummerl. Bummerl galloping through the meadow, Bummerl skirting the shores of Lake Starnberg. Alone, always she was alone. Then she was atop Diamant, climbing the pine-covered hills of Bad Ischl. And then she was on a Hungarian Thoroughbred, racing across the plains of Pest, the loamy scent of the Danube all around her, the wind whipping her face and reddening her cheeks.

And then, unaware whether it was from Bummerl, Diamant, or the Hungarian stallion, she fell. She tumbled from the horse and met the hard, cold ground, a searing pain ripping across her stomach as she landed.

"Mamma!" Sisi cried out. "Mamma!" And she was not certain whether she was little Sophie dying of the fever, or she was herself, falling from a horse. All she knew was that she was terribly frightened, and in need of her mother.

"There, there, Mamma is here." The voice was soothing. A faceless sound filled with familiar warmth.

"Mamma!" Sisi cried out again, longing for that voice once more, and the soft touch to her forehead that accompanied it.

"Mamma is here, Sisi. Mamma is here."

The voice seemed distinct from the dream, as if it were in a world apart from this field, with this heavy horse and the ruddy smell of damp dirt. Sisi opened her eyes, and she noticed that she had slid from one dream to the other, for now she was suddenly in a bed in Possenhofen, her mother sitting beside her. She blinked. No, it was not Possenhofen. It was someplace else. The Hofburg Palace. But her mother was still there beside her. Sisi blinked again.

"Look who finally woke up." Ludovika leaned over the bed, her tired eyes surrounded by a web of fine lines, new since the last time Sisi had stared into those same eyes, years earlier.

"Hello, my darling girl." Ludovika's hand felt warm on Sisi's cheek.

"Mamma?" Sisi tried to sit up, unsure of whether she was still dreaming. "Mamma, is it really you?"

Ludovika smiled now, a weary smile that spoke of both relief and concern. "Your fever seems to have broken, at last."

"You are in Vienna, Mamma?"

"It would appear so." Ludovika laughed now, a familiar, kind laugh. A comfort-bringing sound that ran through Sisi's body like a cleansing rain.

"Mamma!" Sisi reached for her mother, pulling the strong, familiar arms close to hers in an embrace. Tears slid from her eyes. "Mamma!" Sisi held on to her, savoring the touch of her mother's skin, petrified that if she let go, her mother might slip from her and leave her alone again.

"Mamma, I am so happy to see you! I have never been happier to see anyone! When did you come?" Sisi was still crying — tears of delirious relief and joy. She was not alone.

"I came as soon as I received word from Franz. You were very ill, my darling. You almost lost your baby."

That triggered Sisi's memory — she was pregnant. Now Sisi remembered the days leading up to the fever. Her refusal to eat, her inability to sleep.

"You made yourself so sick with worry, my darling. You must take care of yourself." Ludovika was pressing her palm into Sisi's forehead, probing for signs that the fever persisted. "I do believe the fever has broken, but I'd like Doctor Seeburger to see you just the same. Are you up for a visit with the physician? How do you feel, my darling?"

Sisi took her mother's hand in hers. "I feel happy," she answered, realizing that it was the first time in almost a year that she had felt that way.

Under Ludovika's diligent and determined nursing, Sisi slowly regained her strength. She began with broth, spoon-fed by her mother three times a day. Eventually she could stomach bland meals of bread with milk and eggs. And within a week, her appetite had returned and she was taking full meals in her bedroom, eating Viennese beef and chatting happily opposite her mother, whose presence she savored more with each passing day.

At night, her mother slept beside her in the big four-poster bed, so that the familiar face was the first one Sisi saw when she awoke each morning. Sisi's night terrors subsided; it was an unspeakable comfort seeing Ludovika there, being able to reach out and rest a hand on her mother's cheek while she snored, knowing that she, Sisi, was no longer alone.

Summer had bloomed into its full green splendor, and Sisi noticed herself enjoying the warm air, the breeze that glided in through the open windows, the sweet hint of lily and lilac from the gardens below.

"Perhaps you might feel up for a walk today, Sisi? Nothing too strenuous of course, but just to get out of doors a bit?" They were eating lunch in Sisi's sitting room, looking out the opened windows on the midday light of late June.

"Will you come with me?" Sisi asked.

"Of course I shall come with you." Ludovika sipped her beef broth.

Sisi thought about it. Eventually she answered: "All right, then."

"Good." Ludovika nodded.

Sisi turned back to her soup, giving thanks for the hundredth time that day that her Mamma was beside her.

"Sisi?" Ludovika continued, her tone tenuous now. "I've been meaning to ask you something."

"Yes?"

Ludovika paused, taking a fortifying breath. "Do you see Franz — the emperor — often?"

Sisi shook her head, lowering her spoon. "I used to. Before little Sophie . . . well . . . before . . ."

Ludovika reached her hand across the table.

"Before that . . . well, even when things were good between us . . . I barely saw him then. He rises so early, Mamma. He spends his days reading news from around the empire, and getting reports, and meeting with his ministers, and meeting with the generals and the police. When he has free time he often goes hunting. So, usually, I wouldn't see him until dinnertime. Or after that."

Ludovika nodded.

"But then, when little Sophie . . ." Her voice trailed off. "Since then," Sisi resumed speaking, her voice shaky. "I've been awful to him. I'm afraid I told him to stop coming to me."

"And he did? He stopped coming to you?"

"Not at first. At first he tried to reason with me. He was really very patient." Sisi allowed her spoon to slip into her broth, her appetite gone. "But I suppose he finally gave up on me."

"Obviously he did not give up on you entirely." Ludovika pointed at Sisi's growing belly and forced out a quick laugh.

"Oh," Sisi put her hand on the bump. "There was one night."

"And then, since that night, he's been . . . absent?" Ludovika asked, still sipping her soup.

"Yes." Sisi cleared her throat. "I've been so terribly melancholy. I remain in my bed most days. And I wouldn't have allowed him into the bedroom, even if he had wanted to come. But mercifully he did not."

"Sisi —" her mother did not mask her look of concern now — "this can't go on. This retreat from your marriage. You must force yourself to remain dutiful to Franz."

Sisi pushed her bowl away, her elbows landing on the table. "How, Mamma?"

"You simply . . . you force yourself. When he knocks, you welcome him in. Into your bedchamber. Into your bed."

One must always do one's duty. But Sisi

shook her head. The thought was too much. "No."

"Sisi, listen to me," Ludovika said, her tone insistent. "Do you think I *loved* your papa?"

But when Sisi lowered her eyes, unresponsive, Ludovika softened her voice, changing her approach. "Listen to me, Sisi. You are still so young — there can still be many years of children and happiness ahead of you. These are the most important years of your marriage."

"Mother, it's too hard. I tried, really I did. But Sophie is always with us. Even when she's not. And she's had Countess Esterházy in my apartments ever since the earliest days of my marriage."

Ludovika listened silently, her lips pressed together in a tense line.

"And, Mamma," Sisi continued, her throat feeling tight. "Sophie took the girls, and then when little Sophie . . . you know . . . well, since then, she barely lets me lay eyes on Gisela. I fear she is poisoning my own daughter against me with talk of my carelessness and frivolity. Do you know what she said, when I demanded control of my children?"

Ludovika shook her head. "What did she say?"

"That of course I could not have my children to myself. That I myself was only a child — far too reckless and wild to take care of myself, let alone them. As if I couldn't take care of my own babies. I just can't care anymore, Mother."

Hot tears seared their way down Sisi's cheeks, as she stared into her mother's eyes. It was the first time she had spoken these thoughts aloud: "It hurts too much. Loving him, Franz. Loving Gisela. Even this baby. It's better to just remain detached, where I can't be hurt further."

Ludovika no longer seemed hungry, either. They sat at the table, an uneasy silence hovering between them as Sisi wept noiselessly. Eventually, Ludovika propped her elbows on the table and, sighing, answered in a slow, husky voice. "But if you have a boy, everything changes, Sisi. Then you are the mother to the Crown Prince. Do you understand how much power that gives you?"

"Not if Sophie takes him from me."

Ludovika tented her fingers together in front of her face, thoughtful. "How does she take them? Why doesn't Franz protest?"

"I have asked him that so many times that he has grown frustrated — exasperated — with me." Sisi exhaled a short, bitter laugh. "I fought for them at first, I really did. And I fought for Franz, too. And I think, for a while, I had won. Hungary was the happiest time of our lives. But when little Sophie . . . after that, I think Franz truly did believe that Gisela would be in better hands with his mother. And I agreed. I was in no state to be an attentive mother. I gave up. And now it's too late."

"It is *not* too late, Elisabeth." Ludovika pressed a closed fist down on the table, causing Sisi to jump back. "Your daughter is still very much alive, and only a few doors down this hallway. And your husband can be won back. But that rests with you. You must fight, Sisi."

"I feel no strength to fight for them, Mamma. I see no point."

"Let us hope for a boy. A son who will love his mother. That is our best hope. That would change everything."

"I do wish for a boy, Mother, believe me. I can't stand the idea of having any more daughters. It is too sad for me."

A voice sounded from outside, in the hallway. "Let me in *now*!" Just then Sophie entered, unannounced, appearing at the door to the suite.

"Hello, Sophie." Ludovika threw Sisi a furtive look, whispering, "You sit. Finish your lunch. I shall deal with her." With that, Ludovika rose and crossed the room toward her sister, reaching out to give her a dutiful hug. "Good day, Sophie. We are just finishing up our luncheon."

"And I've come to see the little mamma." Sophie looked from her sister to Sisi, her features set in an artificial smile. "Since you two have been avoiding my summonses and notes. Holed up in here, ignoring the entire court. How are you feeling today, Elisabeth?"

"She gets stronger every day," Ludovika answered, stepping between her sister and Sisi.

Sophie shifted, sliding around her sister so that she might look squarely upon her daughter-in-law. "You look much recovered. Mercifully. Franzi and I have been beside ourselves with worry."

"You can visit anytime you like, Sophie," Ludovika said, her hands knit together in front of her waist. "Franz has been devoted, coming to visit often. The door is open, as you know."

"Yes, all right," Sophie said, her glance darting back and forth between her sister and her daughter-in-law. "But Ludie, why have you not been answering my notes? I've been summoning you. The entire court knows that my sister is here, and yet you have failed to appear with me at a single dinner, a luncheon, even as much as a game of cards." Sophie leaned forward now, her eyebrows lifting in two angry crescent moons. "People see how little regard your daughter . . . and now you . . . show to me. They are *whispering.*"

"People always whisper." Ludovika sighed, her head falling to the side.

"Yes, but I won't have it, not when —"

"I did not wish to leave my daughter's side when she was so ill. I thought surely I'd see more of you in my daughter's apartments. I thought you'd be here beside her, comforting her. And bringing little Gisela in to comfort poor Sisi."

"Bring the baby? In *here*?" Sophie lifted her fleshy, ring-covered fingers to her mouth, displaying her horror at the suggestion. "I'd never expose the child to illness."

"She's quite recovered now, Sophie. I think a visit from the child would do Sisi good."

"I've been getting updates on a daily basis from Doctor Seeburger. Of course I've been worried."

Too worried to visit? Sisi wondered. But she did not need to fight with her aunt, not now that her mother was here. Her mother would protect her, and that understanding instantly unwound the tension that had coiled Sisi's nerves at the sight of the archduchess.

"I'm glad to hear that you've been concerned, Sophie. It is your grandchild she carries, after all."

"You think I don't know that?" Sophie's eyes narrowed but she caught herself, pulling her features back into a calm expression. "And how is the child?"

"Franz and Sisi's little baby is doing quite well. We've had a visit with the doctor today to confirm that. You can tell Franz. Have him come visit. Have him bring Gisela, in fact."

"You are now telling me what messages to deliver to my son?" Sophie laughed, a sound with no mirth. "I say, Ludie, you never really did understand what it meant to be a guest in someone's home, did you?"

"I do apologize, Sophie," Ludovika said, pressing her hands together in front of her waist. "I was under the impression that this was the home of the emperor."

"Oh Ludie, let's not argue." Sophie smiled, putting a hand on her sister's shoulder. "Anyway, I'm happy I came to see for myself how well you both are. Now that Sisi . . . Elisabeth . . . is on the mend, will you finally come join me for a dinner? Many in this court would like to meet the mother of the empress. It's poor form for you to be cooped up in here, behaving like a hermit. Behaving like . . ." Sophie's voice trailed off but her eyes, which slid to Sisi's seated figure, finished the thought.

At this, Ludovika threw her shoulders back, standing to her full height so that her long, lean frame now faced her sister's. "Now you listen here, Sophie." Ludovika raised a finger, staring down at her sister. "You may issue orders and summonses to everyone else in this house, but you hold no dominion over me."

"Ludovika, how dare you raise your voice at me. You will stop this or I shall —"

"No, I will not stop until I am finished, Sophie. Now, I have heard quite enough of what you have put my daughter through, and

I am telling you this — it ends right now." Ludovika spoke with none of her usual deference or patience. Her anger was bare and exposed, dripping off her words and as red-hot as her flushed cheeks. Sisi felt even herself trembling; no one, not even Sisi, had ever spoken so forcefully to Sophie.

"I have loved her like a daughter, Ludie."

"A daughter? A daughter, she says." Ludovika turned to Sisi and gasped out a laugh. Sisi did not speak — she simply watched the exchange, transfixed.

"I have given your daughter everything she could ever want, even *after* she has defied me, time and again."

"Sophie, you've done nothing but issue orders to her since the first day she arrived from Possenhofen. Now listen: Elisabeth is pregnant with your son's baby, and I will not allow *anyone* to harass her or punish her." Ludovika, her lip quivering, continued on. "It was not her fault that your son fell in love with her, against your wishes. Nor is it her fault that her daughter fell to a fever. Do you hear me?"

Sophie, who looked cowed before her sister's erect frame, fidgeted, not answering.

"Do you hear me, Sophie? Because if not, I may need to summon Franz in here and have *him* explain. If only your son knew the way his wife has suffered. Blaming herself. Elisabeth almost lost this baby once. If she *does*

lose it . . ." Ludovika crossed herself now.
"Well, that's the future heir of which we
speak. So we *all* must do what we can to
make her comfortable and safe. Do you understand?"

Sophie still did not answer.

"I asked: Do you hear me?" Ludovika
somehow looked even taller than she had a
moment ago.

"I heard you, Ludie. You certainly spoke
loud enough."

"Good. Now, starting today, Gisela will be
permitted to visit with her Mamma. Every
day. We'll have no more of this separation.
It's not good for Elisabeth to miss her daughter so, and it won't be good for the unborn
baby to have a mother who is so sad. Do I
have your agreement on this?"

"You have my agreement," Sophie answered, her mind clearly distracted with trying to make sense of what had just occurred.

"Good. Then that is settled." Ludovika
turned from her sister, sitting back at the
table and calmly scooping herself a spoonful
of broth, as if they had just agreed on the
lovely weather outside. "And besides, I'd like
to visit with my granddaughter."

Whether it was Ludovika's stern warning or
her own superstition that she risked upset-
ting the baby growing inside Sisi's belly,
Archduchess Sophie behaved entirely differ-

ently for the remainder of the pregnancy. She was politely distant — sending gifts and pieces of fruit as she had in the previous two pregnancies. She pulled Countess Esterházy from her post in Sisi's suite, telling the gray-haired woman that the empress wanted privacy with her mother. She advised Franz to visit with his wife, which he did. And she willingly granted the request that Sisi be given time to visit with her daughter each afternoon.

Ludovika was quickly smitten with Gisela. "She looks just like you did, Sisi. Look at these chestnut ringlets. We must order some new bows for them immediately."

"That's what Franz has always said, that Gisela reminds him of me." Sisi shifted in her seat, delicately balancing her growing belly with her squirming toddler.

"She is truly your daughter." Ludovika smiled.

"Down, Mamma," Gisela asked quietly, sliding herself off her mother's lap. Sisi noticed with a sharp tinge of sadness that the little girl never wished to stay in her mother's arms for long.

They were outdoors in the gardens; a picnic sprawled before them on the *tapis d'herbe,* the neatly clipped carpet of lawn. Gisela wobbled tenuously off the blanket, putting one slippered foot on the grass before turning back for reassurance.

"Go on, darling, you may walk. We will watch you." Sisi laughed as her unsteady daughter clutched a bush for support.

"Flowers!" Gisela pointed a chubby finger at the beds of nearby tulips, the parterres brimming with vibrant red and yellow petals.

"Flowers, that's right." Ludovika smiled at her granddaughter, rising from her own seat on the blanket. "Shall we walk over to the flowers and find some butterflies, my little dear?"

Gisela spotted her grandmother walking toward her and ran back to her mother, collapsing into Sisi's skirts. "Where's Grandmamma?" she asked, her little lip quivering.

"Afraid of Grandmother Ludovika?" The duchess leaned her head to the side, staring at the bashful toddler. "She is so shy. In that way she is unlike you, Sisi, you were not shy. A bit dreamy. Sometimes a bit moody. But not timid."

"That's Franz," Sisi said, sweeping her daughter up into her arms for a kiss.

"Indeed." Ludovika agreed. "He was such a timid little boy, I remember that. Of course, Sophie has that effect on most people."

Sisi shifted in her chair. "I wish you had met little Sophie, Mamma. She was so . . ."

"I wish that, too, my love." Ludovika put a hand on her daughter's, noticing how Sisi swallowed hard, fighting the urge to cry.

"But you mustn't let the grief for that lost

child prevent you from loving this perfect little girl in front of you."

"Do you think Gisela will remember her sister? Will she even recall how she loved her?"

Ludovika's eyes softened, reflecting her daughter's sadness. "Perhaps she will. And perhaps she will not. But she will certainly know this baby." Ludovika gestured toward her daughter's belly. "And the siblings to come after."

Sisi sighed, fingering the Sophie-shaped charm she wore on her wrist. After a long silence, she asked: "When does it stop?"

"When does what stop, Sisi?"

"The pain. Of losing a child. When does it stop hurting like this?"

Ludovika's face sagged, her shoulders rising and then falling with a slow exhale. "It never stops."

"But I don't ever remember you suffering like this, Mamma. Even after you lost . . ."

Ludovika winced and Sisi let the question wither, unfinished. Eventually, her mother spoke.

"It becomes something that you learn to live with. You carry it, always, but you learn to enjoy the life that you still have before you. You learn that a beautiful summer day in the garden with your daughter is a gift from God, meant to be enjoyed. And so that's what you do — you enjoy it."

These times, with three generations of Wittelspach women — Ludovika, Sisi, and Gisela — were sweet times for Sisi. Her mother's presence cast a protective cocoon around the three of them, like a holy relic whose presence wards off the haunting presence of dark spirits. Sisi felt at ease, safe in her rooms once more. She found that her days were once again busy: she answered the many letters she had cast aside, she ordered new dresses for after the birth, she walked outside the palace to give alms and attend mass, and she looked forward to the afternoon visits with Gisela.

Franz had started visiting their suite again, and even though he rarely spent the night, Ludovika had moved into a bedchamber adjacent to her daughter's rooms, deeming it appropriate to give her daughter privacy for when the emperor did visit.

Fortunately, though she was installed in a separate suite of rooms, Ludovika was able to hear Sisi's groans on the night in late summer when the labor began.

"Is it time?" Ludovika flew into the room, her hair wrapped in curling papers, her eyes alert.

"It's time." Sisi winced, fighting through a sharp spasm. "Mamma, fetch the doctor."

Agata, Marie, and Ludovika remained by Sisi's side for the entirety of the labor, while Franz paced nervously in the antechamber, surrounded by his ministers, his mother, and a carafe of port. When the baby emerged into the world hours later, a pink, screaming ball of black-haired fury, Sisi heard the words she had been too fearful to hope for.

"A son. You are delivered of a son, Your Majesty!" Doctor Seeburger held the baby high for Sisi to see, as if proffering the screaming body as proof. "A healthy baby boy. Long live the Crown Prince."

Ludovika and Marie erupted in celebratory cheers, clutching one another as they bounced up and down. Sisi allowed her head to drop back onto the pillow, indulging in an exhausted, contented laugh.

"A son," Sisi gasped, closing her eyes to thank God. "A son. A son. A son. Please, someone, fetch my husband."

Agata ran for the door to the antechamber. A moment later, Franz burst into the bedroom, his face taut and his hair unkempt. "What is it? Is it a boy?" He looked from his wife to the doctor.

Doctor Seeburger held forth the tiny, plaintive bundle. "Congratulations, Emperor Franz Joseph. Your wife has just delivered your heir."

"My heir?" Franz repeated it with a tinge of incredulity. Doctor Seeburger, usually so stoic, couldn't help but smile as he nodded. Franz approached. At the doctor's urging, Franz took the baby in his hands, clutching the body and staring down without a word. The little legs looked tiny as they flailed in Franz's trembling hands. Sisi took it in, looking on as her husband stared down at his son, beholding his face for the first time.

"Well, hello there, my son." Franz's eyes roved over every inch of newborn flesh to ensure that all was as it should be. "Is he healthy? Is he strong?"

"Indeed, Majesty." Doctor Seeburger nodded, a satisfied grin on his usually stern face. "A healthy little boy if I've ever seen one."

Franz laughed, turning back to his son's pink little face. "A son!"

"Empress Elisabeth did a commendable job, Majesty," the doctor said, perhaps noting the yearning look in Sisi's eyes. "It was a very difficult labor. Perhaps the hardest one yet. But both mother and son should soon be in perfectly good health."

"Thank you, Elisa!" Franz ran to his wife, holding the baby forward so that his exhausted wife might see her child.

"We have a son." Sisi did not struggle with the tears, but rather let them stream out. "Thank you, God, thank you."

A holiday was declared and the entire empire was ordered to commence a three-day festival, paid for by the Habsburgs. Wine, beer, sausage, fireworks, and more beer were gifted throughout every town in the name of the new heir. Crown Prince Rudolf's first gift to his people. Those who did not partake in the days-long consumption of Habsburg beer and wine attended masses, held in churches and cathedrals throughout the empire, to pray for the health of the new prince and his recovering mother.

Sisi heard it when the birth was announced to the city of Vienna — one hundred and one guns firing off a salute to the tiny Habsburg heir. One hundred and one more years of Habsburg rule. The roar of the rifles ripped through the hot August night like a rainless summer thunderstorm.

"Long live Crown Prince Rudolf!"

"Cheers to Empress Elisabeth!"

"God bless the Empress and the Crown Prince!"

"Listen to that, my little Rudy." The pop of the guns, trailed by the raucous yelps of the mob that stood carousing outside the palace gates, sailed in through Sisi's open bedroom windows and rattled the frame of her bed. Rudolf simpered, irritated by the noisy disruption to his evening meal, and he balled up his little fists and pounded them angrily on his mother's chest. Sisi, at that moment nursing Rudolf, could not help but laugh at her son's temper.

"Those cheers are for you, my prince. They are for you." Sisi kissed his soft, downy little forehead, savoring his clean, baby smell and the rhythmic pulsing of his tiny lips as he drank from her tender breast.

Ludovika sat, sentrylike, at the door to the suite, ready to call out a warning should Sophie approach to see her new grandson. But Sophie would not come tonight. She was with Franz and the rest of his advisors, celebrating and toasting the new prince with the rest of the court. A celebration that Sisi gladly declined in order to have this private moment with her new baby.

"Long live Empress Sisi!" Another cry of revelry drifted in on the warm current, and Sisi smiled; they were using her nickname. The love of her people was now as certain as the continuation of the Habsburg line. The entire empire, it seemed, had exhaled a collective sigh of relief at the birth of Crown Prince Rudolf. And so, too, could Sisi.

Rudolf's birth had been long and taxing, and so Sisi did not argue when her mother offered to take him so that she might have a chance to sleep.

"You must rest, my Sisi. You've done your part. You sleep soundly, knowing that Rudolf is safe with his grandmother."

"Don't give him to Sophie. Mamma, you promise?"

"I promise, my Sisi. I will not let him out of my arms. Now sleep."

"I think I shall, yes . . ." Sisi yawned, softening willingly into the pillows as she shut her eyes. She knew that her son would be there when she awoke. And that her husband would be back to visit. And that her mother was near. And that knowledge was so wonderful that even the thunderclap of the fireworks and the increasing volume of the revelers outside could not prevent her from slipping into a deep and restorative slumber.

She awoke to brilliant summer sunshine and total silence; Vienna, having sated itself with merrymaking, had turned in to sleep off its excesses.

She had a son. A healthy, hungry, rosy little son. The realization washed over Sisi, bringing with it a wave of fresh happiness, and she called out for her mother to bring Rudolf to her.

"How is he?" Sisi asked, taking the bundled little boy in her arms.

"He is just perfect. He's strong; he slept almost as long as you did, Sisi." Ludovika stared at him, as if she'd never have her fill of watching her little grandson.

Sisi slid out of the top of her shift so that her son might feed at her aching breasts. "Tiring stuff, the business of being born. Isn't that so, my little Rudolf?"

Franz had picked the name, a family name, and Sisi had happily agreed. She thought Emperor Rudolf Habsburg-Lorraine sounded just fine.

There was a knock, and then Franz's head

appeared around the door.

"Franz!" Sisi waved her husband toward the bed. "Come in!"

He entered her bedchamber bashfully, looking somewhat haggard after what had likely been a sleepless night of celebrating. But when he saw his wife in the bed, holding his son, he smiled proudly. "You are awake."

"We are, and we awoke with quite an appetite this morning," Sisi chirped.

Ludovika busied herself in the corner, tidying and folding Rudolf's little blankets.

"It's such a wonderful moment." Franz held his hands forward, forming a square shape, as if to make a frame around the image of the new mother and her feeding baby. "I don't wish to disturb it in any way."

"It is a beautiful family portrait," Ludovika agreed.

"Yes, but not without the papa. Come, Franz," Sisi said, wincing at Rudolf's nibbling.

"Elisa, can you believe he is ours?" Franz nuzzled up beside his wife in the bed and joined her in studying the little face.

"All ours," Sisi said. "We did it."

"You know, if you're tired, we can bring in a wet nurse to feed him."

"No," Sisi said, her tone resolute. "I want to nurse my own son."

"Well, if it's what you want, I'd say you've earned it."

Sisi smiled. "Are you happy, Franz?" She turned to him, genuinely interested in her husband's response once more, she realized.

"I am, Elisa. And are you?"

"Happier than I thought possible." Sisi smiled, finding her mother's gaze in the corner of the room before turning back to her son.

"Who does he look like?" Franz cocked his head.

"While his hair is so dark, it's hard to tell," Sisi quipped. "I suspect that it will lighten, to an auburn like his papa's."

Franz beamed at this. "I have something for you, Elisa. A gift."

"Oh?"

Franz removed a small leather box from his pocket, presenting it to his wife.

"You open it for me," she said, still holding their baby.

Franz lifted the lid of the box to reveal a necklace, three strands of magnificent pearls.

"Franz!" Sisi gasped, looking from the necklace to her husband.

"Do you like it?"

"Like it? Well, it's splendid."

"It's nothing, compared to what you have given me," he said, looking toward their son.

"Put it on me." Sisi leaned forward as her husband fastened the pearls around her neck.

The three of them sat silently together, huddled in a collective embrace, as Rudolf ate his fill. Eventually, with one last gasp of energy, the little prince let out a petulant burp, and then he slipped into sleep.

"I could watch him all day. I wish I did not have to go." Franz sighed.

"Then don't." Sisi spoke quietly so as not to wake her baby.

"I must. The emperor does not get the same three days of holiday that the rest of the people do. Not when the Italians are trying to leave the empire."

"Poor Franz. Always carrying the weight of the world on your shoulders."

"See what you have to look forward to, little Rudolf?"

Sisi frowned at the thought: at the thought of this little baby, her son, one day being as besieged and constantly harangued as his father now was.

Franz kissed his son on the forehead and then he did the same to his wife. "Farewell, my loves." Without any indication of when he might return, he quit her room.

As soon as Franz was gone, Sisi regretted not asking him if he'd like to visit her this evening. She missed him already.

In the days that followed, Sisi slowly regained her strength. Eventually, she felt up for walking and dressing and answering her correspondence, beginning with the notes that came in from her Bavarian family members.

A week after the birth, while sitting in bed answering letters, Sisi saw her mother enter. Rudolf rested beside Sisi.

"Good morning, Mamma!" Sisi whispered, not wanting to wake him. "I've had word from Bavaria. In fact, I'm just now reading Ludwig's note. He's sent a toy train for Rudolf."

"And how is he?" Ludovika approached the big bed, hovering beside her daughter.

"Who — Ludwig, or Rudolf?"

"Both, I suppose. But I meant my grandson." Ludovika paused, staring down at the baby's face as he slumbered. He was suckling in his dreams, his lips moving in a rhythmic motion. "He really is perfect, isn't he?"

"Yes, he is," Sisi agreed.

Ludovika lowered herself down onto the bed beside her daughter. "How are you feeling?"

"Very fine, Mamma. Stronger each day." Sisi stole one more glance at her son, his presence like a magnet drawing her continually to him. "Though I can't get through more than a letter an hour. I'm so distracted with him in here. In the best way possible." Smiling, feeling glutted with love for her son, Sisi turned back to the pile of letters.

"And you, Mamma? How are you?"

"Fine. Just fine." Ludovika ran her fingers over the wide skirt of her gown, pressing down nonexistent wrinkles. "Sisi, my darling, there is something I must speak to you about."

"Yes?" Sisi lowered her pen, noting the edge to her mother's tone.

"You and Rudolf are both healthy, and you and Franz seem to be happy once more." Ludovika paused, and Sisi looked up in time to note the expression of sadness that her mother quickly concealed with a smile. "I think my stay is complete. It's time for me to go."

Sisi's entire body tensed, like a clenched fist. Ludovika continued. "I've been here for months. Much longer than I had intended. And I've been receiving updates from Possenhofen. They need me back home. The little ones, especially. But the older ones as well. Helene has yet to accept a proposal, and she is now half a year older than when I came here. And your papa. You know he is not always . . . well."

The happiness Sisi had awoken to evaporated, vanishing like a warm puddle under the scorching summer sun. She understood, of course, that the family back in Bavaria would need Ludovika. Her mother managed the home, and the duchy, for that matter. But how could Sisi go on without her? How could Sisi return to the way things had been before Ludovika had appeared, somehow righting the wrongs and restoring sense to her daughter's life?

Sisi knew her answer: she could not. There was only one solution. "Take me with you, Mamma."

Ludovika looked at her daughter, eyes widening. "Hush, child, don't be silly."

"I'll go to Possenhofen with you."

Her mother spoke in a quiet, scolding tone, as if afraid of what Sisi was suggesting. She threw a glance over her shoulder to ensure that they were alone in the room, fearful that someone else might hear. "Elisabeth, your place is with your children. You know that."

"We'll take Gisela and Rudolf with us," Sisi said, persisting.

Ludovika laughed, incredulous. "Darling, be serious."

"I am serious, Mother," Sisi answered, her voice flat.

"Elisabeth, I can no more take the empress and her children — one of them being heir to the empire — away with me than I can take the stones of the Hofburg Palace. A war would be started before we even reached the outer gates. It's madness."

"I cannot stay here, Mamma." Sisi shook her head. "Not alone."

Ludovika's face wilted. "Sisi."

"Mamma, please."

"Child."

Yes, *child,* Sisi thought. Little more than a petrified child. "I can't be without you, Mamma. You can't go."

"Sisi." Ludovika lifted a hand and stared her daughter squarely in the eyes, her tone steady, resolute. "We all face our own difficulties. But you are a part of this family, and you have a right to be here. And now that you have your son, things will not be as dire as they were before I arrived."

"They will be." Sisi began to shiver, even though the morning was a warm one. "They will be worse, in fact, Mother. Sophie will get her way, and she will punish me for having challenged her all of these months. Don't you see?"

"Then there's only one thing to do, Elisabeth." Ludovika arched her eyebrows, her eyes looking sternly into her daughter's face. "Don't let her."

If they had been in an open, acknowledged battle, then Sisi could have strategized, faced her aunt with every weapon she had, and her determination to win. But their conflicts never happened like that. They weren't battles fought in the broad light of day; they were silent struggles, wrestling matches that occurred without any formal declaration of war, silent coups as silky as the dresses they wore, so that Sophie always carried out her designs before Sisi even sensed that the traps had been set.

This time it took place in the quiet of the night — while Sisi slept. She awoke one morning just days after her mother's departure, much later than her usual waking time. The sun blazed high in the sky, brightening her bedroom, in which a breakfast tray sat, untouched. The birds, lethargic in the midday heat, had retreated into their nests with no further song.

The room was spinning. Sisi felt groggy and disoriented. The previous few nights — the nights immediately following Ludovika's departure — Sisi had not slept at all. She'd been too upset at the loss of her mother. The previous night, however, her body had made up for those sleepless nights, and she had slipped into a deep and dreamless slumber.

She had slept longer than she could ever remember sleeping, so worn down had her body been by the nursing and the insomnia. But how had Rudolf's cries not awoken her? Sisi rose from bed, feeling shaky on her bare feet as she walked toward his bassinet. She felt as if she was ill, her body fighting something off.

She steadied herself on the frame of the bassinet before looking down at her baby. But the bassinet was empty. Rudolf was not in his bed. She ran to the sitting room next door. No sign of Rudolf. He wasn't in her office either, or their dining room. Sisi shrieked, a bloodcurdling cry that brought Marie panting into the suite from the antechamber.

"Marie, he's gone! Where is my baby? Rudolf is gone!"

"Majesty." Marie stared at her.

"Marie, where is Rudy? He's gone! Some-one took him!"

Marie, her features knit tight, asked, "Em-press, don't you remember?"

"Remember what?"

"Prince Rudolf was wailing away this morn-ing but you were too fatigued to rise. Sophie came to fetch him so that you might sleep."

Surely this had not happened; Sisi always awoke to the first sounds of her baby's cries. And she would never have handed him over to Sophie's care. Sisi narrowed her eyes, furi-ous at her lying maid. "Marie, what are you saying?"

"It was about six o'clock this morning, Madame. I came to your room because I heard the crown prince crying. I tried to wake you but you seemed so tired. Then the archduchess came and offered to take Prince Rudolf so that you might sleep. I told her that she could not, not without asking you first. I was surprised that you agreed, but you did."

"I did?" Sisi steadied herself on the frame of the bassinet, feeling even more dizzy. "I agreed to let Sophie take my baby? Did you see this with your own eyes, Marie?"

"I did, Majesty. And like I said, I was surprised, but it was what you wanted."

"What did I say?" Sisi brought her palm to

her temple, where a headache had just begun to throb. She felt dizzy.

"Are you all right, Majesty? You look ill."

"I'm fine, Marie, just remind me what I said to Sophie."

"You didn't say anything, Madame. The archduchess simply came over to your bed and whispered that Rudolf was awake and that she would take him. And you nodded and rolled right back over to sleep. I've never seen you in such a deep slumber, Empress."

Sisi tore through her wardrobe and threw on the simplest dress she could find. Without touching her breakfast or waiting for Agata to brush her hair, she ran to her mother-in-law's apartments, avoiding the stares of the startled and inquisitive courtiers she passed along the way.

"Blessings for the crown prince's health, Empress Elisabeth!" A round-faced noblewoman whom Sisi vaguely remembered as being from Bohemia paused to speak with her.

"Thank you," Sisi answered, and kept clipping down the hallway, her bodyguards struggling to keep their tail of her. Further behind her, Countess Esterházy was trotting to keep apace as well. Sisi didn't even care. Let her trail me, she thought. Let the whole palace see me take my son back.

She halted, panting, only once she reached

the outer doors to Sophie's apartments. "Let me in."

"The archduchess is out." The guards stood outside of the always-closed doors of Sophie's suite.

"Where are they?" Sisi demanded, breathless. She felt the quickness of her heartbeat, felt the blood pounding in her neck, surging with the instinctive need to fight. "Where are my children?"

"The Archduchess Sophie has taken their Imperial Majesties the Princess Gisela and the Crown Prince Rudolf for a carriage ride."

Sisi stamped her feet, aware as several courtiers walked by that she was behaving precisely as Sophie had whispered throughout the palace — saying that her daughter-in-law was too young, too immature, too easily governed by unstable emotions to raise the prince and princess.

"You tell Sophie . . . the archduchess . . . the *instant* that she returns, that I am looking for her. In fact, you tell her that I *order* her to come to my apartments with my son and daughter. Do you understand?" Sisi raised a threatening finger at the guard.

"I shall deliver this message to the archduchess, Empress Elisabeth." Whether or not Sophie obeyed was quite another thing, was his implication. And Sisi knew as well as this guard that that was not likely to happen.

Franz was similarly indisposed, his bodyguards thwarting Sisi outside the entrance to his state chambers. "Orders, Empress Elisabeth, no visits or petitions today."

"I am his wife, not a pestering courtier with a petition. Now let me through!"

"They are in meetings with the Italian ambassador, Empress. We've been explicitly told that it is highly sensitive. No interruptions, Emperor's orders."

Sisi clenched her jaw and marched back to her suite, where she scrawled off a furious letter to her husband. She was back in familiar territory. Alone and powerless to find her children. All she could do was wait.

The fever spread through the city shortly after Franz departed for Italy, on his urgent, last-ditch attempt to stop the Italians from declaring independence. Whether her susceptibility to the fever was precipitated by her despair, Sisi did not know. There were enough reasons to despair: Franz had left Vienna with nothing more than a quick and distracted farewell, with no answer as to when he would return; her mother was gone; worst of all, her two children were once more completely absent from her life.

Her illness followed on the heels of these blows, and Sisi's body seemed as powerless against the fever as she herself was against her miserable situation. Though she eventually beat the fever, a cough persisted; a painful cough, even in the thick heat of the summer.

The words of her mother rang in her ears, a warning and a lifeline: don't let Sophie win. Don't give up. Fight for your family.

Sisi was determined to get her children back, but she knew that as long as Doctor Seeburger still proclaimed her ill, she would never succeed in her suit. So she obeyed the doctor's orders like the perfect patient. As summer cooled to fall and the days shortened, bringing with them the threat of cold, icy winter, Sisi remained in bed under piles of blankets, sweating through layers of silk and wool and cashmere, as the doctor commanded. She sipped bowl after bowl of broth and drank scalding hot tea — so hot that it temporarily thawed her clogged lungs. Yet still, the cough remained. She rested so much that she could not possibly force herself to sleep anymore, and yet she pretended to be asleep every time Doctor Seeburger entered her bedchamber.

"What more can I do?" It was a gray day at the start of winter. Sisi's lungs burned with the lingering cough.

"Nothing, Empress. You are doing everything I advise. Yet I am sorry to say that this cough persists." Doctor Seeburger tapped the tip of his chin, no longer attempting to mask his befuddlement, as he conducted his daily visit. "Your breathing is still too labored to

586

make me think that your lungs are cleared."

"But it's been months now," Sisi growled. Months, in the lives of an infant and a toddler, were an eternity — what important moments of theirs had she missed?

As the days shortened, her health deteriorated even further. While the cough continued, a new, more troubling symptom made itself known. Sisi watched in horror as — daily, it seemed — her wrists and knees swelled, throbbing like overripe fruit. Her body had been seized from her; her once beautiful, celebrated figure was now morphing and reshaping itself before her own petrified eyes.

"Empress, I must admit that this is beyond me." Doctor Seeburger was in her bedchamber, pressing and prodding against the turgid flesh of her knees and wrists. Nothing could be done. Restricting fluids had not brought the swelling down. The daily massages he had ordered only caused Sisi excruciating pain. All the while her joints continued to expand, like skins of wine ready to burst with too much liquid.

"You *must* do something! I appear fit for the circus tents . . ." Sisi wept, avoiding his gaze. Avoiding the accidental glimpse of her disfigured appearance in the mirror. "I can't leave the bedroom. I can't see the emperor."

"If Your Majesty grants me permission, I'd like to ask to bring in a lung specialist. I've worked with a certain Doctor Skoda before and I believe he might have more luck with the diagnosis and treatment."

"Whatever you advise, Doctor Seeburger," Sisi said, her voice frantic. "Just get me well again. I must have my children back."

Doctor Skoda was a formal man, more stern even than Doctor Seeburger, and he set right to the business of listening to the empress's lungs, and examining her swollen joints.

After his exam, Doctor Skoda retreated a distance from the bed to review his findings, and Sisi pretended to drift off into a peaceful sleep. Several minutes passed before she heard the faint sound of whispering — the barely audible conference of the two perplexed physicians.

"A rare condition, indeed." Sisi heard Doctor Seeburger repeat his common refrain. "What could it be?"

Doctor Skoda's response was too quiet for Sisi to hear, but the gasp that followed from Doctor Seeburger was not. Sisi's heart raced in response, but she forced herself to keep her eyes closed.

"But how could she have fallen victim to it?" In his alarm Doctor Seeburger was being reckless with the volume of his voice, a fact for which Sisi was grateful.

"From him, of course." Doctor Skoda answered matter-of-factly. Who was *him?*

Sisi wondered. Rudolf? Perhaps it was some health complication resulting from the labor?

Doctor Seeburger challenged the theory, whatever it was. "But, Doctor Skoda, that's a dangerous assertion, as I'm sure you understand. To venture such a guess is to imply that the emperor has been tainted, as well . . ."

Again, Doctor Skoda's reaction was not loud enough for Sisi to hear it. Perhaps it was not even transmitted as a spoken response — perhaps it was a nod or a look of the eye — a message exchanged between the two doctors, the meaning of which only they could understand.

"Then why does *he* show no symptoms?"

"His body is stronger than hers — it is probably still fighting the disease off. But the empress? Well, she has had three babies in four years. She is weak and depleted. Her mental state, as you tell me, has not always been . . . well, there have been the bouts of deep melancholy and anxiety. Her diet is lacking, her appetite often nonexistent. In addition to the lung condition, I also find her severely anemic. Of course her body would succumb to the symptoms sooner."

Now Sisi could barely keep up the charade of sleeping. She wanted to leap from the bed and demand to know what they were discussing — what dire illness was plaguing her?

"Fortunately, with the right treatment, it is

not a life-threatening ailment. The empress faces no long-term risks," Doctor Skoda explained.

"But how can we treat it, Skoda?"

"I will advise that the empress take a trip, somewhere to the south, to take in the warm air. She certainly should not remain in Vienna for the winter. I will advise a sojourn, somewhere by the sea. If she undergoes treatment, and rests, we may have every hope that Her Imperial Majesty shall make a full recovery."

There was no way she was leaving court without her children, Sisi thought, already prepared to fight the doctor on this.

"But what if the emperor does not wish her to leave?" Seeburger seemed uncomfortable with the developments being discussed. "His Royal Highness is very attached to the empress."

"He ought to do what is best for Her Royal Highness," Skoda answered, his voice suddenly prickly. "He, after all, is the reason she suffers from this."

"Shh! Come now, Skoda, watch yourself! You can't talk like that in this palace. There is always someone listening."

If he only knew, Sisi thought to herself, her blood throbbing between her ears.

The two doctors stood silently awhile, and Sisi knew that they must have been looking at her — her peaceful sleeping figure. This poor empress, they must have thought, pitying her for this illness. But what was it? Sisi wondered. And would Franz suffer, too? How had Franz fallen ill?

Doctor Skoda's next question to Doctor Seeburger confused Sisi. "Who?" he asked, his voice barely a whisper. "Who could it be?"

Sisi did not know what this meant. But she did hear the answer. It was as clear and loud in her ears as if Doctor Seeburger had shouted it to her. And understanding immediately crystallized in her mind, forcing her to open her eyes when she heard the reply.

"It could be any number of them." Doctor Seeburger sighed, keeping his voice low. "But . . . ordinarily, Count Grünne ensures their hygiene — their health — beforehand. There is one, however. That actress, Frau Roll, do you know of her?"

"Yes," Doctor Skoda said. "Go on."

"I hate to place too much store on palace rumors and hearsay. But we'd be fools to shut our ears to the reports . . . the reports that she has the same condition."

There was no confusion remaining. Only the rending apart of Sisi's heart, the latest symptom to add to the list of her ailments.

"How could you not have told me?" Sisi glowered at Marie, her favorite lady-in-waiting, her most trusted and loyal ally. "I would have expected Countess Esterházy to keep it from me. And Paula and Karoline —

even though they can seldom keep quiet on a piece of gossip. But you, Marie? How long have you known?"

Marie stared toward the bedroom door longingly, like a trapped animal looking at the door of its cage. "Majesty, I'm not sure I know what you speak of."

"Marie, don't you dare. I saw the way she looked at him at New Year's, and I know that everyone knows about this, except me. When did it begin?"

Marie looked at her now, the breath catching in the back of her throat as though she might weep. Reluctantly, she said: "I first started hearing whispers of it right around the time you returned from Budapest. Last summer. When you were in mourning over Princess Soph . . ." But Marie did not finish the sentence before the tears welled in her eyes and she brought her hands to conceal her face.

"Save your tears, Marie, you have no right to imagine yourself a victim here." Sisi's voice was cold. "And she's just the latest, from the sound of it. The doctor said there were others. Oh, Marie, why did you not tell me?"

"I'm so sorry, Empress." Marie sobbed into her cupped hands.

"What a fool I am." Sisi smacked the desk, rising to pace the room. "Of course, it all makes sense now. He's been so willing to avoid our bedroom. In fact, even when I invite him, he declines. I thought the man had the patience and self-control of a monk. But no, it's that he's taken that scarlet-haired *actress* for a lover!"

Sisi fumed, her body bristling against the restricting confines of her corset as she huffed. "This man, who promised to be faithful, who promised to come to my bed each night." She couldn't cry, she was too angry for tears. "And you, Marie, I was betrayed by you as well. And Agata, too. Don't even try to tell me you didn't both know. This court is so ripe with gossip, I'm sure you all knew the first night it happened."

"Majesty, please understand. You were ill. You were so ill that I feared for your life. And then you were with child. And then you delivered the child and you were so happy. When in that time could I have told you? I could not bear to break your heart after everything you'd been through."

"Don't give the emperor that much credit, Marie. Broken my heart?" Sisi laughed, a wild outburst of angry laughter. "Too late. That has happened a thousand times already. Gradually, you see? A piece of my heart here, a bruise in my heart there, a gash through it there; so that now it is wasted, useless. No, you cannot break something that is already beyond repair."

The way Marie looked at her — a mixture of fear and pity — was enough to make Sisi go mad. She forced herself to continue talking so that a scream did not issue from her mouth.

"I'd known Franz was gone from me, emotionally. In fact, he never really was mine, fully. I always shared him — with his mother, with the empire, with *Grünne,*" Sisi said, the disgust heavy in her voice. "Always. From the day we married."

Sisi laughed, a bitter, mirthless laugh, and she knew that she sounded mad. "What difference does it make if he gives his body away, also?"

They sat in silence, Sisi's mind running over all the days during which Franz had turned down her invitations to visit their bedchamber. He had always pleaded something: Italians, Hungarians, ministers. He had told her about everyone but his mistresses. And now, here she sat, her body disfigured and her heart a cold, shriveled lump.

Eventually, Marie spoke. "What will you do, Your Majesty?"

Sisi sat up tall, her hands resting firmly on her legs as she massaged her sore knees. "I shall do what the doctors have advised me to do. I shall go abroad. Franz is gone. He has abandoned me. Why may I not do the same?"

PART THREE

XIII.

She leaves her room at a brisk pace, quickly growing short of breath. But she is far from tired. She feels awake and alive, as she hasn't in years.

She knows which door is his; the maid was, mercifully, discreet enough not to ask why the empress needed that information. Slipping out a back doorway, she glides, undetected, through the dark hallways. "It is not right for an empress to scurry about in the halls unaccompanied." If only she knew, Sisi thinks.

She knocks on the door now, quietly. She throws a look over her shoulder, just in case a guard patrols a nearby hall. But she stands entirely alone.

And then he appears at the door, a sliver of candlelight spilling out into the hallway as his face emerges. He stares at her, his shirt unbuttoned, hair disheveled. His features betray surprise; hers was not the face he had expected to see on the other side of his door. "Sisi?"

"May I come in?" Though it's a question, she

doesn't await a reply. She presses the door open, stepping in past him.

"Do you have any idea what time it is?" His breath smells of wine and his room is in chaos. He has clearly been writing, or working, or pacing. Something that her restless mind can understand. "It is well past midnight, is it not?"

She shrugs her shoulders, allowing his question to go unanswered.

"Is this wise?" He looks from her to the door, shutting it. Closing the two of them in.

She walks toward him, her heart knocking against her breast. He appears wild, more handsome than she has ever seen him. Is this wise, he asks? No, it certainly was not wise.

CHAPTER THIRTEEN

*SCHÖNBRUNN SUMMER PALACE, VIENNA
AUGUST 1862*

"Aren't they just adorable? Look at them, so *tiny!*" Sisi clapped, beckoning Marie closer to her where she sat, awash in the golden afternoon light that spilled in through the tall windows of her palace bedchamber. "Marie, bring them to me; let me touch them."

"Please, Your Majesty, be still."

"Sorry, Franziska." Sisi leaned back, allowing her hairdresser, Franziska Feifilak, to get a better hold of her thick hair. As the woman's skilled fingers laced the curls with strands of pearls, Sisi caught hints of the aroma of her hair, freshly washed in rosewater and almond oil.

"Marie, bring them here at once."

The countess obeyed, halting her unpacking to walk from the bed to the seated empress, carrying with her the two new corsets.

"Just arrived from Paris, Empress." Marie

placed one of the corsets in Sisi's outstretched hands.

"It's the new fashion," Sisi said, stroking the smooth bone. She glanced up at her attendant, eyebrows lifting. "What do you think? Can I cinch myself smaller than eighteen inches?"

Marie didn't attempt to mask her creased brow, her downturned lips.

"I know, I know, you disapprove, Marie. But you mustn't frown like that, you'll give yourself wrinkles." Sisi sighed. Then, cocking her head so that she addressed the hairdresser: "Franziska, do you disapprove of my tight lacing as Marie does?"

"I simply wish for Your Majesty to be happy, Empress Elisabeth," Franziska answered, her words tripping over a Polish accent. Franziska, like Marie and the empress herself, was foreign to Austria. An advantage, almost a necessity, for Sisi these days.

But Marie did not like the hairdresser's answer. "I remember how you used to despise even the loosest of corsets, Madame. And I'm not sure that tight lacing to eighteen inches or below is healthy for a mother of three."

"Two," Sisi snapped.

"Yes, but I mean that you have given birth to —"

"Yes, I gave birth to three children. One of whom is dead. And the other two are not with me. So I'm not sure what being a mother has to do with anything, Marie." Sisi regretted her biting tone as soon as she saw the pained look that gripped Marie's face. She sighed, turning her gaze back to her reflection in the mirror.

Eventually, Franziska broke the tense silence. "I think Your Majesty has the right to a little fun."

In the mirror, Sisi noticed Marie's scowl. The countess worried about so many things these days: Sisi's fixation on her diet; her compulsive interest in her wardrobe and beauty routine; her complete disinterest in court life. Sisi's budding relationship with this new hairdresser — a woman who had made her name styling actresses in the theater — was simply the latest cause for fretting.

"Put it back on the bed, Marie. I'll wear it to dinner tonight." Sisi handed the corset over, turning her head to glance out the window.

A dark-haired little boy came suddenly into view, pulling Sisi's attention to where he skipped across the courtyard below. He wore lederhosen, a cap on his head, and a light summer blazer. He ran away from the palace, chasing a small white dog — that terrible creature belonging to her mother-in-law. Sisi's heart stopped. "Rudy?" She leaned closer to the window, pressing her fingers to the warm glass. But he was gone, tucked behind a shrub and out of sight. Her heart hammered against her rib cage.

"Majesty, please, keep your head still." Franziska took Sisi's scalp in her strong, gloved hands, guiding her back toward the chair.

"Sorry." Sisi answered absentmindedly. Her thoughts were no longer in this bedroom, no longer consumed with corsets and hair washing and which dress to select for dinner. Had Franz and the children returned to the palace already?

"Marie?" Sisi shifted her weight in the chair, ignoring Franziska's audible sigh. "What time was the emperor expected back?"

The Hungarian noblewoman paused her unpacking, placing one of Sisi's evening gowns down on the bed. She removed a small clock from her pocket. "I'd suppose any time now," the countess answered. Sisi balled her hands, too restless, suddenly, to remain seated.

Franziska, responding to her fidgety subject said: "Almost done now, Empress. Just the pinning left. I told you already, it would not take so long if you would let me cut a few inches off."

Sisi did not have to think about this. "No."

The hairdresser finished her thick braids, which ran the length of Sisi's back and past her waist. It had taken half a day to get to this point. The routine was always the same: once a fortnight, Sisi washed her hair in a solution that she herself had concocted. The solution had been perfected to maximize the shine of her glossy brown curls — a formula of slick almond oil, brandy, rosewater, cognac, and raw egg yolks. Next, the hair had to dry, which, given its volume and length, required several hours, even on a summer day as warm as this one. Once dry, Franziska — who had been sought after by every Viennese noblewoman in the city before joining the employ of the empress — would weave a series of elaborate braids, wrapping them around Sisi's face like a crown. Finally, Franziska added in jewels, flowers, and feathers, pinning the hair back in a manner that had to appear loose, yet could not actually come loose. Sisi would inspect the finished product, and, if any hairs looked amiss or at risk of slipping out of the coif, her hairdresser was gently but firmly chastised.

"What do you think?" Sisi would ask, as she examined herself in her gold-gilded mirror, scrutinizing every angle.

Always her hairdresser would smile and answer in the same way. "I think, Madame, that you are worthy of your title: most beautiful woman in the world."

And then the hairdresser would slip away, out of sight, to clean her combs; Franziska had learned long ago that seeing loose strands of hair distressed Sisi, even filled her with a gripping sort of panic. As if, in shedding a hair or two, she was at risk of shedding her beauty.

Altogether the process required several hours; on days when the empress washed her hair, her aides knew that she would skip luncheon and be otherwise indisposed for most of the day.

Normally it was a process Sisi enjoyed, and she looked forward to the familiar ritual. While Franziska worked behind her, massaging her scalp and manipulating the thick tresses, Sisi would dictate letters to Marie or supervise the tidying of her bedchamber: the sorting of her lotions and ointments, the organizing of her wardrobe, the ordering of new tonics, perfumes, and clothing.

But this afternoon Sisi felt restless. Being back in Vienna filled her with a sense of unease, even dread. Especially now that she knew Franz and the children were back at Schönbrunn.

Franz had not been at the summer palace when Sisi herself had arrived, days prior. She had expected — had even prepared herself — to see him after her long journey from Possenhofen. But when she had arrived, weary and anxious and tearful, Herr Lobkowitz had received her instead.

The aide, who had greeted Sisi with less hair and a more slumped posture than when she had left, informed his patroness that the emperor, along with the children and his mother the archduchess, had not yet returned from the summer retreat at Bad Ischl. Had any of the court ladies happened to spend the summer at the Kaiservilla? Sisi had asked. The aide had lowered his eyes as he waffled: yes, he believed it was quite possible that perhaps a few of the court's noblewomen had traveled with the imperial retinue to the mountains. Sisi had presumed as much.

Several days later, the previously sleepy, empty palace was abuzz with preparations for the emperor's return. And the imperial party's arrival was precisely why Sisi had planned to devote most of the day to her bathing and beautification rituals. She was expected in the emperor's state rooms that evening, she had been told, where she would meet with her husband before joining him for a private dinner. She had to look her best, she had told Franziska. Not because she harbored any hopes that Franz would return to her, to their marriage, and that they would be like they once were. That childish hope had been quashed years ago when Franz had abandoned her for the Italian campaign, leaving his children with his mother and his wife with nothing but his mistress's illness.

And yet, Sisi felt a certain amount of nervous anticipation ahead of her meeting with Franz. It wasn't every day that she had dinner with her husband after such a long separation. She wanted him to see her as strong, the master of her own fate, even desirable. Why did she still long for Franz's approval? Franz's attention? She did not know, but she did.

Perhaps she wanted him to know that he had been wrong, straying from her. Perhaps she wanted to torment her husband, putting herself before him as an alluring object that he could no longer possess. Yes, she admitted, she wished to arouse him, then reject him. She wished to hurt him. And even if she could succeed in those designs, it would never be enough to pay for the pain — the years of rejection — that she herself had endured.

But the mere glimpse of Rudy had shaken Sisi. It had forced aside the quiet intentionality of the morning like a freight train scattering seeds floating in the wind. Rudy would be four now, she knew. Entirely different from the last time she had seen him. That little figure below had been less of a baby and more of a young boy — running, laughing, playing chase. Would he even know his mamma?

Sisi felt as if she might faint, and she was about to tell Franziska that she needed a break when Herr Lobkowitz appeared at the doorway.

"Empress, good morning!" It was well after noon, but the aide was being polite, Sisi knew, not wanting to seem as if he were judging the fact that it was after midday and still the empress was not yet dressed. "May I impose on a moment of your time, Your Majesty?"

Sisi blinked, steadying herself on the arm of her chair.

"Empress, are you quite well?" Herr Lobkowitz took a tenuous step toward her but paused, heeding protocol. He had not yet been invited to enter.

"I'm fine." Sisi took a slow, deep breath. "Come in, come in. Do you have news of the emperor?"

"Indeed I do, Madame. And in fact, I have a few matters I was hoping I might discuss with Your Imperial Majesty prior to your meeting with His Imperial Majesty this evening. It should be very brief."

"Yes, what is it?" Sisi asked, her mind still teeming with the image of Rudy, even as she forced herself to focus. And Gisela — she hadn't seen her daughter yet. What must Gisela be like now? No longer a toddler, but a proper girl, to be sure. A girl who would not even recognize her own mother.

"I can come back, if there is a better time, Empress?"

"There's no better time. Come in."

"Perhaps Your Majesty is in need of some refreshment," Marie said, gliding forward. Ever solicitous, ever pushing these maternal suggestions on Sisi. "Shall I have some broth sent from the kitchens?"

"No," Sisi said, turning back to her secretary. "Tell me, what news?"

"As you wish, Majesty." Herr Lobkowitz slid his monocle onto the bridge of his nose and looked down at his papers. "As you know, the imperial party returned from the summer retreat this afternoon."

"I think I've just spotted Rudy below," Sisi said.

"Oh?" The aide followed her glance toward the window. "The crown prince was down there?"

"Yes, chasing a dog."

Herr Lobkowitz crossed the room to look out over the meandering, manicured gardens — green, vast, and lit up in afternoon light. "I do not see the crown prince anymore. Nevertheless, I will make sure that his governesses have not been neglecting their duties."

"Yes. Now, what business, Herr Lobkowitz?"

"Of course." The aide adjusted his monocle and looked back at his notes. "As you know, the emperor has ordered a private dinner in his rooms this evening. The menu, which His Majesty's secretary has sent to me, shall include —"

"When can I see the children?"

Herr Lobkowitz looked up, stammering. "On that topic I have not been briefed.

Perhaps Your Imperial Majesty might wish to raise that topic with the emperor this evening?"

"Fine." Sisi nodded. She felt Franziska pinning thick swaths of her hair along the back of her scalp, and her head already felt heavy with the weight of the coronet.

Herr Lobkowitz continued. "I thought it prudent to warn you, Your Highness, that the emperor has not had a particularly good summer in matters of foreign policy."

"I know."

"You know that the Italian kingdoms are officially independent from His Majesty the Emperor?"

"Yes, I know that," Sisi said. Franz had been defeated in Italy. And badly. From what Sisi had read throughout her summer stay in Possenhofen, Franz's popularity throughout the empire — and hers as well, though she hardly cared — was the lowest it had ever been. "What else, Herr Lobkowitz?"

Now the aide fidgeted once more with his monocle.

Sisi sighed. "What is it, Herr Lobkowitz?" She shifted in the chair, arranging and rearranging the folds in her wide skirt.

"As your Majesty no doubt suspects" — the aide paused — "news of your return has spread quite rapidly throughout the court."

"Of course it has. News spreads quicker than the fever in this court." Sisi laughed, a short, bitter laugh. "The disgraced, jilted queen has come back to face her estranged husband, her husband's lovers, and the children who have no doubt forgotten her."

"No, Your Majesty, what a horrid joke!" Herr Lobkowitz attempted a lighthearted laugh. "Everyone is so happy to have you back, of course."

Sisi leaned her head to the side. "I'm sure that's what it is."

"Please, Empress, sit still," Franziska interjected.

"Sorry."

"Indeed we are all so happy . . . *overjoyed* . . . to have you back," Herr Lobkowitz continued, his cheeks flushed. "I beg you most humbly to believe that."

"I believe that *you* are happy to have me back, Herr Lobkowitz."

"Quite, Madame. Especially after you were away for so very long."

"That's very nice of you to say, but I'm sure you must have some point."

"Yes." The aide leaned close, lowering his voice. "I would advise that, given the length of your time away from your family and your . . . *official* duties . . . that perhaps you have some explanation ready. So as to be prepared should anyone dare to ask . . . well, why it was that you were away . . . *ahem,* for so long."

Other than the fact that her mother-in-law

was impossible to live with? And that she had had to heal from an illness transmitted to her from her husband's mistress? Other than the fact that her husband — who had abandoned her — and her children — who had been taken from her — had been the only ties holding her to this suffocating, unbearable court?

But no, she could not speak that bluntly. One did not speak such garish truths — not in Vienna. Not to the bashful, pious Herr Lobkowitz. And certainly not in the righteous Habsburg Court.

"I've already explained to you, Herr Lobkowitz. I was ill . . ." Sisi lingered on that one word, still bitter. "And, seeing as my husband was in Italy fighting anyway, it was advised by the court physicians that I take a tour to the southern countries for an extended period of rest and recovery. And so, like a good patient, I obeyed. I traveled throughout Madeira, Greece, and Corfu. There, will that do for a testimonial?"

"Yes." Herr Lobkowitz considered the answer. "And I've been sure to offer that information to all who inquire."

"And I'm sure there have been many such inquiries."

The aide fidgeted, shifting from one foot to the other. "But that only explains the first two years." And now Herr Lobkowitz paused. "What about the past two years? You've traveled throughout Bavaria, and spent an extended stay at Possenhofen. Do you . . . does Your Imperial Majesty . . . really mean to say that the climate of Bavaria is warm and restorative?"

"I was visiting my family," Sisi snapped. "I had not seen some of them since my wedding. I had not been home in years. And besides, I longed to stay at Possi to see the marriage of my dear sister Helene."

Herr Lobkowitz nodded, digesting the words. "Yes, that should work."

And that *had* worked. That was how Sisi had convinced her parents to let her stay for as long as she had. But even their joy at having their daughter home — their indulgence as she had listed her grievances with Vienna and the Habsburg Court — had reached its limits.

"Sisi, my girl." Duke Max's expression had seemed to darken over the course of the summer, as he had sensed his daughter's desire — her intention — to remain at Possi as long as she was allowed. "As wonderful as it is to see you . . . your place really is with your husband and your children. Don't you long to see your children? Don't you believe that the emperor deserves to have his wife by his side as he weathers these disasters throughout his kingdom?" These refrains had been repeated often, by both Max and Ludovika.

Ludovika's hints and insinuations had

turned to outright insistence once Sisi had seen Helene happily married off to her own husband, a German prince from Thurn.

"Yes, you stayed to see the wedding of your dear sister. People here remember Helene, such a sweet girl." Herr Lobkowitz was scribbling something in his notes, already planning his strategy for the prying, disapproving court. "Good, that's settled then."

"I'm glad you feel more comfortable," Sisi answered, smirking at the fastidious aide.

"And, if I may be so bold, Empress Elisabeth, how long do you plan to stay at court?" The aide held tight to his pen, poised for the answer.

"I suppose until they turn me out," Sisi said, her tone gloomy.

"Empress, such a humorist today." Herr Lobkowitz looked at her appraisingly. "So, I might tell people that you have returned . . . indefinitely?" His voice betrayed his hope that her answer might be in the affirmative.

"Where else can I go?" Sisi sighed. "I've traveled for years. My parents have sent me back here. I suppose you are stuck with me."

"I'm so very glad to hear it." Herr Lobkowitz smiled, and Sisi knew that he meant it.

"Well, in that case" — Herr Lobkowitz rapped his pen against his paper — "perhaps now that you are officially installed back at court, and with the emperor returning for the fall and the coming winter season, perhaps you might like to add to your household? I was hoping I might find you some additional attendants."

Sisi looked at Marie, still busy unpacking and sorting Sisi's trunks from her voyage. Since her sojourn to Madeira four years earlier, Sisi had had Marie by her side every day, but no one else. Marie had been the only lady Sisi had taken with her when she had quit the court. Franziska had been a recent hire, when she'd found the woman and recruited her away from her post at a theater.

Now, back in the palace, Sisi felt the absence of Agata, after years of ignoring the loss. The maid had resigned from her post, years earlier, when the empress had announced her intention to leave court for an extended period of traveling. It was too much for Agata to leave her new husband, the woman had confessed, tearful and red-cheeked. Sisi, still irate back then about Franz's infidelity and Agata's silence on the matter, had let the maid go without so much as a hug. She had told herself that it was for the best. That she wouldn't miss Agata. But still, sometimes, Sisi dreamed about the sweet Polish woman — dreamed that they were back in Bavaria, giggling with Helene and gossiping about Karl. Aggie had been the last link to Sisi's former life.

"Yes." Sisi agreed now, swallowing hard as she nodded to Herr Lobkowitz, pushing the memory of her old friend, Agata, from her mind.

"I'll need a new chambermaid. Someone to tend to the apartments. But that's it. I have you, Herr Lobkowitz, to help me in my duties. Marie, Countess Festetics, is my lady-in-waiting. And Franziska does my hair. I prefer to keep my household small."

Sisi shuddered, remembering the courtiers who had once shadowed her every movement, scouring her space with prying eyes, filling it with the faint scratch of whisper: the Countesses Esterházy and Karoline and Paula. She had dismissed them on the day that she had decided to leave court for Madeira, and had not spoken to them since. "I don't like being surrounded by people I cannot trust."

"A very valid point, Empress Elisabeth. And one I had anticipated." Herr Lobkowitz shuffled his papers, looking over his notes. "I've done the service of scrutinizing the court, looking for young ladies of only the highest caliber of character and discretion." Herr Lobkowitz paused for effect and Sisi did not answer. "Given that you are back at court after such an extended absence, you will most likely be quite busy. I feel very strongly that you should have some assistance."

When Sisi did not reply, the aide added: "I've found two young women whom I'm sure you will find very agreeable."

"Oh?" Sisi reached into her dresser and removed a small tub of her favorite skin cream, a concoction of beeswax, crushed strawberries, honey, and spermaceti. "And who are these ladies who have won your high opinion, Herr Lobkowitz?"

"There's a Countess Frederika von Rothburg, a very quiet young lady from the northern kingdom of Württemberg, and a Lady Ilse von Bittel, the daughter of the Viscount von Bittel. A woman whose virtue, my sources tell me, is above reproach."

Sisi knew so little about the young women at court these days. "I don't wish to be gossiped about."

"I have been assured that these two women are not that type."

Eventually, rubbing in her hand cream, Sisi answered, "I'll think about it."

"You are too kind, Your Majesty."

"As for the chambermaid . . ." Sisi lifted her hand and the aide offered her a cloth on which she now wiped the excess lotion. "That's the most important one. She will be the person in my apartment all day."

"Yes." Herr Lobkowitz nodded.

"I don't want an Austrian," Sisi said, matter-of-factly.

"Oh?"

"No," Sisi said. "No one from this court."

"Who, then . . . might I ask?"

"I want a foreigner. In fact, I've asked Marie to find me someone. Preferably a Hungarian. If she doesn't speak a word of German, all the better. Isn't that right, Marie?"

In the corner, where she stood sorting the empress's shawls, Countess Festetics nodded.

"Very well then. Please let me know if I can be of any assistance in that search, of course." Herr Lobkowitz tapped his pen once more to his notes and bowed. "I shall not impose on you any further."

"Did you arrange the gifts like we discussed?" Sisi asked.

"Indeed, Your Majesty. The dollhouse has been delivered to the nursery for Princess Gisela, and the toy train set has been delivered to the archduchess's suite for the crown prince."

"The archduchess's suite?" Sisi asked, her stomach dropping.

Herr Lobkowitz shifted from one foot to the other. "The crown prince and the princess do still sleep in the nursery off their grandmother's suite."

Sisi bit her lower lip; the certainty that her children loved — even preferred — her mother-in-law made her dizzy with envy.

The aide, sensing she had finished with him, edged backward toward the bedroom door.

"Herr Lobkowitz, one more thing."

"Yes, Your Majesty?"

"Will they know that the gifts come from me?"

"I've made sure to include a card indicating that the presents came from their most devoted and loving mother."

"Hopefully they are told as much," Sisi said, twisting her hands together in her lap. "Fine. You may go. That is all."

The aide took his leave, but before several minutes had passed, he was back. "Empress?" This time he appeared in the doorway with his arms full.

"What is it?"

"Did I not tell you that the joyous news has spread of your return?" He walked into her room, a restrained smile tugging upward on his lips. "It seems that the court is thrilled to have you back." Herr Lobkowitz first deposited a large basket stuffed with jams, sausage, and flowers on the table of her bedchamber.

"Who is it from?" Sisi asked, her hair still in the clutches of Franziska.

"This note is from Baron von Bach," Herr Lobkowitz answered. "He wishes a most warm welcome to Your Majesty. That's quite nice. Shall I write him a thank-you note on your behalf?"

"Please do," Sisi agreed. "And what about that? What is it?" She pointed at the second item delivered to her suite: a heavy wooden crate. Herr Lobkowitz called in several footmen from the antechamber to prize it open.

"It's a crate of Hungarian wine," the aide said, scratching his thinning hairline as he looked down at the wooden box.

"From whom?" Sisi asked.

"Curious." Herr Lobkowitz scanned the note before handing it to Sisi. "It's not in German; I can't make it out."

Sisi read it, the handwriting long and elegant, the language one she now understood. *"The Hungarian people are overjoyed to have their beloved empress in her rightful spot once more."*

"That's nice," Sisi said, touched. And then she saw the signature: *J. Andrássy.*

She breathed in, remembering a night, years earlier. Dancing in a warm hall in Budapest, violin notes swirling around them. Suddenly, for a reason she could not have explained, she felt dizzy once more.

Sisi's bedchamber was still bright and warm when she quit her suite to meet Franz that evening. Herr Lobkowitz and Marie trailed behind her, accompanying her as far as her husband's dark-paneled state rooms.

"One does not go scurrying about alone in the hallways, isn't that so?" Sisi had smirked as she'd repeated the past censure of her mother-in-law.

Walking the halls, the long line of gleaming

windows to her left, the gold gilt and mirrors all around her, Sisi attempted to appear calm, self-assured. She had forgotten the decadence of the Habsburg halls after such a long stay at Possenhofen, so cozy in its threadbare and shabby disrepair. Even the dress of the courtiers here in Vienna appeared riotously decorative, and Sisi made a note to commission new gowns as she nodded coolly to the courtiers she passed.

"Empress, welcome back." A young nobleman in the military uniform looked away from his pretty companion to bow to her.

"Thank you," Sisi replied, and kept walking.

"Empress, God bless and keep you." A thick middle-aged courtier whom Sisi knew to be the wife of a Bohemian count bowed before her.

"Thank you, Countess."

"And God save the crown prince," the countess called after her.

Did Sisi imagine it, or did their eyes widen when they spotted their long-estranged empress? For some of them it had been four years since they had beheld her. Had she changed that much?

Sisi was ushered immediately into the emperor's inner rooms. He had taken this new suite of apartments, she had heard, when she had told him of her plans to leave the court for her travels. It was just as well — the thought of him coexisting with her in her apartments made the court seem even less bearable.

The emperor's rooms were spartan in their appearance, much less decorated than the formal state rooms and reception halls. Inside, Sisi found Franz alone, sitting in a plain wooden chair in the presence of several guards. Sisi breathed out her relief at the fact that Sophie was not present.

Sisi curtsied as her entrance was announced. "Emperor." She lowered her eyes, longing for him to speak, to tell her to rise, so that she might gain a better view of him. Had he changed in these recent years as well?

"Empress." Franz's voice was formal, expressionless. She kept her eyes lowered. After several moments, he rose and walked toward her.

"Elisabeth, rise, please." Franz paused before her and took her hands in his own — gloved, both of them — helping her up to a stand. There, he looked into her eyes and they stood opposite one another, silent. He still wore the officer's uniform, still stood with that impossibly erect posture. But the signs of aging were undeniable. His auburn hair, now laced with gray, had retreated back behind a long and lined forehead. His eyes, the same light blue that Sisi had remembered, appeared sunken, surrounded by a web of fine lines, the cause of which had surely been worry and fatigue and loss. His mustache, once so thin and neat, had been replaced by a full beard, and thick sideburns grew down his cheeks like unruly vines. Had some mistress told him that she liked that more serious look?, Sisi wondered. She didn't know. She knew so little of the life he had led these past years.

Franz spoke first, his stiff features softening into the hint of a smile. "Good to see you, Elisabeth."

"And you, Franz." She noticed the rate at which her heart raced.

"You look ravishing, as always." He sounded earnest, and Sisi felt satisfaction at the compliment. She had, after all, spent the whole day preening for this meeting. She had selected a formal evening gown of cream-colored silk, detailed with silver thread stitched in the shape of roses. With the help of her new Parisian corset, she had tucked her tiny waist into the tight-fitting gown and had covered her wrists, throat, and ears in diamonds. Her cheeks were brightened with rouge. Her brunette curls, fragrant from the perfumed water, were pulled back in a loose coronet, accented with pearls and white petals.

Sisi's beauty regimen had been fastidious and strict for years, but that had been more for the routine and the familiarity of the process; not until this night had she so fervently longed to appear pretty. She suspected that she had succeeded.

"You have not aged a day." Franz still looked at her and she sensed the stirring of his desire. Men were so frail, Sisi thought with bitter satisfaction.

"If only that were true." She lowered her eyes, fluttering her lashes.

"That's not to say that you look exactly the same." Franz still studied her. "This is new." He pointed at her head.

"Oh?" Sisi grazed her heavy bun with gloved fingers. "Oh, yes, I've grown my hair out."

"I had heard that you had hired a new hairdresser. And that, with the way she fashioned your hair, you were the envy of the entire court. Even the other courts of Europe." Franz still looked at her, a wistful smile glimmering behind his serious features. "No longer a young girl with simple braids."

"No."

"It looks nice."

"Thank you." She wondered, in that moment, whether he remembered the fight they had once had over a hairdresser.

Franz gestured toward the corner, where a table was covered in a damask cloth and set with candles. "If you would join me?"

"Indeed." She accepted his arm and he escorted her to the table, set for two.

"How was your journey?" Franz neglected

623

the assistance of a footman, helping Sisi into her chair by himself.

"Which one?"

"That's right." Franz laughed. "You're a world traveler now. I never knew from where your next letter would arrive: Corfu? Egypt? Madeira? But I was referring to the most immediate journey, from Possenhofen to here."

"Fine. Tiresome but fine. And yours, Franz?"

He seated himself opposite her at the small round table, his hands reaching for the crisp napkin with an efficient flourish of the wrist. "You know how it is, traveling with the children."

"No, I don't, really."

"Well it's never quite uneventful. But we made it, that's what matters."

"I hope I will be able to see them soon," Sisi said, masking the urgency that she felt as she said it. Franz had never responded well to her frantic insistence.

He nodded now, lowering his eyes. "They would like that."

A footman appeared then, delivering two bowls of hearty vegetable and pork stew.

"How is your family?" Franz tucked a napkin into his collar and leaned over his stew.

"They are well, thank you." Sisi looked at her stew but had little interest in eating it. Her corset was too tight. And lately she preferred to eat bland dishes, if anything, in the evenings: boiled chicken, flavorless broth.

"What is the latest from Possenhofen, Elisabeth?"

"Karl has a nice new wife. I believe she has improved him, in fact. I think she might be to blame for his gentler demeanor." Sisi smiled as she remembered her brother, and the change that had occurred in their relationship. "No, thank you." She shook her head, rejecting the offer of wine from the footman.

"Yes, you mentioned in one of your letters that your brother had married."

"Indeed." Sisi nodded.

"And Helene as well, you said?"

"Helene married a good man, a prince from Thurn," Sisi answered. "She did not win the argument to end in a nunnery, but she did find herself a kind, gentle groom."

"I hope she received the gift I sent?" Franz wiped the red broth from the corners of his mouth, where it stained his silvered beard.

"Indeed, she was very grateful. It was a lovely silver service."

"Good." Franz nodded, pouring himself more wine. "I'm happy for your sister. Helene deserves much happiness."

They both fell quiet and Sisi wondered if Franz was thinking, as she was, about years earlier; when he himself had been betrothed to Helene. How his love for her, Sisi, had prevented the match. Had he made the right choice? she wondered now. Had they been wise to act so impulsively? To act on what they'd thought, as mere children, was love?

They sat in silence for several moments longer. Eventually, Franz spoke, his words as feeble as thread as he grasped for some way to weave them together. "I read that your cousin Ludwig has ascended to the throne in Bavaria."

"King Ludwig is *our* cousin, isn't that so, Franz?" Sisi cocked her head. "Don't forget, your mother is a Bavarian, just like my mother, even if she would never dare admit it."

Franz slurped his soup, retreating back into silence.

As the first course was cleared, Sisi spoke. "I am sorry to hear about Italy."

Franz coughed into his napkin, wiping his mustache. "That was a blow, indeed." He looked into her eyes now, redirecting the conversation. "Did you not enjoy the soup, Elisabeth?"

"Oh, that's right." Sisi nodded, rapping the table with ringed fingers. "We don't discuss politics. Or military affairs. Or anything of import." She said it with a smile, but her words were without cheer.

"Please don't be cross." Franz leaned toward her. "I simply wondered if the meal had displeased you."

"I rarely eat in the evenings."

"How is that? I remember you having a healthy appetite. This is a change."

Many things have changed, Sisi felt like answering. But she simply said: "It upsets my stomach." Sisi watched as several footmen appeared with plates of breaded veal, beets, green salad, rolls, boiled potatoes, and candied pears.

"Well, then, I'm sorry I ordered so much food." Franz watched ruefully as the plates were delivered to the table. He pointed to the veal. "We had to have *Wiener schnitzel* in honor of your return. Won't you have a bite?"

Sisi obliged him, spearing herself a small serving of the breaded meat. The footmen retreated and they were left alone once more, seated in an uncomfortable, unfamiliar silence.

"Thank you for inviting me to join you for dinner," Sisi said eventually, looking up at him.

"Of course." Franz swallowed a mouthful of potatoes. "I was eager to see you. It has been a long time." He paused. "Too long."

"It has," she agreed.

"Four years," he said, as if she were unaware of the fact.

How much would they actually address of what had happened between them? The reason for her departure? She decided perhaps he ought to be the one to bring it up, to apologize for his part.

"I hope that you are back . . . for good, now?" Franz looked down at his plate, tearing apart his veal with several stabs of his fork.

"I plan to be. I missed the children so very much. I hope I will be able to see them tomorrow?"

Without missing a beat, Franz answered, "I will check with Mother to see what she has planned for them."

Sisi lowered her fork to her plate, attempting to remain calm. It was the manner in which he had said it: casual, oblivious. Unaware of the painful longing that filled her, the rightful mother. Before Sisi could suppress them, the words burst forward from her mouth like bile. "Do you allow your courtesans near our children?"

Franz choked on a bite of veal and immediately began coughing over his plate. Several footmen rushed forward, hovering nearby like solicitous governesses. Franz took several large gulps of wine. Eventually his cough subsided, and with watery eyes and a red face, he looked up at his wife. "Excuse me."

"Do you, Franz?" Though she had spoken to no one at court during her absence, and would have had no spies to give her information on the names or positions of the ladies, Sisi harbored no naïve illusion that Franz had abstained from all female companionship in her absence.

"Elisabeth, please." Looking over his shoulders, embarrassed by the presence of the footmen, Franz leaned forward and whispered, "Our children spend their time with their Grandmamma, my mother. As well as their governesses and their tutors. And with me, of course. No . . . er . . . *courtiers* have much interaction with them, except in the most controlled of capacities."

Sisi leaned back, pushing away her untouched food. Enough with this Habsburg habit of skirting around things: implications and insinuations but never outright honesty. "Oh, come now, Franz, let's not be so squeamish. Everyone knows that I was ill. And that's the reason I had to travel south to Madeira. Your mistress made you ill, and you made me ill."

Franz threw another nervous glance toward a footman in the corner before leaning in to speak. "You went south to heal, Elisabeth, I'll grant you that. But no one, not even the doctors, was perfectly certain what caused your illness. And certainly no one told you that you needed to stay away so long."

"No, that was my decision," Sisi answered. "That point I will concede. And I hope you will concede that your mistress made me ill. I've never heard you apologize."

"Elisa, of course I regret that you were hurt, but if you would only . . ."

"Elisa?"

"It's not as though you've been blameless," Franz said, a rare tinge of emotion — irritation, perhaps? — apparent in his voice. "You were gone, long before. And then you outright left us. I wondered how you could stay away as long as you did. It struck me as highly . . . unnatural."

"Unnatural? And what was natural about our arrangement for me? Losing my children? Spending my days haunted by that . . . that *woman,* Countess Esterházy?"

"Elisabeth, please —"

"Why would I come back? To share you with all of the other women? Your mother, first among them. And then God knows who else?"

"Enough" — Franz winced — "please."

"Oh, I'm sorry, is it too vile? These things may be done, but just not spoken of, is that how it happens? What did you call it? *Repräsentazions-pflicht.* 'Keeping up a fine front.' That's what you told me on our wedding day, wasn't it?"

"I shall not even try logic, Elisabeth." His frustration, his condescension — he sounded so much like Sophie.

"What logic?" she asked, her tone bitter.

"That . . ." Franz paused. "That for an emperor to have a . . . to have companions . . . is a perfectly natural custom. A custom as old as time itself. Especially after you with-

630

drew from me. You never seemed to acknowledge it, but I do have certain . . . rights . . . as emperor. Everyone seems to understand it but you." His hand gripped the napkin, twisting it, as his eyes avoided hers. "It says nothing about how I feel about you, Elisabeth. Nothing. Surely you know that?"

Sisi exhaled an angry laugh. "You'll have to forgive me, Franz. I never did quite catch on to the Habsburg manner of doing things."

They sat opposite one another in a tense stillness. Eventually Franz served himself a second helping of veal. Sisi could barely look at her plate: so rich, so heavy, so *Austrian.*

After he had finished a second serving of dinner and several glasses of wine, Franz broke the silence. "I truly regret how things happened between us."

Sisi didn't answer. Let him offer more than that, she thought, sipping a glass of cold water.

Franz put his forearms on the table, propping himself up. "I do hope, now that you're home, that things might improve between us."

Sisi looked at her husband, head cocked. "How so, Franz?"

"Well, you *are* still my wife." Franz folded his hands and let the words hang between them. When Sisi did not reply, he took a long sip of wine and continued, "I've put a lot of thought into this." He waved his hands toward her then back toward himself. "I've asked myself: What's best for both of us? What's best for the children?"

Sisi stared at him, her eyes unblinking.

"Elisabeth, I'd very much like to return to how things used to be between us. Give . . . this . . . another try. If you would be willing to do that."

Sisi thought about this: *to return to how things used to be between us.* But she was not the girl he had married. She no longer loved him. In fact, she no longer believed herself capable of loving any man. And that was through no lack of effort on her part; that was *his* doing.

"Return to how things used to be between us?" She looked up at him, her eyes cold as she repeated the proposition.

"Yes." Franz pushed himself back in his chair, his full belly now pressing against the restricting confines of his starched military jacket. "You are still my wife. And I'm still very fond of you." His eyes wandered down toward her exposed shoulders, her bare arms. Sisi repressed the urge to shudder.

When she spoke next, her tone was light. She could not offend him until she had the guarantee of seeing her children. "I'm here, Franz, aren't I? I plan to take up my duties as empress once more. I plan to take up my duties as mother. What else do you envision happening?"

His eyelids appeared to be growing droopy,

perhaps from too much wine and meat. "I had hoped that you might be willing to . . . return to the marriage."

Sisi knew how to put him off. "So you are offering to give up your mistresses?"

Franz lowered his gaze, his elbows propping himself up on the table, and Sisi confirmed what she had expected: that he did not expect to have to part with any of his *companions.* Emperors always had mistresses, didn't they? That was what her mother had told her when Sisi had wept over her husband's discovered infidelity. The fact that Franz had waited so many years to take a mistress had been testament to his deep love for his empress. Hadn't Sisi's own father, a mere duke, produced bastards all over his duchy?

Franz switched to port now, pouring himself a full glass. "Please don't be vulgar, Elisabeth."

Franz was not the soft, sensitive boy who had fallen in love with her. He was not the reckless young suitor who had asked her to dance and then presented her with a bouquet of flowers at a ball in Bad Ischl. He was not the love-struck groom who had whispered to her on their wedding day. Sisi saw that. Years of power and pressure had hardened him: years at war, years spent arguing in the council of ministers, years spent bedding pliant lovers.

He was somehow impenetrable now. Haughty, requiring others' submission. More stiff and more certain of his exalted status as Emperor Franz Joseph.

Seeing that she would not answer him on his proposition, Franz changed topics. "Rudolf reminds me of you, Elisabeth. You ought to see him."

Sisi did not answer, but her heart faltered in her chest.

"What? You do wish to see your children, do you not?" He looked up from his port.

"I long to see them with an aching more severe than you know, Franz." Sisi clutched the table and leaned forward. "Please, tell me when."

He nodded, taken aback by the intensity of her response. "I have no doubt that once you see little Rudy, you will join me in longing for more children. More sons, especially."

Sisi winced and Franz noticed. "Oh. Is that such a painful thought to you?"

The thought of having more children petrified Sisi. She would not do it. She could not. And not just for the reasons Franz might have expected: hurt feelings, resentment over her separation from the first three. No, Sisi doubted that she could physically carry more children. She had enlisted the services of her own doctor, a Doctor Fischer, while in Bavaria to help her understand why she often went months without having her cycle. Marie told her it was on account of her strict diet and long hours spent riding and hiking. But that mattered not. She had done her duty — she had produced an heir. She had no further desire to share a bed with her husband, not when he had invited other women into their union. He was the one who had severed that tie, not Sisi.

"Franz, just please promise me that I may see the children."

Franz drained his glass and placed it down on the table, his movements tired. "You may see them, Elisabeth."

"Tomorrow?"

"Tomorrow."

"Where?"

"Come back here in the morning, following breakfast. I will arrange for them to visit me instead of taking their lessons."

"Please." Sisi's voice cracked. "Please just them. Not your mother."

Franz sighed, as if to say: *This again?* But he nodded his agreement.

"Thank you, Franz."

They finished dinner with cordial chatter. Sisi was determined not to anger Franz lest he retract his offer to let her visit the children. And Franz was sleepy from too much dinner and wine.

The gardens outside grew dark and quiet, the only sound wafting through the windows was that of the fountains humming in a low gurgle. Sisi yawned, eager to be asleep so that tomorrow might come sooner.

"You've had a long day of travel, Franz. Perhaps I ought to let you retire."

"Thank you, I think that is best." Franz pushed himself away from the table and rose to a stand, not helping Sisi this time. They exchanged a casual kiss on the cheek before heading for opposite doors.

Franz paused on the far side of the room, hovering for a moment. Sisi turned.

"Good night, Elisabeth."

"Good night, Franz." As Sisi left the room, she could not help but overhear the order given by her husband to his nearby valet. "Fetch the carriage. I shall go and visit Frau Anna Nahowski."

Sisi walked briskly down the long, candlelit hallway, her heels landing in angry stomps on the varnished floor. Her mind was spinning. Just minutes after proposing a marital reunion between the two of them, Franz was off to visit some woman. Did he spend every night with this woman, just as he had once slept in Sisi's bed every night? She shivered as she pictured his once-familiar body twisted up in the sheets, his arms around some other body. She had known that he spent time with other women; she had even arrived at some sort of resignation, if not acceptance of it. So then why did it torture her so to hear it confirmed?

Sisi was fuming, and grateful that the halls before her stretched dark and empty. She passed no one but an alarmed footman, lighting the row of chandeliers that lined the hallway. "Empress." The man bowed quickly, nearly dropping his candles. Sisi kept marching past. Alone. *Scurrying through the hallways alone.*

It was late in the evening. Their dinner had gone so long that the rest of the court would have retired to private apartments by now: laughing over card games, singing songs over the piano, seeking out lovers for surreptitious trysts. How she missed Possenhofen and its quiet, dark familiarity. There, where she was more likely to be woken by the distant howl of a wolf than the giggle of a young, champagne-drunk duchess returning from her lover's apartments.

Sisi didn't notice the man approaching, not until she nearly bumped into him. "Excuse me," she stammered, startled by the tall outline, the figure obscured in the dim shadows where the footman and his candles had not yet reached. "I didn't see anybody there."

"Your Majesty?" The voice was deep, laced with an accent that Sisi immediately recognized as Hungarian.

"Yes?" Sisi narrowed her eyes and looked up into the face opposite her, her eyes still adjusting to the dark. "Count Andrássy?"

"At your service, Empress Elisabeth." Andrássy swept her gloved hand up in his and placed a kiss on it, bending into a deep bow before her.

"Hello, Count Andrássy." Sisi completed a perfunctory curtsy before realizing that, as Empress, she need not bow to him.

"It's a surprise to see you, Empress. And a pleasure."

"And you, Count." Andrássy was her husband's former rival, the leader of the Hungarians who had clamored for independence. What was he doing at Schönbrunn?

"Many people are happy to have you back, Empress."

"Back? But how long have you been here — I am surprised to find *you* at court, Count Andrássy."

Andrássy laughed at her bluntness. "Why is that, Empress? We Hungarians and Austrians are friends now, are we not?"

Sisi thought about this. "Are we?"

"I certainly hope so. After all, it was your husband and I who worked so very hard to ensure that we would be." Andrássy smiled at her, his dark eyes catching the flecks of the distant candlelight. Now he whispered, "As long as I keep my hopes quiet that someday my country will be free."

"Ah." Sisi looked over her shoulder out of habit before smiling, leaning toward him and whispering: *"I love those who yearn for the impossible."*

Andrássy cocked his eyebrows, impressed. "I had forgotten that Your Majesty reads Goethe."

"Daily," Sisi responded, equally impressed that he recognized it. She began to walk, continuing on toward her apartments. Andrássy fell in step beside her.

"Then in that case, I must insist that we be friends."

"Good," Sisi responded, turning a sideways glance toward him. Her eyes had adjusted now, and she saw that Andrássy looked as handsome as he had that night in Budapest, years earlier. He wore a simple black suit that was just a shade darker than his hair and neat mustache. He kept his hair longer than most men in the court, and it fell around his ears in thick, unruly waves. "I am glad of that, Count Andrássy. You are far too agreeable to despise."

"But did you really despise me?" he asked, his eyes darting toward hers with a merry smile.

"Only until I met you, I suppose."

He nodded, accepting that answer. After a pause, he spoke: "You look very well, Empress."

"Thank you, Count."

"I hope that your trip served its purpose? And that you feel recovered from whatever it was that ailed you?"

Sisi bit her lower lip but did not answer. She was grateful for Andrássy's perception; he quickly changed the topic. "I had heard that you returned several days ago. Tell me, did you receive the bottles of wines I delivered to your suite?"

"The wine!" Sisi said, bringing a hand to her lips, remembering the crate that Herr Lobkowitz had brought in earlier that day. "You must think me so impolite. Yes, I did receive them. Thank you, Count."

"But of course," Andrássy said. "The gift comes not from me alone, but from all Hungarians. We have missed you at court. I think I speak for the entire nation when I say that you have become a sort of champion in our collective imagination." He whispered this last part, "You are the most popular Habsburg in Hungary."

She felt her cheeks growing warm.

Andrássy lifted his eyebrows in a playful expression. "Dare I say, the *only* popular Habsburg in Hungary?"

"But the least popular Habsburg among the Habsburgs," Sisi answered. They both laughed.

"They are the same wines we served at my dinner party." Andrássy leaned close to her, as if they were in a crowded room and not an abandoned hallway. "The night you honored me with a dance." Now his dark eyes twinkled with mischief, and Sisi forced herself to look away.

"I'm afraid that fact went right over my head, Count. You give me too much credit when in fact I know very little about wine."

"In that case, why don't I speak to the cooks and plan a tasting for us tomorrow at luncheon? You have a Hungarian countess, Marie Festetics, in your household, do you not? It could be good fun for us, and the emperor should join us as well, if he is available."

Sisi shook her head. "Tomorrow will not be possible, Count. I plan to see my children in the morning, and if everything goes as I hope it will, the meeting won't be over by luncheon."

"But of course that is your main priority, Empress." Andrássy nodded knowingly. "I am sure they have missed their mother almost as much as you have missed them."

Sisi thought about this, pausing her steps. "I fear not," she said, surprised at the overwhelming need to confess. "I fear that there is no place left where I might find a foothold in their little hearts."

Andrássy paused opposite Sisi, looking at her as he considered this. "But no one can ever fill the role of a mother, Empress. I am sure it is just a matter of time. Now that you are back they will get to know you and fall in love with you, as all who know you do."

Sisi looked up at Andrássy, grateful for his kind words, even if he was merely being polite. They continued along in silence, Sisi stealing one more sideways glance toward Andrássy. He really did cut a striking figure beside her, so tall and strong and dark. But it was the intangible characteristic that made him truly attractive: his calm, unassuming self-confidence. Andrássy's was a self-assurance that came not from a military uniform or a title, but a deeper, more immutable aspect. He was a well-liked and respected leader, a good man, and he knew it. He knew it without needing it validated — a truly rare trait in this court.

"Thank you for saying that," Sisi said eventually, her tone quiet.

"I try to make it a duty to speak the truth," Andrássy answered.

"And how about you — have you been well, Count?"

"Indeed." Andrássy nodded, reaching into a pocket and retrieving a small portrait, which he offered to Sisi. "I've recently been married. Here is my Katinka."

Sisi looked down into the face of a serious, square-jawed woman with dark waves and a plain, sensible bun. She wore a jeweled gown, surely her wedding dress. She looked older than Andrássy, and less spirited.

"My congratulations to you, Count." And

then, to be polite, Sisi added: "She is beautiful."

"Thank you, Empress Elisabeth." Andrássy tucked the miniature likeness back into his pocket and looked back at Sisi. "She remains in Hungary."

"You must long for your new bride while you are here in Vienna."

"I have been busy," Andrássy said. Sisi studied him, noticing no warmth or husbandly pride in Andrássy's tone as he spoke of his wife.

"She does not wish to see the court? I would welcome her gladly. She could join my household, if you wished that for her."

"A truly generous offer, Empress." Andrássy frowned. "And I thank you for it. But Katinka has little interest in policy or travel." Turning to her, he said, "You have been quite the traveler of late, have you not?"

"Yes."

"Madeira. Greece. Corfu. I followed your progress as best I could. It sounds as though you've been to some savage places."

"None as savage as this court, I can assure you, Count Andrássy."

Andrássy laughed and Sisi joined him.

"Do you plan to leave again soon, or will you stay some time in Vienna?"

"I plan to stay here as long as I can tolerate it."

"That is how I plan my stays in Vienna as

well, Empress."

They continued to walk beside one another in a comfortable silence. After several moments, Andrássy spoke. "Well, you should know that you are always most welcome in Budapest. It is, after all, your kingdom. Please do let me know if you should ever like to travel there, and I'd be happy to arrange it."

Sisi paused, looking toward him. She remembered the freedom she had felt racing across the plains, hugging the Danube River on horseback. It felt as if it had been in another life. It had been.

"It would be fun to teach my children to ride there," she said.

"The plains of Pest," Andrássy agreed. "No better place."

Sisi nodded and continued her walk. "I am looking for a Hungarian attendant, Count Andrássy. Someone discreet. Someone whom I can trust in my chambers. The less she cares for Austria, for this court . . . the better."

"Would Your Majesty like my assistance in filling this post?"

"I've asked my lady, Countess Marie, to assist me. Speak with her."

"I know the Countess Festetics. I'm certain that, between the two of us, we can find a very worthy candidate."

"Thank you, Count Andrássy."

"It is I who must thank you, Empress. You do great honor to Hungary. And my people see this and appreciate it."

They approached the corner that would lead them down the hallway toward Sisi's suite.

"This is where I take my leave, Empress."

"Wait." Sisi paused, taking a hold of Andrássy's arm so that he, too, paused beside her.

"Is anything the matter, Majesty?" His dark eyes peered down at her, concern suddenly evident in his expression.

Sisi shook her head, no. She was not yet ready to turn the corner and face the guards outside her door. And then, beyond the door, Marie and Franziska would be waiting, launching their questions: Had the dinner been a success? Would she reconcile with Franz? Her heart raced. Oh, she was not yet ready to surrender this quiet, peaceful moment. Not yet ready to leave Andrássy's company and the reprieve it had somehow provided for her.

Before she understood what she was doing, Sisi leaned forward and swept Andrássy's hands up into her own, lifting them to her, squeezing his palms. She clung to him, as if petrified that he might let go. It was a sudden, abrupt movement. An egregious breach in protocol.

Andrássy stood motionless. After a pause, he squeezed her hands once. An unspoken gesture, meant to give comfort, and then he slid his hands free.

Still watching her with his intent, silky-eyed gaze, he took his hands behind his back, crossing them, as if trying to conceal a crime.

"I'm sorry." Sisi lifted her hands and cupped them in front of her face, wishing she could melt into the floor and out of sight. "I'm so sorry. I don't know why I did that. I think I went mad for a moment. Seeing Franz . . . the emperor . . . for the first time in years. And thinking about my children, knowing they are somewhere in this palace, and yet I cannot get to them. And knowing that I will have to face *her* . . . the archduchess . . . again. And wondering at every turn if I might bump into one of my husband's lovers. I went completely mad. And now I am telling you all of this, as if you care, and you must only be further convinced of my madness. Oh, I am so sorry."

Sisi lowered her hands and stared at Andrássy, embarrassed by her decidedly unregal behavior. Reaching for a man like that, clinging to him like a shameless coquette at a dance. He looked at her for several moments, a quizzical expression on his face. And then, the sound of his laughter erupted throughout the quiet hallway. He tried to suppress it, but that only seemed to prompt him further, and Sisi was so relieved that she joined him, allowing her stomach to burst against her corset with full-bellied laughter. She clutched her sides, wincing, but she could not stop herself. The harder he laughed, the louder she did, too. They stood opposite one another, two powerless people in the throes of giddy, all-consuming hysterics.

Eventually, Andrássy spoke: *"We do not have to visit a madhouse . . ."*

". . . to find disordered minds." Sisi finished the Goethe line, *"The world is the madhouse of the universe."*

"A palace is no exception." Andrássy nodded his head, his eyes alight with good-hearted amusement.

"Still, I am mortified." Sisi brought her hand to her cheek, certain it was flushed a deep crimson.

"When you took my hands, Empress, I thought that perhaps you wished to dance with me again? As we did in Budapest years ago."

So he remembers that night, too. Sisi felt heat rise to her cheeks, to her neck, to the flesh of her breast.

"But alas, we lack the music," Andrássy said, his eyes still twinkling.

Sisi swallowed, attempting to compose herself, to rein her features back into an expression of collectedness. "Thank you, Count Andrássy. Really."

"For what?"

"For, well, for your understanding, I suppose."

"I did not mean to laugh at your troubles, of course, Empress. I simply found it . . . unexpected."

"What?"

"Here you are, our beautiful, beloved Empress. Half of your subjects in Hungary believe you are divine by birth. And you're standing before me, spilling the cares of your heart. It comforts me to know that you, too, are troubled by the same woes as the rest of us mortals."

"If you only knew, Andrássy."

"I'm afraid that if you tell me, you might take a hold of me again." He smiled good-naturedly. "And then, being a proper, chivalrous gentleman, I might feel compelled to kiss you in your distress."

Sisi's heart tumbled in her breast, bouncing up into her throat, knocking the words off her lips.

Bowing before her, Andrássy took her hand to his lips and whispered: "Good night, Empress Elisabeth."

"Good night, Count Andrássy." She let him kiss her hand. Another breach in protocol. A harmless enough gesture, yet it prompted a shiver on her skin.

When he spoke, his face was close to hers, his voice barely a whisper. "Will you please call me Andrássy, just Andrássy? I've never really liked the idea of the title."

"That makes two of us."

XIV.

Sisi's tutor: Your Majesty wears her hair like a crown instead of the crown.

Sisi: Except that any other crown is more easily laid aside.

CHAPTER FOURTEEN

HOFBURG PALACE, VIENNA
OCTOBER 1862

"Good morning, Elisabeth." The archduchess did not look up from her breakfast when Sisi's entrance was announced. Sophie sat eating toast and pastries with the children, her waist full and round beside the small nursery table. At her feet her little dog snored.

"Good morning, Sophie. I'm here for the children." It was a clear morning, warm, with the last hint of autumn's softness, and Sisi was eager to take her children out into the gardens.

"They are not yet finished with their breakfast." Sophie turned back to her coffee. She often resisted these scheduled morning outings.

"Well, this was the hour of my appointment. It should come as no surprise."

Sophie sighed and put her cup down on the table. Mumbling some soft censure to Gisela, admonishing her granddaughter to sit up straight, Sophie turned to her daughter-in-law for the first time. "I'm not certain that today is the best day to go off gallivanting with the children. I had planned for Rudolf to see his tutor this morning."

Sisi resisted the urge to scowl, reminding herself to remain calm. "He's four, Sophie. He can play with his toy soldiers at any time. I'm sure his tutor need not supervise such activity."

"My son . . . the emperor . . . began his military training when he was this age. Why, we had him in a military uniform at age four. I don't expect you to understand the importance of this education, or the pressure the crown prince will someday shoulder. Not when your days consist of washing your hair and riding horses and . . . composing poetry."

This stung. Plus, Sisi had not told her mother-in-law of her new hobby of composing poems, and she made a note to have Marie find out who this latest spy might have been. Nevertheless, Sisi let the comment go unanswered — Sophie's barbed words had little consequence since Franz had sanctioned these visits, and both she and her mother-in-law knew that. Clapping her hands, Sisi walked toward the table. "Come, children, Mamma has arranged an outing to the pond. We shall go feed the ducks."

"But I am still eating." Gisela looked up, her bouncy curls pulled back in two tight braids. At six, she resembled her mother, yet resisted Sisi's attempts to get close.

"Mamma has ordered a picnic, my love. We can eat again as soon as we are outside. We must go enjoy this sunshine."

"I'm ready, Mamma!" Rudy rose from his chair and wobbled toward Sisi, landing in her skirt for a full-bodied hug.

"Hello, my darling boy." Sisi leaned over and ran her fingers through his loose brown ringlets.

Sophie stared at Sisi, her eyes taking in her daughter-in-law's tightly corseted waist. Sisi delighted inwardly: her narrow frame was her favorite way of defying her mother-in-law. With a waist cinched to just above eighteen inches, it was clear to all, especially her mother-in-law, that Sisi did not carry Franz's child. She was master of her body once more, no longer living as a breeding mare whose sole purpose was to populate the Habsburg line.

Avoiding her mother-in-law, Sisi said, "Gisela?"

The little girl turned to her grandmother, awaiting her verdict.

Sophie sighed. "Go ahead, my darling."

"But I wish to stay with you, Grand-mamma."

"But your papa says you must go." Sophie scowled and slurped her coffee, now seated alone at the nursery table.

■ ■ ■ ■

Outside in the Burggarten, the sprawling expanse of the imperial gardens reserved only for members of the royal family, the grass was warm from the sun's light. Sisi spread an oversized blanket a few yards from the pond. She reached into a basket and retrieved bread, which she crumbled and handed to Rudy. "Stay close to me, my darling, understand?"

Rudy nodded, then ran toward the water, his hands dropping morsels of food before he had even reached the pond's edge.

Her daughter stood at the far end of the blanket, watching her brother chase a row of ducklings. "Gisela, would you like some food for the ducks as well?"

Gisela shook her head, looking away from her mother. It was painful, her daughter's coldness, but she understood it. This girl had lived almost the entirety of her six years under the constant supervision of her grandmother. Sisi had little hope that what the girl had heard about her absent mother had been positive. Or perhaps — an even more painful thought — she had heard *nothing* about her mother.

"Then how about some food for you? You said in the nursery that you wanted more breakfast."

Now Gisela looked toward her mother, her tiny features still pulled tight in an untrusting scowl. "All right." Gisela nodded.

"What would you like? I have boiled eggs." Sisi riffled through the picnic basket she had ordered. "And cucumbers from the garden."

"I want a cheese tart," Gisela said, walking closer across the blanket.

Sisi shook her head. "We do not have any cheese tarts."

"Then an apple strudel with *Schlag.*"

"I did not bring pastries."

"Why not?" Gisela crossed her arms and puffed out her lower lip.

"Mamma!" Rudy was running back toward them, a terrified expression on his face.

"What's the matter, my darling?" Sisi reached for her son, pulling him into a hug. She saw that, behind him, several ducklings trailed. "There, there, my darling. No need to be afraid. They are simply hungry."

Rudolf looked at her, unconvinced.

"Go now, feed them." Sisi handed him another fistful of crumbs and he reluctantly rose to walk back toward the ducks.

Gisela still looked at Sisi, reluctant to step closer to her and the picnic basket. "Grand-mamma always brings pastries on picnics."

Sisi thought about this. "Gisela, there is a queen in England named Victoria. She has eaten so many sausages and pastries in her life that, now, they say —" Sisi paused, looking into her little daughter's hazel eyes as she blinked, her attention finally turned on her mother. A thought tugged on Sisi's conscience: Was it wrong of her to share with her daughter her own fears, the dread she felt about growing large?

"Oh, never mind." Sisi sighed, waving her hands. "How about this: how about once Rudy has fed the ducks, we go into the greenhouse. You see that building over there? The one built entirely in glass?"

Gisela followed her mother's pointing. "Yes."

"What do you suppose they have in there, my darling Gisela?"

"I don't know."

"They have butterflies. Butterflies in every color you could possibly imagine. Would you like to go pick your favorite?"

Gisela thought about this, her short arms crossed in front of her chest. Eventually, she nodded. Sisi could have leapt up in joy. A small victory.

Just then a carriage pulled up across the yard, stopping at the main entrance to the palace. Sisi watched as a dark-haired man alighted from it, extending his hand to help a woman step out.

Even from this far away, Sisi knew who it was. "Andrássy."

Just then, he looked back over his shoulder, issuing an order to the footman. But there was no way he would see her, Sisi, not unless he knew to look all the way across the gardens. She shielded her eyes from the strong sun to gain a better look at him, and the woman who accompanied him. She didn't recognize the lady, a blonde in a daytime gown of a rich fawn-colored brocade. Her curls were pinned back and partly covered by a matching cap, and Sisi was certain that this was not the wife whose image Andrássy had shown her. Katinka, he had called his wife. This light-haired woman smiled up at Andrássy as he escorted her toward the palace.

"Rudy?" Sisi called to her son, who turned at the sound of his name. "Rudy, come here for a moment."

"I'm still feeding the ducklings," her son protested.

"Just for a moment, I wish for you to see someone." Sisi rose, taking her children each by the hand. "You see that man over there? I want you to remember his name; it is Count Julius Andrássy. Listen for his name, for he is a very good man and I think we all must learn from him."

Just then, as if he heard his name mentioned, Andrássy searched the grounds, his stare landing squarely on Sisi. She stood up straight, tense, as their eyes held one another in a locked gaze, the distance between them suddenly removed.

Eventually, Andrássy bowed his head in her

direction, a smile on his lips. The fair-haired lady beside him noticed this, and her look now fell on Sisi as well. The lady whispered something into Andrássy's ear, as if to pull his attention back from the empress onto herself. Why, Sisi wondered, was she jealous of a woman whom she had never before seen?

Sisi visited the nursery two mornings a week, and attended church with her children and husband each week. On mornings when she was not with her children, she stayed in her rooms, nibbling on a light breakfast in bed and reading poetry and tending to her toilette: brushing her hair, having massages with oil, and experimenting with new creams and ointments that promised to keep her skin youthful and her waist tight.

Her beauty treatments took hours to complete, and she found that she often grew bored while waiting for Franziska to tame and style her long hair. For this reason, she worked on composing poetry and reapplied herself to her study of Hungarian.

"I've been terribly lax with my studies," Sisi sighed to Marie, whom she was using as a tutor once more. She had enlisted Andrássy to find a suitable Hungarian maid with whom she might also practice.

Sisi rarely passed an afternoon without some form of rigorous activity outdoors, regardless of the weather. Her favorite activity was still riding, and the imperial guards assigned to her had had to improve their equestrian skills in order not to lose sight of her when she took off out of the palace walls. Finding that Diamant could no longer keep up with her stringent demands, Sisi had acquired a new, two-year-old Lippizaner whom she called *Vándor,* Hungarian for Wanderer.

Together, Sisi and her companion would wander for hours, racing along the Danube and through the Vienna Woods, oftentimes returning to the palace sweat-soaked and cloaked in the darkness of evening.

Doctor Fischer, whom Sisi had moved permanently to court in order to replace Sophy's ally, Doctor Seeburger, warned her against such a schedule.

"Empress, with the amount of physical strain to which your body is regularly subjected, coupled with what I must call an inadequate diet, your body will be very unlikely to conceive. I think you are jeopardizing your ability to have another son."

"Good," Sisi would answer, unaffected. She did not bother to tell the physician that conception was already made impossible by the fact that she and Franz never shared a bed.

Sisi saw her husband in an official capacity: she stood beside him in the dazzling splendor of the crowded Spiegelsaal, in the frenzied environment of the Burgtheater, in the pious setting of the mass. When they were together, it was easy enough to be cordial. They had settled into an understanding, a way of coexisting in their marriage. She, more popular and beloved by the common people, would accompany Franz when he required her. In return, he ensured that she was given access to her children. Though she sometimes caught him looking at her with a gaze that spoke plainly of his desire for her, Franz had not revisited the topic of a physical rapprochement.

On the evenings when she had successfully evaded Franz's tiresome state dinners, Sisi kept to her rooms. She combatted loneliness and melancholy with a never-ending list of hobbies and tasks, an agenda to keep both her and her household occupied. She kept the candles lit and her attendants busy dispatching her orders until she was ready to fall asleep. But still, insomnia kept its nightly vigil by her bed. The hours after midnight terrified her: lying alone with nothing to do but think proved worse than any nightmare. Oftentimes, struggling against the itch of restlessness, Sisi would pull her bell and summon Franziska or Marie well before dawn.

Herr Lobkowitz had delivered on his promise of finding Sisi the two quietest, most plain and discreet young maidens at the court to attend to the empress. Countess Frederika von Rothburg spoke so softly, and with a northern accent so thick, that Sisi oftentimes found her incomprehensible. And Lady Ilse von Bittel was so timid that Sisi was certain that the withdrawn, frail young girl didn't have the capacity to be a gossip. Andrássy, too, had delivered on his promise and had found for Sisi a kind-faced woman by the name of Ida Ferenczy, a Hungarian, to act as the attendant in her apartments.

It was late spring, shortly before the imperial court would relocate to Schönbrunn, and one of the final days before the afternoons grew unbearably warm and riding became unpleasant. Sisi had paused her afternoon ride, allowing her horse to rest. She was in a rural area, one hour's ride outside Vienna and the palace. She lay on the cool earth beside the Danube, looking up at cloudless blue as her breathing slowed and her body cooled. She would have to bring Rudy to this spot for a picnic, she thought to herself, imagining how he would enjoy seeing the wildflowers that dotted the green fields.

And then, as it always happened, the thoughts of her children pulled her into sadness. An aching feeling somewhere deep inside, between her heart and her gut. Grief over how seldom she saw them, and how little say she had in their upbringing. Over the fact that, in just a couple of months, her sweet, sensitive little boy would be plucked from the nursery and stuffed into a military uniform and subjected to the first stages of drills and training at the hands of stern and unforgiving military tutors. It was no way to raise the gentle, free-spirited little boy. A little boy who shared her love for nature and animals and kisses and stories.

Sisi reached into her sack and retrieved her notebook. Her notebook, where she confessed her hurts and composed lines that spoke of her loneliness; it was the best salve she had. It was the only companion that did not fret, have its brow creased in worry, like Marie, when Sisi unburdened her lonely heart. It would never whisper and repeat her secrets, like an aide or attendant might. This afternoon, while the sun shone bright but her mood listed toward darkness, the words came easily.

She felt the vibration of the horse hooves, trembling in the ground beneath her, at the same time she heard their sound. She looked up from her notebook, shielding her eyes to gaze in the direction of the approaching rider. The horse slowed and the rider came into view. She smiled, in spite of her previous melancholy.

"Hello, Andrássy."

"Empress Elisabeth, I'm so happy I've found you." Andrássy halted his horse and hopped lightly from its saddle, tying it to a sapling beside Vándor. "Please, please, do not get up." He walked toward her and took a seat on the grass beside her. "It's a lovely day for a ride, is it not?"

"Indeed." Sisi looked at Andrássy beside her. He wore lightweight suit pants, the matching jacket discarded, the top buttons of his white shirt undone and the collar open. She herself was in a cool riding habit of blue silk several shades lighter than the sky overhead, and she'd fashioned her hair in a loosely braided bun.

"I see you've slipped your imperial guard," Andrássy noted, looking around at the empty fields surrounding them, his face flushed from the warm afternoon and the exertion of the ride. His hair was windblown and wild.

"Shortly after Vienna," Sisi said, smiling. "It's really shocking to me how slowly they move."

"In the unfortunate event that our two peoples should ever go to war, I shall have to warn my fellow Hungarians that it is *you* they will have to look out for. We won't even notice you approaching and then, all of a sudden, you'll be on top of Buda Hill, claiming the castle and the lands of Buda and Pest."

"Our two people?" Sisi cocked her head.

"The Austrians and the Hungarians."

She half-grinned. "I'm not entirely certain that I wouldn't fight on the side of the Hungarians."

Andrássy leaned toward her. "Let's hope you never have to make that decision."

"Indeed, let's hope that."

"Have I interrupted you?" Andrássy looked down at her notebook, a recently started set of couplets scribbled across the top page.

"Oh, no." Sisi put her hands over her work, self-conscious.

Andrássy began to recite a bit of poetry: *"Every day one should at least hear one little song, read one good poem, see one fine painting and . . ."*

"And if possible," Sisi finished the line for him, *"speak a few sensible words."*

Andrássy looked at her, impressed.

"I think you're the only person at court who might know Goethe better than I do, Andrássy."

Andrássy smiled, continuing: "I'm sorry to say you shall get no sensible words from me. But I see you writing a poem, and here" — he pointed at the river — "is beauty much greater than any painting."

"All we lack is the music."

"I won't offer to sing," he said, winking. "So, what have you written?"

Sisi looked at the notebook, fidgeting to conceal it. "Only a few lines of some very poor poetry."

"May I?" Andrássy lifted his eyebrows.

"You really will not be impressed, I assure you."

"I very much doubt that. I'm always impressed by you."

Sisi hesitated. "All right." She sighed. Andrássy took the notebook in his hands and read aloud what she had started:

"O'er thee, like thine own sea birds,
I'll circle without rest.
For me earth holds no corner
To build a lasting nest."

It was not until she heard the words spoken aloud that Sisi realized how deeply intimate they were. A glimpse into her lonely, unrooted soul. She felt her cheeks redden, embarrassed that Andrássy had seen these confessions on paper, and she took the notebook back in her hands. They sat beside one another, silent, for several moments.

Eventually, Andrássy looked up, his eyes serious. "You carry great sadness, Empress Elisabeth."

She thought about it. There was no use lying to him, not after he'd read those words. She blinked, eyes lilting out over the river. "Yes, I suppose I do."

Andrássy nodded. And then, with a thoughtful expression, he said, "Hungary."

"Pardon?"

"Hungary is my . . . what did you call it? *Lasting nest*. Hungary is why I feel rooted."

Sisi thought about this. Possenhofen was

no longer where she felt roots. Helene was gone. Father's health was failing. Mother had told her that she had no right to flee to Possenhofen any longer. No, that was Karl's nest now, as she had always known it would someday be.

"But then, I suppose it's different for men." Andrássy looked out at the river, apparently skimming the thoughts right from her mind. "We are not forced to quit our homes, our families, to join a new clan."

Sisi nodded, exhaling an audible sigh.

"And your clan is not exactly the most welcoming one, I can imagine." He looked at her, an appraising, inquisitive look.

"I knew, though," she replied, uncomfortable with his intuitive awareness, with his apparent ability to discern her most private thoughts. "I knew, when I married, what I was taking on."

"Did you really? At — what was it — age fifteen? Could you really have known, Empress?" Andrássy seemed skeptical, and Sisi thought perhaps she had better let this conversation wither without a further reply.

"How about you, Andrássy?"

He cocked his head. "What about me?"

"How is the Countess Andrássy?"

He sat still, glancing out over the calm surface of the Danube. "Katinka is a good woman." He offered nothing else.

"Come now, I bet you had ladies from

Budapest to Paris offering you their hearts," Sisi said. "Surely you must have loved her madly to marry her?"

His brows creased toward one another as he thought about this. "I hope God, and Katinka, forgive me someday."

"Hmm?" She arched an eyebrow. "Come now, I've just confessed my private thoughts to you. What do you mean by that?"

Andrássy plucked a blade of grass, tossing it toward the river. "I should not have married her."

"Why not?" Sisi asked.

Not meeting her eyes, he said: "I am not a good husband."

"I am certain you must be," Sisi reasoned. "You are away from home more often than she would like, perhaps."

Andrássy shook his head, plucking more grass blades from the earth beneath him. "That doesn't bother her. In fact, I think we both prefer to have the distance between us. I feel no longing to return to her. And she, it seems, feels no longing to welcome me home."

After a thoughtful pause, he added: "My problem, with life as much as with women, is that I let the perfect be the enemy of the good."

Sisi thought about this. "I see how, if it is perfection that you seek, you find that your wife is lacking. But you must remember, no one is perfect. Not even you."

"There was one girl, years ago. Kati was her name. Perhaps that was why I married Katinka — she had the same name as this other girl. Either that, or because everyone told me that it was far past the time that I take a wife."

Andrássy chewed on the side of his lip, his face heavy in thought. "Oh, but this was another lifetime, it seems," Andrássy said, his voice almost wistful as he ran his hands over the tips of the sun-warmed grass blades. "I knew her when I was in Paris."

That was years before she'd ever met him, Sisi knew, when Andrássy had been exiled by her own husband, Franz Joseph.

"I would have married Kati," Andrássy continued. "I wanted to marry Kati, in fact, and I told her so."

"What happened?" Sisi asked, not sure why she felt jealous of a faceless girl, all of a sudden.

"Kati did not want to marry me."

Fool, Sisi thought, but she refrained from saying it aloud. Instead, she asked, "Did she offer any reason?"

"There was an older Hungarian prince back home. With more land and a more prestigious title. He owned most of Transylvania, and he was not dangerous. *He* had not been exiled from the empire." Andrássy shook his head, grinning sadly.

"I bet she regrets her decision every time she reads about you in the papers. Or sees your likeness."

Andrássy grinned. "I very much doubt it."

"Have you been pining for her ever since?"

"Oh, perhaps." Andrássy turned to Sisi, smiling. "No, no." Now he shook his head. "I'm far too busy to pine."

They sat beside one another in silence, watching a boat glide along the Danube, toward the east. Toward Hungary. After a while, Andrássy turned back to Sisi, shifting his body so that he leaned toward her. "There has been one other since Kati. One other woman whom I've seen and thought to myself: I could love her."

"Not your wife?" Sisi asked. Andrássy shook his head.

The blond woman Sisi had seen him with in the gardens, perhaps? Without understanding why, Sisi felt jealous again. Yet she forced herself to smile and ask, politely: "And what is her story?"

Andrássy bit his lip, thinking before he answered. "Well, she is beautiful. And kind. And every time I speak with her I am left with my mind awhirl. She gives me much to think about."

Sisi looked away, plucking a piece of grass from the earth, which she then released into the breeze. "She sounds lovely. Why did you not fall in love with her, in that case?"

"Because she was not free to be mine. Unfortunately, another man had gotten to her first."

Sisi returned his gaze now, noticing how his brown eyes caught a glint of the golden sunlight overhead. "This is too sad, Andrássy."

"I suppose it is quite sad." He nodded.

"So what is her name — this perfect being, this unattainable lady you admire?"

"The name of the lady bears no relevance," he said, looking away from Sisi, breaking the charge that had passed, a moment earlier, between their eyes. "As she will never be mine."

Sisi nodded, words evading her. For a brief moment, her mind wandered back to the night in Budapest, years earlier. The night she had danced with him, Andrássy. She had done so in front of Franz and a roomful of others: a blameless action, devoid of any meaning or significance. And yet, here, on the grass beside Andrássy, she felt as if there was more meaning. Here, even though they didn't touch. They sat, apart, only speaking. Speaking was a harmless action, was it not? And yet, for a reason she could not quite utter, Sisi would never have wanted Franz to witness this moment.

Finally, she blinked, clearing her mind of the fog that had collected. "It will be dark soon. We should return to the palace."

"You should." He nodded. "I am not going that way."

"No? Where are you going?"

"I will rest in the next town this evening and await my servants. We are returning to Budapest for the summer."

"Oh," Sisi said. He had not told her about his departure until now. "To see your wife?"

Andrássy shook his head. "She will remain up north. She loathes my city in the summer as much as I loathe her isolated and secluded retreat."

"Why must you go?" Sisi asked.

Andrássy sighed, running his fingers through his dark hair. "There is some discontent at home. It seems greater liberties and rights only go so far. They still resent the rule of a foreign emperor. Deák has demanded that I return and help him sort this out."

Andrássy's point of view made sense to Sisi in a way it had not, years earlier, when her husband had griped to her about Hungarian antagonism. "How long until they start to demand their independence again?"

"You must remember it is not 'they' to me, Empress. It is 'we.' "

"Oh . . . yes, of course."

Andrássy sighed. "I hope to quell the disruption, for now. To tell Deák to advocate for harmony, rather than discord. Though I do not know how long I can keep peace for your husband."

Sisi thought about this. "I couldn't bear to think of you as an enemy again. I hope you remain our friend."

"As do I."

"And I shall miss seeing you here." It seemed a horribly selfish thing to say when he was returning to plead her family's cause to an unhappy populace. And terribly bold.

He looked up at her, his eyes creasing in a faint smile. "May I write to you while I'm away?"

Writing in itself was harmless; she wrote to hundreds of people a week. Nevertheless, Sisi suspected that this was the point at which she ought to say no. Perhaps it was her last chance to say no. If Andrássy began to write to her, would she come to crave his correspondence? Here was her chance to halt that need for him before it took hold of her. Knowing this, she opened her mouth to answer. As she did so, she smiled and said: "I hope you will."

XV.

Outside, sun pours down over a summer day in Budapest, the Danube shimmering its way around the base of the hillside. The new *Széchenyi Lánchíd,* the Chain Bridge, stretches across the river like cast iron lace.

They stand atop the hill. The crowds surround them, waving flags and dancing to the Gypsy bands that pop up in small clusters. The people clamor so loudly that Sisi swears she sees the buildings tremble around her. A crash of cannonfire sounds.

"*Éljen Erzsébet!* Long live Elisabeth!"

One man approaches, his steps ushered through the hordes by a minister. He has long brown hair tinged with silver, parted in the middle to reveal a serious face. He alone in this entire multitude does not wear a smile.

"Empress." The minister directs the man forward, but he appears bashful, too timid to step any closer. "Please, allow me to introduce you to our most beloved national composer, a man who —"

"Franz Liszt." Sisi nods, finishing the sentence, beckoning the composer closer. "A man who needs no introduction. Why, Master Liszt, how can we thank you for composing our Coronation Mass?"

She stares into his eyes, momentarily struck by his presence. How she would love to shake his hand, to touch the fingers that play the piano with unparalleled virtuosity. But when he looks up, returns her gaze, she notices. Franz Liszt, the world's most beloved musician, has tears in his eyes. His lips part, and he speaks quietly. In Hungarian, his native tongue. "*Éljen Erzsébet.* Long live Elisabeth."

CHAPTER FIFTEEN

BAD KISSINGEN SPA, BAVARIA
JUNE 1866

Sisi received two letters at breakfast that morning: one from her husband, the other from Andrássy.

Spring in Bad Kissingen had proven a difficult time for Sisi. She missed Rudy terribly. And yet the thought of returning to court filled her with anxiety, and, lately, skull-splitting headaches. Her mother-in-law, though often bedridden with coughs and aches these days, had tightened her grip over the education of the grandchildren, specifically the crown prince. Rather than being allowed to enjoy a longer childhood, as Sisi had advocated, and pursue a well-rounded education including languages, poetry, and arts, Rudy now spent long days studying history, military strategy, and Habsburg protocol. Already his tiny arms and legs were stuffed into the stiff uniform of the Austrian officer, as if he were playing dress-up in some game from which he would never escape.

Franz's notes spoke of the boy's "difficulties" adjusting to his new military tutor, an unforgiving general by the name of Leopold Gondrecourt. Sisi ached to hold and comfort her sensitive little boy. But, knowing that that was an impossibility whether she remained at court or traveled, Sisi had heeded Doctor Fischer's advice and had agreed to spend the winter away from Vienna, in the resort town of Bad Kissingen.

Tucked away in the pristine Bavarian forest, at the base of the pine- and snow-capped Rhön Mountains, Bad Kissingen had been, at first, an ideal place for Sisi to recover her energy and lift her flagging spirits. The air was crisp and clear, the scenery wild, and her schedule free of the official appearances expected of her at court. Having left behind Herr Lobkowitz, Countess Frederika, and Lady Ilse in Vienna, Sisi spent her days now with just the companionship of Marie, Ida the new maid, and the hairdresser Franziska. There, away from the crowds and the protocol that worsened her anxiety and increased her discomfort, Sisi was allowed to rest and take in the mild, therapeutic waters of the nearby Franconian Saale River.

And yet, her poor health persisted. While Marie applauded the talents of their Bavarian cook, Sisi found the food unpleasing, and complained daily that she had no appetite or interest in food. Headaches often accompanied her throughout her long, monotonous days in the rented villa. At night she felt weary, yet sleep evaded her. Restless, yet unable to concentrate on any given task, she rode any time that her head pains were not incapacitating.

The letters from Andrássy were the one bright spot that winter and spring. He wrote her often, describing his time in Budapest, where he and Ferenc Deák were attempting to mollify an agitated and impatient populace. His letters always mentioned politics — he regularly sought her opinion on political matters — but they carried so much more than those updates. He inquired about her health, seeking her reassurance that she was taking care to eat and rest. And he always ended his letter with a piece of poetry or favorite quote.

"Is that all the mail this morning, Ida?" Sisi pushed aside her breakfast plate, having barely nibbled on a piece of dry toast.

"And the new dresses you've ordered have arrived, Empress." The maid answered in Hungarian, as Sisi had instructed her to. Between her correspondence with Andrássy and her daily conversations with Marie and Ida, Sisi now felt as comfortable in Hungarian as German.

"How about my creams?"

"Not yet, Majesty."

Sisi frowned. "I'm almost out." The thought

of passing a night without first embalming herself with ointments and rose-flavored oils frightened Sisi; that was how women invited wrinkles.

"Perhaps your ointments will arrive tomorrow, Empress," Ida answered, always tactful.

Sisi took Andrássy's letter to a chair by the window. There, in a puddle of April sunshine, she sat and opened the envelope.

"Sisi." She smiled as she read his greeting. She had urged him in her most recent letter to call her by her favorite nickname, and he had obeyed, addressing her with the same informal title his Hungarian people had adopted. Nevertheless, she noted, the address came without description. She was not *"Dear Sisi."* Just as he was never *"Dear Andrássy"* in her letters to him. They did nothing wrong; they were simply friends communicating by letter. She continued to read:

Spring has bloomed throughout our city like the opening buds of a tulip. How I wish you could see it: the children fold their school papers into little boats and float them along the Danube. Their thoughts are on birds and sunshine, not school. And how could their minds dwell anywhere else? All around us burst signs of new life. Even now, as I write, my window is open and I smell the perfume of wildflowers, a nearby café serving fried potatoes, and the river. You shall have to plan a visit to this part of your kingdom next spring. There is nothing quite like springtime in Budapest.

Deák and I continue to advocate for a more measured, pragmatic solution to the strained relationship. I know that I have told you, in the past, that it will be independence or subjugation for my people. But I believe that the people begin to see our more moderate side; perhaps not all ties with Austria need be severed. If only we could have some acknowledgment from the emperor that our rights are sovereign and equal, so that the union between our two nations might be more akin to a respectful partnership than a relationship of master and subject.

But enough ink spilled on politics. I read your last letter with relish. I imagine the hills, covered in snow and ice, as they begin to thaw; the first signs of green might now be appearing on the boughs as you, bundled in fox fur, traipse along the wooded paths. Perhaps the ice has melted into a chilly, determined brook that begins its descent down the mountain slope. Do you walk through those wooded hills? I hope so. The air must be good for your lungs, and the views good for your soul.

You included no information in your last correspondence as to when you plan to return to Vienna. I will be so bold as to offer a piece of unsolicited advice on that matter; but I will do it with the words of our favorite philosopher, so as not to risk arousing your anger:

"Things which matter most must never be at the mercy of things which matter least."

Your most faithful and devoted servant,

J. Andrássy

Sisi folded the letter and tucked it back into its envelope. She knew the quote and knew what he meant: Andrássy was urging her back to court. Back to her role as empress and mother. And wife. She had confessed to him, in her last letter, that the thought of returning to Vienna brought on feelings of panic and desperation. And yet, he still encouraged her to return.

Sisi asked Ida to bring her paper and ink and she sat at her desk to begin her letter. Slipping off the heavy rings that weighed on her fingers, she began: "Andrássy."

I love to hear you write about Budapest. I think I shall have to agree with you on one account: that I spend next spring in that portion of the empire. I remember the magic of welcoming spring to Budapest, and it's an awakening that I wish to witness again.

Sisi already knew which quote she would share with him; it had popped out at her, spelling Andrássy's name across her mind when she had beheld it.

I found this in Goethe last night and thought of you:

"The world is so empty if one thinks only of mountains, rivers and cities; but to know someone who thinks and feels with us, and who, though distant, is close to us in spirit, this makes the earth for us an inhabited garden."

Sisi paused. Was she too bold in her selection of the quote? Would Andrássy think it strange — her confession of how deeply she valued his correspondence? She hesitated, tapping the paper with her finger, considering whether to tear this paper in two and begin a new letter.

Just then, Ida burst into the room, tugging Sisi's focus away from the letter. "Empress Elisabeth!"

"Ida? What is it? Goodness, you startled me."

The maid panted, her tall, lean figure impossibly erect.

"Heavens, Ida, what is the matter?"

The maid walked forward, a small piece of paper quivering in her hand. "Empress, it's a telegram. From Vienna, from the emperor."

"A telegram?" Hands trembling, Sisi reached for the paper, reading the hastily typed lines. She lowered the paper, looking into the eyes of her maid.

"Tell Marie," Sisi said, rising from the table. "Begin packing my things. We must leave today."

"Yes, Your Majesty." Ida performed a quick curtsy before sweeping out of the room.

Sisi looked down at the paper once more, reading the last bit aloud to the now empty room.

"Please come home, at once STOP We are at war FULL STOP."

War had been declared by her husband, and even now Austrians were exchanging gunfire with the joint forces of the Prussian and Italian armies. Prussia, having grown more belligerent over the past decade, had been challenging Austrian supremacy in Central Europe since the time of Maria Theresa. But now, with Prussia's dangerous new allegiance with Italy, along with its flagrant disregard for other German duchies and kingdoms — lands that Franz had vowed to protect — Austria could no longer sit idly by.

Sisi's bedroom back in Schönbrunn Palace, however, showed no signs of the war. The room was immaculate: fresh flowers spilled out of the porcelain vases, the mantels were free of dust, the windows were ajar, allowing in a balmy breeze and notes of faint bird-song. On her bed sat a little book, the only item out of place.

Its title was written in Hungarian. Sisi riffled through the pages, noting that it was an anthology of Hungarian poetry. A small card slipped from the front cover of the book and Sisi opened it, intrigued.

You are correct to appreciate Goethe, but our Hungarian poets have earned their place alongside the Germans.
I look forward to hearing your thoughts.
Your devoted and faithful friend,
J. A.

Was Andrássy back at court? The thought caused Sisi's heart to knock against her chest, and she placed the book down on her bedside table. How ludicrous, she chided herself. Her kingdom was at war, and all she could think about was the fact that Andrássy might now be under the same roof? That she might be able to see him — and as soon as that very evening! Just like that, her anxiety at having returned to court skittered aside, replaced by excitement. Even hope.

"Franziska," Sisi called aloud, listening for the clip of her hairdresser's footsteps in the adjacent rooms.

"Yes, Empress?" The wiry woman peeked her head in from the drawing room.

"We must begin dressing now."

"But Majesty, it's only three o'clock in the afternoon."

"I know what time it is. But I must look my best for dinner."

That evening Sisi took her husband's arm, noting the relief in his expression as she did so. "Keeping up a fine front, right?" she said, whispering to Franz, her head cocked sideways. "During wartime especially."

"Thank you, Elisa . . . Elisabeth," Franz said. Worry tugged hard on his features, stitching his eyebrows close to one another in a permanent scowl.

"In we go," she said. Franz nodded.

Escorted into the Spiegelsaal by her husband, Sisi had to temper her delight when, upon entering the glittering hall, she spotted Andrássy's tall outline in the corner of the room. His back to her, Andrássy stood in the midst of a conversation with a short, thickly built man. Deák stood nearby, listening on, but Sisi did not recognize Andrássy's other conversation partner. Andrássy turned only when he heard the emperor's entrance announced. He, like the rest of the crowd assembled in the hall, bowed to the imperial pair.

The fighting so far had been far away, in distant lands with barely recognizable names, and yet, the group assembled for dinner that night seemed to buzz with nervous tension. Andrássy alone seemed cool, even merry.

"Empress." He crossed the room and bowed before her. He wore an immaculate suit, and his wavy hair was longer, more unkempt, than the last time she'd seen him. His eyes held her now, his expression vibrant, direct, hinting at mischief. And perhaps they were entangled in some mischief, the two of them, with the amount that they'd been writing.

"Count." Sisi's voice came out quietly. How funny that, now seeing him in the flesh, she felt shy, even formal. This, after their correspondences these past months had held pages and pages of private thoughts and candid confessions.

"You look quite recovered, Empress." Andrássy stared at her a few moments longer than was proper, but no one noticed. The crowd had assembled around the emperor and the new courtier, whom Sisi had still not met.

"Thank you, Count. You look nice as well."

"I said 'recovered.' Who said anything about you looking nice?" Andrássy winked, and she couldn't help but smile, unaccustomed as she was to such irreverence from a courtier.

Sisi looked stunning tonight and she knew it. Even Franz, irritable and skittish, had been momentarily taken aback upon first seeing her.

She had selected a lightweight gown of ivory-colored silk, with small rose-colored flowers stitched around the neck and sleeves. A matching belt cinched the dress around her famously narrow waist. She wore her hair loose, with just a few pieces pulled back off her face. Franziska had woven strands of pearls and wildflowers into her curls, and she had rouged her cheeks and colored her lips.

"May I escort you to your place, Empress?" Andrássy offered his arm, and she reminded herself to move slowly and gracefully, the cool empress, as she accepted it. Inside, she was teeming.

"Who is that man with whom you were speaking, the one to whom Franz now speaks?" Sisi angled her chin toward the new face.

"Friedrich Beust," Andrássy answered. "Minister of Saxony. Or, I should say, *former* minister of Saxony. He, like so many other leaders of the small German duchies, has been overrun and driven out by Prussia. Beust hates Bismarck — and the whole brutish Prussian government — perhaps even more than your husband does."

Sisi nodded, studying this new man named

Beust: his thick, square frame, the way he spoke with his hands, like a conductor pulling the attention of those around him into the song he led. She could tell that Franz was taken with him; he looked at Beust with the same captive stare with which he'd once looked at her.

Sisi took her place at the opposite end of the table from her husband. Between them sat Sophie, appearing irritable and fidgety in a pumpkin-colored gown. Beside her sat the new Saxon nobleman, Beust, and across from her was the aged minister von Bach. To Franz's right sat Count Alexander von Mensdorff-Pouilly, the foreign minister and a handsome young man with a mustache and parted dark hair. Sisi had heard that he was a distant relative of England's fat Queen Victoria. Grünne sat beside the foreign minister, and two cardinals also joined the party. Andrássy had somehow found himself in the seat immediately to Sisi's left.

Inside the palace the air was warm, and the mood at dinner was tense. Sisi, having been briefed by Herr Lobkowitz during the hours she'd spent prepping her toilette, knew why. To date, the Austrians had met Prussia and its allies in battle four times. Three of the four campaigns had been, technically, Austrian victories. Yet Franz was dissatisfied. Victories that should have been easy and decisive had proven to be the opposite.

Austria was sustaining casualties at an alarmingly high rate. And the most recent battle, fought just a day earlier at the Bohemian town of Gitschin, had been a victory for the Prussians. If this pattern continued, the Austrians would soon run out of supplies. And men.

"What is most troubling to me is how ill prepared they look out there." Beust smoked throughout dinner.

Franz made to answer but Sophie cut him off. "Anyone would look ill prepared next to Bismarck. The man is a warmonger."

Beust shook his head. "Not only a warmonger. A planner. He's been preparing for battle since he was named chancellor. There is something to be said for being well prepared, Archduchess. Even if I do hate the man."

Franz nodded at Beust but Sophie had a retort, which she offered in a brusque tone. "We are the Austrian Empire. We shall prevail."

Sisi discerned quickly over the course of the dinner discussion that there existed two opinions on the progress of the war. Sophie, with dismissive utterances to her son and condescending smirks toward Beust, betrayed no alarm at Prussia's speedy mobilization and superior weapons.

Beust, to Sisi's incredulity, disagreed openly. And, more surprisingly, the newcomer to court was not cowed by the archduchess.

Beust made his concern plain, stating to Franz that a change in strategy was needed, and quickly. "The Prussian guns are mowing us down before our men even have time to reload." Beust looked at Franz throughout the entirety of dinner, his eyes avoiding Sophie. "We must modernize our arms, Majesty, I entreat you."

"They have better rifles, I'll grant that. But our cannons are better," Franz said, looking to his mother for her agreement.

"Indeed they are." Sophie waggled her fleshy index finger, like an approving governess after her pupil gave the correct answer. "And don't forget, we have the Austrian cavalry in our forces."

"I doubt that some well-trained horses shall be enough to compensate for the deficit in men, trains, and gun power." Beust lowered his eyes, sensing that he had pressed up against the outer limit of their patience. When he spoke now, his tone was quiet. "Bismarck's got more troops at his fingertips than anyone else in Europe, even Napoleon the Third."

"Speaking of Napoleon, have we had any word from Paris this evening?" Franz turned to Grünne.

"Not yet, Your Grace."

"Napoleon will come to our aid before too much longer." Franz wiped his mustache with a napkin and spoke in a tone of strained optimism. "Gentlemen and emperors shall always side together against belligerent, brutish upstarts like Bismarck."

Sisi turned to Beust and saw that he had more to say on the topic, but at last he refrained from doing so.

"What do you make of it all?" Sisi spoke to Andrássy in a hushed tone. She had left dinner with the emperor but they had parted ways. Offering a perfunctory excuse about meeting a minister, he had turned toward the courtyard and his waiting carriage, leaving Sisi to make her way back to her own suite. On her way, Sisi had been delighted to meet Andrássy.

The days were at their longest, and the faintest hint of lilac light still seeped in through the palace windows.

"Care to take a long route back?" Andrássy suggested, his head tilted sideways toward the doors that swung out into the gardens. "It's a lovely evening."

"I don't see why not." They stepped outdoors, following a pathway bordered by tight-clipped trees. The palace was quiet, the grounds succumbing to shadow, and Sisi directed them toward the conservatory, a grand building of glass and iron.

"I'm happy to have Beust here, even if your mother-in-law is not," Andrássy said as they walked.

"He seemed quite brave at dinner, did he

not?" Sisi asked.

"He is too new to court to realize the need for a censor."

"That's good," Sisi said. "He'll speak the truth, which is what Franz needs to hear."

They paused, stopping outside the entrance to the conservatory. "After you," Andrássy said, gesturing with an arm. She led them into the building. Inside the air hung warm, rich with the fragrance of dirt and plant life.

Andrássy walked behind her, saying: "What no one dared to acknowledge at dinner is how utterly abandoned we have been by our so-called allies."

Sisi paused, turning to face him. She stood just inches from him now, their faces illuminated by the soft glow of moon, its first light piercing the conservatory windows. *"We need no one."*

Andrássy arched an eyebrow.

"Sophie's motto. *'We need no one.'* We are the Habsburgs, after all. It's what she has always told her son. After he lost the friendship of Russia, and then England. And then Prussia. And now, it appears, France."

Andrássy thought about this, running his hand absentmindedly through his disheveled hair.

"But whom did Franz expect to side with us?" Sisi asked.

"Well, I don't think we had any hope for Italy. Not after they've just fought Austria for their own independence. It makes perfect sense that they aligned with Prussia."

"Is there any chance of France coming to our aid?"

Andrássy cocked his head, considering this. "I don't share your husband's optimism on that score."

"Why not?"

"There are rumors."

"What sort of rumors?" Sisi asked.

"I hear that Bismarck traveled to France specifically to meet with Napoleon."

Sisi sighed.

"It seems that this Bismarck, whom your mother-in-law considers nothing but a belligerent warmonger, is in fact quite the diplomat. It's as Beust said: Bismarck planned for war with Austria. He even hoped for it. I hate to say it, Sisi, but your mother-in-law is wrong."

"No need to regret saying that," Sisi said, crossing her arms. "So then, France will side with Prussia." She now understood the gravity of Franz's position, of Sophie's miscalculations. "How does the emperor not know this?" she asked.

Andrássy smiled, a sad, regretful smile, and quoted to her a line she knew well, *"A person hears only what they understand."*

"Goethe," Sisi said. "But how can the emperor have been blind to these events?"

"When you are the ruler of the most power-

692

ful state in Europe, how can you possibly understand the threat that a lesser German state might pose to you?" Andrássy leaned close now, his tone low and mocking. "What chance do better guns, more men, railroads, willing allies, and better diplomacy stand when you are the Habsburg king? God's anointed heir to the Holy Roman Empire?"

"Quite a good chance, I would imagine."

Andrássy nodded. They stood beside one another in silence for several moments, milky wisps of moonlight slipping into the otherwise darkened conservatory. All around them fern fronds and palm leaves caught the glint of moon, shimmering in a gentle breeze. Even with the mood as heavy as it was inside the palace, out here, in this evening, it was difficult to remain tense.

Eventually, Andrássy spoke. "Did you see the poetry book I left for you?"

"I did." Sisi turned to him, sensing his closeness in the dark more so than actually seeing him.

"I thought of you when I saw it. I hope you enjoy it."

"It's written entirely in Hungarian."

"You are up to it, Sisi."

"Speaking, perhaps. But reading? You give me too much credit."

"You always say that, but I give you precisely the amount of credit to which you are entitled."

Sisi blushed at this, her breath becoming less even. Suddenly, she wished the room they stood in was not made of glass; that she could shut a door and close out the rest of the world. Even in the darkness she was intensely aware of his body beside hers. How she longed to kiss him.

"Well, Empress, it's rather dark. I think I'd better see you safely back to your rooms before we are spied upon. I'd hate to be credited with ruining your reputation, wandering the grounds like this after dark."

"Please, Andrássy." She laughed, a hollow sound. "I stopped caring about my reputation at this court long ago."

By early July, the sick and wounded had started to seep into the capital. Once they started coming, it seemed as if they'd never stop: like an inglorious parade without fanfare or trumpet notes. Bandaged men limped down Vienna's stately, sycamore-lined boulevards, seeking out hospitals and monasteries, begging for food and bearing scars that turned Franz's war from a topic of tense talk into a ghastly, inescapable reality.

Inside the palace, the air hung heavy, stifling and breezeless. Everyone in the halls and state rooms wore an irritable scowl slicked with a sheen of perspiration. After a series of inconsequential engagements, reports came back from the front via telegraph that both the Prussian and the Austrian forces had converged in Bohemia, near the ancient fortified city of Königgrätz. If decisive, this battle could end the war.

Sisi, feeling anxious inside her sweltering palace rooms, asked Franz what she could do to be of service. Sitting still was no longer possible for her.

"Visit the hospitals," Franz said. He sat at his desk behind a pile of papers, maps, reports, and books. "Comfort the wounded and dying. Let them stare at their beautiful empress. You shall be a momentary balm to their misery."

And so, on a humid afternoon in early July, Sisi called for her coach and set off on a tour of the hospitals. It was a day that sapped both her energy and her spirits, but she did her best not to show her horror as she met her wounded subjects, looking on their mangled faces, the gnarled knobs of flesh where limbs had once been.

At the last stop, exhausted, Sisi walked the line of beds in the sick bay. She was attempting to maintain her mask of composure against the stench of emptied stomachs and scorched flesh.

"Empress! Empress!" A nurse in a white starched uniform, sleeves rolled back, rushed toward her.

"Yes, what is it?"

"Please, come quick, if you would."

Sisi was led into a surgery room, where a man lay on a cot, his body writhing in agony. Sisi looked on, horrified, as the blood pulsed from an open wound near his shoulder. He screamed. Then he screamed once more, this time louder.

"He's Hungarian," Sisi said, understanding his anguished words.

"He needs an amputation, Empress Elisabeth." The nurse stood beside her, speaking in a hushed, urgent tone. "But he refuses to have it. You speak Hungarian, Your Majesty, do you not?" The nurse shifted, as if anticipating the look of disgust that would surely ripple across the empress's face.

Instead, Sisi nodded, pushing the lace trim of her sleeves back. "Yes," she said, answering in Hungarian. "Hello, sir." She approached the bed, coming into the line of sight of the suffering man. "The doctor would like to help you. We must let him help you."

"Empress Elisabeth?" The man's eyes widened, his attention momentarily pulled from his pain. "Am I in heaven? I've died, haven't I?"

"If this is heaven, I shudder to think what hell must look like," Sisi answered, offering a comforting smile.

The man still looked at her, unbelieving.

"You are very much alive, sir." Sisi took his hand in hers. "And there's no reason that you should not stay that way, as long as we do what the doctor says."

The man tried, and failed, to sit up in bed. "You're even more beautiful than they say."

Sisi flashed a sad smile, looking to the nurse. To the waiting doctor, the tools nearby and ready. "Please, won't you let the doctor perform his surgery, so that you may begin to heal?"

The man looked to the surgeon, his eyes narrowing.

"Come now. It'll be over quickly," Sisi said, approaching the cot. "I'll be with you. We can speak of Hungary together."

"Oh . . ." The man looked once more, distrustfully, at the gleaming row of surgical tools. And then he nodded. "All right." He leaned back on the bed. Sisi kept his right hand in her own while the doctor and nurse approached the left side, where the wound gaped.

"You must look at me," Sisi said, fixing her gaze on the man's bloodshot eyes. He hesitated, watching the doctor approach, the knife shimmering in his outreached hand.

"Never mind that," Sisi said, her voice assured as she squeezed the man's hand, her tone soothing yet authoritative — the way she would speak to Rudy. "Look at me. We shall have you better in no time. Now, why don't you tell me about your home? From where in Hungary do you come?"

As the man wailed and writhed, biting

down on a wooden block, the surgeon performed his bloody work.

Sisi, her attention so focused on the patient and the crushing grip of his hand, noticed only after it was all over that a crowd had assembled outside of the surgery. There, at the front of the crowd, stood Sophie. Her mother-in-law had watched the entire procedure, and now the archduchess stood, pale, a look of unadulterated horror on her face at the scene she had just witnessed.

As the man slipped off into sleep, Sisi rose, planting a kiss on his sweat-stained forehead before tiptoeing from the room.

"Sophie," she said, nodding at her mother-in-law as she exited the surgery. "I didn't realize you were here." Side by side, the two women began to walk. Sisi felt, for the first time, just how utterly spent her body was.

"Franz told me he sent you down here. I thought I'd come meet you." Sophie looked around the sick bay, her hands knit together in a tight bind, her features taut and ill at ease. "I thought perhaps I'd greet some of the poor fellows myself. Show a united front, for the empire, right?"

"Oh. Yes, yes, of course." Sisi tugged on the lace trim of her sleeves, pulling them back into place. She noticed as she did so, too tired to react, that some of the man's blood now covered the previously immaculate white.

Sophie was still staring around at the sick

bay, her eyes darting listlessly over the rows of invalid bodies. Then she looked back at Sisi. "But you look exhausted." Sophie unclasped her hands, lifted them to her breast. "We should get you home. Shall we ride back to the palace together?"

"Oh? But didn't you say that you wanted to greet . . ." Sisi gestured toward the men, feeling too tired to finish her own sentence.

"I'll come back," Sophie shook her head, a flicker of her wrist. "Another day. For now, let's get you home." Sophie stared once more out over the sick ward, her face unnaturally pale.

"Well, all right," Sisi said, her voice quiet with fatigue. She had put in a full day. "Let's go."

With that, Sophie took her skirt in her hands and sped for the exit.

They sat opposite one another in the carriage, bouncing over the sunbaked cobblestones in silence. Sisi, staring out the window, noticed the intensity with which Sophie looked at her, but she did not return the gaze.

"So much blood." Sophie said it like a whisper, barely audible.

"Pardon?" Sisi turned.

Sophie stared at the stains on Sisi's gown, then into her niece's eyes. "Those men . . . back at the hospital . . ." Sophie's voice trailed off as she swallowed, looking back down at Sisi's bloodstained sleeves. "So many of them. And that was just one hospital." The archduchess shifted in her seat, smoothing the wrinkles of her heavy brocade gown. Sisi turned her focus back out the carriage window.

After a moment, Sophie cleared her throat. "Elisabeth?"

Sisi looked up, noticed the way Sophie twisted the folds of her dress in her hands. Noticed the scowl that pulled down on her lips, the skin well worn after years of that pinched frown.

"Yes, Sophie?"

Sophie bit on her lower lip, then spoke: "That was admirable. What you did back there. Visiting with those men." Sophie's eyes lifted away, glancing distractedly out the carriage window. The evening was a warm one, and people congregated on the streets, their faces bearing the same tense expressions as those worn in the palace halls.

Sisi, stunned by the rare compliment, replied, "Thank you."

"I know that it was Franz who told you to do it. And I'm not sure why it was you he asked, and not me. I would have been happy to go visit those poor fellows, really I would have." Sophie said it as if it was she who needed convincing. "But still. It was good of you to do it."

Sisi scowled. "In fact it was I who asked

Franz what I might do to be of service."

Sophie turned her gaze back on her niece. "Oh?"

"Yes, Sophie," Sisi answered, too tired to mask her annoyance. "If I, as empress, can give even some small comfort to those men, to my subjects who have given so much for the empire, then I am more than happy to do it. And in fact, I plan to visit the hospitals every day, from now until the war is over."

Sophie cleared her throat, shifting her seat in the carriage.

Sisi noticed, as she stared at her aunt, just how much older Sophie looked. Yes, Sophie's was a familiar face. And yet, Sisi saw in that moment how entirely changed she was from the woman who had welcomed them, years ago, to Bad Ischl. The way her eyes, once so sharp, were now hooded in drooping skin. The heavy lines carved into her face, especially around her downturned lips. The way she constantly massaged sore, arthritic fingers. Sophie, without Sisi's awareness, had become an old woman.

"I'm glad that . . ." Sophie pulled her eyes away. "It's a relief, for me, that Franz has you by his side in this. He loves you. Even after all of . . . after everything . . ." Sophie faltered, exhaling before she continued. "It's been . . . difficult."

Sisi nodded, unsure of what, exactly, they were speaking about. These past few weeks of war? This war that was a direct result of the foreign policy that Sophie had advocated for years. Austrian arrogance. Austria standing alone. Austria needing no one. Austria remaining static, stalwart; lulled into the belief that, with God on the side of the Habsburgs, no one else posed a threat. That policy that now crumbled, melting like the ice cones peddled by the street carts in the hot July evening.

"I just . . . oh, I don't know," Sophie said, twisting the folds of her dress as she shifted once more in her seat. "I want what's best for Franz." She looked up now, her eyes touched with a softness that Sisi had never before seen in them. "You know that, right? I've *always* wanted what was best for Franz, from the moment I first held him in my arms. That is my sacred purpose. You know that, right?"

"Yes, Sophie," Sisi said, sitting up straight, peeling her hot skin off the sticky seat of the sweltering coach. "I am a mother, too. I know what it's like to want what is best for one's children. *You* know that, right?"

It seemed that the night was even hotter than the day had been. Sisi sat in Franz's study, having just kissed Rudy and Gisela good night. The windows were opened, but no breeze entered. Even the gardens, usually such a pleasant respite from the palace, seemed unwelcoming to her.

Franz sat nearby, scouring a list of papers on his heavy desk. She waited here each night, knowing that, if news came, it would come here first.

Sisi fanned herself, lifting her hair off her neck. Perhaps Franziska was right — perhaps she *should* cut her hair, she mused unhappily.

The minutes passed, announced at each quarter hour by the clock on Franz's mantel. Just as she was about to rise, to tell Franz she was retiring to her bedchamber, Beust knocked.

"Your Majesty?"

Sisi knew, instantly. She saw it in the tight line of Beust's jaw, the stiff squeeze of his shoulders. The news was not good.

"Beust, what is it?" Franz beckoned him forward. Beust placed the telegram on the desk, where Franz picked it up.

Beust bit his lip, looking on as Franz read the message. After what seemed like an eternity to Sisi, Franz moved, dropping the paper and propping his elbows on the desk. His head fell into cupped hands.

Beust spoke first. "They've broken through our center, Your Majesty."

Franz smacked the hard surface of the desk, landing his fist with a force that caused Sisi to jump back in her chair. "Retreat," Franz said, his voice hoarse. "Order the retreat at once, before they're all slaughtered."

But Beust did not move, did not race to dispatch this most urgent of responses. Instead, he stood still, looking straight into the emperor's eyes as he said, "There's nowhere to retreat to, Your Majesty. The Prussians have us surrounded."

Franz shut himself in his rooms that night and all the next day. Sophie did the same. A still, eerie calm enveloped the palace. The following evening, Sisi ordered a dinner of light broth for herself in her apartments and sat with the poetry book Andrássy had given her. When the sun went down, she began to prepare for bed, slipping out of her gown and letting her curls fall loose. She stood before the mirror, in the middle of her evening ritual of coating her skin with rich cream, when Ida appeared.

"Empress?"

"Yes, Ida?"

"There's a visitor outside your chambers."

"This late?" Sisi looked at the clock and noted that it was past nine in the evening. Whoever it was, this visitor was both late and uninvited; who would dare such a flagrant breach of protocol?

"It's the Count, Your Majesty."

"Andrássy?" Sisi dropped her small tub of cream.

"Yes, Majesty." Ida nodded, looking toward

the new mess on the floor. "Shall I ask him to come back tomorrow?"

"Show him into my sitting room."

"Yes, Empress." Ida curtsied and left the room.

Sisi greeted Andrássy several minutes later, having slipped into a simple dress of white and lemon-yellow cotton. She had kept her hair down.

"Andrássy." She extended her gloveless hand and he kissed it. Another gross breach in protocol, she thought.

"Forgive my casual appearance," she said. He looked formal in a full coat and tails, a top hat in his hands. She wondered, with a pang of jealousy, from where he was coming.

"Sisi." He looked over his shoulder as if to ensure that they were truly alone. Such a visit would cause a flurry of palace gossip, should it become known; the empress receiving a man in her apartments, alone. And so late at night. But neither one of them said it.

"Would you like to sit?" Sisi asked.

He nodded.

She lowered herself onto the blue silk settee, and he took a chair opposite her. It was the first time he had ever been in her private quarters. "Can I offer you something to eat or drink? Wine? Coffee?"

"Nothing for me, thank you." His words were clipped and Sisi sensed his distracted, restless manner. Odd, since he was the one who had appeared at her door so late in the evening.

"Have you heard?" Sisi asked. "Franz will officially surrender."

Andrássy looked up. "Thank you for seeing me so late."

Without thinking, she answered, "I'm always happy to see you." She regretted it immediately. It was the truth, yet it sounded unacceptably bold. "Andrássy, is everything all right?"

He nodded, pressing his palms onto his thighs.

"What is it?"

"I had to see you." He looked directly into her eyes for the first time and she felt her cheeks grow warm in response.

"What for?"

"I had to see you one more time . . . before I leave."

The news hit her like a fist to the stomach.

"Before you leave? But when are you leaving?"

"Tonight. By train."

She turned and looked out the window, out over the gardens, cloaked in nighttime. She waited several minutes before she spoke, though she heard that her voice still cracked when she did so. "Why must you go so suddenly?"

"The war is over after today. The battle was decisive, but not in the way we had hoped it would be."

Sisi understood that much, but not why it meant that he, Andrássy, had to leave her.

"Hungary is now on the verge of outright rebellion. They've watched closely these past few years. My people, they have remained loyal and have waited patiently, unlike Italy and the German states. But they are tired of waiting."

Sisi nodded, knitting her hands together in her lap.

Andrássy continued: "The emperor, your husband, needs us more than ever. Rather than risk losing us, he will finally be willing to negotiate with us. As equals. Deák and I must return. We must prevent our people from declaring outright rebellion. Instead, we must draft our terms. Make our demands plain. And show them that there is another way. That our emperor — but our *empress,* especially — wishes to listen to us, and work with us."

Sisi saw the hope in his eyes. Saw how, even though she felt exhausted, he was alive and energized opposite her. The cause he had been fighting for his whole life — the cause for which he had been exiled and almost killed — was now finally within reach.

Sisi thought about this and sighed. And then, because she did not know what else to do, she spoke the truth. "Andrássy —" Her voice was filled with yearning, and she wondered if it was obvious to him. "I am so very happy for you. And I shall do whatever I can to help you." And now, her voice quivered. "But I don't know how I can stay here, after you are gone."

"Sisi." He put his hand on top of hers. She wore no glove, and neither did he. It was the most intimate gesture they had ever shared.

"I mean it, Andrássy. You are my only . . ." Her voice faltered before she finished, and she lowered her eyes.

"I know." He put his finger under her chin and angled her face upward so that he might stare at her, his lips just inches from her own. She looked into his eyes, dark and earnest, and she wanted to cry. But she could not allow tears.

When Andrássy released her chin, he reached down, lifting her hand and cupping it between his own two hands. Her hand looked so small in his. Without a word, he lifted it to his lips and placed a slow kiss on top of her smooth, white skin. She closed her eyes, savoring the sensation of his lips touching her hand. That was it. That was all he could give her. It was not enough.

When she opened her eyes, he was looking at her, and he spoke. "Perhaps, someday, there will be a way for you to come with me."

"How?" she asked, her voice a faint whisper.

"I don't know," he sighed, looking down at

her. For the first time, his eyes were sad. "But I've always been a champion of foolish hopes and lost causes."

XVI.

We, and not Hungary alone, but the monarchy, can still be saved. . . . For the last time, I beg you in the name of Rudolf, do not let the last opportunity slip by.
> — Letter from Sisi to Franz Joseph
> July 1866

CHAPTER SIXTEEN

Andrássy wasted no time in making his first move, inviting Franz Joseph to Budapest for negotiations, and news of it reached Sisi shortly after the New Year. The court was installed at the winter palace. A prolonged period of cold had settled over the city, bringing with it a dusting of light snow and the promise of long, chilly nights.

One evening in late February, Sisi entered a state dinner on Franz's arm, dressed in a heavy gown of rich crimson brocade. She did her duty, chatting throughout the meal with Beust, who had been asked by Franz to fill the position of foreign minister following the peace negotiations with Prussia. As the final dessert plates were cleared, she sought her opening to slip away and retire to her apartments.

As Sisi rose from the table, Beust followed. "Empress Elisabeth, do you intend to take

711

your leave?"

Sisi turned, pausing. "Yes, Chancellor." And then, so as not to appear abrupt, she offered her routine excuse. "Headache."

"May I be so bold as to request the pleasure of escorting Your Imperial Highness out?" Beust offered his arm.

"All right, thank you." Sisi stole a sideways glance, studying Beust beside her. He always had the air of being in a hurry. Tonight his eyelids hung heavy with fatigue. His hair, a combination of indistinguishable blond and gray, fell in unkempt disarray.

"I hope you enjoyed your dinner, Empress?" The chancellor's eyes darted around the room, at the noblemen and ladies rising from the long dinner table and slowly splintering off into smaller parties to drink wine and exchange gossip.

"I did, thank you. And did you enjoy yours, Chancellor?"

"Hmm? Oh, yes, of course, Majesty." Beust waved his hand as if to indicate that the question of his enjoyment held little importance compared to what he planned to say next. Sisi noted how the chancellor now angled his body to turn his back on the nearby guests, as if to gain privacy. "I was hoping, Empress, that I might be able to seek your advice on a certain matter."

Sisi stood up straighter. Courtiers in Vienna seldom — if ever — consulted their empress on anything of substance. They looked to her for their fashion cues and hairstyles, perhaps. She resisted the urge to smile. "I'd be delighted if you would, Chancellor."

Beust paused at the threshold of the dining room, leaning closer. "May I be quite frank, Empress?"

Sisi nodded.

"I hear that you are a friend" — again Beust glanced over his shoulder — "to the Hungarians."

Sisi thought of Andrássy, gone from Vienna, with a pang of longing. But she kept her gaze steady, answering: "Go on."

Now Beust threw a look in Franz's direction. The emperor sat, smoking a cigar and sipping a glass of port in between his mother and the pretty duchess, the one named Elizabeth, from Modena.

"I was told, Empress, that I might count on you to help me make the Hungarian case to the emperor."

Sisi was now intrigued; it had been years since she'd felt a part of the decisions considered by her husband. That Beust — clearly a shrewd and reasonable man — now came to her meant that he believed her to have some influence.

"What case is it that you wish to make, Chancellor?"

"The emperor must compromise with the Hungarians. And he must do it fast."

Sisi considered this. Coming from Andrássy, a statement such as this would come as no surprise. But the chancellor was as loyal to the Habsburgs as any advisor in the court; Franz had, after all, invited Beust to Vienna after his own kingdom had been devastated by the Prussians. Beust would not advocate any course unless it favored Austria.

Beust seemed to intuit Sisi's confusion. "Her Imperial Highness is surprised by my revelation."

"I had not known you to be a champion of the Hungarians, Chancellor."

"I am a champion of the emperor," Beust declared, his expression serious. "And preserving his empire. At least, what little remains of it. It's the only way to maintain the balance of power in Europe, to keep those Germans from pulling all of Europe into a great war." He reined in his tone, throwing another look in the direction of the dinner table before whispering to Sisi, "They pulverized us in Prague."

It was the Peace of Prague he spoke of, Sisi knew. The recent agreement to end the war with Prussia. Napoleon III had overseen the peace process and had made sure that Austria, as the losing party, had felt the consequences of its ill-advised declaration of war on Prussia. The old German Confederation, the union of dozens of Germanic kingdoms and principalities previously governed by the

714

Austrian Empire, had been abolished. In its place, Prussia was seeking to form a newly imagined German Confederation, an alliance that would explicitly exclude Austria from its membership.

Beust nodded to a group of exiting courtiers before turning back to Sisi, speaking low so that only she could hear. "Venetia is lost, given to the Italians by that generous little Napoleon. We're losing control of Bohemia and the smaller states to the north, and Italy in the south. The balance of power is shifting." Now Beust leaned so close that Sisi could smell his breath, thick with residual cigarette smoke. "If we aren't careful, Hungary will be next to go. It's a crumbling house of cards."

Sisi nodded, understanding the tenuous scenario from her earlier discussions with Andrássy.

"It was my understanding that you are well connected with the Hungarian side." Beust's darting eyes turned back on her. "And that your closest friend is Hungarian?"

Sisi felt a moment of discomfort. Was it so well known, her friendship with Andrássy, that even a newcomer such as Chancellor Beust had heard of it?

Beust raised his eyebrows. "Countess Festetics is Hungarian, is she not?"

"Marie. Oh, yes, Marie. Of course." Sisi laughed, relieved. "Countess Festetics is my oldest friend at court, and a most faithful attendant."

"Right." Beust nodded, retrieving a cigarette from his pocket and lifting it to his lips. "May I?"

Sisi nodded.

"What do you make of that Andrássy fellow?" Beust exhaled two columns of smoke through flared nostrils. "I don't know Deák well, but Andrássy has always struck me as reasonable."

Sisi tempered her response. "Yes. I've drawn the same conclusion."

Beust nodded, flicking loose a spray of ash.

Sisi continued, "I've had the opportunity to speak with Andrássy — Count Andrássy, on the topic, in fact."

Beust cocked his head, intrigued. "Oh?"

Sisi hurried to add, "We first met when the emperor and I had a prolonged stay in Budapest, several years ago."

"Yes, of course." Beust nodded. "And what does Andrássy say?"

"I agree with your assessment that he is quite reasonable. In fact, he tells me that he and Deák have modified their objectives of late. It's compromise they seek — their condition would not be outright independence. And in fact, they recognize there are certain benefits to maintaining the longtime union between Hungary and Austria."

"Yes?" Beust was attentive, the cigarette

hovering between his barely parted lips. "Then what would they ask for?"

"I can't speak for them, of course," Sisi answered. "But it's my understanding that they seek a certain amount of autonomy. They would be willing to recognize Habsburg rule of Hungary if Austria would recognize them as a separate nation. Distinct and autonomous, rather than subjects."

Beust knit his brows toward one another. "How would that work?"

"Franz promised them a constitution back in '49, in exchange for his ascension to the throne. They still do not have one. And they'd also like a separate parliament, from what Count Andrássy has mentioned."

"And what about prime minister? Would they recognize me as chancellor of the entire empire?"

"I fear that I cannot answer that," Sisi answered. "I've relayed what I know."

"And I'm impressed by how much that is." Beust nodded, taking a long pull from his cigarette. "Very useful indeed, Your Majesty."

"I am happy to help, Chancellor." Sisi was ready to excuse herself, eager to return to her bedchamber and write to Andrássy about this exchange while it was still fresh in her mind. But Beust did not appear to be finished with the conversation.

"I might need you further, Empress." He leaned toward her. "If you would be willing?"

Sisi stared at the chancellor but did not answer.

"There are some at this court who, even now, see no need for compromise or pragmatism." Now Beust's gaze flew to the far corner of the room, and Sisi followed it, her own eyes landing on Sophie's reclining frame. There her mother-in-law sat, her legs propped up on an overstuffed ottoman. Face flushed, she stroked her little dog and sipped champagne as she railed to a small cluster of courtiers. Sisi could not hear the topic of her lecture, but she was certain from the expressions on the faces of the courtiers that none of them planned to interrupt the archduchess.

"We are the Habsburgs, after all." Beust spoke in a quiet, mocking tone, and Sisi recognized how much trouble he would face if this conversation were overheard. She as well.

"We need no one," Sisi said, her tone full of meaning as she repeated her aunt's motto. "Isn't that what she's said for so long?"

Beust flicked his cigarette impatiently. "And, hence, we *have* no one."

Sisi nodded. "It's clear that now is the time to compromise rather than risk losing yet another ally, Chancellor."

"But would he . . . can the Habsburgs be made to see it, Empress? The urgent need for compromise?"

"The case you've just laid out is very compelling. You don't believe Franz . . . the emperor . . . would agree?"

Beust sighed. "We are all subjects to the chaos of this crazy world. I learned that all too well when I saw the Prussians overrun my homeland. There is no pride left for me, no delusion of divinely appointed kingship."

Now Beust looked around, at the room scattered with half-drunk, giggly courtiers who swayed to the music of violins. At the gilded wall trimming that caught the glint of hundreds of fresh candles. At the line of impenetrable imperial guards stationed throughout. "But I fear that here, in the Habsburg halls, the illusion of infallibility may linger on."

Sisi turned back to the chancellor. "What can I do?"

"You can speak candidly to him, can you not?"

"I suppose I can."

"Good. Only you and one other person in this court would do so." Again both of them looked to Sophie. "Perhaps you might present an alternative, a more realistic view of things. But would you be willing to oppose her?"

Sisi did not need long to consider her answer. "Quite."

Sisi relished the opportunity to advocate for the Hungarians to her husband. Not simply because in doing so she was directly challenging the calamitous course charted by her mother-in-law, but also because it was a cause that she knew would benefit Andrássy and the people he — and she — loved.

Sisi had relayed the content of her discussion with Beust to Andrássy, and now the two of them were writing more regularly than ever. In order to remain discreet, Sisi did not send the letters directly to Andrássy, nor did he to her. Instead, they were written and signed by both Marie and Ida. Sisi maintained, at least publicly, an image of aloofness.

However, the truth was that their correspondence had taken on a new urgency. They were no longer just friends: they were allies. The Hungarian people had waited on their promised constitution since 1849. Sophie, enraged over their rebellion, had warned Franz against allowing them one. But the myth of Habsburg infallibility had crumbled in recent years. Austria was vulnerable. And many Hungarians were prepared — even eager — for war.

It was only their love for and trust in their national heroes, Andrássy and Deák, that had restrained the restless Hungarians thus far. And they heard, and believed, that the empress loved Hungary in a way that no Habsburg before her had. Surely she was championing their rights in Vienna? Andrássy wrote that he and Deák were putting forward the idea of compromise. Hungary appeared willing to accept a place in the Habsburg Empire, as long as they were recognized as an equal and autonomous partner. Anything less from Franz would force them to declare rebellion. It was Franz's move.

Sisi longed to avoid another war, and to keep Hungary, her favorite region, as part of the empire her son would inherit. But she noted how Franz remained influenced by the conservative bloc at court. The archduchess encouraged the emperor to allow Andrássy's overtures to go unanswered. And so, as the winter dragged on, Sisi realized she would need a strategy if she were to somehow oppose the voices — the *voice* — that had so long held Franz's ear.

As overpowering and persuasive as Sophie could be, Sisi possessed one weapon that her mother-in-law did not, and she knew it: Franz still cared for his wife, even after all these years of coolness and separation. He enjoyed having her beside him, he enjoyed entering a room with her on his arm and seeing the heads turn to behold the beautiful empress. Sisi decided to seize every opportunity that this advantage afforded.

Invitations to join Franz at the Opera House, the Burgtheater, at formal state dinners — invitations that Sisi had often turned down with polite apologies and half-conjured excuses — were now accepted. Franz, delighted by the sudden rapprochement, reacted by inviting his wife to ever more outings. Sisi passed the second half of winter in a busy blur of balls, soirees, and nights at the theater, taking all the time she could with Franz. Whenever politics came up, she advocated in a soft yet firm tone for maintaining the historical and strategic allegiance with Hungary. "Think of Rudy. What empire shall he have left to inherit, if we allow it to disband because of our own willfulness?"

The weather was warming, Sisi would note as they returned to the palace from their outings together. If fighting were to occur, it would be soon. Hadn't Franz better reach out to Andrássy and invite him to compromise?

The court decamped to Schönbrunn for the warm season. Still, Franz extended no overtures to Andrássy. Sisi, growing increasingly agitated by her husband's inaction, made a move.

It was an afternoon in late spring. Around the palace, tulips pressed their way through the green lawn and the sun poured down over a landscape of heavily budded trees.

"It's a lovely day for a picnic. I thought it would be nice to get outdoors for a bit." Sisi's tone was merry as she looked out over the grounds, the nearby Obelisk fountain jutting up out of the gardens. At the base of the fountain the famous Schönbrunn grotto gurgled and hummed with the voice of a dozen fountains. The mountain gods, their muscular forms carved from stone, writhed and wrestled as their opened mouths splashed water into the pool. Swans skimmed its glassy surface, their regal presence a welcome sight after a long, fierce winter.

"Brilliant idea," Franz said, nodding. "I'm glad you proposed it."

A dozen uniformed footmen buzzed around them, sorting silver, draping white linens over a table, and unpacking baskets of meats, cheese, wine, and bread. Not as rustic a picnic as Sisi had envisioned, but that did not matter.

"I confess, I had a purpose in asking you to this lunch, Franz."

Franz looked at her now, his eyebrow tilting upward. "Oh? And what's that?"

Sisi allowed a coy grin to tug on the corners of her lips. She lowered her eyes, blinking. And then, smiling broadly, she lifted her eyes, holding fast to his. "I have something for you."

She waved one of the footmen forward. The liveried man carried a large rectangular bundle, draped in a sheet.

"What's this?" Franz leaned back in his chair, his interest piqued.

Sisi rose from her place and walked toward

the package. With a flick of her wrist, a dramatic gesture like a performer, she tugged on the sheet and its contents were revealed.

Franz gasped when he saw it, a gloved hand coming to his face to conceal his open mouth.

It was a portrait. A portrait of her, Sisi. She had commissioned it specifically for Franz from one of Europe's most-sought-after portraitists.

Herr Winterhalter had captured her alone, in a scene of considerable intimacy. In it, her hair was loose, her long dark tresses tumbling around her shoulders as only her husband had the right to see them. She wore nothing but a thin, white shift, almost like a nightgown. The loose material slid off her, revealing a naked shoulder and a soft, ivory neck.

Herr Winterhalter had captured her in such a way that one got the sense, as they looked at the canvas, that in the next moment, the gown might slip off entirely, tumbling to the ground and revealing the full splendor of the empress's famous figure. Sisi's gaze was quizzical and evasive; she didn't look directly at the observer, but off to the side, as if tempting you to catch her attention, begging you to turn her head.

Sisi had blushed the entire time she had posed for Herr Winterhalter, and she blushed now, as she beheld the finished product. Especially as she saw the speechless awe with which Franz admired her likeness.

She inhaled quickly, standing up tall. "I thought it was about time that I have some new portraits done. And Herr Winterhalter is the master." Sisi slid back into her seat opposite her husband. "It's for you, Franz. And only you."

"Elisabeth . . ." Franz's voice faltered, even as he sat, transfixed, eyes fastened to the large canvas.

"Do you like it?"

He took several moments to answer. "It's . . . it's exquisite."

Sisi smiled, lowering her eyes. "Good. Then it shall be yours. Though I beg you to put it somewhere private."

"Of course." Franz looked at her now. She hoped the real subject wasn't a disappointment after his eyes had held the portrait for so long. "I would share this with absolutely no one, believe me. I want it entirely to myself."

"Good."

Just then the footmen deposited the entree course, a peppery beef stew. Franz looked once more at the canvas, as if reluctant to keep his eyes away from it. Eventually, he gestured for the footman to cover it back up. Turning back to the table, his face composed once more, he took up his napkin and lifted his fork. Sisi forced herself to tuck into her own bowl.

They ate in silence a few moments before

she asked: "How do you like this dish?"

"Quite tasty."

"I've ordered us a Hungarian menu."

"Indeed." Franz looked down at his plate.

"I remember enjoying the food immensely while we were in Hungary."

Franz nodded, eating.

"Didn't you, Franz?"

"I prefer our food here in Austria." Franz was dipping his bread in the sauce. "But every once in the while, Hungarian food makes for a nice change."

"Agreed," Sisi said, already full of the beef after only a few bites. She took a small sip of wine. "How are things going on that front, with the Hungarians?" She knew the latest. Andrássy kept her abreast of every exchange he had with Vienna. But she hoped to hear Franz's perspective.

"We've reached an impasse," Franz said, pausing to wipe his mouth with a linen napkin.

"On what point?" She knew the answer, but she asked anyway.

"Deák and Andrássy . . ." Franz paused, clearing his throat with a sip of wine. Sisi noticed the small lurch in her gut, the flutter that happened when Franz spoke Andrássy's name.

Franz continued: "They insist that Hungary would have its own prime minister. They would like to break from Beust."

"But not a separate monarch, I hope. They would still recognize you as their king?"

Franz nodded.

"And how does Beust feel about that?" Sisi posed the question as if she did not already know the answer.

"He supports it," Franz said, an incredulous frown pulling on his features. "He says: 'Let them squabble over their own affairs; what's important is that we preserve the empire.' "

"That's the critical point." Sisi felt full from the rich meal and lowered her spoon. "Franz, why do you need to be involved in their petty domestic disputes anyway? Let a Hungarian deal with that. Even Beust is happy to allow that. As long as they acknowledge you as their king and they remain loyal members of the empire."

"But Mother suggests that I will willingly cede my power if I allow them a prime minister."

"Your mother really underestimates you so?"

Franz paused, thinking about this.

"Would they be under your military still?"

Franz nodded yes.

"So we would remain one empire. Under one king. You. And one military." Sisi forced herself to pause, to keep her tone measured. To not too wholeheartedly betray her passion on the subject. And yet, it was thrilling, having a voice, and Franz not abruptly dismissing her, as he so often had in the past. She inhaled, continuing: "But we let them take over the tedious and tiresome tasks of their own internal affairs. And no more blood need be shed. It sounds as if we retain the best parts of power and cede to them those of the least importance."

Franz thought about this for several moments before propping his elbows on the table. "It's a compelling argument."

Sisi pressed her case: "Beust seems to feel that it's very important we act, and quickly. He thinks it would be the end of the empire if we lost the Hungarians."

Franz ran his fingers through the auburn beard, traced with gray, that covered his cheeks. "I know what Beust thinks."

"Please, Franz, write to Budapest. Invite Deák and Andrássy to make this compromise."

He looked at her directly now, his light-blue eyes holding hers with a tinge of wariness. "Why are you so eager?"

Sisi was taken aback by the directness of the question. She couldn't answer the full truth. She wasn't even sure if she could have told herself the full truth. Instead, she lightened her tone and glanced out over the view, over the grotto and the Obelisk. "You know I've always loved Hungary."

"I remember." Franz nodded after several moments. "You loved the Hungarians, and the Hungarians loved you."

But she thought of one Hungarian, in particular. She rested her cheeks on her hands, hoping to hide the flush that rose to her skin.

"Do you still study Hungarian?" he asked after several minutes.

She nodded. "Yes."

He looked down at his bowl, his appetite gone.

"Franz." Sisi leaned across the table, putting her gloved hand on top of his. Her silly dining gloves, another Habsburg custom. She swallowed that thought. "Franz."

He looked up at her.

"These are tumultuous times over which you preside." She paused. "But, I hope to tell Rudy someday . . . that we did all we could to preserve his empire."

Franz sighed.

"You've ruled during such difficult and changing days." Sisi's tone was beseeching now, her entire body leaning toward his in a way it had not in years. Like a flower angling toward the sun. "None of those other calamities could have been stopped. But this one . . . this one developing right before our eyes . . ."

Unexpectedly, tears filled her eyes. And then, perhaps even less expected, Sisi bowed forward and placed a slow kiss on his hand. "Please, Franz. Please do not let this last piece crumble."

Franz, moved to wordlessness by her uncharacteristic and unsolicited display of affection, took several moments to speak. When he did, his voice was meek. Even melancholy. "All right, then, Elisa."

Sisi's heart quickened as she looked at him, awaiting his next words. It was a positive sign that he used her nickname, the nickname from the years when he had adored her, and she had adored him.

"I will invite them here." Franz propped his elbows onto the table with a heavy slouch. "But I make no guarantees — it will be up to Andrássy and his side to win me over to this compromise."

Sisi lifted her gloved fingers to her lips to conceal the wide grin that burst across her face. When she had regained her composure, she said, "You are wise, Franz."

"I just hope I don't regret . . . well . . ."

"Regret what?"

Franz sighed. "Inviting Andrássy here might be the most foolish thing I do as emperor."

Andrássy arrived in Vienna weeks later, delayed for several days due to heavy thunderstorms. Sisi saw him for the first time at the formal state dinner the night they arrived, given by the emperor and empress for the Hungarian delegation. Sisi had spent the entire afternoon preparing for the dinner: she appeared now with her hair in a glorious coronet of braids and jewels, her figure tucked into a snug dress of a rich, raspberry satin.

"Welcome to Vienna, Count Andrássy." Sisi greeted him in the receiving line at the back of the Spiegelsaal. It was one of Schönbrunn's grandest halls, opulent with gold gilt and rows of glittery mirrors. Every candelabra was lit, so that the dancing candles illuminated the frescoes that swirled overhead. But Sisi cared about none of the grandeur of the room. Standing there, staring at Andrássy after such a long absence, she longed to smile. Longed to inquire about his arduous, soggy journey. To revel in their joint progress on behalf of Hungary. But she was aware that Sophie stood beside her, listening.

Sophie had worn a scowl on her face ever since Franz had announced his intention to invite Andrássy and Deák for negotiations: *Don't you remember what they did to us in '48? And don't you remember, it was a Hungarian who tried to stab you to death?"* But Sisi had prevailed, perhaps because Franz now saw the painted image of his wife's bare shoulder, her loose and glossy tresses, every time he stepped into his study to consider his foreign policy.

"Thank you, Empress Elisabeth." Andrássy bowed to Sisi now in the receiving line, his dark eyes twinkling as he said her name. The appreciative way in which he studied her appearance filled Sisi with satisfaction.

"It is good to have you in Vienna, Count." Sisi tried to keep her facial expression calm as she beheld him. Inside, her heart clamored, beating so violently that she feared it was louder than the nearby violins.

"The palace feels welcoming and warm after our days on the road, Empress." Andrássy looked as handsome as she had remembered, and in spite of her better judgment, she smiled.

"I understand that the journey was a tiring one, Count Andrássy. I hope you have recovered?"

"I am quite comfortable now, Your Majesty." Andrássy lingered before her, his eyes holding hers, smooth and rich as dark silk.

"Count Andrássy." Sophie stepped forward, impatient in the receiving line.

"Archduchess Sophie, it is splendid to see you." Andrássy peeled his gaze from Sisi to turn and pay his respects to her mother-in-law. And like that, their reunion was over. At dinner, Andrássy was seated beside Franz, at the far end of the table from Sisi. Throughout the meal, they exchanged brief, fleeting looks. Sisi, for her part, chatted with Deák through most of the dinner. Though she longed to let her eyes wander to the far side of the table, she forced herself not to. She could not stare, Sisi knew. Someone would surely notice the pull between the two of them — if they hadn't already.

The following day marked the beginning of negotiations — discussions to which Sisi was not invited. Sisi passed the morning with the children, attempting to remain distracted as she helped Rudolf study his French. In the afternoon, even though the heavy rain persisted, she rode — a long, strenuous ride that she hoped would tire her out and beat back the restlessness that gnawed at her.

That evening, Franz took his supper in his suite and ordered no visitors. Sisi, chilled from her outing and frantic to hear how the day's meetings had gone, felt edgy and without an appetite. Unsettled, she paced her apartment, barking orders at Ida and dismissing Franziska when sitting still to have her hair brushed proved too tedious. At dusk she decided to set out for another walk.

"But, my lady, it's raining out." Ida, who was turning down the bed for the evening, eyed Sisi disapprovingly.

"Then fetch my cloak." Sisi paused at the doorway, allowing herself to be bundled into the hooded cloak.

"It is nearly dark out, Empress."

"I will stay on the terraces."

"Why don't I prepare you a bath instead?"

"I am too restless tonight. I can't stay here." And with that, Sisi set out into the waterlogged gardens. She ordered her guards to leave her, promising them that she would remain within the private grounds. She was too on edge to have to listen to the sounds of their boots pattering behind her, like the echoes of the phantoms that already visited her at night.

The trees shivered as a clap of thunder ripped across the sky. Sisi made her way out onto the colonnade, opting for the covered stone walkways rather than the drenched and muddy lawns. She pulled her cloak tighter around her shoulders, grateful for Ida's insistence that she take it.

How could she find an update on how the day's discussions had gone? she wondered. Franz's abrupt retreat to his chamber seemed to indicate that the day had not been successful. But when would she hear from Andrássy?

Pulling her cloak tighter around her shoulders and head, Sisi quit the pathway and made for the hill. She climbed the sodden slope, pausing only when she reached the top and stood before the Gloriette, the series of archways that boasted, triumphant, across the summit. Out of breath and soaked, she paused, sitting down on a covered stone ledge. There she peered down the hill, at the rain that splashed the endless grounds below her. That all of this existed for one man, and for her, struck her as somehow ludicrous, even after all of these years in her role. She sat — she didn't know for how long — as the gardens sank deeper into darkness.

A shadow of mist appeared just a few feet away. At first, Sisi thought it nothing more than the rain. But then, she smelled its scent: cigarette smoke.

"Hello?" She called out, her voice barely rising above the thrum of the rain that slapped the stone archways around her.

"Hello?" Sisi repeated her call.

Just then, a tall figure emerged from the other side of the arch.

"Andrássy?" The delight in Sisi's voice was apparent, even to her, as she stood up.

"Sisi?" He sounded equally pleased. He walked toward her, reaching her in two long strides. He kissed her cold, ungloved hand.

"Andrássy." She stared at him. "This is a surprise."

"Indeed. It's good to see you."

"And you."

"Please." He helped her back to a seated position on the stone ledge, and he sat beside her. "Or is it too cold out here? Would you prefer to go indoors?"

"I came out here of my own accord," she said, smiling.

"Well then, please, allow me." He removed his stiff white coat and draped it over her shoulders.

"Thank you."

"I had to come see this," he said, gesturing around at the architecture that enfolded them. "It looked to me like a giant wedding cake atop this hill."

She laughed, burrowing into his coat as she looked out over the dark gardens, thrilled at how close he was. At the fact that they were alone. She lived for these stolen moments of intimacy. They were wrong, forbidden, and yet, they had somehow become the sustenance that helped her survive their long and painful separations.

"Trouble sleeping?"

She nodded.

"Me, as well. I doubt I shall be able to sleep at all tonight."

Her glance slid sideways, to where he sat beside her. "How did it go today?"

Andrássy sighed, taking up the half-expired cigarette that he had been smoking prior to her appearance.

"That bad?"

"He seemed to come with his mind already decided against us."

Sisi thought about this, frowning. "What did he say? Did he grow angry?"

"On the contrary. He was quiet. Almost disinterested at times."

"Who was there?"

"He came with Beust. I brought Deák."

"Surely Beust considered your side?"

"Indeed. He did try his best." Andrássy took a long pull on his cigarette. "Things were not exactly amicable, but they were cordial, for most of the day. Until we came to the matter of separate governments."

"What happened?"

"He thinks we are playing a stealthy trick to slowly strip him of his power."

"He said that?"

"Indirectly."

Sisi thought back to the conversations she'd had with Franz on the topic. "He has already lost so much land."

"Through war. Something we are trying to avoid," Andrássy said.

"I agree." Sisi nodded. "War must be avoided at all costs. But he is hesitant to cede his control over the government in Budapest. He fears that it would give the appearance of weakness."

"Yes, but we can't truly be equal members of the empire if we can't at least govern ourselves."

Sisi shivered, pulling Andrássy's coat closer around her neck. She breathed him in, his scent. Damp wool and cigarette smoke and a hint of something sweet — shaving cream?

Andrássy sighed, finishing off his cigarette and stomping it out beneath his boot.

"Is this an impassible difference?" she asked.

"I hope not."

Sisi exhaled. *"Difficulties increase the nearer we get to the goal."*

Andrássy looked at her, his smile apparent

in the murky, waterlogged moonlight. He had recognized the quote from Goethe.

"Who else would know what to say at such a time?"

He nodded appreciatively, taking her bare, cold hand in his; his skin felt impossibly warm against hers. This was indiscreet, she knew, but she could not resist his touch. They sat beside one another in silence, staring out at the rain for a long while, her hand unmoving in his.

For how long they sat like that, she didn't know. Not long enough. Eventually, Andrássy turned to her. "I didn't expect to find the empress of Austria sitting out here, after dark, in the rain."

"My maid proposed that I take a bath, but I couldn't imagine sitting still." She blushed as soon as she said it, as soon as she realized how indecent a topic it was.

He lit another cigarette and stared at her, holding her with a thoughtful gaze. Exhaling, his eyes still on her, he asked: "Who do you think is the more restless soul of the two of us?"

She smiled, taking the cigarette from his fingers and inhaling a puff for herself. "Hard to tell."

"You seem pretty restless." He smiled at her, watching her smoke.

"I am." She nodded, exhaling.

"I didn't know you smoked."

"I don't," she said, her mind still processing his question. "There was a while, right after I first married Franz, when I was content. Or at least, I thought I was. Other than that, I can't really recall not ever being restless. I've never found a horse that could run fast enough."

Andrássy turned, looking through the veil of falling rain out over their dark surroundings. "I wonder if, after we settle the Hungarian question of independence — *if* we settle it — if I will find some peace. In Hungary. Perhaps I might be able to calm down then."

"I was happy in Hungary," Sisi said.

Andrássy turned to her. "Then you should come back."

Her breath caught, suspended in her throat. "I would like that," she said, after several moments. "Would you?"

He slid his body closer to her on the cold stone ledge. He did not speak, but the look on his face answered her.

"Sisi." He was close to her now, taking her face in his hands. His fingers felt warm, almost as warm as the burn she now felt in her cheeks. He hovered before her, his face just inches from hers, their eyes locked. Sisi was hesitant to break the thread between them by speaking.

"Perhaps I don't wish you to come, Sisi. Perhaps I would not be able to survive, if you did." As he spoke, she smelled the cigarette on his breath. "Is this how it would be, I wonder? You, right in front of me. And yet, forever out of my reach?"

"Kiss me, Andrássy." Her voice was pleading. It surprised even her.

The shake of his head was minuscule, barely perceptible. But enough to break her heart.

"No," he said at last, his voice resolute. He dropped his fingers, letting go of her face.

She lowered her eyes, forcing herself to breathe as she fought back tears. He loved her, she felt almost sure of it. And she loved him, it was useless to go on denying it. Her insides clamored, her heart teemed with equal parts love and anger. How cruel a joke the fates had played on them!

"I must go." Sisi rose, sliding herself out of his jacket and handing it back to him. Without it, the night felt unbearably cold, and she brought her arms around herself.

Andrássy stood, resting a hand on her bare, goose-pimpled arm. "May I walk you back?" He seemed hesitant to let her go.

"No, stay here." Her voice had a frantic edge as she slid her arm from his grip.

"At least allow me to explain . . ." He reached for her once more.

"Please, stop. I beg you," Sisi said, willing herself to remain strong. "I must go. Good night." She excused herself, turning back toward the palace. But when she was back indoors, she did not turn toward her own bedroom.

XVII.

"And so begin the days of revelry," she says, as she steps aboard the steamer. This barge will carry her across the river, to the flat plains of Pest, for the first official celebration. She has been, mercifully, allowed to change, and she's exchanged the heavy ceremonial robe of brocade for a featherlight gown of white tulle.

They've decorated the steamer for her, so that blue and white flowers festoon the deck — a nod to her Bavarian roots. They never fail to point out that she, like them, does not come from Vienna.

Meanwhile, the reports already seep out of Austria's capital, reaching her ears. She hears that one of Franz's ministers has railed against today's events, saying that "Andrássy deserves to hang more today than he did in '49."

She smiles. Let them stew in Vienna. Finally, they notice her. They realize the error of their ways, ridiculing and disregarding her for all of these years.

Now the eastern bank of Pest comes into

crystalline view. She longs to squint, the sun is so fierce overhead. As the barge taps the berth, sending the river to lap up against the shore, she spots him. Her heart lurches, a quick intake of breath. Andrássy deserves to hang more today than he did in '49.

He stands there, a hand extended. Without looking to see who watches, she takes it.

"Empress." He stares at her, his lips forming a smile under his dark mustache. "It is done."

"Not done," she says, her head tilting to the side. "Only just begun."

CHAPTER SEVENTEEN

*SCHÖNBRUNN SUMMER PALACE, VIENNA
SPRING 1867*

"Elisabeth?"

"Hello, Franz."

"I wasn't expecting . . . this late . . . is everything all right? Are the children all right?"

"The children are fine, Franz. I am here to see you."

"You . . . you are?" It was the first evening she had knocked on her husband's bedroom door in years, and the shock on his face was apparent.

"Are you alone?" She raised her eyebrows in a suggestive manner.

"I am. Wait one moment." Franz spoke into a footman's ear and the man scurried off — perhaps on his way to intercept whichever young courtier was on her way to the emperor's bed. But Sisi pushed that thought aside.

"I was hoping I might come in." She blinked, her lashes fluttering.

"Of course." Franz stepped aside, opening the door wider. He still appeared surprised, but perfectly willing to welcome her.

"You're not too tired?" she asked.

"Not tired at all." With Sisi in the bedchamber, he closed the heavy door once more, shutting them in. "Furious, but not tired."

Sisi went to the table in the corner and, without invitation, poured them two glasses of brandy. Outside, the rain still continued to pelt the palace windows and walls like liquid gunfire.

"The day did not go well?" Sisi crossed the room, bringing him his drink and sipping hers.

Franz took a long sip, more like a gulp, before answering. "They would have their own parliament in Budapest. A separate prime minister and a separate parliament. What use would they have for me?" With that, Franz drained his cup.

"But you'd still be emperor."

"They would castrate me!" His breath was hot with the liquor and the insult as he spat, and Sisi guessed that it was not his first glass of brandy this evening.

"Hardly, Franz." Sisi rose to refill his drink and hers as well, which she too had gulped in several sips.

"You say that because you'd sign off on it

tomorrow. I know perfectly well what you think."

"I think that Hungary is invaluable to this empire," she answered, staying calm. "I want my son's kingdom to include Hungary, as valuable and rich and beautiful a land as it is. But I hope that there will be no blood spilled in forcing them to stay. They are a separate people and deserve recognition."

"They would cut my kingdom in half."

"On the contrary. It would keep your kingdom whole. They do not wish to leave the kingdom unless you would force them to stay . . . as subjects."

"So they want the option of leaving, and then they will choose to stay. It seems nonsensical."

"It is a question of recognition. They would like to be a partner in the empire, rather than the conquered subjects of the empire."

Franz thought about this as he finished his second glass. After several moments he said: "Andrássy did say there would be a separate coronation in Budapest, where they would formally recognize you and me as King and Queen of Hungary. No longer foreign monarchs, but monarchs of Hungary in our own right."

"That must sound compelling." Sisi cocked her head sideways, sipping her brandy.

"I would be the weak Habsburg, though. Letting them dictate terms to me like that."

"On the contrary." Sisi placed her glass down and faced Franz. "There is nothing weak in a leader who is wise and just to his people."

"You don't think me weak?" Franz looked tired, shriveled somehow.

"I know you are not weak." She stood near to him now and lifted her hand, tracing the line of his cheek with her fingers. She allowed her hand to stay there, sliding down to his neck, so that they stood as close as they had in years.

"Whom do you most admire, Franz? Your grandfather? He was Franz the *Good.* Maria Theresa? She was the *pragmatist.* Nobody thinks fondly back to the leaders who burn them and shoot them and conquer them." She leaned forward now, pressing her palm to his chest. "You would be the wise emperor, Franz Joseph. The emperor who saved the kingdom. They would love you in Hungary for ages to come."

She leaned her head to the side, looking at him in a manner that she hoped reminded him of her in years past, in their happier times. When she spoke, she did so quietly, whispering. "Emperor Franz Joseph and The Great Compromise."

He sighed. "Well, *one* thing was clear today. One point upon which everyone in the room agreed."

"Oh? What's that?" she asked.

"After centuries of detesting their foreign Habsburg rulers, the Hungarians finally have a leader whom they adore. A leader whom they want to keep." Franz paused, his features sagging. Defeated. "You, Elisabeth."

"Oh, come now, Franz." She kept her tone soft, even as her heart raced within her breast. "Don't be distraught. I see great hope for us." She paused, her fingers intertwining with his as she took his hand. Something she had not done in years. "Is there anything I can do . . . to lift your spirits?"

Franz's eyes darted to hers, as if startled by the question. After a moment's hesitation, he put his arm on her waist, pulling her body closer. His eyes held hers, as if questioning her. But she didn't reject him. She allowed him, even encouraged him, by inching another small step toward him. Now their bodies touched.

Franz leaned forward and kissed her, and she closed her eyes, tasting the brandy on his lips. Those lips that she had once kissed so often. The hand he had rested on her waist slid up her midsection, pausing tenuously below her breast. She sidled closer to him, not initiating any new caresses, but not discouraging him either.

Franz responded by kissing her with a new boldness. She kept her eyes shut. And then he was inching their bodies toward the bed. She yielded, moving with him as he lowered her down onto the downy pillows. Had she known, when she came to his bedroom, that they would do more than talk? That he would want to make love, and she would allow it? Yes, she supposed, she had known.

They had been apart for seven years and their bodies, changed in the separation, had all but forgotten one another. It was a brief, wordless encounter. For Sisi, the challenge was not so much in participating — Franz did not seem to need much encouragement once she had allowed him to kiss her — but in forcing Andrássy's face from her mind. When she shut her eyes, all she could see was him as he had appeared out in the rainy courtyard, moments earlier. His dark, expectant eyes. His lips, so close to hers. So she opened her eyes, staring blankly at the room before her. And yet, she could not quiet her mind. What would Andrássy think? But she could not ask that. It wasn't Andrássy's right to think anything. Franz was her husband. Franz had every right to yearn for his wife's touch.

Then why did she feel so guilty?

The day dawned warm and bright, and Sisi slipped from Franz's room before he awoke. Back in her bedchamber, she looked out over the grounds and saw that the rain had stopped. A bold, determined sun shone down, drying the puddles as if eager to reassert itself after days of absence. Sisi pressed her forehead to the window, hoping that the day's talks would mimic the clarity of the blue sky, finally purged of dark clouds and thick, obstructive fog.

Ida swept into the room. "Empress, you're back."

"I am," Sisi said, sitting down at the small breakfast table. She looked disinterestedly at the plate that her maid now placed before her and reached instead for the coffee. She felt the beginning of a headache.

"We were so worried. You never came back last night from your walk."

"I stayed in the emperor's room."

Ida's look was precisely what Sisi had expected: disbelief, mingled with shock.

"It's true." Sisi could not help but laugh at her stunned maid. "Fetch water. I need a bath."

Sisi left the palace in the late morning, riding Vándor along the Danube, toward Hungary.

In the late afternoon she paused to rest at her favorite point on the river, the wildflower-dotted meadow about an hour's ride from the palace. She had slipped her guard and was relieved to be alone, to be free to scowl and fret without worrying about the gossip her sour mood might kindle. The thought of returning to Schönbrunn filled her with dread. She was feeling wretched this afternoon, remembering Franz and the way she had deceived him into thinking she desired him last night. How he had fumbled beside her before falling asleep, his arm on top of her as he snored all night. How she had lain awake, wishing she could flee his room but worrying that in doing so she might wake him.

Her thoughts, however, were interrupted when she spotted a familiar figure approaching on horseback. She fought the urge to jump up, to run to meet him. She stayed where she was, seated by the river, as the rider neared. He stopped just feet from her resting spot.

"I thought I might find you here." Andrássy, panting, hopped off the horse. She could tell, instinctively, that he was happy today, even triumphant. Entirely different from how she had found him the night before.

"Hello." She shielded her eyes as he sat down beside her. "I did not expect to see you out. Has my husband dismissed you again?"

"We did it." Andrássy leaned toward her, smiling as he lifted her hand in his. "Franz . . . the emperor . . . agreed to our dualistic approach. He was entirely changed this morning, Sisi. Assertive, confident. Sisi, we did it. Hungary shall be free!" Andrássy kissed the top of her hand. Not once, but three times.

She smiled, and she meant it, but she pulled her hand away from his grip. "I am so happy for you, Andrássy."

"Not just for me. For *us,*" Andrássy crowed. "For all of us. The empire shall continue. You shall be crowned Queen of Hungary." He looked around; at the meadow, at the river. Then back at her. "I should have brought champagne. I just had to tell you first."

"How did you know to find me here?"

"I ran to your apartments. I was so deliriously happy that I didn't care who saw me, or what they thought. Ida told me you had gone out riding, and on a day such as this, I guessed you would have come here."

She smiled, though she felt dizzy. When she had been with Franz, she had felt as though she were betraying Andrássy. Now, with Andrássy, she felt as though she were being unfair to Franz. It was too overwhelming, the disquiet she felt. A restlessness that couldn't be quelled, not if she raced on horseback until the far end of the earth.

Andrássy, still elated, didn't appear to notice. "You know, Sisi, that the people . . . the Austrian *and* the Hungarian people owe you the credit. It is because of you that this has happened."

If only you knew, she thought, lowering her eyes.

Andrássy looked now over the river. He leaned back to recline on the ground, propped up on his elbows, smiling. The cause for which he had spent his life fighting would now be realized. It was one of the best moments of his life, Sisi sensed, and she watched him bask in it, his figure awash in the afternoon sunlight. She had to pull her eyes away.

After a while, he spoke. "We sat here once, years ago."

"I remember," she said, looking out over the river. It was the day he had left for Hungary, and she had realized how terribly she would miss him. Though she did not meet his eyes, she sensed that he now stared at her. What did he want from it all? she wondered. Did he enjoy torturing himself? Torturing her? She did not know how he managed, but she knew that she could not survive it much longer. Perhaps it was best that he left. But she would never ask him to leave, she would never in fact want him to go.

Andrássy lifted his hands and formed a square shape with his fingers, framing her profile in them. "If I could have this scene painted, I would stare at it every day. The river, so blue in the background. And the foreground, well, that's the most beautiful part."

"What are you doing, Andrássy?" The bluntness of her question jarred them both as she turned to look in his eyes.

"What do you mean?" He sat up, dropping his hands.

"What is happening?" She waved her hands

between them. "What is this? How can you expect me to go on like this?" Her voice sounded wild now, and she was certain her expression matched it.

Andrássy lowered his eyes, his shoulders sagging. He nodded. "I know."

"Do you? Because you seem perfectly fine."

"Sisi."

"How do you do it? How do you stare at love like this and not allow it to either overcome you, or else, break you?"

He closed his eyes, and his face did not show the customary calm that Sisi had always found in him. His voice was quiet when he answered. "It is difficult for me, too."

But Sisi felt like hitting him, railing against him until he offered more of a confession. "I asked you to kiss me. You looked as though you wanted to. You always look as though you want to. And yet, you refuse."

"I cannot say what is in my heart," he said, his voice still quiet, controlled. "Any more than I can ask you now what's in yours."

"Isn't it obvious?" She laughed, a bitter laugh.

"Yes, it's glaringly obvious. But I cannot say it."

"Why not?"

"It would be treason." He took her hands in his, trying to calm her, but she resisted. That was not the touch of his for which she ached; it was not enough.

"Look at me, Sisi. Please, look at me."

She gave in, staring into his dark eyes for several minutes, seeing her own anguish reflected back to her in them. Before she could control them, tears began to rise in her eyes, spilling down her cheeks. She succumbed to the tears, allowing herself to cry with all the force she had used to hold them in for so long. Andrássy wrapped his arms around her and pulled her into an embrace.

She allowed herself to rest on his shoulders. Through her tears, she gasped out her words. "It's so cruel. It's all been so cruel."

"I know." He ran his fingers through her hair. "I know."

He allowed her to cry until she felt she had no tears left. "We can be strong, Sisi."

She pulled away from him, looking up at him through the film of tears. "Must we be strong, Andrássy? What if we decided instead to be honest? To be happy?"

"Shhh." He pressed a finger to her lips, blocking further words from utterance. "I will not put you in danger. I will not. I will not be the cause of your marriage's failure or your reputation's ruination."

She laughed at this. As if Andrássy would be to blame for her marriage's failure.

"I cannot tell you what I long to tell you." He removed his finger from her lips and slipped it under her chin. She loved it when he took her face in his hands like this. She loved it when he angled her face close to his. If only it could be followed with the kiss she craved.

"I once told you," he said, his breath landing gently on her face, "whatever it is that I wish to say, I find that Goethe has already found a way to say it better. Well, I don't think that quoting a little bit of Goethe is treason, is it?"

Andrássy pulled a small book from his pocket, opening it to a page that was folded over. She saw his familiar, elegant cursive scribbled in the margins and knew that he had pored over this passage many times. At the bottom of a long passage he had scrawled, in clear, capital letters: *SISI*. Her heart lurched.

Andrássy cleared his throat and began to read the passage:

"To be loved for what one is, that is the greatest exception. The great majority love in others only what they lend him; their own selves, their version of him . . ."

Her heart hurled itself at her rib cage as he read on.

"This is the true measure of love: when we believe that we alone can love this way. That no one could ever have loved so before us. And that no one will ever love in the same way after us."

He paused when it was over, taking a slow,

deep breath. When he looked up at her, she saw that he, too, wept.

XVIII.

For three centuries we have tried faith.
Time and again we have tried hope, till
only one possibility remained, that the
nation should be able to fall in love with
some member of the reigning house from
the depths of the heart.
— Former Hungarian separatist,
writing about Sisi
June 1867

Chapter Eighteen

BUDAPEST, HUNGARY
JUNE 1867

Sisi did not know how she would tell Andrássy that she was pregnant. She had not even told Franz, and she supposed that he, as the father, ought to be the first to know. And yet, the conversation she thought about most was the one during which she would have to break the news to Andrássy. Every time she thought about him, she recalled the last time they'd been together. The afternoon they had spent together on the banks of the Danube. The afternoon when he had told her that Hungary would be free and that he loved her.

Sisi had arrived for the coronation in Hungary's capital in triumph, the people lining the boulevards, their cheers of "Long live Elisabeth" so thunderous that she thought she saw the buildings tremble. Flowers rained down on her as the coach sped uphill, bound for the castle on Buda's heights. Her coronation would be the proudest of her moments as empress, for she would be officially recognized by the people she loved. Both they — and she — knew that it was Sisi who had brought this dual monarchy about.

And yet, when left alone to get settled into her apartments in Buda's castle, Sisi grew nervous and agitated. She did not know why she suffered from this guilt, this fear of telling Andrássy that she had returned to her husband's bed. It had been one night only, the night she had pressed Franz to compromise on the issue of Hungarian autonomy. Franz, who had so seldom been assertive in their marriage, had asserted his husbandly influence that one night, and to such a dramatic effect. It was odd, that a child could have been made in that brief, unremarkable matter of minutes.

The baby had just barely begun to show the first signs of its presence — just a small swell in her belly, noticeable only because the rest of her frame was so narrow. While traveling, she had concealed her belly by dressing in roomy cloaks and free-flowing gowns. Ida had already taken out the seams of the gown Sisi intended to wear to the coronation. Sisi had sworn Ida to secrecy, so that when she arrived in Hungary, only Ida and Marie knew.

Sophie, who was increasingly unwell and flatly opposed to the purpose of the trip, had chosen not to travel with her son to the Hungarian coronation. Just as well, Sisi thought, though it would have given her satisfaction to see Sophie's face as the Hungarians venerated their beloved queen.

Andrássy welcomed them with a formal banquet the first week in June, attended by hundreds of Hungarian statesmen, ministers, and noblemen. Outside the walled castle, the city was in a state of ongoing revelry, the Habsburgs having donated barrels of wine and ale in honor of their own celebrations. The days were at their longest and the meandering streets of the Buda hillside were aglow as sunlight mingled with candlelight. The people danced and sang, playing an unceasing chorus of Hungarian czardas and Gypsy music. Spontaneous cheers erupted, lauding "Sisi, the Hungarian Queen!" Word had spread that the beautiful queen had been their champion in the Hofburg, and Sisi had secured her place in the Hungarian imagination as the most popular Habsburg. Some even whispered that the queen had fallen in love with the handsome Andrássy, and he with her. Who, it was asked, could blame either one of them?

Inside Buda Castle the mood was merry but more subdued. Sisi saw Andrássy throughout the dinner, smiled as he introduced her to an endless stream of faces as "Our Queen of Hungary, Elisabeth."

But it was not until after dinner, when she strolled the castle complex alone, that Sisi hoped to speak with him in private. She had slipped him the note at the end of dinner, and hoped he would come.

Midnight sounded at the nearby cathedral of St. Matthew without a sign of Andrássy. Fortunately the evening was a warm one. Sisi paced the stone paths, listening to the gurgling of the fountain as she both dreaded and longed for the moment when she would see his face emerge into the dark garden.

They had written since their last encounter, but their communication had primarily been to discuss the coronation and the plans for Sisi's trip. He had not again implied, or outright spoken of, his love for her. Until his most recent letter. He had closed that note by saying: *Know that I think of that Goethe passage daily, for the beautiful truth it makes plain.* Sisi had kept it, along with every other letter he had ever written her, in a locked drawer of her escritoire.

"Sisi." She heard his voice now and her eyes flew in his direction.

"Andrássy." She ran toward him, her gown belling out in the breeze. She wore a flowing dress of filmy vanilla chiffon with gold trim on the neck and sleeves. A cape of the same pattern draped over her shoulders. On her head rested a delicate tiara encrusted with hundreds of small, brilliant diamonds.

"There's my queen." Andrássy took her

762

gloved hands in his and raised them to his lips. "Sisi." He smiled at her, his dark eyes happy. "Sisi, you are as radiant as ever. They love you, just as I knew they would."

She smiled up at him, her anxiety dissipating as she sensed the love *he* felt for her, too. "Andrássy." All she could do was say his name.

Andrássy, still holding her hands in his, looked down at her. "You are every bit the queen we have prayed for."

She gulped. How could she tell him?

"And tomorrow shall be a day . . . oh, do you know what they call you?"

She shrugged her shoulders, no.

"They call you *Hungary's Beautiful Providence.*"

She smiled, but still did not speak. She had never gotten comfortable with the blurred line between the divinity ascribed to her and her own awareness of her many glaring faults.

"Can you believe we did it? Hungarian autonomy! A dual monarchy." Andrássy was overcome for a moment and did not speak as he stared at her. After a moment, he hooked his arm in hers. "Shall we walk, or sit? I was so happy that you wished to see me."

Andrássy moved to walk with her through the dark, quiet garden.

"Wait one moment." Sisi paused. The first hint of uneasiness was audible now in her voice. "Andrássy, I must tell you something."

Andrássy turned to face her. "Yes?" He sensed her tone. "What is it? Is something wrong?"

She hesitated, angling her body away from his.

"Sisi, you know you can tell me anything."

"I know." Sisi dropped his hand and turned her back on him.

"You are frightening me." Andrássy put a hand on her shoulder. "Please."

Steeling herself with a deep breath, she slipped from his grasp. She stepped into a puddle of moonlight where it spilled into the courtyard through an opening in the trees. There, she slipped the cape off her shoulders and turned, looking at him in profile.

Andrássy, watching her with a look of concern, did not at first notice the difference in her figure. Then his gaze slid down to her waist and after several moments, he made a small noise, a barely audible gasp.

But it was loud enough to cause Sisi's heart to drop to her stomach.

Andrássy's mouth fell open. And then, shaking his head, he whispered, "No."

Sisi stared at him, watching as understanding took root. His shoulders sagged first, before his head dropped into his hands. She stood there, motionless. After several moments he looked up at her.

"Well, you certainly have caught me unaware." His tone seemed put out, indignant, and Sisi felt herself step back, away from him. What right did he have to be angry with her?

"I had no idea that you and he still . . ." Andrássy put his hands up, not finishing the statement.

"We don't. We only . . ." She stammered, unsure of what she hoped to say.

"It seems you *do.*"

"It was one time."

He put his hands up as if to keep her away. "Spare me the details, please, Empress."

"Empress?"

He shrugged. When he spoke, his voice was hoarse. "Many congratulations to you and the emperor. Another child. I'm sure you're both elated."

"He doesn't know yet."

"Why not?"

"I haven't told him. I wanted you to hear first."

"Why?"

"Why do you think?"

"I'm not sure, to be perfectly honest. I think the man who had the honor of putting the baby in your belly ought to be the first one to know that it's there."

She closed her eyes, steadying herself on a nearby sapling. "You make me feel so vile for having . . ."

He stared back, his dark eyes catching a speck of moonlight, giving them the illusion of two small, dark flames. "Why did you feel the need to tell me first? Was this some sort of malicious plan to make me suffer? Good God, Sisi, I knew you had grown frustrated with me of late, but I didn't know that you wished to destroy me."

Because I love *you,* she thought. But she swallowed those words.

When Andrássy spoke again, his voice was toneless. "I'm also unclear as to why, months ago, you were asking me to kiss you, when you are clearly very much still participating in your marriage. It is not how you would have had me think it was."

"That's not true, Andrássy. Franz and I never . . ." She stepped toward him, trying to take his hands in hers, but he slid them into his pockets.

"Your belly would seem to refute that, Empress."

"Will you stop calling me that? Please, believe me. The marriage has been over for years."

"No, Empress. Clearly it has not been."

She did not know how to reply.

He spoke again: "At least in my case, I know that I will never be happy in my marriage. I have accepted that and I atone for that every day of my life. I have freed her to live her life, and I live mine. We are apart. Separate."

"Andrássy, please, let me —"

"But you? You have deceived me, Elisa-

766

beth." He shut his eyes now, resting his head in his palm. "Or is it that you can't decide? Torn between Franz and me? Perhaps you want both of us?"

"You are being cruel and you are very much mistaken, Andrássy. You know that I no longer love Franz like that."

"But you are not through with him, that much is apparent."

I did this so that I could be with you, she thought. Indignant anger began to form like a knot in the pit of her stomach. Balling her fists, she stood up, pushing herself off the trunk of the sapling. She looked him in the eyes as she said it, her words defiant: "I did this because it was what was best for the empire. It was what was best for the emperor. Yes, it was even what was best for *you.* Don't you see? *I* am the reason that this compromise was reached. I am the one who made all of this possible."

Andrássy looked down at her belly, his eyes smoldering with anguish. Bitterness. Envy.

"I sacrificed myself for this cause, don't you see? And yet, you punish me." Her voice threatened tears now, but she would not allow them to burst forth.

Andrássy looked away. "I feel deceived, Sisi." He wrung his hands, as if crushing some invisible object. "I feel so sick with jealousy that a part of me longs to run into this castle right now and challenge Franz to a duel. That's right, I dream of killing the man I made into king."

What he was saying was punishable by death, and they both knew it, but he would not be stopped. He stepped closer to her now as he spoke, his voice twisting with anguish.

"My worst nightmare has come true — knowing that that man still possesses you." He put his hands on her arms now, his grip firm as he pulled her close. "At least if Franz killed me, I could be spared the pain that tortures me every single moment of every single day. And if not, well, if I had the good fortune to kill him, then I could have you. Finally. I could love you the way I know I am supposed to love you."

They were both crying now. Sisi dropped her head to his shoulder as she wept. "I want to be free for you, too."

Eventually Andrássy lifted her chin up so that their gazes met. He looked down at her, his eyes softer now, but still tortured. "Sisi." He sighed, his lips just inches from hers. "Do you love me?"

"If I love you, what business is it of yours?"

Andrássy cracked a melancholy, lopsided grin. "How could you quote that to me at such a time?"

"What difference does it make whether or not I love you, Andrássy, when you have made it perfectly clear that we will never be together?"

Andrássy ran his hands through his hair, absorbing these words. He let out a slow exhalation while he paced in front of her, his expression appearing as if he was fighting inside his own mind. Eventually he paused his steps, turning back to her. He was calmer now, his eyes illuminated by the soft, pale glow of the summer moon above them. "You're right." He shrugged as he said it. "You're right." A long pause followed. "I had held on to this wild hope that, if I could get you crowned as Queen of Hungary, that you would come here. That you could be with me here. And that somehow" — he waved his hand forward between the two of them — "that somehow, we would be allowed to be together." He stared at her belly. "I now see that that was a vain and foolish hope."

Sisi nodded, accepting his judgment. Stepping backward, out of his grip and away from him, she said: "If you'll excuse me, Andrássy."

He watched her go, his face still in anguish. She offered no explanation. She reentered the castle but she did not walk toward her bedroom. Instead, she turned toward Franz's suite.

The emperor's bedchamber was lit. Franz was awake and drinking wine, perhaps to settle his nerves before tomorrow's momentous event.

"Elisa?" He was surprised to see her enter,

ushered in by the guard. Franz smiled a bashful smile, his lips stained purple from wine.

"I need to speak with you. May I join you?" Her tone made it perfectly clear: she did not have the same intention for this late-night visit as she had had the last time she had surprised him by knocking on his door. Franz sensed that and sat back down, gesturing for her to take the seat opposite him.

"Of course, please sit. Can I offer you some wine?"

"Please."

Franz poured them each a full cup. He nodded at the guard, dismissing him. It was the first time they had been alone, Sisi noted, since the night they had conceived the baby growing inside her.

"Tomorrow has arrived, at last." Franz stared at her over his cup.

"Indeed."

Perhaps noticing the way she squeezed the folds of her gown in her fingers, Franz asked, "Is everything all right?"

She did not know how one approached such a conversation with one's husband. She had not exactly prepared for this. And yet, hadn't she been prepared for it for many years? She summoned the courage and began, her tone bold. "Franz, you know how much I loved you when we married. Don't you?"

Franz pursed his lips, pausing a moment. Emotions had never been his preferred topic.

"Yes, I suppose I do."

"I adored you, Franz. I wanted nothing more than to be a loving wife. And empress. And then mother."

Franz nodded.

"So quick bright things come to confusion."

Franz arched an eyebrow. "Pardon?"

"It's a line . . . of poetry," Sisi explained. "Shakespeare. *A Midsummer Night's Dream.*"

"The one with the donkey?"

"Yes, the one you hated at the Court Theater. Oh, never mind."

"What is it, Elisa? I'm sure you didn't come here tonight to quote poetry."

"Franz." She took another sip of her wine, pausing to pull her wild thoughts together. "I don't know whether our marriage went wrong because we allowed . . . other people . . . to come between us." She placed her wine cup down on the table between them, lowering her eyes. She did not mean it to be an accusation — another argument over a mistress or her mother-in-law. She simply meant to state the facts. "Or whether it was us. That we, at some point, allowed ourselves to grow apart." She paused, her heart hammering against her rib cage. This was the most candid conversation she had ever attempted to have with her husband. Franz seemed willing to let her continue, so she did.

"You seem fine, Franz. You've always seemed fine, somehow. You seem to have negotiated some sort of peace. Away from our marriage." Now she looked up and saw that he wished to speak.

"Elisa, I am not the one who left, for years."

She nodded. It was true.

"And I have invited you back into our marriage several times."

"I know you have, Franz."

"I still love you." He said it as if it were the most simple fact in the world.

"And I still love you, Franz, I do. A part of me will always love you." She sighed. "But there's only so many times that a girl can allow her heart to be crushed by the same man before that love . . . changes."

Franz looked down at his hands, which he now folded on the table between them. "You have no idea, the demands I've had on me."

"Because you wouldn't share them with me."

"And you weren't always . . . *present.* I had to find comfort where I could — sometimes in other places."

Sisi cocked her head. "But you were not ever mine, not entirely mine, to begin with."

Franz nodded. He knew it was more than just the other women. He had chosen his mother, and his ministers, and his courtiers, on many occasions.

"But I do not mean to say that it was entirely your fault, Franz. It wasn't. I made the decision, at a certain point, to leave the marriage, as well. In my own way."

Franz nodded, his fingers absentmindedly stroking his beard.

"Franz, I am going to have a baby."

Franz lifted his eyes to her now, two wide circles of light blue.

Sisi nodded, but Franz shook his head, as if warding off a fog. "A baby?"

"Yes."

"Is it . . . ?"

"It's yours, of course. There has been no other man. Ever."

"Really?" Franz, his head falling to one side, seemed genuinely surprised to hear that. "Never?"

"No."

"Not even during all those trips?"

She shook her head. "No one but you."

He seemed stunned. Incredulous even. "Well, I am speechless," he stammered. "It's surprising news. But wonderful all the same. A baby."

"Franz, I come to you with a request. It's not a typical request, I would grant that. But then, not much of our marriage has been typical."

"What is it?" He looked at her, his eyebrows knitting toward one another.

Here came the difficult part, and Sisi forced herself to proceed. "I must leave you, for a time. I beg you, Franz, that if our child is a girl, that you will allow me to raise our child in Hungary. At least for a few years. I must have this child away from the Viennese court. And we are, after all, official royalty here now." She pressed on, ignoring Franz's incredulous expression. "If the child is a boy, then I know that you will never allow it. A prince would be in the direct line of succession and must be raised within the imperial court, I know. But if it's a girl . . ." Her voice trailed off, the longing apparent in her tone.

"Franz, if it's a girl, I wish to raise her myself. To be a mother, at last, to my own child. Away from court, away from your . . ." She did not need to finish that thought. "I long to have one child who loves me and thinks of me as a mamma. I long to have one child on whom I can pour out all of the stolen and denied love that I've felt three times over."

Franz drained his wine cup, thinking about this. It seemed an interminable pause, and Sisi felt that her heart might shatter her insides. But then Franz looked up, nodding.

"Fine," he whispered.

Sisi clutched the table with white fingers. "You know that means — away from Vienna. It means, I will stay here."

He nodded, a sad smile on his face. "I know, Elisabeth. I know what you mean."

She sat back, stunned at his acquiescence. At how . . . *easily* . . . Franz had accepted this. But then, she thought, nothing about the years that had brought them to this moment had been easy.

Franz thrummed the arm of his chair as he continued. "Elisabeth . . . I *would* love to see you, once in a while." It was a request, and not an order. "And to know" — he pointed at her belly — "my child."

Sisi nodded. "Of course I will allow you to see your child, Franz. And I will bring her back myself, when I come."

"You really think it's a girl?"

She nodded.

"How can you be so sure?"

Because I have waited long enough, she thought. "I can't be sure. But I can hope."

He nodded, a slow movement. "You really want to stay here?" Franz looked down at her, his eyes bright and blue in an otherwise ashen face.

"I do." Sisi wiped the tear that ran down her cheek.

"So far from home?"

"Franz." Sisi put a hand on top of Franz's. "Surely you must know that Vienna has never much felt like home for me. This place . . . Hungary . . . feels more like home than Vienna, than the court, ever did."

Franz sighed, thinking about this. "So I suppose this is it, Elisa?"

Sisi blinked away the tears as she continued to look into his eyes.

Franz straightened up, rapping his hands

against the armrests of his chair. "I suppose our marriage changed years ago. But I suppose now we both understand one another. It will be different for us."

She looked at him through glassy eyes. "You have been happy for years, Franz. Have you not?"

"Happy?" He cocked his head. "I don't know that happiness has ever been my prerogative. I don't suppose it was ever presented as an option for me." He crossed his arms. "Satisfied, yes, I suppose I have been satisfied. At peace, knowing that I have done my duty."

She took his hand in hers, leaning toward him. "You are a good emperor, Franz."

He nodded, lowering his eyes. For someone who heard flattery all day, this remark appeared difficult for him to accept.

"And I will always love you, Franz. But I want you to understand what I am able to give you, and what I'm no longer able to give you. I need your permission."

He knew what she was asking of him. She was asking him to release her, just as she, years ago, had released him.

"Are *you* happy, Elisa?"

"Not yet," she said. "But I think I can be. Here. Away from it all."

Franz looked sad, sighing as he spoke. "I hope you will know, Elisa, that I only ever wanted for you to be happy. Even if I didn't always make that clear. I suppose, once I learned how deeply I had failed to make you happy, I stopped trying. I gave up. But now, I have the chance to give you your happiness back, and I will not deny you. You have my blessing."

"Franz." Sisi kissed his hands. "Thank you, thank you, thank you." They were both crying now. It was the end of something, and they both knew it. But it was the start of something else, too, and that filled Sisi's heart with hope.

Marie had told Sisi which door to look for. The countess had also been discreet enough not to ask why the empress needed the information. Slipping out a back doorway from her bedchamber, Sisi had walked, cloaked and undetected, through the dark hallways.

She moved at a brisk pace, quickly growing short of breath. But she was far from tired. She turned down the hallway, her footsteps echoing off the stones. She raced down the passageway. She felt awake and alive. At last she reached the spot Marie had described. Mercifully it was well past the middle of the night, and the servants and noblemen alike were retired to their chambers.

She knocked quietly, in case a guard patrolled a nearby hall.

He came to the door, shirt unbuttoned, hair

disheveled. His features betrayed surprise at the disturbance, at the face he spotted staring back at him. "Sisi?"

"Andrássy." She pressed on the door, opening it wider and stepping in past him.

"Do you have any idea what time it is?" His breath smelled of wine and his room was in chaos. He had clearly been writing, or working, or pacing. Something Sisi's restless mind understood.

"Is this wise?" Andrássy looked from her to the door as she now shut it.

She walked toward him and leaned her head on his chest, breathing in a moment before she looked up into his face. He appeared wild, more handsome than she had ever seen him.

"Andrássy, I love you. I've loved you for years."

He put his finger to her lips, his eyes sad. "Sisi, we have discussed this. Our hearts are not free to give away."

She edged his finger to the side. "But that's just it, Andrássy. My heart *is* mine, once more, after all of these years. Mine, to do with it as I choose."

He stood silent, taking her cheeks in his hands, her skin burning at his touch. When he spoke, his voice husky, he confessed, "Mine has been yours, Sisi, for years. Possibly since the first time I laid eyes on you. And certainly since the night, years ago in

Vienna, when you grabbed my hands in your own. Do you remember? I was astounded at how easily I fell in love with you that night."

And with that, she leaned forward and kissed him, her lips meeting his in the embrace she had craved for so many years. He kissed her back, wrapping his arms around her waist and pulling her body into his.

"I love you, Andrássy. I have loved you for so long," she whispered, pressing her lips back into his. And then she began to laugh, and she repeated the words that came to her mind: *"I laugh at my heart, and yet, do its will."*

"Sisi. My beloved, darling Sisi." Andrássy scooped her up into his arms and carried her across the room to the bed, where he lay her down with a movement so tender she barely felt the pillows beneath her. He kept his arms wrapped around her. The way he looked at her, his eyes inches from hers, brought tears to her eyes.

Andrássy's hands rested on her cheek for a moment before moving from her face to her neck, and his lips followed. She trembled in delight as he placed a soft, delicate kiss on her neck. And then his hands were unfastening her gown, unpeeling layers of clothing. She aided him, lifting his shirt so that soon it was just their skin that touched. There was no discussion of what they were doing — the time for discussing had passed. They both knew the crime that they had agreed to, and their bodies led them willingly into their beautiful treason.

As Sisi welcomed Andrássy's touch, she could not help but laugh in rapturous delight. She, who had accepted the fact that her bloom had faded, that her years of passion were a thing of the past, was now loving a man with an appetite and ardor that she had never known she possessed. Her body seemed to be awakening as if from some frostbitten slumber. And this awakening drove both her and Andrássy mad, her desire only increasing under the tender and sure ministrations of Andrássy's affection. They had just begun, but already she was certain that the night would not be long enough. Her lifetime might not be long enough.

She realized in Andrássy's arms what she had been missing all those years — that moment of rapturous delight in which the body and the soul tasted a glimpse of eternity. Franz had never brought her to that moment, though he himself had always appeared to achieve it during their lovemaking. Wasn't that the perfect way to understand her failed marriage? Longing, yearning, desiring, but never tasting the joy. How he'd vowed to give himself to her, but had somehow kept himself out of reach.

This night opened Sisi's eyes to a world she had scarcely known existed. Andrássy loved her in a way that made it plain that her pleasure was more important than his own. And when she refused to let him go, pulling him back toward her, he did not look at her with disapproval, but with boyish delight, as if he were thrilled with how badly she longed for him.

In the quiet, still hours before dawn, Sisi lay in Andrássy's arms. She sighed as he kissed the soft dip where her neck met the collarbone. The first hint of predawn light had begun to filter in through the window. Sisi shut her eyes, willing it to disappear, beseeching the world to remain shrouded in the dark veil that enabled and protected this perfect moment.

Just then, a thunderous peal erupted from outside the windows, shaking the glass panes in their frame. Thunder, on a day that promised to be so clear and sunny?

"It's beginning," Andrássy said.

"What?"

"A twenty-one-gun salute. Up on St. Gerhard's Mount. Your coronation day has officially begun."

Sisi groaned, burrowing into the crook of his neck. "Why must daylight come?"

"Daylight. Terrible daylight." His fingers grazed the bare skin of her back. "I hate myself for having put you in danger."

She looked up at him, her cheeks rosy. "Oh, but wasn't it worth it?"

"But now you are stuck in my bedchamber, Sisi, and it is getting light out." Her hair fanned wildly over the pillow, and he ran his fingers through it.

"If I'm stuck here, I might as well enjoy myself, hadn't I?" She shifted her body so that she might kiss him.

"Empress, I am shocked at your energy." Andrássy laughed in mock indignation. "This poor count needs to sleep."

Sisi's hands slid under the sheets as she reached for him. "You are not allowed to sleep just yet."

"Really, Sisi." Andrássy took her face in his hands. "Hadn't you better go? It will soon be lighter and lighter."

"Then you had better stop wasting time on these arguments. That's an order."

Andrássy stood nearby in a robe, watching as she dressed herself in the murky light of early morning. The closer they came to the moment of her departure, the more anxious he seemed to be.

"Are you certain that you don't wish for me to walk you back?"

"If you're going to do that, we might as well announce it to the entire court at today's coronation," she said. "What if someone saw us together?"

"But I hate to think of you being alone, making this walk."

"I've always *scurried* about alone. It drove Sophie crazy. I will scurry back quickly."

"It's not right. I should have come to your chamber."

Sisi laughed, adjusting the sleeves of her gown. "I hardly think that an empress can have her lover waltz past her guards and into her suite."

"Is that what I am? Your lover?" He pulled her toward him and placed a long kiss on her lips.

"You are my lover, and I am yours." She smiled up at him.

"I like the way that sounds." He kissed her again. "I don't, however, like the fact that I might have put you in danger."

"Andrássy, please." Sisi lifted her curls and fastened them in a loose bun on the back of her neck.

"I mean it."

"Do you regret last night?"

"Not in the slightest. But it doesn't change the fact that I've put you at risk. I've never wanted to be the cause of unhappiness for you."

She leaned into his body, her cheek resting on his chest as she breathed in his scent. "Don't you see that I did not know happiness until I came to you last night?"

"What if I've just ruined your life, Sisi?"

Still resting her head on his chest, she sighed. "Andrássy, I lost my children. I lost my parents and my first home. I never really had my husband to begin with. You wonder if you've ruined my life? No. I've only just decided to *live.*"

Andrássy stared at her and they stood in silence for several moments before he placed a kiss on the top of her head. He held her close. "We won't have to worry any more once you relocate here."

Sisi smiled. "*If* I relocate here."

"You must."

"Just think of it. We would be together, at last." She paused. "But won't you tire of me, seeing me each day?"

"If you behave as you did last night, then yes, I might grow tired."

She laughed at this, her hands still interwoven with his.

"No, my darling Sisi. On the contrary. I shall love you more each day."

"Even as I . . ." She looked down toward her stomach, where the hint of a bump would continue to swell. "Grow big?" It was the first time they'd mentioned the baby since their quarrel.

Now Andrássy put his hand on her belly and spoke, his tone soft. "This baby is a part of you. I could never feel anything but love for it."

"Do you promise, Andrássy?"

"I promise."

"You'll still love me?"

"For the rest of your life."

But that did not satisfy her.

"What? Why are you frowning, Sisi?"

"I've had a man make a promise to me before that was supposed to last a lifetime. And it did not."

Andrássy took her hands in his and lifted them to her heart. He looked down at her now, his dark eyes ablaze as he spoke. "Sisi, listen to me. All of these pieces of you that are broken, I see them. And I love them, too."

Sisi lowered her eyes, starved for — yet frightened of — those words.

"Look at me. I want you to look into my eyes as I tell you this, so you will know how truly I mean it."

"All right," she whispered, her mouth dry.

"Sisi, if you will let me, there's nothing I want more than to be the man who shows you that it is safe to love again."

Tears ran down her cheeks as he said it. She shook her head, looking away.

"Sisi."

"It's just that . . ."

"What is it?" He angled her chin upward with his finger.

"Andrássy, it's just that . . . I've had to be so strong for so long. How can I risk, once more . . ."

"Don't you see, my darling?" He lifted her hand, resting it on his chest so that she could feel his heartbeat, its pace rapid like horse hooves against his breastbone. "Don't you see? Oh, but you know this well enough already. That there is nothing that requires more strength than to allow yourself to be weak for another."

XIX.

The wind whips her face, setting her hair awhirl around her face and matching the urgency of her own uneven breath. All around her the earth smells of springtime: mud and ripened acacia petals.

Beneath her, the horse speeds forward in his even, stately gait. She matches his rhythm, their bodies working together as the world whirs by.

So this is how the swallows feel as they circle, free, she thinks. The blue ribbon of the Danube glistens beside her, its clear waters like an invitation, a seduction. Up ahead the hill of Buda rises, the church steeple visible against the backdrop of a cloudless sky. Skirting the hill are the endless plains of Pest, a sea of green dotted with the purple petals of wildflowers.

My kingdom, she thinks, urging the horse forward. Her body will grow tired, eventually. But her soul? Well, her soul is, at last, awake.

CHAPTER NINETEEN

BUDAPEST, HUNGARY
JUNE 8, 1867

"Ravishing." Franz breathed the word as his wife entered the small antechamber of the castle, just moments before their coronation procession was scheduled to set out. "You look absolutely ravishing, Elisabeth."

"Thank you, Franz."

"Fresh and happy," Franz said, almost to himself, as his eyes stayed fixed on Sisi. "Like I have not seen you in quite some time. Like the girl I married years ago."

"Thank you, Franz." Sisi blushed, lowering her eyes. She was aglow, and she knew it. "I feel fresh and happy." *But I assure you, I am not the same girl you married.*

"You look very fine yourself, Franz."

"Do I? This orb feels too big. I fear I might drop it in the middle of the mass." Franz forced out a feeble smile, and Sisi felt for him. Deep shadows under his eyes testified to his fatigue. The ermine cape that hung

788

from his shoulders, over the ancient mantle of St. Stephen, looked unbearably heavy.

Following tradition, Franz's entire wardrobe had been plucked from the ancient garments worn by the Hungarian kings enthroned before him. The high point of the day would come later when, in the cathedral of St. Matthew, Andrássy placed Hungary's holy crown on Emperor Franz Joseph's head, making him King of Hungary, by the will of the Hungarian people.

Sisi, on the other hand, had ordered everything new for the occasion. Her gown, a masterpiece, had been stitched in Paris, arriving in Budapest as a celebrated royal would — under heavy guard and with its own imperial escort.

It was a work of art, finer even than her wedding gown had been, and Sisi felt unequal to its grandeur. The dress was ivory and silver brocade, with a narrow, black velvet bodice trimmed in diamonds and pearls. The sleeves hung off her upper arms, showcasing the creamy white skin of her neck and shoulders. She wore a diamond choker around her neck and white gloves on her hands. The skirt fell loose, loose enough to obscure the hint of her belly, with a regal train that would trail behind her as she made her way to the front of the cathedral. Stitched into the lace overlay that draped around the bell-shaped skirt were the patterns of delicate leaves and flowers.

Over the gown she wore a cape of white satin.

Her hair had taken the entire morning to style, a fact for which she had been grateful. It had given her hours to sit in the chair with nothing to do but remember the night she had just passed with Andrássy. Franziska, discreet enough not to ask why the empress blushed after her night out of her apartments, had pulled Sisi's curls back into a coronet of loose braids. The hair framed her face before falling gracefully down her back, a simple look that made room for the diamond-encrusted tiara that would be placed on her head: a crown once worn by the Habsburgs most beloved ruler, Maria Theresa.

On the other side of the thick castle doors, the crowds waited impatiently, lined up since before the first predawn cannon salutes. When those doors opened, Sisi and Franz would fall in line at the rear of the processional, trailing a dozen Hungarian noblemen bearing the flags and standards of their royal houses. Clergymen would lead the way, bearing gold-gilt crosses and jewel-encrusted bowls of holy water to bless the royal pair. And Andrássy . . . Sisi's heart quickened at the thought of seeing him. Andrássy would stand before the monarchs — almost their equal — wearing on his tunic the broad cross of the Order of St. Stephen, and carrying Franz's sacred crown on a pillow of red velvet.

"How do you feel, Franz?" Sisi adjusted

her heavy skirt, smoothing the mass of lace and satin that draped over her legs.

The emperor thought about this question. "Fine. A bit impatient, I suppose."

Sisi nodded.

"How about you, Empress Elisabeth?"

"I feel happy," she said, turning to him with a smile. "And full of hope."

Franz nodded, casting his eyes back toward the doors.

"You are a good emperor, Franz Joseph," she said, taking her husband's gloved hand in her own.

"And you are a good empress, Elisabeth." They looked into one another's eyes, a silent communication passing between them. Even after all the years and heartbreak that had come between them, only the two of them could go through what awaited them, on the other side of the doors. A moment only they could share.

"It's time." A short priest emerged in the antechamber, his silken robes aflutter with the haste of his gait. After the requisite bow, he stood and rattled off their instructions. "When I knock, they shall open the doors and you shall process, straight up toward the street. The processional before you will lead the way. You may look from side to side if you wish, but do not pause until you reach the cathedral."

They both nodded. Franz rose from his

chair, standing beside Sisi. She took his hand and squeezed it, one last gesture of support.

"Are you ready?" Franz asked her.

"I am. And you?"

"Is one ever ready to divide his empire in half?"

"Franz," she said, squeezing his hand. "You are keeping your empire whole."

Franz looked forward. "Let us go."

The doors opened and Sisi was stunned by a blast of color, an eruption of trumpets. Hundreds of courtiers lined the route, waving Hungarian flags and looking on with eyes wide and mouths moving in inaudible responses and reaction. They stood plumed in their finest robes and suits, the women with meticulously coifed hair, attempting to mimic Sisi's famous style. Behind them, the common people jostled and cheered, a wall of merchants, peasants, children, and tradesmen, all crammed onto the processional route with one purpose: to catch a glimpse of the king and queen.

In front of Sisi, Hungarian noblemen lifted their banners, charting a course for the cathedral atop the hill of Buda. Imperial bannermen played triumphant notes on glistening trumpets, as guards stood stiff and erect, hemming in the path now intended for royal feet.

Sisi kept her eyes down as she walked, just a few steps behind Franz. She listened as the people cried out her name. *"Éljen Elisabeth!* Long live Queen Elisabeth!" The only noise louder than the cries of the crowds were the roars of the cannons that fired off a steady salvo as the monarchs made their way up the hill.

As they reached the massive doors to the cathedral, the bells clanged so uproariously overhead they sounded as though they might crack the bell tower. Inside the organ vied with the trumpets to play its notes the loudest.

"Here we go." Franz turned to her, adjusting his cape one final time. Sisi nodded.

"Yes, here we go." Her body trembled, as it had on her wedding day, but she forced out the hint of a smile. "After you, Your Majesty, King Franz Joseph."

And then, looking forward, Franz began to walk.

Sisi fell into step beside him, eyes still cast downward. She had yet to catch a glimpse of Andrássy, but she knew he was there. Somewhere in front of her. He was the one who would make her husband King of Hungary.

The walk to the altar seemed to take an eternity, and Sisi reminded herself to keep her eyes down, her features composed. The image of humility, even if the people packed into this cathedral thought her, in some part, divine.

When they reached the front of the cathedral, two thrones awaited. There they would sit, side by side. Two flawed mortals forever memorialized, together, in this moment. How strange, she thought, to be a part of what would surely become history, and yet still worry that she might trip on her heavy skirt.

Her dress was cumbersome, and Franz helped her as she stepped up to the altar. And then she turned to look out over the cathedral, her eyes acclimating to the scene so that the sea of a thousand unique faces blended into one fuzzy tableau. The noise throbbed so loudly around her that she longed to stop her ears, to drown out some of the din, but she knew she could not. A deity does not quake simply because the crowd yells. An empress stands fixed, immutable: the calm that continues on, even as the world rages. Even though, all along, she has found it impossibly difficult to do so.

Beside her, Franz looked composed. Even stiff. And yet, Sisi detected the weariness that lingered behind his calm mask. The human frailty that persisted, even after all of his years of training and emotional mastery. For a brief flash, she yearned to remove those coverings from him; to free him of his trappings so that he might once again resemble the man she knew, the man whose hopes were once so interwoven with her own that she had not distinguished between the two distinct threads.

But it was too late for that now. He had made his decisions, she had made hers. She could not undo the past any more than she could retrace the course she had set for the future. She admitted that to herself one final time, sadly, as if wishing him farewell. Wishing a version of herself farewell.

All around them now, the crowd packed into the cathedral jostled and applauded, vying for a spot close enough to touch them.

"My Queen!"

"My Empress!"

"Long live Elisabeth!"

"Long live Franz Joseph!"

Sisi turned from the crowd back to Franz. He, too, appeared stunned and overwhelmed. He faced her and mouthed the words "good heavens." She smiled, remembering how she had once looked at him and thought that he moved like a god among them. The imperial guards, sensing that the mood of the congregation grew ever more boisterous, pushed back against the crowd, stemming the tide of those people inching their way closer to the two monarchs.

Sisi's eyes did not rest on the emperor for long. Desperately, she combed the scene once more, looking for another face. Where was Andrássy? she wondered. Surely he was there. After the two of them, he was the central figure of this entire day.

Finally, her eyes landed on him. He stood

near the front, the welcome sight of his face almost entirely obscured by the ornate head-piece of a bishop in front of him. He was more dashing than she had ever seen him — his dark eyes aglow, his tall frame outfitted in a traditional coat. He had been watching her all this time. When they locked eyes she smiled. She did not care who saw.

And then as Andrássy approached the altar, she looked out once more at her adoring subjects. They cried out for her. *So this is what it feels like to be a queen,* she thought, feeling that, for the first time in her life, she was up to the task before her. She was in the kingdom she had been meant to rule.

"Sisi! Sisi!" The crowds were enraptured as she knelt beside Franz, tipping her head before Andrássy in preparation for the crown that would be placed atop her famous chest-nut curls. When she lifted her gaze, staring out once more at the crowd, she flashed a coy, beguiling smile. They erupted in cheers.

Sisi stared out over the cathedral, absorb-ing the scene, willing her eyes to take in every drop of color, every smiling face; hearing the music that roared, composed especially for this day by Hungary's own Franz Liszt. Would she be able to remember it all? Doubt-ful. But she'd remember, for the rest of her life, how she felt as she beheld it. Proud of Franz. Happy for Austria. And how, for the first time in years, she felt that she was home.

At home among a people to whom she belonged. Beyond this congregation stretched the fields of Pest, where she would ride her horses; the mountain of Buda, where she would ramble, staring out over the blue ribbon of the Danube; the cheering people who called out for her in the street.

And with the sea of faces swelling around her, her gaze landed once more on the one face she longed to behold. The one man who knew her better than anyone else. The man who knew her and loved her, not because she was his queen, but because she was Sisi.

And here, on this altar, wearing the crown for which she had fought, Sisi made her decision. She hadn't been ready, the first time a crown had been placed atop her head. She hadn't understood, then, what it meant. Hadn't even fought for it, really.

This time, it would be entirely different. This time, she stood ready. She lifted her palm to her belly, to where a baby grew inside. A child that, at last, might be hers.

God, for some inexplicable reason, had granted her a second chance, and she would seize it. She would be a good queen. A loving queen. A queen worthy of the adoration that these people — for some mystifying reason — now gifted to her.

She would be the ruler not only of this land, but of her own life.

A CONVERSATION WITH THE AUTHOR ALLISON PATAKI

Q: *The Accidental Empress* is quite the dramatic story! What was it like, writing a novel about Sisi?

A: Yes, it certainly is full of drama. Sisi, or Empress Elisabeth, was an incredibly complex individual who lived in a fascinating moment in history. And her story — in some ways very relatable, in some ways completely foreign — played out before such an epic backdrop, with all the accompanying glitz of the Habsburg Court and the tumult of the Austro-Hungarian Empire. I was as enchanted by her as everyone else was.

Q: What in this is true, and where does the "fiction" part of the "historical fiction" genre come in?

A: I decided early on that I would be crazy *not* to rely heavily on the historical record for plot and character development in *The Accidental Empress.* The raw material itself was so good and intriguing that there were all of the fixings in there to make a compelling novel.

To begin with, Sisi was not supposed to be Empress of Austria. Hence, the title of this novel. Sisi was a free-spirited girl who left Possenhofen (and a wild, unstructured lifestyle like the one you see her living at the start of this book) at the age of fifteen. She traveled with her mother and sister to support Helene in her coming engagement to Emperor Franz Joseph.

Sisi did in fact inadvertently steal the spotlight when they arrived in Bad Ischl, and, in doing so, inadvertently stole her sister's groom. Archduchess Sophie was not happy to see her plans derailed. Some of Sophie's quotes in this novel lamenting the unsuitability of such a match are exact quotes.

The plot of *The Accidental Empress* begins with their arrival in Bad Ischl, the women dressed in black (after getting separated on the road from their clothing trunks), and that is in fact how it occurred. Subsequent events and details such as Franz Joseph's unanticipated attraction to Sisi, the cotillion dance for his birthday, the preparations leading up to their marriage, the births of their children, and their periods of closeness and estrangement are based on historical fact.

Descriptions of the incredibly difficult hand Franz Joseph was dealt concerning Austria's foreign policy, and the wars that ensued in and around the Austrian Empire, are also based on the facts. Sisi did accompany Franz Joseph on the trip to Hungary in 1857, much to Archduchess Sophie's vexation. While it started out as a great trip for Sisi — one that began her lifelong love affair with Hungary and its people — it was during that time that both her little girls became sick and little Sophie died. The second trip to Hungary described in this book, at which time the dual monarchy was officially established in 1867, was also taken from history.

Many of the most deliciously awkward moments of this novel are plucked directly from the historical record. The *Morgengabe,* or morning gift, was given to Sisi the day after she lost her virginity. I also discovered that Sophie would advise the pregnant Sisi to parade before the palace gates to show off her belly to the public, while she would also warn Sisi not to look at the pet parrot, lest the empress have a baby that came out looking like a bird.

Some of the most overwhelming and august moments are true as well: Sisi undergoing a complete makeover in the months before her marriage (and Sophie's insistence that the bride whiten her teeth and improve her conversational and dancing skills); catalogues of the endless stream of gifts lavished on Sisi by Franz Joseph and Sophie (most likely in an effort to get the "provincial" girl well-dressed enough before her introduction to the highly judgmental Viennese court); descriptions of the magnificent wedding ceremony and protocol-dictated reception; the moment in which Sisi flees in a panic during the Kissing of the Hand ceremony; and Sophie accompanying the newlyweds to Laxenburg on their honeymoon, where she spent entire days with a very unhappy Sisi while Franz Joseph returned to Vienna each day to work.

Descriptions of the court rituals are based largely on fact, such as the customs of wearing gloves while eating, and discarding slippers after only several uses. So, too, are the descriptions of the extreme lengths to which Sisi went with her beauty regimen. Putting slabs of raw meat on her face and washing her hair with egg-yolk solutions are two of my favorites. Sisi was also compulsively preoccupied with her legendary hair and all that went into its styling and upkeep.

Some of the most tragic and troubling moments in *The Accidental Empress* are also taken directly from the historical accounts. Sophie did in fact keep Sisi's babies in a nursery right off of her own suite, largely restricting Sisi from interacting with them on the pretext that she herself was little more than a child. Sisi was not permitted to nurse or take the lead in raising her young children.

And the pressure to have a son? That's historically accurate as well. A pamphlet was indeed left in Sisi's rooms presenting the urgent need to produce a male heir, though historians cannot confirm who put it there. The fight over Rudy's education — a militaristic education like the one to which Franz Joseph had been subjected versus the more well-rounded course for which Sisi advocated — was also a source of great conflict in the Habsburg household.

And, of course, the constant tug-of-war for Franz Joseph's attention and affection was an ongoing struggle for Sisi as a young bride and mother.

Q: Seeing all of these conflicts that Sisi faced, we can't help but ask: Why doesn't Sisi stand up for herself more?

A: Time and again we are rooting for Sisi, and we want to see her stand up for herself. And she does try, throughout. But as twenty-first-century readers, we must resist the temptation to look at Sisi through our modern lens.

The mythology of Sisi that persists today is mostly concerned with the personal tragedies she faced as well as her iconic looks. But there's obviously much more to the character of Sisi than just the beauty for which she is still remembered. She was a human rights activist, an avid traveler, a lifelong student, a devotee of Shakespeare and poetry and philosophy and foreign languages.

But Sisi's was a gradual process of self-realization over many difficult years. It would be anachronistic to expect Sisi, a sixteen-year-old bride with almost no formal education and no idea of what marriage and court life entailed, to adapt effortlessly to her very demanding new role.

Sisi was completely ill prepared for the life into which she was so quickly thrust, and the consequences were as disastrous as you might expect them to be. Franz Joseph, due to both his personality and a lifetime of preparation and grooming, understood the role he was expected to play. He was dutiful and devoted to that role — to the point of coldness at times — for the entirety of his life. In his view, the happiness of the individual mattered very little when compared to one's duties and obligations.

Sisi did not espouse that unwavering devotion to her role or to the many demands of life at the helm of the Habsburg Empire. Sisi was independent and romantic and sensitive and free-spirited. Besides her initial immaturity and inadequate preparation, Sisi appears also to have had precisely the wrong temperament for the job she landed.

In that way, Archduchess Sophie was, oddly enough, correct. You might even say she called that one.

Q: **What do you make of the character of Sophie? How influential was the archduchess in Sisi's life and marriage?**

A: Other than Franz Joseph, that relationship is really the dominating one in Sisi's early life at court. And as you can see, it was an extremely fractious one. One historian refers to Sisi's "almost pathological dislike of the Archduchess" (Joan Haslip, *The Lonely Empress: Elizabeth of Austria*).

It's a dynamic as old as time itself: the overbearing mother-in-law, the smothered and resentful daughter-in-law, and the hapless husband caught in the middle, clueless as to how to negotiate between the two. Throw in the internal and external pressures that this young couple faced, and you have the recipe for a disaster of epic proportions.

Sophie was a powerful figure, looming large over both the court and over most aspects of Sisi's private life and marriage. Sophie did in fact take the children from their mother. Sophie did install her ally, Countess Esterházy, in Sisi's apartments. She did exert influence over her son's conservative foreign policy.

But, like any human relationship, Sisi's and Sophie's was clearly a very complex one with multiple layers and perspectives. Because this novel is written from the perspective of Sisi, I took up a view that casts Sophie in a less-than-flattering light. Sisi was not complimentary of Sophie in her letters and interviews, and those documents have given history a view of the many conflicts in which the two women engaged. Sisi described her mother-in-law in the following way: "I was completely *à la merci* of this completely malicious woman. Everything I did was bad. She passed disparaging judgments on anyone I loved. She found out everything because she never stopped prying." That's a scathing review!

Sisi was much harsher in her writing on Sophie than Sophie was on Sisi. In Sophie's descriptions, you see a devoted — to the point of overbearing and meddling — mother who believes that nothing is too good for her son. What wife can't help but fall short in those circumstances? But Sophie's criticisms of Sisi are subtle and nuanced, what we might call passive-aggressive. Perhaps that speaks to the different personalities of the two women; while Sisi did not attempt to mask her moods and emotions, Sophie was controlled and shrewd and always aware of how things might appear.

Q: **And then the other colossal figure in Sisi's life was Count Julius Andrássy. What do you make of him, both as a character of fiction, and as a real histori-**

cal figure?

A: Ah, yes, Andrássy. He makes me swoon, as he made the ladies of his own time swoon.

Multiple biographers refer to Andrássy as the great love of Sisi's life. Brigitte Hamann is one such example. The sense I got from their own letters and writings was that Andrássy and Sisi shared a deep connection — emotional as well as intellectual — and a profound respect for and devotion to one another. Andrássy seemed to give Sisi the validation she had always craved from Franz Joseph. Andrássy's letters to Sisi show that he valued her input and he sought her involvement in his political and personal affairs. He actively recruited her as a partner in negotiating the Austro-Hungarian Compromise of 1867.

It is clear that there was an intense affection between Andrássy and Sisi. Andrássy wrote, toward the end of his life, that he was one of the few people in the world who knew the true Sisi. He referred to her as "the pinnacle of all womanhood" and Hungary's "Beautiful Providence." Men loved Sisi as soon as they met her. Women loved Andrássy as soon as they met him. What then must the chemistry have been like between the two of them?

Rumors circulated in both Austria and Hungary that they were lovers. Sisi's fourth child (the one she is carrying at the end of this novel) was gossiped and written about in Vienna as "the Hungarian child," a moniker that couldn't help but raise suspicions as to the parentage. Add in Sisi's decampment from Vienna to Budapest, and her flagrant preference for the company of Hungarians over Austrians, and you have the fixings for scandal on an imperial scale.

The relationship with Andrássy was one that gave Sisi hope and purpose. The years in which Sisi worked closely with Andrássy for the cause of Hungarian autonomy were the years in which she came into her own — both as a woman, and also as a leader. So, in my imagining of it, Andrássy was a huge part of that.

Q: **Were there places where you deliberately deviated from the historical record to veer off into fiction?**

A: Yes. And that is probably the biggest challenge for me in writing historical fiction: first wrangling the historical record and then allowing myself the creative space to write fiction inspired by it. Each instance where I altered or interpreted the facts was the result of much thought and intentional deliberation. As this is a novel and not a biography, I had the luxury of pulling not only from the proven facts, but from the mythology and reports as well. Take my fictional rendering of the Andrássy relationship as an example. There were rumors and reports that the relationship between Andrássy and Sisi was a romantic one, and they certainly loved one another, but biographers obviously can't prove definitively whether they were intimate. Additionally, this is the Victorian era we are talking about, so matters as delicate as intimacy were dealt with in those days only through innuendo and gossip, veiled with the secrecy and shame necessitated by the prudery of the time. In my fiction, I chose to imagine and explore the possibilities that were enabled by the rumors, and I gave Sisi and Andrássy the full extent of a romantic relationship. It seemed like the appropriate arc for them as characters of this novel.

Additionally, Andrássy did not meet Sisi for the first time at the opera in Vienna. At that point, Andrássy was still a political opponent of Franz Joseph's (exiled after the uprisings of 1848–49) and was not a visitor to the Austrian capital. But, knowing what a major character he was to be, both in Sisi's real life and in my own novel, I chose to introduce the character of Andrássy to the reader and to Sisi a bit earlier than the actual dates would have allowed.

Another place where I deviated from the historical record was in the treatment of some of the tangential family members. For example, Franz Joseph's father was still alive during the years covered in *The Accidental Empress,* but he was an inconsequential player in Sisi's life and marriage. As my fictional Franz Joseph says in this novel, it was his grandfather, the Emperor Franz, who played the primary role of father figure in his life. Franz Joseph's father was unambitious and weak and played almost no role at court, and no role in Sisi's life.

Franz Joseph also had three younger brothers and a younger sister. But, again, as they played only minor roles in the life of Sisi, I made the strategic decision not to expand the already large list of supporting characters.

On Sisi's side of the family: Karl, Sisi's brother, was not such a bullying menace as I portrayed him in my book. Sisi was actually close to all of her siblings. I needed a mechanism for some early character development for the spirited, plucky young Sisi, and so Karl became an early opponent of sorts.

The imperial trip to Salzburg during Sisi's first winter as empress was entirely fictional. They did travel to Salzburg throughout their marriage, but not at that moment. However, having been to Salzburg at Christmastime, and having witnessed firsthand the magic of that Alpine town over the holidays, I felt that there had to be a scene with them there, in that place where "Silent Night" was composed. And I wanted it to be while they were still happy.

For the purpose of pacing, I've modified the timing of Sisi's fourth pregnancy just slightly. Historians assert that Sisi brought every bit of leverage she had to the negotiating table in order to bring Franz Joseph around to the idea of the Hungarian Compromise; a temporary reconciliation in the marriage was a critical piece of that. Sisi and Franz Joseph conceived around the time of the Austro-Hungarian Compromise, but it was right after the coronation as opposed to right before it.

And finally, individuals who are well-versed in the musical history of this time period will note that there's an anachronism in my mentioning of "The Skater's Waltz." Émile Waldteufel composed that hauntingly beautiful piece several decades later than I place it here. I utilized the license granted to historical fiction to get this great piece into the story because it is so whimsical and moving and lovely, and it struck me as the perfect musical accompaniment for Franz Joseph and Sisi while falling in love. It also happens to be a piece of great personal significance to me, and if there's one waltz that I would credit with providing me with the musical fuel and inspiration needed to write this story, it's that one.

Q: **What about the rest of the cast of**

characters? Are they based on the historical account?

A: I drew directly from the history in creating the characters for *The Accidental Empress.* And I was so fortunate to have such a colorful and complex cast of individuals from which to pull. Agata, the servant, is the only major character created entirely from fiction. Pretty much everyone else is named for and plays a role inspired by the role they played in Empress Elisabeth's life.

Q: What is the biggest challenge in writing a novel like *The Accidental Empress*?

A: Wrangling the historical record. There's so much information out there. And it's so fascinating that I want to use it all. I wanted to include as many facts and events and individuals as I could, until the story was bursting at the seams.

When writing a novel, the story has to flow in a manner completely different from that of a textbook or a straight biography. I can't just list an infinite number of facts. I have to choose what I need in order to tell my fictionalized version of this story.

It was also difficult when I came to junctions in Sisi's life where the historical record is mixed on what exactly happened. For example, when Sisi flees court for the first time, shortly after Rudolf's birth, some historians point to her husband giving her a venereal disease and/or being discovered in infidelity. Others say it was entirely Sisi's depression and other mental health crises that caused her to ail. I can't say who is correct, but, since this is historical fiction, I chose to explore one possibility and what it would mean for the arc of the characters and the plot.

Q:What went into your research?

A: A lot of reading. The names of the biographies and books I relied on are listed in my acknowledgments. I read not only about the characters but also about the world they inhabited and what their daily lives might have looked and felt like. I'm grateful that so many historians have devoted so much time and research to these individuals, and that I get to be the beneficiary of all of that great work.

And then one of the most fun parts of the research process is traveling. It was in Vienna, years ago, that I first stumbled across the image of Sisi. She still looms large in Austria and Hungary as an almost deified figure to this day. The Schönbrunn and Hofburg Palaces are fantastic resources in which to learn about not only Sisi, but all of the Habsburgs. Vienna today still feels so grand

and imperial.

Budapest, to me, feels more whimsical and unruly. Walking around the Castle Hill and looking out over the Danube and the Chain Bridge, I could imagine why the romantic Sisi loved it there so much.

Both places were hugely important locales in her story, so I loved visiting both to learn about Sisi, Franz Joseph, and their life together.

Q: **Speaking of Budapest, the scene of the Hungarian coronation is interwoven throughout the novel. Why did you pick that scene to be both the grand finale and the linking scene that we keep coming back to as readers?**

A: That was Sisi's moment of triumph. It was at that time that Sisi reached the height of her power, her influence, and her physical strength and beauty.

The years leading up to this moment had shown that the policies advocated by Archduchess Sophie and the conservative bloc at court were failing. The disastrous war with Prussia was a clear example of that. And meanwhile, Sisi's power at court was in the ascendency. It was at that time that she began to make demands for herself as an individual and a mother, as well as to assert herself as an advisor in politics.

The Hungarians truly did love Sisi and embrace her as their queen in a way that they did no other Habsburg. And Sisi returned that affection. She did in fact learn Hungarian and infuriated many in Vienna by speaking in Hungarian. And she did choose to surround herself more and more with Hungarians (like her two favorite attendants, Marie and Ida). After years of unhappiness at the Viennese Court, Sisi negotiated a separate peace for herself. Hungary was a huge part of that.

Q: **So the ending is kind of a cliffhanger. Is there a part two in the story of Sisi?**

A: Well, from where I'm sitting, there's a lot more story to be told!

Sisi has a lot more living to do, and I can tell you this much — if you think her life has been tumultuous and dramatic so far, you have to see what happens in the coming years.

■ ■ ■ ■

READING GROUP GUIDE: *THE ACCIDENTAL EMPRESS: A NOVEL*

ALLISON PATAKI

■ ■ ■ ■

TOPICS AND QUESTIONS
FOR DISCUSSION

1. Though Sisi was often referred to as The Fairy Queen, this is not your typical fairy tale, in which a girl falls in love with a prince and the two of them live happily ever after. Could Sisi and Franz Joseph have had a happy marriage? Why or why not? How does Pataki's novel take up the notion of "happily ever after" as it relates to the lives and marriages of the novel's characters?

2. When Sophie learns of her son's intention to marry Sisi, the archduchess has this to say: *"She is not fit. It is as simple as that. She is too young — a child really, too giddy. Unable to fulfill the role and all of its obligations"* (page 249). What was it about Sisi that made her, in Sophie's eyes, "not fit" for the role of empress and wife? Was Sophie at all correct? Why did Sophie prefer that her son marry Helene?

3. As eager as she is to marry Franz Joseph, Sisi quickly becomes overwhelmed and in-

timidated by the amount of work that goes into preparing for her new role as empress (pages 262–70). How would you feel in Sisi's situation? Would you be excited to undergo such an extreme transformation?

4. On their wedding day, Franz Joseph turns to Sisi and says: "Repräsentazions-pflicht. *Keeping up the front. That's what this is. We play our roles today.*" In what ways does Sisi resist this requirement of life at the Habsburg Court? Why does this job requirement bother Franz Joseph less? Would Sisi's life have been easier if she had just accepted "how things are done," as Sophie and Franz Joseph so often urge her to?

5. While Sisi bristles at many of the customs and rules of her new life at the Habsburg Court, perhaps nothing upsets her more in her first few days than when she discovers that Sophie has had her red slippers thrown away. Discuss this moment (pages 327–30). Why do these "tattered red slippers" matter so much to Sisi? What other moments were difficult for Sisi in her adjustment to life at court?

6. Consider the character of Ludovika. What does the duchess's presence at court mean to Sisi? Discuss the various mother figures in the novel. How does Sisi's relationship with

her mother compare to her relationships with her own daughters?

7. What is the most difficult aspect of Sisi's life as empress?

8. Franz Joseph often finds himself in the middle of the conflicts between Sisi and Sophie. How does he do at navigating the tense dynamic? What might he have done differently? Were you in any way sympathetic to Franz Joseph, with the various pressures he shouldered in his roles as emperor, husband, son, and father?

9. Sisi feels dislike for Andrássy before she even knows him. How and why does her impression of Andrássy change over the course of the novel? Did your impression of Andrássy change throughout the book?

10. Throughout the novel, Pataki has chosen to intersperse the chapters with scenes from the Budapest coronation of 1867. Why did the author choose this final scene, in particular, to intersect the rest of the novel? What did this one moment mean for Sisi as empress? As a wife? As a mother? As an individual?

11. Compare Sisi's relationship to Andrássy with her relationship to Franz Joseph. How

are the two men different? In what ways are they similar? How does Sisi behave differently with each of them?

12. Sisi grows more and more consumed by her physical appearance as the novel progresses. Discuss this aspect of her personality. Does her beauty regimen become a true obsession, or is it more of a diversion? Does it make Sisi less sympathetic of a character to see her becoming so vain?

13. Sisi was an avid horseback rider, considered by many to be the best horsewoman in the world during her lifetime. At one point in the novel Sisi tells Andrássy: *"I've never found a horse that could run fast enough"* (page 739). Discuss what riding means to the character of Sisi throughout the novel. Through what other diversions does Sisi escape?

14. If you could pick one character from *The Accidental Empress* with whom to spend a day, which character would it be and why?

15. Consider the two epigraphs at the opening of the novel. Why did the author choose those two quotes? What other quotes are significant throughout the novel?

ACKNOWLEDGMENTS

I am indebted to countless historians, biographers, curators, and fellow devotees of Sisi and her fascinating life. The historical record and writings on Sisi are so abundant and complex that I had a veritable feast of facts, dates, characters, rumors, and reports from which to pluck the makings for this historical fiction novel.

Sisi remains, centuries later, much as she did throughout her life: magnetic, elusive, confounding, endlessly enchanting. She was a figure who inspired mythology even in her own lifetime. As the simplest of stories has at least two sides to it, then imagine how many sides there are to the rich and significant story that is the life of Empress Elisabeth of the Austro-Hungarian Empire.

The books on which I relied in my research were: *The Fall of the House of Habsburg* by Edward Crankshaw; *Twilight of the Habsburgs: The Life and Times of Emperor Francis Joseph* by Alan Palmer; *The Habsburg Monarchy,*

1809–1918: A History of the Austrian Empire and Austria-Hungary by A. J. P. Taylor; *The Lonely Empress: Elizabeth of Austria* by Joan Haslip; *The Reluctant Empress: A Biography of Empress Elisabeth of Austria* by Brigitte Hamann; *Franz Joseph and Elisabeth: The Last Great Monarchs of Austria-Hungary* by Karen Owens; *A Nervous Splendor: Vienna 1888–1889* by Fredric Morton; *Fin de Siecle Vienna: Politics and Culture* by Carl E. Schorske, and *The Swan King: Ludwig II of Bavaria* by Christopher McIntosh. All of these are non-fiction accounts, and all of them come with extensive bibliographies and source references. Especially invaluable were the personal letters and diaries of the members of the Habsburg family and court, translated and transcribed in Brigitte Hamann's work. I thank all of these historians for making my job so much easier.

It was at Schönbrunn Palace, over a decade ago, that I first slipped into Sisi's world, and I've been going back there in my mind since then. Now I hope readers will want to do the same, through their own imaginations and the pages of *The Accidental Empress.*

To my agent and friend, Lacy Lynch: thank you for your instinct, your tireless work ethic, your dedication, your integrity, your humor. Thank you for being on this journey with me, having believed in me and helped me grow since the very first and roughest of manuscripts.

To my editor, Beth Adams: I'm grateful that my work was once again in your capable hands. Thank you for your clarity of vision and for caring about Sisi and her story as much as I do. Thank you for steering the ship with grace, humor, and your keen insight.

To Lindsay Mullen, Katie Nuckolls, Alyssa VandeLeest, and the whole rock-star team at Prosper Strategies: you are untiring and unflappable. There is nothing you cannot do.

My deepest thanks to those who make it possible for me to do what I love: to Jan Miller, Shannon Marven, and the entire team at Dupree Miller & Associates; to Jonathan Merkh, Becky Nesbitt, Amanda Demastus, Brandi Lewis, Rob Birkhead, Jennifer Smith, Chris McCarthy, and the whole team at Howard Books; to Carolyn Reidy and the whole team at Simon & Schuster; to Judith Curr and your team at Atria; to Kathryn Higuchi and your team of meticulous copy editors; to Daniel Decker for your singular knowledge of the bookselling world; and to Rachel Cali for your fact-checking expertise.

Special thanks to friends who have supported me and worked with me on this journey: Ambassador and Mrs. Earle Mack; Ambassador and Mrs. Hushang Ansary; Carolyn Rossi and the Copeland family; Harvey Weinstein; Kathie Lee Gifford; the Yale,

Hackley, and Putnam County communities, who have mobilized with gusto to help me launch my career; Allison McCabe for your friendship and words of wisdom; Leonard Riggio; Pamela Robinson; Lucy Stille; Dana Spector and the team at Paradigm; Pamela and David B. Ford and the team at Princess Pictures; Steve Golin, Doreen Wilcox Little, Paul Green, and the team at Anonymous Content; Zenia Mucha; Fred Newman; Richard Farren; Rabbi Jacob Freund; Sheila Weber; and Desiree Gruber.

To the veteran authors for whom I have such deep admiration and appreciation, your support means more than you know: Mary Higgins Clark, Philippa Gregory, Lee Woodruff, Michelle Moran, and Aidan Donnelley Rowley.

And to the treasured network of lifelong friends who have inspired me, encouraged me around blind corners and through very rough drafts, and shared in the highs and lows: thank you to Marya Myers, Charlotte Lamb, Margaret Hunter, Cristina Corbin, Ali Reed, Cristina Scudder, Kasdin Mitchell, Liz Steinberg, Jackie Carter, Emily Shuey, Dana Schuster, Shannon Farrell, Alyssa Oakley, Cornelia Kelly, Dede Philbrick-Wheaton, Katey McGarr, Blair Golden, Ashley Eklund, Lizzie Garvey, Carrie Wuellner, and so many others.

And last but furthest from least, to my family of siblings, parents, inlaws, grandmothers, aunts, uncles, nieces, nephews, etc. — I love all five hundred of you. Dave, you inspire me every day. Thank you for speaking my language. Thank you for supporting me and being on this great adventure with me. Here's to stepping into our next decade together, hand in hand.

Mom and Dad, the only reason I even know about Sisi is because you took our family on enriching trips and instilled in us the importance of studying history, asking questions, and pursuing our passions. Dad, you are the consummate dreamer. I admire your wisdom and your intellectual curiosity, as well as your love for our family. Mom, you are perpetually undaunted. You are the most devoted and dogged cheerleader, and the way you roll up your sleeves and get to work humbles and amazes me.

To my siblings: Owen, Emily and Mike, Teddy and Emled — you guys make life joyful and exciting. And to my second family, Nelson and Louisa and all the Levys: I don't know how I got so lucky as to win the family lottery not once, but twice. I love you all and am so grateful to call you my own.

ABOUT THE AUTHOR

Allison Pataki is the author of the *New York Times* bestselling historical novel, *The Traitor's Wife*. She graduated Cum Laude from Yale University with a major in English and spent several years writing for TV and online news outlets. The daughter of former New York State Governor George E. Pataki, Allison is a regular contributor to *The Huffington Post* and FoxNews.com. Allison lives in Chicago with her husband. To learn more and connect with Allison visit AllisonPataki.com.

The employees of Thorndike Press hope you have enjoyed this Large Print book. All our Thorndike, Wheeler, and Kennebec Large Print titles are designed for easy reading, and all our books are made to last. Other Thorndike Press Large Print books are available at your library, through selected bookstores, or directly from us.

For information about titles, please call:
    (800) 223-1244

or visit our Web site at:
    http://gale.cengage.com/thorndike

To share your comments, please write:
    Publisher
    Thorndike Press
    10 Water St., Suite 310
    Waterville, ME 04901